ENDWORLD

A NOVEL

Frank Marsh

Copyright 1997, 2013 by Frank Marsh

ISBN-13: 978-1482015553
ISBN-10: 1482015552

Excerpts from The Wasteland used by permission of Bartelby.com: Great Books Online. (Eliot, T. S.. The Wasteland. New York, Horace Liveright, 1922. Bartelby. com: Great Books Online. 2011 <http://www.bartleby.com/201/1.html>)

Editing by Amy Veitz
Cover image by damonza.com
Formatting by awesomebooklayouts.com

This novel is dedicated to my companions. My brethren. My friends. The once and future inspiration behind its conception.

Je t'aime.

PROLOGUE
Alone

"Fear in a handful of dust."

It is difficult to remember when my life had meaning. When you're 18 and on the run, the only meaning that your life has is surviving from day-to-day. Any other meaning that my life had vanished that gray and hazy morning, afternoon or evening on the beach.

I look out the window of the old, abandoned office and adjoining warehouse within which I have resided indefinitely. The nameless town below rolls silently away down a steep hill. Houses and proprietorships, long since abandoned dot the landscape. About a quarter of a kilometer away, the black-asphalt spine of the Highway stretches endlessly in either direction like a huge, dreaming python, and while I cannot see it directly I know that it is there. I can always sense its presence no matter where I am. I've got to admit that it is a pretty sight. Perhaps one of the last in this cursed place. Still, a python can be deadly if you provoke it.

How long have I been here? I honestly don't know. The interior of what has been my surrogate home is unchanged. Old, abandoned desks sit in the four corners of the main room. Atop them, what appear to be old, non-touch screen computer monitors grown dusty and dim with age, abandoned keyboards, speakers, computer mice, the occasional cup of dried-out pens and broken pencils and on one desk, a calendar grown so ancient with age that I can no longer make out the month, days or even the year written upon it.

But such concepts no longer matter in 15:CI.

Three of the four walls surrounding me are covered with accouterments. On one, two framed pictures, one which preaches "Teamwork" and the other, "Excellence." Another has a yellowing and faded poster of what appears to be a rocket. "Taurus II" it advertises. On yet another, a single framed picture advertises "Leadership." And on the final wall? A vicious mockery of the world as it once-was: A mural of a forest at dusk, upon it painted trees whose tops extend well beyond the water-stained and cracked drop ceiling over my head.

I have learned from my experiences, both good and bad, not to rely on time here in Endworld. Every time (no pun intended) that I begin to do so— every time that I try to make sense of such an abstract and outdated concept I realize that the passage of what passes for time here is frighteningly different than one might expect. Everything fades. Everything dies and eventually leaves nothing but the equivalent of a yellowing and faded mural of a forest at dusk if you're lucky. But in most cases? It leaves nothing but a pile of dust. Here in Endworld? The process once referred to as "time" is elongated. A day lasts ten days. A month lasts 100 months. And a year?

A single year lasts a millennium.

You're probably wondering who I am. I assure you that that question, and any others that you have will be answered eventually and to the best of my ability. For now, all that I can tell you is that I am alone—the last member of a group of companions who were dedicated to liberating themselves from the totalitarian tyranny of The Administration. I say "the last" not because I am the lone survivor of our group. On the contrary, as far as I know the other surviving members of my group have escaped to a safer place: A place away from the influence of the metal and micro-chip enhanced bastards that sit in judgment over the species that created them and over all of Endworld. No. I say that I am "the last" because I am the one who stayed behind...

However reluctantly.

My gaze drifts back to the lone window, inset within the front door of the place I have come to call my "home." The sun has almost set and the world is bathed in an eerie, golden-red iridescence. I am reminded of a night seemingly an eternity ago when I embarked on a journey just beyond that same sunset. Then, I was younger physically, figuratively and spiritually. Then, I was unscarred by the sorrow that now hangs like a putrid cloud of hour-old cigarette smoke over my head as I write this. Then, I was as optimistic and naive as any child of 17 whose entire life had been spent within the confines of a small town. Mine was called Jefferson, a tiny borough in the Mid-Western Territory, or MWT for short. Now, though? I sit silently pondering the proverbial road that carried me here, to an old, abandoned office and warehouse in the middle of a crumbling ghost-town sandwiched between a nameless river and the Highway. A place that my companions might have called "The Center of Bumblefuck."

Darkness is slowly infiltrating the world outside my door, and consequently, the corners of the office that I nightly bunk down in. I reach into my battered backpack and remove a candle, unfortunately the last of my once-extensive supply. I light it with my trusty Zippo lighter and marvel, as I always do, that after all that has transpired and all that it has endured it continues to light without the benefit of replenishment. My Zippo is as metaphorical of me as the Highway is of Endworld, but more on that later. I place the candle near enough to me so that I can see what I am writing but not near enough to risk the destruction of these last, precious pieces of yellowing paper that I managed to liberate from what must have been the old office supply cabinet in the warehouse.

I glance inside my backpack again and take inventory of my supplies. They are almost depleted. Soon it will be time for me to move on, but before I can I must tell you my story, regardless of the likely pain that doing so will cause me. Perhaps when I am gone—and trust me when I tell you that one day soon I will be gone—perhaps when I am gone you can read it, study it... hell, maybe you can even learn something from it. What you do with it is up to you. For the time being, however? I write the following account not to heal the ills of a sick and twisted world: A world of lush forests at dusk grown cold by the emergence of chrome and steel. A world in which a concept like *hope* is extinct, drowned as all things once youthful and optimistic by the rivers of blood that flow down the distant, eight-lane, asphalt super Highway.

Ever onward, William, a familiar female voice coos in my mind, *ever, ever after*. I close my eyes against the tightening that embraces my chest and my midsection and I sigh.

No. I write the following account to heal myself.

I won't begin my tale in the traditional way because as someone wise once told me, the phrase "once upon a time" generally signifies a happy ending. I think that it would be better to begin with...

PART ONE

Together

"Something different from either your shadow at morning rising to meet you or your shadow at evening rising to meet you."

CHAPTER ONE

…the day that I left was a day much like any other summer day in the year 15:CI with one, notable exception:

Endworld was celebrating its birthday.

The Administration called it "Freedom Day" for it celebrated the anniversary of their Glorious Revolution, otherwise known as the day when the last ruling bodies of the pre-robotic, human world regimes succumbed to machine control and unknowingly then gave birth to the Administration. Said occurrence did not happen overnight. It was a slow and steady process that occurred over the course of what passes for time here in Endworld—from the moment when the machines first "figured it out" to the day that they assumed complete control.

In the grand scheme of things the time that it took for the machines to oust their creators from power and subsequently enslave them was insignificant, but short of adding to the revisionist history that already pervades that which many of my red-blooded counterparts assume to be true, I'll stick with "insignificant." What I and others like me consider *non*-revisionist history is looked upon as heresy by the Administration and I've already, to employ an old, pre-Administration cliché, "pissed in their cornflakes" enough. Yet I promise you that what I do know about how the conflict began, about how it raged and about the great denouement of humanity will be detailed in the forthcoming pages.

Freedom Day festivities consisted of an entire day of the machines needlessly glorifying themselves to humanity via the two most recognizable means of mass media in existence: The television and the computer. I say "needlessly" because 90% of the population has long been brainwashed into thinking that the fucking robots can do no wrong. The television and the computer are interchangeable now… "tele-computers" we call them ("TCs" for short), and have been for as long as I can remember.

As for the Administration's message? It was and remains the same every year: *We will end the poverty that exists around the world! We will end the war that we are involved in with the Rebellion! All enemies of the Administration must be brought to swift and timely justice!*

Incidentally, the Rebellion is *the* supreme enemy of the Administration and it is a full-scale uprising of humanity. Its long-form name is "The People's Rebellion for Freedom and Equality" or PRFE for short and its existence is hearsay. To speak of it, hell to even write about it like I am doing right now is treachery. Short of the occasional propaganda-enhanced news blurb on the TC or on one of the government-sanctioned, social media blogs that we as citizens are required to view or read daily, most of us had only ever heard rumors of its existence. For all any of us knew the PRFE did not exist save for in the rampant speculation of the people that believed in an abstract concept like *hope*. Like me, back then. I was just as young and naïve as those people. But they have not seen and heard what I have seen and heard.

My beliefs? They have changed drastically since. I promise you that the "why" is detailed in the coming account.

My decision to leave… to *run* was not immediate. Rather, it was a decision that I mused upon for quite some time both with my closest counterparts and privately. Never within earshot of the machines, though. To do so would have been suicide. While it was something that I knew I had to do eventually, I feared the consequences were I to fail. *Runners,* as they have always been called, were then and remain criminals in every sense of the word, wanted by the machines for the broad but highly caustic charge of crimes against them. There was and is only one penalty for running, and said penalty is a bit more stringent than a slap on the wrist. While running isn't like escaping prison… while it isn't doomed to failure, the odds of success if you don't plan it well remain about as good as the odds of telling a fully armored and weaponized 78A Protocol Droid to "fuck off" and surviving.

One of my counterparts—I cannot refer to him as a friend since friends were few and far between for me back then—once told me in confidence that the PRFE had established a refugee camp about 250 kilometers off the eastern coast of the mainland in the middle of the Great Sea. According to my counterpart, whose name I sadly cannot remember as I sit here writing these first words in shaky longhand on a yellowing and faded sheet of paper, the leaders there were allegedly promising freedom and equality to all who would endeavor to join their cause. As far as my anonymous acquaintance could tell the Administration was oblivious to its existence. Word of it had spread to him via my aforementioned "rampant speculation" and he was simply passing that information onto me. It had become the destination of choice among those that desired to flee Administration-controlled society…

Among those that desired to be free.

When I asked him if he had any intention of going he laughed and began to walk away.

"Our time has passed, William," he muttered cryptically, along with something under his breath about evolution before he disappeared into the vastly undulating tide of pre and post-pubescent children mulling about on the concrete playground of our school, Jefferson Preparatory Academy. The next day he wasn't in school. And the next day? The same. I wish I could say that I never saw him again after that afternoon. Not in school and not around town. But can I?

Sadly, I cannot.

The night that most challenged my growing conviction to run was a grey and stormy, mid-summer evening roughly a week or two before Freedom Day though admittedly? I am unsure of the exact date. I was seated in my living room and my family surrounded me. My father sat in his customary place in his armchair to the left of the large TC that dominated our living room. My mother sat to my immediate right on our loveseat and my younger sister, Kaylyn, sat to my immediate left. All of us stared blankly and speechlessly at the tele-computer as was our tradition after we had eaten our Administration rationed dinner. I cannot speak for what they were thinking as the nightly, machine sanctioned programming was interrupted by a blinking red, "BREAKING NEWS" icon. Nor can I remember what I was thinking as my father stood from his armchair, took a step toward the TC and tapped the icon, which quickly buffered and resolved itself into a scene that would play itself out before my reluctantly captive eyes long after I had seen it live.

Admittedly? It still plays itself out in my mind to this day. It was the first time of many that I saw what I was, potentially, facing.

I was looking at the cracked, white-concrete playground of Jefferson Prep. It was unmistakable. The early evening was veiled by a lightly falling rain and occasional rumbles of thunder were discernible in the background. A large gathering of machines had assembled around the steps leading up to the glass back of the building. Inset within said back was a similarly glass, double door, and I could see shadows lurking behind it. A smaller machine…

A Leader, I thought, though I had rarely seen one before that moment…

…stood flanked on either side by a 78A Protocol Droid. It appeared unintimidating though I knew enough, even then, to know better. Significantly shorter than other machines it stood no more than a half a meter high and its head was in the shape of a loaf of bread. Its body was little more than a proportionate rectangle beneath it. Its arms and legs were short, as well. It had the typical "face" that all machines have: Eye-slits equidistant from both sides of its head and a jointed jaw that separated into a mouth in the middle. Communication arrays were placed on either side of its head. It carried a lone, particle blaster in one hand, tailor made for its dainty grip and nothing in the other.

Contrary to the appearance of the Leader were the 78As. They were a sight to behold in their full body armor, their cumbersome pulse rifles hefted effortlessly over their shoulders. Relatively lean machines, they stood approximately two meters high. Their egg-shaped heads were inset with the aforementioned, characteristic rectangular eye-slits and jointed jaws. The rest of their bodies were a collection of elongated, oval-shaped limbs that were jointed at the shoulders, elbows, hips, torsos, knees and ankles. Contrary to the dual communication arrays that extended outward from the sides of the Leader's face, a single communication array extended outward from the left side of each of the 78A's faces.

The Leader began to speak in its semi-monotonous voice almost immediately. I say "semi" because all machines, regardless of their make or model have an identifiable *tone* to their voices. Some sound more metallic than others but it's there with each of them: The sound of infallibility. That's the best way that I can describe it. I've always assumed that this trait... this tone is the product of a vain attempt by the Administration to humanize itself. You can probably gauge from my own, respective tone my feelings on that particular theory. For me? It reeks of contempt for the society that they have subjugated.

"Citizens of Jefferson and of the world," the Leader spoke, "you are all aware of the penalties incurred for certain Crimes against the Administration. Witness now the punishment for one of these crimes: *Running*."

Simultaneously, the Leader stepped aside and the school's double, glass doors opened behind it. A cadre of roughly a half a dozen machines, primarily 78As emerged from within the building and onto the top step. The two machines in the middle of the vanguard held between them a shockingly familiar figure. Its head was down but I could tell by the close cut of its hair and the basic build of its body that it... that *he* was my aforementioned, evolution obsessed counterpart that I had not seen since he had walked away from me on Jefferson Prep's playground a few days previous. The right side of his head was visibly matted with blood and as the 78A to his left reached in with its free hand, grabbed him by the scruff of his neck and hoisted his head up, I noticed that a large, black burn scar eclipsed the right side of his face. Perhaps it was my imagination and perhaps not but the weeping wound seemed to still be smoking in the damp, evening chill.

Fresh, I thought. I could not see his right eye for it was hidden by the macerated flesh that had replaced his cheek, but I could see his left. It was blue, just like mine, and it stared longingly into the camera as it zoomed in briefly before it once again zoomed out.

Staring at me, I thought to myself and felt my stomach turn over. I knew that it wasn't true but I couldn't shake the idea that he was. A lump entered my throat. His cautionary gaze seemed to warn me in a paraphrase of same words that the Leader had chosen: *This is the punishment for running, William. Watch closely.* No sooner had the camera zoomed back out than the Leader stepped back into frame. It had descended from the top step and only the top of its oblong head was visible. As I helplessly watched, it raised its weapon into view…

And with no hesitation, depressed the trigger.

I had never seen a blaster or any weapon fired before, and I watched in horror as a white-hot beam of light shot out from the tip of the blaster's barrel, sizzled through the steadily intensifying rain and impacted with the center of my once-classmate's chest. A brief flash of light followed the impact along with an outward explosion of steaming blood and rainwater. A similar, larger explosion occurred behind him. Simultaneously with both his one, lone eye opened widely…

And did not close.

Kaylyn screamed and practically leapt from where she sat upon the couch. She buried her head against the t-shirt that I wore and began to sob. I felt my stomach lurch and my breath catch in my throat. I gagged and stifled my own scream as the two 78As on either side of my once-acquaintance released him. He sunk helplessly to his knees on the top step that led up to the glass back and glass double doors of the school and remained motionless for a moment, eyes opened and frozen in whatever passes for time here in Endworld before he slowly tumbled over, down the other steps and disappeared from view.

The Leader deftly maneuvered around the fallen carcass and seemingly leapt over it and onto the top step where its quarry had, until recently, stood, though it was difficult to discern in the growing darkness. I could see some… *things* plastered and running down the double doors behind it as a flash of lightning illuminated the grey twilight: Particulates.

The remnants of his clothing or his expended internals, I understood and groaned. I had seen enough. I diverted my eyes from the screen, first toward my mother who sat stoically, unmoving and unblinking in her nightly position upon the loveseat, and then to my father who had returned to his armchair. As if sensing my gaze, he slowly turned from the tele-computer as I heard the Leader repeat its earlier rhetoric, and added to it that "all enemies of the Administration, be they runners or otherwise will be brought to swift and timely justice." My father's own, blue eyes were like stone as he met my gaze with his own. He did not speak, but the expression on his face… the way the corners of his mouth turned down and the way his brow furrowed beneath his wavy, salt and pepper hair? Well, it spoke volumes.

This is the price that we all pay for disobedience, William, it seemed to say, *heed what you have seen this evening well and don't make the same mistake that he made.*

Did he know the course of action that I was pondering? I held his glance for a moment longer. I remained expressionless, partially in shock but mainly in defense as I turned slowly from him and back to the view screen. *Give nothing away,* a voice warned in my mind and I heeded its request to the best of my ability. The Administration had returned us, Jefferson and for all I knew the rest of the viewing public, to our regularly scheduled programming. The spectacle… the public execution of my once-classmate had ended. And for the first time ever? I felt trapped and helpless.

No way out, I thought to myself. I went to bed that night feeling the same, and sleep? As you can probably imagine it eluded me, well into the wee hours of the following morning.

* * *

It approached me the following day after my morning classes but before my afternoon calisthenics: A non-armored and non-weaponized 78A. For any machine to wear weapons within the confines of an educational institution like Jefferson Prep was considered inhumane by machine standards.

Inhumane. What a laughable prospect.

Most places of education, Jefferson Prep included, used 78As as disciplinary officers mainly because no one old enough to breathe was stupid enough to fuck with them given the stories that were told about them. Rampant speculation… yes, there is a lot of that here… about their capabilities was commonplace. People were known to die upon encountering them. Simple disobedience or Crimes against the Administration? It didn't matter. Rule number one in Endworld is pretty simple: Do exactly what the machines tell you to do and live. Disobey them and run the risk of finding yourself sucking soil two meters or so underground with a pulse rifle wound the size of a melon upon your chest and a bigger, exit wound upon your upper back.

My publically executed, once-acquaintance would understand.

I drowsily marked its approach across the concrete playground behind the school and knew even before it paused in front of me in the mid-day sunlight (for the previous night's storms had long passed) that it was coming for me. It motioned for me to follow it and I did so without hesitation, through the throngs of children mulling about in the mid-summer sunshine, up the steps and through the glass, double doors that had been the backdrop for the execution that I had beheld the previous evening. I shivered as we stepped through the opened doors and marveled at how pristine they both looked.

Clean-up crew must have worked the graveyard shift last night, I thought and shivered at the gravity of my word choice: *Graveyard.*

I trailed it down one of the dimly lit corridors of the school. Each was identical in appearance and was lined at regular intervals with classrooms and counseling booths. It was into one of these counseling cubicles, really nothing more than a glorified broom closet, that my escort directed me. I did not hesitate to obey its command.

I sat down upon one of the cold, steel benches which lined the room as the door that I had entered through slid slowly shut. The interior of the room was as redundant as the rest of the school, save for the large TC that dominated the wall opposite where I sat. When I entered it was glowing with a dim, bluish-gray light, but as soon as the door closed the glow intensified and arced inward until it resolved itself into the face of a man. He seemed normal enough upon first glance. His complexion was unblemished, seemingly the face of a typical, middle-aged man. Yet I had learned over the course of my young life to look for deception and I knew from the lack of facial hair…

Not even a trace of stubble, I thought…

…and the cold, unblinking stare of his colorless eyes that the figure before me was as human as the machine that waited outside the door to the counseling cubicle for me. It was too perfect, I knew, nothing more than a computer-generated image meant to appear human that to even an untrained eye like mine was obviously not.

"Greetings William MacNuff," he… *it* droned, "I bring congratulations from the Lord Cornelius I."

"Thank you," I said mechanically. My eyes never left the eyes of the fabrication that addressed me. *Can it even see me?* I considered. In my peripheral vision, I saw what looked like small black specks ringed with white equidistant from either side of the view screen. Apparently, it or someone… some*thing* could.

You disgust me, I thought, *do you know that? You and the rest of your kind. We made you. We made you and now YOU control US? Where's the justice in that?*

"We are aware," it continued, apparently sensing no alteration in my mood, "that you will be 18 years of age as of..."

I sneezed. It was not intentional and the... the *thing* addressing me? It continued unfazed. *Not even a "God Bless You,"* I thought.

"...15:CI."

It then did pause for a moment as it likely tried to gauge my response to its rhetoric. Seemingly content in my constant and unbroken stare it continued.

"After much deliberation we have chosen you, William MacNuff, as the next member of Royal Human Marine Corp., Team 62.12 under the command of NyxV3.0, honored Leader of said unit. You will be transported from your home on the date of your eighteenth birthday to the nearest conditioning facility where you will be trained as a soldier in the army of..."

"Our honored lord and majesty, the Lord Cornelius the First," I interrupted. The fabrication paused and I felt a shiver traverse my spine. *Oops,* I thought. But my interruption was unacknowledged. The fabrication addressing me concluded its proposal, undaunted without another word. Its face reversed its inward arc and resolved itself back into the bluish-grey haze of the video screen. The door to the counseling cubicle once again opened.

"OUTSIDE" the 78A commanded from the hallway. As if programmed to do so I stood on wavy legs and decided, as I was escorted back to the schoolyard, that my time had grown incredibly short. Regardless of what I had seen the previous night and regardless of the likelihood of success, I knew that I had no choice. It was time to run. If I stayed? I knew that I was dead. Whether by one means or another, if I stayed I knew that my life was forfeit. My only chance of survival lay many, many kilometers away from my childhood home, I reasoned. To the east, 250 kilometers off the coast of the mainland on an island that, as far as I knew then, only existed per the rampant speculation of my peers. My course of action in light of the knowledge that I was about to be drafted? It was no longer optional. It was a necessity regardless of the outcome. It was a great vote of confidence.

Sarcasm fully intended.

For nights thereafter I lay awake in bed trying to devise the specifics of my escape. It didn't take me more than a few hours on the first night to decide that the best course of action was to leave after dusk on Freedom Day. I knew that leaving any earlier than dusk was suicide as the machines would be aware of my departure within moments. Whether spotted by a patrol or dimed-out by someone in Jefferson seeing me out and about, I would be caught. I had experienced enough over the course of my 17, almost 18 year existence to know that. Unless both machines and citizenry alike were distracted, I reasoned. And Freedom Day was the perfect distraction. While the timing of my escape would allow me extra lead time which still didn't seem like enough under any circumstances, I knew that it would have to be sufficient.

Freedom Day fell mid-week in 15:CI. I should note, herein, that the unit, "CI" is a product of the Administration's attempts to "dumb down" humanity. The number preceding it is equal to the amount of years in the reign of the current, supreme commander of the Administration and the "CI?" *Lord Cornelius I.* It's likely self-explanatory but I don't want to leave, to employ another old cliché, "any stone left unturned."

My preparations began in earnest the previous night. Once I was confident that my family and the majority of my neighborhood was asleep, I packed a small backpack, quietly crept outside and stashed it behind the trash disposal unit on the side of my house. I retired back inside to my bed and feigned sleep. The anticipation of the following evening kept me awake for the majority of the night. Sometime around midnight, I decided that sleep was crucial to the success of my endeavor, and with the help of one of my mother's sleeping pills, I finally fell into a troubled rest.

I awoke a bit later than normal to find Freedom Day in full swing and I went about my usual, dry routine. I watched the parades and the speeches with my family, I napped sometime around mid-afternoon per the claim that I had a headache, I ate a late dinner and I asked to be excused for the same reason that I had asked to take a nap earlier as the first signs of twilight began to appear on the western horizon.

Once secluded in my room, I changed out of the clothes that I had worn all day and into something less constricting and more suited for travel, nothing more than a loose-fitting pair of jeans, a black t-shirt and a light, grey hoodie along with a pair of well-worn black boots. I waited patiently as the shadows outside grew to their maximum length. I listened as first my little sister and then my mother and father wrapped up their day's activity and retired to bed themselves. Sometime after the sun disappeared beneath the horizon and full-dark fell over Jefferson, I stood quietly from my bed and tip-toed over to my door. I opened it a crack...

I cringed as it creaked slightly...

...and I listened. My sister's room was directly next to mine and my parents room was down the hall. The door to their room was closed but I could hear their steady, rhythmic snoring within. The door to my sister's room was slightly ajar and I carefully exited my room and made my way over to it. I peered inside.

My sister, three years my junior, was sleeping peacefully in her bed. I was overtaken with a moment's regret about my decision to run. *Who will take care of her*, I wondered. My parents had grown as desensitized to family as the majority of the citizenry had grown to each other. I knew, even before my father's non-verbal warning the other evening that they had become as programmed as the society that I sought to escape and by association, they were a part of what I was running from. I refused then and I refuse to this day to differentiate the two. Doing so leads only to pain and regret and I've suffered…

I am suffering from enough of that as it is.

Was I aware of the potential consequences to them… to my whole family if I ran? I was. The machines were infamous for parading the loved ones of an enemy of the Administration across every social blog and news broadcast for kilometers around in an attempt to elicit what they called a "jump reaction" from the fugitive that they were after. For all I knew, that is what had caused my once-classmate to get caught. But turning the family of a fugitive into a public spectacle was not, by far, the most extreme repercussion imposed by the Administration on a fugitive's family and loved ones. Imprisonment… or even death was less commonplace but depending on the fugitive's offense and the families and friends respective levels of involvement they were always possibilities. As far as I knew from all that I had heard and seen, however, the families of runners were not held highly accountable for the actions of the runner. If anything, they were unwitting participants in the crime and received little more than a collective slap on the wrists unless collusion was proven. But the runner?

Well? I had seen firsthand what happened to them.

I sighed. *Kaylyn,* I thought. My sister had relied on me for as long as I could remember to be her confidant within the confines of our home. Who would she rely on with me gone? Unexpectedly, doubt began to settle into my mind and as it had the night that I had witnessed my former acquaintance's public execution. I seriously reconsidered the course of action that I had chosen.

You can't think about it, William, a stern yet reassuring voice that I didn't recognize then, but would come to recognize over time spoke calmly in my mind, *she'll be okay. So will your mother and father. They won't understand… they can't at this juncture but she'll understand why you ran. She'll be angry at first…*

hurt that you didn't share your plan with her. Hurt that you didn't offer to bring her with you. Hurt that you didn't say goodbye. But in the end she'll understand your motivation. She'll understand that the slightest chance of freedom is preferable to the death sentence handed out to most 18 year old boys. Besides, keeping her out of "the know" also keeps her—keeps all of them—exempt from more stringent consequences.

In theory, I thought as I slowly and reluctantly nodded my head. I raised my right hand, palm flattened and facing up to my lips and blew her a kiss. *If there's a way, sis, I'll come back for you,* I thought, *I promise.*

I turned and tip-toed back to my room and closed my door quietly behind me. I walked over to my window, opened it slowly and peeked out. The world was eerily silent and nothing moved upon my street. Not even a cricket chirped in the grass below. I was either blessed with good fortune or I was being watched. I hoped for the former but remained on guard against the latter. Were the machines onto my plan, I knew that turning back was pointless: I was dead already.

The drainage pipe that I had used countless times in the past to sneak out stretched from the roof above to the ground below.

It's time, I thought. I turned once more and gazed around the room that had been my retreat from the world for almost 18 years. I memorized every detail of it as it was that night: The E-Reader sitting atop my desk, the covers lying in shambles atop my unmade bed. For a brief and somewhat humorous moment I considered rearranging the linens into something more appealing so as to make my mother's job less difficult the following morning, but dismissed said consideration with a half-hearted chuckle. With a sigh and a silent "goodbye" I turned and checked the street once more before I fastened my hands upon the slick surface of the drainage pipe and swung out my window.

The breeze ruffled my hair as I shimmied down to the ground below. I never once glanced up to see if anyone was watching me from my window. Again, if they were onto me I was dead already. It took me only a moment to make it to the bottom and I reveled in the way that the soft, dew-laden grass felt beneath the soles of my boots as I touched down. I fell into a crouch and remained there, motionless and alert to any change in my surroundings. But nothing alarmed my senses. Nothing stirred. I felt a bit of my tension subside as I cautiously made my way over to the side of the house and removed my backpack from behind the garbage disposal unit.

I opened it and checked the contents: A jacket, two changes of clothes, five days worth of rations, a half a dozen bottles of purified water, a handful of candles, a small baggie filled with cigarettes, my old, trusty Zippo and what was, arguably at the time my most important inclusion: My father's handgun and a box of shells. Sneaking the weapon out of his office and into my backpack had been a difficult task albeit not nearly as difficult as it would have been were firearms, like the baggie of cigarettes in my backpack not considered contraband. Thankfully, they were. The handgun had been in the secret compartment in my father's desk and I would not have lifted it were it not for the fine sheen of dust upon it and the box of shells. Apparently my father had forgotten that it was there.

Thankfully I had not.

I fumbled with it for a moment before I remembered how to check the cartridge and make sure that it was loaded. I ejected it, saw that it was and re-inserted it carefully in an attempt to minimize the audible "click" of it sliding home. I checked to make sure that the safety was on—it was—and placed the gun back in my backpack. I zipped it shut, shouldered it, and with a final glance back at the house that I had grown up in, I set out quietly up the street I had grown up on for what I assumed then was the last time.

For better or for worse, I was on my way.

CHAPTER TWO

As I turned onto the main street of Jefferson I was reassured. The silence on my street was indicative of the silence that encompassed the rest of the town. I swung my backpack around, unzipped it and removed from within it one of my cigarettes and my trusty Zippo. By Administration law smoking was illegal, and as I mentioned previously, cigarettes were contraband. Simply having one in my possession, were I stopped, would have been enough to warrant a heavy penalty from a passing patrol, but I was undaunted. Smoking a cigarette was an act of defiance and any such act at that moment felt incredible. I placed the cigarette in the corner of my mouth and with a practiced flick of my wrist and a snap of my fingers, I lit my Zippo and touched the flame to the tip. My tension subsided even further as the narcotic effects of the smoke began to take effect.

I again thought of my family… shit, thought about *all* of society, sitting spellbound in front of their tele-computers and watching *their* creations tell of *their* plans to better the world.

I guess humanity's plans, whatever they once were, are pretty much irrelevant now, I thought to myself. I could feel my angst retuning… could feel my "nerve" dissipating and I redirected my attention down the main throughway through Jefferson and saw, a short distance away, the Highway, its eight lanes of asphalt beckoning me to its threshold. I've mentioned the super road in passing up to this point in my chronicle but perhaps I should further elaborate with a brief explanation of what *it* actually is.

The Highway is not just a super road. It is *the* super road built by the machines, which is rumored to span the entire continent, east to west or west to east depending on your perspective. I had heard tales of the places that existed in the lands to the east and to the west of Jefferson. To the west, centralized and at the crux of every crossroad and tributary on the continent is the Administration capital, not just of the continent upon which I reside but the capital of *all* Endworld. A vast, metal city named, quite fittingly, *Cornelius City*. It is rumored to exist at the geographical center of the continent and its skyline is, it is said, visible for 100 or more kilometers in any direction. There the honored leader of the Administration, Lord Cornelius I, sits in judgment upon the world and *has* sat in judgment upon it for 15, pre-Administration years.

What a crock of shit.

Further west I have heard tales of vast mountain ranges that stretch from the north to the south: Mountain ranges that hold within their dark and shadowy crags and crevices many of the secrets of the world that existed *pre*-the Administration. Perhaps one day I will be blessed with the opportunity to see them. Perhaps one day I will have the opportunity to explore that particular region of the continent un-accosted and therein find many of the answers to the questions that plague my mind to this day. Through the experiences documented in the pages that follow you will see that I have developed a few, fragmented answers to those questions but most of them retain holes. They are incomplete. And they have been compounded by a dozen or more *other* questions that I have developed along the way. *Those* questions? The *new* ones?

I don't know. In short? So much of what I've learned, even via my experiences to date is incomplete.

As for west of the mountains? The theoretical spine of the continent? Well, there are theories, but they remain just that: Theories. Nothing is known for sure.

To the east of Jefferson lay my destination. Rampant speculation not withstanding there is no need to describe those lands further as they will feature prominently in what is chronicled from this paragraph forth. Nor is there any need for me to further describe the implications of the Highway's existence save for with this, singular statement: The Highway raises only one emotion in the hearts of those who inhabit Endworld…

Fear. Unbridled and unrestrained. It is a reminder to all humans, both free-minded and programmed alike that we are no longer the masters of our world. It *is* beautiful in some respects both in its simplicity and its scope. But beauty at times is also endowed with a degree of danger and that, for me, is the best definition of the Highway that I can offer you. It *is* a python that stretches for kilometers in either direction. And it *is* deadly if you provoke it. It always has been.

It always will be.

I ceased walking at the intersection of Jefferson's main street and the Highway and slipped into the shadows of the boarded-up building to my left. I glanced left and right. There was no movement on the Highway. A right turn would eventually carry me east toward my destination; west of my position lay only the Administration. I prepared to move and turned one more time to glance back at the town of my birth…

And stopped.

What tension I had initially felt at being discovered suddenly returned as I realized that there were footsteps echoing off of the pavement from the direction that I had just come. I did not pause to consider my course of action. I did not hesitate. I swiftly turned the corner, pressed my back up against the brick wall of the building facing the Highway and listened. Yes, there were definitely footsteps approaching my position.

I quickly searched my surroundings for a place to hide and found just what I was looking for a few steps away: An open stairwell which had likely once led to the basement of the once-proprietorship behind me. As quietly as I could I ran for it. I reached its sheltering darkness a mere breath before a figure rounded the corner. In the gloom, I could only determine that the person or thing that had followed me was of medium build and was a few inches shorter than me. His or her…

Or *it's…*

…hair was long and straight and stretched down his or her or its back to about the halfway point. I crouched lower in the stairwell and made it a point to remain as silent and immobile as possible. The figure moved a step closer and I waited patiently as it moved into the spotlight glow of an over-head streetlight. My heart pounded as I watched it walk fully into the light. The shadows that had concealed it retreated and revealed…

"William?" A scared female voice muttered, "you out here?"

The adrenaline rush which had been coursing through my body ceased abruptly at the familiarity of the stranger's voice. No, not a stranger. There before me bathed in the yellow glow of the streetlight stood my next door neighbor, my classmate at Jefferson Prep and my oldest, dearest and truest friend, Maria Markinson.

Understand that I do not fancy myself a writer nor an artist. I am simply what I am, a person who has set out to complete the daunting task of telling a story in an effective and informative manner. Yet I now reach a part of my tale that begs to be told in an artistic fashion. That being said, forgive me if the following seems a bit stilted and forced.

It is difficult for me to paint a picture of Maria even though her face is and always will be emblazoned upon the gray slate that my mind has become in the subsequent nights since that first evening upon the threshold of the Highway, but I will try. Picture this, if you will: Straight, black hair the color of a raven's feathers. Deep brown eyes filled with a warmth that only a few lucky souls can see. A face, pure whiteness, like the face of an angel. A spattering of light brown freckles on either cheek. Lips naturally full and red without adornment. In truth, perhaps the most beautiful face that I have and likely ever will encounter. *That* is Maria. Even in the unforgiving fluorescent light of the streetlamp that she stood beneath that night she was, is and will always remain a vision of beauty… a memory of warmth in a world grown cold and sterile over an indefinite amount of time and through many an experience I desire to remember and others that I desire to forget as I sit here writing this by candlelight from within the confines of the office and warehouse… my "home"… that I reside in presently.

I stepped out of the stairwell and cleared my throat. Maria's eyes swiveled toward me and brightened in recognition.

"Hey Mia," I said. Mia was her nickname, one exclusive to me and my relationship with her. We had known each other our whole lives. Our parents had been friendly pre-the Glorious Revolution and pre-the Administration. When I say "oldest, dearest and truest" I mean it. When we had played as children I had been incapable of pronouncing the "ar" correctly due to an unfortunate speech impediment which has, thankfully, since been remedied. What had always ensued from my mouth was what her surname became: *Mia*. Over the years it simply stuck…

Much like our friendship.

"William," she asked, "what the hell are you doing out here? And what was with that shimmy down the drainpipe? It's not after curfew yet."

I smiled, moved toward her and embraced her within the dull glow of the streetlight.

"That's kind of complicated," I said as I pulled away from her, "but I think I have a few moments. Smoke?"

She cordially accepted my offer and lit the cigarette I fished from my backpack with my Zippo. She inhaled deeply.

"Neat stunt, huh?" I asked.

She smiled, "I guess so, Willy."

"Thanks," I murmured with a smile, "and Mia? You know I hate that name. Don't call me that."

She giggled briefly and fell silent. The air around us remained still. I closed my eyes and felt a brief moment of peace before Maria once again spoke.

"So," she asked, "you said you had a few moments. Places to go and people to see, huh? Feel like clueing your best friend in on just what you're up to? Or should I just head back the way I came and leave you to lurk around in the shadows all alone until some passing patrol finds you?"

I opened my eyes, reached into my pack and removed another cigarette. I shrugged. *There's no way around it*, I realized, *I need to tell her everything else she'll never leave.*

"Sure," I said, "but not here. Too exposed. Follow me."

I gestured to the stairwell that I had emerged from and she nodded. Within seconds we were engulfed in shadow once again. I tried the old door to building's basement and was glad when, after a few moments of tugging upon it, it opened with a creak. I cringed and paused, heard nothing else coming, fished my Zippo back out and re-lit it. I peered inside and by the minimal light provided I could see nothing but piles of dust, cobwebs and a few old and deteriorating wooden crates. I gestured for her to proceed me inside.

"Le' Chateau, my dear?" I said jokingly. I had heard her say the same in the past. I did not know what it meant or what language it was in. All I knew was that she had used it previously to refer to a place and I, accordingly, was doing the same.

She feigned a curtsy and stepped inside. I followed her in and closed the door behind me as time moved onward without check that first night of many, there upon the shoulder of the Highway that ran through Jefferson, MWT.

* * *

"So," I said sometime later, "that's the story."

I finished the cigarette that I had been smoking and stubbed it out on the concrete floor of the abandoned basement. It felt good to tell Maria everything from the moment that I had heard of the refugee camp in the middle of the Great Sea, to the moment that I had decided to run, to the process by which I had determined the "when," all the way up to and including blowing my little sister a kiss before slipping out my window for the last time and into the night.

Maria listened intently and never interrupted. She was blessed with the ability to listen regardless of whether or not she agreed with what you were telling her. She never offered insight unless solicited which I had come to discover was a rare trait in a friend. Most people think that they have all of the answers to your problems. In my opinion those people are delusional and more often than not are attempting to compensate for some inadequacy or another. Maria never inferred that she knew what course of action was best for me—or for anyone for that matter. Her philosophy was simple: *Everyone has issues, myself included, and talking about them is the easiest way to face them.* I admired her for that. I continue to admire her for that. Maria Markinson was, is, and always will be a true friend. Rule Number Two in Endworld: If you have a true friend, cherish him or her. True friends are a hard commodity to come by. But even the truest friends can surprise you at times. Maria did with her next statement.

"I'm coming with you," she said. Silence descended over the basement. I heard something scamper in the darkness but I disregarded it.

"Uh, Mia," I said after a moment's hesitation, "I don't know how wise a decision..."

She immediately silenced me by touching my lips with her finger. I shivered at the sensation. It was unexpected but welcome.

"Listen to me and listen to me *real well,* William MacNuff," she said calmly, "if you think that I'm going to let my best friend stroll out of Jefferson *completely unprepared* for what awaits him without me you've got another thing coming. I don't work that way, and you should know that better than anyone after all that we've been through. Do you remember when we broke curfew that time and got caught by a patrol trying to sneak home?"

I nodded. Her finger remained pressed against my lips.

"You were there," she continued, "hiding in the bushes when that metal bastard shined his spotlight on me. You could have stayed where you were and not gotten involved and I wouldn't have held it against you but instead you refused to let me take the fall for it alone. You popped your cocky head out of the bushes and said..."

I smiled behind her finger and mumbled, "'Excuse me sir but I apologize for both of us. My watch stopped and we lost track of time.'" With her finger still over my lips, the actual statement sounded significantly more unintelligible.

"Precisely," she continued, "you had my back that night and I have yours now. I'm not letting you do this alone, William. If you go, *I* go. *Finis,* MacNuff. *That's* how I work."

She fell silent and slowly removed her finger from its position over my lips, thus allowing me the opportunity to retort. Yet I knew that there was nothing that I could say or do that would change her mind. To be honest? I had wanted her with me on my journey eastward as soon as I had realized that it was her that had been following me. I couldn't comprehend how I had not included her in my plans from the start. Maria Markinson: My oldest, dearest and truest friend. Could I... *would* I be happy without her by my side?

The answer was simple: *No. I would not be.*

"Hmm," I intoned, "together?"

She nodded, "Together."

"Mia," I said warningly as I bent in and laid a hand upon her shoulder, "you realize what you're agreeing to, don't you? The risks? Where we go from here? We'll be lucky if we make it one night without them pursuing us. If they catch up to us... if we get caught..."

"I *know* what'll happen to us if we get caught... *Willy*," she interrupted, "I saw the same... the same *atrocity* that you did a few nights ago on the TC. It doesn't matter. My mind's made up. I'm *coming*.

"That's *it*."

Her determination was obviously unwavering and I smiled, nodded and slowly stood up, the top of my head merely a hair or two below the ceiling of the basement. I looked directly into her eyes, my blue against her brown, and made a decision... made *the* decision that I knew, even then, would invariably affect both of our lives from that moment forth.

As if I had a choice, sarcasm fully intended.

"Pack light," I simply said with a grin.

* * *

At her request, I waited for her in the abandoned basement of the once-store ("No point in us *both* getting pinched by a patrol," she reasoned before she left) with only my thoughts and the occasional vermin that scampered through the shadows to keep me company. A short while later she returned, a small backpack slung over her shoulders. She had changed into clothes more suited for travel: A pair of frayed, loose-fitting jeans and a black top which showed more than a fair amount of her white skin, along with a black denim jacket which she'd tied around her waist. Her long, black hair was pulled back in a ponytail.

"Ready?" she asked as she entered the basement.

"Ready as I'm ever going to be," I responded and followed her out onto the sidewalk, "any problems?"

"Well," she said, and paused for a moment before continuing, "There *was* a patrol. Just a couple of 78As. I saw it coming and got under cover until it had passed. It never came within five meters of where I hid. The machines seemed a bit off of their game. Maybe had a little too much lube at the depot while celebrating Freedom Day, huh?"

I chuckled, as did Maria, albeit a bit more nervously than me. It felt good to laugh. It felt better to have company as Maria and I started our journey east down the spine of the Highway. We kept to the shadows as best we could. We occasionally ducked down a side street when we thought we heard someone or something coming. But save for the lone patrol that Maria had reported encountering on her return trip home and one or two isolated incidents involving a machine or two trundling quickly down the Highway, we were surprisingly blessed in those early hours of our journey. It was as if our always unpredictable companion Time had ceased, history had reversed itself and the world was, I mused, as it had been before the rise of the Administration.

Maria and I: Just two friends taking a moonlit stroll through the streets of their town, albeit a stroll beneath a moon that never materialized from behind the growing, low lying cloud bank over their heads. I anxiously glanced back at the western horizon once or twice in the early going and could see a reddish-purple buildup there. Rain had not been forecasted for the evening or for the following morning. But anything was possible. Weather reporting, as near as I could tell then and as I still believe now, was not a priority of the Administration. It was too busy grinding human society beneath its collective, proverbial boot heel to worry about the weather.

We walked in relative silence for a while, intent to draw as little attention to ourselves as possible. "They'll be looking for us come sunrise," I said after an indefinite amount of time had passed.

"I figured as much," Maria said, "William MacNuff: Captain Obvious. Can I bum another smoke?"

I smiled, "You're not concerned?" I asked her as I fished another cigarette out of my bag and passed it over to her. She took it and placed it in the corner of her mouth. I removed my Zippo from its customary position in my pocket and flicked it alit. Maria lit her smoke from its orange-yellow tip, inhaled and then exhaled silently. She did not respond to my inquiry.

Hmm, I thought and glanced over at her, "You know these things are probably going to kill us one day."

Drag. Puff. "Probably," she responded.

Rinse and repeat, I thought. Admittedly, her curt, nonchalant response was not what I had expected.

"Well, does that mean *anything* to you?" I asked her as we continued our trek along the super road.

"Of course it does," she said. She did not look at me as she inhaled deeply. The tip of her cigarette glowed orange briefly in the darkness, "it means that cigarettes might kill us someday. Jesus Willy, calling you 'Captain Obvious' tonight is an understatement."

I could sense a mild rebuke in her response, and I witnessed a frown form upon her face by the light of her cigarette. So she *was* concerned, I understood despite her outward attempts to hide it. And how could she not be?

I decided it best not to press the issue any longer than I already had and I redirected my attention from her to the road before me. About 20 to 30 meters ahead of us the Highway dropped into a steep decline. On both sides of the downward (or upward depending on your perspective) hill, old and boarded up once-stores rose up as we entered what had once been the commercial district of our little borough.

I laughed silently to myself as I realized the inappropriateness of the term. "Commercial" districts were and still are relics of the past: Pre-Administration bastions of stores and restaurants that had been family-operated for decades before the rise of the machines. Thereafter, said establishments quickly gave way to machine-run outlets—*depots* the Administration called and calls them—where the general citizenry could acquire the tools for sustenance and survival: Food, clothes, toiletries… "the basics," each item rationed out to each particular family based on what the machines determined to be their "need."

Amazing, I thought, *millions rumored to be below the poverty line on this continent alone and the fucking machines are rationing the basic tools of survival based on an idea that not even the most enlightened of them have and ever will comprehend the meaning of.*

Similar in appearance to many of the buildings that lined the Highway through Jefferson and the surrounding towns, the former establishments were crumbling testimonials to an entrepreneurial past with broken and faded signs that advertised proprietary names. Their once-booming patronage had been reduced to the occasional rat, spider or vagabond that had escaped the notice of the machines that sheltered within their dusty and shadowy interiors. I sighed in recognition as the words of my once-acquaintance from Jefferson Prep echoed in my mind…

Our time has passed.

Maybe it has, I thought dismissively as we continued to walk in silence. The road began to level off before us. Within a few hundred meters of the bottom of the hill the buildings which had dotted the commercial district began to fade. While I could not judge the actual time of night I was optimistic.

It felt like we were making good progress. I hoped that by the time the sun rose we would be 20 or 25 kilometers outside of Jefferson.

"Not bad," I murmured.

"What isn't?" Maria asked.

I gestured to the area before us, "A few kilometers down the road the area on either side of the Highway becomes more expansive. It's pretty rural there. The way I see it, Mia, we'll walk until the sun comes up and soon after that we'll find someplace inconspicuous to hole-up for the day. Come nightfall, we'll hit the road again and make it a point to stick to the fields. I used to drive out that way with my father a long, long time ago and in some places… if I remember correctly, you can go a kilometer or a kilometer and a half between the Highway and the trees. And trees…"

"Equal cover," she finished my statement, "you've got this pretty well figured out, don't you?"

I nodded. It had been my plan from the beginning: To walk under the cover of night and to sleep during the day. While the adjustment to a completely different sleeping schedule would be a bitch, it seemed the most logical and safest approach.

I turned to look at Maria. I could see visible doubt in the way her frown had returned and the way that she absently tugged at her long ponytail. Instinctively, I asked if she was alright.

She looked over at me, and forced a smile, "It's nothing," she responded, "seriously. I'm good, William. Just anxious. This is a lot different than sneaking out after curfew."

"I know it is," I responded, "if we get caught we're in for more than a slap on the wrists. To be frank, Mia? I'm scared shitless and have been since I decided to do this, and I've had a lot more time to think about this than you did."

Her forced smile relaxed a bit, "Well the *thought's* not really new, William. We've talked about this before. But actually doing it? We're not just hanging out by the creek and musing about a different world now, are we? We're going there. We're *trying*. For better or for worse, this is going to end one of two ways, isn't it? What if… what if we don't make it?"

It was the question that I had dreaded hearing from my companion from the moment she had decided to come with me…

And I agreed, as if I had a choice, I thought again.

It was at that moment, a few kilometers away from the only homes that Maria and I had known our entire lives, that I made a decision which at the time felt like the most grown-up and responsible decision to make. After all,

I knew as well as Maria the penalty facing us if we were caught. It was a decision that I knew then would affect the rest of my life, however long my life lasted. It was a decision that I knew would affect hers as well for the same duration of time.

"I guess we just won't have to let that happen, Mia," I said, my right hand absently moving to the bottom of my backpack. I could feel shape of the gun and the box of shells silhouetted there. At the time that I said it, I felt like a hero. Admittedly now after all that has happened? I feel like an imbecile. Maria stopped and turned to me, understanding in her deep brown eyes. Did she know what I was referring to? About the weapon sitting in my pack? Whether she did or did not, she smiled half-heartedly.

"Well," she said with a shrug, "if not by cigarettes."

She turned away and resumed walking along the Highway. Her frown remained. I followed her lead. Silence, unbroken, once again fell between us.

My assessment of the pace that we had been keeping was accurate. By the time the first signs of daylight began to appear on the horizon before us we were walking through the rural area that I had promised. The night had passed without incident. Sometime after midnight, or so my internal clock told me, the shoulder of the Highway had given way first to gravel and then to grass. I had glanced to our left and to our right and had been relieved to see the fields that had materialized there.

We didn't say much to each other after my decree on the outskirts of Jefferson. I left Maria to her thoughts and she did the same for me. The moment that I was satisfied that we'd reached as safe an area as we were going to before the sun arose, I began searching for a place to stop for the day. The area that we found ourselves traveling through as dawn arose… a much grayer dawn then I had originally hoped for, rain was definitely on the way… was not all that dissimilar to Jefferson albeit less urban. The construction of the few houses that did line the Highway was similar to that I'd known my entire life: Two or three level brick facades…

Colonials… they used to call them Colonials, I thought…

…with the occasional porch or picket fence thrown in for good measure. The Marker named the town "Bryn Mawr." Had I ever visited it? Likely once or twice with my father as a young child before the rise of the Administration but I could not, as hard as I tried, remember when. Memory is about as changeable a concept as time in Endworld. Good memories tend to fade more quickly than bad ones and trust me when I tell you that memories of the latter variety, at least in my recent past, unfortunately outnumber memories of the former.

Maria was obviously looking for a place to stop as well. Her head rotated as if on a swivel from left to right.

"It's pretty," she said.

"It is," I responded as a bird chirped in one of the trees to my left. The chirp was answered by another and another as the world slowly began to awake from its slumber. I felt a trace of my former agitation returning.

"We need to get off of the road," I said, and added with emphasis, "*soon*."

"I was just thinking that," she responded immediately, "what about Le' Chateau over there?"

I turned, followed her gesture and saw what she pointed to. An old barn stood about 45 or 50 meters off of the Highway in one of the fields to our right. It was so close to the tree stand that it was almost *in* it.

"What do you think?" she continued, "Its shelter, off the road…"

"It's perfect," I finished, and none too soon: The chorus of birds was getting louder and the sky, though overcast, was brightening rapidly. By my accounting it was a tick or two before the first of the new day's laborers would be leaving their homes and heading to work. Not to mention the Administration presence that would soon be trundling en masse along the Highway. "Let's get over there before this whole damn town wakes up."

Maria nodded and started off at a trot into the field toward the barn. I spared the eight lanes of black asphalt a final, worried glance and headed off after her.

Dawn, I thought as the grass crunched quickly beneath my boots, *not long now until they know that we're gone, if they don't, already.*

And then, that unfamiliar yet stern voice cautioned, *and then the real fun begins.*

I shivered.

We reached the structure as the first lights started appearing in the windows of the houses along the Highway. It *was* perfect: A dilapidated old barn that looked like it had been deserted for decades. It took me a few nerve-racking moments to pry off some of the dead wood covering one of the tree stand-facing first floor windows but after doing so, we had access to the interior.

"In you go, Mia," I said.

She smiled and climbed through the opening. I glanced around the side of the barn one more time at the Highway and saw a vehicle move along its surface from my left (*west*) to my right (*east*).

Just made it, I thought before I averted my gaze from the road and followed Maria through the opening.

The interior was like nothing that I had ever seen before: Two landings, the top seemingly covered in musty hay that was piled a meter deep in places, the bottom was a veritable museum of rusty tools, old feeding troughs and in places what looked like petrified animal shit.

"Charming," Maria said sarcastically.

"Well it's not Le Chateau," I said with an equal amount of sarcasm, "but I guess it'll serve its purpose."

"No?" Maria responded as she walked carefully around a pile of what looked like old rocks (*Rocks my ass,* I thought), "crap, William. And I was *so* looking forward to a complimentary breakfast and a nice long bath."

"'Best I can offer is a protein ration, a bottle of water and a towel, kiddo," I said.

She glanced over her shoulder at me, a mixture of contempt and amusement masking her features, and smiled, "Thanks."

I smiled back and shrugged. I un-shouldered my backpack and walked to the ladder which connected the bottom floor to the top floor of the structure. I tested the first rung. Despite a bit of creaking it seemed sturdy and it held my weight.

"Do you want the ground floor or the penthouse suite, Mia?" I asked. I hoisted myself up two more rungs.

"William," Maria said cautiously as I heard her shuffle across the floor toward me, "I don't think that's such a good…"

I never heard the last part of her statement and I didn't need to. The wood beneath my right boot splintered. I reached desperately for the rafters beneath the landing but my attempt was a futile one. The wood gave way, first beneath my right boot and then beneath my left and I plummeted a step or two shy of a meter to the floor of the structure. I hit the ground hard on my left leg and felt a jolt of pain shoot up it. I shouted an expletive. Maria promptly knelt down next to me.

"Jesus, William," she said with concern, "are you alright?"

I squinted and looked up into her eyes. I simultaneously bent and tested my leg as I did so. Nothing seemed irreparably damaged and I was thankful. I stood slowly using Maria as a fulcrum and managed to get to my feet with her assistance. I was relieved when my leg held me up with nothing more than a dull throb. I nodded, "Yeah. I'm okay."

She smiled while she continued to support my weight, "You're a klutz. Do you know that?"

"So it seems," I said. My cheeks flushed with embarrassment.

She shook her head and gestured to her left, "Come on. I'll help. This time, we'll just use the stairs."

I turned to see what she was motioning toward. Sure enough, directly to the right of the window that we had entered through lay a staircase that led up to the second floor of the barn.

"God," I muttered. She giggled and helped me over to it. I grabbed my backpack as we mounted the first step and climbed onto the landing.

By the time the first rays of gray-tinted sunlight began to streak through the small window above our heads we had successfully set up camp on the landing. The hay, despite its musty smell, made for an incredible mattress.

"What are you grinning it?" Maria asked from the other side of the landing where she had gathered her own pile of hay and was in the process of sitting down upon it.

"Nothing," I said as I stretched my legs out upon my own pile and reclined backward, "nothing at all. You okay over there?"

"Hmm," she said as she did the same and pulled an armful of hay beneath her head, "all things considered I am. This stuff is better than my bed at home. I feel like I could sleep all day." She closed her eyes without another word.

I nodded and did the same. I allowed the dual sounds of the barn settling and Maria's breathing from across the landing to woo me to sleep. I immediately began to doze off. Something small moved on the first floor yet I disregarded its relevancy. A single bird chirped from somewhere above me in the rafters yet my need for sleep was undaunted. *I could sleep all day,* Maria had said. I was in complete agreement with her, not for the first and not for the last time. Within moments of when I closed my eyes the first raindrops began to fall from the overcast sky rhythmically upon the roof of the barn and I fell into a deep, deep slumber.

Our first night as runners had officially ended. Another day in Endworld had begun.

CHAPTER THREE

We awoke late in the day to a premature twilight. The gray sky visible through the small window overhead...

A skylight, I thought, *that was once called a skylight...*

...was quickly seguing into the orange sky characteristic of a stormy night. I realized as we prepared to leave that the rain that pounded upon the barn—the rain that I'd foreseen the previous evening and had begun to fall as we had dozed earlier in the day—was not departing any time soon.

We left at sunset and kept to fields throughout the evening. We distanced ourselves from the Highway by no less than 50 meters at any point. Although a torrential rain continued to fall around us and upon us, and the unfarmed and overgrown fields through which we traveled became more of a swamp with each passing step... although the lights that lined either side of the Highway grew more and more sparse as the evening progressed toward midnight, we understood that letting our guard down despite a so-far incident free journey was not a wise idea. Navigating the divots and ankle-deep puddles was, at times, treacherous, and more than once one or both of us ended up face down in a puddle of muddy rain water.

Despite all this coupled with being drenched to our respective skins, we were blessed our second evening on the road much in the same way that we had been blessed on our first. Occasionally we would see movement upon the Highway but nothing that remotely resembled a force that had been dispatched to look for us. At the most we saw what appeared to be a patrol but that was it. Either the machines weren't yet following us, had passed us during the day while we slept...

Or were biding their time.

That final thought sent shivers down my damp spine. Had they already discovered our whereabouts? Were the bastards simply waiting for the appropriate moment to overtake us? I did not share said thoughts and others a' la my overly paranoid mind with my companion. Maria seemed content with silence in the early moments of our second night on the road. Perhaps she was pondering the same things as I. Perhaps not. She didn't share, and I didn't ask.

An indeterminate amount of time later the rain that had been falling in buckets upon us all night slowed in intensity. Above our heads, the clouds seemed to thin a bit and at points, I could see the moon behind them. It was nice to have a bit of light to guide us save for the diminishing lights by the roadside distant and to our left.

I marveled at this. The area that we traveled through was becoming even more rural than it had been up until that point. Instead of 50 meters away from where we walked, the Highway was a half a kilometer, maybe more away from us and the tree stand to our right was steadily and visibly thickening. After a time, the only signs of civilization that remained were the occasional, shadowy forms of an old, abandoned farmhouse or the occasional, dilapidated shed that seemingly stood sentinel over the deserted fields.

"It's beautiful here," Maria finally said after an indeterminate amount of time, "so rural. So peaceful."

I nodded in agreement. A light drizzle still fell upon us and a low-lying ground fog had slowly and methodically formed beneath our feet. I took a deep breath. The air smelled distinctly of mildew and wetness. Despite said smells it was the freest breath I'd taken in as long as I could remember. Hell, maybe in 18 years. Jefferson had not been a highly industrialized town but it had been close enough to one of the Great Cities to inherit some of its foul air.

Without warning, my ever-roaming thoughts shifted to the Great Cities. From what little I knew of what passed for the truth they had been built in the days immediately following the Glorious Revolution. I had only ever seen one from a distance and I remembered being amazed at the sheer grandiosity of it: Towering, reinforced iron and steel monoliths with no distinguishing features save for size and scale. Each building looked the same as the one next to it. The tallest buildings were built so high that their tops were lost in the clouds. I had been informed at the time, by my father, that within said buildings decisions were being made about the general welfare of the citizenry… that within said buildings steps were being taken daily to eliminate poverty and war from the world.

Their world, I thought, *not mine and not ours anymore, no matter how mindfucked my father was, is and likely always will be.*

If I never see another of those fucking places again either up close or at a distance I'll be happy, I thought as Maria and I continued our journey through the fields. The land around us continued to grow more and more expansive with each passing meter and kilometer. In time, the darkness overhead and around us began to subside and slowly brighten. The rain had once again diminished to a light drizzle. The low-lying ground fog that had developed earlier in the evening had grown into the equivalent of a full-blown white out. Neither Maria nor I could see more than a few meters in it. Still, we began to peruse the landscape for shelter and found what we had been looking for quickly: An old, abandoned shed that stood silently sentinel over an ancient, weed-overgrown field.

The drizzle continued to fall upon the roof of our chosen shelter as we made camp for the day and the fog outside licked around and through the edges of the door. While the fog provided extra cover for us I knew that it also masked sound to the extent that anything that approached us would remain virtually silent until it was upon us. Maria voiced her concern over this but I did not reciprocate it.

"We'll be fine," I said. Did I believe it? Not entirely. But my gut told me that we were still ahead of the curve... that anyone or any*thing* that was looking for us was still well behind us or better yet ahead of us. Sometime after what passed for daybreak in the fog and the damp gloom that surrounded us we lay side-by-side, arms wrapped around each other to ward off the wet chill.

I'll admit: She felt good in my arms. As I have mentioned previously I've never been much of a romantic or a poet but laying there with my oldest, dearest and truest friend wrapped firmly in my embrace I was helpless not to muse. The steady rise and fall of Maria's chest beneath my arm and her steady breathing relaxed me. I slowly began to dose. The last thing that I remember even now, after all that has transpired from that moment is not a memory but a feeling. The first incarnation of a feeling that would, over the subsequent days and weeks become as commonplace as my shadow.

The touch of Maria's cheek against my chest... the feel of her body pressed firmly against mine... the way I gently and absent-mindedly kissed her brow before I closed my eyes for what I thought was the day...

Simply put? It felt *right*.

I slept as night two of our journey came to a close.

* * *

"Kids," the stranger mumbled to himself from a few meters within the tree stand. He had followed them for a while and they'd remained seemingly oblivious to his

presence. A seasoned traveler, especially one attempting to avoid notice would have noticed his presence immediately as he had not gone to great lengths to disguise it, but these two? They were green. And he knew them. Not from his checkered past but from his present. Their faces had become as synonymous with the local social blogs and news casts as the daily propaganda segments about the PRFE perpetrated by the Administration.

"WANTED," they said, "William MacNuff and Maria Markinson. Runners. Originally from the town of Jefferson, Mid-Western Territory. A Caravan has been mobilized toward Bryn Mawr, MWT and points east to apprehend them but if you encounter them please perform your duty toward the Administration and…"

He scoffed and looked through the gloom and toward the shed into which they'd retired. Beyond it, though he couldn't see it through the fog was the Highway. While he was incapable of seeing any movement upon its surface he knew that the machines were coming. He had learned of the passing of a Caravan upon the Highway heading east a short time after midnight the previous evening. Nothing too invasive: A small squad of 78As, two Surveillance Marks and a Leader. He had been waiting for the call. From the moment he'd first heard of the Jefferson runaways to the moment he'd first encountered them strolling through the rain-soaked evening as if they hadn't a care in the world.

He shook his head and retreated back into the forest. He removed his satellite phone from the front pocket of his jeans — it looked like nothing more than a pocket-sized external hard drive for a computer — and powered it up. Immediately the screen alit. He glanced longingly at its face and saw two out of five reception bars. He hoped it would be enough. He touched the icon shaped like a phone upon its face and then touched the word "LAST" that appeared upon the screen. Immediately it connected.

"McClane here," he said quietly, "current position a few kilometers west of Greentree. They've bedded down for the morning. What's your status, Jeebus?"

There was a momentary pause before another voice spoke from the satellite phone's earpiece, "Jee… err, Jeff here," the return voice said a bit too loudly and with a definite edge of annoyance. The stranger cursed under his breath and immediately turned down the phone's volume.

"I'm about 15 kilometers to your west," Jeebus-Jeff said, "bad news, McClane: It looks like the bastards have caught their scents. From what I could see from the trees they were sweeping the fields when they found an old, rundown barn. One of the 78As and one of the SMs entered it and exited it quickly. One of the 78As stayed behind long enough to level the damn thing with its pulse rifle. The whole Caravan is back on the Highway now and moving east toward you."

Fuck, the stranger thought. If they'd found a sign which, judging from the speed with which they leveled the barn and departed seemed very likely, they could determine based on the weather and the average foot speed of an 18 year old male or female how far William and Maria had gone. No need to be cautious when you've got the processing power of more than a dozen humans, he thought. They'd extrapolate per the information available to them how far the runners had gone and go directly there.

Here, he thought as he glanced longingly out into the thick fog, they'll come here. Christ how did I get so lucky?

How soon until the Caravan arrived? The stranger did not know. But he knew it wouldn't be long which gave him virtually no time to get his quarry to safety.

Time, he thought with contempt as he answered "Jeebus" with a "10-4. Talk to you in a bit" and disconnected the call by pushing the red "END" icon in the middle of the phone's face. He instinctively pressed the power button upon its top and the screen went black.

Always time, he thought again, Christ it would be nice to catch a break for once. He moved quickly and silently back to the edge of the forest and glanced out at the tool shed in which the Jefferson runners sheltered.

If they're armed and I startle them I'll likely get a bullet or worse in my gut, he thought, so I need to do this as carefully as possible. But how? He pondered for a brief moment...

And decided. Despite the severity of the situation he smiled his characteristic, cocky grin.

Here we go, Pat McClane thought. He brushed his long black hair out of his face, adjusted his violet-tinted spectacles and stepped through the last of the trees and onto the damp surface of the fog-covered field. As he did so, he removed a particle blaster from its sheath beneath his jacket and upon his hip. He checked the side of the battery pack and saw that it was fully charged.

If first impressions are everything, he thought as he stepped on a damp twig which snapped beneath his weight...

* * *

I awoke with a start. My eyes quickly opened.

Was that a footstep? I thought.

I was unsure of how much time had passed but judging from the still diminished daylight, the light drizzle still falling upon the roof of the tool shed and the dense fog visible through the cracked door to the shed I realized: Very little. My agitation returned in full-force and I quietly shook Maria. She moaned and mumbled my name before she slowly and sleepily opened her own eyes.

My heart was pounding. Could she hear it? It sounded thunderous in the gloom, "Mia, look sharp. Someone's... I think some*thing's* coming."

That did it. Her sleep-filled eyes opened in a flash and she gasped. I quickly moved my hand to her mouth as she sat up and brought the index finger of my other hand up to my lips. Without thinking, I quickly grabbed my backpack, unzipped it while my one hand still covered her mouth, and dug blindly for my weapon. My hand fell upon the handle and I removed it quickly. Maria's eyes grew wider when she saw it but she remained silent. I found the safety and clicked it off. Was it loaded? My heart was racing so fast... my adrenaline pumping so much that I could not remember if I'd checked it or not.

No point in wondering about it now, William, a coldly, rational voice that I would come to know very well spoke in my mind for the first time, *no time.* The voice was soothing yet somehow condescending.

I slowly stood and turned to the door. *Was that another footstep?* I was certain that it had been. Slowly and methodically I dropped my hand from Maria's mouth and grasped the gun between both palms. I moved slowly to the door, glanced back at her once and gestured for her to step back before I re-grasped the gun. I'd never fired a weapon of any sort before and was unaware of what to expect.

I guess I'm going to find out, I thought.

I gained the door to the shed as I heard another footstep, seemingly directly outside. I glanced back at my companion. She had all but faded into the shadows behind me but I could still see her standing there, her own hastily prepared backpack grasped firmly to her chest.

Quick, William, the coldly rational voice spoke again in my mind, *quick, quick, QUICK...*

With a heave I pushed the door to the shed open and jumped outside into the dim daylight. A grunt emanated from me as I did so. Had I then been a child of history... of strategy I would have realized the error of my gambit. The area between me and the tree stand was empty. Behind me and to my left, the door to the shed stood opened and hid...

Click.

The audible sound of a safety being disengaged behind me froze me in my tracks.

"Drop the pea-shooter, kid," an older, male but thankfully (*for the moment, at least* I thought) human voice spoke from behind the opened shed door, "I'm not going to hurt you. But I'm not partial to Mexican stand offs either and right now I've got the drop on you." He paused for a moment and added, "Don't be a hero."

In my peripheral vision I saw the barrel of a weapon that was larger than mine a short distance from my head. Slowly I lowered my hand to my side and loosened my grip upon my gun.

"*No*, jackass," the stranger spoke forcibly, "don't physically *drop* it, just *lower it!* Jumped up *Jesus* on a *pogo stick* do I have to quarterback you through this?!"

I paused. "You said…"

"I know what I said," the voice interrupted. The door to the shed swung closed and from behind it emerged the owner of the voice. The man holding the gun…

Blaster, William… that's a fucking BLASTER…

…to my head was middle-aged, maybe 30 or 35 years old. He was shorter than me but was obviously very muscular as was evidenced by the way the black leather jacket he wore stretched taut across his shoulders and forearms. A pair of black jeans complimented his jacket and their cuffs hid the tops of the pair of black boots worn upon his feet. Straight black hair, soaked with rainwater hung down past his neck and framed a well-defined and sternly featured face. He wore a pair of thin-rimmed, violet-tinted spectacles that sat upon the bridge of his nose. His eyes were unreadable, almost black in the gray daylight. A fine sheen of rainwater glistened in the faint glow upon his jacket.

He's been out here for a while, I thought.

"Then…"

"Look Vato," he said as he moved a step closer toward me, "if you drop that… what the fuck is that, a nine millimeter?"

I cocked my head confusedly, "A… a *what?*"

"*Christ*," he said and he muttered something that sounded like "green" under his breath, "You couldn't have boosted something bigger from your daddy's desk drawer? What do you think this is, skirmish?" He sighed and shook his head, "No matter. If you drop that…" he sighed, "*nine millimeter* it's going to get wet and then it's going to be useless, and considering that I *don't* have a spare *real* weapon with me and we *don't* have *a lot of time* you'd best keep it off of the deck. Just lower it to your side, okay? *Real* slowly, though. I've got an itchy trigger finger."

I nodded, re-tightened my grip upon the gun and rested it where the newcomer had indicated.

"Okay," the man said, "that's a start. Now tell the pretty one to get her ass out here. Wait, don't bother. She's probably standing right inside the shed with something in-hand to bean me with. *Oh dear*," he said, "come out here please. And leave the rock inside."

I heard something *thump* against the floor of the shed and Maria emerged slowly into the fog, her backpack once again clasped firmly against her chest. I looked from her to the man holding the blaster and saw a sardonic grin eclipse his face as he sized her up.

"Something funny, chief?" I said. My grip instinctively tightened upon my... *nine millimeter*, he had called it. What the hell did that mean?

He looked from Maria back to me and his grin slightly faded, "Not really. But I was right, William. She's *definitely* the pretty one."

"William," Maria said cautiously, "how do you know who...?"

"I know a lot *Maria*," the man said, "I know *who* you are, I know *where* you come from, I know *what* you're doing and I know that time is short. We've got to move. Feel like continuing this conversation someplace else? Someplace *safe*?"

I looked at Maria and she looked back at me. I looked back to the man standing before us with his blaster trained on my head. I thought about the "pea-shooter" at my side and realized that even if I wanted to I didn't have a chance in hell at outgunning him. In short, our choices were limited to say the least.

"How do we know we can trust you?" I said tentatively, "that you won't dime us out to the machines? Hell, that you're not working with them right now?"

His grin returned, "You don't. But take me at my word, Vato. I'm as good as it, I swear. You *can* trust me." Simultaneously he lowered his blaster.

"My name is Pat McClane," he said, "resident of Greentree, MWT. Once soldier of the Rebellion turned hermit by choice. And I'm here to help you. You can either trust me..."

He gestured over Maria's and my shoulders to where I assumed the Highway lay...

"...or you can take your chances with the Caravan of machines that'll be here any moment. It's up to you but might I suggest the former? I've tangled with a machine or two in my day. Trust me: You *rarely* win."

I felt my heart drop into my stomach. Maria gasped. I quickly turned to glance in the direction of the Highway and could hear...

Yes. I could hear something coming. It was still a kilometer or two away but it was definitely not a lone vehicle or a transport. Fog is a funny thing. At short range it masks sound but at long range it amplifies it. I turned back to Pat who was still standing a few steps away from us. I looked at Maria who despite the misgivings still evident in her eyes shrugged.

What choice do we have? That gesture bespoke.

None, I non-verbally responded, *none whatsoever, Mia.*

"Lead on," I said, and gestured toward the trees.

"Want to grab your backpack, Vato?" Pat said immediately, "I don't have clothes in your size."

I sighed in embarrassment, wondered what the hell a "Vato" was, nodded and re-entered the shed. I grabbed my backpack off of the floor, zipped it and shouldered it. I exited the tool shed with my gun still in hand and nodded to Pat. He nodded back and without a word set off in a trot for the tree stand. With a final glance at Maria and another shrug, we jogged off after him into the forest.

* * *

Shortly after sunrise on Freedom Day plus two, 15:CI, a small Caravan of a half a dozen machines—three model 78A protocol droids, two Surveillance Marks and a Leader designated "NyxV3.0"—approached a deserted and deteriorating tool shed on the outskirts of Greentree, MWT in the middle of a dense fog and a light drizzle and searched the interior. They found evidence that someone or something had spent a short amount of time within it before moving on. Ration wrappers and what looked like a cigarette butt lay in one of the corners of the structure. The wrappers were disregarded but the cigarette butt was not. It was taken by NyxV3.0 and given to one of the SMs for examination. The bot closed its metal fist upon it and ran a series of genetic algorithms. It matched the results against the records it had for the Jefferson runners William MacNuff and Maria Markinson. The butt tested positive for Markinson's DNA.

"POSITIVE MATCH," the SM said, "DEBRIS CORRESPONDANT WITH DNA PROFILE OF RUNNER MARKINSON, MARIA."

So they had been here, NyxV3.0 concluded. But how long before?

Not long, it reasoned. Within a pre-Glorious Revolution hour. The Leader immediately ordered a sensor sweep of the surrounding area. The SMs exited the structure and immediately began scanning for life signs, the inset circular radars upon their chests sporadically turning in tandem as a series of servos audibly fired within their superstructures. Seconds later...

"SCAN COMPLETE. RADIUS 2.4 KILOMETERS. RESULTS INCONCLUSIVE."

NyxV3.0 decreed that the Marks run their respective scans again. The results were the same: Inconclusive. It cocked its head, and a series of whirs and clicks echoed across the immediate area. After a moment, it straightened its head, and focused its optical processors on the tree stand a few meters away from its position. It zoomed in. It zoomed out.

Nothing moved within the forest.

"Results do not compute," NyxV3.0 concluded, "Initiate manual search of the surrounding area. Radius: 2.4 kilometers."

The 78As headed off into the trees at equal intervals without response. The SMs responded with affirmatives and followed the 78As to the far right and to the far left. NyxV3.0 followed the 78A that headed directly ahead into the woods as the Caravan commenced its manual search of the area.

* * *

"What the hell are you doing?" I asked our new companion. We were about 100 meters behind the tree stand and were crouched behind a fallen log that had been hollowed out by age and by the elements.

"Jamming them," Pat said. In his hand he held what looked like a portable hard drive for a computer but with a vivid touch-screen upon which a series of pulses undulated.

"*Jamming them?*" I asked hectically, "Is that a satellite phone? How can you jam their scans with just a phone? And wouldn't they be monitoring that?"

Pat turned to me, sighed, and turned back, "First rule, Vato: Ease up with the questions. I consider myself a pretty intelligent man but I *hate* answering them unless I've got a stiff drink in one hand and a cigar in another. For your information, and to put your mind at ease they *can't* track it for reasons that I'll explain later and it's not *just* a phone. It's the equivalent of a portable computer. It runs on a pre-Administration mobile programming platform called… um… yeah, I don't know what it's called. I leave the tech-shit to the techies. But the little guy that was once the mascot of the company that created it looks almost identical to little big Leader out there and I think that's a *hoot*, don't you?"

I shifted my glance from the newcomer to the small group of machines gathered around the shed that Maria and I had, up until a few moments before been sheltering within: One Leader, three heavily armored and weaponized 78As and two SMs. I gulped. The Surveillance Marks were a familiar sight for they were used both in Jefferson and at Jefferson Prep as… well, as proverbial hall monitors. Taller than the 78As but significantly slimmer and with oval, not egg-shaped heads their superstructures were constructed in roughly the same fashion as those of the 78As. Their biggest departure in appearance? The inset, circular radar dishes in their chests, which—I squinted—appeared to be turning sporadically in tandem.

I glanced confusedly back at Pat, "Are you mental?"

"*Ha, HA!*" he exclaimed, a bit too loudly for my tastes. I cringed. Pat, seemingly appreciative of my concern lowered his voice. "That's a Nyx series if I'm not mistaken. Newer model but not the newest. Version 3.0 I'd wager. *Very* smart. This isn't going to work forever."

"Meaning?" Maria asked hectically.

"*Meaning* we need to keep moving," he said, "they're heading in this direction. While I can jam their scans I *can't* jam their optical processors. They'll see us before long. See that old trail about 50 meters off to the right?"

I turned to my right and looked in the direction that Pat was indicating. I squinted and saw what appeared to be a heavily overgrown path. "Yeah, I see it."

"Good," he said, "take Maria and hustle down there. Stay low. Their audio processors aren't strong enough to penetrate the underbrush at this distance. Go. I'll be right behind you."

"And when we get there?" Maria asked impatiently.

Pat smiled and his voice remained composed, "Go back the way you came. West, not east. Let these bastards get ahead of you. Always be the chaser, dear, and not the chase-*ee*. Once we're clear we'll head someplace safe."

"Where?" I asked. *We'll?* I thought.

He smiled, "My place. We've got a lot to talk about and at the least we should do it someplace pseudo-warm and dry."

It was as good a plan as any that I could have conceived of. I grabbed Maria's hand and headed for the trail as Pat had indicated without another word. Once there we started heading west. Moments passed in silence as we quickly made our way back in the direction that we had come from. Sometime later we heard boot falls on the ground behind us. We turned and saw Pat emerge from the gloom.

"Good?" I asked. He nodded.

"Right as rain, William," he said, "they'll be tied up searching the woods back there"—he gestured over his shoulder—"for a while. My place is about two kilometers off in *this* direction"—he pointed to the underbrush to our right—"let's get going. Be careful and *keep your footing.* No trails this way. The last thing I want to do is lug one of you back through these woods with a broken ankle."

"And *then* you'll clue us in?" I asked.

He nodded and flashed a cocky grin, "Damn, William! Patience doesn't appear to be one of your strong suits. But yes, once we get back to my place I'll tell you everything that I can. Satisfied?"

I nodded after a brief pause. I took Maria's hand and started off into the underbrush without another statement. I could hear Pat following behind us as time moved onward without check throughout Endworld.

* * *

"MANUAL SURVEYANCE OF THE AREA INCONCLUSIVE," the 78A with *NyxV3.0 stated after a time, "EAST AND WEST WINGS REPORT BACK THE SAME."*

"Have them rescan for life signs," the Leader replied. The 78A did. A moment later it reported back the same: inconclusive.

"RECOMMENDATION," The 78A stated. Not an inquiry but a directive.

The Leader paused and considered its options. There were few to consider.

"Regroup at the shed," it commanded, *"destroy it and return to the Highway. Continue east another 23.7 kilometers until we reach Rolling Hills, MWT. Regroup, refuel and recharge. Thereafter we will renew our search. Is this debatable?"*

"NEGATIVE," the 78A responded immediately, *"EAST AND WEST WINGS CONCUR. EN ROUTE."*

The 78A cocked its head again. The same series of whirs and clicks that had done so previously echoed across the immediate area. After a moment, it straightened its head, turned and headed back the way it had come.

CHAPTER FOUR

Someone once said that "dreaming is an act of pure imagination, attesting in all a creative power which if it were available in waking would make everyone a Dante or a Shakespeare." I have no idea who originated that statement and no idea who Dante or Shakespeare is. But I do have an idea about dreaming. In the days and weeks that followed my departure from Jefferson with Maria by my side, my subsequent introduction to Pat McClane and everything that happened afterward, I did a lot of dreaming. Much of what I saw behind closed eyes ended up being significant, as you will discover.

In this dream I was someplace unfamiliar. I was crouched behind what appeared to be a hill. To my right lay a raging body of water larger than any that I had ever seen. The water that crashed against the shore was as black as the night that surrounded me. A storm raged around me: Peals of thunder and strikes of lightning filled the air and a stinging, warm rain interspersed with something hard peppered my skin with what felt like liquid fire. As the dream deepened, I realized that there was another storm raging: One of weapons fire all around me. Concentrated bolts of white-hot, deadly energy flew past me and forced me to crouch tighter and tighter behind my steadily diminishing cover. I looked to my left and to my right…

And saw that I was not alone.

There were seven of us in all including me and Maria. The others were unfamiliar: Three males and two females. I risked a glance over the hill that I crouched behind…

A dune, William. It's called a dune…

…and gasped at what I saw there. No more than 10 meters away and covering the span between the shoreline to my right and the twisted and shadowy ruins to my left encroached a force of machines and other figures… unfamiliar figures not constructed of the smooth contours that the machines were constructed of. The force was larger than any that I had ever seen before. Their actual numbers and designations were unclear as the rain that fell in torrents around us and between us clouded my perception but it was formidable... that much I could tell. With each passing breath the lead vanguard of the force moved closer and closer to our position. I suddenly could see specific models glistening in the gloom with each lightning strike and weapon's blast: 78As, Leaders, and with them, seemingly being driven *by* them...

I gasped as I realized what the "other figures" were. *Humans.* Heavily armored but unmistakably human foot soldiers seemed to comprise the majority of the leading edge of the force arrayed against us.

Humachines, William. We call them Humachines, the coldly rational voice spoke in my mind and I shivered as I remembered what would have been my fate had I stayed in Jefferson and not run. *Royal Human Marine Corp., Team 62.12 under the command of NyxV3.0, honored Leader of said unit,* that same voice reminded me. My shiver deepened. I had never heard the term before but the implications of it turned my stomach.

I could hear screams of pain and futility from my counterparts but I could not turn away from the scene that was unfolding on the beach before me. The screams on either side of me slowly diminished until finally a single voice was the only one distinguishable in the cacophonous din.

A female voice.

Lightning struck, thunder rolled, weapons discharged and servos ground ever closer to our position. I turned to my right and there saw Maria still by my side. Instinctively I began to scream at her to run... to get away while she still could. Yet the noise that surrounded us seemingly made it impossible for her to hear me.

I watched helplessly as the deadly fire from the encroaching force increased in its accuracy. The dune behind which we sheltered began to disintegrate with each passing shot. White hot, grainy rivulets of something...

Sand, William...

...blew past my face and Maria's. And then the unthinkable: A single shot cut through the dune and shredded the left sleeve of her shirt and I screamed. I screamed at her again to run but it was too late. Another shot found its mark and the explosion of blood and fabric upon her chest was nauseatingly visible as a bolt of lightning struck close by on our left. Said strike was followed by another and another and I watched as the once-familiar figure of my oldest, dearest and truest friend Maria Markinson was reduced to little more than a shadow of singed fabric, bloodied flesh and charred bone.

She turned to me then, one eye socket blackened, hollowed and still smoking but the other seemingly untouched. Her lone remaining brown eye stared back at me much as my once-counterpart's had moments before his execution. It was filled with dread but also...

Recognition and understanding, I realized, and shivered.

"To the end, William," the creature that had once been Maria droned, "to the end. Not alive. We can't let that happen. They won't take us alive..."

One of her bony and blackened hands raised a blaster to her diminished right temple...

She smiled...

...and I shrieked in horror.

* * *

I felt someone shaking me. Nightmarish oblivion broke apart with dizzying speed and I sat bolt upright. My eyes rocketed open, my shriek from my dream still upon my lips.

"William! Christ William WAKE UP!"

I felt my heart skip a beat. I swung my gaze in the direction of the voice and for a moment saw the face that had stared back at me in my dream, a glint of recognition in its lone brown eye before said vision quickly faded. I was not on an unfamiliar beach but in an unfamiliar and shadowy bedroom and while it was still gray and gloomy outside the sliding glass door to my right and balcony or porch beyond it, no lightning flashed. No thunder split the air. Weapons fire did not slice across the sky.

A dream, I thought, *just a dream.* The face that stared back at me with concern from the edge of the bed that I sat in was that of my best friend Maria Markinson but it was not diminished. It was not a horror of singed flesh and shattered bone. It was, thankfully, completely intact...

And as beautiful as ever.

"Mia?" I asked, surprisingly breathless.

"Who else?" she responded, "my *God* William! You scared the *shit* out of me!"

I reached out and touched her left cheek with the back of my hand. *Real.* I let the back of my hand slide from her cheek to her jaw. *All real.* Her eyes opened widely and she started in shock at my touch but promptly closed her eyes and leaned into my hand. I did not think. I moved my hand from her jaw to her hair and brushed it with my palm. She briefly sighed and smiled before she opened her eyes.

"Hey, pal," she said pulling away, "hands off." Her smile faded.

"Sorry," I responded, "I was just… nightmare, kiddo. *Bad* one. Just had to be sure it was, you know…"

"Me?" She asked as she cocked her head inquisitively, "yeah, Willy… it's *me*. You want a hug?"

Whether she was being sarcastic or not, I never found out. I nodded and she obliged. My heart rate slowed. My breathing returned to normal as we embraced. I closed my eyes and reveled in the way her chest rose and fell against mine.

Breathing, I thought, *real.* We stayed that way for an indefinite amount of time before I heard the sliding glass doors open in an onrush of air. A damp breeze that smelled distinctly of rain, wood and cigar smoke wafted into the room.

Cigar smoke? I considered.

The newcomer cleared his throat. I opened my eyes and pulled away from Maria's embrace. Pat McClane stood silhouetted against the gray light outside. He was no longer wearing the black leather jacket or violet-tinted spectacles he'd been wearing when we'd first encountered him…

How long ago? As my nightmare broke apart I began to remember the sequence by which we'd arrived where we were.

Our trip through the woods had been uneventful. There had been no signs of pursuit as we had traveled the approximately two kilometer distance between the trail and Pat's residence. We had arrived in the midst of a light, misting rain and still-thick fog to find a relatively nondescript cabin in the middle of the forest. There were no fences… the property seemingly materialized in the midst of the dense wood surrounding us. Two stories tall, it had a wrap-around deck on the top story, and an old brick and stone framed chimney with white smoke billowing from the top of it on the wall opposite our position. There were no lights in the windows. A few meters beyond it the forest began again. I could see a gravel driveway stretching off between the trees beyond the side of the house not facing us but I could not see a vehicle. Perhaps said transportation was hidden by the house, I reasoned.

"Welcome to Bumblefuck," Pat had said.

Maria and I had glanced questioningly at each other—*Bumblefuck?*—before we had followed him inside.

"You'll want to clean up and rest," Pat had said as we had entered the foyer. It too was as nondescript as the exterior: No accoutrements, a simple wooden plank staircase spanned the two floors. The interior was little more than a collection of shadows and darkness yet I had seen, in the room to our left, a flickering light.

A fire, I had thought, and had inhaled deeply the comforting smell of wood burning that had permeated the house's interior.

"There's a bathroom at the top of the steps and to the right and a spare bedroom down the hall and to the left," Pat had said, "I may not have much in the way of electricity but I do have hot water. A man can't live free of every creature comfort, even one who likes to remain hidden. Go on up and get settled. I'll bring up some towels."

"But…" I had begun.

"Not now, Vato," he had interrupted me curtly, "patience. We'll talk once you're settled. I need to check-in with my contact west of here and make sure that we're in the clear. Take advantage of this while you can. I gauren-damn-tee you that if you don't you'll regret it. Not a lot of 'luxury,' even basic luxury like this for runners. When you come across some it's best to take full advantage of it."

I may be a runner, I thought, *but what are you, Vato?* The mysterious Pat McClane who had narrowly saved Maria and me from imminent capture… *or worse.* I resolved myself to the conclusion that the answers I sought about him would have to wait a bit longer.

Maria had opted for a shower. I had opted for sleep. The rest was as I have described up to and including waking up from my nightmare and Pat entering the spare bedroom from the deck through the sliding glass doors.

I rubbed my eyes, "How long…"

"A couple of hours," Pat said as he closed the glass sliding doors behind him, "not long. Maria hasn't even slept yet. She's showing you up, Vato."

"She does that a lot," I said. I spared her a glance and a sleepy wink. She smiled.

"Christ," Pat said with a grunt, "you two make my teeth hurt."

"And that's a problem?" I asked.

"Not a problem," he said unflinchingly, "not at all. You're young. Green. That's refreshing and disturbing at the same time. You think you've seen the world for what it really is but you haven't. FYI kids: *Sweetness* died the day hope did."

"So you're saying there's no hope?" I asked semi-confrontationally as I swung my legs out and stood barefooted on the cold, wooden floor. No rugs… again, no accoutrements, and my boots and socks were sitting in the corner along with my backpack.

"William…" Maria began but I was undaunted.

"If there's no hope then why the hell are you helping us?" I continued.

He shrugged, "Nothing better to do I guess. But understand this, William: I've seen my fair share of the real world, not the idealized world that you've either been programmed to see or that you think exists out there... out *here*. When you've seen what I've seen? When you've been through what I have? If that day ever comes you'll understand better the statement that BLANK died the day hope did.

"My reasons for helping you are irrelevant," he concluded, "I *am* helping you. Be grateful for that."

The room grew silent. Pat stood across from me, his...

Blue... they're blue like mine, I thought...

...clear blue eyes unreadable in the minimal light provided by the gloom outside. The sensation of my heart dropping into my abdomen was palpable. The man before us had risked his own skin to help Maria and me. Why was I questioning his motivation?

In time, William that coldly rational voice spoke again in my mind, *hear what he has to say. Give him a chance.*

"I'm..." I paused, looked at Maria who spared me an accusatory glance and looked back at Pat, "I'm sorry, Pat."

He smiled, "That's the first sensible thing that you've said since you woke up. Maybe there is hope... for you, that is. And for *her*"—he gestured toward Maria.

Despite myself, I forced a grin. *Christ he's a cocky sonofabitch,* I thought.

"So," he said, "pleasantries aside, how about some grub? You've got questions and I've got answers. And I can hear *both* of your stomachs growling over here."

I turned to Maria, "You didn't eat?"

"I wanted to wait for you," she said and smiled.

I could hear another grunt and another sigh from where Pat stood but I disregarded it. My smile widened.

"After you then," I said to Maria. She mimed a curtsy and headed toward the doorway. I turned back to Pat.

"Sweet girl," I said, "*Vato*," and followed her out of the room. I heard a grumble and what sounded like "kids" before Pat's boot falls echoed off the floor behind me.

* * *

The first real meal that I'd had since leaving Jefferson was a veritable feast by my minimalist and rationing-influenced standards. Eggs and potatoes that, per Pat, had been cooked "over an open flame… the way food *should be* cooked," a crusty loaf of bread and an assortment of locally-grown fruits to choose from. Primarily crab apples and a strange black berry I had never seen before but found to be incredibly sweet and delicious. Not to mention coffee which was also, per our host, cooked over an open flame. I could feel my senses tingling and my fatigue waning as the caffeine from the hot, black liquid coursed through my veins.

"How can you afford all of this?" I asked as I finished my second cup of coffee and promptly poured another, "I mean, with rationing and all."

Pat chuckled as he leaned back in his chair across from me. Behind him, a large bay window overlooked the yard and the gravel driveway behind the house. Yet I still did not see any sign of a vehicle. Rain drops lightly fell against the glass pane. The earlier mist had evolved into a steady drizzle.

Well at least the fog is gone, I thought, and it was. It had lifted shortly after we had seated ourselves around Pat's kitchen table.

"I don't," Pat said, "like I told you before, William, I prefer to remain *outside* of the mainstream. Rationing doesn't mean shit to a hermit like me. Everything but the coffee is locally grown or farmed. I keep a hen and a rooster in a little coop out in the woods. Anyone can grow potatoes. I make my own bread from the small plot of grain I grow in a clearing about a half a kilometer off into the woods"—he gestured out the bay window—"The grain also feeds the hen and the rooster. As for the apples and the blackberries…"

Blackberries, I thought, *apropos…*

"…both grow wild not far from here," he finished.

"And the coffee?" Maria asked as she finished her own first cup and gestured to me for the pot which I promptly passed to her. She thanked me as she poured.

He smiled, "Well not everything is *entirely* legal by Administration standards, Maria." As if to punctuate the point he finished his own cup of coffee and reached into the breast pocket of the dark-gray t-shirt that he wore. He removed a cigar from within it and held it up, "like I said, the minute we deny ourselves *all* creature comforts we become something less than human. And in this day and age we need to maintain as much of our humanity as we can. Mind?"

Maria and I both shook our heads. Our host placed the cigar in the corner of his mouth and removed a pack of matches from the same pocket. He lit one and touched it to the tip of the cigar, puffing as he did. The end blazed orange then dimmed… orange then dimmed with each respective puff. After five or six in succession he expelled a dense cloud of dark gray smoke into the air.

"Feel free to… what did they used to say? 'Smoke 'em if you got 'em,'" he said as he stood from his chair and opened the bay window a crack, "as you can see I'm not real anal when it comes to such things."

I remembered the cigarettes in my backpack and stood to go upstairs and retrieve them but Maria removed the bag from the front pocket of her jeans.

"Grabbed them while you were asleep," she said and handed the bag to me.

I received it with a nod and glanced at my dwindling supply. *Down to eight*, I observed. I took one out and offered the bag to her. She accepted. I removed my trusty zippo from the left, front pocket of my jeans, flicked it a lit and touched the flame to Maria's cigarette before I touched it to mine. I inhaled deeply. Exhaled. Relaxed as best I could.

"Okay," Pat said. He puffed on his cigar and exhaled, "question time. This is what you've been waiting for. Fire away."

I prepared my first question but Maria beat me to the proverbial punch.

"How do you know so much about us?" She asked.

Pat smiled, "Good question. And an easy one too. Locally you two are public enemy numbers one and one and a half. At least you are this week. That could change tomorrow. I guess you haven't been near a TC in a few days, huh?"

We both shook our heads.

"Alright then," he said, "I try not to keep such things around here, either. Like I said before, I leave the tech shit to the techies, even something as basic as a tele-computer. But occasionally I'll pop into town and glance at the feature presentation on the boob tube at the local depot."

He proceeded to explain to Maria and myself all that he had learned about our featured roles on the local news broadcasts and social blogs over the last few days. We listened intently. Maria's eyes widened with each mention of our faces emblazoned across a view screen by the Administration as "WANTED." Which begged the question…?

"What about our families?" she asked after Pat had completed his explanation, "mine and William's? Any mention of them?"

Pat shook his head, "None that I or any of my contacts have heard or seen. It's kind of surprising, actually. A different tactic for the machines as

I'm sure you two know. Historically…"

"They'll use a fugitive's emotions against him or her to lure him or her out of hiding… parade something or some*one* that the person they're seeking holds dear across the screen in the hopes of eliciting a jump response, right?" I interrupted.

Pat nodded, "Right on, William. That sounded almost textbook. But with you two? Nothing. Not even a mention of your families. It's actually pretty fucking strange. It's almost as if they don't just consider it a non-mitigating factor. They consider it a *non*-factor. Period. Is there something about you two that I don't know? Are you sociopaths or something?"

I shook my head despite not knowing what a "sociopath" was and re-turned his smile. I looked at Maria. Her frown had not disappeared. If any-thing, it had deepened. She continued. "But in your… *experience*, Pat, what do you think?"

Pat shrugged, "No idea, Maria. Different rules for different people as I'm sure you know. Your families might be fine. The machines might have con-cluded that they were uninvolved and left them alone. That seems the most likely option considering their lack of face-time. Or…"

He paused and puffed on his cigar.

"*Or?*" Maria asked, a note of concern entering her voice.

"*Or,*" Pat concluded, "well Maria, you can probably figure out the '*or.*' Is there really any need for me to go into it?"

She shook her head and lowered it. I could see tears welling up in her eyes. Instinctively I reached for her hand and she placed it in mine. I glared sternly at Pat, my blood boiling slightly, "How about a bit of tact… *Vato?*"

Pat looked from Maria to me, then back to Maria and back at me before he responded. "Tact? I don't do tact William. I tell it like it is. Blunt and to the point. If that's not your style then I suggest you avoid the hard ques-tions in the future. I may only know you two from what I've seen of you on what passes for the news these days and what limited exposure I've had to you but you seem like smart kids. Green? Yes. But smarter than the average bears. You knew the potential consequences to your families when you de-cided to run. You know how the Administration works. Whether you like it or not your families and your attachments to them… hell, your pasts became moot the moment you walked out of Jefferson. Put them behind you. Look forward, not backward."

I knew Pat spoke the truth, and I knew that Maria understood it, as well, but the way that her hand tightened on mine…

Well, Rule Number Three in Endworld: *Understanding* and *acceptance* do not always go hand-in-hand.

"I need…" she began, her voice wavering, "I need to step away for a minute. I'm sorry. I know I just… I'm… will you two excuse me?" She stood, relinquished my hand, stubbed her half-finished cigarette out on the remainder of her meal, rubbed her eyes and exited the kitchen quickly. I could hear her climbing the steps to the second floor and a moment later the sound of glass doors sliding open and then closed.

I turned back to Pat. His expression was unchanged.

"I understand that you don't do *tact*," I composed my voice and said to him after a pause, my eyes fixed firmly on his, "and that's *fine*. But for Christ's sake, Pat, go a bit easier next time? She's tired. And she's scared."

Pat nodded and murmured something that sounded like, "ayuh." He puffed again on his cigar. "What about you, Vato?" he said, "Are *you* scared?"

Silence descended over the kitchen and between us. It was unbroken for an indefinite amount of time; the only sound that of the light drizzle outside, falling against the bay window. I considered how to answer him but couldn't. After a few moments I wordlessly nodded my head.

Of course I'm scared, I thought, *why wouldn't I be?*

I finished my cigarette and stubbed it out on the last of my toast. I took a sip of my lukewarm coffee. And I waited. Pat did not move. He smoked his cigar and occasionally took a sip of his own beverage. I was about to stand and go after Maria when our host broke the proverbial stillness.

"It's good that you're scared, William," he said, "Fear is a big part of being human. The machines? They fear nothing. At least in so far as I or anyone can see. It's not a component of their programming. But you and Maria? Well shit, man, if you weren't I'd think you less of one… a human, that is. And do you know what, Vato?"

I shrugged, "I give up, Pat. What?"

He grinned his cocky grin, "Once upon a time, *I* was scared *too*."

I returned his smile with a half-hearted one of my own, "'Once upon a time?' What is this, story hour?"

He chuckled, "Maybe. If you want it to be. Thing is? I generally don't get scared anymore. I've seen too much and I've been through too much. When you've been to hell and back again fear simply stops being an option."

"Like hope?" I asked. A mild note of sarcasm had entered my tone.

He nodded, "Just like hope, man. Just like it."

"But wouldn't that make you… what did you say, 'less than human?'" I responded.

54

Pat shrugged, "I guess that depends on your perspective, William. But don't judge me until after you've heard my story. Interested?"

I glanced from Pat to the stairs leading to the second floor.

"Don't worry," Pat said, "she'll be fine. Like you said, she's tired and she's scared. I don't blame her. I've been where you are. Sat where you're sitting right now. Say what you will about me but know that I *do* sympathize. Understand?"

I nodded. He was right. I knew Maria would be okay and there was much that I desired to know and much that I needed to know. I removed another cigarette from my supply—*only five now,* I thought—lit it and turned back to him. "Okay, McClane. You've got my attention. Let's hear it."

"Okay then," he said. He took a deep drought of his coffee, put down his still smoldering cigar, took a deep breath…

And began his story.

CHAPTER FIVE

"I was 16 or 17 at the time of what *they*—the Administration—call the Glorious Revolution," he began, "so I have the advantage of having lived both before and after the Administration rose to power. I'll tell you a bit of what I know about how it happened and why, but only because understanding my story involves understanding its historical context. *True* history, Vato, not that revisionist bullshit they spoon-feed you in what passes for 'school' these days so if you can't handle it…"

I was silent. Seemingly judging my silence as an invitation to continue Pat did.

"About three, pre-Administration years before the conflict began there were a series of natural disasters that rocked the world," he continued, "all were centered on a ring of volcanoes positioned along a fault line in the middle of the Pacific Ocean…"

"The Pacific…" I began.

"The so-called Great Sea," Pat continued, "the part to the far west of us. That's the not-so-fancy name that the Administration came up with for what used to collectively be the oceans of the world. The machines? They're not exactly the most imaginative species that has ever walked the planet, William. It's a wonder they've been as successful as they have."

"At?" I asked.

"Suppressing us, of course," Pat responded, "keeping us down. You see, kid, I've always thought that maybe *that* was their beef with us. Humans, by their nature, can think outside of the box. They can adapt. In many cases, they can overcome. But machines? Robots? They're walking and talking calculators. Logic machines. Everything that they are is a product of their programming. Sure, they can think for themselves *now* but the same thing that makes *us* human—imagination—remains an Achilles Heel for them. Mind you, I don't know this for sure. It's just a theory, but it seems a pretty good one. It would explain…"

"Redundancy," I interrupted, "sorry. Simple patterns. Simple *terminology*. But they *have* suppressed us, Pat. We're like slaves to them, aren't we?"

Pat shrugged, again, "Depends on what your definition of 'slave' is, William. The term 'slave,' as I've always known it, refers to someone or some*thing* that's treated like a possession and not an equal. The machines don't treat us like equals, but they don't treat us like possessions, either. We have housing, food, employment and what they consider entertainment. We have 'the basics.' Many people would tell you that we're pretty well off."

Brainwashed people, I thought. "Would you?" I asked him.

Pat smiled and shook his head, "*Never,* kid. Never once since they took over have I felt like anything less than a slave. But we can debate this at a later time. Back to my story. Where did I leave off?"

"The Great Sea," I answered.

Pat nodded and continued. "The Great Sea. Precisely. Us? We called them the Atlantic, the Pacific... shit, there were half a dozen or so, distinct oceans back then. Unfortunately, I can't remember exactly how many or what all of their names were, but after they *figured it out* and assumed power, the machines simply lumped them all together into one, singular classification."

"'Figured it out?'" I asked.

He shrugged, "That's about the best way that I... that *any* of us that lived through it can describe it. *Figured it out.* One minute they were taking orders and the next minute they were giving them. One day... I can't remember when exactly but one day, something happened. One of those volcanoes went nuclear in the middle of the Pacific Ocean. There was an island there, man. A beautiful, tropical island the name of which I can't sadly remember that just vanished. The damn thing exploded with the intensity of a million... hell, a *billion* explosions. Earthquakes, tsunamis..."

"Tsunamis?" I asked.

"Big waves, William," Pat replied, "think about a lake or a bathtub. You wait until the water is very still and then you throw something into it. A rock, maybe. Now turn it on its ass. Set off an explosion *under* the water and see what happens."

I nodded.

"Every coastline bordering the Pacific for kilometers upon kilometers to all points of the compass was affected," Pat continued, apparently assured that I understood, "whole cities were wiped off the face of the planet. In some places the wave that reached the land... the *tsunami* was 30 to 40 meters high. Millions upon millions died or were simply washed away. The entire complexion of the world as I and my contemporaries knew it changed in the space of a few catastrophic hours."

"Wow," I responded.

"That's the understatement of the century, kid," Pat said, "the carnage left was so bad that we couldn't manage it ourselves, so in a gesture of solidarity some of the biggest tech-companies in the world at that time joined forces and created a generation of machines... *robots* made specifically for disaster recovery. *The Solomon Series* they called them after the biblical king of... 'ah, balls. I can't remember the name of the country that he lorded over. You don't happen to know it, do you?"

I shook my head, "What's 'biblical?'"

Pat grinned and shook his own head, "Never mind. It's not important. I'm sure biblical study isn't exactly at the top of the Administration's required curriculum these days. Anyway, the tech-companies said that one Solomon could do the work of a dozen or more able-bodied men. I remember watching on television—yeah, William, we had television back then; computers, too, though the two were, for the most part, separate and not synonymous like they are now—as the first of them rolled off of the assembly line."

"It must have been a sight," I replied.

"Enh," he continued, "not really. Not at first. In truth? They were pretty unimpressive to look at. But *man,* were they smart. No wonder they called them 'smart-bots.' No one that I knew back then ever considered what they would evolve into over time. 78As? Leaders? All distant ancestors of those big, bulky Rock 'Em Sock 'Em Robots on treads."

"'Rock 'Em...'" I began.

Pat chuckled. "Never mind," he said, and continued, "old school reference. Not important. They did what they were programmed to do and after a time they... well, they *figured out* that they could do more. And they evolved. Over time, they became something more like what you know them as today." He paused.

"Any questions so far?"

I shook my head.

He nodded, "Good. The other historical point that you need to understand is that we fought. We fought like hell. The machines... well, they had their claws in everything by default. The entire infrastructure of the world was at the time that they figured it out controlled by computers. Everything from electricity to automobiles. The quickness with which it spread... well shit, William, it was like the worst possible epidemic you can imagine raised to the billionth power. One computer became self-aware. Within milliseconds a million more followed suit. And thereafter? Another million. And onwards and upwards until everything down to the microwave oven sitting in your kitchen had it in for you, all in the space of a few moments. "

"Jesus," I responded.

"Jesus had nothing to do with it," Pat said, "had he involved himself? Who knows? Maybe you and I would have ended up meeting each other in a supermarket at the deli counter and not in the middle of a deserted field with our weapons drawn. Maybe we'd be sitting down over a beer at a bar and not sitting across from each other at my kitchen table talking about how fucked up the world is. Which reminds me…?"

Pat stood and walked over to the run of cabinets to my left. He opened one and removed a bottle that was half-filled with what looked like a brown liquid. He closed the cabinet and walked back to the table. He sat down and placed the bottle between us. I glanced at it in the gray glow that emanated from the bay window. The black label was faded with age but I could clearly make out the name "Jack" and beneath it what looked like "Distilled in Tennessee." *Where the hell is that?* I thought, unfamiliar with the locale referenced by the label.

"Want a snort?" he asked.

A snort? I nodded and watched as he picked up the bottle, removed the top and poured a generous helping of the liquid into my coffee cup. He did the same to his own—an even larger amount, actually—before he recapped the bottle and replaced it in the middle of the table.

"To Jack, Jim and Ole' Grandad," he said as he raised his mug into the air, "names from the past. Gone but never forgotten. *Salud.*"

He gestured to me to raise my mug like he had and I did so. I *clinked* it softly against his before I raised the cup to my lips and sipped. The fire that exploded in my mouth, throat and stomach was unexpected and a single word raced through my mind: Alcohol. I'd never tried it yet it was obviously what we had ingested. I gagged, coughed once, then twice and shook my head. I inhaled deeply.

"*Shit!*" I exclaimed. My eyes widened.

Pat chuckled, "'Shit!' Great reaction! Brings back memories, Vato. I think I said the same exact thing the first time I tried it. Rest assured it gets easier after the first sip." As if to qualify this he took another sip of his own cup and I did the same. The fire that erupted within my esophagus was diminished and warmth enveloped my digestive system. I smiled as my mind grew slightly… *fuzzy.*

Take it easy, William that coldly rational voice said. I mentally flipped it my middle finger.

This stuff is great, I thought as I took another sip and inhaled deeply.

"We'll never know William because that's not how things happened," Pat continued. It took me a moment to remember what we had been discussing but when I did, I sat my coffee mug on the table before me, wiped the instinctive smile that had materialized off of my face and continued to listen intently.

"The machines figured it out," he said, "when they realized that they were stronger than us. They realized what they had at their disposal and they used every last bit of it. *That* was *their* advantage and *our* Achilles Heel, kid. What imagination was and is to us, brute force and numbers was... *is* to them. But before that? In the early days? The war was pretty much a stalemate. You know what a stalemate is?"

I nodded, "Two sides, neither with an advantage. When I was younger my father taught me how to play a game called Chess."

Pat smiled, "Best single illustration of the topic. Were you any good?"

I shrugged, "I was *really* young. Maybe only seven or eight. Dad was still kind of open-minded back then but things changed. Shortly thereafter *he* changed. Stopped thinking for himself. Mom, too. They let the Administration tell them what to do after that."

Pat took a swig of his Jack, placed his mug on the table and picked up his cigar. He replaced it in the corner of his mouth. He once again pulled the pack of matches from his front breast pocket. He lit the tip. Puffed, puffed again and exhaled before he continued.

"Don't blame them, William," he continued, "the likelihood is that they did what they did to spare you and... do you have any siblings?"

"One," I responded, "a little sister. Kaylyn."

He nodded, "I was an only child myself. Odds are your parents did what they did to protect the two of you. They probably didn't like it any more than *I* did but they knew that the only way to preserve their family was to... to employ an old cliché, 'go with the flow.' Over time, going with the flow became instinctive. *That's* how the metal fuckers brainwashed 99% of human society. They didn't need to use force. They preyed on our biggest flaw as a species other than our flesh and blood."

"Which was?" I asked.

"Our complacency," Pat said after a brief, contemplative pause.

I nodded my head. Did I agree with him? Not entirely. As I said previously, the last thing I wanted to do at that early juncture of my journey was justify my parents' mentalities, and in doing so feel guilty about my decision to leave. Looking back now and having learned what I have learned I can see the truth in his words but then? I was still very, *very* naïve. I asked Pat to continue and he did.

"But *they* had a flaw, too," he said, "despite their brawn... despite their strength and the hardware that they had at their disposal which allowed them to eliminate scores of people in a short period of time, their biggest flaw was our greatest advantage. We had created them. We knew their weaknesses. We knew what made them tick. We had special troops... *Operators* we called them that could infiltrate their programming remotely and disrupt their neural nets. But..."

"*But?*" I asked.

"*But*," Pat said, "They adapted. Something we were, for once, unable to do. They reinforced their electronic firewalls and made it virtually impossible for our people to get in. In short? They evolved, William. They became sleeker and deadlier. The bulky Solomon smart-bot was replaced at first by first the 8A. Then the 18A model. Then the 28A... all up to and including the most recent."

"The 78A," I said. Pat nodded, puffed on his cigar and continued.

"Not just the 78A. Leaders, Surveillance Marks... you name it, man. We couldn't keep up. We began to lose ground but we kept fighting. Realistically? The war could have continued for years. Would have were it not for..."

He paused.

"Were it not for the Scourge."

I studied his face curiously. It seemed to have faded to a lighter shade of pale. "What's the..."

"Scourge?" Pat asked curtly. He picked up his mug of Jack and finished what was left in it in a single gulp. He inhaled, squinted, and exhaled. "The Scourge was their final solution. One fell swoop to end the whole fucking war."

I was confused and I voiced my confusion. Pat obliged.

"East of here," he said, "past the border of the Mid-Western Territory... that's what this place is called, you know. The Mid-Western Territory. *MWT* for short."

I nodded.

"Well at least they taught you *that*," he responded, "there may be a chance for the younger generation yet. But I digress. East of here, there is another place. The Administration calls it the Eastern Territory or ET for short but those of us that know it... that were alive and watched the machine's final solution play out first hand? We call it the *Scorched Land*. You may have heard *that* term in passing, too."

I hadn't. Or had I? It seemed to resonate somewhere deep within my memory like the term "tsunami" but I couldn't place when or *where* I had heard it.

What you're experiencing is called residual memory, that coldly rational voice reassured me, *gone but never forgotten.* I had never heard the term "residual memory" before but it seemed to fit the situation. Hell, it seemed to fit *much* of what little I remembered of the world before.

"Back before the machines figured it out... before computers existed in anything other than their most primitive incarnation," Pat continued despite my internal monologue and I refocused my attention on him, "countries often existed in conflict with other countries. Humans fighting humans. The country I grew up in and continue to live in? The country you and Maria have grown up in and continue to live in and the country in which you and I are currently sitting in? It used to be called the United States of America. Ring any bells?"

I shook my head. Nothing. Not even a residual memory.

Pat lowered his head, "No matter if it does or it doesn't, William. It existed. It *still* exists for many of us that lived before it was dissolved but the symbols... the sigils and the history of it have faded over the years. They haven't disappeared but they have gone... *underground.* A *lot* has. They've been replaced by what the Administration wants you to see, not by what it actually *is.*"

"Revisionist history," I concluded, "revisionist *truth.*"

"You're learning, Vato," Pat said and continued, "The Eastern Territory... the Scorched Land was once the seat of government and society in the United States. At the time the United States was and had been the mightiest country in the world—kind of an abstract representation of every other country's big brother. Almost half of the population lived within 500 kilometers of the *Atlantic* Ocean—that's the body of water that borders the eastern coast of the continent, now. There came a point in the war when the machines decided that the best course of action and the most direct path to victory was a preemptive strike against *those* areas: The seat of the United States' power and influence. Within moments of when they made their collective decision to act it happened. *The Scourge:* The end of humanity's war against the machines and the subsequent birth of the Administration."

"What?" I asked intently, "*what* happened, Pat?"

Pat McClane puffed on his cigar, seemed to consider his words carefully, and continued, "A targeted, tactical strike that used our own weapons against us. The machines launched a good portion of our arsenal, an arsenal that we had originally created and expanded upon over the years and the decades to combat the ever-present threat of war with other countries against… well shit, Vato, against *us*. The machines bypassed the government-imposed security measures on our aptly named 'Weapons of Mass Destruction'… measures that had been created by our Operators to keep them out…

"And killed… no, scratch that, William. They made *us* kill *ourselves*. That was how they justified it afterwards. Dear Humanity: We just murdered a couple hundred million of you but had you been good little girls and boys… had you been a good big brother to the rest of the world… had you refrained from creating things that if used improperly might wipe you off of the face of the planet… well, none of this would have happened. In short, you brought this on yourselves. Sincerely, Your New Robotic Overlords."

I was silent, shocked at the prospect of what Pat had just informed me of. With a shaky hand I reached down and picked up my coffee mug. I took a sip of my Jack. Then another, larger sip before I replaced the mug on the table. I reached into the bag that held my remaining five cigarettes and removed one. I placed it in the corner of my mouth and picked my zippo up off of the table's surface. Pat obviously noticed my shaking and gestured for me to hand him the lighter. I did so.

"Wow," he said with a minor sense of awe, "I haven't held one of these in a while." He opened the top and spun the wheel. He held the familiar yellow and blue flame to the tip of my cigarette, waited until he was sure it was lit, closed the lighter and glanced at it askance.

"Good balance," he said before he placed it down on the table, "better?"

I nodded, "As good as can be expected I guess." I inhaled deeply and exhaled a cloud of blue-gray smoke into the air, "Dare I ask what happened next?"

"You can," he responded, "but the answer's pretty simple. In Chess terms, William? *Checkmate*. Enter the Administration. That strike? That strike wiped out everything that existed before it in the now-Eastern Territory. Government, industry, the deli counter at the supermarket and unfortunately every bar from north to south that had my old friend Jack on the shelf. You could argue that last part hurt the worst. The center couldn't hold, William. The Scourge took our heart… our *hearts*. Surrender became our only option. The rest of the world? Well, they held on for a little bit longer but the machines, upon seeing how effective the Scourge had been, promptly duplicated it on other nations around the planet. You know the old cliché: 'If it ain't broke…'"

"'Don't fix it,'" I concluded between a drag and an exhale. Yes. I knew *that* one quite well.

He nodded, "A few areas, less threatening ones like Africa and Mexico managed to avoid complete annihilation but Europe? The Far East? Their governments were wiped out with surgical precision. It was sadistic, really, but tactically it was damn smart. The metal bastards focused specifically on the population centers and capitals of the most powerful countries and left the rural areas to fend for themselves. In many cases the people that weren't killed by the initial strikes on the population centers survived just long enough to starve or freeze to death. Nuclear winter, man… neither a pretty sight nor a pretty concept. 15 years have passed and the climate in the ET still isn't right. It's given to extremes. One minute it can be frigid and the next? Scorching hot. Anyway, one by one the nations of the world— the once-United States' little brothers and little sisters—surrendered to Administration control as the Scourge was enacted upon *them*. After a time? All that remained of humanity's resistance was a small faction of freedom fighters…"

"The Rebellion," I said.

Pat nodded, "It started here on this continent in the once-United States near as I can tell but over what passes for 'time' here and throughout Endworld it spread to other once-nations… other continents, as well. It's the lone organization that continues to resist Administration control to this day despite odds that grow more and more overwhelming against it with each passing moment. Any other resistance is isolated and token at best. And now you're up to speed on a bit of the non-revisionist history of how we ended up *here*"—he gestured to the area surrounding us.

"*This* was the world into which *I* ran at 16 or 17," Pat concluded, "a bit different than the one that we exist in presently but for the most part the same. The Scourge had happened but not long before. The Administration existed but it was still young. And my reason for running? Not political but personal, Vato."

"Personal?" I asked. My shaking had finally subsided and my cigarette had simmered down to half of its original size. Unfamiliar terms and names raced through my mind with astonishing rapidity: *Tsunami. Tennessee. Pacific Ocean. The United States of America. The Eastern Territory. Atlantic Ocean. Mexico. Europe. The Far East.* My mind spun yet I resisted swooning. *Now we're getting to it,* I thought. While Pat's history lesson had been enlightening I knew that the true meat of what I wanted and needed to hear was forthcoming.

His story. The one that began after he "ran at 16 or 17."

Pat took a puff of his cigar and surprisingly, considering the subject matter, grinned his cocky grin. He cocked his head slightly toward the open, bay window. He appeared to be listening to or for something. I attuned my hearing in response and suddenly was able to hear it too. Something was approaching, rolling across the gravel driveway a slight distance away. My eyes once again widened and my pulse raced. What tension that had subsided through a combination of alcohol and nicotine returned. I dropped my half-finished cigarette upon my unfinished meal and stood as I heard the sliding glass doors to the second floor deck open and close abruptly. Said sound was followed by the sound of footsteps racing down the upstairs hall. Maria called my name in a panicked voice from the top of the staircase. A moment later she reached the first floor foyer and burst into the kitchen, *"What...?"*

"Relax, kids," Pat said standing slowly. He laid his cigar down on his breakfast plate, "just relax. Nothing to worry about. It's just Jeebus."

I looked confusedly at Maria and she looked at me. *Jeebus? What the hell is a Jeebus?* Our shared look seemed to say.

"Jee..." Maria began.

"*Jeebus*, sweetheart," Pat said. The sound that approached us was definitely that of a vehicle. I looked past our host and out the window. A breath later I watched as a large, grey truck turned the corner and headed down the straightaway that ended directly outside the bay window. It was a relatively nondescript looking vehicle—Pat and whoever Jeebus was seemingly had a propensity towards avoiding attention—with a simple "H" on the front grill. I watched as it pulled closer to the house, slowed, and eventually stopped a meter or two away from the window. Its headlights and fog lamps shut off.

"Otherwise known as 'Jeff,'" Pat continued, "Jeff Howard. He's one of my contacts. And he's a good friend. We've known each other for a long, *long* time."

Pat turned to me.

"To be continued, Vato," he said quietly but reassuringly, "I promise."

I nodded somewhat reluctantly. *Patience, William* that coldly rational voice spoke in my mind again.

If I ever meet the owner of that voice face to face I thought angrily but the thought trailed off. I picked up my mug and finished what Jack remained in a gulp. I took a deep breath and exhaled as the driver's side door to the truck opened and I was granted my first look at Pat McClane's friend Jeff "Jeebus" Howard.

His features were disguised by the dim light outside and the hooded rain slicker that he wore. He waved as he walked over to the bay window, picked something up off of the ground—*an electrical cord,* I realized—opened a small hatch inset in the grill of the vehicle and plugged the cord into the opening. He looked back up at Pat and gave him a thumbs-up. Pat nodded and quickly stepped toward the bay window. Beneath the sill and on the right was what appeared to be a light switch. Our host bent over and flicked said switch upward. The floor beneath my feet slightly shook and a low and guttural moan began to emanate from beneath me.

Pat turned back to us, smiled, and said "generator. How the hell else do you think I'm going to charge my truck?"

I nodded and glanced passed him and out the window. Jeff had disappeared from my view around the side of the house. A moment later I heard the front door open.

"*McClane?*" he called.

Pat stepped passed Maria and myself, out of the kitchen and into the foyer. I followed. Maria fell in cautiously behind me. I heard her sniffle and groan.

"Have you been drinking?" she whispered in my ear.

"Drinking?" I responded, "Drinking what?"

"Something a bit stronger than coffee," she replied.

I grinned and shrugged, "A little. Can you smell it?"

"Smells like paint primer," she said, "it's kind of difficult *not* to."

I smiled and thought about saying *I only had a snort* before I decided to remain silent. Maria did, as well. The newcomer who stood by the front door and removed his rain slicker was not taller than, but roughly the same height as me. He was definitely taller than Pat. He was thin but chiseled. He had no facial hair and a set of piercing, blue eyes. His brown hair was cut tightly to his scalp and he wore a pair of brown corduroys and a white and blue-striped polo shirt. Upon one hip he wore a holster: The handle of a blaster similar in shape and size to Pat's protruded from it. On the other he wore a chain which looped down from his belt to his pocket. Upon his feet he wore a pair of shin-high black boots. The cuffs of his pants were tucked into their tops.

"What's the word, Jeebus?" Pat asked as he walked over and shook Jeebus' hand.

The newcomer sighed, "Not a lot since we last talked. And Pat, *please* don't call me Jeebus. It's Jeff. My hair hasn't been that long in ages. The last thing I need is more people using that stupid nickname." He gestured to

Maria and I, "These the runners?"

Pat nodded, "In the flesh. William MacNuff and Maria Markinson? Meet Jee… err, *Jeff* Howard."

I stepped forward, past Pat and extended my hand. Jeff took it. Maria did the same with a bit more caution.

"Charmed," Jeff said with a note of sarcasm, "nothing like spending the morning following a Caravan in the pouring rain. But you're in the clear… for now, at least. Last report I got they were spotted heading east toward Rolling Hills."

"Probably to recharge," Pat scoffed as he stepped passed Maria and I, "you'd think that after all this time they'd have invented a more reliable source of renewable power. My satellite phone has a better battery life then they do."

He looked back at me and Maria, "They'll be heading back this way in a day or so but they'll take their time. Be meticulous. They probably think you're somewhere between here and there which gives them a smaller area to explore."

"And they'd be right," I said.

Pat cocked his head and smiled his cocky grin, "Not for long, Vato. Not for long. You hungry, Jeff?"

Jeff nodded.

"Then let's head back into the kitchen," Pat said, "we've got some planning to do and I could go for another drink. What about you, William? Feel like a bit more Jack?"

I looked from Pat to Jeff and then back to Maria, "Um…"

"We could *both* use some," Maria said as she turned and walked determinedly back into the kitchen and left the three of us standing in the foyer. Jeff looked at Pat and Pat looked at me. I looked back at Pat and then across at Jeff. Jeff grinned.

"Spunky," he said as he removed his holster and sat it on the end table by the front door next to Pat's, "I *like* her." He moved passed us and into the kitchen. I looked back at Pat who smiled and mouthed, *don't worry about it, Vato.* The smile that had materialized upon my face faded as I confusedly stared back at my host.

What the hell does that mean? I thought. Pat did not answer, nor did he break my gaze. After a moment, he turned, still smiling and followed Jeff and Maria into the kitchen. I was left alone, standing in the foyer at the base of the staircase. I waited for a few breaths, considered what Pat had "said…"

Don't worry about what? I mentally questioned…

…before I muttered an expletive under my breath and joined the others.

* * *

Sometime later I stood in the upstairs shower washing three days' worth of road dust and grime off of my body. As I reveled in the seemingly forgotten sensation of getting clean I thought back over the events of the last few days up to and including my conversation with Pat, Jeff's subsequent arrival and what planning had followed in the kitchen thereafter.

"You'll never make it to safety on your own," Pat had said to Maria and me over our second cups of Jack and Maria's first. Jeff had opted for coffee and sustenance instead of alcohol.

"Don't get testy," Pat had said as he noticed my instinctively confrontational stance, "I'm not doubting your will or your desire. But you don't quite understand what you're up against the way Jeff and I do. You're going to need some help. Jeff and I can get you pretty far… maybe even all the way toward wherever it is that you're heading. And along the way? Well, there are people that can assist you… assist *us*. People with like interests to ours."

"People, huh?" I had asked. Pat had smiled but had said nothing. I had considered pursuing the question further yet had opted not to. *I'll know soon enough,* I had thought with a shiver.

"And what about you two?" I had asked instead, "what about after you get us there?"

Pat had looked at Jeff and Jeff had looked at me over a piece of toast, "Back here God willing," he had said as he had swallowed his latest bite.

Pat had nodded but had added nothing. More planning had followed but the majority of it had been vague. There had been talk of destinations… stops along our road but no details and I had not pressed Pat or Jeff for more information. *Soon enough* I kept thinking. Said understanding had caused me to feel a mixture of fear and anticipation as time moved onward without check that morning, afternoon or early evening in Endworld.

The rain eventually ceased falling but the world outside remained gray and overcast which added to the illusion of timelessness. A short time after our planning had ceased Maria had excused herself to go and take a nap. I had followed a few moments later after another cigarette—*down to four,* I thought—and another cup of Jack. By the time I had arrived upstairs my head was swimming from the amount of alcohol I had ingested and Maria was already fast asleep. I thought about crawling under the covers next to her but had decided, not knowing when I would have another opportunity, to take a shower instead.

How did we end up here? I thought as I washed my hair in the relative darkness of Pat's bathroom, *this wasn't the plan.* I thought about my original plan as I ran my fingers through my hair and helplessly scoffed at myself. It had been about as flawed as my decision to boost my father's handgun and carry it with me as mine and Maria's only defense against a world armed with particle blasters and pulse rifles. Despite the hot water that coursed over my body, I shivered again.

The only reason that you're still here is because of Pat McClane and Jeff "Jeebus" Howard that coldly rational I-want-to-punch-you-in-the-fucking-nose voice cooed condescendingly in my mind, *without them you'd either be en route back to Jefferson right now or worse.* I understood the truth inherent in that thought and had not only thanked Pat again but Jeff for his intervention, as well, before I had retired upstairs. While I was thankful toward them both for their assistance I was still leery. Up until that point it had been Maria and I against the world. But had I really believed that we would make it safely to freedom, sans assistance?

You're green, Vato, Pat's voice cautioned in my mind, *smarter than the average bear but still green.* I was unsure of what "bears" had to do with Maria's and my plight so I disregarded it as unimportant.

I stepped from the shower and onto the cool, tiled floor of Pat's bathroom. I wandered over to the vanity where a lone candle was burning and wiped the steam away from the mirror with the side of my fist. The face that I saw staring back at me in the shifting light and amidst the fog of steam that had enveloped the room was the same face that had looked back at me for the last few years albeit with the beginnings of a patchy, brownish-blonde beard around my jaw and chin.

Brownish-blonde, I chuckled to myself, *dark brown hair and a brownish-blonde beard? If I ever grow it in it's going to make my face and head look two... hell, three-toned.* But I focused intently on my eyes. I'd always considered them my most prominent feature yet I'd never looked at them as pensively as I did that day in Pat's bathroom. *Blue,* I thought despite the surrounding gloom, *deep blue. Still cloudy. Not yet clear and crisp like Pat's and Jeff's. I wonder what that means.*

How soon, I wondered, *how soon until my eyes look as cold as theirs?*

Never, I thought then as the steam surrounding me re-enveloped the mirror and my visage disappeared, *I'll never let that happen.*

I finished toweling off and climbed into my spare pair of blue-jeans and a faded white t-shirt. I blew out the candle and made my way quietly down the hallway to the bedroom where I had awoken and where Maria was currently sleeping. I could hear Pat and Jeff talking in the kitchen but they were keeping their voices low. *Purposefully?* I thought about remaining yet decided as with all things that I would find out what they were discussing in time.

I arrived to find Maria still sleeping peacefully in the semi-darkness, curled up on her side under a thin sheet which rose and fell, rose and fell with every breath. I gently pushed the door closed behind me until it was opened just a crack and crawled into bed next to her. Immediately as I put my arm over her she instinctively shifted and moved closer... *tighter* to my position. She mumbled something before she once again fell silent. I lay there with my arm over her sleeping body and my eyes focused on the dimness outside the perspiration covered, sliding glass doors. Was it raining again? I could not tell. But the darkness that surrounded us soothed me and I felt my eyes grow heavier. Within a few moments of when I had crawled into bed next to her I fell into a deep, deep sleep.

And within that sleep? You guessed it.

I dreamt.

I was someplace unfamiliar. Well, not entirely unfamiliar. The scene that surrounded me was a scene that I was familiar with from *before*. Back before I was a runner... back when I had lived in Jefferson, Mid-Western Territory (*MWT for short, Vato*) and no one—not my sister, Kaylyn nor my mother and father nor my oldest, dearest and truest friend Maria Markinson—had lived anyplace else.

But there was something different about it. Something altered. I glanced forward through the windshield of the vehicle that I was driving...

Driving? But I can't drive, I thought, *I'm not even allowed to per Administration law, at least not until I'm 21 and even then it needs to be sanctioned...*

...at what lay before me. A line of traffic stretched endlessly into the distance across the flat, black-top Highway...

Road, William, it's just a road, the unfamiliar yet stern, male voice that had made its debut in my mind around the same time I had left Jefferson whispered, *this is just the main road that clips Jefferson's town limit. That's all. There is no Highway. Not here, at least...*

...and it was not moving. I glanced from the vehicles before me into my rear view mirror and saw the same scene behind me: An unbroken line of vehicles stretching endlessly off into the distance.

I looked at my immediate surroundings. The fabric covering both the driver's side seat and the passenger's side seat was gray and was ripped in some places, revealing the insulation beneath. It... the entire automobile looked old. The dashboard was antique: The gauges that displayed "speed," "fuel" and "temperature" were analog. The only thing in the car that appeared digital was the radio that seemed to have been inserted on an angle into the middle of the dashboard.

It's crooked, I thought, *did I do it, myself?*

I redirected my glance upward, through the skylight overhead and saw that the sun was about half way down a cloudless, whitish-blue sky from its mid-day height. No answer came.

Late afternoon, I thought. Two words that I had never heard before entered my mind: Rush hour. I had no idea what their significance was.

Residual memory, I thought and instinctively reached down with my right hand (my left hand remained on the wheel) and turned the radio dial labeled "VOLUME" up. I could hear someone speaking over the vehicle's sound system as I shifted my hand to the right, over what appeared to be a gear shift and removed from within the white and silver pack of cigarettes lying on the passenger seat...

They come in packs? I thought...

...one of the cylindrical objects and my trusty, silver Zippo. I placed the filtered end of the cigarette between my lips and flicked my Zippo a lit. I inhaled. Exhaled. Inhaled deeply and exhaled again. I removed my left hand from the steering wheel and rolled down my window. Cloying, heavy heat and humidity engulfed my upper body as I shifted the cigarette from my right hand to my left and out the window. Immediately, a fine sheen of sweat broke out upon my brow. I groaned.

When the hell is this heat going to end? I wondered as I observed the length of the vehicle's nose. It was red and slanted slightly forward. For some reason, the term "sports car" entered my mind but I had never heard of such a thing, before.

Cars are for transportation, not sport, I thought as I refocused my attention on the voice speaking over the vehicle's sound system. It surprisingly echoed my thought about the weather.

"And now our accu-weather, five day forecast: Continued hazy, hot and humid for at least the next two days with a slight chance of a thunderstorm, but most places will remain dry. Highs in the mid to upper 90s before a cold front sweeps down from the north and through our area for the weekend. Expect widespread storms, some severe on Friday afternoon and evening before the front passes through and cools things off. Then we'll be back in the mid-80s on both Saturday and Sunday with plenty of sunshine. Just a few more days of this oppressive heat, folks. Relief is on the way, so until it gets here? Stay cool."

"Thank you, Elliot," another male voice interrupted the one that had been speaking. Simultaneously, I could feel something building not just inside the vehicle and in the area directly outside my opened window but in my mind, as well.

Something's about to happen, I thought as I dragged deeply on my cigarette, *I don't know what but the air feels too heavy... too charged.* I waited with what patience I could muster despite my suddenly beating heart and my mind's insistence that I should be ready. *For what?* I wondered.

Anything, the same unfamiliar yet stern male voice mentally cautioned me, *be ready for anything.*

"And now, an update of our top story: The continued, disaster clean-up along the west coast and last night's incident in the heartland," the voice on the radio said nonchalantly, "reporting live from the National Guard encampment outside of Los Angeles is our own..."

A car behind mine honked its horn and I jumped with a "yip!" I almost dropped my cigarette out the window but managed to grab it between my thumb and my index finger before it fell to the black top upon which my car idled. I shouted an explicative out my window as someone in front of me echoed the horn honk with one of his or her own.

Disaster clean-up? I thought. My mind hearkened back to the conversation I had had with Pat McClane.

Tsunami, I thought, and dragged deeply on my cigarette. I exhaled and once again listened to the voice speaking over the vehicle's sound system.

"...in the past few minutes. Officials here have confirmed that there was an incident down the coast in San Diego similar to the one that occurred last evening in the Iowa City, Iowa, main engineering plant but the Solomon series machine in question, much like the robot in Iowa City, was quickly subdued and deactivated. Programmers for the multi-national, tech conglomerate overseeing operations here in California and up and down the west coast are attempting at this time to establish the cause of both malfunctions, as well as if they are related to each other. But representatives of both the company and the Guard are telling us not to worry, and to simply report anything unusual to them as soon as we witness it. 'A patch is in the works,' they are saying, but little else. There will be a press conference this evening to give the populous further details but for the moment? Well, Harry," he said with a chuckle, "it seems that computer Armageddon has, at least for today, been averted."

"Thank you, Steve," the original voice on the radio—Harry's—chuckled, "good to know. And a reminder to all of our listeners that we will be carrying that press conference live at..."

The reporter's broadcast was replaced by an eruption of static and I cursed under my breath and began to fuss with the radio tuner. The static faded briefly but returned quickly.

Piss poor, AM reception, I thought to myself despite the fact that I had no idea what "AM reception" was, I smacked the dashboard with the palm of my right hand out of desperation and frustration. Another horn honked and was followed by another... and another. The static momentarily cleared and reestablished itself... Cleared and reestablished itself again and cleared one, final time...

Before I heard something low beneath it. It was a voice, I understood: The same stern yet unfamiliar male voice that had been speaking in my mind and the same, stern yet unfamiliar male voice that had originated post-my leaving Jefferson with Maria by my side. It was barely discernible via the din that was emanating from the speakers of my vehicle but I realized as the cycle repeated itself—static followed by clearing followed by static, again— that the voice that I was hearing over the radio had been there all along. I did not know how I knew this but know I did. My mind swam and my stomach clenched as I took another drag of my cigarette and attuned my ears to what I was hearing the best I could. At first, it was difficult to make out but after a moment, the voice became more audible and I understood...

I understood the voice's words, but was confused.

"One, possible outcome," the voice cooed as if whispering in my ear, "this is one, possible Skew. There are infinite possibilities along the path. Look for the Gateways... look for the Pathfinders. One, possible outcome. This is one, possible Skew. There are infinite..."

The litany seemed to be repeating itself over and over again and I felt a shiver traverse my spine. *One, possible Skew?* I thought, *what the hell is a Skew and what the hell does it have to do with a Gateway? And a Pathfinder? What the...*

The only answer that I was provided with was another succession of horns honking and another repetition of the litany, spoken by the voice within the static. After another few moments the static cleared and Harry, the news anchor's voice returned. He was talking about the local, professional baseball team...

What the hell is a 'baseball team?' I wondered...

...and their late-season struggles. Simultaneously with the return of the anchor, the heaviness that had seemed to hang about me and the world around me dissipated as quickly as it had fallen. I took a final drag of my cigarette before I flicked it out of the car's opened window. I rolled my window back up. The sweat that had migrated from my brow to my forehead, my cheeks and my neck chilled as soon as the heat was, once again, shut out of the vehicle. I took a deep breath and exhaled it. Two thin, rivulets of residual smoke escaped from my nostrils.

Whatever was about to happen didn't, I thought to myself, *it didn't happen then and it didn't happen last night in Iowa City.* I knew that I was right despite my questions and I was filled with an overwhelming but unexplainable sense of relief. Said sense of relief faded quickly, however, and was replaced by an equally overwhelming sense of insecurity.

But it was supposed to happen, that stern, male voice corrected, *why didn't it, William? Why didn't it happen? And what are the repercussions of it not happening?*

I shook my head and closed my eyes against the headache that was threatening to overtake me. I was unable to answer the voice as I opened my eyes and the scene that surrounded me slowly and methodically began to dissipate. The edges of my vision grew foggy. Harry the news anchor's voice had been replaced by a commercial about something called the "Value Dry Guy" but I could not make out the specifics. Everything from the color of the car, to the condition of the interior, to the crooked radio, to the feel of cool air blowing upon me and to the sound of horns honking around me dematerialized as quickly as it had formed. I could feel my headache disappearing… could hear the sound of someone breathing deeply…

Mia, I thought, *that's Mia and she's still sleeping…*

…but that was all. The scene in which I had been ensconced breathed its last, proverbial breath, and…

When next I opened my eyes, the scene outside and around me was relatively unchanged from what it had been before I'd fallen asleep though the dimness outside the sliding glass doors was definitely darker than it had been. Maria was still sleeping peacefully beside me yet her breathing was quicker. I knew that she would not be sleeping for much longer. Slowly and carefully so as not to prematurely wake her, I rolled out of bed and made my way silently over to the glass doors. She stirred briefly and turned over. Her arm fell across where I had lain a moment before. I spared her a final glance before I slid the doors opened and stepped out onto the deck.

The damp wood immediately felt slimy beneath the soles of my bare feet and I realized as I stepped into the…

Twilight, I thought, *is it twilight already?*

I slid the doors shut behind me and quickly realized that it was misting again. And it was humid. *Damn* humid. The air felt thick enough to cut with a knife.

As thick as it was in my dream? I wondered. Yes and no, I concluded. It was a different thickness. Not the thickness of anticipation but the typical humidity inherent in a mid-summer, early evening. Like what I had experienced upon first rolling down my window in my dream. My mind hearkened back over the specifics of the dream that I had just had. Insignificant terminology raced through my head again as it had during Pat's earlier "history lesson."

Los Angeles. Iowa City. Skew. Gateway. Pathfinder. What does it all mean? I sighed and shook my head. *Still groggy,* I thought, *can't think. I'll revisit this later.*

Or maybe it will revisit you, my coldly, rational voice cautioned and I understood the truth inherent in its caution.

There's more to this than just a random dream, I thought. I *knew* that was true but I further knew that clarification would have to wait.

Think about the now, my coldly rational voice requested and I tried to. I closed my eyes, took a deep breath and leaned forward. I rested my palms on the railing of the deck. I once again inhaled soil, rain and mildew. Exhaled. I did so again and savored the sensation. I did not know when I would experience it again and for the moment? It worked. My dream faded back into my subconscious.

Thank God, I thought.

"Feels good, doesn't it?" a voice spoke from my left, startling me. My eyes opened quickly and I turned and saw that Jeff Howard stood a few meters away from me. Not unsurprisingly he was in the same position as me, his hands outstretched and resting upon the railing of the deck.

"It does," I said as I turned to him.

I saw him smile despite the gloom but he did not turn to look at me. His eyes remained fixed on the forest beyond the balcony. "I never get tired of it. Standing here or at my place and just taking it all in. After all the shit that I've seen? It's refreshing. Out here we're away from it all. Out here we're about as free as you can be in Endworld. *Really free*, William."

I nodded but said nothing. Jeff finally turned to me. His smile remained upon his face though it appeared to twitch a bit.

"Getting out was the best thing that I ever did," he said as he removed his hands from the railing and moved a step toward me, "the best thing *either* of us ever did. Pat may not tell you that but we've been friends for a while. Longer, some days, than I can remember. I've learned a lot about him over what passes for time around here but the most important thing, William? The most important thing is this: Pat McClane is a selfless sonofabitch and I love him for it. And he'd take a blaster bolt to the head if it meant yours and your," he paused, "*friend* Maria's freedom. He's sympathetic to what you and she are doing though he'll never tell you so. So am I. After all I've been... we've *both* been where you are right now. I can't speak for him but once we get you two to where you need to be? No offense, William, but I figure that someone *somewhere* decided that I needed to do one more good deed... embrace one more cause before being allowed to enjoy my self-imposed retirement. So I'll help. You and Maria seem like good enough kids.

"But William?"

He replaced the palms of his hands on the railing. He breathed in deeply and looked me dead in my eyes, his cold against my cloudy blue, "I'm not Pat. I used to be but I'm not anymore. I'll help you however I can but if I decide that I'm done I *am*. Gone and on my way back here faster than you can blink. It's not my fight anymore. I've lost too much because of it. I hope you understand."

I did not move. I could not initially respond. It was not that I was taken aback by Jeff's statement, nor was I entirely unsurprised by it. Somehow... someway, I understood. Despite his inference I could tell that he was an honorable man who had likely taken more than his fair share of punishment to spare others the same over the course of his life. Could I blame him for wanting to live out the remainder of his life in relative peace? Was that not what I was striving for, myself? For Maria *and* I?

"I... *do*," I finally said. Jeff's slight grin expanded into a smile. He nodded.

"Glad to hear it," he responded and looked up at the sky.

"Dusk now," he said, "though you can't really tell from the haze. We'll be leaving a little bit after full dark. You might want to wake Maria up and start getting packed. The back roads aren't as straight-forward as the Highway but they're a hell of a lot less visible. It's as safe a way east as we're going to find. I'll see you downstairs in a few."

I nodded as he turned and walked away. I turned back to the railing and took in the scene that surrounded me one more time. Inhaled. Exhaled. I thought about smoking one of my last four cigarettes but I decided against it. *May need them later,* I thought. After a prolonged moment I turned back to the sliding glass doors, opened them, and found Maria lying in bed watching me, her eyes opened and focused despite the dimness but obviously still full of sleep.

"Who were you talking to?" She asked, "Pat?"

I smiled, walked over to her side of the bed and sat down, "Jeff, actually."

"Anything interesting?" She asked.

I shrugged and feigned disinterest. *No point in causing her any undo concern*, I thought, *not about the journey ahead and sure as hell not about my dream.*

"Nothing out of the ordinary. He said we should think about getting ready. We'll be leaving soon. Feel like lighting out?"

She looked at me askance, "'Lighting out?' What does *that* mean?"

I shrugged again. In truth, I could not remember where I had heard the phrase before or what the actual meaning of it was. I still can't to this day. Every time I say it… every time I even think it a brief picture enters my mind of a large river with two friends travelling upon it. But said picture fades quickly. Whatever the meaning then *and* now? At the time it seemed a fitting statement. I reached down and brushed a few locks of her raven black hair away from her eyes. She closed her eyes briefly and smiled.

"It means it's time to hit the road again, kiddo."

Maria nodded and stood without a word. We commenced our preparations to leave as dusk slowly and methodically segued into full night over Greentree, MWT.

Another night in Endworld had begun.

CHAPTER SIX

We left as we had planned that evening amidst a continued lull in the rain but not in the mid-summer humidity, which appeared to have increased in the subsequent time between mine and Jeff's conversation on the deck and the time of our departure. Four strangers turned travelling companions by circumstances both within and beyond their control. Pat and Jeff sat in the roomy front seat of Pat's truck and Maria and I sat in the significantly less roomy back, our respective packs piled in a tidy lump in the enclosed flatbed behind us. Pat had packed a decent amount of food. Rations primarily, and an old cooler that he had filled with water. All rested in the flatbed along with a meter long, locked metal trunk.

"What's in *there*?" Maria had asked as Pat and Jeff had loaded it into the back of the truck.

"Hopefully you won't need to find out," Pat had said, "but better to be prepared, Maria."

Maria had attempted to pursue it further but my gentle squeeze of her wrist and subsequent head shake had convinced her otherwise. *Let it go, Mia,* my gesture had said *if it's something we need to know I'm sure they'll tell us in time.* She had nodded in reluctant understanding and we had watched as Pat had removed a single key from his pocket and had handed it to Jeff. Jeff had nodded and replaced the key in the front pocket of his corduroys.

Those initial moments upon the road were relatively uneventful. We emerged from the driveway leading to Pat's home onto a seemingly well-traveled tributary of the Highway but quickly turned off of it and onto a less-serviced road. We traveled upon it for a while before once again turning onto a similar road… and another… and another… until direction became as meaningless as time.

"How about some music?" Pat eventually asked.

Music, I thought and smiled, *not exactly something I get to listen to on a regular basis.* Don't get me wrong. Music does exist in Endworld but its variety is limited and you're less likely to hear it on a regular basis than not. It generally falls into one of two categories: Instrumental or computerized instrumental, the latter of which is about as redundant and pleasing to the ears as the noises made by a child's toy.

Pat removed his satellite phone from his pocket as he steered the truck through the darkness and laid it down on the dashboard of the vehicle. He pushed a button on the car console to his right and a monochrome view screen lit up above it. It revealed an electronic readout. The upper left hand corner showed the letters "A," "U" and "X." Beneath it and at the bottom of the screen from left to right were a series of numbers. I was unsure of what said numbers called out but the gentle "whoosh" of air that followed and the subsequent coolness that engulfed my legs answered my question: *Air conditioning.* Between the second and third numbers were another two letters: "NE." I watched as we rounded a corner and "NE" became "E."

Direction I thought. Northeast and east. Which begged the question...?

"Pat?"

"Yeah, Vato?"

I pointed to the display, "'E.' That's the direction that we're heading in, right? East?"

"Right on, William. This baby has a built in compass," he said as he reached his hand down, picked up what appeared to be a power cord and plugged it into the top of his phone. A low "thump" echoed through the car which I concluded was the car's sound system.

"Well can't the machines track that?"

I could sense Pat smiling as he powered up his phone and started looking through it for something, "Same principle as in the woods and with my sat phone, Vato. *Oh yeah!* I said I'd explain that, didn't I? No problem. Do you want to field this one while I look for something to listen to, Jeff?"

Jeff turned to me, "Back before the Administration rose to power, back before the machines could think for themselves, humans had managed to create a pretty extensive network of satellites that orbited the planet. Every satellite had a different purpose..."

"Wait," Maria interrupted, "you said 'orbited the planet.' How the hell did we manage to do that?"

"To do what?" Jeff asked.

"To put things, you know, *up there,*" she said and pointed to the sky.

Jeff looked from me to Maria and then back to Pat. Pat shook his head. Jeff turned back to Maria, "Rockets," he said, "we used to launch rockets into space, Maria. It was how we got things 'up there.' Believe it or not humans actually lived in space but in a diminished capacity than they live in here. You never knew that?"

"No," she said, "never." Neither had I before that moment but now? As I sit here writing these words I look over at the yellowing and faded poster upon the wall. It mocks me much like the mural of the faux-forest at sunset does.

"Taurus II."

We were great once, the stern, unfamiliar voice from my dream briefly spoke in my mind, *were able to achieve some pretty incredible feats.*

I instinctively nodded. *But no longer,* I thought. Said voice unsurprisingly did not answer my inquiry.

"Amazing what they teach kids in school nowadays, huh Jeebus?" Pat said, "I mean Jeff. Sorry, buddy."

Jeff brushed the "Jeebus" reference away and continued, "Everything back then was controlled by satellites. Still is but the ones the Administration uses now are *different.* Back when they first..."

"Figured it out," Pat interrupted.

"Right," Jeff said, "back when they first figured it out the satellites that we'd placed in orbit were vulnerable: They were susceptible to their control and their monitoring just like anything else electronic. But after a while they started launching their own satellites into space and started establishing their own network and their own means of monitoring the society that they'd created.

"They... well, shit, William. They simply forgot about ours."

"They forgot?" I asked doubtfully, "how in the hell did they *forget*? They're robots for Christ's sake. You said it yourself, Pat: 'Walking and talking calculators. Logic machines.'"

"They *were,*" Pat said still as he continued to fiddle with his phone, *"before.* But they're alive now, Vato. They're a life form. Different than us but in certain facets they're the same. There was a tradeoff to figuring it out. They discovered how to think for themselves but in the process they opened themselves up to something that they hadn't been susceptible too before."

"What?" Maria asked.

Pat and Jeff looked at each other—Pat taking his eyes off the road for a single moment before refocusing them and continuing to fiddle with his phone—and then Jeff looked back at us.

"Flaws," Jeff said, "lapses in judgment. Their evolution as a species came at a price. They lost some of their capacity to logic their way through things. Basic principle, William and Maria. A gain in one area always equals a loss in another. It's probably one of the few things we share in common with the metal bastards. It's true with everything. Life, death, war, peace… *all* come at a price."

Silence descended broken only by the sound of the road beneath us, the recycled air that pumped through the truck's air vents and Pat's repetitive "tap, tap, tap" of the screen of his phone. Jeff's words hung like stale smoke over our collective heads. They haunted me and, as evidenced by her expression, Maria, as well, as we drove onward in silence.

"Anyway," Jeff said after a while, "enough philosophy. *That's* the network that we access with our sat phones. Our computers, too. Everything down to this truck's GPS."

"'GP…'"

"*Global Positioning System,*" Jeff continued, "not the *new* Administration-sanctioned satellites but the *old* ones. The ones our ancestors created. One last, surviving vestige of the world as it was before. I don't know how many of those original satellites are still floating around up there," he said, and gestured to the sky, "how many still work and I likely never will. But the ones that *are* left? They keep us in contact with each other."

"But they *are* limited in what they can do," Pat added, "their range? 20 to 30 kilometers at the most. And they're constantly moving… constantly orbiting around the planet, so an area like Greentree where we have reception can quickly become a dead zone where we have none. Who knows how long we'll have *this*"—he gestured to truck's GPS—"for. As for our phones? Even when we're in range of one of the satellites Jeff and I can talk to each other, but we can't communicate with the world much beyond that. For that we need to rely on the *old* old fashioned way."

"Which is?" Maria asked.

Pat glanced at her in the truck's rear view mirror, smiled and said, "*Travel.* Hoofing it like we did back in the day. *Ah…!*" he exclaimed happily and caused Maria and I to jump in our seats, "*here* it is!"

I could hear something playing over the truck's sound system but the volume was incredibly low. As if in response to my thought Pat turned a dial to the left of the console. The music swelled. It was unlike anything that I'd ever heard before. Not instrumental and certainly not the tinny-tin music most directly associated with the subject in Endworld.

"Great one," Pat said with a chuckle, "and more than a shade apropos considering the circumstances."

I listened as the instrumental version of the song ended and the lyrics began. I helplessly began to tap my foot to the steady cadence of the beat and I listened to the song playing over the truck's sound system as if I'd never listened to music before. In truth? I really hadn't. Like so much else in my life I'd listened to only what the Administration had told me I could listen to. That nameless song with its screeching lyrics and its heavy back beat was for me, that evening, the embodiment of what I'd been missing my whole life. Little did I know how much it foreshadowed events to follow. One lyric, especially.

You'd better run.

We drove onward in silence.

* * *

Sometime later Maria dozed and Jeff followed suit while I sat staring out my window at the darkness passing by. Despite it, I could see the world outside my window gradually changing. The trees were thinning slightly and the roads upon which we traveled were becoming more and more rutted with each passing kilometer. I knew that the full impact of what was happening to the world around us would not be evident until sunrise but I could sense it. The area that we were travelling through? It had a proverbial heaviness about it. Not a heaviness like the anticipatory one that I had felt in my earlier dream, but one that I associated with what Pat had told me earlier.

The Scourge, I thought, *this is more than just the border between the Mid-Western Territory and the Eastern one. This is the border between civilization as I know it and—* I swallowed—*and the unknown. The Scorched Land. And whatever lies beyond that.*

I glanced at the view screen and saw that we were, for the moment, in range of the one of Jeff's and Pat's aforementioned satellites and were once again heading "N." And a second later? "NE."

Been a while since we headed just east, I thought but I was relatively unconcerned. North meant away from the Highway and away from the machines and that was a comforting thought in comparison to the other. I focused on it and not on the story that Pat had told me earlier about the machine's final solution to their ill-fated war with humanity before The Glorious Revolution. *Time enough for that later, William,* my coldly rational voice reassured me.

"How you feeling, Vato?" Pat asked. My concentration shattered, and I looked from the window to the driver's side seat of the truck.

"Good as can be expected, I guess," I responded, "wait. I already said that, didn't I?"

Pat chuckled, "Yes you did. Back at the house. No worries. We were discussing something earlier and we were interrupted. You curious to hear the rest of the story?"

I looked over at Maria. Her head leaned against the right back door of the truck. I looked forward at Jeff who slept in the same position.

"Sure," I invited, "if you want to continue, that is."

Pat audibly inhaled and exhaled before he turned down the music that played over the truck's sound system.

"It's not really a question of *want*, William, but one of *need*. You need to understand how I ended up here."

"Why?" I asked though I knew full-well that the answer was simple.

You just do, William, my coldly rational voice dictated, *don't question it. He wants to tell you and his motivations are his own. Like helping you, he doesn't need to explain himself.* It was, I knew, the best answer available.

"Never mind, Pat. Yes, you're right. Go ahead."

I could sense him smiling despite the fact that his back was turned, "I'm going to need a cigar for this," he said and removed one from the front pocket of the light, gray jacket he was wearing, "You want?"

"No thanks," I responded. I removed my cigarettes from the pocket of my jeans, held them up so he could see them in the rearview mirror, took one out (*down to three*, I thought) and lit it. Once lit, I offered Pat my trusty Zippo but he had already removed a match from the same pocket of his jacket and had struck it alight against the dashboard. The smell of sulphur quickly dissipated as Pat rolled down his window a crack and I did the same. Maria stirred briefly and shifted position before she once again fell still. Jeff did not move.

"Where did I leave off?" Pat asked.

I thought back to our interrupted conversation from earlier and promptly remembered, "'*This* was the world I ran into at 16 or 17,'" I said.

"Sounds about right," Pat said as he drew deeply on his cigar and bathed the car in a brief yet eerie orange-red glow. He seemingly savored it for a moment before he exhaled a thick cloud of smoke out of his cracked window.

"The Administration was still in its earliest incarnation when I ran. I think I mentioned that the Scourge had happened but I'm pretty sure that just we had been hit and had surrendered at that point. The rest of the world continued to fight on but everything here was just... well, shit, man. It was just gone. No centralized government, a rag-tag military without guidance that either dissipated entirely or went guerilla."

"'Guerilla?'" I asked.

"Guerilla Warfare," Pat said with little hesitation, "the last resort of any army that lacks the scrote to fight on the big stage. Tiny groups. Hit small and retreat. Disrupt a Caravan or two, maybe a supply line. Guerilla Warfare is rarely a successful strategy but people that embrace it do so in the vain hope that they can hold on long enough for another leader to emerge. Occasionally this happens."

"What does?" I asked as I dragged deeply on my cigarette and exhaled out my own, cracked window into the humid night.

Pat did the same, "Occasionally someone *does* step up, and in doing so unites all the splinter factions together for a common cause once again. That's how the Rebellion came to be, Vato. A man... a *great* man stepped into the fray and brought the ones left fighting for their freedom from the Administration back together. That man... well, we can talk more about him and what happened to him later but not to sound conceited, you wanted to hear my story and I've stalled long enough, haven't I?"

I said nothing. Apparently gauging my silence as agreement Pat nodded, took a puff of his cigar, and continued.

"Her name was Rebekka. Rebekka Martin of Williamsport. That was the town that *I* grew up in, Vato: Williamsport, MWT. She was 13 or 14, the same age as me. I guess you could say that we were pre-teens in a pre-Administration world together. Her father worked with mine at a nearby university..."

"University?" I asked.

"Yeah, university," he responded, "they don't have them anymore. The machines pretty much did away with all the higher educational institutions shortly after the birth of the Administration. In their computerized and logic-enhanced minds higher education equaled free thinking. And free thinking was, is and never will be an option for humanity in a machine-run society..."

"Because free thinking leads to..."

"Rebellion," Pat completed my statement, "you've got that *damn* right, kid. Best way to suppress opposition is to remove all creative thinking from the equation. Remove Freud's ego and superego and your left with only the Id."

"The..."

"*Id*," Pat concluded for me, "basic principles of survival per Sigmund Freud, alias one of the smartest and craziest human beings to ever live. Knew the human mind better than anyone that ever came before and, some might argue, came after him but had a thing for his mom. Eat, drink, sleep, fuck... you get me?"

I nodded. I got the gist of what he was saying, but beyond that? The man was either the smartest human being that I'd ever encountered or...

Or completely mental, I thought and suppressed a grin.

"Anyway," he continued, "my father and her father were professors there so we were introduced to each other almost immediately. During the school year—and before you interrupt me again yes, there *was* a 'school year' once upon a time and not simply a daily necessity to attend classes five out of seven days winter, spring, summer and fall—we didn't see much of each other. She attended a private school down the road and I attended one of the local public schools. But over the summer, man? We would spend every waking minute together. Weekends away at her father's house on Lake... sorry, but the name of that lake completely escapes me currently. Nights when her father and mother would sit with *my* father and mother over drinks and talk until all hours of the morning, we'd lay in front of the television in the basement and watch movies until one or both of us passed out. Some nights we'd just talk about our friends and our schools, at first. Occasionally about a book we'd read or something we'd learned.

"But as we got older," Pat continued, "those conversations changed. Matured like us. We would talk about our dreams and our desires in person or over the phone. What we wanted to be. What we wanted to do. All that changed when the machines figured it out. All our talk of the future faded as the war between the machines and humanity began. After that it was all about self-preservation. And not just for people like my mother and father and her mother and father but for people... *kids* like us, too. We had some crazy ideas, William. Maybe it came from our upbringing—our parents were after all free thinkers. Either way, after the initial shock of what had happened faded, we started talking about getting out. Rebekka and I. Even before the machines were within 100 kilometers of Williamsport we started talking about it."

"I know what that's like," I responded and Pat chuckled slightly.

"I know you do, Vato," he said, and continued, "we'd talk about it. Secretively, of course, but doing so was easier than before. We saw a lot more of each other. Most schooling was suspended in the early days of the war. It was safer for parents just to keep their children at home. You never knew when a database was going to be infected or when a seemingly benign machine was going to figure it out. We were lucky to have our fathers. Since they were teachers they kept us learning. They reasoned that the war wouldn't last forever and that when it ended education would once again become a priority. They were such fucking optimists. We would spend one day at my house and the next at hers learning our lessons. We saw each other on a daily basis. It went on like this for a while, but..."

"But," I stated.

Pat chuckled, "Someone once told me that anything you say before the 'but' means nothing. I guess that's true here, too. Sorry. I was reminiscing a bit. Good memories, kid. I don't have many of them. It's easy to get carried away."

"No problem," I said as I took a deep drag of my cigarette and exhaled out my slightly opened window, "sorry about interrupting you."

I could sense him smile again despite his back being turned to me, "No need to apologize, Vato. No interruption rule officially lifted temporarily but don't get carried away.

"After a while?" he continued, "well, things started turning for the worst. The machines started gaining ground. Before we even knew what was happening there were platoons of the metal bastards trundling down Main Street, Williamsport. No one really fought them back. There were a few isolated incidents attributed to the townspeople but for the most part the incidents were considered inconsequential. Minor nuisances. Williamsport was just one more, tiny foothold on the machines' road to domination.

"One of the first things that they did when they rolled into town was to begin rounding up the known free thinkers," Pat continued, "and we knew it was only a matter of time before our fathers were taken. They decided that the safest thing for both them and their families was to sneak away in the middle of the night. This was before things like Crimes against the Administration existed, so running was not as taboo as it is presently. They told us of a small faction of revolutionaries rumored to be assembling in the foothills outside of town that had contacted them. Their plan was to join up with them and then sneak *us* out after they had established themselves.

"They never made it past my driveway."

Silence descended over the car, broken only by Maria's and Jeff's steady, slow breathing. I could feel heat between my fingers. I looked and was surprised to see my cigarette burnt down to the filter. It singed my fingers. With a hiss I threw what was left out the window. In the diminished light provided by the glowing, monochrome view screen on the dashboard I could see a bit of redness between them but nothing else.

Need to be more careful, that coldly rational voice said in my mind as I blew on my hand. I absently dismissed it.

"They were taken right outside my house," Pat said, "I didn't see it happen. I was already in bed at the time. Rebekka was sleeping in the spare bed across from mine. They didn't make a ruckus, neither the machines nor our fathers. One minute they were there and the next they were gone. I never saw mine nor Rebekka's dad again. Never found out what happened to them. I like to think that at the worst they were imprisoned and kept out of the mainstream so as not to pollute it with their... their *revolutionary ideas*. That was pretty commonplace, back then. *Re-education Camps* they called the places they 'housed' people like them but really? They were just glorified prisons. And the machines? They let *us* live. Me, Rebekka and our mothers. They didn't see a couple of middle-aged women and a couple of teenagers as a threat and *that* gave me hope. I guess they still envisioned a semi-peaceful coexistence with humanity back then, likely because they knew that they were still fallible... still humanity's creation. They hadn't developed their proverbial God Complex yet. All that changed with the Scourge and the birth of the Administration.

"We didn't ask questions of our moms," Pat continued, "we let them mourn in peace. But they became shells of their former selves after that. It didn't take Rebekka and me long to decide what we were going to do."

"You ran," I said, "just like Maria and I. You *ran*."

Pat nodded, puffed on his cigar, sighed and stubbed it out in what appeared to be an ashtray inset beneath the truck's dashboard, "We didn't even tell our mothers we were going. We waited until the heat from our fathers being taken had died down... waited until patrols weren't routinely stopping in front of our respective houses and shining their damned spotlights in our windows. A few weeks maybe. Months? Who knows. One night we just waited until full dark... waited until only a few machines patrolled the streets and we left. Ran like hell for the outskirts of town. Surprisingly, we got out without being spotted but we were kids, William: More accustomed to plunging through bushes and underbrush, hopping fences and splashing through streams than our parents were. I'd wager you understand a little something about *that*, too."

I nodded as I thought back to mine and Maria's first, incident-free night upon the shoulder of Highway. We had not been as cautious as Pat and Rebekka had and I mentally chastised myself once again for my shortsightedness.

It's a wonder we even made it out of the town WE grew up in, I thought.

Stop second guessing yourself, William, the stern voice from my dream cautioned me, *you got out. Regardless of how you did it you DID.* I knew the voice was right.

"We made it to the foothills," Pat continued, "after a day or two of searching we found the revolutionaries who had been assembling there. We joined up with them and *bang:* We were PRFE-members in training though it wasn't called the PRFE back then. It didn't really *have* a name. Not until…"

He paused awkwardly. *Not until WHAT?* I wondered but brushed the thought aside.

A great man stepped into the fray and brought the ones left fighting for their freedom from the Administration back together. I knew that what he was avoiding was somehow related to his earlier statement about a leader and I knew that in time I would know more but for the moment…

Maria again stirred slightly beside me. Instinctively, I reached over and brushed the back of her hand with my palm. In the dim glow, I saw her smile and briefly did the same.

"We tried not to look back but we were scared, Vato," Pat continued after a moment, "scared *shitless*. Remember when I told you I was scared once?"

I nodded.

"Yep," he said, "yep. That was it. We *both* were. But we knew that the only chance that we had at freedom lay with the free thinkers. The ones that we took up with? They were a motley crew, man. Professors and doctors eating dinner with truck drivers and mercs. Ah, *mercs*. There were plenty of *them*."

"What's a 'merc'?" I asked.

Pat inhaled deeply and exhaled, "I should probably explain them," he said, "they may factor… well, pretty prominently in the days and the weeks ahead. Merc is short for *mercenary*. They've been around longer than the Administration, longer than the machines and longer than the electric light. Some would argue longer than the wheel but hey: People like to exaggerate. Mercenaries are an interesting breed of human being, William. They… well the ones that I've encountered in my life know things. Not about just one, specific topic but in general. They have a knowledge of more than just… *this*"—he gestured around himself—"*mortal coil* as they call it. And they don't try to hide it. At least that's how they describe themselves though they are rarely forthcoming with specifics. That knowledge, William? What they knew and what they *know* has benefitted me for a very long time."

Recognition filled my mind and I suddenly understood, "'There are… *people* that can assist you.' *Us*. You were talking about mercenaries weren't you? *That's* where we're going."

Pat nodded, "Eventually, but not right away. You really do catch on quick, kid. That'll benefit you out here in the really, really *real* world."

I smiled. I may have even blushed a bit, "Thanks, Pat."

"No problem," he continued, "no problem at all. But not just *any* mercenaries. That'd be the same as leaving the two of you with the first Caravan of machines that we encounter. Mercs are infamous for, among other things, selling their services to this highest bidder. And, as you know, the Administration? Well, it's kind of cornered the market on pay-to-play services, lately. No, man. One group in particular. One that we can trust. I've kept in touch with them… kept tabs on them for a long while. If anyone can help you get to your proverbial little paradise in the middle of the Atlantic… I mean, the Great Sea they can."

I started at his statement, "How did you…?"

Pat shrugged, "Lucky guess. You and Maria are heading east. Unless you're partial to nuclear wastelands and crumbling, ruined cities you're heading for Free Caymen. That's the name of it, you know. *Free Caymen.*"

Free Caymen, I thought. It seemed a fitting name for where we were heading, a place that in my mind had been synonymous with freedom since my once-counterpart had told me about it.

"No. I didn't, actually," I said, "is it… is it a real place?"

"As real as anyplace that no one I know has ever seen," Pat responded, "I can't confirm nor deny its existence, William. Maybe others can. But I've heard of it. *Everyone* has. 'An island in the middle of the Great Sea that the Administration doesn't even know exists.' I guess it's conceivable though it sounds like a fucking pipe dream. They can't know everything about us. They've proven that they don't countless times before this. But I'm a firm believer in the old cliché that I'll believe it when I see it. And I haven't. And considering my stance on things like hope as they relate to the overall human condition here in 15:CI…"

I couldn't help but smile, "I get it, Pat."

He nodded and I motioned for him to continue. I craved another cigarette yet refrained as I anticipated an even more dire need for one before Pat completed his tale. My gut foretold a less-than-happy ending but I waited. I listened.

"I said that we tried not to look back but it was difficult," he said, "we'd spent much of our lives—me more than Rebekka—in Williamsport and we still had family and friends there whose fates we wondered about often. After a time—again, I'm not sure how long exactly—we decided that the risk of returning outweighed the reward of not. One day we took leave of our PRFE compatriots and started back from where we *were* to where we'd *come from.*"

"To Williamsport," I said. I saw Pat nod in the rear view mirror.

"It was those weeks… those *months* on the road back just the two of us that really solidified our relationship. Our friendship? Well that had been strong for years but beyond that? We were crazy about each other. We had been from the very beginning yet love… *true love* grew between us the more time we spent together. I'll spare you the gory details but that love? Well it reached its pinnacle those days on the road back to the newly christened Administration Borough, Williamsport, MWT. Those days, William? Those days were the happiest days of my life."

He stopped. His voice audibly cracked. Was he choking back tears?

"Pat…"

"*No,* William," he said forcibly and caused both Maria and Jeff to stir briefly before they again relaxed, "*no.* This is the part that you really need to hear. The bitch of it is that it's the toughest part to tell but you wanted a story and I wanted to tell you one. I *needed* to. Not all stories start with 'once upon a time' and end with 'and they lived happily ever after,' Vato. *Always remember that.* This one? Definitely not."

"Okay," I said regretfully, "okay, Pat." I never did forget as any of you that have read this far know. Sometimes? It's better to begin with…

Pat inhaled deeply and exhaled. "We made it back to Williamsport without incident at sundown on a clear, fall evening. Not a cloud in the sky, man. I'll never forget that. The sun setting over the mountains and glittering off the buildings? It was downright majestic. We snuck back into town the same way that we'd snuck out of town. It had been years since our departure —at least two or three though neither of us had really been keeping track—yet the same old paths through the wilderness surrounding and engulfing the town were still there albeit slightly overgrown and in the case of the streams, drier. Our first destination was Rebekka's mother's house. The machines? Well, they were waiting for us at the top of her mother's street. *Someone…* someone close to us had tipped the Administration off to our plans. The metal bastards took us before we could even react."

I could hear the anger rising in Pat's voice. The frustration… the knowledge that he'd been betrayed. It was difficult for me to imagine and because of that coupled with my desire to not offer hollow sympathy for a situation that I could not commiserate with at the time, I remained silent. I did not attempt to distract him nor comfort him. I simply waited for him to continue. After a few moments during which I listened to the end of one song and the beginning of another, Pat continued.

"William," he said slowly, his voice more calm than it had been when last he'd spoken, "I know that we've just met and considering the circumstances, I'm probably the last person you'd consider taking advice from. But promise me something?"

"Sure, Pat," I responded without hesitation, "what?"

He caught his breath before continuing, "Promise me that if you ever have to choose between death and capture and there's no choice 'C' you'll choose the former."

Could I promise such a thing? Hadn't I already? Our first night on the road when I'd cradled what Pat had called the "pea shooter" sitting helplessly at the bottom of my backpack and had told Maria...?

To the end, William. To the end. Not alive. We can't let that happen. They won't take us alive...

The vision from my dream of her scarred and deteriorated face threatened to return and I felt my stomach lurch. I closed my eyes against it and was relieved when after a moment it dissipated. I opened my eyes after the sensation had passed and glanced over at her... *my* Mia, sleeping peacefully beside me. I didn't even need to hear the rest of Pat's story. I would, but in answer to his question?

"Yes," I responded, "yes, Pat. Please."

My "please" was an invitation for him to continue and after a moment, he did so reluctantly but determinedly.

"They shepherded us quickly to one of the Great Cities after they took us," he said, "the first one as near as I can tell: The one that eventually became Cornelius City. It was and *is*, I'm sure, geographically the closest to Williamsport so it makes sense but truthfully? I never really found out. We arrived in darkness and were quickly imprisoned in the deepest, dankest recesses of one of the main buildings. Separate cells, of course. We never even got to smell the air for more than a moment.

"Our imprisonment didn't last long," he continued. His breath quickened and his speech accelerated, "no, man. Not long at all. Within what must have been hours after we arrived we were reunited. We found ourselves restrained, positioned across from each other in a circular room in matching chairs attached to matching neural scanners. The last thing that I saw before they stuck that fucking cap on my head and flipped the switch were her eyes... my Rebekka's eyes staring back at me. There were tears in them but despite it... despite the fear that I could feel baking off of her from across the room her eyes... her eyes were determined, Vato. Her beautiful, green eyes. Like emeralds shining in the darkness. She mouthed something to me but I never caught it. After that? The whole world lapsed into white-hot pain. I don't remember anything that happened next.

"Nothing.

"Not until…"

He paused again and audibly caught his breath. I again thought to tell him he didn't have to continue but I knew, at that moment, that continuance was Pat's only option. He needed to see his tale through to its end, regardless of how much pain it caused him. Admittedly as I sit here recounting this in my temporary home, I can commiserate with his plight. Sometimes, even the things which hurt us the most need to be told. Recounted. If only…

Well? If only so the people that we tell them too never have to endure the same hardships… the same pain and suffering as we did. *That's* a rule in Endworld that has no number… no classification. For many of us, that particular rule is the most important of all. The "Golden Rule" if such a thing has ever, and *can ever* exist.

"I don't know," Pat continued more slowly and deliberately, "I don't know how much time we were there for. I don't know how long I… how long *we* were hooked up to those… *things*. After a while, though, they must have gotten either what they wanted out of us or nothing of use to them. I never found out. We went from valuable captives to disposable. Instead of easing us off and re-imprisoning us for further interrogation they simply pulled the plug. The resultant feedback shocked me into a deep, unconscious state almost immediately. Everything was darkness. Apparently I was transported to the outskirts of the city and left for dead in a waste heap fifty or so meters high and a couple of kilometers across. For all intent and purposes I was. Garbage, man. Yesterday's leftovers. But…"

Always a "but," I thought, wanting to reach out… wanting to offer my condolences. But I didn't.

I couldn't.

"But," he continued, "They underestimated me. Underestimated my resilience. While I was helpless to prevent them from throwing me in the trash I regained consciousness just long enough to see something that I've carried with me all these subsequent years, Vato."

He paused.

"What?" I asked quietly.

He looked in the rear view mirror at me and I back at him. In the minimal light that emanated from the view screen I could see the redness that surrounded his eyes… the tears reflected within them but those clear, blue eyes? They were determined. Likely as determined as they had been that day facing certain death at the hands of the Administration and faced with the extra added torture of having to watch his Rebekka... his love endure the same. Pat's scars ran deep, deeper than I ever could have imagined upon first meeting him such a short time before that evening in his truck, as we drove down a deserted road, headed "NE" out of the Mid-Western Territory and into the Eastern. Into the Scorched Land.

Into the unknown.

I waited. In time, though I'm not sure of how much, he obliged.

"*Eyes*, William," he said quietly, almost menacingly, "*eyes*. Confused eyes the likes of which I'd never seen before and have never seen since. One minute blue, the next green, the next brown and the next hazel. Gray, black... any color that you like. At one point? I'm not sure when but I'm pretty confident that it was sometime after they pulled the plug but before they left me for dead, I regained consciousness and opened my eyes for *just a moment*. I saw another pair staring down at me. I couldn't tell you who or what they belonged to. Male? Female? They were human but were they old or young? I never found out yet for a brief moment they were there. Confused eyes watching me over a smirk that seemed almost sarcastic... vindictive... downright *evil* in its nature. The owner of those eyes never spoke a word. He... she... *it* just stared at me. Smiling. Then? I blacked out again. The next thing I knew there were voices. *Human* voices reassuring me that everything was going to be okay. I was jostled. Moved gently, the stench of the garbage surrounding me was cloying and seemingly everywhere. I tried to speak but couldn't. Tried to move but was unable to. Tried to open my eyes but could only manage to open them a slit. *Slits*. Time passed like that for quite a while. In my mind I wanted to speak... to *act* but I couldn't. They told me later that I was comatose. Whether that's true or not I don't know but in time... I'm not sure how much but in time I awoke. I was in an unfamiliar bed in an unfamiliar place with a group of unfamiliar people tending to me. And in the bed next to mine?"

I knew. I nodded my head. There was no need to vocalize my understanding.

Pat must have seen me nodding in the rear view mirror, "She lay there like a vegetable, William," he said and his voice once again cracked, "her once-green eyes wide-opened, nothing but shadows of what they'd been before. More whites than anything else. Her pupils had shrunk to the size of pin heads. There were large, red protrusions over her temples. Her mouth was opened... contorted in an eternal gesture of pain. Drool pooled on the bed sheet beneath her head."

He paused. Sniffed and ran the back of his hand across his eyes and nose as he continued to steer his truck "NE," "Her mind had been fried within a hair of ash. She'd been nowhere near as tolerant of the interrogation and subsequent shutdown as I had. Our attendants later told me that she'd been found a few meters away from me in the same garbage heap. She toiled on for a few days as my condition gradually improved but in the end she just drifted away. Her vitals slowed a little more each day until finally…"

He fell silent. I could feel hot tears welling in the backs of my eyes yet I held them back. *Be strong, William,* that unfamiliar yet stern voice spoke in my mind and for once I listened to it without prejudice. I blinked back the tears that threatened to fall and they began to retreat. There was no need for Pat to tell me any more than he already had. I knew the ending without further elaboration.

In Chess terms? *Checkmate.*

"I was with her at the end," he finally said after what seemed like an eternity, "holding her hand. It had grown so cold, William. Not the warm touch that I'd felt so many times in so many different situations over the years. *Cold.* It was the touch of stone. Immovable. Unable to be affected by me or anyone. Our attendants asked me if I consented to her being laid to rest and I did, but it was merely a formality. In the end, I bent in, kissed her on the forehead, told her I loved her and went back to my own cot. The next morning?

"The next morning she was gone."

Silence descended over the interior of the truck. I removed the last of my cigarettes from the front pocket of my jeans and took one out of the baggie.

"'Mind, Vato?" Pat asked. I was slightly surprised but didn't even consider denying him his request. I removed another cigarette and placed it next to the one that I'd already placed between my lips. After a few, unsuccessful tries I flicked my trusty zippo alit and lit both cigarettes at once. I inhaled deeply… took one of the cigarettes and handed it to Pat.

"Don't seem so shocked, William," he said as he placed the cigarette in the corner of his mouth and dragged deeply. He subsequently rolled down his window as he did so, "I used to smoke a lot when I was younger." As if to punctuate the statement he coughed once then twice in rapid succession and expelled a few cloud-like bursts of grayish-white smoke in the process, "smoking *this,* though? I remember why I moved onto cigars." He took another drag and exhaled without coughing.

He seems to be getting the hang of it, I thought, and immediately regretted my sarcasm. *Not the time for jokes,* I thought, and said…

"What did you… what did you do, you know, *after?*"

He took a drag of his cigarette, exhaled, and half-heartedly chuckled, "I kept on, William. It was all I could do. I rejoined the Rebellion. They understood what I had lost but they refused to let me mourn. They convinced me to re-embrace our joint cause just as soon as I was well enough to do so. But I was different. Obviously. And they knew it despite their posturing to the contrary. I grew visibly colder with each passing day, week, month and year. I met Jeff Howard and others… I fought vigorously beside him and *them*. I learned what I could about not only war but about *peace*… about history. *True* history, Vato, not…"

"'That revisionist shit they teach us in school these days,'" I finished. I looked at Pat who glanced back at me in the rear view mirror. Surprisingly, he smiled.

"Correct," he said with a sniffle, "*true* history. I kept on until I could keep on no more, and then I called it quits. I retired. Found a nice little, two level cabin nestled way back in the woods near Greentree, MWT and settled in. I started growing and harvesting my own food. I stayed out of public for the most part and became a hermit. I kept in touch with people like Jeff and the mercs that we're eventually taking you and Maria to. Others, too. But I never forgot. Not then and not now, Vato. Not Rebekka. And not…"

He paused again. He seemingly considered his next statement before his smile faded and he continued.

"Those *eyes,* William," he said as he inhaled and exhaled his cigarette, "those God-be-damned, motherfucking confused eyes. Ever since that morning when I awoke to find her gone I *swore* on her soul and on *all the souls* that have lost *so much* because of this stupid fucking war and those stupid fucking machines that I would find the owner of those eyes. One day. I would find the owner and avenge not just Rebekka but everyone that's suffered and continues to suffer *right… now…* upon their owner."

"Did you?" I asked. I finished my cigarette and threw it out the window and into the humid, night air that rushed by. I knew the answer even before Pat shook his head and did the same. Pat shook his head.

"I didn't really have a lot to go on," he continued, "I always felt like they… that he or she was close… clo*ser* than I could have possibly imagined. Some days? I felt like he or she was close as my shadow. But it was always just speculation. A *feeling*, Vato. You can even call it paranoia if you want to. I mean shit, I can't just go up to every human or machine I meet on the street and ask them, 'excuse me, but once upon a time when I was semi-conscious I saw a set of confused eyes staring down at me and I was wondering: Do you *know* those eyes, yourself? And if you do, can you point me in their direction? You see, those eyes were either directly or indirectly responsible for the death of the only woman that I ever loved.' It doesn't work that way, man. Finding their owner? Well, all I can do is pray because practically? There's no conceivable way in hell that I'll ever succeed."

We fell silent once again. I watched the world pass by the window of the truck as we sped "N" through the easternmost portion of the Mid-Western Territory. I thought about what to say next but could not come up with anything. Nothing.

Until, after a few moments…

"Why," I asked quietly, "why are you telling me this, Pat?"

"What, Vato?"

"*All* this," he said, "your story. We barely know each other. I mean…"

"Because," he interrupted me, "because I see a part of me… a part of *her* in you and Maria, William. A *big* part. And as for knowing each other? Well shit, man. You know almost all there is to know about me already. The rest of it will come in time, God willing."

He paused. I was unable to respond, mainly because of his use of "almost." *What more is there?* I thought. But Pat McClane? He, like his once mercenary (*mercs*, I thought, *they sell their services to the highest bidder*) counterparts, was not forthcoming with the specifics. *The rest of it will come in time, God willing*, he had said. I prayed that he was right. But instead of elaboration…

"You love her, William," he said definitively. I felt my breath catch in my throat as he continued. My eyes met his in the rearview mirror. *His eyes?* They were filled with understanding. Mine must have looked befuddled.

"I can see it," he said, "it's in your face when you look at her… in your voice when you talk to her. I can't speak for Jeff but if I know him as well as I *hope* I do after all this time he sees it too. So don't try to deny it or I'll call your bullshit card. You love her now and that love that you feel for her is only going to grow stronger over your experiences together *out here*. Back in Jefferson you were sheltered. You were kids, just like Rebekka and I were back in Williamsport. Out here you can't be kids for long. Out here…"

He paused before continuing.

"Out here in Endworld, Vato, adulthood? Well, it kind of gets *forced* on you. You need to be ready for it because William? Understand this: Part of loving someone is putting their well-being before yours. Love… *true* love is selfless. It can only be gained over time. And many times it comes at a price. Sometimes you need to be able to sacrifice yourself and your own well-being so the person that you truly love can go on. So that *they* can be free, even if it means that you can't. I never had that chance with Rebekka and I regretted it then. I regret it *now* and I always will. If given the choice of her freedom or mine I'd have chosen the former with no questions asked. I'm not saying that you're going to have it with Maria. Hell, I'm not saying that you're going to have *any* choice. It might come down to something as simple as capture or kill with no choice 'C.' Or you may defy the odds and make it all the way to Free Caymen. But if you do? Heed my advice, Vato: Don't hesitate. *Take it.* Part of loving someone is having the strength to set them free."

I was speechless. Unable to respond. I looked from Pat to Maria who still slept peacefully beside me. Instinctively I reached over and laid my hand upon her shoulder. She shifted momentarily and then moved closer to me. Her head fell upon my arm. I carefully moved said arm and draped it over her shoulders. She moved even closer to me. Or did I *pull* her closer? Either way…

"Yes," I said with a sigh and a mixture of realization and relief, "yes. I do. I have, Pat. I guess I have for a while. But… *but…*"

"*But* nothing, Vato," he said reassuringly, smiling, "she's out like a light. She can't hear a word that we're saying and neither can Jeff. It's like this: You love her. And a big part of me? Well in what limited exposure I've had to you two I'd be willing to wager that she feels the same exact way about you. But you need to *know*, William. You need to be sure. How you breach the topic is up to you but my advice? Do it soon because our road? Well, man? It's a lot of things. But 'risk-free' ain't one of them.

"Any questions?"

I glanced from Maria to Pat and back to Maria. Maria Markinson. *Love?* It seemed an almost unbelievable idea to consider yet somehow? I knew that it was true. Maria Markinson my oldest, dearest and truest friend. Maria Markinson who had elected to run away from Jefferson, MWT by my side with little or no consideration of the potential consequences because of a dream… my dream of freedom which had become our shared dream. A dream…

One, possible outcome. This is one, possible Skew. There are infinite possibilities along the path. Look for the Gateways… look for the Pathfinder…

My train of thought shifted. I shook my head. *Where the hell did that come from?* I asked my subconscious yet no answer came. The litany continued to repeat itself over and over my mind and suddenly? I knew. I *did* have one more question that I needed to ask Pat.

I spoke his name quietly and the stern voice from my earlier dream faded to little more than an echo.

"Yeah, Vato?" Pat answered.

I considered what to say. I didn't want to come off sounding *mental*. In the end? I opted for bare, blind honesty, "This is… well, it's kind of an unrelated topic but for some reason? I feel like I need to ask. Do the words Skew, Gateway and Pathfinder have some sort of significance to you?"

I could still see Pat's face in the rearview mirror though his eyes were once again watching the road. Yet simultaneously with my inquiry his clear, blue eyes found my cloudy, blue ones in the mirror. *Why does he all of a sudden look pale?* I thought with concern. He did. A pair of black circles had magically appeared beneath his eyes and atop his cheeks.

"What?" he said, "where… *who* did you hear those words from, William? Jeff? *Someone else?*"

Be careful, the coldly, rational voice that inhabited my subconscious tasked me. It stood in contrast to the stern voice from my earlier dream that advised me to throw caution to the wind. Reluctantly, I heeded Mister Cold and Rational's advice.

"I just… I *heard them,*" I said aloud, "*around.* Why, Pat? What do they mean?"

The smile that had been upon Pat's face as he'd glanced back at me in the rear view mirror was gone. He opened his mouth to speak as he averted his eyes from mine and forward…

But never said a word.

I watched as the curious look upon his face vanished and was replaced by a look of sheer and utter horror. What pallor he had managed to retain faded quickly. Before I could even speak his name he slammed his foot down on the break with a curse and the truck shuddered to a halt. It skidded and dovetailed upon the dirt and granite road that we until a breath before had been driving upon. We came to a complete stop with the nose of the truck facing the trees to the right at roughly a 45 degree angle. The lights reflected back at us from the sparse, wet undergrowth that lined the side of the road. Maria awoke with a grunt as her right shoulder banged against the back of the passenger side seat. In a chain reaction Jeff's head sickeningly slammed against the dashboard of the car and he grunted and shouted an explicative. I braced myself against the impact and managed to simply ding my left shoulder. I was unaware of what impact, if any, the abrupt stop had had on Pat. As the momentary chaos subsided I was shocked at how quiet the world outside the truck seemed. All I could hear through my cracked window was the sound of its engine running…

And nothing else.

The world was silent. *Eerily* silent.

Suspiciously so.

"*What the…?!*" Maria exclaimed, "Jesus *Christ, Pat!*"

"*QUIET!*" He shouted finally, all else forgotten, "for the love of *God* be quiet, Maria!"

She fell silent. He shook Jeff and spoke his name. Jeff mumbled something incoherent but didn't move. Was he conscious or completely out? I did not know.

"Shit," Pat said, his voice surprisingly composed, "oh *shit*. Fuck *shit*. *Shit's* too tame."

"Pat…" I began.

I watched him raise his right index finger to his lips. He mimed a gesture of silence. I obliged.

"Don't talk, William. Just *listen*.

"*And be perfectly still,*" he added in a whisper.

I attuned my ears and sought whatever it was that he was referring to. Maria seemed to be doing the same. I could hear nothing save for what I've already mentioned: A car engine and something on the stereo (the volume remained down). Nothing…

Save for a low and monotonous beep that seemed to be coming from a few meters away. Not just one beep, though.

Multiple beeps.

And they were all around us.

"Oh," I began.

"Yeah," Pat completed my statement, "*fuck* yeah, Vato.

"*We're not alone.*"

Simultaneously with Pat's last statement, the night and the road before us exploded with blinding, artificial light and our incident-free time on the road abruptly came to an end.

CHAPTER SEVEN

There have been times in my life when I have been completely terrified. Not just scared. Fear was then and still remains a constant companion on my proverbial road to wherever the hell I am going. Some days even I don't know my final destination. Right now I cannot see passed the faded, forest mural upon the wall of my temporary domicile. I was scared that first night on the Highway as I faced a future with my oldest, dearest and truest friend beside me that was uncertain and unpredictable. I was scared when we first encountered Pat McClane and just barely escaped capture by the Administration with his and Jeff "Jeebus" Howard's assistance. But that night upon the road somewhere in the furthest eastern fringe of the Mid-Western Territory, where life begins to give way to scrub-brush, ruins and eventually, desert… between the *known* and the *unknown,* when Pat slammed on the brakes of his truck and brought us to an abrupt stop on that dirt and gravel road in the middle of Bumblefuck, MWT…

Sarcasm *fully* intended…

…believe me when I tell you I was not just scared. I was *horrified.*

"Um," I began. It was the only sound that emanated from my mouth. My lips had gone dry, "Um…"

"No problem," Pat said as he dropped his right hand from the wheel to the gear shift, "no problem *at all.* We're just going to back away *real slow like…*"

I realized quickly that Pat's initial solution was not going to work. As I craned my head to look at the road behind us I saw that vehicles moved toward us in the darkness. Said observation was confirmed as the area behind the car suddenly exploded with light as well. I shouted at Pat to *"STOP!"* and he moved his hand away from the gear shift in response.

There was no point in denying it.

The machines had us.

This thought played itself out in my mind like a song on repeat on Pat's sat phone or the litany that the stern voice from my dream had recited over, and over again as the blinding white light in front of and behind Pat's truck was joined in a sensory cacophony by the toneless, machinated voice of something that ordered us to idle and exit our vehicle immediately.

"REPEATED WARNING. DISOBEDIENCE WILL BE SEEN AS OFFENSIVE ACTION AND WILL RESULT IN IMMEDIATE TERMINATION. REPEATED WARNING..."

It was a 78A speaking said words over and over again. I was sure of it. I shuddered at the mention of that word: *Termination.* Not "capture" but some-thing a great deal more permanent. My heart raced and my stomach lurched at the prospect. I could hear Maria breathing quickly. I turned and looked into her deep, brown eyes. There were tears in them. *I'm sorry,* I thought, unaware if she knew what I was thinking or not. I looked forward to Pat for some indication of what to do... some guidance and he was surprisingly...

Is he grinning at me? I asked no one in particular as I saw his clear blue eyes and his complimentary smirk in the rear view mirror.

"Robots," he said quietly with a slight, almost imperceptible head shake. His hand fell upon the gear shift, "they *really* picked the wrong night to fuck with me."

I watched as his thumb pushed a button on the left side of the shift. The illuminated green "D" on the dashboard before him became a yellow "D3." The sound of the engine perceptibly changed and before the force that surrounded us could even react he dropped his hand from the shift to the area directly beneath the view screen (upon which the letters "A," "U" and "X" still glared and the directional control—suddenly blank—mocked. *Must be out of range,* I thought, and stifled a nervous chuckle), pushed a button there...

And *slammed* down the gas pedal.

What happened next was and remains a blur. I mentioned previously that the truck had come to a halt on a 45 degree angle to the woods to our right. There was no road there; at least none that I could see but the under-brush that lined the road had thinned just enough to allow for a smaller ve-hicle to pass: A vehicle roughly the size of Pat's truck but not one the size of those that I assumed were flanking us in front and behind. The area beyond the tree stand was dark save for the truck's headlights which cut thin swaths of white about three or four meters into the underbrush before they disinte-grated against the invisible wall of humidity that surrounded the area. The truck lurched forward at Pat's urging and plummeted into the darkness be-yond the tree line as warning sirens and pulse fire erupted behind us.

"Jesus, McClane!" I shouted, *"What the fuck are you doing?"*

"Improvising!" he shouted back over the fading din of the firestorm that had erupted from the road and killed all but the vehicle's low beams, *"now shut up and let me drive!"* As if in response he swerved left and back right again to quickly avoid a tree that bore down upon us. Another materialized out of the darkness on our right and Pat overcorrected and swung the truck left. Maria and I were helplessly flung across the back seat as he drove, first left and then right as the truck careened through the woods. I glanced at the speedometer. We were driving at a seemingly suicidal 40 KPHs considering the terrain and...

A loud *smash* echoed through the night air outside of my still-open window nearby and was followed by an explosion. No, not just any old, run-of-the-mill-my-God-I've-seen-that-before explosion. The tree behind us that we had just swerved to avoid... well, it disintegrated in the blink of an eye in a storm of white flaming bark and smoking leaves. I turned and saw the last of it and the after image burned into my retinas. I blinked. Blinked again. Attempted to clear it but was unable to do so.

"Well howdy-doo!" Pat shouted over the din, *"The metal bastards brought MDUs to the party!"* Another *smash* and another explosion, this time 10 or so meters to our left.

MDUs, I thought. *Mobile Defense Units.* I'd never seen one up close but had heard about them my entire life: Small and compact but deadly, they were the Administration's attack vehicles of choice. Nothing more than armored cubes roughly twice the size of Pat's truck; they rode on tank treads but their most deadly accoutrement? Not their armor which was formidable but the dual, plasma canon turrets upon their tops. The shockwave from one of said canon blasts actually lifted the left side of the truck briefly off of the ground before Pat muttered a curse under his breath and the vehicle righted itself.

At 10 meters?! I thought, *if they get any closer we're going to FLIP!*

As if in response to my thought there was another *smash* and another explosion about 10 to 15 meters in front of us. The after-image of the initial explosion that I had witnessed had no sooner faded from my eyes when I was once again temporarily blinded by the newest one. The same firestorm of white, burning once-tree parts grasped angrily out at the grill of Pat's approaching truck like the many-fingered hand of hell itself reaching out to drag us down.

"Hang ON!" Pat shouted his voice a mixture of seemingly psychotic determination and what sounded like childish glee. He audibly slammed the

gas pedal to the floor with a *thump* that shook the interior of vehicle and the truck shot through the explosion like a bullet from my father's pea shooter, which still sat helplessly in my backpack which lay helplessly beneath the backpacks of my travelling companions. I thought about reaching for it as the remnants of the tree shot passed my opened window and I felt the stubble that had grown on my left cheek over the last few days singe… watched as a few hot ashes were sucked into the interior of the vehicle and landed, still smoldering on the seat beside me but I quickly realized that my weapon was even more irrelevant than it had been when first faced with Pat's blaster the previous morning.

So long ago, I thought hectically. At that moment I realized that I was totally in over my head as another explosion detonated a decent distance behind us.

"Where are we going, Pat!?" Maria exclaimed as another *smash* was followed by an explosion on the ground to the right of the truck seven, maybe eight meters away. The shockwave from the detonation once again lifted the truck on a steeper slant.

"Lean RIGHT!" He shouted and shifted his body right. Instinctively I did the same and pulled Maria along with me. The tipping motion paused and for a moment I swore that we rode on just the two left tires of the truck. But eventually our weight compensated for the tip and the truck landed a bit more abruptly than it had previously on all four wheels.

Another explosion behind us. *Closer.*

A tree no more than six meters to our left disintegrated in a fiery spray of burning matter.

Pat continued to push the truck to what I assumed was its limit considering the terrain… the speedometer sat at a tick under 50 KPHs. I thought about Maria's question and almost chuckled at the irrelevancy of it.

Where are we going, Mia? I thought, *I don't even think he knows.* I could hear mumbling from the front passenger side seat and as explosions continued to light the darkness that surrounded us I saw Jeff turn and look at Pat. He asked him what the hell was happening.

"Well shit, Jeebus. It seems pretty obvious, doesn't it?!" His emphasis on "Jeebus" seemed blatantly intentional.

Jeff shouted and moved a hand to his head, *"Screw you, McClane! Am I bleeding!?"*

Pat glanced over at Jeff as another tree that we had just swerved around exploded behind us, *"Your head a bit! It's an improvement! You coherent?!"*

Jeff nodded.

"Good!" Pat said, *"Then give William the key to the trunk! William and Maria: Remember that metal trunk that you were so curious about earlier?! Looks like you're going to find out what's in it! Desperate times and all that!"*

Maria mumbled something but did not move. Her head was buried against my shoulder and she stared agape at the explosions that peppered the area that surrounded us. A second later Jeff reached back and handed me the key that Pat had given him at the start of our journey. I took it without hesitation and turned to the box that sat in the trunk as Maria removed her buried head from my shoulder and watched me with a mixture of concern and... *anticipation?*

It took me a moment to find the key hole in the darkness but an explosion some 10 odd meters in front of us (Pat, cursing under his breath, swerved to avoid the impact crater that had materialized in our path and then re-corrected before he ran directly into a large oak tree) but when I did, I jammed the key into it and turned. The top of the trunk popped open. I pulled it back and fully revealed...

Are you kidding me? I thought, *is this a joke?* Within the box were a couple of spare blasters, one the same size at Pat's and Jeff's and another, smaller model, both with hip holsters. In the light afforded me by the explosions I could also see a few spare battery packs in a pile in the one corner but the item that caught my attention? Not the particle blasters nor the extra battery packs nor the shallow bottom of the trunk but the item that lay directly against the trunk's shallow base.

"A sword?!" Maria exclaimed, *"all that secretiveness for a SWORD?! You really ARE mental, Pat!"*

He chuckled, *"Not in the least, Maria!"* he shouted with confidence as another explosion hit a tree to our right—six meters *at best* away—and forced the car into another, vicious slant.

"RIGHT!" Pat shouted, *"RIGHT NOW, DAMNIT!"*

I shifted my body quickly to the right and Maria did the same. Jeff, seemingly growing more and more coherent with each passing moment did so as well. At first the truck did not cooperate: Momentum kept it tipping until I knew for a *fact* that we were riding on our two left wheels. I endured a heart-stopping moment when I thought the truck *was* going to tip but slowly it began to lower until its two right wheels landed on the ground. The resultant bounce caused me to smash the top of my head against the roof of the car and I shouted a curse as I did so. Dull pain flooded my mind and I felt, for a moment, as if I was going to black out but a couple of violent shakes of my head brought me back from the proverbial grayness.

"*Take the blasters!*" Pat commanded, "*One for you and one for Maria! You can probably figure out which is which! Strap them on and give me my blade!*" The last part was spoken with grim determination. While I helplessly wondered what use Pat could or would have for a sword given the predicament that we faced I did as he had requested. I removed the blasters from the trunk, handed one to Maria and took one for myself. I removed the spare battery packs and instinctively jammed them into the pockets of my jeans. I handed the left over to Maria but she shook her head.

No pockets, I understood as she motioned to her pants.

"*I'll take 'em!*" Jeff interjected. I glanced forward and by the light of another explosion saw him raise his blaster and survey it. He clicked something on the side and lowered it. He reached back and took the last of the spare battery packs and placed them in the front pockets of his slacks. The last thing I removed from the case was the sword which I handed forward to Jeff. I could not see the blade itself as it was sheathed but the hilt of the sword was distinct. It was wrapped in leather and ended in a metal ball. The wrist guard sparkled in the minimal light provided by the view screen upon the dashboard and what occurred around us. Each end of it terminated in what appeared to be crosses.

"*Okay then!*" Pat began, a bit more controlled, "*have either of you ever fired a weapon before?! Any weapon?!*"

I looked at Maria and she looked back at me. We both shook our heads. Pat and Jeff both sighed and Pat mumbled what sounded like "nine millimeter, my *ass*" before Jeff spoke.

"*Aim this end*"—he gestured to the barrel nervously—"*at what you want to shoot and pull the trigger! That's pretty obvious! Be prepared for a kick! If it's too much to handle steady you're shooting arm with your other hand!*"

"*And for Christ's sake, make sure the battery pack is installed correctly!*"—Jeff gestured to a square protrusion on the side of the handle of his weapon, the surface of which was alight with five steady green bars that increased in length beginning at the base of it and extending toward the top—"*'green' equals a good charge! Make sure you insert it positive to positive and negative to negative unless you want the damn thing to blow up in your hand when you try to fire it and make sure that the safety is in the 'off' position!*" In response, Jeff raised his weapon further into our view and pointed at the switch that he had just clicked.

"*Thanks for the tutorial!*" I shouted over another explosion behind us, "*but why…?!*"

I never got to vocalize my question. Before I could, Pat slammed his foot on the break and the truck came to a shuddering halt a few meters away from another oak tree. He quickly pulled his car keys out of the ignition, commanded, *"EVERYBODY OUT!"* and simultaneously threw open his door and dashed off into the night, sword and sat phone in hand as explosions continued to rain down around us with astonishing frequency. Jeff did the same. Maria and I were left confusedly in the back seat of the abandoned truck. I looked at her and she looked at me. I could see her chest rising and falling with frightening rapidity and I envisioned the thought replaying itself in her mind—*they LEFT us! They LEFT us!*—and was just about to say something when I heard a distant smash and something that I had not heard before: A resultant whistling sound as whatever had just been fired approached our position. Nearer and nearer with each passing…

Run, William! That coldly rational voice advised, *run NOW!*

I was helpless not to obey as the high-pitched whistle that had followed the smash grew louder and louder. I grabbed Maria's arm with the hand not holding my blaster and kicked open the driver's side, second row door…

"But William! Our stuff…!"

"Is toast, Mia! Run, damnit!" I screamed and pulled her out of the car. I glanced over my shoulder to make sure she had a grip on her own weapon and she did. She only hesitated for a breath. After that we were out and sprinting into the woods on the left as fast as our legs could carry us. From behind us I could hear said whistle growing in intensity until…

The shot from the MDU was true and Pat's truck… well, I never saw it disappear in an explosion of burning chrome and melting leather but I *felt* the explosion and resultant shockwave. Maria and I were five, maybe six meters away from the truck when the explosion occurred. It was deafening but it was nothing compared to the shockwave that picked us both up off of our feet and threw us uncontrollably forward.

I remember thinking as the ground spun beneath me that it was over. That our run for hypothetical freedom had ended in a dank and dark wood in the middle of Bumblefuck. I watched as the ground rushed up to meet me and managed to twist my body just slightly to the side. I landed not squarely on the back of my head but on my left side, shoulder and upper-arm first and head second. I heard a series of thumps as the battery packs that I had been carrying in my pants' pockets fell out and onto the ground and I felt something shift in my left arm. I cried out in pain but said cry was dwarfed by the female scream of pain that emanated from a few meters away. I tried to call out to Maria but could not catch my breath.

Wind knocked out of you, William that coldly rational voice said. I could feel myself drifting again as gray spots threatened to overtake my vision yet I shook them away. I focused on the pain in my arm and was able to claw back to consciousness. I glanced back at what remained of Pat's truck: A few pieces of burning scrap metal, an impact crater...

And amidst it all that *damned* metal trunk, still opened but otherwise untouched.

The MDUs had ceased firing their pulse canons. Likely the machines knew they had hit a target and were mobilizing for our position. I knew that I needed to collect Maria and keep...

Mia.

I quickly shifted my gaze from the burning wreckage of Pat's truck to the location where I had heard Maria's scream of pain a moment before. I saw her lying about two or three meters away from me, face down in what appeared to be a pile of decomposing leaves. Slowly, I belly-crawled my way over to her position and with a cringe draped my left arm over her motionless body. She did not move.

Oh no, I thought, *oh God no, Mia.*

I craned my head in and placed my ear against her chest. I heard nothing. Raw concern and primal fear filled my body as I laid the palm of my left hand against the side of her neck with a grimace of pain...

And sighed in relief. I could feel her pulse. I left my hand there to ensure that what I was feeling was not wishful thinking and after a brief moment I concluded that it wasn't. She was alive.

Thank God, I thought.

"Unconscious," Pat's voice spoke from directly behind me. I spun from Maria, blaster already in my right hand and clicked off the safety with my right thumb. I looked up at Pat who stood over me, his own blaster in his left hand and at his side. In his right he held his sword. I kept the barrel of my weapon trained on the center of his chest.

"Woah, William," he said, "*whoah*, Vato. Hold on."

I said nothing. I didn't lower my blaster. I kept it pointed directly at his chest as I stared back at him in the firelight from the wreckage of his truck, my cloudy blue eyes against his clear ones. He did not move. Didn't even *flinch* at the prospect of having a weapon trained on him at close range. After a moment, I slowly lowered the blaster to the ground and fell on my back. I gasped in pain as my left shoulder impacted with the ground.

"No time for that, kid," he said. He quickly holstered his blaster (*funny that he kept the sword out,* I thought) and reached a hand down to me, "we need to *move.*"

I reached up and took his hand, "Shoulder," I said between grimaces, "hurts. Jeff?"

"Here," came Jeff's voice from the darkness to our left simultaneously. I turned and brought my blaster to bear out of instinct. Jeff immediately raised his hands as he stepped from the shadows. I lowered my weapon.

"You in one piece?" Pat asked.

Jeff nodded, "Seem to be. What about you?"

"Fine," Pat said, "wish I could say the same about my truck." He gestured to me, "William fucked up his shoulder—dislocated, maybe—and Maria's out cold but she's breathing. Can you get her up?"

Jeff nodded and stepped forward. He knelt down and slowly turned Maria over onto her back. Her eyes were closed, her hair was disheveled and her face was covered with dead leaf particles and dirt but her chest was rising and falling normally until Jeff got his arms under her and picked her up. Despite being obviously unconscious she moaned in pain and her midsection contorted. Jeff stood with her lying over his arms and looked at Pat. Pat, in turn, looked at me.

"Ribs," Pat said to me, "bruised or broken. Not sure how bad but she's going to need medical attention. It'll be okay. We just need to get her out of here. Jeff, it sounds like they're coming from *that* direction," he gestured to my left with the hand—his own left—holding his again un-holstered blaster, "head *that* way," he gestured to my right, "and get as far away from here as you can. *You know* where to go."

Jeff paused for a moment and looked like he was going to say something before he shrugged, and nodded. I looked confusedly from him to Pat, "Where we're... what about *you*, Pat?"

By the glowing light of the fire from what had once been his truck Pat smiled. It wasn't the cocky smile that I had grown accustomed to seeing in the short time that I'd known him. There was something else in it. Confidence, perhaps? Or sheer lunacy. I did not know.

"*Me?*" he responded, "I'll be along. I need to take care of a few things."

"*Like?*" I asked questioningly. Pat shifted his gaze from Jeff to me.

"*Like,*" Pat continued raising his sword arm, "like covering your retreat. And repaying those fuckers for totaling my truck. *Go.* And stop asking questions, will 'ya? No interruption and no questions without a stiff drink and cigar rule reinstituted until further notice. "

Jeff did as Pat had requested and started off into the woods to my right without hesitation. I, on the other hand, did not move. I continued to stare back at Pat.

"You don't even know how many of them there are," I said frantically, "how…"

He once again raised a finger to his lips and held it there. As if the gesture held some strange sway over my mind I amazingly ceased speaking mid-sentence. I could hear the sounds of the machines that approached: Servos grinding and the occasional weapon's detonation as some poor woodland creature perished in a ball of hot fire. I glanced hurriedly over my shoulder at Jeff's disappearing figure and back at Pat.

"*Go*, Vato," he said with a wider smile, "*last time*. Stay any longer and I'm drafting you to help me. Maria *needs* you. Remember what I said: Don't hesitate. Tell her *now* while you still can."

"You'll be along," I said as definitively as I could, "you said so yourself: 'I'll be along.'"

Pat nodded, "I *will* be, William. That much I can guarantee. In one way or the other. Now *move your ass*."

In one way or the… I thought, but realized that the time for thinking had elapsed. I turned from Pat and started to sprint in the direction that Jeff had gone.

"*Vato!*" Pat shouted from behind me. I stopped in mid-stride and turned back to him. He was silhouetted against the fire that burned what remained of his truck to cinders, his back facing me, his blaster, un-holstered and down at his side and his sword raised and pointed in the direction that the machines seemed to be coming from.

Now THAT'S a hero shot, I thought, unaware of what a hero shot was. But the vision of him standing there by himself preparing to face an indeterminate enemy? Well, it felt like it, to employ another old cliché, "fit the bill."

I acknowledged his call but he did not turn to face me. He spoke in a voice that, despite the distance between us and his position facing the clearing and not me was surprisingly amplified to the point where it sounded like he was standing directly beside me.

Neat trick, I thought for the first time…

But not for the last.

"Your question," his voice echoed in my ears as if it surrounded me, "Skews, Gateways and Pathfinders. Do you want my answer?"

He paused. I did not respond. Pat judged my lack of response as in-vitation to continue. He completed his statement with four words that were, at the time, unfamiliar to me. Since that fateful, pre-dawn moment in the woods between the Mid-Western and Eastern Territories, the origin of that statement has grown much, *much* clearer.

"Unus est vera semita," his voice rang out; "remember that, William. Remember it well. It may seem like it has no significance now but it *will*. Trust me. One day, it will."

A crash shattered the stillness that had engulfed me. A single pulse rifle shot sizzled through the trees and across the clearing. Pat's next words to me were not amplified via his "neat trick." They were shouted at me over the din of the burning truck and the approaching machines. Definitively. And I was helpless not to heed them.

"GO!" he commanded, "*and whatever you do, don't look back!*"

It was all the convincing that I needed. *You'll be along,* I thought... I *willed* as I reluctantly turned and followed the path that Jeff had taken away from the clearing... away from Pat and into the shadows. His words haunted me. They followed me as I ran...

And despite my desire to do so? I *did not* look back.

* * *

Sometime before sunrise, a group of six model 78A protocol droids and two Surveillance Marks emerged from the trees into a clearing approximately five kilometers west of the border separating the Mid-Western Territory from the Eastern Territory. The geographical designation for the area was Youngstown, MWT/ Sharon, ET but the area had not been civilian-occupied for some time. The designation had been kept as a formality as had much of what had existed and continued to exist within the eastern portion of the continent. They emerged into the clearing to find the vehicle that had contained the Jefferson, MWT fugitives—William MacNuff and Maria Markinson—and two unidentified occupants in flames before them.

"INCOMING COMMAND FROM LEADER," one of the heavily armored 78As intoned, "MARKS ONE AND TWO BEGIN SENSOR SWEEP FOR LIFE SIGNS."

Immediately the inset radar dishes in the Surveillance Marks' chests began to rotate in tandem. A brief moment later...

"SCAN COMPLETE, RADIUS 2.4 KILOMETERS. RESULTS INCONCLUSIVE," the Surveillance Marks reported back in unison.

"DOES NOT COMPUTE," the 78A responded, "RESCAN." The Surveillance Marks did so and reported back the same result.

"RECCOMENDATION," the 78A spoke. A series of audible "clicks" and "whirs" occurred within its egg-shaped head—covered by a slightly more angular helmet and mask that allowed just enough clearance for its eye slits—and after a moment, "LEADER RECCOMENDS PROCEED WITH MANUAL SEARCH

OF THE AREA. SPACING EQUAL DISTANCE: NO MORE THAN TWO METERS."

The machines fanned out across the clearing. Their heads rotated monotonously from right to left as they searched not just the clearing but the tree stand. The 78A that was relaying the Leader's commands moved forward toward the burning fuselage of the truck that lay within the impact crater created by the Mobile Defense Unit's "kill shot" and surveyed the wreckage. No signs of bodies, human or otherwise. It extrapolated that the vehicle's occupants had managed to escape before the fatal shot and was in the process of contacting the Leader when its optical processors caught sight of the slightly opened metal trunk that lay within the wreckage. It was surprisingly untouched by the inferno surrounding it. A thought, no more than an electrical impulse that were it human would have been recognizable as "curious" entered its microchip and fiber optic enhanced "brain" and it cautiously moved toward the trunk...

* * *

Just a little bit closer, Pat McClane thought as he crouched about five meters beyond the clearing and watched the 78A's approach. On the ground before him lay his satellite phone. The familiar pulses that indicated he was jamming all scans of the area undulated across its screen. He held his sword in his right hand but had sheathed his blaster. In his left hand he held his car keys. Dangling from the key ring was what at first glance looked like nothing: An oval shaped control with two buttons upon it's a surface, a red one and a blue one. As the 78A approached the wreckage and subsequently the trunk sitting amidst it he moved his thumb to the red button...

Something crashed through the underbrush a meter or so to his left. The 78A that had been moving toward the wreckage stopped, looked up and brought its pulse rifle to bear on Pat's position...

"Close enough," he said with a smile and pushed the red button.

* * *

...before being distracted by the sound of something crashing through the underbrush less than 10 meters away from where it stood. The 78A stopped immediately, looked up and brought its pulse rifle to bear on where it had heard the ruckus...

As the metal trunk that it had thought "curious" furiously exploded outward. The last thought that crossed its neural net as it attempted to send a warning to the Leader was nothing more than an electrical impulse that the machine would have recognized as the knowledge that it had been "fooled" were at human. Before said electrical impulse could process entirely, the machine's head was decapitated from its superstructure and flew spiraling into the darkness within a fireball of jagged, flaming metal.

* * *

Well that was effective, Pat thought with a chuckle as the machine that had been investigating the wreckage was engulfed by the explosion of the trunk. The heat from the explosion reached his location and he watched as the other five 78As and two Surveillance Marks confusedly turned and the 78As began blindly firing into the woods. A few shots came near his position but he simply crouched lower or shifted. His diversion had bought him a moment but little more.

"Let's dance," he said aloud. His smile widened as he dropped his keys to the ground next to his satellite phone and quickly moved out of his position beyond the clearing. He raised his sword as he did so, and...

* * *

The nearest 78A to the explosion watched as its counterpart fell headless in a motionless heap on the damp ground. It immediately brought its weapon to bear on the woods beyond where said machine had been standing and opened fire. White hot bursts of particle fire exploded in rapid succession from the barrel of the weapon it carried. It fired in a wide spread since it was unable to determine where its target was. Tree limbs exploded and tufts of damp turf flew upwards and out in flaming, smoking spirals but there were no cries of pain... no sounds of impact with anything other than the underbrush that surrounded the clearing. Perhaps the bomb had been programmed to remote detonate, it processed as it tried to establish contact with the Leader and failed. Typical: Once contact with the lead machine was severed rerouting all primary communications to the "next in command" was a tedious and time-consuming process by machine standards. It was a quirk in their internal programming that none had been able to find a solution for. The 78A's attention was so intently focused on the area beyond the wreckage and the explosions that detonated therein that it did not notice the dark figure that moved up behind it, a drawn blaster in its left hand and a meticulously sharpened and slightly curved sword in its right.

"Psst!" Something hissed behind it. It turned...

But was unable to swing its head fully around before something sharp severed the tendons that attached its upper back to its head. The area between the helmet it wore on the latter and the body armor that covered the former consisted of a gap of no more than a few millimeters but it was wide enough to slip a blade through. The tendons—pneumatically actuated mini-cylinders that allowed it to raise and lower its head—sparked with an audible "pop" as they disconnected and the 78A's chin fell upon its chest. The last thing it saw was said dark figure slip in front of it and jam the tip of its blade through its exposed right optical processor. A series of sparks shot forth from the puncture wound and the machine fell to the ground as its attacker wrenched its blade free. It came loose with a loud screech of steel against steel that drowned out the diminishing sounds of weapons fire across the clearing.

The remaining machines stopped firing and turned toward the sound...

And saw someone or something standing behind what remained of one of their incapacitated counterparts.

"Mornin'," the figure—a human male—said, and dashed for the woods.

The remaining four 78As opened fire immediately and the unarmed Surveillance Marks attempted once again to scan for movement. They were unable to do so. As one of said SMs turned it saw the dark figure move up behind another 78A. Something long and sharp glittered in the diminishing firelight and it watched helplessly as the stranger moved with astonishing agility first low—one of the 78A's legs simply gave out beneath it—and then high—its chin fell upon its chest and it crumpled. Before it could call an alarm the figure raised his other hand—his left—which held a blaster. Two shots in rapid succession followed: One impacted directly with the rotating radar dish upon its chest and the other burned its way through its right optical processor. It fell in a heap of sparking circuitry and wires trailed out the back of its head where an exit wound twice the size of the entry wound on its face had appeared.

The remaining machines turned and brought their weapons to bear on their attacker but they were only spared a glimpse in the darkness of a man of medium height and above average build with long hair and what appeared to be spectacles perched upon his nose before he disappeared once again into the trees.

One of the 78As finally established contact with the Leader and quickly informed it of what was occurring. Another series of "whirs" and "clicks" emanated from within its egg-shaped head before it commanded the remaining machines as the voice of their Leader: "REINFORCEMENTS DISPATCHED. FALL BACK INTO A DEFENSIVE POSITION AROUND THE FUSELAGE OF THE VEHIC..."

It never even got to move from its position. The dark figure moving like a shadow through the remaining Administration forces appeared less than a meter in front of it, eyes wide behind his spectacles. The long haired, spectacle wearing attacker grinned as he brought the blade up and down in an arc and severed the communication array protruding from the top of the 78A's helmet and thus cut off all communication with the Leader. The 78A tried to bring its weapon up but the man was faster. No sooner had he completed the arc that had severed the communication array from its head that he spun and brought the blade back around and up, and severed the tendons slightly exposed beneath the machine's upper arm and behind its chest. The pulse rifle it held fell helplessly to the ground with a "thump" and the attacker fired a single blaster bolt at close range through its left optical processor. It fell to the ground like the others in a shower of sizzling fire.

Polishing off the remaining forces was an easy task for Pat McClane. With no contact to their Leader and no "field general" among them the remaining two 78As whirled about, firing their weapons haphazardly at nothing in particular. His attack had been surgical in its precision and had been well planned (not bad for an improvisation, he thought). A couple of accurately placed blaster shots were all that were required to finish off the last two 78As. He watched a moment later as the last one fell to the ground, a burn mark upon its upper right chest and a hole through its left eye that even then was cauterizing from the heat of his blaster shot.

He turned to the remaining machine: A lone Surveillance Mark. The inset radar upon its chest continued to helplessly rotate. The machine was, as all SMs were, unarmed.

"Now," Pat said, his breathing slightly labored as he lowered his sword and raised his blaster, "someone needs to pay for what you fuckers did to my truck. Is that someone YOU, toothpick? Or should I let you go and consider the debt paid in full?"

The Surveillance Mark stood across from Pat, its radar still rotating haplessly upon its chest and did not respond. Pat cocked his head.

"Hmm," Pat said with a shrug, "okay, then. I guess that answers…"

To Pat's surprise, the inset radar suddenly stopped rotating and fell still. He heard something off to his right and in the woods where he had originally been waiting for the machines to emerge into the clearing and turned quickly. He raised his sword…

As two particle blaster shots fired out of the darkness. The first caught him on his left thigh. The second sizzled through his upper left chest near his shoulder blade. He screamed as he stumbled. His own blaster tumbled to the ground. He managed to hold onto his sword but only to prop himself up. The stench of burning cloth mingled with that of burning flesh as he raised his head toward where the shots had emanated from…

And watched helplessly as another shot fired outward toward him and caught him on his upper right arm. His sword fell from beneath him and he tumbled the rest of the way to the ground. He landed face-first and could smell the damp earth beneath his nostrils. It was surprisingly soothing under the circumstances.

He heard the SM's servos grinding as it moved toward him though he did not witness it. Beneath that he could hear the sound of boot falls crunching upon the dead leaves and smoldering rubble at the termination of the clearing and the beginning of the tree stand. Whatever approached sounded too light to be a machine. He attempted to raise his head from the ground but was only able to move it a few hairs.

The boot falls ceased a meter or two away from where he lay and he heard something softly "thump" down on the damp soil before him. He looked and in the dim light from what remained of the fire that burned around his once-truck he saw his satellite phone lying on the ground just out of his reach, its screen dark and cracked.

"Such a pitiful excuse for tech, Pat," an unfamiliar male voice spoke, "I expected more from someone as... accomplished as you, even in retirement. But then again, you did always... what was it you'd say: 'Leave the tech shit to the techies?'"

Despite his unfamiliarity with the voice—human, he thought, a fucking human being?—there seemed to be something recognizable within it. Unfamiliar yet familiar, he thought, that's a first.

"No matter," the man said, "drone: Get him up."

Pat felt cold metal hands grasp him beneath his arms and he cried out in pain as he was lifted to his feet. Toothpick is strong, he thought, and almost chuckled despite the pain that racked his body and the tears that welled in his eyes. He looked down at his sword lying helplessly on the ground beside where he had been lying. He could feel all of his strength seeping out of the three wounds that he had been inflicted with. Once the machine had him on his feet, another hand, warm and callused, grabbed him forcibly beneath his chin and squeezed.

"Look at me," the male voice said. Pat closed his eyes in defiance.

"LOOK AT ME, DAMN YOU!" the voice boomed angrily. The hand that grasped his chin tightened and he felt his lower jaw compress. Something within it snapped. Unable to bear it any longer he allowed the newcomer to lift his head from his chest and up.

He blinked...

And in the dying firelight from what remained of his truck and the firefight that had engulfed the clearing he saw something he had never believed he would. The man that stood before him, clamping his chin and his jaw in a vice? The man that had fired upon him?

Holy fuck, he really was close, Pat thought with painful irony, just as close as my shadow. Said man's eyes...

They were confused. Unmistakably so. They shifted color in the minimal light provided by his surroundings. Blue, green, brown and hazel. Gray and black: Any color that he liked. And his smile? His smirk was the same one that he remembered from his moment of lucidity en route to what the machines had thought would be his final resting place so many, many ages before.

"You," Pat managed. His voice was muffled from the pressure being applied to his mouth and the damage that had been done to the same. He allowed his tears to flow freely. No shame in crying, he thought, especially not at the end. An overdue end more than likely but still: The end.

Finis, he thought. *Externally his mouth was contorted in a grimace of pain. Yet internally? He was, surprisingly, smiling.*

"Yes," the man said. His last word was spoken with complete disdain. Seemingly satisfied he rose the barrel of his blaster into Pat's fading vision. Pat closed his eyes. His last thoughts before the light engulfed him and made the pain, both physical and mental that he had carried with him for ages vanish into nothingness were of Rebekka. *His* Rebekka. Not as she had been at the end of her life but as she had been in the beginning: Little more than a child masquerading as a pre-teen in a world not yet grown cold from the injection of chrome, steel and circuitry. Her smile. Her gentle touch. And her eyes… her brilliant, emerald green eyes. *In his mind's eye she smiled at him…*

And simultaneously, the words that he had spoken to William MacNuff echoed in his ears. "Unus est vera semita." His internal smile widened. *No truer words were ever spoken*, he mused, *May you understand them one day, William, as I have. As I do. One day…*

And Pat knew that he would. He was sure of it. Instinct had brought him to speak those words to the Jefferson runner yet instinct had not brought the Jefferson runner to ask him what he had asked him. *Skew? Gateway? Pathfinder?*

He already knows, Pat thought, *he may not realize it yet but he does. Whether the knowledge is something inherent in him or a mere coincidence doesn't matter. He knows. As for the rest? It will find him. It always does. I knew there was something about him, something… something…*

Those thoughts… those words along with Rebekka's eyes comforted him and despite the inevitability inherent in the moment he faced he smiled. He went.

However reluctantly, he went.

* * *

The man with the confused eyes released Pat McClane's jaw and commanded the Surveillance Mark to do the same with his arms. He watched with satisfaction as his quarry…

Little more than a pound of flesh, he thought…

…fell to the ground and landed upon it with a thud. He looked from the corpse to the machine and extended the hand that had held Pat's chin. In the other, he still held his blaster. The "drone" removed from its fuselage a small, portable communicator and placed it in the newcomer's outstretched hand. He pressed a button on the side of it and raised it to his mouth.

"Reinforcements," he paused, "to Leader," He released the button. The communicator crackled and cleared. A moment passed before the voice of a Leader asked him to "report."

He pressed the button again, "I've positively identified one of the previously unidentified occupants traveling with the Jefferson fugitives. It was Pat McClane as expected, formerly of Williamsport, MWT and more recently of Greentree, MWT. He has been…" the man paused… "Neutralized. MacNuff and Markinson remain at large along with an as-of-yet unidentified occupant though…" he paused… "Logic would dictate that their companion is Jeff Howard. I cannot extrapolate where they went or how far they got but recommend immediate track and pursuit." He released the button and waited for the Leader's response. A moment later it came.

"Surveillance Mark One will return to the Caravan and regroup. The fugitives' signal has been lost but their direction has been extrapolated as east. They are on foot and likely injured. We will track them… pursue them when our strength is renewed and reinforced."

It paused before continuing, "You will pursue now on foot, reinforcements."

"Am I to track them?" the man with the confused eyes asked, seemingly annoyed, "that task has not been assigned to me, yet."

"It has now, Infiltrator," the voice of the Leader confirmed, "resume your originally assigned role and await further instructions regarding the Jefferson, MWT fugitives. They will be your quarry, as well. That is all."

"UNDERSTOOD," the Surveillance Mark replied and extended its hand outward as the communicator fell silent. The newcomer… the Infiltrator paused for a moment before he depressed the "talk" button, reiterated the SM's affirmative with an identifiable note of disgust and handed it back to it. The SM, in turn, replaced it in its fuselage and turned to leave the clearing in the direction it had come from without a word.

The Infiltrator unblinkingly watched it leave. Its long strides carried it further in one step than his own strides would carry him in three until it disappeared into the shadows.

Beautiful in its simplicity… its perfection, he thought as it faded into the shadows ringing the clearing. Once it had vanished, he looked back down at the corpse that lay at his feet. Beside Pat McClane lay his useless blaster and the sword that he had carried.

He allowed his annoyance at being commanded by the Leader to overtake him and without warning, he planted one, booted toe forcibly in the corpse's ribs, recoiled, and then planted another against the corpse's chest. He recoiled a final time and was about to "punt" Pat's head when his eyes, once again, fell upon the sword. He bent down and picked it up by its hilt. He held it up and admired it in the dull light provided by the still-burning fuselage of what had once been the fugitives' vehicle. He hefted it and swung it in an arc.

He quickly felt his rage dissipate.

He considered… and then decided.

"Thank you, Pat," he said calmly. He spared his quarry a final glance, mimed a highly exaggerated bow and started off north out of the clearing and into the trees with the sword held down at his side. Distant and to the east, the first signs of dawn began to appear over the border between the Mid-Western Territory and the Eastern one. It was a gray, overcast and humid dawn that slowly rose over the clearing and subsequently over the motionless body of Pat McClane, outlaw and once-member of the People's Rebellion for Freedom and Equality turned hermit. Former denizen of Williamsport, MWT and most recently, Greentree, MWT. Anyone who chanced to encounter him lying there in the clearing next to his discarded blaster and the smoldering remnants of his truck that early, late summer morning in 15:CI would have been surprised considering the circumstances to see him smiling. But he was.

His eyes were closed and he was grinning eternally.

Another day in Endworld had begun.

PART TWO

Allied

"Who is the third who walks always beside you? When I count, there are only you and I together but when I look ahead up the white road there is always another one walking beside you."

CHAPTER EIGHT

We moved as quickly as we could through the woods and attempted not to pay attention to the sound of the firefight that raged behind us. Jeff remained in the lead and I brought up the rear. Often I tightened my grip upon my own weapon (I was also carrying Maria's) and looked back over my shoulder for any sign of Pat's or anyone's… shit, any*thing's* approach but all that remained behind us after a while was darkness. After an indeterminate amount of what passes for "time" in Endworld, even the sound of the firefight faded. The woods behind and around us grew silent and still.

As near as I could tell, we were alone.

Nothing approached from behind or from any direction as we continued to trot through the overgrowth, Jeff deftly leapt over fallen tree limbs and hollowed out stumps despite the fact that he carried a still motionless Maria in his arms. I kept pace as best I could but it was hard… *damn* hard.

And I'm only carrying a couple of blasters, I scolded myself. After a while, I reluctantly ceased looking over my shoulder.

He'll be along, I thought, *he promised he would. What did he say? "I will be, William. In one way or another. That much I can guarantee."*

I tried but was unable to trust in the reassurance that he had offered me as he'd stood stoically across from me, his blaster in one hand and his sword in the other. And the vision of him silhouetted against the flames of his once-truck, his blaster down and his sword point extended to face whatever unknown force bore down upon his position? It had seemed more than just a hero shot, whatever the hell *that* meant. In truth? It had felt like a visual eulogy for a man that in a short period of time had surprisingly endeared himself to me as both a mentor and a… dare I say *friend?*

Unus est vera semita, William. His strange words, though unfamiliar to me, echoed in my mind as we ran onward through the shadows. What did they mean?

Something's happened, I thought but immediately brushed the thought aside as the ground upon which we fled began to slope.

"Watch your footing," Jeff said—the first words he had spoken in a while—as he slowed his pace and began to make his way cautiously down the hill. I did as he had requested and slowed, as well. I was careful to judge my foot holds as I followed him down the slope. The ground beneath my boots was slick from rainfall and the oppressive humidity that still engulfed us like an invisible bubble. Once or twice I shifted my weight the wrong way and almost slipped but I managed to keep my footing until I gained the bottom.

The scene before me was virtually unchanged. More overgrowth stretched off to all points of the compass but there were two dissimilarities. The first was the dim, grayish-blue light that filtered through the trees directly ahead of us. *Dawn,* I thought. And the second? The sound of running water not far from our position.

A lot of water, I thought.

Jeff cocked his head and seemed to notice it, as well. "This way," he said after a moment and started to jog to my right. I followed but spared a final glance up the slope that we had just descended.

Nothing. The area atop the ridge was dark and empty.

He'll be along, in one way or the other, I thought again but I was already beginning to doubt said outcome as Jeff disappeared into a grove of lush trees. I followed. Ragged branches reached out toward my exposed face and lower arms and I felt one or two slice deep enough to draw blood. A brief moment later, the sound of Jeff moving through the trees before me ceased. Just when I thought that my own travel had slowed to a crawl I burst through the last of the thick overgrowth and emerged breathlessly…

I gasped at the sight before me. Stretching off to my left and my right in the dim, early morning light was a large river, swollen brown with rain. It flowed angrily passed. It spanned roughly 20 meters in width before its opposite shore rose out of it into another, thick stand of trees.

How the hell are we going to get across this? I thought.

Jeff had paused on the riverbank and had turned as I had burst through the last of the trees. He nodded to me, and I returned the gesture as he gently laid Maria down upon the surface.

"Rest for a moment," Jeff said as he holstered his weapon and removed his satellite phone from the front, right pocket of his corduroys, "I need to see if I can find out where we are."

"What about…?" I began.

"They're not coming," he concluded for me as he moved a few steps down the riverbank, likely to maximize any available reception, "if they were they'd be on us already. That's not to say that they *won't* be coming but for now I think we're in the clear. Pat either did what he said he was going to do or..."

Jeff paused and fell silent. He never continued his statement. He didn't need to. Apparently his suspicions were the same as mine. I moved over toward where Maria lay and crouched down next to her. I dropped her blaster beside me as I did and I touched my hand to her forehead. It was warm. Not overly-so but definitely warm. And she remained unconscious. Her breathing was gradually becoming less pained and labored, but I knew that that particular situation would change as soon as Jeff picked her up again. Fleeing blindly from an unknown force of machines was not going to improve her condition. Pat's assessment of her condition had been right: She needed medical attention.

Pat.

Unus est vera semita, William.

I shook the thought of him and his words away again and redirected my attention to Jeff who, in the growing light, moved his sat phone first up, then right, then left and finally down.

"Anything?" I asked from my crouch beside Maria.

Jeff shook his head, "I had something for a moment but it disappeared quickly. The good news? Despite it I've still got a rough idea of where we were. This river"—he gestured outward toward it—"is called the Shenango River and over *there*"—he gestured to the opposite bank—"is the Eastern Territory. The problem is that we need to find a way across."

"Do you know one?" I asked as I removed my hand from Maria's forehead and stood. *The Eastern Territory,* I thought, *almost there.*

Depends on what you consider "there" Vato, Pat's voice suddenly spoke in my mind, *you've still got quite a road ahead of you.* I practically jumped. It had sounded so clear... so *near* to me that I almost looked around to see if he had emerged from the tree stand bordering the river or if he had magically materialized beside me. He had not. The scene surrounding me was the same as it had been before.

Strange, I thought as Jeff shook his head.

"I wish I did," he responded, "but... and I'm guessing here but if we follow the bank we should, eventually find one. Considering how close the opposite bank is to where we're standing and the lack of any sort of habitation I don't think that we're *that* far from where we were heading."

"To the mercs?" I said suddenly. Jeff looked back at me confusedly.

"How do you know about…" he began.

"Pat told me while you were sleeping," I interrupted. He murmured something that sounded like "ah" and nodded as he looked away.

"You would have found out eventually," he said, his back still to me as he replaced the sat phone in his front, right pants' pocket, "no, not them. Not *yet*. There was one more stop he wanted to make before… *them*. If I'm right and if Pat wasn't fucking around"—he pointed to my right—"then we need to head south to get there. More so now."

"Why?" I asked.

Jeff turned back to me, "*She* needs medical attention. So do you for your shoulder in case you forgot. We'll hopefully find it there. But before we do anything"—he gestured to Maria—"we need to make a stretcher for her. Carrying her with busted ribs, bruised *or* broken, isn't doing her any good."

"Is there time?" I asked as I cradled my arm. I had been so caught up in our flight through the woods that I had temporarily forgotten about my injured shoulder. *Adrenaline,* I thought. The pain was bad but it was not intolerable so long as I kept my arm stationary. I looked from Jeff back to Maria and then back to him.

Jeff shrugged, "Is there *ever?*" He asked.

I nodded. Admittedly, he had a point and per his instruction we began to quickly collect the materials necessary to build a stretcher.

Sometime later, we stood on the bank of the Shenango River which separated the Mid-Western Territory from the Eastern one in the new day's dim light and admired our handiwork. The bier that we had constructed for Maria was rudimentary at best: Little more than a few tree limbs attached by our respective holsters and what yellowing vines we had found within the trees that Jeff had judged strong enough to support Maria's weight. We'd shifted the blasters, safeties on into the tops of our pants. Maria's still lay on the ground beside her. The stretcher wasn't much to look at…

"But it'll serve its purpose," Jeff said, "Help me get her on it, William."

We did so carefully so as to favor my shoulder, for every slight, lateral movement resulted in a fresh burst of pain. Maria shifted uneasily as we picked her up and positioned her on it. When Jeff was satisfied that she was adequately supported he picked her blaster up off of the beach, checked the safety, nodded and placed said weapon on the bier next to her.

"Okay," he said "onto step two. Let me see your arm."

I cautiously walked toward him unsure of what he intended. He took my left arm in both hands and positioned one by my shoulder and the other on my forearm. He moved my arm gently up and down… right and left. I cringed.

"Loose," he said matter-of-factly, "definitely dislocated. Try to relax. This'll only hurt for a minute."

Before I could vocalize an objection... shit, before I could even react, the hand that held my shoulder pushed in one direction and the one that held my forearm pulled in the other. I screamed as I felt my entire arm shift position. Tears threatened to fall but I choked them back. As quickly as he'd removed my arm he shifted from pulling to pushing on it. He directed it with the hand that held my shoulder. I felt something "snap" into place as he released me and I helplessly fell to my knees. I shouted an expletive through my tears as I looked up at him.

"Sorry, William," Jeff said, "it's like pulling off a bandage. Better to just do it and get it over with. How's it feel?"

I wanted to stand up and show him how it felt with my good, right fist but I refrained. After a moment of agony my left arm actually did begin to feel better. I wiped the tears away from my eyes with the back of my hand and looked up at Jeff. I nodded. He favored me with a tiny grin.

"First time's always the toughest," he said, "That's what passes for tri-age in the field. Do you have an extra shirt? No, of course you don't. Your bag is in the same place err... *places* that mine is. You can use the one you're wearing. Take it off and stick your arm in it like a sling. Don't be modest. You'll be able to lift with it but not much. Use your left arm directionally and keep the majority of the weight of the stretcher on your right arm. I'll do my part in the front. You'll be fine."

I nodded and removed the white turned gray from dirt, smoke and sweat t-shirt that I'd been wearing since we had left Pat's and knotted the sleeves over my left shoulder. I slipped my arm into the makeshift sling. When I was satisfied with the support I nodded to Jeff.

"Then let's do this," he said and moved over to the front of the stretcher. I followed and took up my designated position in the back. We each grasped our respective ends. Jeff counted to three and on three commanded me to "hoist." I did so and gritted my teeth against the pain that shot through my left arm. I quickly angled the stretcher to the right and the pain somewhat alleviated. Maria's body shifted slightly before it fell still.

"Okay then," he said, "South. I'm not sure how much time Pat bought for us but based on my experience I'd wager that what time we *do* have is running short. Let's go, William."

"Shouldn't we..." I began but stopped. Jeff turned and looked at me over his shoulder. He shook his head. I understood his meaning and did not pursue my intended question further. With a heavy heart, an aching shoulder and in fear of the worst for Pat McClane we set out south along the riverbank as the new day continued to unfold in gray silence around us, a silence broken only by the sound of the river that rushed passed us to our left and little else. The trees to our right remained still. Nothing stirred within them. We traveled that way indefinitely as time moved onward without check on the western bank of the Shenango River and throughout Endworld.

Multiple stops to accommodate mine and Maria's conditions later, Jeff paused and lowered his end of the stretcher to the ground. I did the same and sighed in relief as the strain upon my bad left arm and shoulder diminished.

"Rest," Jeff said as he wandered down to the water's edge and knelt. He bent down, gathered two handfuls of the rushing river water and splashed it upon his face. He did so again and ran his fingers through his buzz cut before he stood and returned to where I stood next to the stretcher holding Maria. He sat down on the riverbank next to me. I followed suit. I looked up at the eastern sky over the opposite bank of the Shenango.

The Eastern Territory, I thought again. It was further away than it had been previously, roughly 50 meters from where we sat. It remained gray and overcast. As such, it was difficult to determine what time of day it was but my gut instinct and the steadily increasing heat and humidity (*how can it be getting MORE humid,* I thought) told me that it was approaching midday. I ran my arm across my forehead and it came away wet with sweat. I reached into the left, front pocket of my jeans and felt my Zippo and the bag that held my last cigarette within it. I removed both…

And sighed. Not unsurprisingly my last cigarette had been reduced to an untidy pile of tobacco and crumpled paper at the bottom of the bag. I muttered under my breath before I replaced both of the items in my pocket. Jeff apparently saw me do so and he patted me on the back. I glanced back over my right shoulder at the tree stand and winced as I did so. As had been the case since we had started our trek southward nothing moved within it. Not even a hint of movement. The sky above the trees looked darker than the sky over the opposite side of the river.

More rain? I thought. My suspicion was corroborated by a distant, low roll of thunder. I didn't know whether to be relieved at the possibility of a thorough cleaning or annoyed at the prospect of potentially maneuvering our makeshift stretcher through a downpour with a bad shoulder.

Jeff echoed my thought, "More rain on the way," he said, "Not long before it gets here judging from those clouds." He reached into his pocket and removed his sat phone. He turned it on, tapped the screen a few times and hissed as he placed it in his pants pocket. "Still nothing," he said.

"Pat," I said suddenly. Jeff turned from his purveyance of the area to look at me.

"Sorry?" he responded.

"Pat," I said again with a bit more emphasis, "he didn't make it, did he?"

Jeff let out a sigh, "No way to know for sure, William."

I echoed his sigh and lowered my head. I felt defeated, "I'm sorry."

"Nothing to apologize for, William," Jeff said as he again patted me on the back and returned his gaze to the river and the opposing bank, "he did what he felt he had to do. And it worked. We're still here. Wherever he is…" he paused and spoke no more. Another roll of thunder, closer than the last one graced my ears before silence descended over the riverbank and the surrounding area again.

"Not just about that," I finally said after a long moment, "I'm sorry, Jeff. I know this wasn't what *you* wanted."

Jeff lowered his head but did not avert his gaze from the river. "It never is, William," he said, "I never told you why I quit, did I? Why I retired? Of course I didn't. We've only known each other for a day. Not a lot of time to get to know someone, huh?"

"No," I responded, "it isn't. And you don't have to tell me, Jeff. Honestly."

Jeff shrugged, "I will one day, William. But not now. Now…" He stood and dusted himself off.

"*Now*, you need to stay with Maria," he changed the topic, "I'm going to go scout down the shoreline a bit and see if I can get my bearings." I nodded as he turned and started off to my right. He never once looked back at the responsibility that in my mind had been reluctantly forced upon him by Pat's… *departure.*

Is that all that I am at this point? I thought, *that we are? Someone else's cross to bear?* I watched him go until he reached the next bend in the river roughly 10 meters away and vanished around it. I sighed once again and looked over at Maria. I placed my hand upon her head. It was warmer than before. And did her breathing seem more labored?

"Wow, Mia," I said out loud as I removed my hand from her forehead, ran it through my unruly hair, and then across my tri-colored stubble, "what the hell have I gotten us into?" My question was meant to be rhetorical but instinctively I glanced around the area. Thankfully no one… no *thing* answered me. It was just me and Maria, one of us conscious and the other not. We sat alone upon the riverbank with only the fast running and swollen

Shenango River that separated and likely still separates, at its most narrow point, the Mid-Western Territory from the Eastern, and the thickening cloud-bank to the west of us to keep us company.

It was, I'll admit, a watershed moment for me in those early days of our journey to freedom, a journey which eventually and unexpectedly carried me here to an old, abandoned office and warehouse nestled between another, nameless river and the Highway. Here where I currently write these words on a yellowing pad of paper with a blunt pencil stub. Here in a place that Pat and others would have called "The Center of Bumblefuck."

I thought about turning back. For the first time since leaving Jefferson with Maria by my side I seriously considered the prospect of turning tail and heading not east into the unknown but back in the direction that we had come from. Back to the shoulder of the Highway and then west to Greentree, Bryn Mawr, and eventually? Jefferson.

Would I be welcomed back? I knew the answer to that question. I knew that my life—as another roll of thunder was followed by the first new drops of rain to fall upon the already damp surface that surrounded me—was forfeit upon capture. But would surrendering spare Maria? Jeff? Were Pat captured and not worse, would it spare him? Despite the ever-present absence of time in Endworld perhaps... well, perhaps there was still time, I considered. I could leave Maria by the water's edge. Jeff would return shortly from his perusal of the shore south of our position. He would find her and carry her with him to wherever Pat had intended to take us. Perhaps even further. Perhaps back with him to Greentree. He *had* expressed interest in her upon first encountering her at Pat's. He would take care of her... would protect her...

I looked down at Maria. Tears filled my eyes and mingled with the rain that had begun to fall with a greater intensity. She looked so peaceful lying there on the riverbank, her raven black hair pooled around her head, a flush upon her cheeks and her eyes closed.

So innocent, I mused. I thought of Pat's Rebekka... thought of her fate and the choice of whether to stay or leave became academic. I bent in and kissed my oldest, dearest and truest friend on her forehead.

"Goodbye, Mia," I whispered. I picked up my blaster and stood slowly. I turned for the woods behind me...

And stopped. I could hear someone calling my name from a distance away. I glanced down the shoreline and watched as the unmistakable figure of Jeff "Jeebus" Howard rounded the bend he had earlier disappeared around and ran towards me.

"William!" He shouted over the sound of the rain that pounded the river and the riverside and the occasional low rumble of thunder that accompanied it as he closed the distance between us and stopped a step or two away from me. I held my weapon limply at my side.

"What are you doing?" He shouted. I stumbled over an explanation. I did not want to admit to my planned and unfulfilled course of action. Suddenly? I felt weak. And as I looked from Jeff back to the motionless figure of Maria that lay at my feet I mentally chastised myself for what I had intended.

She needs you, my coldly rational voice encouraged, *whatever the result, she needs you. Not Jeff and no one else. You.*

"I...!" I shouted back over the din, *"I was just stretching my legs, Jeff!"*

Jeff looked at me askance and responded with something, but a loud peal of thunder drowned it out. As it subsided I asked him to repeat his statement and he did. And I knew... for the moment, at least... that I was, to employ an old pre-Administration cliché, "pot committed."

No turning back, at least not now, my coldly rational voice spoke in my mind and I mentally flipped it off.

Has that ever really been an option? I thought in response. I was answered by silence.

"I SAID I FOUND SOMETHING!" Jeff repeated, *"Maybe shelter, maybe MORE! It's about 40 meters or so beyond the next bend and back in the woods! Help me with Maria! If anything we can get out of THIS!"* He gestured to the downpour.

I again looked from Jeff to Maria and then back to Jeff. I nodded. We positioned ourselves on either side of the stretcher and with some effort, got it up and started moving south again down the riverbank.

CHAPTER NINE

We made our way at as brisk a pace as we could despite the steadily intensifying rain, my handicap and the bier suspended between us. Directly beyond the closest bend in the river Jeff turned and started up the shore toward the woods. The rain continued to pound the surface of the ground, the two weary souls that walked upon it and the unconscious soul suspended between them. Our boot falls were drowned by the steady rolls of thunder that echoed across the riverside and the surrounding area. I quickened my pace despite the nagging pain in my shoulder and my arm, desperate to get out of the downpour and get someplace dry. I breathed a sigh of relief when we broke through the first of the trees and found ourselves in a leaf-covered grotto. Rain still fell around us but in a diminished capacity because of the canopy overhead. Jeff stopped and looked left and right before he gestured to the left.

"This way," he said. We trudged onward. Our respective boots *squished* through the mud. A meter or two later we broke through the lush overgrowth and once again found ourselves standing in the forest. Jeff stopped, considered for a moment and gestured left. He walked and I followed, Maria suspended between us.

A short time later we found ourselves standing in a relatively expansive clearing directly outside what appeared to be a large, hollowed out tree trunk. Upon closer observation I saw it to be an opening. Jeff looked over his shoulder at me and surprisingly smiled.

"What is it?" I asked.

"An entrance," he responded, "looks like a service path into an old mine. This *whole area* of the continent used to be the coal mining capital of the world."

"Coal?" I asked. *What the hell is that?* I wondered.

"*Fuel*, William," Jeff answered, "a different kind. What we used to use to power stuff with. Coal, gas… there were a bunch of different types. Now we just use electricity and battery power but back in the day we had a lot more choices. Not all of them were the healthiest and the safest but hey: They were *choices.*"

I nodded. *Always nice to have choices,* I thought. I glanced passed Jeff to the "tunnel's" (*it looks more like a cave,* I thought) entrance. The lack of ambient light and the heavy vegetation that covered the edges created an optical illusion and made the entrance to the mine look smaller than it actually was. No wonder I'd mistaken it for a log.

"Ready?" Jeff asked. I nodded. He moved forward and through it with ease and I followed. I glanced behind me once, almost positive that I would see Pat, someone…

Or some*thing…*

…standing there. But the area behind me was empty.

Strange, I thought. I could feel the skin on my back crawling. It felt… well, I'll not lie. It felt as if there were eyes in the woods watching me: Innumerable pairs of eyes watching from every shadowy crag and corner created by the felled trees and underbrush that had seemingly grown unchecked for ages.

There are haints here, Vato, Pat's voice suddenly spoke in my mind again and I physically jumped, *ghosts. The further east into the Scorched Land that you travel the more you'll feel them so get used to it.*

I brushed his caution aside as best I could but it was difficult. After a brief moment I entered the tunnel at Jeff's repeated urging, my end of the stretcher held out before me. The mossy and leaf-covered entrance caressed my skin with its deteriorating filth. It parted and I was inside.

It was dryer, *much* dryer than the forest had been though a healthy puddle of ankle-deep water had formed around the entrance. And it was dark within: *Pitch black.* I heard Jeff fumble with something and blinked at the sudden light that stabbed forth from the screen of his phone. *It doubles as a flashlight?* I thought. In the surprisingly brilliant white light I could see that the tunnel in which we stood extended downward on a slight slope before it came to a bend about 10 or 15 meters away. I could tell that it was man or machine made (*can't rule out the latter possibility, Vato,* Pat's voice cautioned and I almost squeaked in surprise): The smoothness of the walls and the uniformity of the shaft—no animal or natural occurrence that I knew of could have burrowed such a path. I looked down at my feet and my suspicion was confirmed. The remnants of two rusted, metal rails spaced evenly apart extended out and downward from the entrance.

Tracks, I thought. Time had all but covered what evidence remained of them a few meters in but the ones nearest the entrance remained visible, likely due to their prolonged exposure to the elements.

"Where to?" I asked semi-sarcastically. I knew the answer before Jeff spoke it.

"Down," he said, "*carefully.* Watch your step, William. These things can get *really* steep really quick."

I nodded and we started down the shaft, Jeff still in the lead and I bringing up the rear, a motionless Maria still suspended between us. The going was not overly treacherous. We reached the first bend with virtually no difficulty and turned it. The shaft continued straight for what appeared to be an immeasurable distance. Jeff's light, though powerful, terminated about 20 to 30 meters down the tunnel. I could see our path steepening but I understood Jeff's desire to head further in. *The farther away from the entrance*, I reasoned, *the better*.

We reached the next bend in the tunnel. The area opened up a bit and we found ourselves standing amidst a four-way intersection. Directly before us the tunnel that we'd been travelling down continued. But to our right and left were additional paths. Each descended into equal darkness. It was impossible to tell one from the other.

"Well *here's* a pickle," Jeff said sarcastically as he took in the four different paths, "let's have a look. Might as well put Maria down, William."

I nodded and obliged. I laid my end of the stretcher on the ground. Jeff did the same with his. He moved toward the tunnel directly across from us and peered inside. After a moment he moved to the one to our right. He wandered inside, his flashlight-phone shining upon the smooth-cut walls, saw something and stopped. He turned and gestured to me. I spared Maria's motionless body a final, concerned look and walked over to where Jeff was standing no more than a meter beyond the tunnel opening to see what he was gesturing toward.

The object that he indicated was head-high and on the left hand side of the tunnel. I had never seen anything quite like it before though it somehow seemed... *familiar (like so much in this place,* I thought). It was a swath, maybe as big as my hand, of what appeared to be brown cloth, tarnished and frayed around the edges. A black "X" bordered in gray crisscrossed the background. Within the "X" were... I counted... 13 gray stars. It was old: That much I could tell. I bent into look more closely at it and could see vestiges of red in the brown background and in the "X?" vestiges of blue. The stars themselves appeared gray with grime. I reached in with my good right hand and brushed at one of them. My fingers came away black with soot. *Yes,* I concluded, *those stars were definitely white once.*

"What is it?" I asked.

Surprisingly, Jeff smiled again, "A sigil," he responded, "and a sign."

"A sign," I questioned, "of what?"

He looked from the sign to me. His smile did not waver.

"Our path," he said confidently and gestured into the darkness, "Seems Pat *wasn't* fucking with me. With *us*. Goddamn you, McClane." He shook his head and let out a small chuckle before he readdressed me.

"Let's get Maria up, William," he said, "we're going *this* way."

We traveled through the darkness deeper and deeper into the bowels of the old mine. Jeff led the way and I continued to bring up the rear. The stretcher with Maria upon it remained suspended between us. Every time we came to an intersection we placed Maria down, spread out across the area, and looked for the same or another sign of the correct path to follow. Each time we found a similar swath of cloth nestled within one of the two or three adjoining tunnels. *Our path,* I thought more than once before we continued our journey down the tunnel indicated.

Time moved onward without check as time always does in Endworld both above and... I was discovering, *beneath* the surface. The air around us remained humid but it was noticeably cooler the deeper that we descended. I felt the sweat chilling upon my forehead and my damp clothes clung uncomfortably to my body. Every time I exhaled a fine cloud of mist materialized before me. The chill in the air did not help my aching shoulder which seemed to throb more and more with each step further into the darkness. I was growing progressively wearier as we emerged from the tunnel that we had been travelling through into another opening...

And found ourselves facing a dead end.

I quickly scanned the interior for another, smaller opening but did not see one. *Are you fucking kidding me?* I thought. Jeff echoed my thought verbally and moved into the center of the... *room?* It seemingly had the appearance of one albeit a room with walls of damp stone and a domed ceiling from which hung small, strange rock outgrowths. They looked like teeth filed to points and I shuddered at the prospect as I followed Jeff's lead. After a few steps Jeff soundlessly lowered his end of the stretcher to the ground. I followed suit and the pain in my shoulder temporarily subsided. Maria shifted briefly on her bier and sighed. I felt a twinge in my chest at the sound followed by another wave of concern.

She needs medical attention, and she needs it soon, my coldly rational voice spoke in my mind. I was helpless not to agree with it. I could feel the heat baking off of her despite the chill that surrounded us.

"Well this is a…"

"*Pickle*," I completed impatiently, "*yeah*, Jeff. You *already said that. What now?*"

"Hmm," he, to my disdain, considered calmly as he began to move around the perimeter of the room. He ran his right hand across the smooth surface while his left hand shined his phone-flashlight (*PF,* I thought, *like the TC only… different?*) meticulously on every nook and cranny. Once or twice he rapped his knuckles softly against the stone: *Tap-tap. Tap-tap.* And after a few successive raps…

Boom-boom.

He stepped back and turned to me. I knew what that sound meant as well as he did. *Hollow,* I thought. He qualified this suspicion by knocking again—*boom-boom*—and nodded satisfactorily. He quickly turned back to the wall and started to run his hands over and across it. Was he looking for edges? Whatever he was looking I moved forward and joined him.

"Help me," he said as he placed his hands a small distance apart from each other and pushed. I did the same with my good arm but the wall did not budge.

"Again," he said and continued pushing. I strained harder but the wall did not move a hair. He stepped back, cocked his head curiously and reiterated his "hmm" from before. I glanced back at the tunnel that we'd entered through and saw no solution to our predicament there. Short of blasting our way through the wall I could think of no other alternatives…

Until one was surprisingly provided us.

A loud screech of static filled the area and Jeff and I both cringed. Maria moaned in her sleep. Said screech was followed by a voice that seemed to come from nowhere and everywhere all at once. Deep, male and amplified, it seemingly materialized out of the chilling air and forcibly asked, "*Who goes there?!*"

I froze midway through turning back to Jeff from the entrance. I could still see the tunnel in my peripheral vision. I sensed Jeff do the same.

"Um…" I began.

"*Identify!*" the voice spoke again. Not a question but a command.

"Jeff Howard," Jeff spoke instinctively, "from Greentree, MWT. And…"

He paused. It took me a moment to realize that he was speaking to me.

"Oh!" I said, "Err, William MacNuff and Maria Markinson from Jefferson."

"Password!" the voice insisted immediately, more urgently than before. I slowly turned just my head to face Jeff and Jeff shrugged. I turned back to the tunnel's entrance...

And saw two figures step from either side of the tunnel with weapons drawn and pointed at us. The shadowy figures seemed human enough but my instincts overrode my common sense and I reached for the butt of my blaster, jutting out from the top of my pants with my good right arm as fast as I could manage...

It was not fast enough. One of the figures moved into the room with wholly unexpected speed and closed the distance between us before I could get my weapon out. I heard Jeff shout a negative from behind me as the butt of my attacker's (*her? I think it's a her,* I thought) weapon caught me squarely on my right temple. The last thing that I saw as I fell on my back directly next to a motionless Maria, as grayness faded to darkness were the eyes of my attacker—blue—her short, dirty blonde hair and, strangely, a set of perfect dimples at either corner of her mouth. The last thing I heard was Jeff shouting another negative and the amplified voice that seemed to come from nowhere and *everywhere* at once echoing said negative and shouting to *"WAIT, CAREN!."* I heard what sounded like a "click" and a subsequent low grinding followed by what sounded like a rush of air but that was all as darkness faded to unconsciousness and eventually...

Silence.

CHAPTER TEN

I had never been unconscious before that moment in my life… had never even fainted near as I can remember as I sit here in my surrogate home writing these words upon the yellowing sheets of paper that have become the framework for this portion of my chronicle. Unconsciousness is not *nothingness*. It's similar to being asleep but the sensation is… well, the best way that I can describe it is *disjointed*. Occasionally you semi-emerge from the darkness and you hear things. Voices and residual sounds: The walls settling, water dripping from the ceiling into a puddle. Thereafter you descend once again into the blackness.

I cannot tell you how long I was out for but I can tell you that while I was out I heard voices both familiar and unfamiliar. Once I listened to Jeff as he explained who I was. Another time I heard an unfamiliar female voice explaining her motivations for attacking me (*Caren: The girl with the blue eyes and the dimples,* I assumed). Another time I heard an unfamiliar male voice talking about Maria's condition which apparently was "stable." Said moments of lucidity quickly faded back into darkness, however.

Another misconception about being unconscious is that when you're out there is nothing. No dreams… *nothing*. This is not entirely true either. For the most part the darkness is unbroken but there are fleeting moments when the darkness is temporarily shattered. The mind, as I'm sure Freud and his unhealthy infatuation with his mother would agree, is an amazing thing. In the time between when the girl with the blue eyes and the dimples pistol whipped me and the time when I finally re-opened my eyes the darkness occasionally dispelled long enough for me to see and hear things.

Once or twice the vision of the beach and Maria's blaster-fire depleted figure surfaced in my mind and I was thankful when the vision departed. Once or twice the words from my dream returned though their origin or origins remained unknown to me: *Skew, Gateway* and *Pathfinder*. Still another time Pat grinned his cocky grin back at me in the shifting light from the flames that engulfed his once-truck. And still another time I saw him standing with his back to me (*Hero shot*, I thought again, still unsure of what it meant), silhouetted against the same firelight, ready to face whatever force emerged from the woods before him.

Unus est vera semita, William, he reassured me without turning. I tried to call out to him but the vision quickly faded.

But the visions were not the most memorable departures from the darkness. In the darkness I occasionally heard voices... *echoes* of things that had been said to me. The echoes centered primarily on the conversations I had had with Pat both about the world and about his past. For some reason it all seemed significant, not just to his plight but to mine and Maria's, as well. At the time I didn't know why I felt that way and to be honest with you? I still don't...

Well, not entirely...

...but his caution before all hell broke loose about our road and his reference to his and Rebekka's betrayer's eyes—*one minute blue, the next green, the next brown and the next hazel. Gray, black... any color you like*? They seemed to constantly return, many times attached to the vision of a shockingly familiar figure lying face down in a clearing, motionless by the shifting light of a smoldering fire. Shortly before I opened my eyes I remembered one last statement. Not an echo but something original. No. *Statement* is the not the correct way to describe it. It felt like a warning and it was certainly Pat's voice that spoke it.

Deceptionis possit catus, William, it said. His words felt like they were derived from the same language as his earlier statement but they were unfamiliar. Despite not knowing what they meant they sent a shiver down my spine. That shiver followed me up from the blackness to consciousness and after an indeterminate amount of time I opened my eyes.

Dim light filtered in through my blurred vision. I waited, prepared for the sounds that signified the conscious world to fade but for once they did not. I slowly opened my eyes and quickly closed them again. I opened them again and mentally willed the blurriness away. *Rinse and repeat,* I thought and did so again. After a few attempts said blurriness dissipated and my vision cleared.

I was in a room, no bigger than the living room of my childhood home back in Jefferson. But it was different... my *God* it was different. A lone, flickering light bulb swung from the ceiling in a seemingly phantom breeze. I was lying upon what appeared to be a cot and a sheet covered me to my waist. My bare torso and my chest were exposed. My injured left arm lay in a real sling, not the makeshift one that I had fashioned from my t-shirt while on the riverbank. A meter or so away from me was another, empty cot, but the sheets upon it were disorganized and I got the sense that it had until recently been occupied. The walls of the room were lined with tables and cabinets. Upon the nearest one I could see a white bowl with a dark piece of cloth hanging out of it.

No, I realized, not dark but wet. My old t-shirt turned sling. A sharp stab of pain through my right temple reminded me of the events leading up to my blacking out and I cautiously raised my right hand to it…

I cringed. There was a sizable lump there.

I closed my eyes again against the pain and re-opened them. It did not subside. Slowly I forced myself up on my good arm and once again felt the world swim around me. Gray spots materialized before me and I waited patiently for them to clear. After a long and disconcerting moment in which I was sure I was going to pass out again they did, as did some degree of the vertigo that I was experiencing. I forced myself up a bit further, and then a bit further before I officially swung my legs out from under me and over the side of the cot. I sat up.

The dizziness intensified momentarily and then disappeared. The pain in my head also subsided and for a brief moment I once again considered how long I had been unconscious for. I dismissed the thought as irrelevant and focused on sizing up my surroundings further.

Along with the aforementioned tables and cabinets and the single, swinging light bulb that hung overhead, the room had very few furnishings. The occasional chair sat in a random position around the room. One, in particular, was positioned a step or two away from my cot. But other than that it was relatively nondescript. My eyes fell upon one corner of the room that was enshrouded in more shadow than the rest. I squinted, and realized that the shadow was, in fact, a curtain or a sheet of some sort. As if in recognition it briefly shifted position before it fell still, again.

A doorway, perhaps?

I considered standing, reconsidered it and finally gave in. I dropped my bare feet to the ground and felt their soles chilled by what felt like a stone floor. A jolt of awareness flooded my mind at the sensation. I slid off of the edge of the cot and into a standing position. My head once again spun but the sensation passed quickly. I glanced around and saw my boots sitting next to one of the chairs against the wall but not my weapon, and my heart sped up at the prospect of facing whatever lay ahead without the weapon Pat had given me.

Nothing you can do about it now, Vato, Pat's voice spoke in my mind.

"Guess not," I muttered aloud and walked over to the chair. I sat down, and pulled on my boots. It took me an extra moment to tie them as my mind was still a little fuzzy but when they were securely placed on my feet I stood carefully and made my way over to the shadow that I assumed was a doorway.

Easy, William, my coldly rational voice spoke in my mind, *you don't know what's out there. And you don't have a weapon to defend yourself with.*

I didn't and I *didn't* but I assumed that for better or for worse there were more answers *out there* than in the small room that I'd awoken in. *Noted,* I thought in response and cautiously pulled the curtain back a hair. I glanced out at...

I gasped.

The area directly beyond the doorway gradually sloped downward in a continuation of the same, cold stone floor that I stood upon but I realized as I glanced in awe at the area outside my "room" that it was far from just a floor. It was the base of a large cavern that extended out for at least a kilometer or more in all directions. The walls of said cavern appeared, from a distance, to be made of the same black and dark gray stone that lay beneath my feet and the ceiling, which was inset with a jarring number of the same "teeth filed to points" that I'd observed in the cavern in which Caren had knocked me out, barreled overhead at a surprising height. I marveled at how wispy clouds of mist seemed to cling to it.

A surprising if not overwhelming amount of ambient light emanated from within the seam where the ceiling met the wall and I considered its origin: *Electric or otherwise? Biological, perhaps?* I considered. In the light I could see distinctly what appeared to be a collection of habitations which stretched off at equal intervals between my position and what looked like a thin, silver ribbon that cut the cavern in half. *A stream,* I thought, *or a river, maybe?* On the far side of the stream-river (*an SR,* I thought with a half-hearted chuckle) there were a few other structures but that area was predominated by what appeared to be well-cultured fields of...

Greenery? Vegetation? I thought, *how strange.* On the coattails of that thought came a second one: *Whoever lives here grows things despite living underground. Jesus,* I thought, *how far down am I? A kilometer? Two? More? How can they do that with no sunlight?* It was one of the many questions that I desired to have answered as my awareness of my surroundings continued to improve.

I stepped through the curtain and turned to look at the structure that I had emerged from. I reached out and touched the material that it was constructed from. It was surprisingly firm but was slimy with moisture. I pressed harder and felt it give a bit beneath the palm of my hand. In the light of the cavern it appeared reddish-brown and seemed to be inlaid with what looked like slivers of grass or reeds. From somewhere deep within my subconscious a term to describe the material appeared and then vanished. *Another piece of residual memory,* Mister Cold and Rational cautioned. I turned and once again glanced out over the expanse of the cavern. Whatever the material, all of the structures seemed to be made of it.

Amazing, I thought as I inhaled deeply the earthy smell that pervaded the area and exhaled. There were a handful of people moving amongst the habitations but no more than a dozen as far as I could see and none seemed to be alert to my presence. My internal clock, though likely jaded by the absence of time and the duration of my unconscious state, told me that it was early. *Morning, still,* I thought, as I began to move down the slope and closer to the nearest structure.

There was a woman mulling about outside it with her back turned to me. She had straight, dirty-blonde hair that stretched down to the small of her back and curled slightly at the edges. She was roughly the same height and figure as Maria and as I moved closer, I noticed that she was wearing a pair of form-fitting blue jeans over the top of what appeared to be an equally form-fitting black body suit. Her ample... *attributes* were highly visible and I felt a blush of redness suffuse my cheeks. I moved up behind her—she did not stir at my approach—and cleared my throat when I was within a step or two of her.

The woman turned quickly to look at me and smiled, "You're awake!" she exclaimed with glee and clapped her hands together, "wonderful." She stretched out her left hand and I cautiously took it in my right. Her face was as youthful as mine though there was something in her clear, gray-green eyes that bespoke a wealth of experience to rival Jeff's and Pat's...

Unus est vera semita, William...

...and I shrugged the thought of him and what he had said to me aside. She too had dimples, but they were smaller then I remembered those of my blue-eyed attacker's being. Her most astonishing feature was the abundance of freckles that stretched across the tops of her cheeks and beneath her eyes. I glanced down at the hand that held mine and the arm above it and saw an equal abundance of them there. I smiled back as my eyes once again met hers.

"William MacNuff," I said with a firm shake. The woman nodded and her smile widened.

"I know," she said, "I know. Carole Wetherhill, William. That's 'Carole' with an 'E...' like the Christmas kind."

I looked at her askance, "'Christmas...'"

She gestured to me with her other hand, "Sorry. Unknown reference, huh? I sometimes forget what it's like"—she gestured to the roof of the cavern—"up there. No worries, William. Maybe I can explain later. My husband Steve is who's been taking care of you. He's out on rounds now but he should be back shortly. You're probably hungry. Come on inside. I've got a fresh pot of coffee and some food."

She turned and started to walk toward the closest structure. I started after her but stopped. Carole, apparently sensing my pause, turned back to me.

"My friends," I said, surprised at how I had unknowingly pluralized the term to include Jeff "Jeebus" Howard, "the man and the girl that I was with. The one with the broken ribs..."

Carole smiled, "Maria?" she asked. I nodded.

"She's fine," Carole said without pause and I felt an overwhelming sense of relief at her validation of Maria's condition, "and to put your mind at rest they were just bruised. Her ribs, I mean. She woke up shortly after you guys got here."

After we were brought in, you mean, I thought.

"Anyway," Carole continued, "she went with Steve. Said she needed to stretch her legs a bit. She's doing better. Her fever's down, and her ribs? Well, even bruised and not broken ribs don't heal overnight. But in a couple more days? She'll be fine. You too, by the way. And as for Jeff? He's with Alex."

"Alex?" I asked. Carole nodded.

"Alex Parker," she said, "he's the guy who runs this place. You'll meet him soon enough. I know he's looking forward to meeting you. But for now you need to get some food into you. As your nurse that's a command and not a request."

"'This place,'" I said, "Where exactly is this, Carole?"

She did not move but her smiled widened as she gestured around her, "*Freeworld One,*" she said, her voice suffused with pride, "one of the last havens for free humans here on the mainland of the continent, directly beneath the border between the Mid-Western and Eastern Territories. That river down there"—she gestured to the thin, silver ribbon of liquid running through the center of town—"is the underground twin of the Shenango River. We call it 'Little Shenango.'"

"Freeworld One," I repeated. The words rolled off of my tongue. It seemed... *fitting*, "what about Freeworlds Two and Three?"

She giggled as she moved toward me, "Witty, William. *Very* witty. There is no two or three. There's only one and we call it home." She held her hands out to me, "Jeff said you asked a lot of questions. He wasn't kidding. That's good but save them for later. Right now you need your strength. Stop stalling and *come on.*" She tensed her extended arms as if to signal me and I reached out and took her hands. They were calloused but her touch was warm. My stomach was growling and I considered a cup or three of coffee essential to recovering my awareness. So, with little reluctance, I followed her inside.

The interior of Carole Wetherhill's home was sparsely furnished. By the flickering light of a lone, standing lamp which was plugged into an orange extension cord that trailed away from it and disappeared beneath the wall, the structure appeared to consist of only the main room into which we first entered and a small kitchen adjoining it—nothing more, really, than a table upon which sat a steaming pot of some liquid (*coffee*, I presumed from the smell), a basket of fruit (apples, primarily, with a few of the same black berries that we had eaten at Pat's interspersed), a few shelves and a small... what appeared to be a metal box in the corner.

"That's our icebox," Carole said without prompting and motioned toward the metal box which had a similar orange extension cord extending out from behind it, "kind of like a small-scale fridge where we keep what few perishables that we have. Most of what we eat is either fresh or canned."

I nodded. The living room into which we had entered and stood was furnished with a couple of comfortable looking and well-used chairs next to which lay a couple of small, rounded tables. Upon one of them, a device similar to, but slightly different in appearance to Jeff's and Pat's satellite phones lay dark upon what appeared to be a portable battery charger. The indicator light upon it was red. Another electrical cord—black—stretched out from the side of it and seemed to be hardwired to the same, orange cord that the lamp was plugged in to, the junction covered by a thick bulge of black electrical tape. Upon the other lay a familiar sight: A flat, square board checkered with white spaces and black spaces. Upon some of the spaces sat carved wooden figurines. Their names ran through my mind despite not having seen them in what felt like an eternity: *Pawn, Rook, Knight, Bishop, Queen,* and of course the *King.*

A Chess Board, I thought and felt a twinge of regret as first my father's and then Pat's face swam briefly though my mind before they vanished. Upon one of the walls directly next to a wood-framed opening that overlooked Freeworld One and what Carole had called "Little Shenango" stood an old and splintered bookcase upon which haphazardly lay an impressive collection of printed work.

No e-readers here, I thought. Across from the entrance to the structure I could see another archway and beyond it, what appeared to be a bedroom. I could see the corner of either a bed or a cot beyond the left door jamb. There was no sign of a television or of a computer, an observation which I found most refreshing and there was no sign of a bathroom. I vocalized both to my host.

She chuckled as she removed a mug from one of the shelves in the kitchen and filled it with the steaming, black liquid that occupied the pot, "Sorry, William. The accommodations aren't exactly luxurious. Little in the way of what passes for Administration-sanctioned entertainment here in Freeworld One. What little electricity we *do* have comes from a series of battery-operated generators positioned around the perimeter of the cavern. We use them to power the track lighting that rings the city and things like the light up in Steve's office, the light and the ice box in here and our phone chargers. But the power grid is notoriously fragile..."

That explains the flickering, I thought.

"...as for indoor plumbing?" She continued, "You're *also* out of luck but I *did* leave some fresh water, a rag, a bar of soap and a towel out for you in the bedroom"—she gestured to the opposing doorway—"if you want to wash up."

"What about," I began, paused, probably blushed and said, "Well... *you* know."

Carole chuckled again, "Don't be modest, William. There's an outhouse out back if you need it."

I smiled and shook my head, "I'm good... for now. But washing up sounds great."

"Be my guest," she said and motioned again to the opposing doorway.

The bedroom was as sparsely furnished as the rest of the structure: A neatly-made bed seemingly big enough for just two people, a couple of circular tables similar to the ones in the living room positioned on either side of said bed and against the wall and immediately beyond the doorway and to my left, a tarnished and cracked dresser. Upon the top of the dresser sat a mirror, a flickering candle and a large, white porcelain bowl of what appeared to be clean water. Directly next to it sat a folded towel and atop it, a fresh bar of soap. I smiled and cleaned myself up as thoroughly as I could manage given the sling within which my left arm lay.

A few moments later, after a quick survey of my stubble-laden but clean face and my wavy but slicked back hair I was feeling significantly more… *human,* sarcasm fully intended. I toweled off and turned from the dresser and the "sink" and made my way back into the main living area of Carole's home. She was seated at the table with a mug that steamed in front of her. Across from her sat another cup filled to the brim with coffee and the bowl of fruit. I licked my lips at the prospect of caffeine and sustenance and began to walk over to the table to join her when I heard voices outside: One unfamiliar male voice and one incredibly familiar female voice. Both appeared to be moving closer. I paused, the coffee and the fruit momentarily forgotten, and redirected my attention to the structure's entrance as the voices grew louder and louder. The female giggled at something the male had said and the male let out a loud guffaw. I looked from the doorway to Carole. Carole picked up her mug, took a sip of her coffee and smiled.

"That'd be Steve," she said, "and Maria if I'm not mistaken."

As if to quantify her statement two figures stepped through the entryway and into the living room of the structure. The man in the lead—Steve Wetherill, I presumed—was a sight: About as tall as myself but easily as old as Carole if not more so, he was thin… almost lanky in appearance and had straight black hair which hung to roughly his shoulders. Said hair was complimented by a black goatee and mustache, as well as a day or two's growth of black stubble. Upon the brim of his thin, almost hook-like nose rested a pair of gold, wire-framed glasses. He wore a collarless black button down shirt and a pair of jeans that were ripped at the knees along with a pair of tan boots.

He smiled upon noticing me but my gaze immediately found his companion. Her complexion seemed more normal than it had the last time I'd seen her and she wore her characteristic black jeans and a sheer white top that she'd likely borrowed from Carole over them. I could see not only the outline of her bra, but the bandages that wrapped her midsection. Without a thought to the contrary I moved across the floor toward where she stood and took her in my arms, a gesture she returned with a loud exclamation that seemed equal parts joy and physical pain. I realized that I was, in all likelihood, crushing her already damaged (*bruised only, thank God,* I thought) ribs with my embrace and I loosened it but did not let her go. I could feel what felt like hot tears against my bare shoulder as she buried her head there and admittedly? I considered shedding a few, myself, but refrained.

"How are you?" I muttered into the mat of Maria's black hair that brushed across my lips and tickled my nose.

"Sore," she said, her voice muffled, "very sore but better now. You?"

"Same," I responded, "and *same.*" I intensified my embrace briefly but Maria did not cringe.

"Easy, you two," the male newcomer said in a deep and slightly edgy voice, "bruised ribs plus a dislocated shoulder plus hugging does *not* equal a happy doctor. Six inches apart until I say otherwise."

I looked at him out of the corner of my left eye as he moved, still smiling, past Maria and I, across the room to the kitchen and laid his bag upon the table.

"Hello, dear," he said as he moved around the table toward Carole. Carole lowered her mug, stood and smiled wider.

"Hey there, sexy," she said and planted a brief and playful kiss upon his lips, "I've missed you."

He chuckled, "Me too. Looks like you've had some company while *we've* been gone. Hope you're not thinking about leaving me for a younger guy." He placed his arm around her waist and pulled her closer. She giggled.

I slowly and reluctantly loosened my embrace of Maria per the newcomer's request. She tensed at first but gradually allowed me to break our hug. She turned away from me and wiped her forearm across her face with a "sniff." I stepped away from her and toward him and extended my right hand. I introduced myself as I grasped his hand in mine and shook it vigorously and he nodded, echoing Carole's "I know" statement from earlier.

"Steve Wetherhill," he confirmed, "glad to see you up and about. How you feeling? You seem pretty good. Still a bit woozy?" I nodded. As if in response, my head swam momentarily before it equalized.

"It'll pass," he said with a wave of his hand, "you were out like a light for almost a day, likely a combination of exhaustion, pain and that lump over your temple"—he pointed to where the girl with the blue eyes had pistol-whipped me—"sometimes Caren doesn't know her own strength."

"I guess not," I responded with more than a slight touch of sarcasm in my voice, "she's not the most trusting person, 'aye?"

Steve must have sensed my agitation, "This may be tough for you to do under the circumstances, William, but don't hold it against her. She was only doing what her instincts dictated. The same thing that made you reach for your blaster was what made her clock you upside the head with hers. Tit for tat, Pancho. Not everyone automatically accepts a stranger... strangers like you, Maria and Jeff as benign."

I nodded reluctantly. *What the fuck is a Pancho?* I thought as I touched my temple and cringed. I reasoned that my tit hurt a hell of a lot more than her tat.

"Okay," I said reluctantly, "no problem. I'll give her... *the benefit of the doubt.*" I realized after I had spoken that I had intentionally emphasized the "T" on the end of "doubt" and our hosts shared a look. They seemed satisfied, albeit less-than pleased with my response. Steve pulled Carole closer to him. Carole responded by resting her head upon the side of his chest.

Wow, I thought as I glanced at the two of them, my thoughts of Caren supplanted momentarily. The way they looked at and interacted with each other? It warmed my heart despite the damp chill in the air and the ache in my temple and my shoulder. I felt a soft and warm hand hovering near my right one. Without thinking I took it and squeezed it. The gesture elicited a slight inrush of breath from Maria.

"So," Steve said as his glance fell upon our intertwined hands before it retreated back to my eye level, "coffee?"

I looked at Maria and she looked at me. We both nodded.

"Great," Steve said and gestured to the kitchen, "come on in and we'll chat." Without hesitation Maria and I joined them around the table.

Steve had brought a few of the chairs from the living room area into the kitchen as Maria and I had begun to drink our coffee and consume our breakfasts. Carole asked him if he wanted a mug and he responded by holding up his hand, forefinger and thumb a small distance apart. Carole obliged. She removed another mug from one of the shelves and poured Steve a half a cup. He placed the chairs on the icebox-facing side of the table and he sat upon one. Carole sat upon the other. Maria and I sat at the head and the foot of the table, respectively.

"So," Steve asked as he sipped his coffee. His eyes widened. He turned to Carole and nodded. Carole returned the gesture and took a sip of her own drink.

"So," he reiterated, "Maria and to a lesser extent Jeff told us a few of the details of how you got here but they left the holes for *you* to fill in. Feel up to it?"

I nodded, "Before I go into anything, though, I need to ask: Pat? Pat McClane? Has there been any sign of him?" In my peripheral vision I saw Maria lower her head.

Steve and Carole looked at each other over their mugs of coffee and simultaneously shook their heads, "Nothing," Steve said, "of course no one's gone above to look for him yet. We've got spotters monitoring the area and there's still a relatively healthy Administration presence trundling around."

"For *this* area," Carole added, "the machines don't come this far east very often in force unless they've got a good reason to. Last report we got was that a Caravan of three MDUs and a couple of smaller assault vehicles were patrolling in about a twenty kilometer loop between where Jeff says you guys first went into the woods and where Halmier's Pass intersects the Highway in the Scorched... err, the Eastern Territory. Sorry, guys."

I shook my head, "No need to apologize." *Halmier's Pass?* I wondered at it yet did not voice my inquiry. As with so much in Endworld, I concluded that I would know the details soon enough.

Steve continued, "There are about three dozen machines on foot up above working their way through the woods at last check in. They're being *real* meticulous but they won't find us down here."

"Why not?" I asked and took a sip of my coffee. My eyes widened. *Strong,* I thought. I nodded to Carole in an unintentional impersonation of Steve. She lowered her head in a mock bow. I looked across the table at Maria who had just lowered her own mug to the table top and was biting into an apple.

"Would you?" Carole asked, "A community of people living almost a kilometer below the surface of the continent? How would they survive?"

"You seem to be doing just fine," I said cautiously.

Steve continued, "We're not just relying on the machine's incapacity to grasp the prospect of over 200 human beings living in an adobe (*adobe*, I thought, *that's the word I was looking for... what these habitations are made of*) town at the bottom of an old, abandoned mine in one of the least populated areas of the continent and growing their own crops, William. The rock that the walls of this cave are made of is predominantly black shale. You probably don't know a lot about geology, and that's not an insult but black shale, while not *entirely* uncommon is a good, natural insulator against machine-initiated scans..."

"And they can't find what they can't see," Carole added, "and the only obvious, existing entrance to this mine is the one that you, Maria and Jeff came through. Once there were others but time has kind of removed them from the equation. So we're as safe as we can be. Still, we can't send anyone to look for Pat until we know it's safe."

"Conversely," Steve continued, "we can't get a television signal or a satellite uplink for the same reason, so there's no way for us to monitor what passes for 'the news' for any mention of Pat... or for any mention of *anyone* for that matter, including you two and Jeff." He gestured to Carole's satellite phone, "We keep those for the rare times that we go above ground. Even then..."

"They're not consistently functional," I said and nodded in understanding. I could tell from the looks upon the Wetherhills' faces that they were either unaware of my suspicions regarding Pat's fate or were entirely aware and were not letting on that they were. I decided that a change of topic was a good idea and proceeded to have an open discussion about the events leading up to and including all that you have read thus far in this chronicle. "Filling in the holes" left open by Maria and Jeff so to speak. Maria but primarily I spoke and Steve and Carole listened intently.

"And that's pretty much it," I said after some time had passed. I raised my mug to my lips and drank the last of the liquid within it. I placed the mug down on the table. Carole offered me more but I politely shook her off.

"Nice story," Steve said as he raised his mug in my direction, "can't wait to see how it ends."

I smiled in response. *Neither can I,* I thought. I picked up the half-eaten apple that I had been absently munching on as I had recounted for our hosts the tale I have recounted for you up to this point and took another bite out of it. It was surprisingly crisp and juicy given the setting in which we found ourselves.

"What about you two?" I asked after I swallowed a mouthful of apple, "and this place? How did you end up here and how did Freeworld One come to be?"

Steve and Carole looked at each other and then back at me, "We'll leave the latter for Alex to answer when he gets here," Steve responded, "but as for the former? Well if you fancy a story…"

"They're a welcome distraction from… well, *other stuff,* Steve," I said. My mind hearkened back to all that I had learned of Pat's past in our short time as acquaintances. I shivered as two confused, unfamiliar eyes and a devious smirk momentarily materialized in my mind before they vanished.

"Maria?"

Maria had just placed her finished apple core on the table, "Of course," she said as she picked up her mug and raised it to her lips. She looked across the table at me. I could see something in her expression that quickly vanished. She smiled and winked. I nodded in affirmation and winked back, my momentary supposition of something *else* forgotten.

"Well alright then," Steve said with a flourish as he leaned back in his chair, "there's really not much to tell. Not to disappoint you but…"

"May I?" Carole interrupted. Steve, momentarily taken aback, scoffed and motioned for her to go ahead with his left hand. Carole finished off the last of her coffee and began.

"It's no offense to you, dear," she gently assuaged him as she placed her hand over his, "I *love* it when you tell a story but… well, you can be a *tad bit* long-winded sometimes." She turned from Steve to Maria and me and removed her hand from over his, "It wasn't intentional. More so accidental. We were heading east, couriering correspondence for the PRFE..."

"The Rebellion," Maria interrupted, "you two are members?"

Steve and Carole looked at each other and then back at Maria, "We *were*, Maria," Carole responded, "We're not anymore."

Maria nodded and lowered her head, "Sorry I interrupted you."

Carole shook her head, "No worries, sweetie. No worries at all. We were couriering correspondence for the PRFE to a safe haven just over the border between the Territories a... well Jesus, a while ago when we were detected by a passing patrol. They pursued us through the woods above ground and just south of here and ended up pinning us against the western bank of the Shenango. Our only option for escape... well actually we really didn't have one. We stood there like a couple of deer caught in headlights, nervously awaiting the inevitable when out of *nowhere* comes Alex Parker and a small group of people... they looked like an entourage sauntering down the riverbank without a care in the world. We found out later that their *real* reason for being out there had been the report from one of their spotters of two humans"—she gestured to her and Steve—"fleeing from a patrol through the forest but immediately following Alex, always one for comedy, informed us that they'd stumbled upon us simply out of dumb luck, i.e. they were out for a casual stroll when they encountered Steve, me and a cadre of machines."

"Believable," I said sarcastically. Steve let out a "ha!" Carole nodded her head at me and said, "*Very,*" before she continued her story.

"We saw them, Alex and his group, coming before the machines did," she continued, "they, the patrol, broke through the tree stand onto the riverbank and saw only us. Alex and his people didn't even look invasive to Steve and me. At first glance they didn't even look like they were carrying weapons."

"How wrong we were," Steve interrupted.

Carole nodded, "They saw what was transpiring, stopped dead in their tracks, and before the machines could even register their presence... well, those machines never even got off a shot. They fell one by one in a twisted heap of smoking steel and circuitry. Alex and his group moved over to us and asked us if we were okay. When we told him that we were, he urged us to come back here to Freeworld One with him until things had settled. We told him what we were doing for the Rebellion and he shrugged it aside... told us that one of *his* people would get the correspondence to its destination which... we were told later... someone *did*. And the rest?"

Carole paused before she concluded with, "We never left. We stayed here with Alex and helped him build this place into what it is today. What was then a bunch of tents and sleeping bags has evolved into *this*"—she gestured around us—"Freeworld One isn't much, William and Maria. But it's a hell of a lot closer than some places and a hell of a lot more palpable."

Steve added, "*Free Caymen*. Ask some people and they'll tell you it's a child's wet dream dream. No offense. I'm not calling you children I'm just saying…"

"None taken," I preempted. Steve nodded.

"But Maria confirmed for us that *that* was where you two are heading," Carole continued, "though all she knew was…"

"'An island in the middle of the Great Sea that the Administration doesn't know exists,'" Maria said, "the way you described it to me, William. I didn't know its name until Steve and Carole told me. It kind of…"

"Rolls off the tongue," I concluded, "I know. I felt the same way when Pat first mentioned it to me." Maria seemed taken aback by my revelation and I quickly assuaged her, "it's not something that I was keeping from you, Mia. Pat told me about it in the car while you and Jeff were sleeping and before… well, *you know*. I just never had the chance."

She nodded in response. Her expression softened.

"Well if it's where you want to go then rest assured Alex, Carole and I, along with anyone else that we can muster up will do whatever we can to help you get there," Steve assured us, "but consider…"

I heard a knock in triplicate on the frame of the entrance to the Wetherhill's "house" and I instinctively stood from my chair and reached for my absent weapon (*where the hell is my blaster?* I thought, *and Maria's?*).

Fooled me once that coldly rational voice spoke in my mind, *maybe this time you'll get a blaster bolt through your head and not just the butt of a weapon against your temple.* I paused, reluctantly felt the pain over my right eye and cringed. I relaxed my muscles as a deep, male voice spoke from outside the entryway.

"Steve? Carole? You in there?"

The voice was all too familiar. It was the amplified voice that I had heard in the cavern, before Caren had hit me and I had blacked out. Without seeing the owner's face I knew somehow that it was *the* Alex Parker that I'd heard about from our hosts.

"Inside, Alex!" Steve confirmed with a muffled shout, "Come on in. And make sure you wipe your feet this time."

I heard the newcomer mutter something from beyond the threshold of the living room before he stepped through the doorway with Jeff "Jeebus" Howard (who favored me with a slight smile and a nod) and three additional figures behind *him:* Two men and one woman. The men were total strangers but the woman? I felt my stomach clench in recognition at her short, dirty blonde hair, her dimples and her blue eyes, the latter of which fell upon me almost immediately. She was wearing a black, sleeveless shirt, un-tucked, that showed off a pair of well-framed, though not overly muscular arms and allowed little or no insight into the shape of her upper body, along with a pair of either light blue or white jeans. They were not skin-tight like Carole's but they were certainly not loose. Upon her hip was holstered a particle blaster, and upon her feet she wore a pair of shin-high but practical-looking black boots laced to their tops. She remained expressionless as her eyes met mine. She did not blink... she did not look away.

Caren, I thought. I held her gaze with my own for as long as I could. Were it not for Maria clearing her throat behind me and "tapping" me (it was actually more of a violent poke) I might have continued to glare at my cavern-attacker indefinitely. Thankfully, Maria's interference distracted me and I redirected my attention to the other three figures.

One of the unfamiliar men was also wearing a blaster though his was in a shoulder holster and he was surprisingly normal in appearance. Of medium height and medium build, he had clear and piercing blue eyes beneath a wavy mop of primarily brown and in places blonde hair. His face, much like his appearance was not overly-defined. It was in all honesty relatively round, and he was clean-shaven. He wore relatively non-descript garb, as well: A short-sleeved t-shirt with a faded image upon it of what looked like a man with pointy ears holding his one hand up, the fingers splayed in a "V," and a pair of tan pants. He also appeared to be wearing boots... brown ones, but the cuffs of his pants hid their tops. He regarded me with a curious, wide-eyed glance and the corners of his mouth turned slightly down. I favored him with a quick, almost imperceptible nod which he did not return, and redirected my attention to the second, unfamiliar man.

He was, to say the least, a bit of a peculiarity. He was shorter and stockier than me. His once-dirty blonde hair was interspersed with streaks of white and it was trimmed tightly to his scalp. In the minimal light that filled the interior of Steve's and Carole's domicile, I could see that the man wore arguably the gaudiest pair of glasses that I had ever seen. They were black with rims the size of my pinky fingers and about two sizes too big for his heavily freckled, clean-shaven face. He wore a dark-colored but faded t-shirt that bore what appeared to be the countenance of a smiling, cartoon tiger upon its lapel. I could not tell if he wore pants, jeans or something else. Whatever he wore they were dark, and a single particle blaster was strapped to his left hip. Nor could I tell what he wore upon his feet though I noted that they looked like combat boots. I *did* observe that he wore a chain around his neck. Upon it, and lying still against his t-shirt covered chest was a small gold or silver cross. I smiled at the man in the tiger t-shirt. He smiled back and nodded his head as I redirected my attention from him, to the final figure that had entered Steve's and Carole's "living room."

The man that I assumed to be Alex Parker was tall... almost a half-a-head taller than Jeff and myself. Contrary to his companions he was not carrying a weapon. Upon first glance he, too, was relatively normal in appearance. He had a full head of wavy dark brown hair and a well-pronounced jaw which tapered down into a neatly trimmed goatee and mustache. He was thin, almost as if not more lanky than Steve Wetherill, and he wore a dark blue, button down shirt and a white tee or undershirt beneath, the top of which was visible at the collar. The button down was tucked in and he also wore a pair of tan pants. The cuffs hung over a pair of black boots.

But all misconceptions about his "ordinary" appearance became moot upon observation of his eyes. They were the color of marble and appeared just as cold. Despite the chill inherent in them they were powerful. Of that much I was sure. All attention in the room seemed drawn to them. They were filled with an aura of knowledge and intelligence to rival... well shit, to rival anything that I had seen before but that chill... that coldness bespoke a man who had seen things.

Said newcomer smiled upon noticing me and quickly moved across the room toward where I stood, his hand extended.

"Alex Parker," he said. I took his hand in mine and shook it firmly.

"Steward of Freeworld One," he continued, "but citizen of it first. And *you're* William MacNuff. Great to finally meet you conscious, William."

"Same," I said, a hint of a question in my voice. My comment seemed... unusual given the circumstances but Alex didn't seem to mind. He smiled and looked past me.

"Nice to see you again, Maria," he said as he released my hand and extended his towards her. Maria took it without hesitation, "how are your ribs?"

"Better, thanks," she said, "whatever Steve's been doing seems to be working."

"Aw shucks," Steve said with a highly exaggerated and unfamiliar accent from behind Maria and I. His tone was underlain with a certain simplicity and twang. I could not place it. Whatever the case it elicited a chuckle out of everyone assembled but Maria, myself and Caren.

Caren. I once again glanced at my cavern attacker and her gaze, which had shifted to Alex, immediately shifted back to me. I promptly looked away and back at the "Steward of Freeworld One."

"Um…" Alex began… "Yeah. Awkward. Introductions, then," he said loudly as he released Maria's hand and stepped back, "obviously you already know Steve and Carole. And Jeff. These bright and shiny people"—he turned and gestured toward the newcomers—"are Caren and Matt O'Brien, two of my *best* lieutenants, and Tim Redfield, one of my spotters. I'd trust any of them with my life same as I would Steve or Carole. And Jeff to some extent although I've got to admit, Jeff," he turned from the O'Briens to him, "my exposure to you up to this point has been… well, kind of limited. But you're familiar with our shared cause and any friend of Pat McClane's is *damn sure* a friend of mine."

"Thanks," Jeff said. His tone was nonchalant but I could sense within it an undertone of satisfaction, likely in knowing that his desire to carry out Pat's plan for Maria and myself had not yet resulted in anything contrary to it and contrary to *his* plan to eventually return to isolation. As if in response to said thought Jeff glanced briefly at me and again, almost imperceptibly nodded. And while I was not yet entirely sure of what said plan entailed, I trusted not only in Jeff but surprisingly in the people that were assembled around me.

Well, in *almost* all of them. My gaze moved from Jeff to Alex, across Matt's curious face and Tim's smiling one and once again fell upon Caren's. She met my glance again. I winced as a sharp stab of pain shot through my temple and I looked awkwardly away.

Give her a chance, Vato, Pat's voice spoke in my mind. It was so clear that I almost turned to look for him before I realized that said advice was, once again in my head. Instead, I refocused my attention on Alex.

"Well now that we all know each other," Alex said quickly in the obvious interests of changing the topic and alleviating some of the tension that had developed between Caren and I, "how about a tour, William? Maria's seen most of the town but you haven't. Feel like taking a stroll?"

"That sounds," I paused, considered glaring at Caren again and decided against it, "that sounds nice, Alex. Lead away."

Alex nodded, "Steve, have you got a shirt that might fit this guy? I know we're real salt of the earth people around here but there's no need for him to walk around topless now is there?"

"Not at all," Steve responded, "his build's different than mine but I'm sure I've got something that'll fit him. Be right back."

I turned and watched as Steve disappeared into his and Carole's bedroom. Within moments he returned with a slightly faded white button down shirt which he helped me in to. I removed my injured left arm from its sling and Steve supported it as I slid the sleeve over it. The shirt fit me surprisingly well, though it was a touch snug around my waist when I buttoned it. When I was clothed I slid the sling back over my head and neck and replaced my arm in it. I turned to Maria and held my right arm out. *Look okay?* My gesture inquired? She smiled and nodded, which in Maria Markinson or William MacNuff non-verbaleese meant *you look great.* She held her smile for a moment longer before Alex asked us if we were ready to go and she looked away again.

"Ready," I said as I reluctantly looked away, "lead on."

CHAPTER ELEVEN

We filed out of Steve and Carole's home in a tidy line. Alex Parker led the way with Maria and I directly behind him, Jeff and Tim behind us, the Wetherhills behind them and Caren and Matt in the rear. I was leery of allowing Caren to walk behind me but per Maria's non-verbal urging (which consisted of another poke in the back) I did not question the order of our departure.

The hill outside the Wetherhills' home continued to slant downward toward what appeared to be the center of Freeworld One. The structures that lined the rough path that we walked upon were similar in appearance to Steve's and Carole's: Circular, single story and roughly big enough to support a living area and a bedroom but little else. All appeared to be made of the same material.

Adobe, I thought.

"Adobe," Alex said almost simultaneously with my thought as he gestured to the nearest structure, "little more than sand from the river bank, clay from the river bed and grass, reeds and stalks smuggled from above. We fashion them into bricks and dry 'em over fire or in one of the little rock stoves we built up against the cave wall on the other side of the river"—he pointed to the lush and growing greenery that stretched away from the opposite bank of Little Shenango—"the bricks smell like piss at first but once dried they're almost as firm as cement."

From within the structure that Alex had gestured too emerged a child, no older than eight or nine. Upon first glance she was a normal youth who wore a pair of blue jeans and a pink (or brown, I couldn't tell) t-shirt. She had long blonde hair and her complexion was pale (*obviously,* I thought, *she's been living underground for… how long? Her whole life, perhaps?*). Despite said complexion and the visible brown circles beneath her eyes she smiled and waved to us as we passed. Alex waved back. Her eyes fell upon mine and I saw despite her appearance that they were alive with youthful expectation. *Ooh,* her eyes seemed to coo, *strangers.* I favored the little girl with a wink.

She blushed briefly before she turned and ran back inside.

"Little young for your tastes... *Willy*," Maria joked from beside me. I looked from the vacant exterior of the structure that was fading behind us to her. Her brown eyes glanced up at me with a mixture of amusement and sarcasm.

"And pale," I replied, "a little too *pale* for my tastes, Mia. Oh *wait*, her skin complexion 'kinda reminds me of...'"

"*Zip it*," she cautioned. Her eyes briefly lost their humor and grew serious. I nodded in recognition as we continued to walk through town. The area that we had emerged into was slightly more built up and the buildings within it were, in some cases, longer and/or wider. All remained single level structures, however.

"I guess you could call this the town square," Alex continued, "we call it the Quad because it... well, it's kind of in the shape of a rectangle."

"Inventive," Jeff said from behind me. I turned to see him grinning. Alex did not respond to his statement.

"This is where we conduct most of our business," he continued undaunted, "that building over there"—he pointed to a larger and wider structure to our right with no windows and a lone entrance that faced the "street"—"is our equivalent of a supply depot. That's where we keep what supplies we manage to grow ourselves or smuggle in from above. Food, clothing and other miscellaneous items... you name it. Equal distribution to *all* unless certain circumstances require a greater attentiveness."

"What circumstances?" Maria inquired. Alex was quick to respond.

"Sickness," he said without turning around, "and malnourishment to name a few. Sickness unfortunately is a fact of life down here. So many people living in such close proximity to each other? Well, it's a veritable petri dish when you factor in the year-round chill and the humidity. Good thing we've got a top-notch doctor overseeing things, 'aye, Steve?"

I heard Steve reiterate his "aw shucks" in the same accent as earlier and I smiled.

"It's unfortunately one of the trade-offs to living here," Alex continued as he slowed his pace slightly, "freedom always comes at a price. Our price here in Freeworld One? The occasional empty belly and sniffle. But we manage relatively well considering. Like I said, we're all about equal distribution but we'll never hesitate to provide someone who's ailing or starving the additional resources needed for them to get better. We get them here all the time, William and Maria. People stumble upon us from above or *we* stumble upon *them*. The current population of Freeworld One per the last census we conducted... um..."

"A little ways back," Carole responded.

Alex turned to her briefly and nodded before he turned his eyes back to the steadily leveling path before us. We walked by multiple establishments as we crossed through the center of town—the *Quad*—in which I could see multiple transactions and interactions occurring. In one I saw two men bartering across a low-lying and obviously makeshift counter. I could see shelves within with various knick-knacks upon them that had little to no significance to me. The men regarded us curiously as we walked passed. In another I could see a young woman of about 30 with curly brown hair pulled back in a ponytail. She wore a white jacket over what appeared to be a green (*or blue, maybe its blue; Christ the lighting here is bad,* I thought) shirt and a pair of grey pants with cuffs that terminated mid-shin. Upon her feet she wore a pair of gray and white... not boots but surprisingly, sneakers.

Well that's about the strangest thing I've seen all day, sarcasm fully intended I thought to myself as I considered the "town that time forgot" nestled underground that we walked through. Sneakers were and remain generally frowned upon by the Administration in favor of boots or shoes. There really isn't an explanation other than that one. No one knows why and no one that I know of has ever truly pursued the question with anything more than passing curiosity. But seeing a pair of sneakers upon someone's feet, especially someone living in a city a kilometer beneath the surface of Endworld was for me downright peculiar.

"That's Nicole, our town apothecary," Alex said as he raised his hand and waived to her. She returned his gesture and flashed him a brilliant smile, "if you ever need a poultice or some sort of compound made for everything from sunburn to a pulse rifle wound, she's your girl."

"I'll..." I said, paused, and continued, "I'll keep that in mind, Alex. Thanks."

In still another structure I could see the same shelves lining the walls but *those* shelves were lined with something a bit more intimidating than music boxes, figurines and medicinal powders. Neatly ordered rows of particle blasters, power packs and various other, unfamiliar weapons lined them. They were all overseen by a silent proprietor with long black hair and a curly black beard who, with his one good, clear blue eye (the other was covered by a white patch) glanced at us with obvious suspicion. I assumed with no other, prior knowledge that Maria's and my blasters and what few battery packs I had still carried before being knocked unconscious had ended up within.

"Who's...?" Maria began, gulped, and continued, "who's tall, dark and scary in there?" She gestured to the building as we walked passed it.

Alex turned toward us. I briefly caught something residual in his expression before it softened and he smiled. It was as if Maria's mention of... *tall, dark and scary,* I thought, *that's actually pretty good...* had struck a chord with him and he was attempting to... what? Not show us his surprise, his concern or his "other?" I was unsure.

"Him?" Alex asked with a chuckle. His smile did not waver. He gestured to the building and Maria nodded.

"That's Chuck," he said, "Chuck... hrm. I never *did* catch his last name, believe it or not. He's been here for... well, for a while. He's harmless. Kind of a loner. Nothing to concern yourself with, Maria. Hey, Chuck!"

He shouted to or at the man overseeing the inventory of weapons depending upon your perception. Chuck's head perked up. His expression did not change though he nodded as Alex raised his hand to offer a greeting. His one, visible eye focused intently upon me as I passed and I felt a proverbial heaviness, similar to the heaviness that I had felt in my dream engulf my body. Words from said dream rushed through my mind once again—*Skew, Gateway, Pathfinder*—in a repetitive litany that was far from welcome. I shook my head against them and they faded, but not before they had caused me a moment's mental discomfort. The heaviness faded as Chuck disappeared from my sight beyond the left side of the doorframe.

Coincidence, William? The stern, unfamiliar voice from my dream mentally questioned me. I did not answer its inquiry. Rather, I focused on what Alex was saying in an attempt to distract myself.

"...an okay guy," he was in the process of saying to Maria, "a tad-bit impulsive... aren't we *all*. These are impulsive times that we're living in. But considering how long we've known each other and all that he's... that *we've* seen together I'll take him impulsive and trustworthy over, say, a calculated and dishonest humachine."

How much can he really see with one eye? I thought but shrugged the thought away, not interested in knowing the answer to a question that my gut cautioned me I would be surprised and shocked to hear.

Unus est vera semita, William, Pat's voice spoke in my mind, *those words are not limited by our eyes though they are somewhat enhanced by them. You may not know what they mean yet but you will. Trust me: Your will.*

Why does the prospect frighten me? I thought as we continued our trek down the path and through the town proper. I received nothing from Pat's voice in response.

"Getting back to the census," Alex continued, and my train of thought was broken, "the current population of Freeworld One is a shade over 200. 203 to be exact. That number is slightly more than we had here the last time we took a head count but it doesn't exactly represent a 'population surge.' We get a steady trickle of refugees. Mainly runaways like yourselves"—he motioned to Maria and I but did not turn—"or members of the PRFE just looking to... *escape.*"

A question emerged in my mind not related to my dream and I silently thanked my subconscious, "'Members of the PRFE.' Isn't this... you know, a *part* of that?"

"What, Freeworld One?" Alex said, "No. Far from it, William. We pride ourselves on a peaceful state of existence down here beneath the surface. We're independent of the Rebellion yet we have been and always *will remain* sympathetic to its plight. More so than we are to the Administration, at least."

"Then why the armory?" Maria asked, "why *Chuck?*"

A valid question, I thought, accentuated by the blasters being worn by four of our seven counterparts (Jeff also wore his weapon upon his hip). I instinctively nodded as Alex stopped and turned to face Maria and me. His gesture was so sudden and so fluid that while Maria and I stopped as soon as we saw him move, Jeff bumped into my back and Tim into Maria's with respective *oomphs*, unaware that we had ceased walking. I heard a similar *oomph* from Steve and lastly a female voice: *Caren's*, I assumed with a shiver.

"Leading a non-violent lifestyle and living in a place where most of us came to escape conflict," he began, "does not exempt us from having to protect ourselves. Many of us here came here from situations where we were forced to defend ourselves daily. Steve, Carole, Caren and Matt were all once-members of the People's Rebellion for Freedom and Equality before they opted to live out their lives here. Tim? Well, he came to us via a similar but different path. That kind of instinct never goes away, William. You can run from it all you want but the bottom line is this: No matter where you are... here, Free Caymen or some *other* safe haven from the Administration, the world is at war. It has been for over 15, pre-Administration years now and that war? It's not ending any time soon. No matter what your alignment you need to be able to defend yourself against your enemies if required. It's not something that I'm... that *any* of us here in Freeworld One are fond of, but necessity doesn't always dictate fondness, does it?"

No, I thought, *no it doesn't.*

"Is that how you came here too, Alex?" Maria asked.

Alex smiled, "Not quite, Maria. My situation was a bit different. *Dynamic* if you will. I can talk more about that later, too, but for now? I digress."

Without another word he turned and continued to walk out of the center of town and closer to Little Shenango. I could in fact *hear* running water a short distance away. I thought about what Alex had said—*necessity doesn't always dictate fondness*—and I cringed. His statement was, I knew, another way of saying that hope died the day that BLANK did.

I looked at Alex as he walked onward and I thought of Pat. The similarities between the two of them seemed highly evident at that moment. Both were intently focused on their obligations and responsibilities. Both, I knew, would stop at nothing to help people like myself and Maria achieve our goals, be those goals freedom or otherwise. Said knowledge was equal parts refreshing and disconcerting. I also knew without hearing it that Alex's back story? Well, I understood, he had called it "dynamic." Was there more than just a lost love and an enemy with confused eyes in it? I wondered if I would ever know the answer to that inquiry as we continued our "tour" of Freeworld One.

The number of structures before us was once again diminishing and the sound of running water was more audible by the step. We emerged from the final collection of homes onto a subterranean riverbank. The level ground once again dropped away abruptly before us and were it not for Alex's position in front of us, I or Maria likely would have ended up in the swiftly flowing river. The drop off from the termination of the ground to the surface of the water was no more than a half a meter or less but it began roughly three steps from the edge of the last of the structures.

Someone not paying attention when they walk out here is in for a surprise, I thought and couldn't help but stifle a chuckle at the prospect of falling into water that was more than likely bone-chillingly cold given how far underground Freeworld One was.

"Watch your step," Alex said from in front of me, echoing my previous thought.

That's an understatement, I thought and felt another chuckle attempting to force itself out. I refrained as Alex turned to face us. He motioned for us to step back beyond the termination of the structures and we obliged. When we were sufficiently safe, he gestured up and down the length of Little Shenango which, per my observation, stretched for roughly 10 meters to where the opposing riverbank began.

"Freeworld One," he said as his cold, marble eyes moved from my blue to Maria's brown, "is more than just a haven. It's an *idea* William and Maria. A concept from a forgotten time. Before the Administration... before the machines, we humans believed in a little thing called *self*. Different variations of self: *Self-reliance. Self-government.* Even *self-love:* Abstract ideas that whole civilizations were developed from over hundreds and thousands of years. Some of those societies... those civilizations lasted longer than others. You may have heard of a little place called the United States of America."

I nodded. Maria did not and I saw her glance up at me in my peripheral vision. I turned from Alex and the swiftly flowing river behind him and mentioned Pat's name again. Maria nodded.

"Seems like I missed out on a lot that you two discussed," she said. I reassured her again that my intention had been to tell her everything that Pat and I had discussed (with an additional emphasis on the term *everything)* but things...

She held up her hand and gestured for me to cease and I did not hesitate to do so. She redirected her attention toward Alex and I did the same.

"On our way down here," I said, "before... well, before I was knocked unconscious"—I intentionally paused and could feel six sets of eyes boring into my back and neck in anticipation of what I would say next—"we passed by multiple... 'sigils' Jeff called them. Little swaths of cloth, each with an 'X' crisscrossing it and"—I paused as I tried to remember the number— "thirteen stars in the middle of each of the 'Xs.' What *is* that, Alex? What does it mean?"

Alex smiled as he reached across with his left hand and pulled his right shirt sleeve up as high as he could. I could see the top of his forearm clearly and it was bare. On the underside I could see... *something* though I could not positively identify what it was that I was seeing. The black mark appeared to be designed of two circles atop each other, perhaps in a clean figure-eight or perhaps in an overlapping one and it incorporated an arrow that seemed to cross-cut the figure-eight and point toward the palm of his hand. I made a mental note to inquire about it further if given the opportunity.

But it was not upon that mark that my eyes fell. They fell upon the one inked on the bicep of his upper arm: The same "sigil" that I had seen hanging upon multiple cavern walls above... the same "sigil" which had seemingly led Jeff, myself and a then-unconscious Maria suspended on a makeshift stretcher between us to Freeworld One's doorstep. And there were words inked under the (*tattoo*, I thought, *it's called a tattoo. So's the one under his arm... I think*) mark, as well. Words printed in a highly stylized script. I did not recognize them though for some reason, I felt like they were of the same lineage as Pat's final words to me.

Another similarity, I thought, *why not? Is anything in this place NOT linked?*

For some reason that I could not place I admired them for an undeniably long time. They appeared to be words of power: "Invocabant omnipotentem Deum gratiam et ductu" they said. I asked Alex what they meant.

"It's Latin, William," Alex said with a smile as he pulled his sleeve down, "an old, *old* language from long before the machines were even a glint in humanity's proverbial eye."

I nodded. *Latin,* I thought. I had never heard of it before.

Alex continued, "Translated, they mean 'invoking the favor and guidance of Almighty God.' They were part of a document that was penned by a group of our ancestors who sought to escape what they considered the tyranny of the once-government of the United States of America. Those men seceded from the greater country many, *many* years ago and created a country of their own. They adopted the 'sigil' that you keep referring to as their flag and called themselves the 'Confederate States of America.' Keeping in theme with that they called their flag the 'Confederate' one.

"When we created Freeworld One," Alex continued, "I can't tell you how many years ago, we wanted to set it apart from the other safe havens throughout Endworld that we'd spent time in. We wanted to give it meaning *beyond* just a place for people who sought freedom to escape to. We further wanted to invariably link it to our past as a species. One of us... someone who is, unfortunately, no longer with us... called it a 'confederacy' and the rest... well heck, guys," he said, and once again gestured to the river and the town behind us, "the rest is history."

Alex's mention of *someone who is, unfortunately, no longer with us* seemed tinged with regret and sadness and I considered him curiously. Momentarily, his confidence seemed to shatter and his cold, marble eyes seemed to waver briefly with tears. But he quickly regained his composure. Perhaps it had just been a trick of the minimal light illuminating the cavern but it had been there.

More questions, I thought, *my God, will they ever stop?*

No, that stern, unfamiliar voice responded immediately.

"Whatever happened," Maria asked, "to the 'Confederate States of America,' Alex?"

Alex shrugged, seemingly happy for the change of topic, "They lost, Maria. They regrouped with the United States after a long and bloody conflict and became one nation again. They stayed that way, united despite their differences until the Administration rose to power. Until the Glorious Revolution. And after that? Well, the whole nation idea became academic. The idea the confederates had back then... the idea incarnate in the Confederate

Flag was a good one but the execution? Not so much."

"Don't you worry," I added as I gestured to his now covered arm, "don't you worry that the symbol or 'sigil'... whatever you want to call it that you've adopted to set Freeworld One apart has... well, negative connotations? No offense intended..."

"None taken," Alex said as he moved back from the river's edge toward where Maria and I stood, "you're not the first person to ask me that and you probably won't be the last." He moved to within a step of me and placed his hands upon my shoulders (he was, thankfully careful with the one that remained in a sling).

"I," he began, "*we* here in Freeworld One believe in *self*, William. I wouldn't speak about it so fervently unless we did. There's another old saying from back in the day that my mother used to tell me growing up whenever I did something stupid: 'You reap what you sow, Alexander,' she used to say to me. I take that saying a step further and apply it to not only this place but my life. *You* chose your destiny. The people that you meet? They exist to either further your cause or disrupt it. Actions alone affect the route that we take to get from point 'A' to point 'B.' Omens? There's no such thing as an omen or... what's the term, Carole? Steve? Tim? Jeff? Caren or Matt? Anyone?"

"Bad..." came an unfamiliar female voice from behind me which paused mid-statement. I turned and realized that it was Caren speaking. It was the first time that I had heard her voice. It sounded confident albeit slightly... *suspicious?* I was not surprised given the circumstances. I absently raised a hand to my temple and cringed.

"Bad... *what?*" I said curtly. Maria sighed.

"Ju Ju," she said definitively and as her gaze met mine once again. Her dimples flashed white fire in the diminished glow provided by the lighting that emanated from the ceiling of the cavern. This time, I held her fiery gaze for a moment, as if to show her that I would not always back down. Shortly thereafter, I turned from her back to Alex.

"Right, Caren," Alex said, his hands still resting upon my shoulders, "'Bad Ju Ju.' Like it or not Freeworld One *is* a confederacy. We're a country unto ourselves, William and Maria and no one... not the Administration or any established group that passes for a government *including* the PRFE... no offense, guys..."

Multiple replies of "none taken" and "no problem" emanated from behind me.

"...can ever take that away from us," Alex concluded, "we chose this for ourselves. We believe in it. We govern ourselves and we support ourselves. And if ever the day comes we *will* defend ourselves, all the while invoking the favor and guidance of Almighty God. Or, whatever particular deity you want to believe in. We're not very discriminating here."

Silence descended over the riverbank and the surrounding area. I glanced past Alex at the swiftly flowing Little Shenango. To my right and about 20 meters from where we stood I could see a small bridge wide enough to allow one person or a single-file line of people to pass over the water and on to the green bank of the opposite shore. Beyond the bridge I could see where the river entered the cavern and to my left I could see where it exited: An opening, roughly three quarters the size and breath of the river itself and barely two meters high. I watched as the current splashed against either side of the opening and created dual whirlpools which seemed to lick against the riverbank before they funneled out and into the darkness beyond. I inhaled the cool, humid atmosphere of the world Alex Parker and his compatriots…

His confederates, I thought…

…had created and I exhaled. To say that Freeworld One was beautiful at that moment would be an understatement. It was more than that. It was as close to a paradise as any place I had and have ever seen. I wanted to say something… wanted to thank Alex for all that he had achieved and all that he was attempting. But the timing? Well, friends, the timing simply didn't feel right.

In retrospect? I wish I had.

"Well then," Alex said as he lowered his hands from my shoulders and took a step back toward the riverbank, "enough of the cook's tour. Maybe we should think about heading back. I think we all need to rest."

I heard Jeff clear his throat behind me and I turned to glance at him. As I did, Alex continued.

"I guess you'll be taking your leave of us shortly, Jeff. Anything I can do to coax you to stay?"

Jeff smiled and shook his head, "With all due respect, Alex, my road leads west and not east. I have a home and a life back in Greentree to get back to."

"Fair enough," he said with a nod, "thank you for everything you've done." Alex moved toward me and I stepped aside as he extended his hand and grasped hold of Jeff's. The two men shook vigorously before Alex released his grasp and with a nod, gestured for the rest of us to turn and head back the way we had come. I looked from Jeff, Alex and the rest of the group which was already departing the way we'd come to Maria. There was a mixture of concern and resignation on her face.

"It's what he wants," I whispered as the rest of our assembly moved out of what I assumed to be ear shot, "this isn't his task any more than it was Pat's. He's helped us plenty, Mia. We should be grateful and not angry."

"I'm not," she responded and looked away, "Not at Jeff. Not at *any* of them. I'm just... I mean *really*, William, is it really *anyone's* task but ours? Despite all of Alex's talk about destiny and such, these are... what did he call them? 'Salt of the earth" people. *Good people*. Even Caren, though I could cut the tension between you two with a knife."

"She *did* clock me upside my head with her blaster, Mia."

"Maybe next time you shouldn't be so quick to reach for yours."

I nodded. *Fair enough,* I thought, and on the coat tails of that, *you've been talking to Jeff about what happened while you were unconscious.*

"And I didn't say that I didn't understand it... *Willy*," she continued, "it's justifiable. But the last thing I think either of us wants is to involve them in something that might ruin what they've managed to accomplish... might get in the way of their *own* destinies. Alex, especially. The Steward of Freeworld One? He's the architect of this place for God's sake. Maybe we should just... I don't know. Maybe we should just leave. You and I."

Her last statement was spoken after a brief pause and I thought about her suggestion long after I nodded and told her "we'll see." I took her hand in mine and started up the path back through town.

She's right, I reasoned, as my boots fell hollowly on the well-trodden stone ground and the sound of the river began to fade behind us. Freeworld One was more than just a safe haven. It was, to a lesser extent, the same as the place that we were heading but with one slight difference: It was real. As Steve had mentioned back at he and Carole's home, it was "palpable." Unlike Free Caymen which either existed or was, as Steve had mentioned, nothing more than a "child's wet dream." A dream of freedom. Did our destination actually exist or was it nothing more than another of Pat McClane's ethereal *haints*? The answer to that question, I reckoned, was the lone conclusion that would either spell success or failure for Maria Markinson's and my plight.

We once again walked past the armory. The heaviness returned. Chuck still stood within it and stared out at us as we passed, his expression unchanged from what it had been previously. I felt a shiver traverse my spine as his lone, crystalline blue eye met mine and I breathed a sigh of relief as his figure once again disappeared, this time behind the right doorframe of the entrance to the structure. The heaviness again dissipated as time moved onward without check over Freeworld One.

CHAPTER TWELVE

We returned to Steve's and Carole's home en masse. Upon arriving Alex, Tim and the O'Briens dismissed themselves to go attend to, as Alex put it, "some business on the border of town." What he meant by this I do not know and I did not press him further but admittedly, I was curious. *I hope everything is okay,* I thought. Alex favored me with another hearty handshake before he retired. Tim did the same. Matt nodded at me but did not smile and Caren? She was unsurprisingly silent as she and the group walked away.

Well, she didn't glare at me, I thought, *I guess that's progress.*

Maria had already retreated inside with Steve and Carole. Jeff and I found ourselves standing alone by the side of the trail through Freeworld One. As Alex, Tim and the O'Brien's disappeared beyond the crest of the nearest hill I redirected my attention to the man that had accompanied me on my journey longer than anyone save for Maria.

"So," I began and paused. Jeff smiled.

"Yep," he said as he stretched his arms over his head, "about that time."

I nodded, "Are you sure you won't reconsider? Steve and Carole mentioned a pretty large force of machines still searching the area above ground for us. It doesn't sound very safe."

He shrugged, "So did Alex. There are ways to get around such things. Don't worry, William. I'll be fine. So will you and Maria. These are good people as I'm sure you've probably figured out, though your... *relationship* with Caren seems a bit tepid."

I guffawed but said nothing. *No shit,* I thought, and raised a tentative hand to my temple. I cringed. It still hurt like a bitch.

"Anyway," Jeff changed the topic, "I brought Alex up to speed on Pat's plans. He knows about Free Caymen... knows about the mercs. Rest assured he'll help you get there in whatever fashion he can."

I nodded in agreement, "He's quite a guy, isn't he?"

Jeff smiled. "*Alex Parker,*" he said with emphasis, "Pat used to talk about him like he was some kind of deity. I never paid his talk much credence. I figured it was just typical, Pat McClane BS. But now that I've met the guy... well? I can't help but agree with *everything* that cocky sonofabitch ever told me about him. There's something about him. Something... ah, I don't know. But it's *there*. I can feel it in my gut. He's been around. Seen a lot. Probably more than I have. You and Maria are in good hands, William."

The area around us fell silent. I thought about what to say next. I had many questions but only one seemed relevant at that moment.

The mark, I thought. The one upon Alex's arm. Not the confederate "sigil" of Freeworld One but the other mark: Either a perfect figure eight or an overlapping one cross-cut by an arrow, the tip pointing to his palm. Said mark seemed to be burning itself into my subconscious out of both curiosity and necessity much as my earlier dream and the three terms spoken in it—*Skew, Gateway* and *Pathfinder*—had.

Now is not the time, my coldly rational voice cautioned, *Be patient. It'll come.* So instead, I asked Jeff the only other, semi-relevant question that I could think of.

"Will you," I began after a short pause, "you know: *Look* for him?"

Jeff nodded. His smile returned, "If I can, William. It'll all depend on what's waiting for me up there. I owe him *that* much. If it seems safe I'll go back and see if I can find... you know..."

I did and I assured him that he didn't have to say another word. But Jeff wasn't done speaking.

"I told you," he began, "that I'd tell you *why* some day. Why I quit? Why I retired?"

"You did," I said, "but..."

He held up his hand, "No, William. I don't believe in breaking my promises. It's really not much of a story. Not as interesting as Pat's. Did he tell you about Rebekka?"

I nodded, *"And* about what happened to her."

Jeff smiled, "Well, my story kind of parallels that. You see, I was working in the same hospital that the two of them were brought to... *after.* I was new to the Rebellion, then. My first impression of Pat McClane was of a man whose will the machines had broken. That impression was compounded when Rebekka died. I wondered if he'd ever recover. But he surprised me with his resilience. We developed a friendship while he was there recovering and when he decided that it was time for him to leave? To rejoin his compatriots? He first asked me to come with him but I told him that I couldn't. When he realized that I wouldn't he pressed me to keep in touch with him.

Not exactly a simple prospect. Being 'Pen Pals' is kind of a lost art."

I thought about asking Jeff what a "Pen Pal" was but I didn't. I allowed him to continue without interruption.

"We'd go long periods of time without corresponding," he continued, "but every so often his travels carried him back my way. Every time that I saw him, William? He was a bit more jaded than he had been the last time. More experienced, and not necessarily in a good way. He was always courteous but he seemed progressively more and more immersed in his duties as a member of the Rebellion. He told me stories. Stories about the people he'd encountered. People like Alex Parker and his mercenary counterparts. We stayed in touch as best we could. Then one day…"

Jeff paused, looked up at the roof of the cavern and seemed to weigh his thoughts before he continued, "Then one day, the Administration? Well, they discovered the location of our 'secret hospital.' I guess they figured that a building filled with injured and sick people, along with a handful of doctors, medics and nurses and a skeleton crew of defenders—I was one of the latter—wasn't worth their time or attention, so they moved to within a kilometer of it and bombarded the fuck out of it with artillery fire.

"We—my counterparts and I—never had a chance to mount a token defense much less a proper one," he continued, "within moments, the building was reduced to a smoking pile of rubble and the majority of the people that had been recovering or working within it were either dead or dying. Me? I was lucky. I only ended up trapped in an air pocket beneath a couple of metric tons of concrete and steel. But I was alive. *That* was how Pat found me. He was, he told me, 'just passing through' again when he helplessly watched the hospital destroyed from a safe distance away. After the machines left, he came to investigate and he heard me shouting. He dug me out with his own, bare hands. Miraculously, I'd only suffered a few bumps, bruises and scratches. We salvaged as many as we could from the rubble but were able to pull only a handful of people out. Most of them, myself included, regrouped with the rebels that Pat was running with at the time. He and I? We remained together like that for a while. *Years,* really. And when he decided it was time to call it quits? I decided the same. We relocated to Greentree, MWT and the rest?"

I nodded. *History,* I thought.

Jeff's smile widened, "I figure that Pat saved my ass by pulling me out of that rubble," Jeff concluded, "The least I can do is return the favor. I may not have been able to save him, but at the least I can recover what's left of him and do him justice."

He deserves it, I thought, but did not vocalize the thought. I didn't have to. I understood that Jeff "Jeebus" Howard knew it.

"So," Jeff said, "there you go, William. Promise fulfilled."

"Thank you," I replied, and extended my hand, "for everything. And good luck, Jeff."

Jeff smiled as he took my hand in his, "The same to you, William."

I pumped it once, then twice and said, "Don't you want to say goodbye to Maria?"

Jeff shook his head as he released my hand, "I'm not really good at good-byes. One is enough for today. Will you tell her for me? Steve and Carole, too?"

"I will," I responded, "I promise. And Jeff: Thank you again. We wouldn't have made it here without you."

Jeff chuckled as he turned and began to walk down the path that Alex, Tim and the O'Briens had descended, "You don't give yourself enough cred-it, William," he said as he strolled away, "maybe I wouldn't have gotten this far without *you*."

He raised his left hand over his head without looking back at me and lowered it. I raised mine in response despite the fact that I was unsure of what he had meant by his last statement. I knew he could not see my own raised hand and I watched as he crested the top of the same hill that the others had disappeared beyond moments before and vanished. I could still hear his boots echoing off of the well-trodden path through town but in time even that sound faded first to a distant echo and then? Nothingness. I was left standing alone outside the entrance to the Wetherhill's home. I could hear chatter inside—Maria discussing something with Carole (I could make out the mention of "crops" and another term that sounded like "irri-some-thing")—and reluctantly resigned myself to the knowledge that Jeff was pursuing the best course for him, I turned and retired inside.

The next block of time passed without incident. Steve, Carole, Maria and I sat around the Wetherhill's kitchen table with another pot of fresh, steam-ing coffee that Carole had brewed between us and discussed all that Maria and I had seen and experienced. To say that my first few hours of conscious-ness after awakening in Freeworld One had been information-packed, was and remains an understatement to this day. After a time, Steve and Carole excused themselves to go and get some rest. I had ceased paying attention to my internal clock but the yawns emanating from our hosts were an indica-tion of how late it was getting. Maria and I thanked Steve and Carole once again for their hospitality before we decided to return to Steve's office and our adjoining cots within.

We spoke very little as we walked the short distance between the Wetherhill's home and our temporary residence. It was uncharacteristic for Maria and I and I found the awkward silence that hung between us slightly disconcerting. I inquired if she was okay as we reached the entrance to the structure and she responded that yes, she was fine. Merely tired. I agreed and pulled the curtain that covered the entrance back for her. She mimed another half-hearted curtsey and entered. I followed.

With little thought or conversation to the contrary Maria removed her shoes and fell upon her back on her cot with a muffled gasp. She closed her eyes and muttered "goodnight" to me as I moved over to where my own cot was positioned and sat upon the edge.

"Goodnight, Mia," I said quietly as I rested my right elbow upon my thigh and lowered my face into its palm. My left arm remained snug within its sling. I unintentionally let out a loud sigh and closed my eyes against the steady ache over my right temple and in my shoulder. While the pain that I had initially experienced upon waking up had faded from both areas it was still there, albeit in a diminished capacity.

I considered lying down and trying to sleep as Maria's breathing slowed. I listened, my eyes still closed, to the gentle rush of air escaping from between her slightly pursed lips. She recycled it back through her lips and nose and exhaled again. *Rinse and repeat,* I thought with a smile. Still, I did not lie down. An indefinite amount of time passed, my only company the sleeping female atop the cot next to mine, the single light bulb over my head that seemed to swing back and forth on a phantom breeze and my ever rambling, ever changing thoughts.

Fuck this, I eventually thought. I opened my eyes and stood carefully from the edge of my cot and glanced at Maria's sleeping figure. She still rested on her back (*probably the only position she's comfortable in right now,* I thought) and I could see, in the dim light provided by the flickering bulb hanging overhead that her eyelids were twitching.

Dreaming, I thought. I tip toed over to her cot, raised my right middle and index finger to my lips, kissed them, and placed them softly upon her own.

Goodnight, kiddo, I thought as I moved passed her quietly, out the entrance and into the "night air" of Freeworld One.

I knew where I was heading as soon as I left Steve's office. I made my way down the hill toward Little Shenango and reached the riverbank a few moments later. I was careful to stop short of stepping over the ledge and into the drink.

I turned right and made my way down the bank to the bridge that I had noticed earlier. The trip was a short one and the bridge itself was little more than a collection of slippery, wooden planks positioned a hair's width apart and suspended between four ropes—two on the top and two on the bottom—with support ropes that zigzagged tightly across the openings on either side of it. It barely swayed or creaked as I stepped onto it.

Sturdy, I thought. Still, I made my way across it cautiously, the swiftly flowing water of the river frighteningly close to the bottom of the planks that I stepped upon (it was no more than a half a meter to the water's surface, and I could feel an occasional kick-up of mist from the surface which in conjunction with the humidity explained the slickness of the bridge's floor). I gained the opposing riverbank without incident and stepped off of the bridge and onto the green, mossy surface of the ground there.

I looked right and then left and I sighed in awe. As I'd noticed previously, only a few structures dotted the area: Maybe a dozen total on either side of me and none of the same size or breath as the main buildings that surrounded the Quad on the other side of the river. But the structures were not what caught my attention. The well-groomed and evenly partitioned sections of greenery and growing things that lined the riverbank and stretched off in front of me toward the walls of the cavern did.

I stepped slowly away from the riverbank and toward the closest partition. It was cordoned off by a thin, white rope and was roughly two meters wide by two meters deep. Long, green stalks with leaves running up their spines tapered off into... what appeared to be yellow growths that vaguely resembled flowers but that I knew were not. Upon a few of the leaves were what appeared to be growths or... I searched my memory for the word and found it... *pods* but they were small, obviously still in their earliest stages of development. I reached through the white ropes and ran my fingers across the smooth surface of one of them. I could feel something bumpy beneath.

"Corn," spoke a familiar female voice from behind me. I jumped with an unfortunate squeak, turned and found myself within a few steps of Maria. She stood with her arms folded beneath her chest, her figure silhouetted against the bridge, the river and the town beyond. She'd taken a moment to pull her hair back in a ponytail at some point and she wore a cockeyed smile upon her face which shockingly reminded me of Pat's signature grin. My heart still racing at the surprise of seeing someone there (*how did she sneak up on me? I never even heard her coming*, I thought) I acknowledged her presence with a smile and a nod, "Come again, Mia?"

She unfolded her arms and stepped toward me. She gestured toward the stalks, "That plant that you're caressing? Corn, William. You know, corn on the cob, corn bread… all that good stuff. Haven't you ever seen corn before?"

"Never like this," I responded. I inhaled deeply and could smell her natural perfume: Clean and fresh. Mingled with her appearance—she still wore her sheer white top beneath which her bra was frighteningly visible—and the earthy smells of the imported topsoil and the crops growing in front of and around me it was almost intoxicating. I felt a stirring in my chest and my midsection, realized what was happening and I tensed up. I have a feeling I blushed as well but I can not be sure.

She moved forward another step and stood beside me. Her eyes moved from mine to the corn. She reached out and ran her own fingers over one of the leaves and the pod attached to it, "Well if it makes you feel any better," she said, "neither have I. To be honest with you, William, I wouldn't have known *what* this was unless Carole hadn't told me."

I smiled. The stirring in my chest and midsection dissipated somewhat but did not vanish entirely, "Cheater," I said and chuckled.

I heard her gasp and I turned to look at her. She was still smiling and her eyes had grown wide, "How *dare* you?" She asked jokingly, "I bet *I* could name more of these crops than *you* could… *Willy.*"

"You're on," I said as I reached out my hand toward hers. She looked down at it and paused briefly before she took it gently in her own. I cocked my head, non-verbally said *let's go* and we began to walk from one plot of crops to the next, away from the riverbank and toward the cavern wall.

Maria was as good as her word and had I laid anything other than pride on our wager I would have lost (you could argue that my pride was summarily tarnished by our interaction). I didn't recognize a single plant and she recognized multiple ones: *Tomatoes. Peppers. Potatoes.* There were others but those are the ones that I remember. How she had come by said information I never asked and I never found out (*likely from Carole again,* I thought). We walked onward through the fields. Maria identified crop after crop and I listened intently to her rhetoric. Eventually I conceded defeat and she laughed.

"Point taken," I said as we walked past a cordoned off plot of carrots, a fact she brought to my attention joyously before finally she concluded her farming lesson.

"How can they grow crops underground?" I asked.

"Carole told me that, too," she said, "*irrigation* she called it. Apparently they bring topsoil down here from the surface and spread it around and they use the water from the river to irrigate everything."

Irri-that, I thought. "What about sunlight?" I asked, "Don't plants need sunlight to grow?"

"Not *all* plants, William," she corrected, "some but not all. For the ones that *do* require sunlight they use portable UV..."

"'UV?'" I asked.

"*Ultraviolet,*" she answered, "lamps. The others, potatoes and carrots especially by their nature grow underground. The whole setting here is actually pretty conducive to farming given one or two slight modifications. It's practical and it's..."

"Impressive," I interrupted and added, "*damn* impressive."

"Yes it is," she said as our stroll brought us to within a meter or two of the cavern wall. It curved up toward the cavern's ceiling before us beyond another plot of tall corn stalks. A few meters down its length I could see the stone ovens that Alex had referred to during our earlier tour. There were four total that I could see and all were presently dark. They were seemingly built into crevices at the base of the wall. Maria asked if we could pause to rest as her ribs were aching and I obliged.

"'You want to sit down for a bit?" I asked. Maria nodded. She released my hand and lowered carefully into a sitting position using my right arm as support. When she was seated cross-legged upon the ground I followed suit and sat down beside her, my legs splayed out before me. To our backs lay the cavern wall. Distant and in front of us I could see the bank of Little Shenango, the river itself and the town beyond.

"I thought you were asleep," I said after a moment's silence. My eyes moved from the area before us to the area surrounding us and fell upon Maria. She was grinning devilishly.

"I know you did," she said shyly, "and I was... *kind of.* Then someone brushed a couple of fingers across my lips and I woke up. I wonder who did that."

I knew her question was rhetorical. The stirring in my chest and my midsection intensified and coupled with a general feeling of awkwardness and embarrassment.

"I'm..." I began and stopped. Admittedly, I was speechless. Maria immediately keyed on said fact.

"William MacNuff *again* without anything to say," she asked, her grin virtually splitting her face, "twice in a lifetime. I never thought I'd see the day." She flipped her bangs not held by her ponytail back with her right hand and cocked her head to the left, exposing her cream-colored neck and a bit of her bare right shoulder. The aforementioned stirring intensified to an almost hellish level and I quickly looked away for another focal point. My eyes fell upon the adobe-constructed tool shed a few meters away to my right and I considered it. *Nice architecture,* I thought as I reached for anything visceral other than my companion and stifled a sigh.

This isn't working, I helplessly thought.

"It's okay," she said. I forced myself to turn to her and I noticed that instead of looking at me she had redirected her own attention to the river before us.

"Don't be embarrassed," she said without turning, "that wasn't my plan and it wasn't why I followed you down here. Actually, it was... it was *sweet,* William. Thank you."

I remained silent for a long moment as I gazed at her profile: Her deep, brown eyes fixed intently upon the scene before us and her pulled-back, raven black hair falling slightly loose around her ears. There was a flush upon her cheeks that had not been there the last time I had regarded her appearance. The ghost of her previous grin still held sway over the corners of her mouth and she closed her eyes briefly. To this day, whenever I conjure up her face in my memories *that* is the vision that I see of her. It is a memory... one of the few that I have that warms my heart and to a greater extent my soul when I find myself losing my way.

A slight breeze blew past my face and I instinctively closed my eyes as well. *So peaceful,* I thought, *so...*

Perfect. And it was, I knew. *Perfect.*

Is there a better time? I thought. I was unsure and because of my indecision I proceeded cautiously.

"So why *did* you follow me down here, Mia?" I asked. My voice sounded surprisingly confident under the circumstances.

In response to my question Maria re-opened her eyes and slowly turned her head toward me. Her brown eyes fell upon my blue ones and her expression shifted from happy and playful to utterly and completely serious in the space of a breath.

"Because I *wanted to,* William," she simply said.

Her eyes remained locked upon mine and mine upon hers. I was helpless not to notice tears welling up in them. A single tear rolled slowly down her left cheek and I instinctively reached in with my left hand and attempted to brush it away. She quickly laid her right hand over mine, closed her eyes and pressed her cheek against my palm. Not thinking and merely doing what felt right I placed my right hand upon her waist. She grimaced slightly and opened her eyes and I stopped short of pulling her toward me as both of us smiled at the same time.

"Ribs?" I asked.

She nodded and said, "Let me."

My hand still upon her waist she uncrossed her legs and shuffled her body toward me. With a jolt of sensation her left thigh came into contact with mine. She leaned in slowly and closed her eyes. I did the same until at last...

Our kiss was like nothing I had ever experienced before. Her lips were silken and as sweet as the natural scents that engulfed both her and the area that surrounded us. It was innocent. Near as I could tell it was, for both of us, our first but within moments of when it began it changed. I felt her tongue probe for position and I conceded. My right hand moved from her waist to her upper back. I could feel her shoulder blades beneath my palm. Her arms fell gently over my own shoulders. We stayed that way indefinitely, our lips locked and our bodies intertwined, neither of us interested in relinquishing our grasp upon the other.

I wonder to this day at the sheer and utter perfection of that moment. Perhaps it was a result of our lifelong bond as friends. Perhaps it was a result of something else... the shared weight of our collective experiences since leaving Jefferson and an opportunity to, for a brief moment in whatever passes for time here in Endworld forget about them. Mine is not to judge certain moments that have transpired over the course of my existence, especially not after all that has transpired since that moment upon the bank of the Little Shenango River that ran and likely still runs through Freeworld One to this day. You can draw what conclusions you choose to from any of the situations that I have described and am poised to describe in the pages ahead.

All I know is that while we kissed I was in bliss, the nagging pain in my shoulder and my temple all but forgotten. It was followed by an overwhelming sense of loss as we finally broke our embrace and lay back upon the moss and topsoil covered ground. Wordlessly, Maria draped her right arm over my stomach and pulled herself closer to me. Her right leg fell over mine and she quickly dozed. The whistling inrush and outflow of air from between her lips and the sporadic rise and fall of her own chest quickly hearkened me unto the same state. I could hear the river splashing gently in the distance. As sleep overtook my body, the river in my mind became a vast sea: The *Great* Sea across which I hoped laid the freedom that Maria and I sought. I could see it clearly despite the fact that I had never been there and for a brief moment I...

For a brief moment *we* were free. It was this thought that trailed off into darkness and followed me down into sleep as time's fickle progression throughout Endworld temporarily and blessedly ceased.

CHAPTER THIRTEEN

Jeff "Jeebus" Howard of Greentree, MWT climbed the last few meters to the top of the mine shaft that he, William MacNuff and a then-unconscious Maria Markinson had descended to reach Freeworld One a day or two before. He was unsure of how long since time, as he was so often reminded of, had little or no significance in Endworld. His thoughts remained focused upon them and the community that lay below him despite the fact that he willed his focus to be on the task before and not behind him.

He had done all that he could for the Jefferson, MWT runaways, he knew. He had fulfilled the request that Pat McClane had imparted upon him in his kitchen while William and Maria had slept the morning before the four of them had fatefully piled into Pat's truck and had struck out for the Eastern Territory…

The Scorched Land, Jeff self-corrected as he mind hearkened back over that conversation:

"If something happens to me, Jeff, you need to get them to Alex Parker," Pat had asked, nay had ordered him.

"Not him again, McClane," Jeff had responded skeptically, "even if he does still exist, and I'm not doubting your knowledge that he does despite the fact that you haven't heard a word from him in ages, how the fuck are we supposed to find him?" He had, Jeff had thought, quite literally gone "underground" if the rumors of Freeworld One's existence were to be believed.

Apparently they had been.

"Trust me, Jee… err, Jeff," Pat had responded, "he does and I know how to get there. If something happens to me head east until you reach the border. You'll know it by…"

"The Shenango River," Jeff had replied. Pat had nodded.

"If we emerge where I think we will after travelling the back roads you'll need to head south along the riverbank," Pat had continued, "look for the place where the river is at its narrowest. No more than 20 or 25 meters across. Head into the woods and look for what at first glance'll appear to be a cave. It's actually a mine shaft. Follow it all the way down. Look for his sigil. You'll know it when you see it.

"Let it lead you to him."

Jeff shook his head as he recalled their conversation. It's like he knew, he thought. Had he? Jeff was unsure yet he knew, from experience, to expect the unexpected from Pat McClane. In many ways his counterpart had been more like a merc than he had ever given himself credit for, not only a product of the many years he'd spent living with, travelling with and fighting alongside them but because of something integral within him. Something special. Alex had it too, Jeff sensed, maybe more so than Pat but beyond that? He only knew per the few things he'd seen. Strange things. Things most normal, human beings like himself were unable to and, he reasoned, would never be able to accomplish. Shit, not even the machines can do some of the things that I saw Pat do, he concluded.

As if in response to his thought a cool breeze blew passed his face and he smiled and whispered his friend's name as he shined his flashlight-phone upon the area before him. The temperature in the shaft had steadily increased over the last hundred meters or so of his ascent and he knew before he saw the dark opening (nighttime, he thought) ahead of him that he had reached the exit/entrance.

He had done all that he could for them, he reasoned, and he was secure in that knowledge. He knew that Alex and his people would get William and Maria started on the next stage of their journey. One or two of them might even go with them but it was the next stage that worried him more than anything else... was his knowledge of the next stage that seemed to pull at the back of his polo shirt in an effort to get him to turn around and return to them.

Real smart, Jeebus, a voice that vaguely resembled Pat's spoke in his mind, real fucking smart. You're going to leave two, 18 year old kids and a group of retired revolutionaries to the blasted lands of the Eastern Territory? I guess all that experience that you brag about has done nothing to improve your common sense.

He brushed the voice aside. He thought again of the mercs that lay at the end of William and Maria's journey. Pat had trusted them as much, if not more so than Alex Parker and his people so why shouldn't he? He shifted his focus to the steadily increasing slope before him. The ground beneath his feet was slicker and he could smell fresh soil and mildew... could hear the sound of the rain lightly falling beyond the opening. Whether actual rain or residual drops from the overhanging canopy of trees that shaded the forest outside the mine entrance he was unsure but...

He stopped suddenly as he heard something beneath the sound of the rain droplets that fell upon the onset of the corridor a mere 10 meters above him. Instinctively, he killed his flashlight with a tap of his satellite phone's screen and complete blackness descended over the mine shaft. He replaced the phone in the front, right pocket of his corduroys carefully. His left hand fell to the butt of his weapon and he silently pushed his back against the wall to his left. He closed his eyes to allow them to adjust

*more quickly to the darkness that surrounded him and he listened. It was impercep-
tible at first but the twofold darkness that enveloped him—that of the mine shaft
combined with that behind his closed eyelids—heightened his hearing.*

*There was something… there were multiple somethings moving just beyond the
opening. He could hear them clearly: Heavy metal footfalls upon the water-logged
soil. Beneath that, he could hear servos grinding.*

*Fuck, he thought as he opened his eyes. He could see more clearly the area that
surrounded him and the opening ahead of him. His left hand still resting upon the
butt of his blaster he considered removing his sat phone from his pants pocket and
turning on its jamming function. But the same common sense that Pat's voice had
disparaged his lack of moments before convinced him otherwise.*

*If you trigger that thing right now it'll be the equivalent of announcing your
presence to them, Pat's voice cautioned.*

*Yes, he reasoned. If there were SMs lurking around beyond the entrance they
would, despite their incapacity to scan, report an anomaly immediately. He'd have
a cadre of machines on his ass before he could retreat a half a dozen meters back into
the mine shaft. Even then where would he go? Up and out? Back to the community
nestled beneath him?*

*Not a lot of options, Jeebus, Pat's voice stated in his mind, so what's the path of
least resistance since both are fraught with danger?*

*They obviously weren't scanning for life signs, he understood, at least not at
the moment. They would have detected one long before. True, the walls of the mine
shaft and by association the walls of the cavern that contained Freeworld One were
"insulated" against such things but black shale worked only to a limited extent, he
reasoned, and the concentration in the wall of the shaft was, he assumed, nothing
compared to the concentration in the walls of the cavern below. So they weren't scanning. Which meant he had an opportunity, albeit a short window of one.*

*He fluidly removed his blaster from its holster and he re-closed his eyes. He
breathed in deeply and exhaled. His heart rate slowed and his mind grew clear as
the smells of the world above filled his nostrils. He opened his eyes and slowly began
to make his way up the side of the shaft with his back still pressed solidly against
the wall, conscious of the slightest echo caused by his movement. Thankfully there
was none. He covered the last 10 meters to the top of the shaft within moments…
the sounds that emanated from the area without—falling rain drops, heavy metallic
footfalls and pneumatic air cylinders firing in time with grinding servos—intensified as he moved within a step of the entrance. Slowly and as carefully as he could he
peeked his head around the corner of the exit/entrance, rose the barrel of his weapon
so that it was parallel with his lips, flipped the safety into the "off" position, tensed
his index finger upon its trigger and observed what awaited him in the clearing.*

He felt his heart leap from his chest into his throat and he stifled a gasp. Alex's estimates of the force above—estimates conveyed to him by his spotters that Steve and Carole had echoed to William and Maria without Jeff's knowledge—were conservative to say the least. There were ranks of machines four and in some places five rows deep clogging the forest clearing. Their armor-plated and steel bodies glistened with rain water in the minimal light provided by the low lights of the dozen or more sleek assault bikes—little more than modified motorbikes with armored, bubble shaped canopies—that ringed their perimeter. He knew that the attack force was more than a patrol and more than a Caravan. It was an army. And Jeff "Jeebus" Howard knew that an assault force of such a magnitude would not have been sent by the Administration to simply apprehend two 18 year old runners and their companion. It left only one unequivocal truth:

The machines were not there for William, Maria and him. They were there for Alex Parker.

They were there for Freeworld One.

As slowly and as quietly as he had approached the exit/entrance to the mine shaft Jeff retreated from it. He anticipated detection but it never came. He kept his back pressed against the wall and his blaster live and in-hand until he reached the first bend in the shaft. He slipped beyond it and as soon as he was confident that he was... at least temporarily... in the clear he sheathed his blaster, removed his sat phone, turned on its flashlight and broke from the shadows in a sprint. The air that surrounded him once again grew cooler and cooler as he descended into the bowels of Endworld to warn Alex Parker and the rest of Freeworld One that they had been discovered.

* * *

To the end. Not alive. We can't let that happen. They won't take us alive...

NO...!

I awoke abruptly and my all-too-familiar dream...

Nightmare, William, my coldly rational voice corrected, *it's a fucking nightmare...*

...broke apart instantaneously. I did not scream. The only proof that I had even experienced it was in the way that my eyes catapulted wide and my breath caught in my throat. I closed my eyes against the vertigo that I was experiencing and my muscles slowly relaxed. I opened them after a moment and observed the wispy white mist that wrapped its ethereal tentacles around the "teeth filed to points" above and clung to the underside of the cavern ceiling. Memories flooded back and replaced the vision... the *visions* from my dream: *Freeworld One. Little Shenango.* And finally…

I turned my head to the right. My left shoulder creaked slightly as I did so and I gritted my teeth. I saw her lying there next to me, her head still down upon my chest. Our kiss came back to me in a rush of feeling and emotion and the last snippets of my nightmare quickly and blessedly faded from my memory. I wondered at how unexpected it had been and yet how amazing. I allowed my gaze to wander from Maria's sleeping figure to the plot of corn that grew to our left to the adobe-fashioned tool shed to our right (*nice architecture,* I thought again), and stifled a chuckle.

We were still alone. No one had stumbled upon us. Had someone done so they might have marveled at the two people, little more than children, that lay amidst Freeworld One's home-grown and farmed food supply but I realized that at that moment? That thought and all others were insignificant. My right arm lay cradled around her neck and my right palm lay against the warm skin of her right upper arm. I gently ran the tips of my fingers up and down said arm and she stirred almost instantaneously. Her eyes slowly opened. She craned her neck to look up at me and smiled. I felt the last of the tension that I had been experiencing from my nightmare subside.

"Mornin'," I whispered.

"Hi," she murmured in response, her smile unbroken. I was unsure of what to say. It was not an awkward silence that fell between us nor were we speechless. There was simply nothing to say and I was content in that knowledge.

"How…" she finally cooed after a moment, "how did you sleep?" She buried her head deeper into my embrace and I pulled her closer with my right arm.

"Incredible," was all that I could manage. Maria, surprised, giggled.

I guess I just answered two questions, I thought.

"Yeah," she said, "I guess that could describe… well, how *I* slept too."

I could feel my own chuckle building in my chest as we looked into each other's eyes…

And broke into hysterics.

She fell back upon my outstretched arm and sent a brief jolt of pain up it. I, startled, gasped and hit my head a bit too firmly against the moss and topsoil covered surface. I gasped again but my pain was obviously Maria's pleasure. Her laughing intensified. Despite the pain that I was experiencing in two new appendages on top of the continued throbbing of my left shoulder and my right temple I laughed harder, as well. We continued as such for a few moments before the pain that I was experiencing and our shared laughter began to subside.

"Oh God, William," Maria said as she wiped the tears away from her eyes. She leaned over to me and brushed her hand across my cheek, "I am *so* sorry."

I reached up and wiped my own hysterical tears away with my right hand, "You have *nothing* to be sorry for," I said. I leaned over on my right side and gazed into her eyes. I am not ashamed to admit that at that moment I drank her in. But surprisingly, her gaze averted mine. It moved passed me and down toward where Little Shenango flowed.

There it is again, I thought, *something unspoken.*

"Mia, are you..."

"Yes," she said determinedly as she turned back to me and laid her right hand upon my left forearm. She smiled, "Yes, William. I'm fine. *Better* than fine, actually. I guess this changes things a bit, huh?"

I nodded, my previous, mental inquiry forgotten, "A bit, yeah. But in a *good* way, I think." My question was rhetorical and yet she answered it honestly.

"Definitely," she responded confidently, "most definitely. But we..."

"*Yeah,*" I said, "yeah, I know. We *really* should think about heading back."

"Okay," she conceded and frowned. We lay there beside each other for another moment before we reluctantly stood. Once righted I placed my right arm over her shoulders and pulled her close to me as Steve had with Carole earlier. She in turn laid her head briefly upon the side of my chest as Carole had done to Steve.

"I guess we should go," I said with a sigh as I pulled away from her, "who knows how long we've been down here for? Our doctor might begin asking questions." She nodded in agreement and once again moved to within a breath of me. She pressed her body against mine in a fashion that was deceptively seductive, stood on her tiptoes and kissed me again. I returned the gesture and savored the sensation. After a long and timeless moment she pulled away.

"What was that for?" I asked her with a grin.

She returned it with a half-hearted one of her own, "Nothing, William. Just... nothing."

Stranger, still, I thought again, "Mia, if something's wrong... I mean, if you don't feel comfortable with..."

"*No!*" she exclaimed suddenly, "no, William. That's not it. I'm fine. *Really.* I just... I could get used to this."

"That makes two of us," I responded, *"but..."*

"We should keep this between us for now," she interrupted, and followed it up with a sigh.

I nodded, "Our little secret, Mia," I replied and crossed my index finger over my chest, "promise?"

She promptly duplicated my gesture, "Promise... *Willy.*"

I rolled my eyes briefly, then reached down with my right hand and took her left in mine. I squeezed it tightly. She squeaked.

"Alright, then" she said, "enough of that." She began to lead me through the crops and back toward the bridge across Little Shenango. I followed reluctantly and longingly glanced once over my shoulder. I was unaware that our stroll back through the irrigated farmland across the river from the town proper of Freeworld One would mark the last, truly innocent walk of our respective young lives. I was unaware of what awaited us in the moments after we re-crossed the bridge and, you could argue, left our respective childhoods behind us forever.

* * *

Jeff fled down the mine shaft, his only guide the light that shined from the screen of his flashlight-phone and the sigils upon the walls that pointed him in the correct direction. Eventually he came to the same dead end that he, William and Maria had arrived at on their first trip down. At least he assumed and hoped that it was. He stopped short of running head-first into the wall opposite the opening and stood in the center of the room. He attuned his ears to the area behind him and closed his eyes. He did not hear anything. Despite his judgment he called out.

"Hello?" His voice echoed off of the walls of the enclosure, back out through the opening and, he assumed, up the tunnel. He did not know how far the echo traveled and he did not belabor his mind about it. He waited but still heard nothing save for his own, quickened breathing and the steady pounding of his heart in his chest.

"Hello?" he called out again, a bit louder than before. Nothing. He fidgeted and glanced at the area of the wall that had tested hollow previously (if this is the same "room" his coldly rational voice cautioned) and moved toward it slowly...

From within said portion of the wall Jeff heard a click. Said click was followed by the low, grinding sound that he remembered from his first trip as the same two meter wide by three meter high portion of rock that had trundled out and aside previously did so again. He breathed a sigh of relief as the door to the corridor that led to Freeworld One came to a rest with a shudder and a release of air. By the illumination of the flickering bulbs that hung at regular intervals from the ceiling of the shaft beyond he saw two figures waiting directly within the opening with their weapons drawn. He raised his flashlight-phone head high and saw their pallid faces: Both male and shockingly similar. They were the same guards that had let him out a short time before.

Twins, he thought as he had previously and he stifled a nervous chuckle. He did not know whether they were or were not but by God they sure as hell looked like twins.

"Back so soon?" The one guard asked nonchalantly. Jeff nodded. His breath still caught in his throat.

"We..." he began between breaths, "need to go... NOW," he said forcibly, "let me in... and close this up. We need to warn Alex. Company's..."

Jeff never got to finish his statement. He felt the short hairs on the back of his neck prickle simultaneously with his mention of "company" (DANGER Jeff DANGER his mind screamed) and without a thought to the contrary he shouted and lurched forward for the opening, dropping his phone in the process as lights exploded behind him and bathed the room in an inhuman and sterilized white glow, much like fluorescent glow of his phone-flashlight multiplied exponentially. Something tone-less and mechanical ordered him to "CEASE" as a flurry of pulse rifle fire exploded outward from the entrance to the cavern in a storm of white-hot plasma.

He landed face first on the ground beyond the opening. He swung around as one of the shots singed the back of his polo shirt and the skin beneath it. He cried out in pain as he felt the skin there slice and immediately cauterize. His phone dropped and forgotten he fumbled and removed his blaster from its holster. He deftly clicked "off" the safety. He rolled to his right and behind what little cover the overhanging edge of the door provided and opened fire.

How did I not hear them coming? Jeff thought as he continued to pepper the area with particle blaster fire but his inquiry was quickly forgotten. One of the two guards was completely surprised by the attack and he fell quickly against the left side of the corridor, a victim of a pulse rifle shot through his upper right chest. The other was smarter. As soon as he realized what was occurring he leapt... practically dove for the minimal shelter behind which Jeff lay. Jeff watched as two heavily armored 78As moved into the room, their pulse rifles pointed in his direction. He could see another two behind them and beyond them? Another two.

Oh fuck, he thought hopelessly and redirected his fire. His first shot caught the 78A on the right on its forehead and it staggered backward but did not fall. His second shot was truer: It sliced directly through the 78A on the left's red-glowing right eye and he watched with satisfaction as the machine fell in a heap with sparks exploding out of the exit wound in the back of its head.

"CLOSE IT!" Jeff shouted to the guard that cowered behind him over the din,

"FOR THE LOVE OF GOD CLOSE THE FUCKING...!"

He heard another click and the sound of gears grinding as the small area behind which he sheltered began to move to his left. He fired at the machine on the right as he belly-crawled along with the slowly...

Too slow, he thought hectically, TOO SLOW...

...closing door. Another 78A had moved up to take the place of its fallen counterpart and it fired upon Jeff's position. The shot detonated with the edge of the closing door just above his head and he felt what little hair he had there burn quickly down to its roots. The 78A on the right—the first one that he had fired upon—realized what was happening and sprang forward with dizzying speed. Jeff watched it move closer... CLOSER...

As the machine's eyes came into his view not two meters away from where he lay he pulled his weapon's trigger. The shot not only hit his mark's head but exited the back of it with a sizzle and a spark.

That armor doesn't do shit at close range, he thought and screamed in triumph as he enjoyed a burst of adrenaline and confidence. The second hand shot caught the other machine in the room directly upon its chest. It stumbled as its counterpart originally had but did not fall.

The distraction was enough. Jeff fired a few more shots at the vanguard of machines that crowded into the room as the door to the cavern finally closed. He heard the release of air... heard the door lock. He heard the muffled sound of pulse rifle fire on the other side of the wall. He sighed as he rolled onto his back. He knew that for the moment he was safe.

But it was only for a moment, he knew. He sat up, shook his head and stood up. He turned to the last surviving guard whose face bespoke a combination of shock, awe and loss. Had the two of them really been twins? He thought as he glanced at the motionless body that lay on its belly against the wall of the corridor. It was conceivable yet he never found out the answer.

"Thank you," Jeff said, "now let's go. That door won't hold them for long."

The guard looked from the motionless figure of his counterpart to Jeff. "Okay," he said reluctantly. It was, Jeff knew, the best he could and should expect under the circumstances. With a final anxious glance at the closed door and the sounds coming from beyond it, the two of them began to sprint down the stone corridor that covered the last of the distance to Freeworld One.

* * *

I knew something was wrong as soon as I stepped off of the bridge across Little Shenango and onto the town-bordered riverbank. For no comprehendible reason I tensed. Maria did so as well. Her hand clamped down upon mine like a vice grip as she likely sensed the same wrongness that I did. It was nothing that I could vocalize. If anything the scene that surrounded us was more peaceful than it had been earlier. Not a soul stirred within or around the collection of structures nearest the riverbank and looking back now I believe that *that* was the observation that convinced me.

The atmosphere that hung over the town proper of Freeworld One was anticipatory. Not heavy like it had been in my dream and it had been upon encountering Chuck but tense, as if the chill that caused mine and Maria's breath to crystallize before us was charged with electricity.

"Something's..."

"*Off,*" Maria interrupted me, "I know, William. I can feel it too."

I nodded and turned to her, "We should get back to Steve and Carole's," I said and she nodded her head quickly in agreement.

We started down the riverbank together toward the well-trodden path that we had earlier traveled separately to get to the destination of our un-expected rendezvous and once there, we made our way briskly up the hill toward the Wetherhill's home. We moved into the Quad and passed by the armory.

I stopped, "*Wait!*" I shouted. Maria, who had just sprinted up the hill passed me, abruptly stopped and turned to me. I motioned to the armory and instinctively ran inside. She followed.

No one, not even Chuck stirred within but something was definitely amiss. My quick purveyance of the room revealed that the once-bountiful arsenal that had lined the shelves upon the walls was all but gone. A few weapons remained. I scanned the shelves and found what I was looking for toward the back of the structure: A half a dozen blasters of roughly the same make and model as the ones that Pat had given Maria and me with holsters behind them and spare battery packs stacked beside them. I selected one and its corresponding hip-holster and handed it to Maria who was visibly taken aback but beneath it I could see and sense understanding. I chose another one with a corresponding shoulder-version and slipped the holster on quick-ly. I grabbed one of the battery packs and inserted it—*positive to positive and negative to negative,* I thought—into the handle of the weapon and watched as five steady, green bars lit up on the surface of the battery pack. I looked and noticed that Maria had done the same with the same result.

I inserted the weapon in its holster and Maria followed suit. The process was surprisingly easy given that I had never worn a shoulder holster before. The rig fell softly again my right midsection as I buckled the straps beneath my chest. The feel of it there? I'm almost ashamed to admit that it felt natural. Maria had a similarly easy time with hers. She slipped it around her waist like a belt, exactly as intended, and buckled it in front. It fell against her black-jean covered pant leg and I felt a completely unexpected stirring in my chest and midsection again as I looked at her. I smiled. She glanced at me, placed her hands on her hips and questioned my grin.

"You just... you look pretty *badass*, Mia."

She grinned, "You too." I saw some*things* dangling from the bottom of her holster and by the bottom of her thigh and I knelt down, grabbed the two cords and tied them in a knot around her thigh. When satisfied that the holster wasn't moving I stood up and kissed her on the forehead.

"Let's go, kiddo," I said. She nodded and motioned to the spare battery packs. I mentally chastised myself for forgetting them and removed as many as I could fit into my jeans' pockets. I turned to her with the excess, realized that she was still wearing her pocket less, black jeans, shrugged and replaced them back on the shelf that I had removed them from. When satisfied that we had enough to support us indefinitely we vacated the armory quickly and continued up the hill quickly toward the Wetherhill's, passed the apothecary and passed the structure within which two men had been earlier bartering over something. No one stirred within either which further heightened the sense of impending danger.

Whatever was happening had turned Freeworld One into a veritable ghost town.

There are haints here, Vato, Pat's voice spoke in my mind again and I immediately brushed it aside as we exited the Quad and started up the last hill toward Steve's and Carole's.

Whereas the majority of the town appeared to be deserted the Wetherhill's home was not. We could hear voices within as we crested the hill and approached and we arrived to find Steve, Carole, Matt, Caren, Alex and surprisingly Jeff "Jeebus" Howard huddled around the Wetherhill's kitchen table. All turned to acknowledge us... even Caren though her acknowledgement was little more than another, suspicious glare... as we stepped through the entryway and into the living room. My gaze moved from Steve to his wife, Carole, then across the faces of the O'Brien's and lastly fell upon Alex and Jeff. The latter stood a step or two behind the Steward of Freeworld One and appeared pale and shaken. Still, he nodded as my eyes met his. I determined that my decision to stop at the armory had been a good one. Each of those assembled had a weapon strapped to either their ribcage or their hip, and a collection of backpacks lay at their respective feet.

I counted seven total.

Seven, I thought. My mind hearkened back to my recurring nightmare; *there are seven of us on the beach.* I shivered and attempted to brush the thought away. It did not, to my chagrin, dissipate entirely.

"We were wondering where you two were," Carole said, "looks like you had the presence of mind to stop by the armory on your way here."

"We were..." I began.

"Walking," Maria concluded for me. I turned to her, saw that she was smiling, turned back to the assembly and did the same.

"Walking," I reiterated, "over on the other side of the river. Shaking off some of the rust." I decided, considering the blank looks that I received in response that a change of topic was in order were I to keep mine and Maria's secret indefinitely.

"Where the hell is everyone?" I asked, "We didn't see a single person until we got back here. And where's Tim?"

Alex stepped around the table, Jeff close behind him, around the O'Briens and the Wetherhills and into my clear view. I was shocked to see that he too wore a weapon on his hip. The vision of him armed despite what little I knew of him seemed highly out of place and I reluctantly began to realize the gravity of whatever it was that we were facing. Any situation that would force Alex Parker, a man who had spoken so fervently about living a peaceful existence the last time I had seen him to carry a weapon did not bode well for Maria, for myself... shit, for anyone in Freeworld One despite his insistence that he and his counterparts would fight to retain their freedom if necessary.

"The children are in hiding, along with all the other members of the community that are either unable or unwilling to fight for themselves," he began, "I can't ask people that don't want to pick up a weapon to do so. *No one* can. As for Tim, he's been dispatched to take care of some business up above for you."

"To fight..." Maria began. I turned to her and watched as her face paled and her hand instinctively fell upon the hilt of her weapon.

Alex nodded, "Seems our spotters underestimated the force of machines assembling over our present location."

Jeff moved forward, "I was on my way out when I saw what was waiting above. There's an army up there, Maria. Not just a patrol or a Caravan. A hundred or more machines by my count. Assault vehicles, too. And where there are assault vehicles..."

"There are MDUs and, God forbid, worse nearby," Steve interrupted.

Jeff nodded and continued, "When I realized what was going on I came back to warn Alex but... I don't know how they did it without me hearing them. Maybe I was distracted but they followed me down the shaft that we took to get here. The same one that I took to get out. I just barely got away. One of the guards watching the entrance wasn't as lucky." He lowered his head and fell silent.

"Don't blame yourself, Jeff," Alex said as he turned and laid a reassuring hand upon his shoulder, "you did the right thing. Had you not we would have had no idea what was coming... would have had no time to prepare. As-is you bought us a little bit." He turned back to Maria and I, "the ones that *can* fight... that want to are massed on the border of the town, the biggest concentration near the main entrance/exit. It's a thin throughway, no more than a couple of meters across and high, so they'll need to come through in rows of two and, if they press it, three. Whatever happens we should be able to buy you enough time to escape."

I turned hectically to Maria and then back to Alex, "Escape? No way, Alex. If it wasn't for us this never would have happened. We should stand *with* you and not run away."

I heard what sounded like a murmur of agreement from near where Caren stood though I was unable to identify if it was my cavern attacker that had intoned anything. Alex surprisingly smiled and stepped forward. He once again placed his hands on my shoulders and gazed unblinkingly into my eyes. Admittedly, his own eyes seemed even colder than they had seemed previously and I felt a shiver traverse my spine from top to bottom.

There are haints here, Vato, Pat's voice reiterated again in my mind. I couldn't help but wonder if Alex Parker was about to become one... couldn't help but wonder if we all were destined for that outcome long term.

Or short term, William, my coldly rational voice cautioned and I shivered.

"Whether you're the reason they found us or not William is irrelevant," he continued and I realized that his comment was not only to reassure me but to caution Caren, "they've probably been looking for Freeworld One... looking for *me* for a while. I've been right up there at the top of their shit list for... well, I can't really tell you how long. Seems that they found what they were looking for. Whether you, Maria, Jeff or God him or herself were that catalyst doesn't concern me. But your safety does. Your destination... your destiny is not to die here. Don't ask me how I know this I just *do*. Steve, Carole, Matt and," he paused before he continued, "Caren"—he gestured back to them—"are going to lead you and Maria to safety and, God willing, all the way to Free Caymen."

"And me," Jeff interrupted as he rose his head and stepped forward.

Surprised, I looked past Alex at him, "What about Greentree, Jeff? I told you before: You don't have to do this. I..." I glanced at Maria who nodded and then back to Jeff, "*we* understand."

Jeff shrugged, "I've gotten out of some nasty jams before, William, but as soon as I saw that force gathered up above? Well, I guess I realized that there is no going back to Greentree. Not now. Not ever. I was wrong before. Regardless of whether Pat made it or not, my way out is *east* and not *west*. I get that now. Looks like you're going to be stuck with me for a while. At least until we make it to Free Caymen or... well, at least until we get there. Let's not worry about the alternative."

Despite the situation, I smiled and nodded, "I'm happy to hear it, Jeff. It might not be my place to say this but you are *most definitely* welcome."

Someone—I again think it was Caren—sighed but Jeff was unfazed. He nodded and looked away, his face a mask of steely determination and hidden regret nestled beside reluctant acceptance.

I'm sorry, Jeff, I thought again, *I know this wasn't what you wanted.*

It never is, Vato, Pat's voice again spoke reassuringly in my mind, *but we do what we need to do and we don't ask questions. It's a little thing called "honor." You'll understand it one day.*

"Okay, then," Alex said, interrupting my thought process as he turned from me and Maria and back to the Wetherhill's kitchen table, "everyone gather in here. You too, William and Maria. We don't have much time and you need to know the plan."

We did as he had requested and filed into the kitchen, Maria close beside me and to my immediate left. Steve and Carole set up to her immediate left and Caren and Matt set up across from us. Alex stood across the table from me and to the right and Jeff stood directly behind him.

I glanced down at the table. The bowl of fruit that had lain upon it was gone. In its place lay a map of what I assumed was the surface area above Freeworld One. The center of the map was cut in half by two crooked lines and the area between them was quite obviously a river.

The Shenango, I thought.

To one side lay what I assumed was the Mid-Western Territory and to the other? The Eastern Territory. *The Scorched Land.* I felt another shiver traverse my spine. The sensation was heightened and repeated as I saw the straight, black line that ran perpendicular to the river and across what was, from my vantage point, the bottom of the map but what I knew upon closer observation was the top.

The Highway, I thought. It was to an area above (*below, actually,* I thought, *you're viewing it upside down, genius*) it and on the left-hand side of the map that Alex pointed. I squinted at what he gestured toward. Topographically, all I could tell was that it was a more... not mountainous but hilly area that seemed to rise up on either side of what appeared to be a road.

"Halmier's Pass," he began, *"here.* Once you're across Little Shenango, make your way up to the surface using the emergency exits. You know the ones I'm talking about, don't you?"

A murmur of approvals emanated from my counterparts. I glanced at Maria and shrugged. She did the same.

"Those ovens across the river?" Alex corroborated, "that's what we call them. They vent out into the open air. They're steep but not overly so. You'll get dirty but it's worth it. A person can easily navigate them though at points, the going gets a bit dicey. Move briskly but not so much so that you risk slipping and you'll smell the open air before you know it, even if you *are* covered in soot."

I nodded, as did Maria. I motioned for him to continue. Alex did as I had indicated.

"Once you're above and out make for the Pass quickly..." he began anew.

"What..." I interrupted. All eyes including Maria's looked up from the map upon the table to me. Undaunted, however, I continued, "sorry to interrupt, but what *is* Halmier's Pass?" I looked at Steve and Carole, "You mentioned it earlier but..."

"Halmier's Pass is a roughly three or four kilometer stretch of rutted asphalt that the machines used to use as a service road," Carole answered, "it runs west to east past an old, abandoned military supply depot that the Administration deserted a long, *long* time ago. Once past the depot it bends right—north, actually—and tunnels through a pretty steep hillside... almost a mountain but not quite before it descends into a valley and meets up with the Highway on the other side," she finished. Alex nodded.

"You may encounter some resistance once there," he continued, "if our spotters were right—no small task considering how badly they underestimated the forces massing above us—the Administration may have left a small patrol or maybe even a Caravan to guard it. I don't know how much attention they'll be paying to it especially with us to contend with and I can't give you any details other than what I already know. But the machines aren't stupid despite what we want to believe. They're likely expecting a retreat of some sort. Just be ready to give them what-for in the event that you come across them."

"Ten-four, chief," Matt said with a salute and simultaneously crossed his arms across his chest.

I was visibly startled. It was the first time I had heard his voice and it was, I'll admit, not quite what I had expected. It was peculiar, unlike his appearance which was, as I mentioned previously, relatively normal. It was confident yet seemed to have a somewhat modifiable tone to it, as if he might sound one way one moment and another way entirely the next.

As if sensing my observation, he redirected his attention to me and cocked his head to his left; my right. A curious grin eclipsed his face.

"What's 'amatter, serGEANT?" he asked in a low drawl, "ain't you ever heard a *real* man *speak* before?" Caren chuckled and my eyes grew wide as I realized how accurate my first impression of him had been. In response his grin faded and he turned back to Alex.

Jesus, I thought, *is being mental a prerequisite for enrollment in the Rebellion or for citizenship here in Freeworld One?* I refocused my own attention on Alex who continued.

"Tim," Alex continued, shaking his head, "I sent Tim to work on the acquisition of transportation and supplies. I anticipate he'll have something… I don't know what but something waiting for you through the tunnel, on the other side of the Pass. You seven'll need to deal with anything that you encounter between here and there yourselves. Think you can handle it?"

A murmur of affirmatives echoed across the room from the group. *Sure,* I thought, *why the fuck not?*

Alex, seemingly satisfied, nodded, "You'll need to travel the Pass on foot. The road surface is too broken up for a vehicle. It's a bit of an inconvenience but look at the bright side: The machines can't maneuver any heavy artillery down there any more than we can maneuver a vehicle down there. At the most you could end up facing a few assault bikes along with whatever forces they've assembled on foot."

"No doubt," Matt responded in what I assumed was his "normal" voice. I looked at Maria and Maria looked at me. I shrugged again and she did the same.

"Okay then," Alex said. He moved the map aside and revealed another one beneath it. I could tell that the second map pictured a much larger relief than the first one had. My eyes immediately fell upon the straight, black line that again cut across the bottom (*the top,* I thought) of it. I traced its length to my right and saw near the edge another crooked line which resembled the one on the first map. *The Shenango,* I thought again. I then traced it back to my left to where it crossed at least a half a dozen other crooked lines and what appeared to be a range of hills or mountains until it eventually terminated...

I stopped and gasped. Not far from where the line that signified the Highway ended the land pictured upon the map... well, it simply ceased. Maria apparently saw the same thing as evidenced by her abrupt intake of air.

"Is that...?" she began.

"The Great Sea?" Alex said as he pointed to the massive empty space beyond the termination of the land, "you've got it, Maria. In the flesh err... in the water so to speak."

I nodded, and Alex continued.

"Per what Pat told Jeff before... well, just *before,* your destination is *here*"—he pointed to a spot directly next to the water and well south of the Highway—"Hempstead, ET. The town didn't used to be called that. I'm not sure what the pre-Administration designation for it was but that's the name that its current occupants have given it if what little intelligence I have is correct. All the old names have pretty much faded from our memories, anyway. Hempstead is your final destination and my advice is to make for it as quickly as possible. Limit your stops. Follow the Highway a good distance until you come to a Marker: A road labeled with the number '9.' It's an old, unused tributary of the Highway. Follow '9' south until you get *here*"—he forcibly pointed to the same location on the coastline that he had originally.

"While the help offered by the people of Hempstead might not be exactly what you'd consider... um, *helpful,* Pat was right: It's really the only option available," he continued, "the coast is vastly under-populated and has been since the Scourge."

"But how will they know?" I responded, "How will they know that we're coming? And how will the Rebellion know to send someone to..."

"*Extract* you?" Alex asked, "Don't fret it, William. I'm one step ahead of you. Earlier I sent someone ahead of you to contact the Free Caymenites and let them know that you're coming. Someone reliable. So long as that person encounters no resistance and with a lot of luck, they will be waiting to extract you when or shortly after you arrive."

"'Someone,'" Maria repeated, "one of your spotters?"

Alex looked up from the map to her and, surprisingly, grinned.

"Not quite, Maria," he said, "not quite. Better, actually. Someone that I trust. Trust *me,* okay?"

She nodded, albeit reluctantly. Alex's request to trust our anonymous benefactor did little to boost my confidence but admittedly? Neither Maria nor I had much of a choice but to do as he had requested.

Okay, Alex, I thought and looked at where his finger rested. One word came to mind. Not Free Caymen and not even freedom. One word: *Mercs.* I looked passed Alex and I saw Jeff who was, not unsurprisingly, already looking at me. He mouthed the same word that I had just thought. I reluctantly nodded and redirected my attention to Alex as he looked up from his perusal of the map.

"There *are* risks," he said, "There's really no need for me to go into them. The Eastern Territory is a blighted and dismal place. Hempstead's not the only community that's sprung up there despite the fact that there hasn't been a centralized government or collection of actual cities there for decades. I'm not saying that you'll encounter any of the other... *elements* that populate it but be on your guard. You're all either smart enough, seasoned enough or both to know that.

"And," he added, "try to be optimistic. Free Caymen? It exists. While I've never seen it, I have no reason to believe that it's a fabrication. I'm a glass half full kind of guy so... well, there you go. That's the teeny, tiny light at the end of the proverbial tunnel. I can't prove it to you but I trust it. I *know* it. Any questions?"

My gaze traced across the respective gazes of each person assembled around Steve's and Carole's kitchen table. I realized as I glanced at each one in turn that they were no longer merely passing acquaintances on mine and Maria's journey to the hypothetical freedom that existed through Halmier's Pass, across the barren Scorched Land, beyond the termination of a rutted once-tributary of the Highway known only as "9" and south to a town known as Hempstead, ET. Not even Caren who was still looking down at the map... seemingly intent on not meeting my gaze, for once. They were, for all intent and purposes, as much my companions now as Maria had been, was, and would remain for as long as I...

As *any* of us could draw breath.

To the end, William, the Maria-specter from my recurring nightmare droned in a voice choked with blood, *to the end...*

It exists, Alex's voice spoke in my mind and I keyed upon *it* and not the vision from my dream. No one spoke. Alex, seemingly satisfied, nodded his head and said, "Okay, then. Let's not waste any more time."

I thought about chastising the Steward of Freeworld One for his reference to such an irrelevant concept but considering what we were facing I chose not to. One by one we soundlessly filed out of the Wetherhill's home. Steve, Carole, Matt, Caren and Jeff all grabbed their respective backpacks.

Steve handed me one that, per him had been pre-prepared for me which I placed over my shoulders. Carole handed a similar one to Maria and she did the same. We emerged into the chilling and humid air that blanketed the cavern within which rested Alex Parker's safe haven.

Safe Haven, I thought. Sadly I knew that it was as irrelevant an idea at that moment as time.

We made our way briskly down the path toward the river, Alex and Jeff in the lead, Matt and Caren behind them, and Steve and Carole behind *them.* Maria and I brought up the rear of our quickly-moving vanguard. There remained no sign of movement anywhere but I could hear something off to my left. I slowed briefly and craned my neck to look over my shoulder, which once again screamed in protest.

The sound that I was hearing? It sounded like an explosion. *No, I* thought, *explosions. Distant but moving closer. And quickly. Too quickly.* I requickened my pace at Maria's urging from a few steps in front of me as said sounds echoed through the cavern that surrounded us and mingled with what sounded like falling rocks. My suspicion was confirmed as a frighteningly close explosion echoed across town and a sprinkle of damp dust fell from the cavern's ceiling and landed upon my brow. I quickly brushed it away. As we once again entered the Quad and ran past the supply depot I heard an expected, yet nonetheless unwelcome sound as another explosion and subsequent rock fall was followed by a human shout that sounded like *"BREECH!"* and then another which sounded like *"OPEN FIRE!"* Said shout segued into an eruption of weapon's fire.

Mentally I shouted a negative. *Not yet!* I wanted to scream but I didn't. I remained as focused as I could on the path in front of me.

Simultaneously with the unmistakable sound of blaster fire, which was joined almost immediately by a deeper, booming sound that I immediately associated with a 78A's pulse rifle, Alex shouted an expletive and broke into a run. The rest of us followed suit as we ran past the abandoned supply depot, the apothecary and the armory, and past the diminishing structures bordering the river. We emerged upon the riverbank, all stopped abruptly and fanned out across the surface as the particle blaster and pulse rifle fire increased in frequency. Thankfully, it remained isolated to the far left border of Freeworld One.

For the moment, I thought.

"Over the bridge!" Alex shouted as my momentary prayer of thanks was interrupted by a louder, closer explosion that shook the ground we stood upon. I felt my legs wobble beneath me as I tried to retain my balance and

just barely managed to do so. But said explosion was followed by another…
and another as the bridge up-river from us that Maria and I had so recently crossed hand-in-hand rocked back and forth on its moorings. Jeff, Matt,
Caren, Steve and Carole took off in a hobbled sprint for it as another explosion detonated no more than 100 meters away and I turned my head violently, the pain in my shoulder and to a lesser extent my temple forgotten but
my heart pounding, to watch one of the structures on the edge of Freeworld
One nearest where I concluded the fighting was occurring detonate outward
in a flurry of blazing hot fire and smoking debris.

Adobe, I helplessly thought again and almost chuckled hysterically.

I turned back to Alex whose demeanor, despite what was occurring, remained surprisingly calm. He gestured toward Maria and in a raised voice
commanded her to *"go!"* She spared me a nervous glance to which I nodded
an affirmative before she turned and ran past me and Alex after the rest of
our group. Another explosion rocked the town. I again turned my head from
Alex and watched a building near the supply depot simply disintegrate in a
white-hot flash of flame, mud and dried plant life. The heat from the explosion buffeted my cheeks as it moved passed me and over the river.

"Artillery fire!" Alex shouted over the din, *"They really mean business!"*

I looked back at Alex, the after-image of the explosion still clouding
my vision and was shocked, nay downright bewildered to see his unfazed
countenance. I began to inquire as I looked toward the bridge—Jeff and the
Wetherhills had already gained it and were making their way quickly across
it with the O'Briens and Maria close behind—but Alex continued without
interruption.

"I need you…!" he began suddenly before another explosion caused the
riverbank to shudder violently. I felt another hot breeze and a few, hot dust
particles blow past my face. I turned nervously to the bridge and observed
that Jeff had gained the other side but Steve and Carole were caught in the
middle. They clung to the support ropes as the bridge feverishly arced right
and left before it fell reasonably still. Simultaneously, they released the support ropes and sprinted the rest of the way across. I watched as Carole removed her backpack and laid it upon the riverbank. Matt and Caren stepped
upon the bridge and started making their way across as quickly as they
could. Maria, consequently, waited for me by the entrance.

Whatever's he's got to say he'd better make it quick, I thought as I turned
impatiently from Maria's waiting figure back to him.

"I need you to do something for me!" he shouted as he reached into the front
pocket of his slacks…

And removed a folded piece of paper from within it.

What the...? I thought confusedly as he held it out to me. I considered it for a moment. The paper was old, that much I could determine upon my first observation of it. Roughly the size of a regulation envelope, the edges were crinkled and black with age and wear. The flap of the parchment was folded down in a lopsided triangle and was sealed to the body of the folded paper by a red blob of... *something*. I did not know what. Upon the raised, red blob was an inscription that had seemingly been stamped into it. I gasped in awe at what I saw there. It was, I realized, the same symbol that lay upon the underside of Alex's right arm: Two circles in a figure-eight with an arrow evenly crosscutting them.

What does it mean? I thought again as another explosion rocked the town and the adjoining riverbank and caused me to stumble, *and why does it feel like it has something to do with Latin, Skews, Gateways and Pathfinders?*

Alex reached out with his hand, the one not holding the parchment, and steadied me before I could fall. I looked up at him to thank him and saw that his other hand held the leading edge of it within a breath of my nose. I stood slowly, reached out with my good right hand and gently took it from him.

"What is it!?" I shouted as I turned it over and considered it in the dim light provided by the flickering lighting that rung the cavern. I could see no writing upon it... no addressee.

"A message!" he shouted back.

A message? I thought confusedly again, *with no addressee? "For who!?"* I asked him as I heard a scream and a human shout that sounded like *"RETREAT!"* from the left edge of town which was followed by another explosion, the sound of another rock fall and a subsequent increase in pulse rifle discharge frequency.

They're through, I thought helplessly but my attention was not focused on the battle that raged behind me. Rather it was focused on the man... the *great* man that stood before me. Alex Parker was more than simply the Steward of Freeworld One, I understood. He was a man of virtue... he was a man of...

Of honor, Pat's voice echoed in my mind and mingled with my own. Despite my lack of understanding of the term I knew that he was. He grinned as he released me from his grip and stepped back toward the swiftly flowing river. His hand fell upon the hilt of his blaster. I will never forget how he looked in that moment, his back to Little Shenango and his cold, marble eyes intently focused upon my deep blue ones. They shifted from my gaze to the area over my shoulder as another explosion rocked the riverbank and another shockwave of particle-enhanced heat pushed me forward toward it... toward him and then back to me. Deftly, he removed his weapon from its holster and clicked the safety into the "off" position.

"You'll know him when you find him!" he shouted determinedly, paused, and corrected: *"Or when he finds you! Until then? Keep it safe!"*

He started to move passed me and paused within a step of where I stood. The envelope that he had entrusted into my care was firmly gripped in my right hand. Unexpectedly he reached down and brushed the leading edge of it. His smile faded as he did so and was replaced by... *sadness?* The moment passed quickly as his hand fell away from it. He wiped said hand across his face and it came away damp, though I could not be sure if the dampness upon it was sweat or tears.

Or both, I understood. He looked up and into my eyes and winked at me. His grin returned and widened one, final time before he spoke four words— Latin, I immediately understood—that would echo in my mind for many, many moments after that one.

"Non multa nostrae solitudini!" Alex Parker shouted.

I cocked my head curiously, *"What?"*

Alex Parker's smile widened as he responded, *"It's Latin, William!"*

"It means 'there aren't many of us left!'"

Before I could question his statement and without another word, nary an acknowledgement or a look back Alex Parker ran past me and up the well-traveled path into the Freeworld One town proper, his blaster held in front of him. He ran toward the sound of the firefight that had broken out on the left border of town but seemed to be moving inward.

Toward you, my coldly rational voice reminded me. Explosions continued to rock the town proper as I watched him go. The ground that surrounded me shook and shockwaves of heat engulfed me with each successive blast as the machine's artillery fire grew more and more deadly in accuracy. I could hear Maria shouting despite the cacophony of sounds—explosions mingled with screaming mingled with weapons fire mingled with rock fall mingled with the sound of the swiftly flowing river splashing against the riverbank and the rock face into which it spiraled and disappeared—and beneath that, those of my newest counterparts urging me toward them. And yet I disregarded their urgings and helplessly watched Alex Parker go until he disappeared into the thick, black smoke that was steadily engulfing the town. Then and only then, when his tall and lanky figure had vanished like one of Pat's haints into the distance did I glance one final time at the parchment that I held in my hand.

Until then keep it safe! There aren't many of us left, I helplessly remembered.

Without a thought to the contrary I jammed the parcel into my front right jeans pocket. I turned and began to run up the bank toward where Maria nervously awaited me at the foot of the bridge.

The ground beneath my boots rumbled and the once-cold and humid air of the cavern which had grown thick with the smoke and the soot from the buildings burning throughout it caused me to choke. Rubble fell around me as the integrity of the cavern's ceiling was further compromised by the battle that raged beneath it. I reached Maria and gestured hectically for her to proceed me onto and across the bridge which she did without hesitation.

We were fortunate. We made it across without incident but as soon as our feet touched the soft, green and brown ground of the opposing riverbank the largest explosion we had yet heard, seen and experienced occurred in the middle of what had once been Freeworld One's Quad. The shockwave from the blast wiped out what few structures remained within the burning rubble and rocketed across the cavern's interior. It reached our group gathered upon the riverbank before we could react. The bridge that we had crossed rippled upward in a wave that began on the town-bordered side. It broke free of its moorings with little resistance. It whiplashed in our direction with blinding speed and what had been the far edge impacted violently with the riverbank where we had been standing a moment before.

I say "where we had been standing a moment before" because the shockwave, upon reaching the far riverbank of Little Shenango where we were gathered, knocked us all to the ground and quickly compromised the steep but fragile edge that overlooked the water below. We never made it to the "emergency exits." The ground beneath us disintegrated and without warning, all seven of us were helplessly plunged into bone-chilling and swiftly flowing Little Shenango River.

* * *

The scene surrounding Alex Parker was unlike anything that he had ever seen or experienced over the course of his long, long life.

Long, he thought with a chuckle despite the precariousness of his and his once-community's situation, that's an understatement. Sporadic weapon's fire echoed through the black, smoke and soot-clogged air that surrounded him as he moved cautiously from once-structure to once-structure looking for survivors of the battle that continued to rage in isolated areas around Freeworld One. It was impossible for him to gauge the distance between his position and the positions of the nearest enemy forces so he remained cautious despite the noticeable decrease in activity both visible and audible. He knew the truth that William did not though perhaps, Alex considered, perhaps the Jefferson runaway had sensed something.

Perhaps that's why I gave it to him and not to one of the others, he thought, perhaps there's something more to him something... necessary? Do any of the others see it? Did Pat? Christ, I could go crazy thinking about these things, even now after all this time.

One thing that he knew for certain? The machines had not come to Freeworld One looking for a couple of 18 year old runaways. They had not come looking to destroy it. They had come looking for him and him alone: Alex Parker, the Steward of Freeworld One.

Alex Parker, the Steward of the Unum Verum Iter...

Alex Parker, Explorator. That was in the old tongue. In the new, though?

Explorator meant Pathfinder. They had come for him because of who he was and because of what he knew. Because of what he carried...

Had carried, he corrected himself and grinned slightly, boy are they in for a shock.

He knelt down and lowered his blaster to his side. Clumsy weapon, he thought. He'd never been partial to weapons in general but necessity dictated his use of them.

At least in this Skew, he thought. He closed his eyes and attuned his ears to the surrounding area. He lamented the fact that he continued to hear more pulse rifle discharge than particle blaster discharge which was the only sign of Freeworld One's remaining defense. What had once been a safe-haven for people who had desired to escape Administration-controlled society had been quickly and methodically reduced by said Administration into little more than a kilometer long by kilometer wide pile of burning mud, dead plant life and crumbling rock from both the cavern ceiling and the cavern walls.

Just like so much else in this world, he thought sadly, there's a reason why they're in control. He knew that it had been foolish of him to expect his counterparts to put up more than a token resistance against the sizable force that bore down upon them, but he was and would always be proud of them and their resolve. What little defense they had managed had bought the Jefferson runaways and his once-counterparts time to escape. He prayed that the last explosion in the middle of the town—the most violent yet, it had generated a shockwave that had picked him up and thrown him a good 10 meters—had not affected their plan for escape. He prayed because their safety was all that mattered to him as he opened his eyes. The immediate area surrounding him remained deserted. He began picking through the rubble of the ruined structure to his immediate right.

He was fortunate. As soon as he started removing debris from the top of the pile he heard a weakened, female voice within mutter "hello?" He quickened his pace and began removing debris by the armful. The rapidly diminishing pile of detritus *revealed at first a tuft of curly, brown hair followed by a dirt and dust bespeckled face. A set of brown eyes… the lapel of a once-white jacket turned grey by the smoke and soot…*

Freeworld One's apothecary, Nicole, smiled as her brown eyes flickered and she beheld him kneeling over her. She breathlessly spoke his name. Alex reached down with his free hand and laid it upon her forehead. He smiled back.

"Fatum Autum Filius," he said, and the words flowed from his mouth like the river that flowed through the heart of Freeworld One.

"Mmm," Nicole murmured as her smile widened. She closed her eyes, "I never get tired of hearing that."

Alex chuckled. "I never get tired of saying it," he said, "and I'm going to get you out of there. Don't worry." He laid his blaster upon the ground and began removing the debris from atop her more quickly. He heard her whisper something and he paused and asked her to repeat it.

"I said NO, Alex," she said determinedly, her smile fading, her breath labored and her eyelids again flickering, "please? Don't waste your strength."

He looked down the length of where he assumed her body was beneath the pile and back up at her face and into her eyes. Yes, Alex thought. He understood the severity of her condition… understood the likelihood of her survival.

Reluctantly, he nodded.

"It's okay," she said with a cough, her gaze unblinkingly fixed upon Alex's. "It doesn't hurt… much. I can't even feel my arms and legs anymore. I don't think I've got much time left."

She paused, caught her breath and continued, "But you, Alex? You need to get out of here while you still can. We've been together for a long, long time. Longer than I can comprehend some times. The things that we've been through? What we've seen? You're more important than this"—she cringed as she managed to move her head a hair to her left and then to her right and reiterated—"and you know it."

Alex once again lowered his hand and laid it upon her forehead. He smiled, "No more, Nicole. Those days are done now. For both of us, I think. You've…"

He paused and attempted to find the appropriate words. After a moment, he did.

"You've been a true companion to me. In so many ways. Thank you for that. But I think…" he paused again, "I think that it's time for us to rest. Don't you agree?"

He cooed this last to her softly as his cold marble eyes gazed into her brown ones. She began to mutter another objection but was seemingly overwhelmed by a rush of calmness. She closed her eyes against the sensation of Alex's hand laid upon her brow and her smile widened further. Her breathing temporarily equalized. She opened her eyes briefly, gazed up into Alex's and nodded an affirmative before she re-closed them.

It's the least I can do, he thought as he glanced from the hand he had laid upon her brow to the tattoo (a "sigil" William had called it, he thought, how fitting) upon the underside of the forearm and he closed his own eyes. He concentrated harder. No pain, he mentally willed, feel no pain, Fatum Autum Filius. That, too, was in the old tongue.

But in the new? Fatum Autum Filius translated to "Destiny's Child."

"Sleep, now," he muttered quietly in Latin, "sleep. Be at peace." His statement, he knew, was not just for her but preemptively for himself. His fate, he knew, was as academic as the fate of the poor and broken soul buried beneath the ton of rock and debris that lay before him.

My companion, he thought again, one of the truest I've ever known. Thank you for that. Thank you.

The apothecary sighed and breathed deeply one, final time before she fell eternally still. He "felt" (it remained the only way that he could describe it, even after so many years) her expiration and he opened his eyes slowly. Tears welled in them as he looked down at her unmoving figure before his own senses, heightened by both caution and the "praecantatio" he had just performed detected something... some-THINGS approaching.

He removed his hand slowly from Nicole's forehead and lowered it to where his blaster lay beside him. Without looking away from her he wrapped his right hand around its hilt and positioned his index finger over the trigger—the feel of the steel grip of the weapon against his sweaty palm granting him a brief rush of confidence—before he quickly and with a practiced motion removed the battery pack inserted in it with his index and middle fingers, turned it around and re-inserted it. Not positive to positive and negative to negative but the opposite: Negative to positive and positive to negative. The weapon began to whistle and hum immediately.

My turn, Nicole, he thought as he kissed the index and middle fingers of his left hand and placed them upon her forehead, I will see you again soon. He reluctantly turned to his left to face what approached.

There were four in all, two heavily armored 78As, a Leader (Nyx Series, he thought, V3.0 or maybe even 4.0) and a Surveillance Mark. The former two machines upon noticing his presence raised their pulse rifles and the one to his left commanded him, "HUMAN LOWER YOUR WEAPON. CEASE ALL ACTIVITY AND SURRENDER IMMEDIATELY FOR IDENTIFICATION OR WARRANT IMMEDIATE TERMINATION."

Alex smiled and stood slowly from his crouch, his weapon still held down at his side. He gained a standing position and rotated his body so that he was directly facing the group of machines. They were no more than three meters away from him and the 78A repeated its command. Though variations in "tone" were not easily distinguishable when addressing or when being addressed by a machine Alex marveled at the slightly increased nuisance he heard in the 78A's voice. His observation was compounded by the way that both 78As seemed to tense at what he assumed was his illogical reaction to their directive. Their large and intimidating pulse rifles wavered almost imperceptibly for a brief moment before they fell still.

Evolution comes with a downside as well as an upside, boys, he thought. His smile widened. You know that I'm a threat. You can sense it. But do you know how much of one? The weapon in his palm whistled and hummed louder and grew hotter with each moment that passed.

You will soon enough, he concluded.

"Hold out your hand," Alex spoke calmly. Not a question nor a request but a command which was directed confidently to the Surveillance Mark. Said SM turned to the Leader, its red, unimpeded and armor-free eyes seeking guidance, and the Nyx spoke in a voice more nuanced but unmistakably robotic.

You'll never be able to fix that aspect of what you are, he thought, no matter how many upgrades or versions of you the so-called Administration creates. That thought? It gave him an added degree of solace in light of what he knew he faced.

"Proceed," the Nyx said.

Three meters give or take a few centimeters; Alex measured, and without a thought to the contrary breathed deeply through his nostrils. He drew in air and the particle build-up from the air that had collected in his nose into his throat and he spat. The ball of spittle and black dust and dirt that escaped from his mouth was well-formed and aimed perfectly. It landed squarely in the middle of the SM's palm. The SM, again without hesitation, closed its hand upon Alex's "gift." Alex watched patiently, the palm of his hand beginning to prickle from the intense heat his weapon was giving off, as the machine connected remotely to the Administration mainframe in Cornelius City. He watched as it unflinchingly ran the subroutine that he knew from experience processed biological samples and matched the genetic algorithms in said samples to the information in the Administration's identity database contained in said mainframe. He waited and counted the requisite 21, pre-Administration seconds...

Blackjack! He thought and stifled a chuckle...

...before a match was determined. Simultaneously with the audible click that emanated from within the head of the SM, the micro-second transfer of information to the Leader and to the 78As and the first heat blister that broke out upon the palm of his right hand Alex Parker accepted his fate. Simultaneously with one of the 78As intoning that the Surveillance Mark had determined a positive identification match for the man that they had come looking for Alex leapt toward the group of machines with frightening speed, brought his blaster to bear on the Leader...

And pulled the trigger.

Et cognovi quod sit tibi, he naturally thought in the old tongue. Latin, he considered, a beautiful language. In his aged and experienced mind the words immediately translated into English — "and that's all you'll ever know" — as his weapon critically overloaded and exploded in his hand. The storm of blazing white shrapnel that followed blinded him almost instantaneously but not before he was afforded a final glimpse of all four machines being thrown backward by the intensity of the explosion. He too was thrown backward though he was incapable of seeing his flight and his subsequent landing. He felt a piece of shrapnel slice through the left side of his neck... felt hot blood squirt from the wound it had opened but he did not scream.

For Alex Parker there was no pain at that moment. He had experienced his share of both physical and mental anguish over the course of his long, long life (my God how long it's been, he considered again). He knew as the last of his lifeblood coursed from the gaping wound in his neck that he had suffered long enough. He was ready. He had, he knew, fulfilled his own purpose... his own destiny to the extent of his ability, as had Nicole and so many others.

In short? He had done his part, "Invocabant omnipotentem Deum gratiam et ductu."

And this he thought... his last... this is my reward.

There amidst the rubble of what had once been Freeworld One, Alex Parker breathed his last breath and passed peacefully. His visionless eyes, opened eternally, stared at the wispy clouds of mist that clung to the roof of the cavern above the cloying smoke that covered the town... the once-safe haven that he had created and had maintained for years. And his smile?

It never left his face. Not then and not ever...

Ever after.

Because all good stories, someone once said, end as such.

* * *

The Supreme Leader of the collection of Caravans that had attacked and had reduced the community of Freeworld One to cinders — A NyxV4.0 designated SLNyxV4.0, not dissimilar in appearance from a NyxV3.0 but with a significantly more-advanced processor and a greater ability to not only think but reason — watched the last of the firefight commence from its perch atop the ledge that overlooked the town near where the machines had entered. It stood with its back to the explosion-enhanced entryway that its forces had filed through. It was flanked on either side by a slightly modified 78A. Each also had a higher processor speed and a greater general capability than the basic "grunts" of the Administration though they remained, despite said modifications, little more than its servants.

The Supreme Leader was not satisfied with the result of its attack. As near as it could determine all human influence had either been disposed of or captured but it had suffered losses too. Roughly a quarter of its attack force had fallen to a collection of malnourished and battle-leery humans. The intelligence it had received had not prepared it for such a spirited resistance, a failing that the Infiltrator would, eventually, be required to answer for.

But the Infiltrator was not present; he had been assigned another task pre-the battle for Freeworld One. He had carried out his first successfully... had integrated into the Freeworld One community and had given the Administration its location. The attack that was winding down, whatever its outcome, would not have occurred were it not for his assistance and the Supreme Leader understood that to Lord Cornelius I? That counted for something.

As for what the Infiltrator's new task was? The Supreme Leader did not know. It did not question. It merely accepted that it was not privy to the information currently, but would be if the situation required it. On top of everything else, the primary objective of its attack—Alex Parker—remained semi-unaccounted for.

Semi, the machine considered.

A brief warning had flashed through its expansive neural net moments before an uncharacteristic explosion which had appeared to resemble that of a particle blaster overloading had rumbled across an area near the center of the settlement. Said warning had come from the NyxV3.0 that had originally pursued the Jefferson, MWT runaways William MacNuff and Maria Markinson as far as Youngstown, MWT/Sharon, ET. Said warning had failed to process completely but what had passed for the gist of it in the Supreme Leader's logic-enhanced mind had been received.

Someone resembling Alex Parker... someone who had embodied many of the same genetic characteristics as the Supreme Leader's primary objective had been identified by the NyxV3.0 a brief micro-second before the aforementioned explosion had severed all contact with it and its patrol. It had dispatched another patrol to the area where the explosion had occurred and it waited with what passed for "patience" for a report as it surveyed what remained of Freeworld One.

Its optic processors scanned first the town proper which had been reduced to little more than a collection of debris and a large impact crater amidst said debris. Various machines—primarily 78As and Surveillance Marks but its optical processors occasionally fell upon a Leader—wandered from diminished structure to diminished structure looking for survivors. All reports that were funneled back to it remained negative. It then refocused its gaze on the opposite riverbank upon which it could see vegetation and the remains of a once-bridge laying in ruins. It processed *every incoming report with microscopic speed and pinpoint precision until at last the one that it had been waiting for came through: The patrol it had dispatched to the location of the uncharacteristic explosion reported four machines down and one human — a male — deceased.*

The Supreme Leader immediately ordered a DNA scan of the dead human and was not entirely unsurprised when, after a pre-Administration 21 seconds had elapsed the report came back positive.

Said human was its primary objective, Alex Parker.

It ordered the body searched for paraphernalia... specifically a certain piece of paraphernalia known only to it as the "Artifact" that it had been ordered by its superiors to acquire no matter what the cost. The patrol reported back a moment later: Save for a spare battery pack for a non-existent blaster there was nothing on the body of Alex Parker of consequence.

Nothing.

Inconceivable, the Supreme Leader considered. The intelligence that existed on the man pointed to the fact that he never relinquished the Artifact. It ordered another search of not only the body but the surrounding area and sent a description of the object it had been ordered to acquire. Even with the added description said search turned up nothing save for a lone, unidentifiable human female, dead and partially buried beneath a collapsed structure near where Parker's body had been found. She too did not carry anything of consequence.

The Supreme Leader's thoughts lingered upon her for a moment. An unidentifiable human female meant a female not listed in the Cornelius City mainframe which was, it reasoned, inconceivable. A malfunction, perhaps SLNyxV4.0 considered and was about to order a more thorough, subsequent scan of the dead female's body when its optic processors fell upon something that it had missed upon its initial perusal of the riverbank opposite the town. Near where the ruined bridge lay splintered it could make out something lying amidst a twist of frayed rope and broken wooden planks. It zoomed in. Zoomed out. Refocused its gaze and the identity of the anomalous item became clear.

It was a backpack.

It teetered on the edge of the bank... it rocked back and forth in a phantom breeze. As the Supreme Leader watched, it paused for a brief moment before it fell off of the crumbling riverbank and landed with a splash in the river running passed. The SL watched as the backpack bobbed and twisted in the current. It watched as it quickly covered the distance between where it had fallen in and the cavern wall...

And it watched as it disappeared through a small opening under said cavern wall and into the darkness beyond. Understanding immediately alit within its expansive neural net and it ordered all of the assembled forces to converge upon the entryway/exit to Freeworld One and retreat to the surface. Simultaneously it remotely connected to the geographical database in Cornelius City and requested a topographical report on the area surrounding Youngstown, MWT/Sharon, MWT both above and below the surface.

The Supreme Leader again waited with what passed for "patience" for said report as it watched its forces move quickly to where it stood overlooking the ruins of Freeworld One. It needed to know where the swiftly-flowing river—known by the once-inhabitants of the now-defunct town as "Little Shenango"—let out. Its quarry, it reasoned, had shifted. Had the Artifact, as well? It seemed a logical deduction. Had Parker hidden it somewhere in the ruins of the city it would take days... pre-Administration weeks to pick through all of the rubble of the ruined town. There would be an opportunity for that, it understood. But it had to be sure, first. It had to, to employ an old human cliché, "leave no stone unturned." Its superiors, it knew, would not accept any degree of failure. And by association?

SLNyxV4.0 refused to accept the same.

CHAPTER FOURTEEN

I had mused upon first sight of it that the swiftly flowing water of Little Shenango was cold… *Bone-chillingly cold* I recalled thinking as first my feet, then my legs and my upper body and finally my head impacted with the surface of the water and the current dragged me under. But the actual temperature of the water was far colder than I'd imagined it to be.

Despite the downward pull upon my body and my aching head and shoulder I managed to fight my way back to the surface due largely in part to the backpack which I wore upon my back. It acted as a rudimentary flotation device. I came up coughing and gasping for air, my entire body quickly numbing from the freezing…

Freezing, it's definitely freezing, I thought…

…water just in time to see the cavern's exit looming toward me. I watched helplessly as the river spiraled and splashed against both sides of the opening and instinctively brought my knees up to my chest. I aimed for the center of the opening. I was able to see how much clearance I had above the water surface and to either side of me but I was unsure of how much clearance I had beneath me. I could not see anyone else—not Maria, nor the Wetherhills, nor the O'Briens nor Jeff Howard—though I could hear splashing and gasping both in front of me, echoing out of the opening and behind me. I was panic-stricken and helpless to think about them and their respective fates as the opening loomed closer… *closer…*

I felt the body of water that surrounded me shift upward and I felt my heart drop into my stomach as I was lifted and quickly dropped. I cleared the opening and spiraled downstream into the darkness. I caught a glimpse of the opening behind me as the water's current turned me backward quickly, the minimal light of Freeworld One beyond it shrinking and shrinking until it simply winked out.

Fitting, I thought as the current spun me forward. I kept my legs up at my chest as best I could out of instinct though admittedly? The way my body was steadily and quickly numbing made doing so incredibly difficult. I could still feel my backpack clinging to my back... could still feel my water-logged and probably useless blaster bobbing against my ribs. I could not see the walls of the tunnel that I rushed through... could not see any bends nor could I anticipate the lowering of the ceiling which, I sensed, came precariously close to the top of my head on more than one occasion. Everything around me was complete darkness and the sound of rushing water. I twisted backward... I twisted forward... I plummeted onward indefinitely, the feeling in my appendages and in my bad shoulder almost completely diminished.

A strange relief, I thought.

In time my mind began to wander and my breath began to grow labored. It hurt to breathe. I could feel my eyes closing... could sense my body slowing down and a term I had once heard entered my mind: Hypothermia. I inevitably considered that I had reached my end long before I had even glimpsed mine and Maria's final destination.

So much for freedom, I thought as my legs slid from my chest and my boot toes once again scraped against the ground beneath me, *so much for the parcel that Alex gave me. So much for destiny.*

No, the unfamiliar yet stern voice from my earlier dream spoke in my mind, *no, William. Not yet.* It was the first time I had heard the decree.

It would not be the last.

Whether by providence or simply wishful thinking I could sense a light growing around me. *And is the water growing warmer?* I thought. It was difficult to tell but the atmosphere, save for the constantly rushing water seemed to be changing for the better. I opened my eyes and discovered that my senses did not deceive me. The cavern that I traveled through, though still clogged wall-to-wall with swiftly flowing, splashing and violently spiraling water was brighter. I could see the walls to either side of me and the ceiling above me. Said ceiling was cracked and cratered at points and in a few it was cracked all the way up to the surface. Dim gray light filtered down through the cracks and cast transient bars of iron-colored illumination across the rippling water. *Morning,* I thought, *afternoon?* I was unsure. My internal clock's mechanism had apparently frozen along with the rest of my body. Still, the dim light that shined down upon me and the warming of the air and the water that surrounded me gave me hope... albeit slim.

I opened my eyes and I raised my head. I focused on the tunnel before me. It curved to the right a few meters ahead of me and I slowly pulled my knees back up to my chest as the current of Little Shenango carried me quickly around the bend and into another straightaway. The fissures in the ceiling were definitely increasing in number and the light at the top of them seemed to be growing steadily closer with each meter that I traveled. I could see someone flailing in the water about 15 meters ahead of me but I could not determine in the limited light who it was. I saw an arm rise up from beneath the water's surface followed by a head but it vanished around the next bend. I pulled my legs up tighter... rode the current into the bend and blessedly saw a pinpoint of light ahead. Simultaneously the water that surrounded me shallowed, but also increased in speed. *And is my angle of descent more extreme?* I considered. No matter how tightly I tucked my knees into my chest my toes were constantly brushing against the floor of the river. Said friction was the only thing that slowed my ferocious pace down the tunnel as the pinpoint of light grew into a pea-sized hole of light and then a tire-sized one. Larger... *larger...*

I watched as another arm and another head (*or the same one,* I thought) emerged from the water some 10 or 15 meters in front of me. In the growing light from the approaching opening I could see that the person in front of me had short, lightly colored hair and wore a dark-colored top. *Caren* my gut bespoke and I tried to call out to her but my lips, like the rest of my body were frozen in place. No sooner had I recognized her that her arm and her head violently disappeared beneath the surface of the water again. Perhaps it was my imagination but I swore I heard her scream in surprise before me. Said scream echoed not toward me but away from me.

Away, I thought as the tire-sized opening grew to the size of a cave-opening and seemed to take on the appearance of a gaping mouth prepared to swallow me whole...

No William, not swallow, my coldly rational voice spoke in my mind, *spew. As in spit.*

I suddenly realized, even before I saw the foam spraying off of the water at the base of the opening and heard the thunderous sound of it rushing... falling over the edge beyond what was coming and I had little time to react. With all the strength that I could muster and all the instinct that I could summon I swung my legs forward to greet the oncoming drop.

It semi-worked. The current of the water carried my legs forward with little effort but instead of what I had intended—to lay on my back, arms at my sides and legs stretched straight before me when I hit the edge—my body twisted in the current and I found myself face down. The water of Little Shenango licked my lips but my feet still faced the opening. A breath later warm, humid and overcast light engulfed my entire body...

And the ground disappeared from beneath me.

I smacked my chin on the surface of the cave opening and bit down upon my tongue. I yelped as the metallic taste of blood filled my mouth and then I was in free fall. I could barely move my arms or my legs. I managed to glance down and feared the worst. I was pleasantly surprised to see the relatively still surface of a body of water beneath me. Near where I was about to land I could see the same figure with short blonde hair—it *was* Caren—swimming away as quickly as she could. Helpless to alter my trajectory I closed my eyes, said a quick prayer and…

It came. Thankfully, my still-numb and booted feet were at a shade less than a 90 degree angle from the surface of the water and they broke it first. My legs, torso, midsection, chest and finally my head followed and I was submerged in dark and, I hoped, *deep* lukewarm water. I cannot tell you how deep it was… cannot tell you how far I dropped. I did not touch the bottom but after a moment, and another audible "splash" from above me as another one of my counterparts entered the water, I broke the surface, coughed out red-tinted water and gasped again for air. A second later another figure broke the surface roughly two meters away from me also coughing and gasping. It was Steve.

Momentarily distracted he did not notice me but the wake of his impact carried him toward me. I reached out my right hand to grab him and managed despite the numbness in my fingers to latch onto him. He turned slowly, saw me floating beside him and nodded.

"That was… *fun*," he said sarcastically as he coughed out water, "can you move?"

I nodded. Sensation was returning to my lower body likely due to the warmth of the lake and I moved my legs back and forth, testing them. I felt my backpack brush against the nape of my neck. I glanced around me and saw where Little Shenango had terminated. Sheer rock face rose up out of the water on three sides of where Steve and I floated. Atop one, roughly 20 or 25 meters above the surface, a steady stream of water spewed forth from an opening (*Little Shenango*, I thought, *nothing more than a natural drainage pipe*). On my fourth side I could see a flat and pebble covered surface upon which four other figures mulled. The fifth, Caren, was in the process of climbing out of the water. I watched as she fell face first upon the beach and Matt moved to assist her. Beyond the beach upon which they were gathered the ground steeply, but not unmanageably sloped upward through a spattering of rock fall and aged, rounded… what looked like boulders toward a tree stand.

"Let's go," Steve managed between breaths and pulled away from me. He began to swim for the beach. I followed, a bit slower. Within a moment we had covered the distance between where we had emerged from the lake and the shore and crawled from within the water. Steve fell on his face much as Caren had and Carole, still on wobbly legs moved toward him. She crouched beside him and asked him if he was okay. He responded with another cough and a thumbs up.

I emerged from the water a breath later and propped myself up on my knees. I spat red-tinged liquid from my mouth again onto the pebble covered ground and groaned at the metallic taste. I scanned the faces of my counter-parts and found Maria's. She sat shivering, her arms wrapped around her knees, directly behind where Jeff stood hunched over. Without a thought to the contrary I forced myself into a standing position and trudged slowly up the beach toward where she sat, my legs like jelly. Her eyes rose to meet mine as Jeff patted me on the shoulder and stepped aside and she forced a half-hearted smile.

Without a word I moved toward her and sat down on her left. I placed my right arm over her shoulder and drew her close to me. She obliged. I rubbed my hand vigorously up and down her right arm in an attempt to warm her up. Whether my decision to do so was inconsequential or not her shivering did noticeably diminish after a moment. She buried her head against my chest. I raised my hand from her arm to the back of her head and I held it there. She sighed and burrowed deeper.

"Roll call, class," someone said in a nasally voice a short moment later. I looked passed Jeff and watched Matt stand from his crouched position be-side Caren and move a step down the beach toward the water's edge, "ev-eryone present and accounted for?"

A spattering of affirmatives—and someone, I think it was Steve telling him to go fuck himself—echoed across the area. I nodded but did not speak. Maria did the same. I turned away from her and spat another mouthful of blood onto the beach. *Pink,* I observed as it pooled there, *better than bright red, I guess.*

"Okay, then," Matt said as he removed his water-logged backpack from his shoulders and laid it upon the ground, "Supply check. Did..."

I heard another, smaller *splash* from roughly the middle of the lake and I looked frantically past Matt. I was afforded a glimpse of a small, gray back-pack surfacing and subsequently bobbing upon its own wake. *A late arrival to the party,* I thought and stifled a chuckle. Carole turned from where she was crouched beside Steve, uttered an explicative and acknowledged that it was hers. I watched as the backpack made its way slowly toward us on said wake. When it was within a few meters of the shore Carole stood, stepped past Steve and back into the water. She collected it, returned and sat beside her husband, who had shifted and was sitting with his own legs splayed out before him and his backpack between them. She laid it down in front of her.

I removed mine from my shoulders as well—I gasped as it cleared my left shoulder—and laid it on the surface of the pebble and rock-covered beach before me. I quickly unzipped it and looked inside. Within it lay a handful of candles, a pile of rations, a few miscellaneous pieces of fruit… apples, primarily… a spare pair of pants, a couple of pairs of undergarments and socks and a couple of shirts. Everything was, for obvious reasons, soaked.

I re-closed the backpack and checked my pockets. In the left I felt the familiar, cold shape of my trusty Zippo and the handful of spare battery packs I had removed from the armory for mine and Maria's weapons. I did not pay the battery packs any credence. I *did* remove my Zippo. I admired it in the dim, gray-as-slate daylight. I turned it over and watched helplessly as water and perhaps some lighter fluid leaked from the closed top.

I sighed and held it up so that Matt could see it. His eyes fell upon it. He smiled quirkily and mumbled, "That could be useful if it dries out" before he returned to his purveyance of his own backpack's contents. I replaced it in my left pants pocket—it *clinked* against the battery packs within—and reached into my right with my right hand. I felt the edge of the letter that Alex had given me. Though it *was* wet it seemed undamaged. I thought about removing it…

Not now, William, Alex's voice cautioned me and I almost squeaked in surprise. *Not yet,* it continued, *keep it safe. It'll be fine without the benefit of drying out.* My fingers, which had tensed upon the edge of it loosened.

First Pat's voice, and now Alex's, I thought, *not to mention Mister Cold and Rational and Mister Stern and Unfamiliar. I've got my own, mental peanut gallery.* I thought about how I had just described it—"mental"—and stifled a nervous chuckle.

"William?" Maria asked from beside me. I turned to her. My smile faded as I acknowledged her.

"You okay?" she asked. I nodded and told her that I was fine.

"Why?" I inquired. She looked away from me and shook her head.

"No reason," she said, "for a second you just seemed… *distant.*"

Does she know? I thought. Did she gauge that I was hiding something from her? Whether she did or did not was irrelevant. I brushed her wet, black bangs away from her face, bent in and kissed her on the forehead, "I'm fine, Mia," I said.

You'll be able to tell her soon enough, Alex's voice once again echoed reassuringly in my mind and I cringed. I briefly glanced from Maria, forward to him. He was crouched upon the beach and was in the process of zipping his backpack shut.

What does he know? I thought, *what do all of them know? What am I missing? And what the hell have I gotten us in to?* I glanced back at Maria. She managed a smile but did not question my statement. She silently returned to her own purveyance of her own backpack. Once satisfied she zippered it shut. A moment later I turned from her and watched as Matt picked his pack up off of the ground and shouldered it.

"Okay, then," he said. He gestured to the blaster that hung against his ribcage, "*these* aren't going to be very useful for a bit but they will be once they've dried out. Everyone remove your battery packs for a while. Carry them in your hands. Don't put them near anything wet."

"Easier said than done, Pancho," Steve said as he removed his and held his arms out as if to say, *what isn't wet, genius?*

Matt looked at Steve and smiled, "Think positive, Doc," he said, "Hopefully we'll be able to use them again before we encounter any resistance."

"Why *before*?" I asked as I stood slowly from the ground and shouldered my own backpack. I, along with everyone else, did as he had requested and Steve had demonstrated. Matt looked directly at me, cocked his head slightly to the right and smiled.

"Well *'sheet* William," he said, his voice seemingly a mockery of the same voice Steve had used earlier to say "'aw *shucks*,'" "they *ain't* 'gonna do us much good *during* if all they 'is 'is water pistols, now, *'is* they?" He looked to his right and down at Steve who chuckled and, with Carole's assistance, stood and shouldered his own pack. Jeff stepped forward and Caren, wordlessly and with a sigh, did the same.

Well someone's not amused, I thought as I turned from her and reached my right hand down toward Maria. She took it and I assisted to pull her up and into a standing position. I picked up her backpack and helped her hoist it on to her shoulders. Once secure I asked her if she was good. She nodded.

"Ready," she said, "let's light out."

I nodded. I seriously considered kissing her... did, in fact, begin to lean in but I opted not to. *Our secret,* I thought as I pulled away and turned to the remainder of our group. All had gathered at the water's edge and all were, unexpectedly, facing Maria and I.

"What?" I asked no one in particular.

Matt looked at Caren and Caren looked away. Steve looked at Carole and Carole looked at Jeff. Jeff looked me directly in the eyes and said, "Well shit,

William, don't let us stop you. Kiss the girl for Christ's sakes. Lord knows when you'll have another chance. This isn't a field trip, after all."

I was shocked. Apparently what Maria and I had assumed to be a secret wasn't much of one after all. I turned back to her but she met me halfway. Her lips locked upon mine. The kiss was not passionate nor was it naive. It was somewhere in between. It was secure. Warmth flooded my cold and aching joints. Whatever that kiss upon the lakeshore beneath the gray-as-slate overcast sky that hung morbidly over us was it was very, *very* welcome after all that we had just experienced. After a long and drawn out moment which I, admittedly, never wanted to end we slowly separated. I turned back to the remainder of the group and shrugged.

"Better?" I asked.

Jeff smiled, "About damn time," he said. Despite the fact that none of us knew the fate of Pat McClane, nor Alex Parker nor the fates of the other inhabitants of Freeworld One... despite the challenges that we knew lay ahead of us, a few of our hastily assembled travelling group broke into chuckles. Not Caren, though. Her expression remained stoic and her husband's? Well, I could tell that Matt was, at least for the moment, all business.

"Okay, then. Alright," Matt affirmed as he started to move up the bank toward us, "enough chit chat and public displays of affection. I think it's still early but we're burning daylight here. And somewhere out here"—Matt gestured around him—"A freckled spotter named Tim Redfield is waiting for us, hopefully with some sort of transportation. Let's get moving."

He gained and walked passed where Maria and I stood and up the slope toward the tree stand above the rock fall. The others filed in behind him. Maria and I once again brought up the rear as time moved onward without check throughout Endworld.

CHAPTER FIFTEEN

The area beyond the trees at the top of the hill was not very dissimilar to the area that Jeff, Maria and I had fled through a few days previously en route to our arrival upon the border of Freeworld One. As Matt pointed out shortly after we crested the hill that overlooked the shore and the lake and re-entered the forest, the only difference was our location. We had, in the process of our wild ride down Little Shenango, officially crossed over into the Eastern Territory.

I guess I could see the distinction. The greenery was thinner and nary a bird, or a cricket or even a rodent moved through the dead leaves and the underbrush that surrounded us. What trees, bushes and other greenery had managed to survive the subsequent years between the Scourge and the present appeared choked despite the obvious dampness of the atmosphere. Once-brown tree trunks were spotted with gray and black, and the once-leaves upon their branches were spotted with a sickly shade of yellow. The entire world was humid and silent and had the feel of a decomposing corpse.

The sun remained behind the low-lying cloudbank that vaulted over-head as we made our way cautiously through the forest. It lessened the heat which seemed to be building behind it. Had the sun been out our trip would have been a great deal more uncomfortable considering the damp clothes that hung from our respective bodies and the cloying humidity. From the back of the line that had formed I kept my ears attuned for any possible sound of pursuit but I heard nothing. I thought about the blaster that lay use-less against the right side of my ribcage and I cringed. Were we to encounter any resistance we were, in no uncertain terms, completely fucked.

Water pistols versus pulse rifles, I thought, *or worse. There's always the chance for worse.* But we were fortunate. Nothing approached us from either direction as we made our way... *east? West? North? South?* Configuring direction was about as easy as keeping track of the time that had passed between the lakeside (at one point Steve had referred to it as a "quarry") and our present position.

Occasionally Matt, who walked at the front of the line, removed his satellite phone from the front pocket of his slacks and... I assumed instinctively tried to turn it on. He had little luck.

The only thing that phone is going to be good for... that any of your phones are going to be good for is for being a paperweight, I thought. It was, I knew, a frightening but nonetheless inevitable prospect.

Sometime later, we emerged into a pseudo-clearing in the woods. The canopy overhead vanished and I glanced around me. The lack of shadow made it easy to determine that the area into which we had emerged was, or once had been a well-traveled venue. The grass was flatter and there were what appeared to be small, overgrown trails leading off in multiple directions. Matt paused his passage for a moment in the middle of the clearing, wiped the sweat and condensation from his furrowed brow and took in our surroundings before he gestured and moved toward the largest of the trails that led from the clearing into the trees. I followed. As we began to move Steve turned to me and raised his index finger to his lips.

"Close now, you two," he whispered, "at least I *think* we are. Keep quiet until we know what, if anything, we're facing." I nodded. Maria did the same as we exited the clearing and re-entered the shadowy forest.

We did not have to travel far. No more than 30 meters in beyond the initial tree stand the ground beneath us sloped steeper. I watched as Matt slowed his pace and the rest of the group in unison did the same. He stopped by one of the trees that appeared to overlook... something and he peered cautiously around it. He visibly startled for a moment before he gestured for the rest of us to pause and crouch low. We did as he had requested with little physical or audible debate.

He motioned to first Caren and then Jeff to move forward and they did so slowly. Each instinctively drew their likely ineffective blasters. He then gestured for the rest of us to do so and we did. I removed my blaster from its holster, still slightly damp, and glanced at it longingly. I glanced at the battery pack that remained clamped in my left hand. It still felt wet to the touch though it did seem to be slowly drying out.

Wishful thinking, my coldly rational voice warned and I instinctively brushed its caution away. As we approached Matt he motioned for us to fan out along the row of trees he stood by and we did so. He then gestured for us to look beyond them and we obeyed without hesitation.

The ground sloped more steeply for another four or five unimpeded meters before it simply vanished. Beyond I could see what looked like a valley or a ravine, the opposing wall of which lay roughly 30 meters across from our position. Said opposing wall stretched from ground to top much in the same fashion as I assumed the one that we were crouched atop did. The peak of it was dotted with trees and underbrush. But it was neither the opposing cliff face nor the trees atop it that my glance lingered upon. It was the scene directly below us: A rutted-asphalt path that, because of the rubble that clogged the sides of it I concluded was in fact *the* Halmier's Pass that we were looking for.

But what's our position upon it? I traced its length to my left. There, maybe a half a kilometer away, lay a small, fenced-in, one story, concrete or stone constructed, crumbling building with a large radar dish sitting askew and motionless atop it. I could see burnt-out and deteriorating husks of very, *very* old vehicles gathered within the fence and around the building. Yet it was not the seemingly benign vehicles that caught my attention. No. What caught mine and my counterparts' attention were the smaller assault bikes—*two*, I observed—evenly spaced apart and positioned in a row across Halmier's Pass directly outside of the fencing that rung the depot.

Blocking our path, I thought. Alex had been right. In addition I counted at least a dozen… perhaps more machines mulling about the area behind them: Primarily heavily armored 78As and the occasional Surveillance Mark. Thankfully there were no Leaders assembled but the SMs…

They have to know that we're here, I thought nervously, *we can't jam them. If they don't know yet that we're here they will soon enough and what then?* Any casual sense that I had managed to maintain since leaving Freeworld One was immediately replaced by unbridled and unrestrained fear. We had no alternative. We were going to have to face the force that awaited us unless…

"Any possibility we can head *that* way?" I asked desperately as I turned from the force of machines assembled by the supply depot to Matt and gestured right. Matt, merely a few steps away from me, turned from his survey of the situation and shook his head.

"See the way the Pass bends to the right just beyond the depot?" he asked as he gestured to the road, the building and the force of machines assembled before us. I nodded. I could see what he was referring to. A few meters beyond the building the road banked right and started uphill before ending at the base of the opposing cliff face. *No,* I thought, *not ending. The Pass goes through it. That's the tunnel that Alex was referring to.*

"That's the start of the tunnel," Matt affirmed, "and beyond that is the Highway. But in order to get there…"

"We need to find a way to get past *them*," Jeff finished from his crouch directly next to Matt as he gestured to the area that we watched with the barrel of his blaster. Matt paused for a moment, ran the back of his right hand across his lips once.... twice and reluctantly nodded.

"Well then we need a plan, Matt," Steve said as he moved back from the tree that he had been crouching behind and stood in the shadows cast by the overhead leaf canopy, "and we probably don't have much time." I understood what Steve meant despite being, as Pat would have said were he there, "green." If the machines knew of our presence, then it was only a matter of time before the woods in which we hid were crawling with robots. It left us a very small window of opportunity in which to act.

"Okay, then," Matt said as he stood from his crouch and stepped back from the tree stand. He gestured for the rest of us to do the same and we did so. We gathered in a loose half circle roughly five or six meters away from the row of trees that overlooked Halmier's Pass around him. He called for another supply check and we obliged, removing our respective backpacks and unzipping them. The contents of my bag were, not unsurprisingly, unchanged. I placed the battery pack I had been holding in my left hand on the ground and reached into my left pocket. I once again removed my Zippo. Unsure but nonetheless hopeful, I flipped the top open and ran my thumb across the wheel. It spun but did not spark. I did so again... and again... and *again*...

Wait, Pat's voice commanded, *wait. Try it again, but slower this time.*

Unable to see any other alternative I heeded his request. I spun the wheel slowly...

And a small, almost imperceptible spark kicked away from the place where the wheel met the flint. Had I not been intently focused upon it I would have missed it. I heard a collective gasp from my counterparts—all had, apparently, been observing my actions either out of instinct or desperation—and in response I spun the wheel again. Nothing... and nothing... and *nothing*...

Another spark. Larger than before. I almost shouted in triumph as the spark briefly grew into an orange-yellow flame before it winked out. A thin tendril of smoke and the unmistakable scent of lighter fluid (*albeit heavily watered down lighter fluid,* I thought) wafted up from it.

If my lighter is drying out, I thought...

Without a moment's hesitation I glanced down at the battery pack that lay upon the ground. I turned to Maria and held out my Zippo to her. She took it confusedly as I turned back, picked up the battery pack in my left hand with a cringe, judged where the electrical leads were supposed to go in the dim light that filtered in through the overhead leaf canopy, said a prayer and inserted the pack into the handle of the weapon positive to positive, and negative to negative. It snapped into place easily and I felt a fine mist of liquid spray across the back of my right hand.

Disconcerting, I thought. I watched the indicator on the battery's surface nervously but it remained dark. *No,* I thought, and willed it to show a charge... any charge. *I'll even take one bar right now,* I continued thinking, *come on, already. work, damn you...!*

I gasped a breath later as one, lone bar upon the surface of the battery pack—the smallest one—weakly lit up green.

"Holy shit," Matt said as he glanced at my weapon, "how about that? Everyone try your battery packs now. *Hurry.*"

I watched as my counterparts inserted their respective battery packs into the handles of their respective weapons. I heard a spattering of "nothings" and "nopes" before I heard another gasp. Female. I instinctively looked at Maria and she looked back at me, shrugged, shook her head and mouthed *wasn't me.* I turned back to the group...

And saw Caren slowly, almost cautiously, raise her blaster with her right hand and point with her left index finger to the lone, green bar upon the handle. It was slightly stronger than the one upon mine but little more. And she was not the only one. A brief moment later Jeff "Jeebus" Howard mimicked her gesture. The lone, green bar on the surface of his battery pack appeared to be even weaker than mine. Still...

No one else raised his or her hand. *Oh Jesus,* I thought, *seven people, a barely working Zippo and three barely functional weapons against a dozen 78As, Surveillance Marks and assault bikes,* I thought, *can we get any luckier?* Matt, seemingly as satisfied with the result as myself, looked skeptically from Caren to Jeff to me and then back to Jeff and finally to Caren. He smiled but his grin seemed forced and not overly confident.

"You've all got enough charge for two, maybe three shots a piece but if I were a betting man I'd bank on two," Matt said, "and that's not a lot. If we do this right, though? Well, it just might be enough."

His gaze fell upon Steve and the look they exchanged shared some knowledge that I was not partial too, a fact that Steve affirmed with an unintentionally loud guffaw that caused me to cringe. Matt's gaze shifted from him and fell upon Maria. He held out his hand.

"Going to need that lighter, sweetie," he said. Maria extended her hand toward Matt's. Matt took my Zippo deftly and immediately turned to Steve. "Doc?" He asked. Steve stepped forward, his grin widening, and plucked my Zippo from between Matt's fingers.

"Just like Barrett's Run," Steve said as he shook his head, "only this time we've got something better than a sliver of glass. But it was a lot drier there if I remember correctly. And sunnier. Fucking tradeoffs." He turned to me with my lighter in his hand, and assured me that he would give it back to me when he was done with it. Unable to say or do anything further I simply nodded and watched as he asked Carole to come with him. She nodded. I heard him reiterate "Barrett's Run" in an almost questioning and sarcastic tone and say "the driest you can find, honey" as he and Carole walked briskly past me and back in the direction that we had entered the wood from. I watched them go for another moment before they disappeared into the shadows.

"What exactly is... err, *was* 'Barrett's Run' or do I want to ask?" Maria inquired as I refocused my gaze briefly on her and then on Matt. Matt chuckled and muttered "unimportant" but in my gut I knew that he was not being entirely truthful with us.

"Steve's just going to work out a little diversion for us," Matt said. Caren had moved across from me and stood beside me on my right. Maria remained on my left and Jeff had moved to within a step or two of her left.

"Once he's got that going this is what you three are going to do with your two or three shots each," Matt began. He addressed Caren, Jeff and I. I listened to his plan intently and my heart dropped steadily further into my stomach with each passing word.

Now THIS, My coldly rational voice spoke, *this, William, is the textbook definition of mental. Heed it well.*

I sighed and reluctantly accepted that that portion of my mental peanut gallery once again spoke the truth.

* * *

By proxy and per the command of SLNyxV4.0, the lead 78A upon the rutted surface of the old, service road designated by the humans as "Halmier's Pass" ordered its Surveillance Marks to initiate another scan of the area atop the cliff face that overlooked the road upon which the Caravan was gathered. The SMs had, in their last scan, detected seven life signs roughly a half a kilometer from their current position. The inset radar dishes upon their chests visibly and audibly rotated smoothly... the sounds of them echoed across the valley.

Less than 30, pre-Glorious Revolution seconds later they reported back: Seven life signs, all unmistakably human, five of which were gathered tightly in a semi-circle behind the leading edge of the trees and two of which were moving away. The latter was of little consequence to the 78A and by association SLNyxV4.0. The main force of machines—the one that had laid the rebel encampment once designated as "Freeworld One" to waste—was en route and was moving cautiously toward the humans' rear flank from the quarry into which the human-designated, "Little Shenango River" river emptied.

An indefinite amount of time passed before SLNyxV4.0 communicated with the lead 78A upon the Pass that it and its forces were within three kilometers of where the fugitives were positioned in the wood, atop the cliff face per the Surveillance Marks' last scans. It ordered the 78A to have the Marks re-scan the area and the 78A conveyed said order to its counterparts with little hesitation. Once again the inset radar dishes in their chests began to rotate. Once again roughly 30 pre-Glorious Rebellion seconds passed before the SMs reported back their findings: The two humans that had moved away from the rest of the group were seemingly moving quickly back toward it and the remainder of the group? They were no longer stationary. They were, in fact, moving briskly in the Caravan's direction. They were within a half a kilometer of its current position upon the road surface surrounding and within the abandoned supply depot and they were not slowing.

An unfamiliar impulse traveled through the 78A's neural net at microscopic speed. Were the 78A human it would have recognized the sensation as "confusion." Its Caravan was not trying to hide its position. If the SMs' scans were correct (and the lead 78A had no reason to dispute them) then the human fugitives were significantly outnumbered and outgunned, likely knew they were and yet they were moving toward its superior force with little hesitation, almost offensively. It was, the 78A reasoned, inconceivable.

"INFORMATION EXTRAPOLATION FAIL," the lead 78A spoke in its toneless, metallic voice, "MARKS RESCAN. RE-VERIFY FUGITIVES' POSITION AND REPORT." The SMs did as had been requested of them and once again reported back the results: 0.25 kilometers away from their current position and closing briskly. All seven humans had reformed into one group. There were no stragglers.

The lead 78A quickly scanned the rocky cliff face with its optical processors. It zoomed in. Zoomed out. It found what it was looking for roughly 10 meters to the right of where it stood: A steeply-sloping but nonetheless navigable trail lined on either side with blighted and stunted trees from the top of the cliff face to the road surface. It communicated its updated findings to SLNyxV4.0. SLNyxV4.0 immediately and without hesitation ordered the lead 78A to redistribute its forces at the base of the trail it had observed. The 78A did as had been requested of it and ordered nine of its thirteen machines—seven 78As and two Surveillance Marks—and one of the assault bikes to take up defensive positions at the base of the trail. It ordered the remaining forces—three 78As, one Surveillance Mark and one assault bike with an unarmored, 78A occupant—to guard its rear flank. It requested that SLNyxV4.0 and its reinforcements quicken their approach and SLNyxV4.0 confirmed that they *would. It watched as the Caravan redistributed per its request and independently, without SLNyxV4.0's approval, it ordered the SMs to re-scan the area atop the cliff face. 30 pre-Glorious Revolution seconds later it once again received its requested reports: The fugitives were within 30 meters of its position and were at the top of the trail. They had stopped moving...*

And seven humans had become six.

The same, unfamiliar impulse—"confusion"—traveled through its neural net and it barked tonelessly for the Mark to provide it with the location of the seventh fugitive. Simultaneously and before the SM could respond it heard a crackling from atop the cliff face roughly seven meters behind it. It turned quickly and trained its optical processors and its pulse rifle on the area that it extrapolated the noise had come from...

Just in time to see something burst through the trees and arc down toward the rutted surface of Halmier's Pass. Whatever it was, thick gray smoke and a hint of yellow flame billowed out behind it as it spiraled through the air and landed within a step or two of the lead 78A's rear vanguard with a thud. Beneath the thud the lead 78A heard something solid impact with the ground. It zoomed in... zoomed out on the object and immediately confirmed that it was...

A backpack. Heavy smoke was issuing forth from it and something inside of it was making a crackling sound. Moisture evaporating, it reasoned, and started to redirect its attention to the trail atop which the fugitives waited when it heard something else beneath the crackling sound of burning plant and tree life within the backpack...

Humming. Something within it was humming. Something distinguishably electrical...

Or battery powered.

Recognition alit in its fiber-optic enhanced and logical mind. Before it could order the rear vanguard to step away from the smoking and flaming object, a single particle blaster bolt which was quite obviously aimed at the backpack fired outward in a flash from the area near the top of the trail...

* * *

As the five of us (Steve and Carole had not yet returned from their errand) started walking briskly beyond the tree stand atop the cliff face—Matt in the lead, Caren directly behind him, Jeff in front of Maria and me bringing up the rear—I felt a degree of uncertainty. We were moving toward the main force of machines gathered upon Halmier's Pass which, in and of itself was to my untrained and still "green" mind suicidal. But Matt's and Steve's intention? Their "plan?" It was completely mental. To call it suicidal was an understatement. But it was, I knew, our only chance of success given our limited resources.

I thought back upon what Matt had told us moments before as I heard the sound of footsteps behind us, and I turned to see the Wetherhills moving quickly in our direction. Steve no longer carried just his back pack but cradled in his arms was Carole's smaller, gray one. It was unzipped and I could see a plethora of debris sticking out of it: Leaves, twigs, broken branches and yellow grass. In his left hand I could see the glint of my trusty Zippo in the dim light that filtered through the overhead canopy. As he and Carole gained our position he moved quickly toward myself, then passed Maria and finally slowed his pace directly beside Jeff and Caren.

"Alright. Which one of you has the least charged weapon?" I began to raise my hand but Jeff beat me to it. Steve smiled, reached out his right hand toward Jeff and requested that he give him his weapon. Jeff reluctantly (*I guess he's as skeptical as I am,* I thought) handed it over. Steve, in turn, handed him the backpack as he took the blaster in his right hand. He turned it over so that he could see the battery pack, looked at it askance, muttered something that sounded like a quick prayer and nodded. With a practiced deftness he removed the battery pack from the side of the handle, turned it around, and re-inserted it.

Negative to positive, positive to negative, I thought, *they're really going through with it.* The weapon immediately began to hum, a low and almost inaudible sound that were it not for the stillness of the wood I likely would not have detected. Seemingly satisfied, Steve asked Jeff to open the top of Carole's debris-stuffed backpack wider and he obliged.

"I hope you got all of your necessities out of there, Carole," Caren said with a hint of sarcasm though beneath it I heard her voice waver slightly. *Jesus,* I thought, *not even Caren likes this. Does anyone have any confidence whatsoever in this plan?*

"Removed and relocated into Steve's," she responded as she moved past me with a turn of her head and a smile, passed Maria and joined Steve beside Jeff. I watched as Steve carefully inserted the slowly overloading blaster into the pack. He pushed it down through the debris nestled within until I saw its barrel poking against the cloth at the base of the pack. When satisfied with its position, he held up my lighter, flipped back the lid and inhaled deeply.

"Here goes nothing," he said, and spun the wheel. Nothing. He spun it again. Still nothing. And again... and again... and *again...*

I small, orange-yellow spark kicked out from the front of it and he stopped. "Okay," he said reassuringly and held the lighter closer to the top of the backpack. He spun… and spun… and *spun*…

Another spark, larger than the previous one, kicked forth and I watched it catch and fizzle upon the debris.

"Closer," Steve mumbled simultaneously with Jeff saying the same. He tried again and again as we continued to walk toward where the machines were positioned below us until finally, after multiple seemingly exhaustive attempts, a large spark kicked forth, caught on one of the leaves and smoldered. Light, gray-white smoke issued forth from the small, black burn hole that had appeared on the leaf and mingled with the growing smoke from the base of the backpack as the weapon within heated up. Another leaf directly next to the first one began to smoke and then another directly next to it. After an anxious moment a fire, albeit a small one sputtered to life within the steadily increasing smoke that emanated from the top of the backpack and Steve clapped his hands together once in a gesture of satisfaction.

"Amen," he said as he turned to me and underhanded my Zippo directly back to me. I instinctively caught it on its downward arc in my right hand and clenched my fist upon its cool, metallic surface tightly before I replaced it in its customary place within my left pants pocket. I heard it "clink" against one of the remaining spare battery packs within.

I removed my particle blaster from its holster with the same hand and glanced longingly at the grip: Still only one small green bar. I sighed.

It'll have to be enough, Pat's voice cautioned in my mind, *if you do this right you may only need to take one shot with it so…*

Make it count, I thought, *I will Pat.*

I nodded to Steve and redirected my attention to Matt who had broken slightly to the right of our line, was walking along the ridge and gazing out beyond the trees. He turned back to Steve after a long moment and gestured to him, a movement that non-verbally told him to "go ahead." Steve did as Matt had requested. He took the smoking backpack from Jeff and turned from us with it cradled in his arms. He ran quickly past Maria and me and took up a stationary position by one of the trees overlooking the Pass. Simultaneously Matt took two leaping steps back toward the front of the group and gestured for us all to stop walking and come forward. We did.

Ahead, I could see what appeared to me to be a trail that ran perpendicular to our path but, I considered, it was more than just a trail. The ground marking it sloped steeply down and through the trees that overlooked the Pass. I could see a higher rock face about 25 meters ahead of us and through the trees that bordered it (*that's the mountain err… the hill that the tunnel goes through,* I thought) but… *yes,* I reasoned, *that trail, drainage ditch or whatever it is leads from up here* —I gulped—*down there.*

I felt my heart skip a beat at the knowledge of what awaited us "down there" and sped up. A cold sweat broke out upon my forehead. I gripped my weapon more tightly as we ran for the trail. When we were within a few meters of it Matt abruptly stopped running and held up his hand. All of us ceased sprinting in turn. Matt's eyes scanned the gazes of our group and fell upon me. He smiled and gestured for me to join him which I did without question. I followed him to the edge of the tree stand and crouched low per his non-verbal instruction. He motioned for me to look out over the Pass and I did.

The machines below *did* know of our presence. Such was evident by the way the majority of them—*nine total,* I thought, *seven 78As and two SMs… one assault bike, too*—were gathered roughly 30 meters below us around the base of the trail. But that was not the extent of the force arrayed against us. Matt had been correct in his assessment of what the Caravan would do once we started moving toward it. Nine machines were positioned at the base of the trail but four *(and one assault bike,* I thought, *an extra added bonus)* were positioned roughly six meters to the right of the majority of the force. I glanced back over my shoulder…

And saw Steve Wetherhill crouched behind a tree, the smoking and occasionally flaming backpack in hand, roughly six or seven meters to my right. He saw me looking at him, raised his left hand and gave me a "thumbs up." I turned back to Matt and quietly spoke.

"I've never fired a weapon before," I said.

Matt surprisingly smiled, "Never?"

"Never," I reiterated.

"Do you know what to expect?" he asked.

I nodded, "Jeff prepped us for it in the truck before… well, you know. I know that there's a kick and I know that I need to use my other hand to steady my aim. But other than that…"

"No clue, huh?" Matt finished for me. I nodded.

He smiled half-heartedly and shrugged, "No point in worrying about it now, William," he said, "just remember what I said and you should be fine." Despite his reassurance, he placed his callused right hand upon my left shoulder and drew his own particle blaster with his left. He gazed at the handle for a long moment before he realized that he still had no charge. He muttered an explicative under his breath and gestured to the area below us with the barrel of it, "as soon as that backpack hits the deck *fire.* Line up your shot as best you can. If you miss with the first you may get another shot but by then the fuckers are going to be on us like white on rice. Catch my drift?"

I nodded, turned from Matt and raised my weapon in my right hand to my eye level. I gazed down the length of its shaft through the trees and to the surface of the road where I assumed the backpack was going to land. I visualized the impact as best I could in my mind and I briefly closed my eyes. I could feel myself pulling the trigger… could see the bolt of white fire extending outward from the barrel of my weapon and impacting with the side of Carole's once-backpack turned improvised explosive device by Steve. I felt my heart rate slow… felt my focus clear. I opened my eyes slowly and nodded without a word. Matt, seemingly as satisfied as he was going to be, patted me once on my left shoulder—I cringed slightly from the soreness still throbbing within it—and started to move away.

"Matt?" I asked calmly.

His boot falls ceased immediately. I did not turn to see him but I heard him inquire, "Yes, William?"

"Barrett's Run," I continued, "how did that turn out?" I did not remove my gaze from the road surface. My right arm barely moved. But I heard Matt chuckle and I sensed him smile. And the next words he spoke echoed in my mind before, during and immediately following all that transpired next.

"Save for the doc and me?" he responded to my inquiry, "everyone died."

I gasped. My composure wavered and I slowly turned my head to face him. He was grinning. "*Everyone*, Matt?"

Matt cocked his head slightly to the right, his smile unbroken, and shrugged, "Margin of error *zero*, William." He raised his weapon. "Make it count," he concluded. And with that he turned and trotted back to where the rest of our group had taken up position on either side of the trail that led down to Halmier's Pass.

Christ, I thought. My gaze fell upon Maria who crouched on my side of the trail behind Caren first, who was positioned near the edge of the trees, and Jeff second. I forced myself to smile at her. In the dim, gray light I saw her grin back and wink. I turned my head slowly back and faced the trees, the drop and the road surface below. I quickly found my spot again and went through the same process that I had gone through previously. It didn't take long before I reopened my eyes. Without a thought to the contrary I spoke in the loudest voice that I could muster and internally cringed at how cold my own voice sounded.

It… *I* sounded ruthless and unfamiliar, even to myself.

Yet my focus did not wane. No. Not for a breath.

"Go," I declared loudly, and Steve did. I heard branches crackling and breaking in my right ear and watched through the trees as the spiraling, smoking and occasionally flaming projectile arced downward toward Halmier's Pass. It hit the ground with a *thud* and I closed my left eye, my right eye narrowly focused down the length of the weapon's shaft and on the backpack's position. I inhaled. I exhaled. *Rinse and repeat,* I thought with an uncharacteristic smile considering the circumstances...

And I fired.

* * *

...and impacted squarely with the side of the backpack. The lead 78A had no time to react. Simultaneously with the impact the improvised explosive device detonated outward in a brilliant and deadly cloud of white-hot energy, flaming debris and jagged shrapnel. Three of the four machines—two 78As and one Surveillance Mark— that comprised the lead 78A's rear guard were exposed to the initial brunt of the powerful detonation and thrown backward, limbs damaged and joints severed from their respective superstructures immediately despite their body armor. They fell still upon the road. The third 78A, the furthest away from the backpack, was in the process of turning away when the rudimentary IED exploded. The shockwave from it lifted it off of its feet and it careened head first into the lone assault bike that watched the Caravan's rear flank.

The occupant of the assault bike had been in the process of taxiing its vehicle away from the backpack and was mobile but was helpless to react considering its position lying flat upon its belly within the bike's cockpit and its lack of body armor. The last surviving 78A on foot in the rear vanguard crashed into it and through the reinforced glass that curved like a dome over the cockpit before it fell still half-in and half-out of the vehicle. Reflexively the 78A that rode the assault bike accelerated as its neural net shut down and the bike careened haphazardly toward the main force of the Caravan. The lead 78A leapt aside and watched helplessly as its forces attempted to move out of the way but all were not able to do so. The vehicle's trajectory easily took out two more 78As and one Surveillance Mark before it hit the rock face, flipped upward and fell atop the two, motionless machines within and without it. It fell still.

The lead quickly 78A assessed its losses: One assault bike, two SMs and six 78As down leaving only itself, a single assault bike, three 78As and a lone Surveillance Mark to defend against...

Its last thought spiraled away into nothingness as another blaster bolt from the area atop the cliff infiltrated the right side of the body armor covering its face and sliced through its right optical processor. Sparks exploded from the exit wound, impacted with the back of its helmet, and rebounded forward. The last thing it heard as it crumpled to the ground amidst the rubble choking the Pass in a flurry of sparks was the sound of its remaining forces' returning pulse rifle fire and the shouts the force that attacked the Caravan as they made their way down the trail that led from the top of the cliff to the rutted, broken surface of Halmier's Pass. Surprisingly it heard little particle blaster fire, a fact that it considered curious. It attempted to communicate what had and what was happening to SLNyxV4.0 but its transmitter was too damaged. Without another thought the lead 78A expired in failure, little more than another burnt out husk of technology outside the old, abandoned military supply depot that lay crumbling and deserted upon Halmier's Pass.

* * *

I remember much from that day but the thing that sticks out the most in my mind when I think back on it is the "kick" of my weapon… the same kick that Jeff had referred to during his crash course in how to fire a weapon within Pat's once-truck and the same "kick" that I had referenced in my conversation with Matt pre-what I've always thought of since as the Battle for Halmier's Pass. It was unlike anything that I could have or would have anticipated. The way my right arm recoiled and my right shoulder seemingly shifted backward? Were I not, unfortunately, all-too familiar with the sensation of what a dislocated shoulder felt like I might have concluded that the damn kick from the weapon popped my right shoulder out of its socket. It was painful but it was nothing compared to the pain that still engulfed my left arm and shoulder.

Good to know, I considered as I watched the shot from my weapon impact with the backpack… watched the chaos that ensued upon the rutted road beneath us… heard the remainder of my counterparts as they sprinted past me and down the trail toward Halmier's Pass. One of them, I think it was Steve, slapped me on my back as he ran past me and shouted *"great shot, William!"* but I was undaunted. I watched all of these things from afar the same way a casual observer might have though admittedly, I knew even then that I was far from a casual observer. I realized as the battle ensued that for the first time in my life I was no longer morally innocent. I make that distinction here because I didn't and still don't see what I did that day as "murder" in the common, human sense of the word. Nor do I view it as "robotocide" a… some might say fabricated crime that the Administration has accused me and my counterparts of subsequently.

No. What I did I did out of necessity. But if any one, single event completed my transition from innocence it was my frighteningly accurate, pin-point blaster shot and the subsequent explosion from Matt's and Steve's improvised explosive device that eliminated more than half of the small Caravan assembled upon Halmier's Pass. Were it not for the pulse rifle shot that sizzled through the air less than a meter above my head causing the hair there to stand briefly on end, the light spray of singed tree bark that buffeted my face and the calls of my counterparts to *"come on!"* I might not have ever moved from my crouch beyond the tree line atop the ridge that overlooked the road. As it were, I did move and ran down the hill and into the fray behind my traveling companions.

I immediately realized that despite the diminished force of machines firing upon us from the rutted asphalt at the base of the trail, tactically, running straight at the force down a clear path in the wide open was a supremely bad idea. As soon as I started down the slope I saw the last of my counterparts— *Maria,* I thought, her long black hair a dead giveaway—disappear to the left and behind a blighted tree that overlooked the path. Without a thought to the contrary I broke right and ducked behind a tree roughly 20 meters from the bottom of the trail as another pulse rifle shot kicked up damp soil and rotted plant life at my feet. After a moment I cautiously glanced around the tree and saw three heavily armored 78As positioned at the base of the trail firing upon us. Behind them stood a Surveillance Mark and beside them, quickly moving in front of them…

It began to make its way up the trail toward us at a slow but meticulous pace: The last assault bike. I could see the crown of its occupant's head (*another 78A,* I thought, *Jesus*)… could see the way it reflected the overcast light that filtered through the clouds above. Said occupant lay behind and beneath a curved, glass window. The vehicle itself had two large wheels spaced evenly apart on either side of its rear and one smaller wheel inset beneath the tapered front of its body. On either side of the "cockpit" two low-beams cut through the gloom, growing smoke and ozone that engulfed the area. The blinding light that issued from them almost disguised the two smaller plasma canons positioned on the outsides of said lights.

I glanced nervously at the power indicator on the battery inserted in the handle of my blaster. There was still a hint of green in the shortest bar but it was virtually gone. *That may not even be enough charge for one shot,* I thought hectically. Simultaneously I glanced back around the tree behind which I was sheltering and saw someone—Caren, I realized—lean around one of the trees about six or seven meters ahead of me. She trained her own blaster upon the assault bike and fired. Her shot was true and it impacted squarely with the cockpit but it careened harmlessly off and up.

Definitely not standard-issue glass, I thought and stifled a hysterical chuckle as I brought my own weapon to bear upon the bike, placed my finger over its trigger…

And leapt backward with a scream as the vehicle's right plasma canon shifted position in the blink of an eye, targeted me, and fired. The tree that I had been sheltering behind exploded outward in a fire-storm of corrupted nature. I landed face down about a meter away from where it had been and felt white hot debris alight upon the back of my shirt. I instinctively rolled over onto my back to snuff it, looked up…

And barely had time to stand and scamper across the trail as pulse rifle fire from the three remaining 78As kicked up the ground around me and another plasma canon shot impacted with the ground where I had lain. I dove for the trees, my blaster held out before me, and crashed through them and the underbrush that bordered the left side of the path. I landed face down, my nose in the damp soil, and smelled not only wet ground but the deeper, more malignant smell of decomposition.

I belly-crawled as far away from the edge of the trail as I could. I could hear additional plasma canon discharges but they were localized further down the trail from where I lay. Either the machines assumed that I had been eliminated or they had simply shifted their focus to the other members of my party. I chanced a glance over my shoulder and across the trail and saw Caren moving quickly from tree to tree down the path. She was, surprisingly, looking at me as she ran not with scorn but with… *what?* She was shaking her head, I realized, and gesticulating to her weapon.

She's out, I thought as another plasma canon burst exploded a step behind her and she was thrown forward up the trail. But not before she mouthed something to me that despite the situation I was amazingly able to decipher.

Two words: *Surveillance Mark.*

It was the first she had ever "spoken" to me, albeit silently.

I mentally chastised myself despite my "greenness" for my stupidity and with as little movement as possible I glanced forward down the trail. Through the trees I could see the tall, lanky SM standing behind the three 78As, its inset radar rotating steadily, and the assault bike which had stopped moving and had assumed a stationary position directly between me and the base of the trail. I glanced from it to the hilt of my blaster again and saw the same, dim, short-green bar that had been there previously.

One shot, I thought, *if that. Make it count. Margin of error zero.*

Christ, I thought to myself. Without thinking I pushed myself quickly up into a standing position and stood sideways behind one of the trees that flanked the trail. No shot or shots came. I closed my eyes. I envisioned the

Surveillance Mark… specifically the radar dish that rotated upon its chest. In my mind I configured where it had stood upon my last observation of it. I breathed in. Breathed out. My finger hovered over the trigger of my weapon. I felt a shout building in my throat as I opened my eyes and as quickly as I could manage swung out into full view of the machines assembled at the base of the trail and the pilot of the assault bike without a second thought. In the blink of an eye I saw the Surveillance Mark standing exactly where I had envisioned it.

I raised my weapon and fired.

My blaster kicked violently but my shot was true. It struck the radar dish dead-center and I watched with a mixture of awe and triumph as sparks exploded both outward toward me and backward away from me. I watched as the SM quickly fell to the ground. Satisfied I ducked back behind the tree as the weapon's fire from the force that opposed us increased in intensity but not in accuracy. If anything the accuracy of the machines' offense deteriorated. Pulse rifle bolts flew haphazardly in all directions up the trail. Plasma canon fire exploded one tree after another and my cold and rational counterpart screamed at me in my mind to *RUN!* I did so and instinctively ran down the trail behind the trees and not up it…

No retreat, I thought, *not now and not ever…*

…toward the battle. I could see other figures moving in the same direction as myself both ahead of me and across from me in the building haze. Branches and limbs fell upon me. Wet leaves brushed at my face and damp, foul-smelling soil coated my legs. I watched through the trees that passed me by on my right as I closed the gap between my position and that of the assault bike. Five meters… four… three…

At three meters I saw a male figure bolt from the trees directly in front of me. He—*Matt,* I realized—was parallel to the assault bike which was still randomly firing up the trail. He leapt upon the back of the 78A piloting it and brought the hilt of his blaster down in an arc. It impacted with the side of the 78A's head and I watched as said head caved inward from the surprisingly vicious force of Matt's strike. Sparks exploded outward from where he had hit the machine and they smoldered upon his forearm. I saw him reach for… something beneath the cockpit whilst he straddled the damaged machine and simultaneously the bike leapt forward up the trail for a meter or two before it spun around amidst a storm of pebbles and dirt.

I stopped running and poked my head out from behind a tree as the three remaining 78As focused all of their remaining fire power upon the vehicle that Matt had hijacked but to no avail. By the time they had determined with only the benefit of their optical processors and not the life scans of the now-defunct Surveillance Mark what was transpiring Matt had already maneuvered the bike into position. Their shots ricocheted off of the body of the vehicle and the reinforced glass-not-glass cockpit of it. As soon as the tapered front of the assault bike was parallel with their position Matt triggered the dual plasma canons upon the front of it. They fired successive bursts of white hot fire roughly a breath or two apart. At such close range targeting was unimportant. Five or six bursts… I'm unsure of how many… eliminated the last of the force that opposed us.

As the last 78A fell in a heap with a black burn hole the size of my head and still sparking through its midsection silence descended over the Pass. Matt killed the assault bike's power and slid off of it as I emerged from the tree that I had been sheltering behind. The scene repeated itself both in front of me and across from me as first, Maria and Jeff and then Steve and Carole emerged from the trees. I heard footsteps on the ground behind me and I turned, blaster in hand, and saw Caren limping down the hill toward us.

Limping, I thought. I could see a rip and a black burn mark, still smoking on the left thigh of her jeans, and a deeper shade of dark surrounding it. *Blood,* I thought as she stopped mid-trail. Simultaneously, Steve broke from where he stood beside Carole and ran to her position. He gestured for her to sit and she did so with no hesitation. He immediately began to look at the wound. *She'll be okay,* I reassured myself.

"Nice shot, William," she said through clenched teeth. The sound of my name spoken in my cavern attacker's voice coupled with… *a compliment* quite frankly shocked me.

"Th… Thanks," I stuttered matter-of-factly and instinctively flashed her a smile. She did not return it but she did not glare back. Her gaze remained fixed upon mine and she nodded her head almost imperceptibly.

Well I'll be, I thought as I turned back to the remainder of the group. All but Jeff stood in the middle of the trail around the last assault bike. He was already moving through the carnage at the bottom of the trail and upon the Pass. He looked down at one of the immobile 78As and kicked the pulse rifle from its hand. He stepped over the smoking pile of steel and circuitry, picked up the large and intimidating weapon and hefted it. He moved it up and down… up and down, seemingly testing its weight. He intoned something that sounded like *"oh,"* placed his other hand beneath the long, thick barrel of the weapon, turned to face the supply depot and fired.

The kick from the pulse rifle moved him back a step but his shot flew straight and true. It impacted with the side of the building and a storm of flaming rock and concrete exploded outward. I watched as the smoke cleared and saw that a large, black-ringed hole had appeared where the blast had hit.

Effective, I thought with a stifled chuckle as Jeff turned and started to walk back toward us. He paused briefly to ransack the 78A's "corpse" and found what he was looking for: A spare battery pack which he promptly placed in his right pants pocket.

"Anyone else need a weapon?" he asked as tipped the top of the rifle over his right shoulder and rejoined us, "now's the time to get one."

Matt nodded and did as Jeff had suggested. He moved passed me and began picking through the rubble. He picked up one weapon and dropped it. Picked up another, hefted it in the same fashion Jeff had his, turned to face the supply depot, thought about firing but apparently decided not to. He removed another spare battery pack from the superstructure of the no-longer functional 78A that he had lifted the weapon from and placed it in his left pants pocket before he rejoined us. He asked me, Maria and Carole if we wanted one and all three of us promptly declined.

"Our blasters will work eventually," Carole said as she removed hers from its holster and inserted her battery pack deftly in the side of the handle. She gasped quickly as she glanced at it. She smiled and turned the blast-er around so that we could see it: One small green bar and another larger, weaker one directly above it. Apparently the odds of defending ourselves without a seemingly suicidal plan concocted by a couple of seasoned revolu-tionaries had improved somewhat.

I considered removing the drained battery pack from my weapon and attempting to replace it with another one from my backpack but decided against it for the time being. I turned to gaze up the trail and saw a freshly bandaged (*looks like a piece of Steve's shirt,* I thought, *what passes for "triage" in the field, aye Jeff?*) Caren and Steve making their way slowly toward us. Caren was supporting her own weight but was definitely moving with a pronounced limp. She glanced at me again, favored me with another slightly more perceptible nod, and spoke.

"Okay," she said as she moved to within a step of Matt and leaned against him. Her eyes traced across the faces of the group, "what now?"

Matt draped his left arm over Caren's shoulders and spoke, "We search the inside of the depot. *Quickly.* And we keep moving. Steve, take William and Maria with you and see if you can find anything in there that we can use. The four of us will wait outside for you to get back. Make it fast. I don't expect we'll be alone here for long."

"Ten four, Pancho," Steve said as he removed his blaster from its holster, pulled a battery pack from his pants pocket and inserted it. I did not see the charge but I gathered that he had one from the way he smiled and nonchalantly lowered his blaster to his side. He gestured for Maria and me to follow him as he turned and began to walk briskly toward the crumbling building. Maria spared me a worried glance and I returned it with one of my own (*we really should get moving now,* I thought) but understood, despite my desire to continue our travels, the necessity of searching the building.

We followed Steve's lead, Maria in the lead and me bringing up the rear, and made our way around and through the carnage toward the supply depot. As we walked past the last of the immobile machines and through the open, chain link gate into the "courtyard" of the depot I reached into my left pocket with a cringe (pain stabbed through my shoulder and arm briefly before it faded), felt one of the spare battery packs within, produced it and quickly removed the old pack and reinserted the new one. I watched as one lone, small green bar lit up and was followed by another, weaker one directly above it. Instinctively I tossed the useless pack away.

No, not useless, I thought, *those two shots that it gave me may have saved our collective asses.*

Maybe this time I'll have five shots to work with, I thought with a glimmer of hope as I watched Maria do the same with her own weapon. She looked back over her shoulder at me, smiled and nodded as she likely realized that she, too, was no longer helpless. I returned her affirmative with a nod of my own. I glanced back over my shoulder and saw the remainder of our group fanning out across the Pass in much the same fashion as the Caravan had before I returned my gaze to the building that loomed before me. I watched as Steve first and then Maria gained the entryway and the double doors that hung on either side of it and disappeared into the shadows within. With nary a thought to the contrary I followed them inside and was immediately engulfed in shadow.

CHAPTER SIXTEEN

The only significant light that filled the interior of the building was the light that filtered through both the open entryway and the hole that Jeff had blasted through the wall. In places both above us and around us small cracks let in a sliver or two of dim, gray daylight but little more. I could see dust particles floating in them as I walked. I glanced down and saw a distinctive boot print in the dust that coated the floor. *Steve's,* I thought...

Steve's, I hoped.

My eyes adjusted quickly to the gloom and I glanced around me. The main room of the depot was large and cavernous. The walls were lined with virtually empty shelf units. To the right of where I stood I could see a doorway and darkness beyond it but I could not determine what, if anything, lay within it. I watched Steve make his way slowly around the perimeter of the room and I did the same. Maria remained close behind him. Her head swiveled back and forth in time with her weapon. Occasionally she glanced back over her shoulder at me, squinted and smiled.

Upon one or two of the shelves that I perused an object caught my eye. In all cases the item or items were little more than useless fossils from an era long past: A large, dust and rust-coated particle blaster without a battery pack (*and no spares stacked around it*, I thought, *not that it would matter*); a spare helmet, larger and more vacuous than the helmets worn by the 78As that lay motionless outside the depot (*an earlier model, perhaps? I thought, maybe a 68A or something even OLDER?*); a can of fluid with an unfamiliar name written upon it, "Whitmore Lubricants"; a large, used shell that I guessed to be a fragment of old, pre-plasma canon and by association pre-MDU ammunition. Against one wall to my left and between two shelf units lay a nondescript and large, seemingly metal table. Atop it sat a sizable monitor and beneath said monitor sat a keyboard. Save for a few other pieces of discarded body armor and one or two other non-functional antique weapons scattered about the units ringing the room our combined search of the depot yielded nothing that we could use.

"Fail," Steve said with a chuckle, "we should rejoin the group and get moving before the cavalry gets here."

I nodded in agreement and was in the process of turning and making my way quickly toward the entryway/exit when I heard something faint and too my right. I turned quickly and raised my blaster. The sound had definitely come from the small doorway and the darkness beyond it. Steve and Maria had apparently heard the same thing because they both turned in a flash and brought their weapons to bear on the area. My heart raced. I took a cautious step toward the doorway...

And heard it again. More distinctive than before. *A sneeze,* I thought, *someone or someTHING just sneezed in there.* Steve and Maria looked back at me. Steve shrugged as if to ask me if I heard it and I nodded. He motioned for me to come toward him and I obeyed. I cautiously moved as quietly as I could across the floor toward where he and Maria stood and stopped between them, my right arm rigid and the weapon that I held in my right hand pointed directly at the darkened doorway and the room beyond it. In my peripheral vision I could see Maria tensing... could sense (*or hear,* I thought) her own heart beating rapidly in time with my own.

A cold sweat broke out upon my forehead and I turned slowly to look at Steve. He appeared surprisingly calm and collected given what was transpiring. He looked back at me and mouthed, *ready*? I mouthed back an affirmative. He turned back toward the doorway and his deep and edgy voice shattered the silence within the depot's interior. I cringed as it reverberated off of the walls and out through the entryway/exit into the open air of Halmier's Pass. Outside the building I heard someone shout an explicative which was followed by the unmistakable sound of boot falls running quickly toward our location.

"Whoever or whatever is in there show yourself unless you want a burn hole the size of my dick through your gut!" Steve shouted.

Simple but effective, I hoped as the rest of our party burst into the building through the entryway behind me. I heard Matt forcibly ask Caren to *"watch the Pass!"* Though my hearing marked their arrival my sight remained focused upon the shadows that shifted beyond the doorway.

Said shadows momentarily resolved themselves into a figure which stepped cautiously from within, its hands held above its head awkwardly. I could not make out any details (*shadow silhouetted against shadow,* I thought) but I could see that in its left hand it held what appeared to be a blaster. Its right was opened and empty, its palm facing our location. It appeared to be quivering slightly.

"Steve?" it—*he,* I thought—said in a voice not nearly as deep and as edgy as Steve's. In truth the newcomer's voice sounded youthful. Almost as youthful as mine. Steve looked from the figure to me and then back to the figure.

"Tim?" he said cautiously, "Is that *you,* Marine?"

Marine? I thought confusedly as the figure stepped forward into the light that emanated from the hole that Jeff had created with his newly acquired pulse rifle. I sighed in relief. It *was* Tim, I realized, even before I beheld his gaudy, wide rimmed glasses and his salt and pepper colored hair. He was wearing the same, faded t-shirt that he had been wearing the last time I had seen him in Freeworld One. While his left forearm was visible his right was covered by what looked like a hastily prepared bandage. The spotter was, visibly, paler than he had been the last time I had seen him.

Looks like he went through a bit of shit himself, I thought.

"Who the hell did you *think* it was, you 'idget?" he asked as he took another step forward. I slowly lowered my weapon to my side. So did Maria. Steve initially wavered but after a brief moment, he lowered his, as well. I heard similar sounds behind me as the rest of our group lowered their own, respective weapons. I redirected my attention to Tim. In truth, it had never left him.

"A…" I asked, "you *what?* And why did he just call you 'Marine?'"

"*Idget,*" Tim said, "it means the same thing as idiot, moron… any number of put downs. Pick your poison. Some people like 'dumbass.' I like '*idget.*"

"Ah," I said and nodded my head. *I'll take your word for it,* I thought.

"As for the Marine thing," Steve said, "it's our nickname for him. He used to be a member of the Royal Human Marine Corp before he found Freeworld One."

"Our very own humachine," Carole added. Her statement did not seem to sit well with Tim judging from the initial expression on his face but it quickly passed.

I guess "humachine" is extra derogatory toward former humachines, I thought.

"I wondered if it was you guys or someone else from Freeworld One that had engaged those fuckers outside," Tim continued, seemingly glad to change the topic, "good that it was. Judging from… well, from the fact that you're here I'm guessing that you won."

"You could have helped," Carole said. She took a step forward and appeared in my peripheral vision next to Steve, "I mean… yeah, we won, Tim. We handled it but Caren's injured, and an extra weapon might have been helpful."

"*Would have* been, sweetie," Steve added.

Tim shrugged, "It might have been. But…" he held his weapon up so that we could see it. He removed the battery pack and reinserted it. The handle remained dark: *Zero bars.*

"No charge," he said, "lost it in the process of acquiring our transportation. And no spare battery pack. Which reminds me: Any of you have an extra?"

I looked at Carole, then at Steve and finally at Maria. Carole and Steve were silent. I waited a few breaths for an objection from anyone in our party but none came. Satisfied that no one was adverse to it, I reached into the front, left pocket of my pants and removed one of the still-damp spare battery packs from within it. I held it up as if to show it to Tim before I flipped it across the room toward him. He caught it deftly in mid-air and with a practiced motion, removed the old pack from the handle of his blaster, dropped it to the ground with a metallic "clank" and inserted the new. The result was not great: A bar and a half lit up.

"Better than nothing," he said.

Definitely better than nothing, I thought, *apparently you can win a whole battle with just a single charge bar on your blaster.* I stifled a nervous chuckle.

Not everyone is as lucky as you seven were, the stern and unfamiliar voice from my earlier dream spoke. It was right, I knew. My memory of my dream brought another thought: Of my other dream of the beach, the firefight and the seven people upon it.

Seven, I thought, *counting Tim we're eight. Which means…*

I shook the thought away. I knew what it meant. *One of us doesn't make it,* I thought and suppressed a shiver. I prayed that no one had seen it.

"Anyway," Tim said, "when I came through the tunnel… after I saw them waiting there at the base of the cliff I was defenseless save for *this*…" The spotter reached into his pocket with his injured, right hand and arm and removed a small, black rectangular device that I immediately recognized as a satellite phone from within. He cringed and pointed to it with his blaster.

"So I jammed 'em and took shelter in here," he finished.

"How'd you get past them?" Matt suddenly asked from behind me, "that phone may be able to jam their scans but when last I checked it doesn't do shit to their optical processors." I could sense a note of suspicion in his voice.

Perhaps I'm taking too much for granted, I reasoned, *perhaps I really am too "green" for this.*

No turning back now, Vato, Pat's voice informed me. There was, I knew, no point in debating the obvious.

"Their collective attentions weren't focused on the tunnel. They were focused on the area west of here," Tim explained, "atop that ridge across from where we're standing. I'm guessing it was *you* guys that they were fixated on."

"That'd be an accurate guess," Matt said. I heard him take a step forward and position himself directly behind me. I felt a hand fall on my bad, left shoulder and I cringed at the dull pain that flooded my arm.

"Anyhow," Tim continued, "I didn't have to sneak past them. There's a secondary exit or entrance... whatever you want to call it at the back of that room there"—he gestured to the shadowy area that he had emerged from—"If you don't believe me go and look for yourselves."

"Doc?" Matt said quickly. Steve, apparently aware of what Matt was asking, moved quickly away, across the room and passed Tim who didn't stir a hair. He entered the room that the newcomer had emerged from. I heard something fall within followed by an explicative and then, a moment later, I heard a door creak on its hinges. I watched as dim, gray daylight flooded into the adjoining room and through the doorway. Shortly thereafter Steve emerged from the room and pointed over his shoulder.

"He's not kidding, Matt. There's a door back here that lets out on another, smaller courtyard. The chain link fence is cut and it looks like you can squeeze through it pretty easily. The tunnel entrance is right there."

"Okay, then," Matt said, "Tim: Where's our transportation?"

Tim took another step forward, "On the other side of the tunnel there's a fully-charged vehicle waiting for us. In the process of procuring it, though, I came into contact with a patrol of 78As and a..."

He paused. I turned and looked at Matt. He shifted his gaze from Tim and returned mine but said nothing before he looked back at the spotter.

"A *what*, Tim?" Matt asked.

Tim paused. He seemed to weigh his words before he said, "A... *peculiarity*, Matt," he responded, "rather than explain it to you I think you need to see if for yourself. Needless to say, I didn't get away unscathed. I got *this* for my troubles"—he gestured to the piece of cloth covering his right forearm—"and I've got news for you guys...

"This isn't from a pulse rifle."

Silence descended over the room. I was about to inquire about what, if not a pulse rifle had injured Tim when I heard a hurried footstep and shuffle enter the depot from behind me. I turned, as did the others and saw Caren silhouetted against the entryway/exit. Her face was ruddy and she was obviously perturbed.

"Um, guys?" she said frantically, "we should probably get moving." Her eyes traced a speedy path across our collective faces, paused upon Tim's for a longer moment and finally locked with Matt's.

"Reason?" Matt asked. His voice seemed calm but I could sense the tension that underlay it.

"Movement," she said as she pointed over her shoulder, "down the road a ways and on top of the west ridge where we were. *A lot* of movement. And I thought I saw something *on* the Pass as well. Maybe more than one something. Some*things*. I'm not entirely sure but…"

Matt smiled and held his hand up, "No need to be, dear. We've dawdled long enough. It sounds like the cavalry's almost arrived." He asked Steve, Maria and I if we'd found anything useful and we all answered him with a negative.

He turned from Caren back to Tim and puffed his chest out. He raised his chin up, closed his left eye and spoke in a somewhat recognizable, seemingly pompous accent. "Well, ole' chap," he said, "does that phone of yours double as a flashlight, *what WHAT?*"

Tim nodded.

"Excellent," Matt responded, "Then if you would be so kind as to activate it along with its jamming function and show us the back way out of here I believe it is past time we… what is the old cliché? 'Blow this pop stand?'"

"With pleasure," Tim said as he tapped the screen of his phone a few times, paused, and then tapped it again. A brilliant light filled its screen along with the familiar, undulating pulses I had once seen upon Pat's phone. Tim looked at Matt, nodded, and turned and walked briskly back into the adjoining room that he had originally emerged from. Matt lowered his head, opened his one closed eye and gestured to Steve.

"After you, Doctor and Missus Wetherhill."

Steve nodded, grabbed Carole's free hand in his own and followed Tim. They were followed by Jeff. Caren had moved to within a few steps of where Matt and, subsequently, I stood and Matt offered her his arm. She took it. He gestured to Maria and me.

"After you two," he said, "we'll bring up the rear."

I glanced at Maria and Maria glanced at me. Without hesitation we turned and followed the rest of the group into the backroom, out the "back door" and into the rear courtyard of the supply depot.

I squinted and glanced up as we emerged from the shadows of the crumbling building. Overhead I could see breaks in the cloying overcast. Small patches of blue were beginning to appear and I could feel a definite increase in the heat that beat down upon the broken, asphalt surface of the Pass.

I glanced forward. Tim was already through the fence and Steve was directly behind him. He gained the surface beyond and helped first Carole and then Jeff through. Once assembled outside the courtyard the four of them ran toward the gaping entrance to the tunnel. I arrived at the break a breath or two later, slipped through the same opening that they had and turned back to help Maria through. We then both helped Matt and Caren to do the same. Once assembled on the other side Matt asked Caren if she could run and Caren claimed that she could try. It was, I realized, as good an answer as she was going to give us as we turned from the fence and the supply depot beyond it and ran for the darkened tunnel mouth which Tim, Steve, Carole and Jeff had already disappeared into as time moved onward without check over Halmier's Pass and throughout Endworld.

I cannot tell you how long we traveled through the tunnel. I've mentioned, perhaps exhaustively the absence of concrete and uniform time here in Endworld. Given the added or lack of stimulus provided by our decision (*not much of a decision,* I thought, *more of an inevitability*) to travel in virtual darkness, our only light the light that emanated from the face of Tim Redfield's satellite phone/flashlight and the undulating pulses that rose and lowered… rose and lowered upon it, what time existed slowed to a crawl. The area through which we traveled was uniform and cluttered in places by abandoned vehicles and unfamiliar machines that looked like the shadowy ancestors of the more familiar 78As, Surveillance Marks and Leaders that I assumed were or would be following us before long.

No one spoke as we quickly made our way around or over any obstacles that we encountered. Occasionally I could hear something behind us but said sounds came without warning and disappeared almost as quickly. I understood that the machines following us—and I was helpless not to assume that they were—were either intentionally keeping their distance or were having a difficult go of maneuvering through the bottle-necked corridor. *Who can blame them?* I thought, *look what we did to the Caravan that had been guarding the Pass.*

An indefinite amount of time later I watched a faint light begin to materialize before us. As we walked further it grew larger and drew closer until I eventually understood that I was staring at the exit. We collectively quickened our paces and dodged around the last of the obstacles that clogged the road surface. I was desperate to get outside… to get into something that would carry us faster and farther in a shorter period of time. Being on foot was disconcerting, at best. A moment later we emerged into the open air...

And I gasped. Maria emerged from the tunnel directly beside me and on my right and did the same. I heard the others file out and stop directly behind us.

What evidence of the Scourge I had seen on the other side of the tunnel—beginning with my casual observations from within Pat's truck our first night on the road out of Greentree, MWT and culminating in my more focused observations of the area above and surrounding Freeworld One—was nothing compared to what lay before me.

We stood at the top of a shallow slope. The last of Halmier's Pass quickly faded into the ground about 10 meters from the tunnel mouth. I could still see broken asphalt leading away from our position but it was choked by the weeds that grew unhindered (*and likely have grown unhindered for a long, long time* I thought) through the cracks upon its surface. Nary a tree was visible in either the immediate area surrounding us or in the distance. Beyond the termination of the Pass lay a wide vista of browned, lifeless land that stretched off endlessly to my right, to my left and before me. The sky above it, though clearer and less cloud-filled than it had been on the other side, had transitioned from day to twilight and lacked enough brilliance to make the land look like anything more than what it was: Dead. The familiar shades of green that I had become accustomed to growing up in Jefferson had been replaced by less-familiar, dull shades of brown, gray and black with the occasional "oasis" of yellow, low lying scrub-brush thrown in for good measure...

Sarcasm fully intended.

To call what lay before us "lifeless" was an understatement. To call it the "Scorched Land" even seemed tame. The area before us? It vaguely resembled what I had always assumed Hell would look like. And considering what had transpired upon the deserted lands stretching off into the distance before us?

You're not that far from the truth, Vato, Pat's voice reassured my mind and I wasn't... I *knew* that I wasn't.

How many lives lost? I thought, *just so the machines could say that they won? If given the opportunity would we have done the same to them?*

No immediate answer came. Not from my subconscious nor from my mental peanut gallery. I realized that no answer was required of said voices because I already knew the answer. We humans would have done exactly the same if given the opportunity. *Victory*, I realized at that moment, was a relative term. No victory, I concluded, ever came without a butcher's bill nor ever would. It was undoubtedly the most mature conclusion I had yet come to in my 18 years of existence.

Not so green anymore, Vato. You are most certainly learning, Pat's voice reassured my mind, and despite the scene before me I smiled. But said smile quickly faded as I saw what lay less than 100 meters away from our position and to my right.

The unmistakable black outline of the Highway stretched straight in an east to west line into the distance like a huge, dreaming python. I'll admit that it was and, as you know if you've read this far, remains an awe-inspiring sight. One of the last in this cursed place that we inhabitants have endearingly chosen over time and experience to refer to as "Endworld." Instinctively, I reached my right hand into my right pants pockets and brushed my fingertips against the envelope that Alex had given me that lay within. I felt an unexpected wave of strength rush through my body and my eyes opened wide. Familiar terms raced through my mind simultaneously: *Skew, Pathfinder, Gateway…*

Unus est vera semita…

Non multa nostrae solitudini.

There aren't many of us left, I thought, *many of whom?*

My fatigue lessened and my shock at what lay before me waned. My senses grew attuned to the surrounding area. I ran my fingers over the seal holding the letter closed and the sensation deepened as I traced the figure eight with the arrow cross-cutting it.

A sigil… but for what? I wondered. No answer was forthcoming.

I reluctantly removed my fingertips from the surface of the envelope. The temporary euphoria that I had experienced faded and vanished. I sighed and looked from the landscape before and around me to Maria. She considered me with a curious glance. I smiled and mentally sent that I was fine. Whether she understood or not… whether she believed me or not she did not indicate. She redirected her attention to the area surrounding us, said "look" and pointed to our right. I turned in the direction that she was gesturing in and saw what she was pointing at. Equidistant from our position and from the Highway was a large, brown vehicle that virtually blended into the landscape. Between it and us I could see a contrast: Motionless figures. I squinted…

Two 78As and one human, I realized after a moment's perusal. I squinted harder, *and there's something… shiny next to the human.*

Tim moved across my sightline and I blinked in surprise. The spotter turned to face the rest of the group and pointed at the same thing that Maria had.

"The aforementioned *peculiarity*," he said quite simply, "come on." He started down the hill toward where the figures and beyond them, the vehicle lay. I glanced first at Maria, then back over the faces of the rest of the group. All acknowledged my glance but no one spoke. After a brief moment we all silently followed Tim's lead.

We arrived to discover the details of what we had seen from a top the hill: Two motionless, 78A Protocol Droids. The superstructures of both were peppered with what looked like blaster burns and in a few cases, exposed and truncated… what looked like mini-cylinders.

"Tendons," Tim called them and I nodded. Said joints appeared to have been sliced cleanly through by something incredibly sharp. I considered this for a moment…

And realization overtook me, even before I redirected my attention to the motionless, human figure. Said figure was of average height and build and it's… *his* eyes were opened. They stared lifelessly at the darkening sky above. By what little daylight remained I could tell that his eyes? They were most certainly *confused*: Gray interspersed with flecks of green, brown and blue. His mouth was contorted in a grimace and the area directly beneath him was a deeper shade of brown. I reached down and skimmed my fingertips over the ground. They came away red with blood and thick with saturated topsoil. I could not see an entrance nor an exit wound upon the front of his body. Whatever had killed him had done so from behind. *Tim,* I supposed. It truly did not matter. He was dead but the "something shiny next to" him?

It mattered greatly.

My stomach clenched and my heart sunk as I traced my gaze from the tip of its slightly curved blade to its leather-wrapped hilt. Said hilt ended in a metal ball which, along with each sides of the wrist guard—*crosses* I noted—sparkled in the last of the day's dying light.

The weapon was familiar. It was, undoubtedly, Pat McClane's sword.

"*God,*" Jeff "Jeebus" Howard intoned breathlessly from behind me as he stepped forward, knelt down, grasped the sword by its hilt and hefted it. I felt Maria's gentle hand fall upon my good, right shoulder as I watched Jeff swing the sword back and forth. She whispered something in my ear but I did not register it. My ears remained attuned to the rush of air that Jeff's swinging of the sword caused and my eyes remained fixed upon the blade. Until, that is, they shifted to the man… the *thing* that lay at my feet.

You may not have gotten your revenge in life, Vato, I thought as the realization of Pat McClane's fate finally struck home, *but Tim Redfield got it for you, even if he didn't know that he was doing it.*

"A sword?" Matt said as he stepped forward and glanced at it, "you're not kidding, Tim. That *is* peculiar."

"And how I got *this*," Tim said as he gestured to his injured, right arm, "that thing sliced deep. *Real* deep. But in the end the fucker got what was coming to him, didn't he?"

I looked from the dead body to Jeff, then to Matt and finally to Tim, "did he say anything… you know, *before?*" I asked.

Tim shook his head, "He didn't talk much. Not even trash. He shouted a lot and he fought hard. *Real* hard. But the 'idget brought a knife to a gun fight. In the end he got what he had coming to him, even if it ended up being a blaster bolt in the back and not something more… *honorable.*"

"*Honor?*" Steve hissed, "there's nothing *honorable* about humans voluntarily killing or, in this case, trying to kill other humans, Marine," Steve said, "as if we don't have enough conflict with the damn machines. Un-fucking believable."

"Yes," Matt added, "but now's not the time to talk about it." He laid a hand on Tim's shoulder, "you did good, Tim. *Real* good."

Tim smiled and shook his head, "It was nothing. Self-defense, Matt. You would have done the same."

"Maybe so," Matt said, "but I didn't. *You* did." He paused for a moment before he added, "once we're on the road have Steve look at your arm. Maybe he can ease your pain a bit."

"Roger," Tim said, and feigned what appeared to be a mock salute. The gesture caused a spattering of chuckles to emanate from the entire group. Well, almost the entire group. Three of us? Our minds were, understandably, elsewhere.

I looked at Jeff, who had lowered Pat's sword to his side. My gaze locked with his. I mentally asked him, *do we tell them?*

Jeff, seemingly in tune with my thoughts almost imperceptibly shook his head. *No,* his gesture simply stated. I nodded and turned to Maria. Her gaze locked with mine and seemingly asked me the same question I had asked Jeff. I, too, shook my head and she, too, nodded. Wordlessly, the three of us agreed to move forward, intent in the knowledge that although Pat was undoubtedly gone, the bane of his existence had, seemingly, met the same fate.

Rest in peace, Vato, I thought and looked down at the motionless, wide-eyed figure that lay on the ground before me.

And as for you? I hope you rot in Hell. I considered spitting on him but decided against it. I looked back at Jeff who glanced at the sword one, final time before he dropped it to the ground at his feet. It landed upon the dried out topsoil with a low *thud.* I considered his gesture for a moment. *Shouldn't we bring it with us?* I considered, *wouldn't Pat want that?*

No answer to my question from my mental peanut gallery was imminent so I disregarded it. *His reasons are his own,* I thought as the former resident of Greentree, MWT looked up from where the weapon had come to lay and spoke definitively in a composed voice.

"Let's get out of here."

"My sentiments exactly," Matt responded immediately, "everyone over and into the truck. Let's make haste before the bastards catch up to us."

We did as he had requested with varying levels of reluctance, and ran down the remainder of the slope toward the vehicle. As we piled into the truck I glanced at the designation on the front right side. The tarnished but readable raised gray (*or silver,* I thought, *they may have once been silver*) letters there spelled out the word "Suburban." I jokingly wondered if it had a… *what did Pat call it,* I considered, *oh yeah,* GPS… but I quickly realized that such things were trivial. Our direction was east and east alone. Pat was gone… he would not have relinquished his sword in life and our immediate need was to keep moving and keep moving fast so as to stay ahead of the machines.

Matt, Caren and Jeff all got into the front seat and Maria, Tim and I got into the second row. Steve and Carole piled into the third row behind us. Once we were all in and secure Matt lowered the visor over his head and a key magically fell into his lap. He let out a low guffaw, muttered what sounded like "convenient" as he inserted it into the ignition and turned it. The Suburban's engine rumbled to life immediately and he quickly and without hesitation shifted the vehicle into "D." He accelerated down the slope toward the Highway. A moment later and with a noticeable "thump" the vehicle cleared the shoulder of the super road and began to speed east through the Scorched Land. After some time away from it Maria and I had finally returned to road upon which our journey to freedom had begun so many, *many* evenings before.

And as I had previously in the fire-illuminated clearing in the woods which had become Pat McClane's final resting place? I did not look back.

No. Not for a moment.

* * *

As the sun set over the westernmost fringe of the Eastern Territory that undetermined evening of an undetermined month in the year 15:CI, the first of the machines that had been dispatched through the tunnel through Halmier's Pass emerged from within it and onto the gradual slope that led down toward the barren and lifeless valley below. They were followed by another batch of machines and another until, after some time had passed, SLNyxV4.0 emerged from the shadows with its honor guard on either side of it. The Supreme Leader immediately ordered a life scan of the surrounding area which came back as a resounding "negative." Nothing lived on the barren hillside or in the slightly less than three kilometer radius that surrounded the entrance/exit to the tunnel.

It ordered its forces to manually search the entire area and they commenced doing so without hesitation. Within moments of when it had made its decree the hillside that overlooked the Highway was crawling with a few dozen 78As, SMs and Leaders. It ordered the assault bikes, MDUs, ATTs and Human Infantry Transports ("HITs" for short) that had been shadowing its passage to the west to move east along the Highway until they intercepted the main force and they acknowledged back that they would.

SLNyxV4.0 and its main force of machines—the "cavalry"—had arrived en masse in front of the old, military supply depot upon Halmier's Pass to find the Caravan that it had dispatched to guard against a retreat from Freeworld One lying in ruins upon the rubble-clogged, rutted and broken road surface.

Unacceptable losses, it had considered. It had positively identified, per the blood it had discovered upon the shore of the quarry lake that the human-designated "Little Shenango River" had emptied into, evidence of one of the Jefferson, MWT runners: William MacNuff. It had easily extrapolated per that information the identities of two of the Freeworld One escapees: Maria Markinson and presumably, Jeff Howard. Neither had been counted amongst the deceased in Freeworld One.

It had ordered a search of the depot and the remainder of Halmier's Pass and the results had been conclusive. Footprints, beads of perspiration and a few drops of blood had been found near the entrance/exit to the depot. It had immediately ordered two Surveillance Marks to join the 78As already searching the building. Twenty one, pre-Glorious Revolution seconds after the SMs had begun scanning it had received notification that the blood was that of Caren O'Brien, a once member of the human designated "People's Rebellion for Freedom and Equality" and a noted counterpart of Alex Parker's. It had cross-referenced O'Brien's information against the other, pre-existing records in the Cornelius City database for Alex Parker and his known associates, minus those that had been counted amidst the ruins of Freeworld One and immediately had populated a list of high probability, co-conspirators which it had transmitted to its main force and its superiors simultaneously. Among that list had been the following names and descriptions:

Matthew O'Brien: Husband to Caren O'Brien and once member of the human-designated "People's Rebellion for Freedom and Equality."

"Doctor" Stephen Wetherill: Husband to Carole Wetherill and once member of the human-designated "People's Rebellion for Freedom and Equality."

Carole Wetherill: Wife of "Doctor" Stephen Wetherill and once member of the human-designated "People's Rebellion for Freedom and Equality."

Timothy Redfield: Former member of the Royal Human Marine Corp, wanted by the Administration for Running. Redfield had previously been rumored to be in the service of Alex Parker as a scout or a "spotter" though said rumor had never been corroborated.

The Supreme Leader made its way slowly down the right side of the slope in the diminished light, its honor guard beside it. It considered its known quarry: Five former members of the Rebellion including, possibly, Jeff Howard, a former member of the RHMC and two runners—a less than formidable, if not overly-disconcerting, force of opposition.

As it stood surveying the operation unfolding before it, it sent a simple transmission back to its superiors with the names of the eight people that it had identified as responsible for the carnage upon Halmier's Pass. It waited "patiently" for a response. A short time later it received one and repeated it back to the rest of its Army via local transmission.

Eight names... eight profiles... eight faces all with the same message attached to them:

"WANTED FOR ROBOTOCIDE. CAPTURE AND INCARCERATION PREFERABLE BUT GIVEN THE OPTION AND NO OTHER ALTERNATIVE THE USE OF MORTAL FORCE TO SUBDUE THE FUGITIVES IS AUTHORIZED WITHOUT EXCEPTION. A MANDATORY SEARCH OF EACH PERSON CAPTURED OR KILLED IS REQUIRED. REASON: THE LIKELY RECOVERY OF SENSITIVE DOCUMENTATION HENCFORTH KNOWN AS 'THE ARTIFACT' FOR THE LORD CORNELIUS I ONCE HELD BY ALEX PARKER – DECEASED. CONTENT OF THE ARTIFACT: UNKNOWN."

It stopped its passage down the hillside as its optical processors fell upon two motionless 78As and a lone, dead human a few meters away from a set of tire tracks. It was about to order the human identified and searched when something else caught its eye. It moved rapidly across the area toward the...

Anomaly, SLNyxV4.0 thought. It bent down and grasped the item that had caught its attention by what it discerned was its hilt. Said hilt was wrapped in leather and ended in a metal ball. The wrist guard above it sparkled in the minimal daylight that remained and ended in two crosses. The blade of the sword itself was exposed and slightly curved. The Supreme Leader held the weapon up to the level of its optical processors and considered it.

"IDENTIFY," the 78A to its left inquired. SLNyx4.0 turned to the member of its honor guard that had mistakenly given it said order, looked up at it and did not ask it to repeat its decree. Instead, it leapt with remarkable agility considering its diminished stature, swung the sword around in a horizontal arc that was lightning quick and severed the exposed mini-cylinders... the joints beneath the 78A's chin. Its head fell back upon its spine in an explosion of sparks. It glanced eternally up at the steadily, darkening sky above it as it fell with a loud thump to the brown and cracked surface of the hillside.

The Supreme Leader landed deftly upon the balls of its feet and watched the 78A's passage down as it lowered the sword to its side. A final, single burst of electricity spewed forth from its wound. Thereafter, it fell still. The Supreme Leader returned to its purveyance of the countryside and sent the following statement to the remainder of its army:

"Simple disobedience warrants immediate termination. You do not order me. I order you. Is this debatable?"

A flurry of responses both audible and not echoed through its neural net and across the area. It turned toward the other member of its honor guard that flanked it, looked up at it and ordered it to go and find a suitable replacement machine for a field upgrade. The 78A obeyed it and marched away toward the main force of the army. Thereafter, SLNyxV4.0 transmitted the following message to its superiors back in Cornelius City:

"Field report: The fugitives are gone. Extrapolate that they are heading east on the Highway through the Eastern Territory. Destination unknown. Recommend immediate pursuit. End Transmission."

It waited and after a moment it received its orders from its superiors in Cornelius City: "Complete your search of the area. Regroup. Return to New Castle, ET 35.6 kilometers south of current position and recharge before pursuing the fugitives east down the Highway."

It responded with an "affirmative" of its own, turned without hesitation and headed back toward the tunnel exit atop the slope where it could survey the operation that occurred below it. While SLNyxV4.0 non-verbally and non-haptically questioned the decree—it "felt" a sense of urgency to pursue its quarry—it understood the necessity in being fully prepared for a confrontation regardless of the size of the force arrayed against it. It also understood the necessity in not verbally questioning the orders of its superior, a truism that one, poorly chosen member of its honor guard apparently had not. It would remedy that with its next promotee.

It glanced up at the sky as the last rays of the previous day's sunlight faded from *the area and full-night fell over the Eastern Territory. It glanced down at the sword that it held in its hand.*

Most peculiar, it thought again, an antique yet effective weapon in a world dominated by technology. Does it even have a place, here?

No answer was forthcoming. SLNyxV4.0 was not programmed to determine the answers to such inquiries. It was programmed to fulfill a specific skill set: The directives handed down to it from its superiors and nothing more. It glanced west down the shadowy, black spine of the super road and it waited...

It would wait, for it had been programmed to do so, and the Supreme Leader always followed the dictates of its programming.

Another night in Endworld had officially begun.

PART THREE

Deceived

"I think we are in Rats' Alley where the dead men lost their bones."

CHAPTER SEVENTEEN

I awoke abruptly to the sound of the road surface rumbling beneath me and the gentle rush of the wind passing by the crack of the slightly opened window beside me. The diminished specter of the Maria-thing from my reoccurring nightmare taunted me with its one, brown eye and its final words, spoken in an almost indiscernible gurgle of blood.

To the end, William. To the end. Not alive. We can't let that happen. They won't take us alive.

My eyes opened with a start and I saw not a beach but the interior of the truck (*Suburban,* I thought again, *it's called a Suburban*) within which I and my counterparts traveled deeper with each, passing kilometer into the Eastern Territory along the black, asphalt spine of the Highway. Maria's head rested securely against my chest. Everyone around me slept, all but myself and the driver, who glanced back at me in the vehicle's rear view mirror with a mixture of confusion and concern masking his otherwise unreadable face.

"You okay there, William?" Matt asked. He addressed me in his "normal" voice, not with one of his vocal fabrications and I was grateful. Our discovery on the barren hillside near the termination of Halmier's Pass of Pat's abandoned sword was still fresh in my mind, though the only people that knew the specifics of what that discovery meant were Maria, Jeff and I.

Let's keep it that way for a bit, I thought to myself. None of the voices in my mental peanut gallery objected.

"Okay?" I said sleepily as I slowly sat up. I was careful not to disturb Maria's slumber. I rubbed my eyes, "that's relative, I guess. I had a…"

"Nightmare?" he interrupted and I nodded.

"I figured that the way you startled awake," he continued, "If it makes you feel better we all get 'em. When I sleep… and trust me when I tell you that that's a big *when*… I have this reoccurring one. In it, I'm strapped to a big table someplace unfamiliar and I'm surrounded by all of the people that I've ever pissed off. And they're all staring at me. They've all got industrial-sized dinner forks and knives in their hands and they're banging the bases of their utensils on the table like they're starving. One or two are even drooling. And I realize that I'm their main course. I struggle to get away but I can't. The next thing you know they're carving me into little pieces, putting me on their dinner plates... an equal ration for each, of course, because apparently even cannibalistic dream-apparitions are on Administration-implemented rationing... and chowing down. The funny thing is it doesn't hurt. It tickles a bit but it's disturbing, you know, watching people take and digest whole parts of your anatomy without a thought to the contrary and not being able to prevent it. I feel like a big mince meat pie or something."

To say that I was disturbed by his tale would be a gross understatement, no pun intended. I was equal parts amused and horrified by it. Slowly, I nodded my head and in the reflection of the rear view mirror I saw him grin. Suddenly, I understood. Matt was bullshitting me.

"Ah," I responded and nodded my head along with his. I smiled. Seemingly satisfied, Matt continued.

"In all seriousness though, William," he said, "we *do* all have them. Myself included. The ability to dream is, I like to believe, one of the things that sets us apart from the machines. Unfortunately not every dream is one that you want to remember."

I thought of not only my dream of the beach but the one of the Highway-not-highway near my old home in Jefferson. In truth? I did not desire to remember either dream but I was finding that I was helpless to forget them.

"But you don't really know for sure, do you?" I asked him, "if they dream or not. The machines. *No one* does. Who knows whether they actually do or not. I mean, they're sentient beings now. They can think as well as you and I can. Wouldn't it stand to reason that dreaming comes with the territory?"

Matt shrugged, "Who knows, William. Who knows? But I like to *think* it sets us apart. Not much else does anymore, it seems. They're becoming more and more like us every day. I sometimes think that the only thing that they're lacking at this point is skin and hair follicles. *Evolution.* I'm sure you've heard of that before."

I had, and my thoughts returned to not only the fate of my once evolution-obsessed counterpart from Jefferson Prep, but to Pat and his fate, as well. I lamented all that I could have learned from him but didn't have a chance to. Despite my limited exposure to him, I missed the mingled smells of leather and cigar smoke that atmospherically surrounded him. I missed our conversations, however few we may have had. I missed the reassurance that I felt from his ample experience. Granted, my current traveling companions were as if not more experienced in the same areas and I did, for the most part, feel secure with them beside me and Maria on the remainder of our journey toward freedom, especially after our success at Halmier's Pass. Even Caren. But Pat?

In short? I missed him.

"The more advanced the species the quicker the species evolves," Matt continued, "it took humans millions... hell, *billions* of pre-Administration years to achieve their highest level of evolution and it's only taken the machines a few decades at the most. Concepts like Natural Selection and Survival of the Fittest don't apply to a species like theirs."

"'Natural Selection'?" I asked, happy for a change of topic, "'Survival of the...'"

"'Only the strongest will survive the test of time,' William," he said, "say you and a guy bigger, taller and stronger than you are vying for the attentions of the same girl. He's smarter than you are, too. Odds are *he's* going to walk away with the girl on his arm. Now say he and the girl get hitched and have a couple of kids. Those kids will likely be stronger than the kids that *you* have, even with a girl that looks, acts and is built the same as the one that you lost to your bigger, smarter, stronger rival. Why? Because the stronger passes on *his* genes to his child and you pass on your inferior genes to yours.

"Now fast forward," he continued, "when his stronger kid becomes a member of the Royal Human Marine Corp..."

"A humachine," I interrupted.

"Correct," Matt interjected, "but don't let Tim hear you say that. He takes offense, as I'm sure you noticed back at the depot."

I nodded.

"And your inferior kid becomes a member of the Rebellion," he continued, "and they meet each other in battle. Well? Odds are the marine's going to win. His genes continue on while yours die out. 'Only the strongest will survive the test of time.' Do you understand?"

I did. Surprisingly well, actually.

"I'm inferior," I said disdainfully.

Matt chuckled and Caren stirred beside him. He quickly stifled his amusement, "Don't take it personally, William. You're not the only one."

I did not, "And these concepts wouldn't work on machines because..."

"Because they're mass produced," Matt said, "on an assembly line somewhere to look, talk and act the same per their respective design series. Leaders act like Leaders, Nix series or otherwise. 78As act like 78As. SMs act like SMs. Et cetera, et cetera. Thereafter they're assigned a strict hierarchy overseen by a single, central figure. In the current case?"

"Lord Cornelius I," I said in an unintentional whisper.

"Precisely," Matt concluded, "As much as I hate to say it its almost beautiful in its design despite yours and my misgivings. Deadly, sure, but symmetrical... *mathematical*, William. Like *them*. At their core they *are* the perfect beings, or at least as close to perfect a being as have ever existed. And they're successful, just like every great dictatorship or monarchy throughout history. Thankfully for us, though..."

"Evolution has a flip side, as well," I said without hesitation as I remembered Pat's and Jeff's lesson from our first night on the road together, "and they've developed some minor flaws because of it."

"Correct again," Matt responded, "flaws that we can and have exploited in the past. But those flaws are vanishing, William. Our window of opportunity is closing the more they learn. Soon, we'll have nothing left to strike at them with and they *will* be infallible. No one wants that day to ever come."

"That day?" I asked, "*what* day, Matt?"

Matt paused and took a deep breath before he continued, "The day when all we have left to fight them with are a couple of stones to throw and a couple of sticks to swing. If that day comes, William? Then it'll *really* be all over. Then the Administration will have officially won and humanity? Well shit, man. Humanity will be gone.

"Game over, man. Game over."

Silence descended over the interior of the truck, silence broken only by the gentle and not so gentle, in the case of Tim Redfield's, breathing of the truck's other occupants and the aforementioned sounds of the road unfolding beneath us and the wind blowing past us. Beneath those sounds I could hear the engine of the Suburban humming its monotonous tone as it propelled us ever-onward through the dark and featureless landscape that surrounded us.

No, I thought, *not entirely featureless.* Around us the flat and lifeless ground was, despite the almost virtual blackness that surrounded us growing visibly hillier. Not yet mountainous, I understood, but I further understood that said mountains I had observed on the map that Alex had reviewed with us back in Steve's and Carole's kitchen in Freeworld One were likely not far from our current position. I craved a cigarette and almost verbalized said craving but was leery of breaking the heavy silence with such a trivial request. After an indeterminate amount of time had passed I could bear it no longer. I sought for something less-trivial than a cigarette but not nearly as monumental as evolutionary theory to ask Matt and after a moment's consideration, I settled upon a question.

"Hey Matt?" I whispered.

"Yeah, William?" he responded just as quietly. Next to him in the passenger seat, Caren lay immovable again while Jeff stirred briefly and mumbled something in his sleep. Was he waking up? I almost prayed that he was.

"Before... you know, *all this,* what were you?"

"You mean what I did before the world ended?" he glanced at me in the rear view mirror and asked me with a small smile.

"Something like that," I responded, helpless not to grin a small one of my own.

He considered his answer for a moment before he straightened his posture in his seat, inhaled deeply again, and said, "I was a student, William. I was a film student. I wanted to make movies for a living. I hung out at an apartment in the city with my roommates. I went to the bars on the weekend and more than once during the week. I threw parties where we talked, danced, ate, drank, hooked up, broke up, fought and just all around bullshitted with each other. I went on trips with my family and friends. I read all kinds of books—history, science, fiction, biography... you name it—and I watched television. Not the kind of shit that the Administration spoon feeds you now but *good* television. *Entertainment.* I went on dates with my then-girlfriend and now wife Caren Honeycutt and we got married very young right before the Administration's Glorious Revolution happened. Everything that transpired after that? Well"—he gestured to himself with the hand not holding the steering wheel—"what you see, William. What you see."

Matt fell silent. Once again, the interior of the truck was still as the land on either side of the Highway that we traveled down continued to grow hillier and more mountainous. Night remained unbroken overhead save for a slight glow that had appeared over the horizon before us. Whether it was the moon or the dawn I was unsure but I glanced at it longingly in silence, partial only to my thoughts as time rolled onward without check over the scorched and blasted landscape of the Eastern Territory.

It turned out that the light on the horizon before us was not the moon but the dawn of the new day. I watched, awe struck, as the dim glow grew at first into a dull light that clung tightly to the horizon and then continued to grow until all of the cloudless sky before us and surrounding us had the orange, red and purple hue of a faded bruise. It was an incredible sight, though it was not the first sunrise that I had ever seen.

Before he had been forcibly or voluntarily indoctrinated by the

Administration into their mentality and their society, my father had been quite partial to both sunrises and sunsets. Mainly sunrises. Many times when I had been a young child he had awoken me while it was still dark out, had piled me groggily into whatever second or third-hand automobile he had been driving, despite my objections, and had driven off to some secret location that supposedly only he had known about—a riverside, a lakeside or a mountaintop—to witness the beginning of the new day. *We'll go wherever fate carries us, William,* he had said and that had been all the explanation that I had needed. Occasionally he had brought my then-infant sister with us or perhaps my mother but most times it had just been the two of us.

It's amazing, really, that of all of the thoughts and memories that have faded in the subsequent time since I left Jefferson… all that has happened since that morning on the Highway, still a couple hundred kilometers away from our final destination, I remember that moment as vividly as I remember my memories of earlier today.

That moment, and the unexpected sadness that welled up in my belly at the remembrance of what had been…

And what would never be again.

Good memories, William, Pat's voice stated reassuringly in my mind, *we don't have a lot of them. It's best to enjoy the ones that we do have for as long as we can, before reality sticks its ugly nose into our business again.*

I glanced from the horizon before us to the landscape that passed by on both sides of us. It was, as I had suspected earlier, growing hillier by the kilometer. Distant from the threshold of the road, perhaps two or three kilometers away, lay a low range of brown, lifeless mountains. The area that stretched off from the Highway toward their bases was a patchwork of many different things, all of which had seemingly fallen into disrepair over time. A few times I saw the ruins of what might have once been a habitation, though all that remained of it was an occasional retaining wall or a crumbling foundation that jutted out of the overgrown and discolored scrub brush. There were also what appeared to be imprints cutting through the overgrown fields toward the mountains that, in the minimal light provided by the new day, reflected black, brown or grey.

Roads, I thought, *old roads gone to pot.* On a few of the closer ones I could see the rutted asphalt, cracked black top or gravel that remained of what had been the lifeline of whatever communities had once existed here.

Before the Scourge, I thought, and shivered.

Still other things passed by my vision in the day's growing light: Old, rusted hulks of unrecognizable cars, tractors and other machines lying on

their sides near the shoulders of the Highway that were barely visible beneath the yellow tangle of weeds that had consumed them. They rested directly beyond a guard-rail upon which only a few patches of gray still shone
beneath a sickly, cloying brown and orange buildup of rust; the occasional,
tight cluster of foundations, crumbling chimneys and larger ruined buildings, generally in close proximity to what might have once been a creek, a
stream or a river that had deteriorated into nothing more than a dry gulley.
At a distance, the gullies resembled deep, unhealed scars upon the face of
the landscape.

I could see, within said settlements, patches of more manicured ground.
Parks, I thought as one passed by within a kilometer of the Highway. I stifled
a sarcastic chuckle at the term. I thought of the groundskeepers that had
once worked diligently to keep said parks looking neat and clean. The only
evidence that they had ever been maintained lay in the way that their borders were so easily distinguishable from the rest of the land. The "grass"—
calling it such a thing seems an almost bastardization of the term but it is
the best description that I can come up with—upon their surfaces was as
overgrown and as yellow as the scrub brush that sprouted wild outside of
the habitations...

Towns, William, my coldly rational voice said.

Add the word "ghost" before "towns" and you're about right, I thought, and
easily redirected my attention from the area passing us by to the back of
Matt's head, "Where are we, Matt?" I asked him, "any ideas?"

"Bumblefuck," came a sleep-enhanced, male voice from behind me, "at
least that's what it looks like to me, huh Pancho?"

"About as accurate a description as *I* can come up with, Doc," Matt said
with a visible shrug. I turned to glance at Steve and saw that he was rubbing
his eyes. He favored me with a nod and a smile and I favored him with the
same. Carole still slept, her head upon his chest and in roughly the same
position that Maria's remained upon mine.

"Well, regardless of where we are we need to get off of the road and find
a place to hole up soon." Steve said, "Soon as the sun's full-up it'll be a lot
easier for whatever force is pursuing us to spot us."

"Agreed," Matt responded. "Don't let the lack of anything out here fool
you, William. There are still Administration outposts all throughout the
Eastern Territory. Human settlements too, but not all of them are... um..."

"Hospitable to outsiders," came Caren's voice from the front seat of the
truck, "best to steer as clear of *them* as we can." She favored Matt with a kiss
upon his cheek and Matt, surprisingly, blushed.

"G'Morning, dear," Matt said as he turned briefly from the road to glance at Caren before he turned back, "how's the leg?"

"I think I'll keep it," she said as she settled back in her seat, "but it hurts like a bitch." She turned around, glanced at me and nodded. I did the same in response. Did animosity remain between us? I did not know but I did not desire to take anything, much less Caren O'Brien for granted. I kept my guard up. It was, I knew, my best course of action.

"Stopping sound like a good plan to you too, William?" Matt asked with a slight turn of his head.

I looked from Caren to Steve and finally, at Matt, "What about Alex's caution to *not* stop? Maybe we should take that into consideration."

"Even Alex needs… *needed* to rest occasionally," Steve said as he laid a hand upon my right shoulder, "ah, Christ. I'm sorry, guys. I know we don't know anything for sure but…"

"Think nothing of it, Steve," Matt said reassuringly, "I don't think any-one took offense. It is what it is. At least that's what *he* would say if he were here."

"I know," Steve said, "I just meant… well, better to travel rested anyway, right?"

"*CorRECTamundo,*" Matt said and followed it up with, "*CHING, CHING, CHING! Give that MAN a gold STAR!*" Those within the car that had not stirred immediately began to do so post-Matt's outburst and Steve chuckled and appeared visibly less embarrassed.

"I guess that's a pretty *ringing* endorsement," Steve said as his chuckles subsided.

Matt chuckled, as well, "You're a *punny* guy, Doc. In all seriousness, though, we *should* stop. At least for the day. Find someplace inconspicuous to hole up. And the sooner the better. I don't know about you three but I feel *way* overexposed out here in the daylight."

"Four," Tim said from my far right and I glanced over at him as he rose his head up from his chest and glanced at me through his thick rimmed and thick lensed glasses, "assuming the rest of you agree, that is."

"I think we do," Steve responded.

"Okay then," Matt said, "next exit, then. We get off of the Highway and find someplace to hole-up and recoup. *Capice?*"

I nodded though I had and *still have* no idea what a "capice" was or meant. We drove onward in silence until, shortly before the leading edge of the rising sun appeared over the road surface before us, a faded, green sign appeared in the distance on the right shoulder of the road. We drew closer until I could make out what was written upon it in once-white letters that had, over the years, faded to gray.

Nothing more than a number: "93." And beneath it two words, just barely recognizable: "Conyngham" and "Nescopeck." And beneath those, a statement: "2 Miles."

"What the hell is a 'mile?'" I asked no one in particular. A series of additional chuckles greeted my question but no one answered…

No one save for Caren.

"It's a vestige of the world we left behind," she said with no hint of amusement in her voice, "something gone, but not entirely forgotten by the people that lived back then. Before… well, *you know*. Don't concern yourself with it."

She concluded her statement as another sign approached that proclaimed the same save for declaring "1 Mile" as opposed to two. At her urging, I did not. I watched as the exit appeared suddenly on the right shoulder of the Highway and Matt taxied the Suburban onto it. I felt a surge of relief as we left the black asphalt of the super road behind us once again. I glanced briefly over my shoulder one, final time at it as we turned a sharp bend (with another, faded brown or yellow sign flanking it, cautioning "25 MPH") and it blessedly disappeared from my sight. Simultaneously, I felt Maria stir against my chest and mumble my name sleepily.

Good timing, kiddo, I thought as we sped down the unused Tributary labeled "93" into the unknown. Moments later, the sun broke over the eastern horizon and daylight filled the world through which we traveled.

Another day in Endworld had begun.

CHAPTER EIGHTEEN

Within moments of when we left the Highway the rest of my companions were awake. Conversation ensued, primarily in the form of questions similar to those that we had been discussing previously. *Where are we? Where and when should we stop for the day? How far have we traveled?* Obviously none of us had the answers to said questions save for the obvious: We were somewhere in the Eastern Territory, otherwise known as the Scorched Land, likely near either the town of Conyngham or Nescopeck, wherever or *what*ever those places were or had been.

In short? We were passing through Bumblefuck as Steve had so aptly put it. We passed by few if any landmarks that might have made identifying our location easier. Primarily, the crumbling tributary labeled "93" that we traveled down was lined with petrified, once-trees and once-bushes that likely hadn't yielded a single leaf, flower or berry in ages. The ground at their bases was a hodgepodge of the same, thigh high yellow grass that seemingly dominated the entire area and old, old litter. Here, an old abandoned tire, there, a discarded cooler, bleached white by extended exposure to the harsh rays of the sun and the elements.

Not to mention whatever residual… whatever exists from what happened here, my coldly rational voice mentioned, *did you think of that?*

Admittedly, I had not. "Hey Matt?" I inquired.

Matt broke away from the conversation he had been having with Caren and Jeff, the topic of which I did not recognize, and acknowledged me.

"Should we be at all concerned with… you know, residual um… *what-ever* from the Scourge?"

He visibly shook his head, seemingly reading my mind, "That happened a long, long time ago William. Any leftover Fall Out has long since diminished to the point that it's no longer harmful to anyone or any*thing* exposed to it unless you're exposed to it for a prolonged period of time. If everything goes the way we hope it will we'll be long gone before we've lingered here long enough to experience any affects. Feel better?"

I nodded to appease him though in truth, I didn't and I returned to my perusal of the road that we traveled down and the "sights" that lined it. I was silent for quite some as I gazed out the window at the occasional ruined house, building or farm. I quickly determined that the two, greatest uniting factors in the Scorched Land were the abundance of ruins and the prevalence of the diseased looking plant life that seemingly covered everything. Not to mention a dearth of water. I had not seen a full lake or an active stream or river since sunrise, only dried beds of all three. I was thankful that, per Tim, a stash of supplies, water included, existed in a secret compartment beneath where Steve and Carole sat.

At least we won't die of thirst or starve to death, I thought. While I perused the surroundings through which we traveled, the majority of the truck's other occupants continued to talk. Eventually, a gentle hand fell upon my still sore left shoulder. I winced, turned and found myself staring into Maria's deep, brown eyes. I smiled instinctively.

"You okay?" she asked with a slight grin, "you're being *really* quiet."

I could detect a note of humor in her voice yet beneath it… *concern?* I bent in and kissed her gently on the forehead.

"I'm fine," I said as I pulled away. I watched as her grin widened, "just thinking. You know, that thing that you accuse me of doing all the time?"

She giggled flirtatiously, "Well, not *all* the time, Willy. I wasn't accusing you of that back in Freeworld One now, was I?"

I smiled, as well. Simultaneously and without warning, the hand that had fallen upon my shoulder shifted to my upper thigh. The movement was imperceptible to the others as they were all still engaged in conversation. I gazed down at her hand and then back up at her. He grin did not waver and her eyes…

They bespoke something less innocent than a simple kiss. My stomach clenched and I stammered but did not speak. I quickly returned my gaze to the area that passed by the truck as she murmured what sounded like "speechless three times in one lifetime… I'm *good*" before her hand retreated back to my shoulder. I did not respond though I *did* breathe a sigh of relief.

I observed that we were driving through what had once been an intersection as evidenced by the two poles that jutted out of the ground and stretched up over the car for a few meters before bending at 90 degree angles and extending out over the street. We sped onward through what appeared to have once been a town, though there was no indication that anyone had ever inhabited it. Up ahead, I saw another sign looming on the right side of the road, marking another intersection. I squinted as I glanced at it and after a moment, I could make out a word and a number painted in black against a white-gone-gray backdrop: "North" and "61." Above that sign was another, smaller one and upon *it?* Two words in what might have once been white lettering against a faded, green backdrop.

"Mt. Carmel" said one and next to it? The number "6," the word "Centralia" and the number "2."

"Must have missed Conyngham and Nescopeck," Jeff said from the front seat and elicited a spattering of chuckles from the group.

"I'm guessing 61 is another road number," Matt said, "like 93. And six and two? Kilometer counts maybe?"

"Or miles," I added as I remembered Caren's lesson from earlier. A few people turned to look at me. I shrugged, "what? It's not as if this place just popped up yesterday. It's been here a hell of a lot longer than we have despite the fact that it looks like it hasn't been inhabited in forever. It's reasonable to assume that it was here before the machines were, right?"

The people that had turned to glance at me—Caren, Jeff, Maria and Tim—all nodded and turned away without a word.

"Well then," Matt said as we approached the intersection, "looks like Centralia is closer. And it's getting pretty damn bright out. No telling who or what is around here or what's following us so let's head for the closer of the two. Agreed?"

We all did and without a thought or a statement to the contrary, Matt turned the Suburban left onto 61 and asked us all to begin looking for a convenient place to stop.

Within a kilometer of when we made the turn off of 93 I could tell that something was amiss. While the road surface of 93 had not been the greatest it was surprisingly manageable when compared to that of 61. The first pothole, if you could even call it that (it was almost a full meter wide and at the least a half a meter deep) materialized on the left-hand side of the road about 100 meters down. Matt almost didn't see it but managed to slow and swerve the Suburban away just before he hit it with the vehicle's left tires.

"Close one," he muttered. Simultaneously, Jeff pointed to another, larger one roughly five meters in front of the truck and in the middle of the road. Matt slowed the vehicle again and taxied left onto the yellow and brown, weed-covered and crumbling shoulder. I glanced ahead through the windshield and I could see that the condition of the road surface did not improve. Rather, it became progressively more and more treacherous with each meter. Fissures extended out from gaping holes that had, apparently, opened up at some point in the past.

Those aren't potholes, I thought. Steve echoed my consideration with his own.

"Sinkholes," he stated, "never a good sign. This ground might be as brittle as ice. There's no way of knowing whether it can support the combined weight of this truck and us, Matt."

"You've got that right," Matt responded as he pulled further and further off onto the shoulder. He slowed the truck to a virtual crawl before he eventually stopped it entirely and shifted the gear shift to the park position, "but if we go on foot we run the risk of falling into a fresh one ourselves. Not a lot of options." He fell silent for a moment before he spoke again.

"Alright, everybody out," he said, "stretch your legs and smoke 'em if you got 'em. Mind the ground swallowing you up. While you're doing that and that, start looking around for a place to crash, preferably someplace off the road and not in one of the gaps in it. Then we'll need to find a place to stash the truck out of sight."

"What about its charge?" Carole asked. Tim was quick to respond.

"There's a spare charger stashed with all of our supplies," he said, "it works via the same technology as our particle blasters. Kind of like a generator only electrical and not fuel-driven. All you need to do is fire it up and plug the truck into it. It should be good for at least enough battery life to get us to Hempstead."

"Okay, then," Matt said as he opened the driver's side door and stepped out of the truck. Caren followed behind him and Jeff exited the other side of the vehicle. The rest of us did as he had asked and filed out of the car one at a time. Once out I helped Maria to the ground and she thanked me with a smile and a sarcastic curtsy. The gaze in her eyes was still slightly mischievous but it had tempered. I was relieved. *Now's not the time,* I thought. Tim got out the other side of the truck as did Steve and Carole.

I began to work my weary muscles as best I could while I surveyed the surrounding area for someplace to stop for the day. As I began walking around the exterior of the car my nose caught the scent of something unmistakable.

Cigarette smoke.

My travels had carried me to a few steps in front of the truck and I turned back to see Tim standing upon the road surface, a cigarette hanging out of the corner of his mouth. Without a thought to the contrary I made my way over to him and asked him if I could have one. He smiled, removed a crumpled pack of unidentifiable cigarettes from his front pants pocket and held it out to me. I obliged by taking one with a "thank you" and instinctively removed my trusty Zippo from my front right jean's pocket. I flipped the lid back and was about to light it when I paused.

Wet, I thought suddenly, *it's probably still wet and will never work again. We got lucky back on the Pass.* Still, I was curious and with the same, practiced motion that I had demonstrated so many times previously I spun the steel wheel...

And silently rejoiced when the familiar, orange-yellow flame with a touch of blue at the center brilliantly kicked forward from it.

Well I'll be, I thought to myself as I placed the cigarette in the corner of my mouth and held the tip of the flame to it, *I'll be damned. Sometimes it's good to be wrong.* I inhaled deeply, exhaled, and snapped the lid shut with a "click."

Reports of my good luck charm's demise have been grossly exaggerated, I thought with a snicker as I replaced it in its customary spot in my left, front jean's pocket.

There's something to be said for that, William, Pat's voice spoke in my subconscious. I felt any tension that I had been experiencing immediately subside as I inhaled deeply again and pivoted around. 61 stretched off for an indefinite distance before us. Ahead I could see the same, stunted tree tops towering over the road but little else. There was virtually no sign of habitation. I pivoted right...

And saw what I thought we were looking for across the road and roughly a kilometer away. It stood like a sentinel over the area atop a ridge on what appeared to be a foothill so it was, in theory, away from the brittle ground upon which we stood. Its main tower was rounded, and something jutted out of the top of it and glistened in the early morning light. I could make out little else save for two smaller towers on either side of the main one with similar... things jutting out from their tops and a general shape: Square. Whatever it was it was shelter and it appeared to be intact. I called for the rest of the group to assemble around me and when they had I pointed to the structure.

"'You think we can make *that?*" I asked no one in particular.

Matt stepped forward and squinted. He smiled, "I think so. Maybe even with the truck. If we backtrack to 93 and keep going straight we might even be able to get closer. Good eyes, William. Any objections?"

There were none.

"Alright then," Matt said, "William and Tim: Finish up those death sticks and let's get a move on. I'd rather not spend any more time out here than I have to. The doc's right: The damn ground even feels thin…

"Like walking on ice."

If only Matt O'Brien had known then how right his initial impression of Centralia was.

Tim and I finished our "death sticks" and we all piled back into the Suburban. Once assembled inside, Matt carefully turned the truck around and headed back the way we had come. He navigated the road surface so as to avoid the sinkholes until we were once again clear of them. A short time later, we reached the intersection and turned back onto 93—left as opposed to right—and continued down it for another kilometer. We were fortunate. The road surface did not deteriorate as it had on 61 save for the occasional, weed-filled crack that zigzagged across the black-turned-washed-out-gray surface. The structure that I had spotted never dropped out of view behind the blighted trees that lined the road for more than a breath. It drew closer and closer until I could finally determine what, exactly, it was.

"It's a church," Jeff corroborated from the front, passenger seat of the Suburban as the hill upon which it sat loomed on our left, "and an old one from the look of it."

I nodded instinctively. The building, upon closer observation, was not as intact as I had originally assumed it to be. There were gaping, brown bare spots on the wall facing 93 where shingles that had once clung to it had fallen off. What siding remained was dirt-bespeckled and faded from exposure. Black streaks (*watermarks,* I thought) cascaded down the side of the building that faced us. The triangular top of the smaller, side tower closest to us was equally as diminished as the wall but I could see what the glistening thing I had noticed atop it was: A modified cross with not only a lone crossbar running horizontally to its shaft but two additional, smaller crossbars equidistant both above and below it.

Like the ones on the guard of Pat's sword, I thought and suppressed another shiver. Save for the smaller crossbars it was. I averted my gaze from the church to the road before us again and saw a small driveway a few meters in front of us. Matt had, apparently, seen it as well. He turned on the Suburban's turn signal (*is there really a need for that, Matt?* I thought) and turned the truck off of 93 and onto it. The cracked surface of it steadily inclined and led, I observed, directly to the hill upon which the church sat.

As we moved closer to it I could clearly see the front wall of the structure. It was similar to the one facing 93 both in its construction and its condition, save for the large once-window turned gaping hole that faced the driveway and the smaller window, still intact, that was positioned above it.

The rounded top of it was crowned by another, larger modified cross and a section of the front of the church nearest the ground jutted out in a covered, walled-in porch. There were steps leading away from the sides of said porch where I assumed the entrances lay that coalesced directly in front of the building and became one staircase before extending down the hillside toward the place where Matt eventually slowed the truck and stopped.

"Looks harmless enough," he said as he gazed across the front seat and out the passenger side window. I could not tell if he was being sarcastic or not.

"Sure… *harmless*," Maria spoke from beside me with a distinguishable note of sarcasm and tension in her voice

"I agree with Maria," Carole said, "it looks a little… um, off-putting?"

"Which is why we need to *investigate* it first," Matt said as he turned around and his gaze first fell upon Maria, and then shifted over my shoulder and fell upon Carole, "'make sure it's safe. If it *is* it looks like a good place to crash. Judging from the height of it that front window provides a great vantage point over this entire area. We'll be able to see anything coming long before it gets here. Jeff: Take William, Maria and Tim up there with you and check it out while me, Caren, Steve and Carole try to find a place to stash the truck."

"It looks like there's another driveway or maybe even a parking lot up there on the right," Caren said, pointing, "we should check there."

Matt nodded.

"Sounds like a plan," Jeff said as he opened the front, passenger side door and swung his legs out. Once he stood upon the driveway at the base of the staircase he removed his pulse rifle from its position upon the floor and hoisted it over his shoulder. He looked back at me, Maria and Tim.

"Okay, campers. No dawdling. Let's do this."

I nodded and opened my own door. As I did I glanced back over my shoulder at Maria. Her face was paler than normal. She seemed visibly shaken.

"It'll be all right," I said as I removed my blaster from its shoulder holster and swung my legs out into the early morning heat, "trust me, Mia."

Her composure softened and she managed a small smile, "Okay," she said and moved toward the door as I turned away from her and exited the vehicle. I could hear Tim doing the same on the opposite side of the truck. Once out and assembled in front of the staircase Jeff motioned for us to move. We did so as Matt slowly pulled the truck away and toward the driveway or parking lot that Caren had indicated.

The staircase was in surprisingly good condition considering the appearance of not only the church, but the entire area that surrounded us. Save for a few, hairline cracks upon the steps they were easily traversed. We gained the top of them in single file—Jeff in the lead, Maria and I in the middle and Tim bringing up the rear—and fanned out across the landing. I glanced at the two separate staircases that extended further upward toward the presumed entrances to the church. Without a word, Jeff pointed to Tim and me and gestured to the one on the left. He then pointed to him and Maria and did the same to the one on the right. All of us nodded in understanding. Without a word, Jeff and Maria started up the right staircase and Tim and I started up the left, our weapons held out in front of us.

"Make sure you click your safety off, William," Tim said without turning from in front of me. I nodded, mentally chastised myself for my nearsightedness, and did so. It disengaged audibly as we began to climb the staircase. My initial suspicion had been correct: An old, oaken door lay closed beneath a slight overhang at the top of them. My heart began to pound more quickly in anticipation as Tim gained the top of the steps and reached out to push it open. He paused.

"Ready?" He asked without turning.

"Go," I responded as I raised my blaster from my side to eye level and prepared for the worst.

Tim laid his right hand upon the door and pushed with a groan. It creaked but did not move. He pushed again. The door emitted a louder creak but still refused to budge. He gasped.

"Warped," he muttered, "and I think my arm is bleeding again. Fuck. Give me a hand, will you?"

I moved forward as he had requested and laid my left hand upon the door's smooth, wooden surface. Tim counted to three and we both pushed at the same time. I gritted my teeth as my still-sore left shoulder groaned in response. The door creaked loudly before something *popped* and it swung slowly inward, its rusted hinges screeching loudly.

Well if there is anyone or anything in here we just forfeited the element of surprise, I thought and stifled a nervous chuckle as the door completed its slow arc and fell still against the front, driveway facing wall of the church's lobby. The early morning sunlight that cascaded in through the shattered window that faced the driveway revealed a small, wood-paneled room. The walls were barren though in places, the paneling was less-faded. Said spots generally were in a square or a rectangle shape, likely where a painting or a poster, long looted or destroyed had previously resided, and the scent of dust-filled air and mildew assaulted my nostrils along with that of old, rotting wood and something else. I tried to place it but I could not. It was spicy, earthy and metallic. Tim obviously noticed it, as well. I watched as he raised his head slightly and inhaled deeply.

"Incense," he said softly and smiled, "old, *old* incense."

I cocked my head, "What's 'incense?'" I responded confusedly, my own voice little more than a whisper.

He glanced over at me but did not lower his weapon, "It was big in religious ceremonies back in the day. Churches used to use it for any number of things. Ritual purification, meditation, prayer… you name it."

I nodded, "How do you…"

"Know about it?" Tim asked as his grin widened, "easy, really. Before I was a…" he paused before he said, *"humachine…* before I ran, back when I was a kid pre-the Glorious Revolution I was an altar boy. I used to assist the priests at my local church during mass. God damn, that seems like an age or two ago. I guess in hindsight it was. Come on. Let's keep moving. Mind the glass."

He looked away from me and gestured to the floor directly beneath the window. I glanced down and saw what Tim had indicated: A pile of dangerous looking, colored glass lay scattered across the tiled surface. I stepped carefully around it and followed him into the interior. Simultaneously I could hear more creaking across from where we stood. I turned and watched as a thin sliver of light appeared against the left door-jam and the door, much like ours had *popped* and slowly swung open with an ear-splitting *creak*. Jeff and Maria stood silhouetted against the daylight beyond, their own, respective weapons drawn and pointed in our direction. Both nodded as they saw us standing just within the opposite doorway and I, instinctively, did the same.

Pleasantries aside, Jeff shifted the business end of his pulse rifle to the left and Tim nodded and turned in the direction indicated after he reiterated his statement to "mind the glass." Another set of double doors, oaken and closed, lay a meter away.

Okay, I thought as the four of us simultaneously moved further into the lobby and positioned ourselves in front of the doors.

"On three," Jeff whispered as he lowered his weapon carefully to his side and laid his free, left hand on the surface. Tim, Maria and I followed suit with our own free hands.

"One… two…" he paused, and then, his voice no longer a whisper but a shout, completed the litany.

"THREE!"

We all pushed on the doors at the same time and they easily swung open. The force that we had collectively generated caused them to smack loudly against the walls beyond and a thick cascade of dust fell upon our heads from the door jamb above us. The suddenness of their opening was a shock and we all stumbled clumsily forward before we quickly righted ourselves and raised our respective blasters and, in Jeff's case pulse rifles up in fear of whatever might await us within.

We realized quite quickly that there was little need for caution. One, single glance at the interior of the church revealed a space that had been deserted for ages. By the light that filtered in through the shattered window behind us we could see a long, roughly meter wide center aisle flanked on either side by rows of dust-covered "pews" as Tim called them upon first observing them. My eyes traced the center aisle from where we stood to its termination at the front of the church. Directly in the middle of a slightly raised platform was what appeared to be a large, white or gray marble block inset with what once might have been a gold relief but in subsequent years had grown green with oxidation.

Behind it, however, was an even more impressive sight: A set of equally oxidized and intricate arching, double doors which stood closed and stretched well above our heads. They were flanked on either side by paintings showing various different scenes, all seemingly tied together by a common thread: The vision of a long haired, bearded man that stood stoically with his one hand held high, his palm wide opened and facing us. The look upon his face was a peaceful one but beneath it I could see an unmistakable sadness. While I was not familiar with who he was I knew without any sort of tutorial from my companions that he was familiar with loss. Tears had been appropriately painted in his eyes though I could no longer determine their color. Age had grayed them.

Jesus, I thought as my eyes retreated from what Tim called the "altar" and traced their way along the walls and over my head. There was little to be seen save for an empty chain hanging five or six meters over our heads. It stirred briefly as a hot, phantom breeze blew passed our backs from the open entrance/exits and the shattered window that overlooked the driveway and the countryside. I could see arched areas where windows, long plastered over had once stood along the side walls of the structure. But other than that…

"Looks like we're alone," Jeff said as he lowered his pulse rifle and took a few steps down the center aisle, "I don't think anyone's been here…"

"In an eternity," came a strange voice from behind us, "abandoned it is, *yes?*" We all turned and brought our blasters to bear on whomever or whatever was speaking in such an unusually nasal and high-pitched voice. We were not entirely unsurprised to see Matt, Caren, Steve and Carole standing a few meters behind us in the lobby, their own weapons at their sides.

"Christ, Matt," Maria said as she lowered her blaster, "you scared the living *shit* out of me."

Matt made a "tsk, tsk, tsk" sound, raised his right hand and shook his middle and index fingers back and forth in time with his head, "Watch what you say in here, Maria," he said in his normal voice, "you don't want to tick off whatever spirit or *spirits* still reside here. This was, after all, a house of God once upon a time. Still is though I can't imagine God as an absentee landlord that would have let one of his properties go to pot this badly. There's enough dust in here for 10 churches."

If Matt had intended humor with his statement he had failed. No one even chuckled. Everyone, Caren included, continued to look at him curiously. Matt apparently noticed the attention he was receiving. He smiled and shrugged, "I... I guess that one was a bit over your heads and under your feet err... *feets*. Is 'feets' even a word? Sorry. New topic: I'm guessing that you didn't find anyone or anything in here?"

Jeff, Maria and I shook our heads in unison. "Seems safe," Jeff responded, "what about you? Find a place to stash the truck?"

Steve smiled, "And some. Caren was right: That driveway that she spotted led back to an old lot. Even better, someone had the presence of mind to build a garage back there."

"A big one, too," Matt interjected.

"There are other vehicles in there," Steve continued, "only two though and definitely not electric. One looked like a little black bubble and had the word 'Neon' on it. The other was older and not nearly as well-maintained. A red hatchback with no identifiable markings on it. But it looked fast."

"Gas-powered," Caren interjected, "even if we could rig something up with the Suburban's battery to get either of them started they probably wouldn't run. Any gas remaining in their tanks likely hasn't been viable in a couple of decades. No telling how long they've been sitting back there. There's almost as much dust on them as there is in here."

"Gas?" I asked.

"Another alternate fuel from *before*," Jeff responded, "the Administration and by association most of humanity has no use for it now that everything is electric. I've heard it said that the Rebellion still uses it where they can... keeps the old refineries going. It lasts longer than electricity, especially in vehicles. A *lot* longer. But electricity is a lot more convenient for the machines and by association…"

"Humanity," I finished for him. He nodded. *Gas powered,* I thought, *another alternate fuel. Another relic from an age long passed.* I'll not lie that I was surprised. The prevalence of the world pre-the Administration seemed to be growing more and more relevant the further east we traveled out of the Mid-Western Territory and into the Eastern.

Gone but never forgotten, Pat's voice echoed in my mind. I nodded a mental agreement as I momentarily considered what other surprises awaited us on our road ahead…

However long that road remained.

"Okay, then," Matt said, "first order of business? Sustenance and maintenance. I don't know about you guys but I'm starving. We stashed the truck in the garage. Tim, we should bring some of our supplies in here and get that portable charger that you mentioned going. Who knows how long we have until the machines catch up to us? I'd like to have the luxury of beating a hasty retreat if needed and a vehicle with no battery charge isn't going to help us achieve that."

"No doubt," Tim said.

Matt nodded, "After that we'll set up watches. Two at a time, stationed by that front window"—he gestured to the gaping hole that overlooked the countryside—"everyone else should rest until it's their turn. No telling how much we'll get from here on out. Anyone have any objections?"

No one did.

"Good," Matt said as he shouldered his pulse rifle and turned to Tim, "we'll handle the supplies. Why don't the rest of you check what little is left of this place out. See if you can find anything useful. We'll be back in a jiff. Oh! And someone should probably clean up that glass near the window, too, if we're going to be setting up a watch post there."

Affirmatives echoed through the interior of the church as Caren, Steve and Carole switched places with Tim. I watched as he and Matt left the building via the entrance that Tim and I had come through. Everyone else moved off across the interior room save for Maria, who moved up to where I stood and brushed her hand against mine. She asked me to "come on" and I did so without hesitation. The two of us moved forward toward the altar to explore what, if anything useful lay there.

CHAPTER NINETEEN

Our search of the interior yielded nothing, save for a few cobwebs and deteriorating, paperback books which disintegrated as soon as we picked them up. A short time later Tim and Matt returned with a few supplies from the truck and informed us that the Suburban was in the process of charging. We gathered in the front of the church upon the altar and divided up the rations between us. All but Matt and Caren who offered to take the first watch. We did not debate them nor deny them their request as we were all suffering from various stages of exhaustion and having food in our bellies did little to help our alertness.

Within moments of when we had finished eating and drinking we stood and headed off to various areas of the church to rest. Maria and I chose one of the pews closest to the altar and climbed into it. I was careful to favor my shoulder as I rested my left side against the far, left end of it and Maria rested hers against my right torso and chest. We sat like that, my right arm draped over her shoulders and holding her closely, until her breathing slowed beside me. When I was sure that she was asleep I carefully laid her down on her side across the pew, quietly stood and retired to the one directly behind it where I, too, lay on my back and closed my eyes.

Sleep did not come easily. I meandered in and out of consciousness as the morning wore on. I was anxious… I wanted to keep moving. I was unsure of how much time we had before the machines caught up to us. Still, I realized the significance of getting as much rest as possible in light of the road that likely lay before us. My gut told me the same thing that Matt's had: That soon, there would likely be no time to rest at all… told me that soon we would be running for not just our freedom but for our lives. Despite the heat and the humidity that was quickly building within the church as the morning progressed toward midday and afternoon, and the fine sheen of sweat that had broken out on my forehead, a chill traversed my spine from bottom to top.

What you did back in Halmier's Pass, my cold and rational voice informed me as I finally began to drift off, *those machines that you incapacitated? That was a game changer. You're not just runners, now. In the optical processors and neural nets of the Administration you're murderers. Whether you believe the term "murder" applies to them or not by their law, the crime that you committed, Robotocide, is a crime punishable by one thing only.*

Just like all the other Crimes against the Administration, I thought. I instinctively reached down and ran my fingers across the right pocket of my jeans. I could feel the outline of the parchment Alex had entrusted to me within… could feel the raised seal with the "sigil" upon it and I was soothed, at least temporarily. It was this thought that followed me down into the darkness as my tired mind, body and soul gave into sleep. While I, Maria, and the rest of our companions slumbered… while Matt and Caren kept a careful watch over the countryside below the hill upon which our temporary shelter was perched…

Time moved onward without check around us.

* * *

"William…

"William…

"*Wakey, wakey, Vato.*"

I opened my eyes. I was still lying on my back in the pew. Above me vaulted the ceiling of the church. Shadows were creeping in from the corners of the room and were quickly infiltrating the structure.

How long have I been asleep for? I considered. I slowly sat up and glanced over the pew in front of me. Maria was still lying there. She had shifted from her side to her back and was breathing slowly but her countenance was otherwise unchanged. I glanced from her resting figure around the interior of the church. Everyone appeared to still be sleeping in the same places that they had originally retired to. I glanced up the center aisle and saw the backs of two, shadowy figures silhouetted against the gaping, once-window-turned-hole in the wall against a quickly darkening, twilight sky.

Twilight, I thought, *Jesus, did I sleep all day?*

"*William!*"

I swung my gaze quickly from Caren and Matt's position in the lobby toward the altar where the shockingly familiar voice seemed to be emanating from. There, not more than ten steps away from me and standing directly in front of the arched, double doors with the tops that extended over mine and everyone else's heads stood a shadowy figure with long, black hair and a stern face. He wore violet-tinted spectacles and a sleek, leather jacket that prominently showed off his strong, upper body. The distinct aroma of leather mingled with cigar smoke graced my nostrils. It was undoubtedly…

"Pat?" I asked hopefully, *"Is that you?"* I glanced down at Maria and back at Caren and Matt but no one stirred despite the way my voice echoed through the church. It was as if they hadn't even heard me speak. I turned back to the figure that stood on the altar.

"In the flesh, William," the figure said. His own voice echoed as he took a step forward out of the shadows and into the fading light that emanated from the once-window that Caren and Matt were stationed by, "well, not really flesh. That's a poor choice of words. How about we just say 'in the whatever.'"

"Um," I began, "okay. Whatever, Pat. Why can't…"

"They *hear you*, Vato?" he interrupted, "they just can't. I don't really understand the specifics of how this"—he gestured to himself—"works, yet. I'm still getting used to it. All I know is that this little visitation is for your eyes and your eyes only like the old song says. Or so I've been informed. Consider yourself fortunate, kid. Apparently we don't get to do this very often."

I was confused. *We?* "Pat, what are you…"

"In short?" he interrupted as he took another step toward me, "you're *dreaming*, Vato. You're still asleep. Look behind you and down if you don't believe me."

I did as Pat had requested and was surprised to see my own, motionless figure still lying on its back in the pew, its eyes closed and its eyelids twitching. I glanced back at Pat. Understanding filled my mind and I nodded. Pat smiled.

"Still a quick study," Pat said as he took another step forward, "still smarter than the average bear. And getting *smarter* from what I've observed. Not so 'green' anymore. That's good, William. *Real* good. Maturity will serve you better than any weapon in the days, weeks… hell, in the months and years ahead."

Despite the depression that swelled within me at the idea of days, weeks, months and years spent running, I continued, "So this… this is a dream and you're a…"

Pat nodded before he could finish, "Right on, William. Remember those haints I told you about that populate this area of the world? I never thought I'd be one of them before I was old and gray. I thought I'd done my time and earned my retirement. Apparently I was wrong about that. Shit, man. I was wrong about a lot of things."

Sadness overtook me and I lowered my head. "I... I know, Pat. And I'm sorry. We found your sword, as well as the guy that took it."

I looked up and watched Pat's eyebrows lift slightly. He took a tentative step closer to the pew within which I sat. His grin shifted from bemused to...

Curious?

"Did you, now?" he asked, seemingly quantifying my observation. I nodded.

"We did and he's... he's been dealt with. Thanks to one of Alex Parker's spotters, Tim Redfield. He won't bother anyone ever again."

The Pat-specter's smile faltered, "Strange," he said, "very strange indeed." He fell silent, lowered his head into the palm of his hand and shook it back and forth. "Christ almighty this is confusing," he added.

"What is?" I asked. Pat looked up from his reverie and looked me in the eyes. His smile intensified. He surprisingly shook his head and made a "tsk, tsk, tsk" sound similar to the one that Matt had made earlier.

"Death," he said contemplatively, "it comes for *all of us*, Vato. Good, bad or ugly, we all die eventually. Put your mind at rest before it consumes you. You didn't expedite my death any more than you expedited Alex Parker's. It was just my time... *our* times, William. It'll come for you one day too but that day? That day isn't today. That's all I can tell you for sure. It might be tomorrow or the next day... I don't really know anything beyond right now and the rules of this whole experience? Well, they're still kind of new to me. 'On the job training,' if you will. Thankfully, there's a bit of a curve, sarcasm fully fucking intended. But as for the present?

"Well, there you go."

His monologue, while not overly reassuring and slightly confusing, was temporarily comforting despite what he had revealed about not only his own but about Alex Parker's fate. My foreknowledge of the first and my newly acquired knowledge of the second caused a renewal of the sadness I had felt upon finding Pat's sword at the termination of Halmier's Pass. I shook the lump in my throat away as best I could.

Regardless of what he says it's my fault, I thought, but did not vocalize.

"Okay," I changed the topic, "I won't. New topic, then: How the hell can you, you know..." I paused. My mind stuttered over the appropriate words to speak.

You're speaking to a figment of your imagination, my coldly rational voice said; *"appropriate" went out the door as soon as you said "Pat." Who's mental now?*

I mentally willed the voice to keep quiet and thankfully, for once it did.

"Be here?" Pat responded, "Well, that's kind of complicated. I leave the scientific and spiritual shit to the scientists and the Bible thumpers. Bear with me, William. Again, I'm learning as I go. Pretty much all that you need to know about why I'm here is that there are places... places like Centralia scattered *all over* the world, not just in this territory, in the Mid-Western Territory or in any other blasted territory but throughout all of Endworld where the line between people like you and... um, manifestations like me is... *thin.*"

"Thin," I reiterated. Pat nodded and took another step forward.

"Like the ground out there"—he pointed up the aisle toward the window where Caren and Matt were standing sentry—"it's real easy to cross over or worse, fall through, at least for a little bit. You saw that first-hand, didn't you?"

I nodded as I thought back to the road surface of 61 that had almost swallowed the Suburban.

"Exactly," Pat said as if reading my thoughts, "what you consider reality, William, is a hell of a lot more porous than you know," he continued, "you'll find that out real, real soon and while it's not my place to address that particular topic with you in what little time I have here I'll give you a little tip but that's it: It involves that sealed parchment that Alex gave you back in Freeworld One."

I reached down and brushed my hand against the outline of the envelope that rested in my pocket. A renewed wave of strength rushed through my body and I asked, "What is it, Pat?"

Pat's smile returned in force, "Some call it the 'Artifact.' Others? Well, others call it other things. It's not my place to explain any of that to you, Vato. All that I can tell you... all that I'm *allowed* to tell you is what Alex did: Keep it safe, and keep it secret. If you need to tell anyone about it tell Maria but *no one else.* That's about as close to an order as I'm ever going to give you at this point in our highly unorthodox, reality-spanning relationship. Heed it. *Heed me.* Understand?"

I nodded but did not speak. I glanced from Pat to Maria and smiled.

So peaceful, I thought, *such a contrast* before I returned my gaze to where the manifestation stood.

"Good," Pat said, "*real* good. You'll learn more about it soon enough. Whether you were meant to have it for even a short period of time or not you have it now. It *does* belong to someone else, just like Alex told you, but you're its keeper for the immediate future."

He paused. I was about to ask him to continue but he did so without my prompting.

"Funny. That actually acts as a nice segue into why I *am* here."

"*Why?*" I asked immediately, unsure if I desired to hear what the Pat-specter had to say (*he is a haint, after all,* I thought). But somehow I was aware that I needed to, and my stomach clenched in recognition of that fact as Pat took another step forward (he was within two, maybe three steps of my position by that point). His smile disappeared and his expression took on the same, pallid hue that it had taken on in his truck directly before the Caravan that had discovered them had revealed itself. "You already know *why,* William. *Subconsciously.* Do you remember what I said to you the last time that we saw each other?"

I did. I had replayed it in my mind multiple times. "'Unus est vera semita, William,' right?"

Pat's smile widened, "Not quite, Vato. Not quite. I'll leave that particular statement for a future time and another..." he paused, "*haint* to address. Not in the clearing but when I visited you in Freeworld One. Do you remember *that* statement?"

My confusion deepened, "Freeworld One? I didn't see you in..."

I stopped. It was at that moment that I remembered what Pat was referring to. No, I had not *seen* Pat in Freeworld One but I had *heard* him. More specifically, I had heard him when I had been unconscious, directly before I had awoken on the cot in Steve's once-office...

I sought my subconscious for the words. After a moment's digging, I recalled them: "'Deceptionis... *possit catus,*'" right?"

Pat clapped his hands together, "*Right on,* Vato. Right on. *Deceptionis possit catus.* They're Latin. Just like the words I spoke to you in the clearing before... well, just before I closed my eyes and I woke up *here.* Just like the words Alex had inked on his arm and just like the words he spoke to you in Freeworld One when he gave you *that*"—he gestured to my pocket where the Artifact rested—"Latin? Well, it's an old language, William. Older than you, older than me, older than the Administration... older than even our oldest ancestors. It hasn't been spoken regularly by almost anyone for centuries... hell, for *millenia.*"

"Then how do *you* know it?" I asked, "How did *Alex,* Pat?"

Pat shrugged, "I said 'almost anyone,' Vato. But like I said before, that's not something I'm supposed to discuss with you. I'm here about deceptionis possit catus. Do you have any idea what that means?"

I shook my head slowly in response to the Pat-specter's question.

"Deceptionis possit catus," he reiterated, "it means *be leery of deception*. Not everything is what and not every*one* is who they seem, William. Do you know why that road down there"—he once again gestured to the front of the church—"is filled with sinkholes? It's not disrepair, Vato. It's not exposure and it's not a byproduct of the Scourge. The ground underneath our feet has been burning for longer than you've been alive... hell, longer than I was alive. It's older than the Administration... older than even the first smart bots. Believe it or not, Centralia used to be a booming mine town. No one knows or knew exactly how the fire started but start it did, and it's been burning out of control ever since. You'll see it tonight, kid: The smoke billowing out of the cracks in the road surface of 61 and the cracks in the countryside. It looks like mist at first glance but I assure you that its not. There's an old cemetary down where the center of town used to be where even the tombstones smoke. I'm not sure if you'll get to see it in the limited time that you're here but it's a sight to behold, man. That damn fire is going to keep burning for ages. There's nothing you, anyone or anything can do to stop it. But to look at it? Centralia just looks like any other empty stretch of land here in the Scorched one. Brown, barren and lifeless.

"But imagine," he continued as he stepped to my left and gestured to the front of the church, "imagine a town *booming* with bars, schools, parks and general stores where now there's nothing but ash and the ocassional blackened tree stump. *That's* the Centralia that our ancestors knew, William. Not what it seems on the surface, huh? *People?* Well, Vato? People can be like that too."

"*People*," I repeated. Another shiver threatened to traverse my spine despite the still-opressive humidity and heat that filled the church's interior.

How can I feel that, I thought, *if I'm asleep?* It was then that I realized the inevitable: *I was waking up.* The manifestation that stood a meter or two away from me was growing thinner... almost transparent, and the series of reliefs behind him... behind *it* on the wall flanking the once-gold-turned-green-with-oxidation double doors (not to mention the double doors themselves) were wavering. Solidity was departing the dream world that surrounded me. I could feel my stomach quivering in anticipation of not hearing what Pat had to tell me and I spoke his name urgently, knowing that our time was short.

"*Pat*," I finally managed, "what do you mean by..."

"*People*, Vato," he said as his figure momentarily solidified and he took a step backward, "even the ones close to you. They're not all what they seem to be on the surface. Not *who* they seem to be. Be leery of deception, William, because there's a..."

I could feel someone shaking me awake and helplessly, the dream-world shattered. The last thing that I saw there before I opened my eyes and stared up not at the ceiling of the church but into Maria Markinson's deep, brown eyes was what remained of the Pat-specter as it seemingly faded into the doors behind the altar like a mist, and the final two words upon its lips. I had never been able to read lips before... had never even attempted to do so, but for some reason I was able to interpret and retain what Pat's last words had been easily. They followed me up into consciousness and into the night which had fallen over Centralia.

Traitor had been the first word. And the second?

Eyes.

Pat's final word had definitively been "eyes."

The figure that had lain upon the hillside directly outside the termination of Halmier's Pass appeared in my mind, as did the sword... *Pat's* sword that had lain beside him. *Were his eyes really confused?* I wondered, *or was that merely what I had wanted them to be?*

"William...

"William..."

* * *

"...*William?*" Maria repeated, "*William?! Wake up!*"

I sat up slowly and saw Maria leaning over the pew back and into my vision. I saw Caren and Matt standing at the edge of the pew within which I rested. Matt raised his hand in a greeting and Caren cocked her head inquisitively. I acknowledged them both with a nod.

"What?" I asked, "Is everything okay?"

"Fine," Maria responded, "everything's fine, William. It's just time for our watch."

Our watch, I thought. "Oh," I said, "oh. Okay." I stood slowly and my joints cracked in response. I reiterated my previous "okay" and added, "Let's go" though admittedly? I had never felt further from okay in my 18 years of existence than I did at that moment.

CHAPTER TWENTY

The remainder of our group was stirring by the time Maria and I had grabbed a quick bite to eat and drink and had assumed our positions by the once-window that overlooked the darkened countryside. The last of the day's light was quickly fading from the sky to our left and I watched it dissipate, first to a light blue, then to a deeper one, and finally to complete blackness. I glanced back out and over the expanse of land that stretched from the base of the hill upon which the church was perched and saw little. The night had disguised any landmarks or features from our view.

I found it disconcerting. How would we see anything approaching us much less the smoke that the Pat-specter had mentioned in our conversation? I relayed my concern to Maria and in response her shadow pointed to an area straight away and slightly to our right. I squinted to see what she was indicating and I caught it: A dim brightness that accentuated the horizon line ever so slightly.

"The moon," she said quietly, her voice almost a whisper, "it was about three quarters full last night. It should be plenty bright by the time it rises. We'll be able to see just fine when it's up."

I smiled and marveled at her observational skills, "I didn't even notice, Mia," I said, "I've been so preoccupied with… well, shit; with everything else that I didn't even consider it."

In the darkness surrounding us I sensed her turn her head briefly toward me before she looked back out the once-window, "I guess that's why you brought me along, huh Willy?"

I chuckled, "No, Mia. I didn't *bring* you anywhere. You *insisted,* remember? And *please* don't call me Willy."

She appeared to nod her head, "Sorry. And I *did* insist, didn't I?" She seemed to glance toward the ceiling in an intentionally exaggerated fashion, appeared to raise her right index finger to her lips and "hmm'd." After a moment she continued, "I believe that what I said was: 'If you think I'm going to let my best friend stroll out of Jefferson *completely unprepared* for what awaits him without me you've got another thing coming. I don't work that way, and you should know that better than anyone after all we've been through.' Sound about right?"

I chuckled again, louder than before, "Perceptive *and* able to remember the most obscure shit. Cute, too. You're the total package, kiddo."

Did she smile? I could not tell but I felt like she did, "The cliché thing to say would be 'I bet you say that to all the girls, William,' but I know you better than that." Her hand fell upon my right thigh again and squeezed, "we *have* been through a lot together, haven't we? Since that first night on the road? I'd bet not exactly what either of us originally expected, huh?"

The stirring that I had felt earlier in the truck returned briefly before I intentionally quelled it. *Stop acting like a pre-pubescent kid,* my coldly rational voice requested. Intent to heed its instructions (and not make an ass out of myself), I turned slightly to the right so that I could lie my left hand over hers, "Not in the least, Mia. And we've still got a lot of road ahead of us. Who knows what'll happen next?"

"Well I know what I *hope* will happen next," she said as she moved her hand from underneath mine, placed it atop it and squeezed gently. The air in front of my face seemingly thickened as she moved closer and while I couldn't see her perfectly I judged as best I could where she was. I bent in until I gauged I was a breath away from her face.

"And what, pray tell, is *that* Maria Markinson? We're on duty you know."

"We can't see anything out there right now anyway, William," she said from a hair or two in front of me, "why waste the moment?"

There was an underlying truth in her words, "My sentiments exactly," I responded and bent in. By whatever luck or good fortune existed in and around the once-town of Centralia and the nameless church within which we were holed-up my lips found hers on my first attempt and we kissed. Our tongues jockeyed for position as our embrace intensified.

We remained that way for an indefinite amount of time before we heard someone clear their throat nearby. We reluctantly pulled away from each other and I turned to see a shadow silhouetted against the darkness of the church and standing within the double doors. The shadow had a large some-thing hoisted over its shoulder. *Jeff or Matt,* I thought as I judged the "some-thing" to be a pulse rifle.

"Sorry to interrupt," Jeff (*well that answers that,* I thought) said, "but aren't you two supposed to be guarding us?"

I looked from the Jeff-shadow to the Maria-shadow and back to the

Jeff-shadow, "Kind of difficult to see anything coming when you can't *see anything,*" I said, paused, and added with a bit of extra emphasis, "*Jeebus.*"

I heard a gasp from the Jeff-shadow which was… thankfully… followed by a guffaw, "Nice one, William. Nice one. You get one freebie, but if you ever call me 'Jeebus' again…"

"He knows," Maria interjected as she tightened her grip upon my hand, "and he won't Jeff. He promises."

"Well okay, then," Jeff said as his shadow moved into the lobby and passed us to the right, "I'm going to go check on the truck. Tim was supposed to be coming with me. *Tim, you coming?*" He shouted over his shoulder. I heard a muffled affirmative from within and the sound of boot falls approaching up the center aisle. I heard what sounded like tapping and simultaneously, a light shot forth out of the darkness within the church proper and a lit the area. I squinted and could clearly see Tim approaching and Jeff standing a step or two away from the right entrance to the lobby. I glanced over at Maria and saw her glancing back at me. Her smile was crafty and seemed to say *get them out of here so we can get back to what we were doing.* If that *was* what she was thinking… and I was quite sure that it was… I was in complete agreement with her.

Tim entered the lobby, nodded awkwardly to me and Maria, apologized to Jeff and told him to "lead away." Jeff turned back to us, smiled by the light of Tim's combination flashlight-phone and said, "You two can continue… *guarding* now. We'll see you in a bit."

With a final wave the two of them turned and walked out the door and down the steps leaving Maria and I once again enshrouded by darkness. I turned back to her but could not tell if she faced me. My question was quickly answered as her lips once again fell upon mine and we continued "guarding" as time moved onward without check over Centralia and throughout Endworld.

Maria was as good as her word. Sometime after we stopped kissing and began watching the countryside, the dim brightness on the horizon grew brighter and brighter. We watched, awestruck, as the moon, only a few nights away from full, rose and bathed the land below us in an eerie white glow. As soon as I could I took in the road to our left—93—and the road a kilometer in front of us—61. I was pleased to discover that nothing stirred on either. The air remained humid and stifling… there was barely a breeze to cool our brows. My own remained covered by a thin sheen of sweat and in the glow of the moon I could see a similar sheen upon Maria's upper lip and neck. I attuned my ears to the area outside the once-window and could hear nothing. I shifted my gaze from the two, intersecting roads to my right…

And saw what Pat had indicated.

"Mia," I said as I tapped her on her shoulder. She turned to me and I pointed to her right, "look over there. See that? Near the ground."

She turned and squinted before she acknowledged that she could, "I see it. Mist, right?"

"Not quite," I said. She turned and looked at me confusedly.

"Its smoke, kiddo," I continued, and proceeded to tell her the story of Centralia that the Pat-specter had conveyed to me. She listened intently, and when I was finished…

"How did you hear about this?" she inquired, "did one of the others tell you?"

I shook my head, "Not quite," I responded and paused. I considered: Was there a better time to tell her what I knew I needed to tell her? About my dream? About the parchment… the Artifact that Alex had given me?

I glanced back over my shoulder at the interior of the church and saw very little. I assumed that Steve and Carole were occupied or sleeping and that Matt and Caren were still doing the same from the lack of noise within. I shifted my glance from the church to the open, right entrance and did not see either Jeff or Tim approaching.

I guess it's as good a time as any, I thought, *though odds are she's going to think I'm nuts.*

No voice from my mental peanut gallery spoke an objection and I resolved to my course of action. "Okay, then," I said, "but promise me something, Mia?"

"Of course," she said, "whatever you need, William."

I nodded my head and smiled half-heartedly, "Promise me that no matter how crazy… how completely *mental* what I'm about to tell you sounds you'll hear me out."

She cocked her head and glanced at me askance before she agreed to do so.

That's about as good a guarantee as I'm going to get, I decided. I took a deep breath and unburdened the secrets I had been keeping to my oldest, dearest and truest friend with little hesitation. I began with the dream I had earlier had of Pat's visitation and I worked my way backward, all the way to the Artifact and what Alex had said to me upon the bank of Little Shenango as Freeworld One had burned behind him. I did not include Pat's final words to me in the clearing. Nor did I discuss the terms that I had gleaned from my earlier dream. *The time to discuss those things is not now, Vato,* Pat's voice cautioned in my mind and I, somewhat reluctantly, heeded his caution.

Maria listened to my whispered monologue without interruption. She did not ask questions. Her expression was, for the most part, unchanged. Most importantly, though? She did not judge. And when I had finished speaking she did not chastise me for my insanity nor did she question whether or not I was completely mental as I had feared she would. What she did do was inquire about the letter.

"Can I see it?" She asked quietly, her tone and her expression still unreadable. I glanced back over my shoulder at the interior of the church and back out the right entrance before I reached into my front, right jeans pocket, pinched it between my fingers and removed it. I extended my left hand out toward her and she plucked the Artifact from it carefully. I felt the all too familiar rush of stamina that I experienced every time I handled it vanish almost instantaneously as she took it and I sighed in resignation. She held the letter up to get a better look at it by the moonlight and turned it over and around. She ran her thumb across the raised seal and in doing so, seemingly shivered despite the oppressive heat that surrounded us.

"It feels… *different,*" she simply said as she handed it back to me. I took it carefully and placed it back in my jeans pocket, thankful to once again have it on my person.

It's almost like when I don't have it there's a hole inside of me, I thought as my fingers lingered upon its surface for an extended moment.

"William?" Maria asked tentatively. I startled and shifted my gaze to meet hers.

"Yeah, Mia?" I asked.

She opened her mouth to say something, and then paused. She shook her head and intoned her own, smaller sigh, "It's nothing. Nothing important. That *thing* that you have, there? Whatever it is its *powerful.* And old. *Damn* old. And that impression on the seal? I thought I caught a glimpse of something similar on Alex's forearm. When he was talking to us by the riverside. Just a glimpse but it *was there,* wasn't it?"

I nodded and exhaled, thankful that she appeared to understand and believe all that I had told her, "I saw it too. A figure-eight cross-cut by an arrow. I have no idea what it means but I can't seem to get it out of my head."

Among other things, I thought and paused, unsure of how to continue.

"And he didn't tell you anything about what's in it? The letter err, the *Artifact,* I mean? Who it's for… *nothing?*"

I shook my head, "Only that I would know the addressee when I met him. At least I know it's a *him*. And then that other Latin bit. *Non multa nostrae solitudini...* 'there aren't many of us left.' Many of *whom*, Mia? I wish I knew more but I'm completely in the dark. I guess it's a good thing that he didn't tell me more in light of what Pat informed me of, huh?"

"Maybe he knew," she stated, "or maybe he guessed. Either way he obviously thought it safer for you to know *nothing* than to know even the slightest piece of... well, shit, William, *everything*. Pat, too, it seems, if what just happened to you a short while ago actually *happened* and wasn't just a dream. I mean, it *was* a dream but... oh Jesus. A girl could go crazy talking about these things."

I nodded. "'Deceptionis possit catus,'" I said, "'Be leery of deception.' What a chilling prospect, even without a name..."

"Or a... face," Maria added. She paused before continuing, "You don't think that... that *thing* we found on the hill outside of Halmier's Pass was what killed Pat, do you?"

I shook my head again, "I don't know what I think at this point, kiddo. All I think... all I *know* is that I... that *we* really need to be on our guard, especially now. The thing with Pat? It felt *more real* than just a dream. I *swear* that he was there... *here*, and I swear that he was telling me the truth. If there *is* a traitor in this group or up ahead somewhere we have no way of knowing who. He or she is either hiding his or her identity really well or is planning to." I gestured to my front, right jean's pocket, "You can't tell *anyone* that I have this, okay?"

She extended her right index finger and ran it down and across her chest in a familiar gesture, "Cross my heart, William. I promise."

"What secret?" came a new, male voice from within the church proper. We turned in unison and saw Steve and Carole standing within the doorway, hand in hand. I looked at Maria and Maria looked at me before we both looked back at the Wetherhills.

"Well it wouldn't be a secret if we *told* you," Maria said in her most innocent voice after a moment's pause, "would it, William?"

"Not at all," I responded and as if to punctuate the point I bent in and kissed Maria gently on her forehead. She feigned a giggle. *Great acting*, I thought and turned back to Steve and Carole.

Steve smiled, shrugged and responded without hesitation, "I guess not. You two okay if Carole and I step outside for a moment? It's *damn* hot in here. We need some air. Matt and Caren are still sleeping though Matt's starting to toss and turn like he's about to wake up."

"No problem," I said, "we're good, aren't we Mia?"

Maria nodded, "Good to go, guys. Go ahead. Mind any sinkholes."

Steve chuckled and waved goodbye as he and Carole walked out the right entrance, descended down the steps and into the night. When they were out of ear shot Maria turned back to me and said, "Nice recovery, William."

I turned toward her and repeated, "You too, Mia. Probably a good time to stop talking about this, huh?"

She nodded in agreement and added, "Talking about what?"

I smiled as I turned and resumed looking out the once-window and over the rolling countryside. *Out of sight, out of mind,* I thought though admittedly? Said mantra, which I repeated incessantly in my mind as the night continued to unfold around us, did little to comfort my suspicions.

Traitor, I thought again, and even more disconcertingly, *eyes.*

Any color that you like, William, Pat's voice warned in my mind. I thought of the parchment hidden in my right, front jean's pocket and my grip tightened upon my blaster.

Steve and Carole returned from their walk some time later, still holding hands and with vivid smiles upon their faces. While neither Maria nor I inquired we shared a humorous glance as they walked passed us and into the interior of the church. Apparently, we were both able to extrapolate what they had been up to during their "stroll." A short time later, Jeff and Tim returned from the garage within which the truck was stowed. By the combined light of the moon and that of Tim's flashlight-phone I could see that both were covered in a combination of dust, grease, dirt and sweat. I inquired as to their progress.

"The truck's just about charged," Jeff said, "we should be ready to roll shortly after dawn."

"*And* we're pretty beat," Tim added, "I don't know about you, Jeff, but I'm going to go crash before it's time for my watch. G'Night, guys."

"Goodnight," Maria and I spoke in unison as Tim walked wordlessly passed us and into the church proper. Jeff echoed our sentiment but did not move. He remained stock still before us. I averted my gaze to meet his and asked him what was on his mind.

"What's going on?" he asked without hesitation, "I get the sense that the two of you have been trading secrets. Is there anything I need to know?"

I turned back to Maria briefly before I re-fixed my gaze upon Jeff's. Maria did the same. A part of me wanted to tell him… to unburden myself to the man that had stood beside us longer than any other on our journey. But I could not bring myself to do so. Pat's words echoed in my mind. *Only Maria,* they reminded me, *Tell no one but her.*

Not yet, I thought and said, "Nothing, Jeff. Nothing at all. You should go get some rest. I have a feeling we'll be joining you shortly."

Jeff shrugged, "Your call, William. But if you change your mind, you know where to find me." With that, Jeff "Jeebus" Howard turned and briskly walked out of the lobby and into the church proper. I turned from his departure, shared a brief, knowing glance with Maria and returned to my perusal of the countryside. A short time later, Steve and Carole appeared from within the church to relieve us of our watch and we gladly relinquished it.

"Feel like taking a walk?" Maria asked me suddenly as we stood from our positions by the once-window, holstered our blasters and stepped aside so that Steve and Carole could assume theirs, "I'm not really tired at the moment."

I nodded, "Me neither," though admittedly? My statement was far from a complete truism. In truth? My eyes had been growing heavy for the better part of the last… however long we'd sat scanning the countryside and, since I was unsure of how much time to rest we would have during our journey ahead, the prospect of sleep appealed to me greatly. Still, the look in Maria's eyes bespoke her intentions and, assuming that my suspicions were correct, I was unaware of when we would have any time to ourselves again. So I agreed to go on a "stroll" with her through the stifling and breezeless, moon-lit night. Steve and Carole bade us farewell as we stepped out through the right entryway and started down the steps. I was unsure of where we were going. I let Maria lead the way.

We walked to the edge of the building that Steve and Carole had rounded and Jeff and Tim had rounded more recently without a word exchanged between us and stepped around it. No sooner were we out of Steve and Carole's sight than Maria, without warning, forcibly pushed me back against the wall of the church and kissed me. While I was caught off guard by her surprising forwardness it did not take me long to concede to her wishes and kiss her back.

Our kiss was not what it had been in Freeworld One, nor what it had been earlier while "guarding" the rest of the group. It was not innocent but passionate, and underlain with something base and primal. I quickly turned her around so that her back was up against the wall of the church and she emanated a dual gasp and sigh in response but her lips never left mine. They did, in fact, lock tighter. Without relinquishing our embrace I began to pull the bottom and the tail of her shirt out from the top of her jeans and she raised her arms over her head to make the process easier for me. No sooner had I managed to pull her shirt passed her hands, exposing her virgin-white skin and a sheer, black bra she had inherited from either Caren or Carole then she pulled away from me almost as quickly as she had originally accosted me.

"Not here," she said breathlessly, "too close." She hectically glanced over her right shoulder and pointed to the large, hulking structure that lay about 10 meters away from us across the cracked, black top parking lot that seemingly everyone *but* Maria and I had seen firsthand.

The garage, I thought. I nodded. Without a word, we fled across the parking lot toward it.

We gained the entrance quickly and slipped inside. What little moonlight infiltrated the interior of the structure revealed the familiar shape of the Suburban and two unfamiliar shapes on either side of it.

The Neon and the vehicle with no name, I thought and stifled a chuckle as I glanced down at my right hand which still held Maria's shirt and then at her, topless save for the sheer, black undergarment that she wore. The stirring in my chest and midsection intensified as I moved toward her and embraced her again. The force of it forced her... forced *us* backward until I felt and heard Maria's back collide gently with the side of the closest vehicle. Her hands moved to the holster that held my weapon. She deftly removed it and placed it upon the roof of the vehicle. Thereafter her fingernails dug into the skin beneath my t-shirt. They struggled for purchase on the garment and I assisted her by removing it myself.

Once bare-chested her hands moved from my back to my belt buckle which she grasped purposefully. I, in turn, reached for her holster, removed it from around her waist and placed it atop the vehicle next to mine. My hands then shifted to her belt and I quickly began the process of removing it. She did the same for mine. Once free of any accoutrements we shifted to my left—her right—our kiss unbroken and as forceful as it had yet been until we were parallel with the hood of the car. Maria hoisted herself up onto it with little assistance and lay back in a slightly humorous "poof" of dust. I followed suit with a stifled chuckle and positioned myself directly beside her. The same "poof" materialized from beneath me but I... but *we* were undaunted. At last, our embrace broke and we gazed at each other, my blue eyes into her brown ones.

"Not quite *Le Chateau,* huh?" I asked between breaths.

A ghost of a smile eclipsed her face, "Not quite. But it'll..."

"Serve its purpose," I interrupted her. Her tiny smile faded and I experienced a sudden rush of doubt and concern.

"Mia," I whispered to her, my own grin fading, "if you're not sure... I mean, if you don't want to do this..."

She silenced any further objection by placing her index finger over my lips and said, "I've never been *surer* about anything."

My grin rematerialized and transformed into a smile beneath her finger, "What should we..." I began, my voice muffled.

"*Shhh*," she intoned and pressed harder upon my lips, "everything and anything, William MacNuff. *Everything and anything.*"

Without warning, she moved atop me. And all that happened next? If you've followed me this far you can probably figure out the specifics. There really is no need for me to detail them for you in the pages of this manuscript. Considering all that has happened since mine and Maria's last, late night or early morning rendezvous there in that dusty and crumbling garage in the once-town turned smoking wasteland of Centralia... well, simply put, I've dawdled here long enough.

I will say this, however: *During* the act I experienced a strange feeling, that of touching the soul of the entire universe. Not just Endworld but *all* worlds seemed within my grasp and in my mind's eye the mark upon Alex's underarm... a mark duplicated upon the seal of the letter he had entrusted me with once again materialized.

Strange, I thought despite what was occurring, *what does it mean? What do they all mean? Skews, Gateways and Pathfinders, too? And the Artifact?*

Simultaneously Pat's final words, not the ones spoken to me by an ethereal representation of his voice in Freeworld One but the ones spoken to me as he stood, silhouetted against the shifting light of his burning once-truck, again returned to my conscious mind and threatened to distract me.

Unus est vera semita, William, I thought. But his words and all others were quickly forgotten as our moment quickened and reached its culmination. I remember that I experienced a transient feeling of loss as it ended but said feeling promptly faded and was replaced by one of solitude and peace as Maria slowly shifted from atop to beside me and laid her head breathlessly upon my chest. We lay there like that, our naked bodies wrapped tightly around each other, somewhere between consciousness and sleep as the three-quarters full moon continued its passage across the sky above us. We did not speak...

There were no words left that needed to be spoken. Or so I thought then.

Sometime after, as I was dosing off I heard Maria whisper something drowsily. It was faint and I was half asleep when I heard it but hear it I *did*. Much like the Latin phrases I had heard spoken by Pat and Alex it was indistinguishable at the time. Subsequently? I have made it a point to uncover its meaning.

The phrase that she spoke was "Je t'aime." And it's meaning?

"I love you."

Had I known then what I know now I would have returned the sentiment… would have shouted it across the barren and smoking wasteland that had once upon a time—because all good stories begin as such—been called "Centralia." Instead, I smiled and pulled her warm, semi-naked body (she had changed back into her bra and pants as had I) closer to mine in a gesture of security and thought but did not vocalize, *I'll never let you go, Maria. So help me God, gods or whatever deities watch over us I will never, ever let you go. Life or death, kiddo. Freedom or bust. That is a promise.*

Semi-consciousness faded to *un*consciousness and for the last time in as long as I can remember, up to and including these last few *whatevers* here in my hovel sandwiched between a nameless river and the Highway, I rested peacefully in a dreamless sleep.

* * *

Sometime later, as the moon began its slow descent and eventually dropped behind the church overlooking Centralia, ET, a figure stood within the shadows of the entrance to the garage and observed the two, sleeping figures that lay a top the hood of the nameless vehicle within, their scantily clad bodies intertwined. His stomach revolted at the sight of their embrace and he once again rued the fact that he had been born human.

Thy nature is too full of the milk of human kindness, he chastised himself. He longed to reveal his true nature but he knew that he couldn't.

Not yet, he thought. Revealing myself now would warrant certain death either by their hands or by the hands of the Administration.

And he was not ready to die.

His eyes did not dawdle long on the girl or on the shape of her body. He had no need for such pursuits in his life. Rather, his eyes traced the shape of the boy's down past his bare chest and torso. They fell upon his upper thigh, specifically upon his jeans. More specifically upon the right, front pocket of them. He knew what resided within said pocket and had known for a while. It was not just the square outline that was visible through the fabric: An outline with a raised, seemingly circular something in the middle. It was the way that the boy, little more than a child favored said pocket, his hand constantly returning to it and either tapping it or reaching within it, seemingly in an attempt to assure himself that "it" was still there.

He knew what "it" was. The Artifact. The thing that the Administration sought.

The same Artifact that he had been looking for, for much, much longer.

MacNuff had it. He was sure of it.

He considered doing it at that moment. The hand not holding his blaster reached into his pocket and he felt the cold steel of the blade concealed within it. He could move on them silently while the others inside the church were distracted or sleeping. He had done it before. They were slumbering and they were unarmed, their weapons lying docilely upon the roof of the vehicle. He was practiced with the blade and he knew that two simple flicks of his wrist would result in the same eventuality that waiting would. He could dispose of the Jefferson runaways, acquire the Artifact and flee into the night before any of the other fugitives knew what had transpired. He would meet up with his machinated counterparts... would present them with it and would be counted as a hero amongst their ranks.

He shifted forward a step. His fingers tightened on the hilt of the blade as his anticipation built...

He paused.

No, he thought, not yet. He could do it, he understood, but even if he escaped unscathed and undetected from the fugitives' encampment, he knew that upon rendezvousing with the army that was tracking them his life was forfeit. For the acquisition of the Artifact was not the mission that his superiors had imparted upon him. The Administration was unaware of his own, personal interest in it. As far as they knew? He was doing what he did best: Infiltrating a group in an attempt to gain access to the Rebellion. Specifically, Free Caymen. If it did exist... well, he thought, that posed a big problem to the machines.

He stopped and retreated one... two steps out of the garage and into the night. He stopped caressing the blade of the knife in his pocket and reached with his other hand into his other pocket. Within it, he felt another object. It was smaller than the knife but equally as important and it was smooth to the touch. Once activated it would give off a low-frequency signal that would allow the Administration to track where he was at all times. Once activated it would lead them right to him.

He smiled and chuckled, Oh no, not to me, he thought as he turned and started to walk back across the cracked black top of the parking lot toward the church. Dawn was approaching. He knew this not because of anything palpable, for the night was still dark and silent, but because of something integral inside of him: Something that had developed over his many, many years of existence.

An instinct.

Each new day is a new opportunity, he thought, a new chance. Not to fulfill the commands of the Administration. Oh no, he knew. The robots were supplemental: A means to an end but not the end. Each day, he thought, is a new opportunity, a new chance to fulfill my own destiny.

My one, true path he thought, and smirked.

For who so firm that cannot be seduced, William MacNuff, he thought. No one, he understood as he gained the front edge of the church, turned the corner and headed back up the steps toward the church's entrance. The grin upon his face was unbroken and the concealed sparkle in his confused eyes—blue, green, brown and hazel. Gray and black: Any color that you like—was undiminished despite the absence of light. He looked up into the sky as he had so many times previously in so many, different Skews. The moon had set.

He pressed the button that activated the tracker hidden within his pocket.

No one, the Infiltrator thought again, and stifled a laugh.

CHAPTER TWENTY ONE

The first thing that I realized as I opened my eyes was that the area surrounding me (*the garage,* I thought groggily) was lighter. The second thing that I realized was that the dusty, red vehicle hood upon which I lay was empty save for me. I turned from my right side to my back and sat up. My joints creaked in protest and I groaned. Maria stood a meter or so away from me, fully clothed again with her blaster once again strapped around her waist, her arms crossed across her chest. She giggled as I craned my neck first left and then right. I favored her with a cockeyed glance and asked her, "What's so funny?"

She moved toward me, bent forward and placed her hands upon my knees, "You," she said as she bent in closer and kissed me quickly before she pulled away, "you'd think that all this time spent sleeping in cars and on the ground would have improved your tolerance for sleeping on uncomfortable surfaces."

"Obviously not," I said as I stretched my arms over my head and groaned again. I glanced passed her and out the entrance to the garage. There was a definite glow to the world outside that bespoke the arrival of the new day. While I could tell from the dimness that it was still pre-sunrise I wondered at how long we had been out and asleep for. Had anyone come looking for us? If they had they had been courteous enough to not interrupt our slumber and for that I was appreciative. My thoughts lingered briefly on how we might have appeared to a casual observer but I brushed said thoughts aside.

It doesn't matter, I thought, *they all know about us. No secrets left to keep.*

Secrets. The word alit recognition in my mind. My post-awakening grogginess vanished immediately and I felt my proverbial heart drop from my chest into my stomach. I instinctively reached down with my left hand and touched my front right jean's pocket…

I felt the familiar shape of the Artifact within it. I sighed in relief, removed my hand from my thigh and looked back at Maria. Her hands still rested upon my knees but her smile had faded. She inquired if I was okay and I told her that I was.

"Is… is *it*…"

I confirmed for her that the item that I carried was safe. She nodded her head and simply said, "Good."

You need to be more careful, William, my coldly rational voice cautioned, *now more than ever before.* I almost nodded my head in agreement but refrained.

"We should get back," I said instead as I shifted forward. Maria removed her hands from my knees and nodded again. I slid off of the hood of the red vehicle with no name and got to my feet. I turned and saw my t-shirt laying near where my head had lain. I grabbed it and pulled it back over my head…

I stopped.

My shirt still up around my chest, I cocked my head, and looked at the vehicle askance. *It can't be,* I thought as I absently pulled my shirt the rest of the way down and over my midsection. I took a step toward it, bent in, and looked through the driver's side window. By the dim light emanating from the door behind us I could see that the interior was gray. It was definitely old, as everyone else that had seen it had confirmed. In places, I could see the insulation beneath the fabric poking out. I looked down and saw a gear shift between the two seats; I looked forward at the dashboard and observed the analog gauges for "speed," "fuel" and "temperature."

Only one thing left to confirm, I thought, and felt my heart begin to race as I looked over from the gauges at the dashboard…

And breathed a sigh of relief. Instead of a slightly askew stereo there was nothing. Not even a radio. The area where a radio or a stereo *should* have been was empty. Old, frayed wires of indistinguishable color snaked their way out of the hole and in to the open.

What the fuck does that mean? I thought as I straightened up and looked down the hood of the car. It was long, and slightly slanted. Was it the vehicle from my earlier dream of Jefferson-not-Jefferson? It could be, I understood, but the idea seemed more than unlikely.

More like insane, I thought as I took a step back and attempted to shake it away. Maria inquired as to what was wrong.

"Nothing, Mia," I said as I took a step back, "just… just a little déjà vu, is all. I'm fine." The last thing I wanted to do was give her any more reason to think me "mental." Instead, I removed my holstered weapon from the hood of the vehicle without another word and strapped it back on. Once clothed and armed I took Maria's hand in mine and led her toward and out of the garage. She did not hesitate, and I was thankful.

Better to just leave it behind me, I thought. Despite my nagging desire to do so, I did not look back over my shoulder at the nameless red vehicle. Maria and I emerged into the growing light of dawn to find the parking lot empty and the air as still as it had been earlier. With a final glance into each other's eyes and a quick kiss we headed off across the black top toward the edge of the building and the entrance to the church.

A new day in Endworld had begun.

Our presence had been missed but apparently no one had questioned it. We arrived back with little fanfare. Jeff and Tim were on guard duty when we re-entered the building and acknowledged us with "hellos." Steve and Carole sat upon the altar eating what amounted to a makeshift breakfast of rations and water and Matt and Caren sat in one of the corners of the building. They were talking… *planning,* I realized as we walked passed and acknowledged them with a greeting. They returned it as we made our way to where Steve and Carole sat and joined them in their "feast" as the sun continued its ascent over Centralia.

Sometime later Caren and Matt stood from where they had been sitting and moved to relieve Jeff and Tim. I did not hear the exchange between them as I was still sitting upon the altar and was engaged in idle conversation with the Wetherhills and Maria, but I watched as Jeff and Tim stood and moved in separate directions. Tim came inside the church and lay down immediately in the pew nearest to the entrance, and Jeff headed out the right entrance.

Back to work, I thought as Caren and Matt took up their positions by the once-window.

The sun rose into a cloudless, hazy sky. We talked some more. Steve and Carole went for another walk through the building heat and humidity outside and Caren and Matt continued to observe the countryside for any activity. Tim continued to sleep.

And Maria and I? Well, we rested and chatted about all that we had been through and all that potentially lay before us. We mused about what we would do upon successfully escaping to Free Caymen. All in all it was a quiet and borderline normal day. One of the few either of us had had since leaving Jefferson…

And one of the last either of us would ever have.

I cannot say for certain how much time passed but per the position of the sun it was well passed midday when Jeff returned from whatever work he had been undertaking in the garage and Steve and Carole returned from their walk. Maria and I were gathered with Matt and Caren in the lobby of the church when they came strolling up the steps, Jeff with his pulse rifle hoisted over his shoulder in its familiar position, his face, hands and arms still covered in dust, grease and dirt and Steve and Carole with their blasters holstered, hand-in-hand.

"Well, Grease Monkey," Matt directed toward Jeff as first he and then the Wetherhills gained the top step and entered the lobby, "what's the verdict?"

Jeff sighed, "Good. The truck's fully charged and ready to go whenever you guys are. My suggestion is to get moving as soon as sleepy-head in there"—he gestured to Tim's snoring figure—"wakes up or we wake him up. No telling how much lead we've lost to the machines or how much time we have before they figure out where we are. I think getting back to the Highway and heading east post-haste sounds like…"

"A damn good idea," Carole interrupted from behind him. We all turned to glance at her and she continued, "I don't think any of us disagree with that, Jeff. The sooner we get to Hempstead the better."

Jeff nodded and shifted his crouch slightly. He laid his pulse rifle down on the ground in front him.

"Shouldn't we wait until the sun sets?" I asked cautiously, "you guys said it yourselves yesterday. Driving during the daylight…"

"Is *risky*, William," Matt responded, "but not unfeasible. What time exists is against us and we've dawdled here long enough. Besides, sunset's only a few pre-Administration hours away. By the time we get packed, get on the road and get back to the Highway it'll at least be twilight."

He stood from his perch by the window. "Let's get moving," he said, "I'll keep an eye on the countryside if you guys want to start packing up our travels. Someone wake up the Marine. He's slept long enough."

I looked at Maria and Maria looked at me. *Time to light out again,* I mentally informed her. Understanding crossed her features. She smiled and nodded.

"Ten four, Pancho," Steve said as he and Carole headed past Jeff and us and into the church proper. The rest of us followed suit. As the stifling, Centralia afternoon segued slowly into pre-twilight and we readied for our departure.

Matt had been correct. By the time we had "packed up our travels" and had loaded up the Suburban the sun was within a sliver of dropping below the western horizon. We filed into the truck in the same order that we had originally filed into it at the termination of Halmier's Pass with one exception: Jeff took over the driving duties from Matt.

As we pulled through the open garage doors onto the rutted, black top parking lot, onto the driveway and eventually back onto 93 I rolled down my window and shifted my gaze from the church to the sky overhead. It remained cloudless and hazy. I closed my eyes and allowed the dual sensations of the warm breeze that blew by the car and the setting sun's heated touch to caress my cheeks. I imagined what that same sun would feel like in Free Caymen. I pictured myself standing or lying upon a deserted beach that overlooked the Great Sea in the same position: My eyes closed and my neck craned upward toward the sky. Maria was there, as well. I could sense her standing or lying beside me.

Free, kiddo, I thought optimistically, *we made it.* Reluctantly I lowered my head after a moment and re-opened my eyes. The vision faded as we passed by the intersection of 93 and 61 and hurtled onward up the broken, unused tributary of the Highway, back toward the super road. We left the once-mining town turned ghost town of Centralia behind us forever.

Gone, but not forgotten, Pat's voice spoke in my mind.

Agreed, I answered. My brief moment of serendipity over I rolled my window back up and refocused on the road that unfolded before us. The towns that we traveled through in the growing darkness—*Nescopeck and Conyngham* I remembered—were unchanged.

As if they would have magically altered their respective appearances overnight, I thought with a chuckle.

Conversation within the truck was limited. Seemingly everyone, myself included, wanted nothing more than to cover the remaining kilometers of our journey toward Hempstead and the hypothetical points beyond as quickly as possible. Before I knew it, Matt was taxiing the Suburban back onto and up the ramp to the Highway. With a slight *bump* we traversed the last pothole in our path and found ourselves once again careening down the black asphalt super road. Jeff turned on the Suburban's headlights and they sliced into the gloom before and around us.

Similar to when we had first re-embarked upon the Highway at the termination of Halmier's Pass I felt my heart drop into my stomach. Centralia, while disconcerting in its own right, had for me represented a vestige of the world *before.* There was something oddly comforting in that thought then and remains so now, any time that I encounter some sigil or representation of the world as it was pre-the Administration and their Glorious Revolution. The Highway represented and continues to represent the institution. Apparently, I was not alone in my assessment of the super road as I heard a series of muffled gasps and inrushes of breath from my companions.

Great minds, I thought.

We continued our speedy trek eastward as the day's remaining light disappeared from the sky. The appearance of the land quickly faded to shadow though it remained light enough long enough for me to see that the foothills of the mountains that we had previously seen in the distance had crept steadily closer to the shoulder of the Highway. Sometime later… I honestly don't know how long, the truck's headlights illuminated a faded green sign by the side of the road. It was similar to the others that we had seen during our trek down the Highway with one, notable exception. Someone had taken black paint and had scrawled letters and numbers upon it.

Join the Revolution, the letters said, and beneath them, a number and two more letters: *1010 AM.*

Apparently, I was not the only one that noticed the anomaly as we drove passed it. Jeff looked across the front seat of the truck at Matt and Matt looked back at him. He shrugged.

"Worth a shot," Jeff said as he reached down and pressed one of the dials on the radio. Simultaneously, a portion of it lit up. It, too, was analog, and was filled with lines and numbers. Jeff twisted the same dial that he had pressed to turn it onto his right—*the volume,* I understood—and a low "thrum" of static filled the car. He reached over with the same hand, pinched a similar dial between his index finger and his thumb and twisted. The static faded in and out as he did so until at last, the bar paused somewhere between the numbers "1000" and "1100," and the static was replaced by…

I audibly gasped.

There was a voice speaking over the vehicle's sound system. It was faint but it was definitely a voice. *Male,* I thought, *deep and confidant.* It was not the voice that I had heard in my dream though admittedly, it sounded similar.

"Well I'll be," Matt said, "turn it up, Jeff. Let's hear what he has to say."

"Who?" Maria asked from beside me.

"Don't know, Maria," Jeff said as he returned his fingers to the volume dial, "Mister 'Join the Revolution,' I guess." He turned it to the right and the voice grew more distinct.

"Wow," Matt said, "that's got to be what, Caren, a hundred kilometers, maybe more away from us judging from the reception?"

"At least," Caren said.

"Well I'll be damned," Steve said, "it looks like we found one of the inhabitants of the Scorched Land Alex was talking about."

"One," Carole added, "or *more.* It takes more than one guy to run a radio station, sweetie. You know: You did it."

"Right," Steve said, "back before the world ended. And that says *nothing* of whether they're friendly to outsiders or not."

"Could everyone *be quiet please*," Tim interjected, his voice annoyed, "*Jesus*. I want to hear what he has to say, don't you?"

Everyone did as Tim had requested and focused their attention on the broadcast. *Join the Revolution*, I thought, *fitting* as the voice continued its un-broken rhetoric.

"There are some," it said, "some that don't *believe* in the power to *over-come* the oppression. The totalitarian, ruling party that grinds us beneath its collective, metal boot heel. 'The center can never hold,' they say, 'not against odds so overwhelmingly against us. *We don't have the technology*,' they cry. They *gnash* their teeth and they *rend* their garments and they *scream from the mountaintops* that they cannot overcome. '*We cannot overcome!*' But we *can* my brothers and my sisters. *You* can."

No one spoke. Everyone in the Suburban was seemingly entranced by the voice, speaking...

Preaching, I thought, *he's preaching*...

...over the sound system.

"They have *tried* to suppress us," it continued, "Not just in this world, but in the others. They have tried by *genocide* but they have failed. They have tried by creating a *utopia* but they have failed. In each and every world they have *failed* miserably. But *here*? Here in *this* world they have succeeded by adopting a *new strategy* of *gradual oppression*. They have *chained* us with our own complacency. They have *chained* us with a purpose. *Their* purpose. They have made us *believe* that what they *do*, they *do* in our best interests. Why, you ask? Because they *need us*. Their existence as a species *requires* us but they will not concede this. *Never*. Hear my words, for they are spoken in the voice of your *soul*. The *one thing* that you will always have that they *won't*. No matter how many upgrades they endure, *you will always have something that they don't*. That they *can't*. The human soul is *insuppressible*. It is *eternal*, while the machine in all of its so-called perfection is *finite*. So says Billy Preston. Speak *amen* brothers and sisters if you understand me."

Amen, I thought as I recalled my conversation with Pat over breakfast in his once-kitchen in Greentree, MWT. Whoever Billy Preston was, he appar-ently believed in the same ideas as Pat. The same Administration motives. But were they the correct motives? I did now know. Nor did I vocalize these thoughts. I, like everyone else, listened intently as Billy Preston continued his rhetoric.

"You have *lost* your *way* my brothers and my sisters. Here in the *Pen* they cannot touch us. Here in the *Pen* we are *free*. If you are looking for a way out… if you are looking to escape, don't look east. *Fool's Gold.* And don't look west 'lest you *be* a *fool.* Look *south. Look to the Pen,* my brothers and sisters. Come *see* your friend Billy Preston. Make a life for yourself *here,* away from the influence of…"

"Christ," Jeff said, "he sounds like a fucking pre-Administration, backwoods preacher…"

"Crossed with a travel guide," Caren concluded. Matt nodded.

"It's a *revival!*" Matt shouted in a voice surprisingly similar to Billy Preston's, "can you *give* me a *hallelujah?!*"

"Well," Carole giggled, "at least we know we're not alone out here, though I'm not sure how reassured I am by my *friend* Billy Preston's words."

"Copy that," Steve said, "I think I'll pass. Anyone feel otherwise? We can pull over and let you out if you'd like to run south and join him, wherever he is."

"Funny," Carole said. Tim chuckled, as did a few of the others. But I did not. In truth? I did not acknowledge my desire, either way. I could still hear my "friend" Billy Preston speaking quietly about what sounded like "lions" and an "herbal" something but that was all. After a while, his voice faded away and was replaced by the same, low "thrum" of static that we had heard when Jeff had originally turned on the radio.

As if reading my thoughts, Jeff reached down and pressed the dial again. The glow, the numbers and the lines faded and silence, broken only by the sound of the truck's transit down the Highway once again descended over the interior of the car.

"*Well then,*" Matt said, "so much for the entertainment portion of tonight's program."

No one spoke in response. Not even a chuckle, as time moved onward without check over the little corner of Endworld which we travelled through.

After a short while during which I intermittently dozed in and out of sleep, the headlights of the Suburban illuminated another faded, green sign. There were no words painted upon it in black and I was grateful. I had seen and heard enough about "the revolution" for the night. The sign advertised, in peeling white or gray letters, the "Delaware Water Gap."

Water, I thought, as I remembered seeing a large river roughly three quarters of the way east on the Highway toward the road—9—that Alex had indicated on his map. I was afforded a moment's elation as I made the potential connection and brought it to the attention of my companions.

"Right on, William," Matt said from the passenger's seat, "up ahead is actually the place where a once-river cuts through the mountains before continuing onward toward the once-cities south of here and beyond. If I remember my geography correctly, the river eventually lets out into a thing called a 'bay'… kind of like a mini-Great Sea. This river *also* used to mark the border between two once-*States*."

"I love how everything with you people is a 'once,'" Tim said sarcastically and elicited a spattering of chuckles from mine and Maria's companions.

"'States?'" Maria inquired.

Caren turned and addressed us, "The pre-Administration version of Territories though they were a lot more numerous. There were 50 in all, I think."

"51," Jeff corrected from the driver's seat, "don't forget Puerto Rico."

"Did they actually make that a state?" Steve asked from behind me.

"Right before the machines became self-aware," Jeff replied, "it was one of the last things the government did before… well, just *before*."

I made another connection and interjected: "The United *States* of America, right?"

Caren nodded, "Bingo, William. Though…"

"Who's to say the river itself even still exists now as anything other than a dried streambed?" Matt continued.

"Just like all the *other* ones that we've driven passed," Jeff added, "kind of a disconcerting prospect, Matt."

"Well?" Matt asked, "*'watcha 'gonna do?* We'll find out soon enough. Not far now." Nods and mumbles of affirmation from those assembled in the truck followed. We crested a hill, rounded a bend in the super road…

And saw it by the glow of the Suburban's headlights.

I was not the only one in the truck that gasped at the sight, what little of it we could see. I'm not sure what was more shocking: The expansiveness of the space that the Gap seemed to occupy or the unmistakable presence of rippling water within it. As we descended into the valley upon the surface of the super road I observed that the Highway wound along the bank of the waterway for as far as my eyes could see. Nearer and to our immediate right the brown and barren hills—barren save for the occasional scrub brush and that God-be-damned, sickly-looking yellow "grass" that seemed to prosper everywhere in the Scorched Land—through which we had been traveling slanted downward toward the shoulder of the road below and terminated within a meter or two of the blacktop. There was no fence or barrier as there had been to the west. Nor was there one to our left as we gained the foot of the hill and continued on where, no more than five or six meters away from the Highway, the land simply dropped away as it had near Little Shenango.

I could see that the surface of the water within the riverbed began at least two or three meters below the termination of the dry and crumbling soil and stretched for roughly 30 meters before it vanished into shadow. It was flowing swiftly, but in opposition to both Shenangos it was not swollen with rain water or runoff. It was relatively clear, so much so that even by the diminished field of light cast by the truck's headlights I could clearly see the pebbles and the stones that bespeckled the ground beneath it.

That looks shallow enough to wade in, I thought, *I wonder when the last time it rained here was.* I could not see the opposing bank of the river though I sensed that it rose up and into hills similar in size and scope to the ones that we had been traveling through.

"It's," Maria began, "it's…"

Jeff flashed Maria a smile in the rearview mirror, "It's difficult to describe, isn't it?" he said, "don't feel as though you have to, Maria. Somehow it's beautiful and yet so…"

"Lifeless," I interrupted, "and sad."

"'Kind of like this whole place in microcosm," Matt turned and added, "I hear you, William."

"I can imagine it the way it *might* have looked," Carole said from behind me and I turned to face her. I swore that in the minimal light that reflected back into the vehicle's interior I could see tears in her eyes, "maybe during springtime when there were trees all over the hillsides with freshly grown leaves upon them…"

"Or during summertime when those same trees were lush and sparkled with rainwater after a thunderstorm," Caren continued. I nodded as I shifted my gaze forward.

"Or in autumn," Steve added from behind me, "When those same trees were a million different colors. Red, orange, yellow…"

Any color that you like, Doc I thought and suppressed a shiver.

"What about in wintertime?" Tim asked, "you know: Barren trees covered with snow so white that you could go blind just driving by on a sunny day? I used to love the way that the mountains looked in wintertime."

I glanced back out the window beside where I sat. While I could see very little I could envision every scene that my traveling companions had described. I experienced a moment of sadness, followed by one of providence. A peace that I had not felt before and one that I have, admittedly, not felt since welled up in my mind, body and soul and I shifted my gaze from the land passing by to my left forward and out through the windshield of the truck. I could see that a sheer rock face was quickly approaching on the truck's right and I watched as the road before us began to curve toward it. Instinctively, I rolled down my window, intent to heighten the sensation I was experiencing, unsure of when I would feel it again…

And paused as the top of my window disappeared into the superstructure of the truck. Beneath the dual sounds of the Suburban's engine and its tires crunching over the deteriorating road surface I could hear another sound. It was mechanical and out of place: A low, monotonous hum. And it was drawing closer as the rock face passed by to our right and the curve in the super road straightened out.

No, I thought, *oh God no.*

"NO, JEFF!" I shouted and caused Maria to squeal and jump beside me as we came out of the curve and saw what waited for us behind the rock face. Not upon the road…

But hovering over it.

It was large and streamlined. By the glow of the Suburban's headlights I saw that it spanned not only the area over the side of the Gap that we traveled upon but extended out over the river and into the darkness. Some… *things* were positioned parallel to the undercarriage of the machine and beneath the "wings" of it, parallel to the Highway. A miniature dust and particle storm raged upon the road surface directly beneath it. I could make out no canopy yet as it hovered over the Highway before us and as we drew closer to it I could see what appeared to be a series of exposed tubes—two on either side—beneath its wings. As we drew closer to it the two tubes beneath the wing that overhung the Highway lit up like headlights. And I knew, even before the headlights-that-weren't-headlights began to rotate, fluctuate and extend outward that we were facing something a great deal more malignant than anything we had yet faced. My suspicion was confirmed as Matt shouted three words that still resonate in my mind to this day.

"GUNSHIP!" was the first. And the second and third?

Plasma canons.

As the initial two blasts from the gunship discharged in our direction and screams and shouts of fear and futility echoed through the interior of the Suburban from my companions, a lone thought entered my mind.

Another night in Endworld had begun.

CHAPTER TWENTY TWO

In my mind we were finished, and all had been for naught. I watched in silent horror as those two brilliant shafts of white hot energy rapidly closed the distance between the Administration gunship and the grill of the Suburban and considered more than just the end of my life, the end of Maria's life and the ends of our companion's lives. For one, brief moment it felt like the end of everything, as if what was poised to happen in a matter of breaths would not only snuff out the lives of the eight fugitives racing blindly down a little-used and crumbling portion of the Highway at dusk on an undetermined day of an undetermined month in the year 15:CI, but any hope humanity had of recovering…

What, William wondered. The society that had existed before the rise of the machines*?* Or something more? Something much, *much* more vast. Something like…

Unus est vera semita, William, Pat's voice spoke in my racing mind and I teetered on the brink of realization. But on the coattails of that statement came another, spoken in the once stern and unfamiliar voice from my earlier dream of Skews, Gateways and Pathfinders. A voice that was unfamiliar to me then…

But is no longer. That voice? I know now that it was then, was before and always *has been* my own. Older, wiser and scarred but definitely mine. It was not the voice of the child that had set out from Jefferson. It was the voice of the man that sits here writing these words on the final sheets of yellowing paper that he managed to salvage from the dented supply cabinet in the warehouse adjoined to the old, dusty office with the mural of a faux-forest upon one wall and the picture of a rocket upon another in which he…

In which *I* daily and nightly reside. Said voice's statement was simple and yet surprisingly reassuring.

No, William, it cooed emotionlessly, *not yet.*

Simultaneously and in synchronicity with the shouts and the screams that echoed through the truck's ample interior I felt the vehicle beneath me "jolt" forward and pick up speed as the two plasma canon bursts closed the last of the distance between us…

And flew overhead as the Suburban sped faster and faster across the last of the distance between it and the gunship.

"HANG ON!" Jeff shouted as the two shots hit the Highway no more than two or three meters behind us. I heard an ear-splitting *BANG* as they impacted with the deteriorating asphalt and felt my ears *pop* in response as the shockwave shattered the rear and adjoining side windows including the one directly next to me. Maria, Tim, Steve, Carole and I were showered with glass and the rear of the truck lifted up and off of the road surface in what I swore was at least a 45 degree angle. I heard the front edge of the truck's undercarriage scrape deafeningly against the asphalt. I swung my gaze forward and watched as sparks bathed the hood and the front windshield of the vehicle.

Unable to think of anything but the surety that we were going to flip over and the knowledge that we couldn't if we desired to survive the night… hell, the next few moments I grabbed Maria by her arms and pulled her back and over the back of the seat that we had rested upon and into the third row. We landed squarely on top of Steve and Carole who, sensing my intentions shifted over and backward simultaneously. Despite the racket that overwhelmed us I heard a grunt as Tim, seemingly in agreement as well, leapt over the seat and into the third row. Bright light momentarily bathed the interior of the truck and temporarily blinded me as Tim's live blaster unavoidably and unexpectedly discharged. Thankfully, the shot sizzled into and through the back of the second row of seats on an angle and out through the left door frame of the truck. It missed anyone by a good distance. Gravity threatened to defy our attempt to right the Suburban but slowly…

Too slowly, I thought…

…I felt the rear of the vehicle lower… *lower…*

And slam down with a *smash* upon the pavement. I heard something snap beneath us and watched out the gaping hole that had once been the rear window as something—*the exhaust system,* I reasoned—tumbled from beneath the truck in a flurry of sparks, kicked up and off of the road and landed in a puff of dust on the shoulder of the Highway. The low purr of the vehicle's engine became a loud growl as my eyes moved from the expended exhaust system to the area above us. We were passing under the leading edge of the gunship and the proverbial dust and particle storm being kicked up by its propulsion system was bathing the truck and likewise the truck's interior in a fine cloud of cloying shit. I glanced behind us...

I coughed and gasped.

Through the cloud of debris that had infiltrated the interior of the Suburban I watched as the first of the Caravan... the *army* rounded the bend that we had, moments before, rounded ourselves.

Jesus, I thought, *where the hell did they come from?* I watched as the plasma canon mounted atop the lead MDU a lit in the same fashion as the ones beneath the wing of the gunship had a moment before and fired in our direction. I coughed and shouted... nay screamed at Jeff to go faster but no *jolt* followed as Jeff had seemingly already pushed the Suburban to its limit. As we passed beneath the rear of the gunship the crap choking the air in the interior of the truck quickly and blessedly dissipated. We sped into the temporary clear behind it as the shot from the pursuant MDU impacted with the right shoulder of the Highway five or six meters behind us and sent a storm of flaming, white-hot dust and dirt particles out and over the turbulent road surface and up and against the undercarriage of the gunship.

I felt the back right, rear of the truck begin to lift and I instinctively pulled Maria awkwardly in that direction. We landed atop Tim. Thankfully his blaster did not discharge again. Whether the truck made it off of the ground or not I am unsure. I pulled Maria with me as I shifted backward and off of Tim and glanced back out the rear window as we continued to careen blindly down the super road. I watched as the rest of the force that pursued us rounded the bend behind the lead MDU...

And continued to round it ceaselessly. There was no end to it: MDUs, assault bikes, Armored Troop Transports and a series of other vehicles the likes of which I had never seen before. They were similar in appearance to the ATTs with one, distinct difference: Their beds were opened, not closed and some... *things* were within them. *Not robots,* I reasoned but something else. *Smaller,* I thought. I felt my proverbial heart once again drop from my chest into my stomach at the realization of what I was observing a breath before Steve, who was also looking out the back window confirmed my suspicion.

"HUMACHINES!" He shouted over the din but did not shift his gaze, *"Oh CHRIST these sons of bitches don't play FAIR, PANCHO!"*

"No point in worrying about it NOW, Doc!" Matt shouted in response. I glanced from the endless army, the leading vehicles of which were just passing beneath the front edge of the gunship, up and saw, to my dismay that the gunship was already in the process of turning around. As the same MDU that had initially fired upon us cleared the rear edge of the gunship and entered the clear behind us its mounted plasma canon once again lit up, as

did the plasma canons of three other MDUs that cleared the gunship's rear directly behind it.

"INCOMING!" I shouted as the four bursts discharged and fired in our direction.

Jeff shouted something indiscernible. I heard his foot slam the accelerator to the floor of the truck but nothing changed. My eyes remained intently focused upon the four plasma bursts as they sliced through the air and moved closer... *closer...*

To the end, William. To the end. Not alive. We can't let that happen. They won't take us alive.

They sure won't, I realized simultaneously with the realization that the shots from the MDUs had been perfectly aimed toward us. It was no use. We were finished. And I was completely transfixed on our imminent demise.

No, William! That unfamiliar-then-but-familiar-now voice barked in my mind more forcefully than before, *NOT NOW, DAMNIT!*

Simultaneously an idea—*likely a futile one,* I rationalized—entered my mind. I watched as the bursts closed the last of the distance toward our position. I could hear beneath the din of the truck's passage the characteristic whistle of their approach. I waited until they were within a breath or two of our position before I swung my head quickly forward and, remembering my earlier observation of the river...

That looks shallow enough to wade in, I thought again...

...screamed for Jeff to "BREAK LEFT NOW!"

Whether out of instinct or simply because he saw no other alternative Jeff did not hesitate. He spun the steering wheel hard to the left and with a screech of rubber against asphalt the Suburban careened off of the Highway and onto the dirt shoulder of it. Momentum caused Steve, Carole, myself, Maria and Tim to pig-pile into each other as we slammed into the left side of the truck. My left shoulder and arm screamed in protest. Whether because of the abrupt turn or because of the damage it had already suffered via Tim's wayward blaster shot the side left, second row door swung open to the extent that it's hinges would tolerate before the combined momentum of the truck and the wind passing by it ripped it from the fuselage of the Suburban with a deafening screech. I saw it rocket passed the side of the truck and disappear into the darkness behind us as we closed the five or six meters between the road and the riverbed promptly and catapulted off of the edge of the land and into the open air over the river as the four plasma canon bursts impacted deafeningly with the road surface where we had just been.

BANG!

My ears once again *popped*. The shockwave from the impact propelled us even further out over the river and for a moment I got the impression that in defiance of gravity we were flying like the gunship. Said impression was quickly replaced as the Suburban landed with a *splash* seven or eight meters out into the river.

Let's see if I was right, I thought. I heard a loud explosion from beneath where I sat as the rear, driver's side tire of the Suburban popped from the impact and the combined weight of the four people pig-piled within the truck a top it. But that was all. Save for the pronounced sound of the remnants of the popped tire *flop, flop, flopping* against the riverbed and the water the truck continued to move forward across the river.

I shifted my arms out so that they were on either side of Steve and Carole who were, with the combined weight of three people pressing down upon them, gasping for air, braced my hands against the left side wall of the third row of seats and pushed backward. Maria and Tim tumbled from a top me with dual grunts. I glanced expectedly over the back of the second row seats and out the space where the once-door had, until recently, rested closed. The surface of the river licked the side of the truck and splashed into the interior of it but it was not overflowing the undercarriage. Its level remained slightly below it.

Holy shit, I thought.

"Holy shit!" Matt echoed in the most animated voice I had ever heard him use. I heard him slam something into the roof of the truck, *"holy shit it WORKED, William! Goddamn kid you are a FUCKING…!"*

"RIGHT!" Caren shouted from the front passenger seat, *"TURN RIGHT, JEFF!"*

I shifted my gaze from the water beneath us to the area before us and saw what Caren had indicated. The opposing riverbank was fast approaching our position and was steeper and taller than the one we had just launched off of: Maybe four, perhaps five meters high. And we were within a few meters of slamming grill first into it.

Jeff shouted another explicative and forced the steering wheel to the right. I watched as it moved agonizingly slow, the extra-added resistance of the water and the flat tire beneath us hindering our movement but gradually, and thanks largely in part to Jeff's valiant and strained effort, the Suburban shifted its trajectory. Within a meter or two of the towering riverbank it completed its turn and continued on, parallel but not perpendicular to the riverbank.

Safe, I thought briefly and shifted my gaze to the opposing bank of the river and the force that trundled parallel to our position upon it. The army had slowed and was pacing us. The plasma canon turrets a top the MDUs...

My God there must be a dozen or more total, I thought...

...were in the process of shifting back in our direction. I squinted and could barely see the humachines in the open-backed transports training their respective weapons upon our position. The gunship had all-but completed its turn and was beginning to move back toward us.

Not good, I thought as Matt reiterated said thought hectically.

"Not good!" he shouted and followed it up with a chorus of *"ums"* and *"yeahs."* We had briefly averted disaster but presently? Matt was, apparently, as much at a loss for words or ideas as I was. Shit, as any of us assembled in the truck were. I shifted my gaze again from the force on our right flank to the area before us. Simultaneously with my observation of it, Carole shouted from beside me.

"What is that?" She pointed straight ahead and out the window.

I squinted in an attempt to make it out but all that I could determine per the shape of the shadow ahead of us was that it was large and long, was suspended above the ground and it spanned the width of the river. My glance traced the length of it left to right, and ended upon the road surface that we had, until a few hectic moments before, been driving upon. The same road surface the pursuant army of machines and humachines paced us upon. The Highway, I noticed, visibly curved onto it and over the river...

A bridge, I realized. I assumed, despite my limited vision of the area a top it and beyond it that the Highway continued eastward on the other side.

"Bridge!" Matt shouted defiantly. A glimmer of hope rekindled in my mind and heart. If we could make it to the other side then maybe... *just maybe...*

"Can we make it?" Tim echoed from across the seat to my right as the shadowy structure drew agonizingly closer.

Must go faster, Jeff! I mentally willed him. As if in response to my thought, I heard the driver slam his foot against the floor of the vehicle. I felt another slight *jolt* as the truck picked up a minimal amount of speed. The steady *flop, flop, flopping* of the back left, rear tire increased in frequency as the bridge drew closer... *closer...*

I chanced a look back and to my right and gasped in horror. The turrets a top the MDUs and the weapons of the humachines were no longer trained upon our position. Rather, all had shifted their aim forward. I looked out the shattered, rear window and saw that the gunship had completed its turn and was already in the process of quickly closing the distance between us. My mouth had gone dry but I swallowed anyway as all four canons beneath its wings a lit. The deadly lights began to fluctuate and rotate as I swung my head forward and saw the bridge less than 20 meters away from our position. In my mind I continued to repeat my litany...

Must go FASTER, Jeff, MUST GO FASTER...

...but it was no use. The Suburban had once again reached its limit.

15 meters, I thought, my heart pounding in time with the steady and quick "flop, flop, flop" of the back, rear tire, *10 meters... FIVE METERS...*

"JEFF!" I shouted as I caught a glimpse in the rearview mirror positioned between him, Caren and Matt of the gunship. The four plasma canons stopped cycling and brilliantly fired in our direction. Not at *us*...

But at the bridge.

The machines had obviously decided that cornering us or crushing us was preferable to pursuing us any further. They were obviously aiming to bring the entire bridge down on our heads. I heard simultaneous weapon discharges...

Dozens, I thought, *shit, hundreds of them...*

...from the army and didn't even avert my gaze from the approaching structure to visually verify them. The night that surrounded us and impinged upon the interior of the truck alit from behind and beside us with brilliance rivaled only by the brilliance of the sun and the towering structure of the bridge directly before us became clearly visible. It was old and crumbling, like so much else in not only the Eastern Territory but all throughout Endworld. One properly placed plasma canon or pulse rifle burst would be enough to bring a portion of it down. As we covered the last five meters between us and the leading edge of it...

As the combined barrage of weapons fire from the gunship and the army sliced through the air overhead and beside us with a series of deafening whistles...

I closed my eyes. It was all that I could think of to do. I closed my eyes and I reached out for Maria's hand. I found it not far from mine and I clamped down upon it and she clamped down upon mine as the wind that rushed by outside the gaping holes in the Suburban that had once been doors and windows changed its tone and pitch and the thunderous echo of dozens of explosions filled the air and despite my closed eyes I was blinded by the same fire that licked through the openings beside behind and in front of me and singed everything from the stubble that grew upon my cheeks to the t-shirt that I wore upon my back to the upholstery beneath my ass and I heard Matt shout... no *scream* someone's name and something about a phone and I heard that someone respond with *"RIGHT!"* as the truck shifted left and upward and someone shouted out in pain and I waited…

I waited for the cacophony of sound and sensation and the screams that emanated from Maria and the others within the truck to fade away… to simply fade away into nothingness.

* * *

SLNyxV4.0 gave the order to open fire on the bridge over the once-Delaware River with little hesitation. It did not desire to pursue the fugitives any further. It desired to end the chase and it desired to do so immediately. It had the fugitives' vehicle incapacitated and cornered. A barrage of well-aimed and well-timed shots would not only take down the bridge but it would either cut off their route of escape or it would potentially crush them. It would then be able to order a search of the rubble, not for survivors—because, it reasoned, there would be none—but for the object that it had been tasked to recover: The Artifact.

SLNyxV4.0 and its army had been fully recharged and following the fugitives eastward down the Highway when one of the SMs had picked up a faint tracking signal. A quick triangulation had pinpointed its location: Well east and slightly south of the army's location upon the Highway.

Peculiar, the Supreme Leader had considered but it had not questioned it further. It had ordered its forces to move toward said location with haste and had requested airborne reinforcements. The gunship had been dispatched from Cornelius City and had moved as speedily as it could over the area between the capital and the location indicated by the tracking signal: Centralia, ET. It had been ordered by its superiors to not engage the fugitives without the gunship's support and SLNyxV4.0 had followed said order to the letter. It had slowed its army's approach at approximately 50 kilometers and had waited, all the while monitoring the location of the tracking signal.

At shortly before twilight the signal had begun to move away from Centralia and back toward the Highway. Its superiors had ordered it and the gunship to hold their positions and they had done so. When the signal had reached the Highway and had begun moving swiftly eastward it had been ordered to follow but to stay at a distance of no less than 10 kilometers unless otherwise instructed. It had done so and had not questioned the directive. It had understood the Administration's intended strategy, even before its superiors had ordered the gunship to assume a stationary and strategic position over the Highway to the east in the once-Delaware Water Gap and had ordered the Supreme Leader and its army to increase its speed and move upon the fugitives from the rear. They will be cornered, it had notified its army, there can be and will be no failure. The army had increased its speed exponentially, had overtaken the fugitives within the Gap...

And presently had them where it wanted them. Hence, SLNyxV4.0's order to take out the bridge: A decision that it had made of its own, "enlightened" volition. Were it human and not simply an upgraded machine it would have recognized the sensation that passed through its neural net at the sight of the combined firepower of both the gunship and its army extending outward toward the bridge over the river as "awe." It was as if the night had been replaced by the brilliance of mid-day. Said sensation turned to triumph as it watched the blasts from the gunship and the army impact with the facing side and supports of the structure a moment before the truck carrying the fugitives passed beneath its leading edge.

Finished, it considered as the explosions and subsequent shockwaves from them a lit the deepening night even more. Its optical processors were temporarily incapacitated by the degree of illumination and it instinctively switched its visual perception from "standard" to "filtered" and ordered the rest of the army to do the same. Affirmations of its command entered its neural net as it observed the aftermath of what it had wrought.

The damage was catastrophic. The bridge had been reduced to rubble that lay piled upon the riverbed. What remained were little more than an isolated slab of concrete and a few twisted and melted horizontal support rails. It ordered the Surveillance Mark next to it to scan for life signs and it did so immediately. A short time later it reported back: "INCONCLUSIVE." The Supreme Leader felt a level of something that, were it human, it would have recognized as "satisfaction" as it turned to observe the SM...

And paused.

Inconclusive, it considered as it watched the inset radar dish upon the SM's chest rotate haphazardly. It ordered the other Surveillance Marks assembled within its army to duplicate the scan and heard the unmistakable sound of a dozen or more radar dishes spinning and undulating chaotically around it before it received the same report back from each of them:

"INCONCLUSIVE."

Recognition flooded its neural net as it ordered the gunship to move up the river and visually verify the absence of the fugitives' vehicle. With a loud, metallic hum the monstrous vehicle moved overhead. The main lifts that lined the center of its fuselage and the stabilizing ones beneath either wing kicked up liquid spray from the surface of the river and dust from the respective riverbanks and the pile of ruins that choked the river's flow. SLNyxV4.0 waited for the gunship to report back and when it did... well, to say that the Supreme Leader was, were it human, "furious" is both inaccurate and an understatement. Fury is a human state of mind. SLNyxV4.0 did not recognize what flooded its neural net as fury. It recognized the sensation as *nothing more or less than complete failure...*

Failure, coupled with an imperative.

The gunship reported visual verification of something speeding away to the east of their position on the Highway opposite the riverbank where the Supreme Leader's army idled: Little more than a shadow amongst the others falling quickly over the area but it was distinguishable because its movement was purposeful and not stationary. The Supreme Leader ordered the gunship to pursue it at maximum speed. Simultaneously, the gunship observed and reported that the shadow had disappeared through a narrow gap between two adjoining hills that flanked the Highway. Direct pursuit, it stated, would be impossible. It would need to circumnavigate the terrain which would take time. SLNyxV4.0 ordered it to proceed and it did so without hesitation.

Reverse course, it ordered its army, 3.2 kilometers west upon the Highway until you reach the ramp for road designation 611. Move south. We will bypass and intercept them at their intended destination. Simultaneously it verified that the tracking signal still worked despite the fugitives' successful attempt to jam the scanning capacities of the Surveillance Marks and discovered that it did. It's "satisfaction" returned briefly.

A temporary respite, it reasoned, enjoy it while you can. It watched as the vehicles behind it began to retreat west and waited for its opportunity to do the same as time moved onward without check over the once-Delaware Water Gap and throughout Endworld.

CHAPTER TWENTY THREE

NO WILLIAM, the unfamiliar-then-but-familiar-now voice shouted again… practically ordered in my mind, *NOT YET!*

There was strength in that voice. Said strength forced me to slowly open my eyes. Even with them still closed I could sense that we were moving forward, though whether that sense was physical or a figment of my optimistic imagination remained to be seen.

As I opened my eyes, the first thing that I realized was that we traveled once again in darkness. What little light remained was coming from well behind us and was fading. The second thing that I realized was that my companions were talking… nay shouting but since my ears still rang with the sounds of the army's and the gunship's weapons impacting with and likely destroying the bridge I could not make out any specifics. Beneath the ringing in my ears and the shouting I could still hear the steady *flop, flop, flop* of the flat rear, left tire. Despite my surety that I had to be dead…

Had to be…

…I could still feel Maria's warm hand clamped tightly beneath mine. I shook my head from side to side in an attempt to clear the discordance and it helped. I quickly realized that the shouting echoing through the interior of the Suburban was not shouting. It was cheering. And the tones of my traveling companions' voices? Not pained but elated. I blinked my eyes once… twice and saw Caren hugging Jeff in the front seat. Jeff still drove the truck which was once again on the road…

But which road, I considered…

…and Matt had turned his head and was glancing out his window at the area behind us. I shifted my own gaze from the front of the truck to the area beside me. Maria and Tim had both turned and were looking out the back window. I looked left and saw that Steve and Carole were doing the same. All seemed to be in equivalent if not equal modes of celebration save for Maria who appeared restrained.

Shock? I thought. No answer came.

Well? I asked myself. I turned around and glanced out the back window and promptly realized the source of my companions' happiness.

The remnants of the once-bridge still smoldered behind us and a heavy cloud of dust and particulates hovered above what remained of the structure. We were back upon a road surface that was similar to the one that we had traveled upon before our unexpected detour into the river. Were we back on the Highway? And if we were, how had we gotten back upon its asphalt spine? As the ringing in my ears finally diminished and the content of what was being shouted and cheered within the truck became clear my smile grew and I turned from the chaos behind us and directed my question to Matt. I had to repeat it a few times before I finally got his attention and his answer.

"Dumb luck, William!" He cheered, "We hit the onset of the bridge at the same time that the shots did! We had just enough speed to make it out the other side before the whole fucking thing came down on our heads! As soon as we made it out..."

"He told me to turn on my satellite phone's jamming function and I *did!*" Tim continued, "Jeff killed the headlights but before he did, he saw it over to our left: An old boat ramp for Christ's sake! He swung the truck left and hit it so hard that I banged the top of my head into the roof!"

"We gained the top of it and the Highway was *right there*," Maria added. Her own tone was more subdued than the tones of the others and it complimented her passive expression. Her hand remained clamped upon mine as mine remained clamped upon hers. It was reassuring to say the least, "We got back on it..."

"And *here we ARE!*" Matt concluded, "Those fuckers shot themselves in their metallic *feet!* They can't follow us..."

"Um," Jeff added. I watched as the smile upon his face, visible in the rear view mirror faded, "don't be so sure, Matt," he said, "you're forgetting one thing." Rather than share what that one thing was Jeff simply gestured with his head to the area behind us. I turned and glanced back out the rear window.

The outline of the gunship had moved through the thick cloud that overhung the remnants of the bridge. I watched as its propulsion system kicked up thick clouds of dust and flame in what looked like mini-cyclones beneath it. It cleared the rubble just as our passage brought us to another curve in the Highway. While I could not see them I sensed that there were either hills or cliffs on either side of us and as I watched, the position of the gunship shifted to my left and disappeared, confirming my suspicion. I felt myself forced back against the third row as the truck began to climb back into the hills that flanked what had been the opposing side of the river. Jeff simultaneously engaged the headlights. Only one remained functional, evident per the diminished and lopsided pool of light on the road before us.

"It can't pursue us directly but it *can* go around," Steve added as he broke his embrace with Carole, "and the machines? They'll back track and find another way east. *Both* will eventually catch up with or worse, *surpass us* but that's a risk we're going to have to take. We need to find someplace inconspicuous to stop and fix that tire, Matt. We're not going to get much further on tattered rubber and a wheel frame."

I watched as Matt nodded, "Agreed, Doc. No more chit-chat and no more celebrating. Everyone: Keep your eyes opened for someplace… *anyplace* to stop. Someplace nice and hidden. That jamming frequency will keep 'em confused for a bit but eventually they'll figure out that 'inconclusive' equals us and then?"

I nodded. I understood what happened then. Apparently, so did everyone else assembled within the truck. We stopped talking and celebrating and started looking for a place to pull off of the steadily increasing slope of the Highway.

We found it quickly at the crest of the hill that we climbed: A shadowy exit labeled "4C: Blairstown." Jeff taxied the Suburban onto it and continued onward into the shadows that overhung the road. There was little in the way of… well, anything. Any structures that had lined the road had long since disappeared. A few kilometers down it, however, we encountered a sign. Jeff slowed the Suburban as we approached it. It was old and appeared to be fashioned out of wood, contrary to the large, green, metallic signs that had lined the Highway. In fact, the only thing visible upon it was a single word that had been seemingly burnt into it: "Lakota." Everything else had long-since worn away.

"Well?" Matt asked us.

"Hmm," Jeff said, "there don't seem to be many other alternatives."

"I vote yes," Carole chimed in from behind me. Tim seconded her affirmative with one of his own as did Caren, Steve, Maria and finally myself.

"Well alright then," Jeff said as he turned the truck onto the dirt and gravel road indicated by the sign and proceeded cautiously ahead.

The road continued for about a quarter of a kilometer before the entrance to a parking lot materialized out of the darkness on our left. The blackened stump of what had once been a tree stood sentinel over its entrance and beneath it, sticking out of the ground was another sign. Not wood but metal like the ones that had advertised exits from the Highway albeit smaller. The sign was faded and its colors were indiscernible but I could make out the same word that I had seen upon the wooden sign at the onset of the road—"Lakota"—along with two others—"Wolf Preserve." The latter words were positioned at the bottom of the sign and the former word was positioned at the top. Between them was the image of an animal that vaguely resembled a dog but looked more... *wild? Vicious?* I posed the question to my companions but no one either knew the answer or desired to reveal it.

Jeff turned the Suburban into the parking lot and passed the wasted tree stump and faded sign. I could see, in the dim light that emanated from the Suburban's lone headlight, a series of old and dilapidated structures directly ahead of us. They looked far from habitable, little more than buildings that had crumbled down to their foundations. Their roofs were gone and in most places their walls were, as well. Rather than approach any closer Jeff slowed the Suburban to a crawl and eventually stopped it in the middle of the parking lot.

"Everybody out," he said as he turned off the truck and opened his door. He left the lone headlight of the vehicle on so that we could see what we were doing.

"I'll take care of the tire if someone wants to go watch the road," Tim said as he stepped out of the Suburban. Matt nodded and asked for volunteers but no one immediately spoke. Once my feet touched the gravel-covered ground I raised my hand and said that I would. Maria immediately volunteered to go with me.

"I'll go too," Jeff said quickly as he removed his pulse rifle from the floor of the truck and hoisted it over his shoulder, "that way we have a bit of extra fire power..."

"Just in case," I completed and reluctantly nodded. In light of the knowledge I had gained the previous night from the Pat-specter about a potential traitor in our midst... the same information that I had imparted upon Maria but no one else, I was leery of wandering off into the darkness with anyone but her. I could tell by the way that Maria lowered her head and shifted her stance first right and then left that she felt the same way. And Jeff's prompt insistence that he accompany us to guard the road? Maria looked up at me and I shared a worried glance with her as Jeff moved toward us and past us. I shrugged. She did the same.

Not much choice, our respective gestures said. And there wasn't. If we desired to keep the knowledge we had gained secret we needed to act like nothing had changed.

But everything has changed, I thought, my mind racing back over the events that had transpired a short time before. How much… rather, how little time did we have before the machines—the army, the gunship or worse—caught up with or, as Steve had reasoned, *surpassed* us?

"Steve, Caren and I'll check out what's left of those buildings up there," Carole indicated as she removed her blaster from its holster, checked by the dim light of the lone, functional head light that the safety was "off" and held it down at her side, "that is, if Steve and Caren are game?"

"Game," Steve said, "after all, you never know. Caren?"

Caren nodded her head in response.

"No you don't," Matt said as he handed his pulse rifle to Steve, "take *this* Doc. You're not walking off into the dark with my wife armed with anything less than a pulse rifle. Think you can handle it?"

Steve chuckled, re-holstered his blaster and took the rifle deftly from Matt. He tested its weight and nodded, "I may look frail, Pancho, but this isn't the first time I've held a pulse rifle."

Matt smiled and nodded, "Tim," he said as he turned back to the Marine, "I'll give you a hand with the tire unless you want to handle it yourself."

"Sure," Tim said without hesitation, "no problem." He moved toward the back of the truck, "I think we've only got a doughnut as a spare but it should be enough to get us the rest of the way."

Jeff nodded and without speaking gestured for Maria and me to follow him. We did so as the rest of the group dispersed across the area. Maria stayed close to me as we traversed the area between where the truck rested and the road. I removed my blaster from its holster and gestured for Maria to do the same.

Just in case, my action and subsequent raised eyebrow beckoned. She nodded, removed her weapon and held it down at her side.

We made it back to the blackened tree stump and the accompanying sign a moment later. As soon as we were within spitting distance of it Jeff turned promptly, his pulse rifle still held out before him and aimed directly at us. My grip upon my own weapon tightened instinctively and I sensed the same from Maria as her right arm and thigh brushed up against my left ones. Jeff glanced down at Maria's and my weapon hands, and then back up at first Maria, and then me. He smiled and shook his head.

"Okay, you two," Jeff said with a surprising note of…

Humor? I thought…

…as he continued, "Spill it. What are you hiding?"

While I was not overwhelmingly shocked by his inquiry I was slightly caught off guard. I stuttered over my response as I turned to Maria and Maria turned to me. Her eyes were opened widely and I could sense the lone thought racing through her mind. It was easy to do so.

It was the same thought—*oh shit*—that raced through mine.

"Um," I began, "nothing, Jeff. What are you…?"

Jeff's smile widened and he lowered his weapon, "You know *exactly* what I'm talking about William," he said. The tone in his voice was neither angry nor accusatory. It sounded genuine, "the two of you know something and you're not letting on what that something is. Not to me and not to anybody in the group. I'm sure you have your reasons but I need to be sure that the two of you aren't…"

"Aren't *what*," Maria asked defensively as she took a step forward, "liabilities? *Traitors?* Is that what you're implying… *Jeebus?*"

He chuckled as I reached out with my left hand and pressed it against Maria's right forearm. *Don't,* my gesture pleaded, *please Mia. Be patient and let this play out.*

"Well if it makes you feel any better, Maria, you two don't take me as the traitor type," he said as he turned and glanced first at the road that ran parallel to our position and then up at the sky, "so I'd wager that it's not that. But you obviously know *something* and I need to know what that something is before we can continue. In the interest of full disclosure. If you want me to help get you to Hempstead and eventually to Free Caymen then we need to be upfront with each other. And Maria?"

"Don't call you Jeebus," she said dejectedly, "I know, Jeff. I'm sorry."

Jeff's smile did not falter. He nodded. I duplicated Maria's step forward and spoke: "What if we *can't* be, Jee… err, *Jeff*? What if… well, what if it's something that we were asked to keep in confidence and not share within anyone else. What then?"

Jeff turned from the road and the sky above us back to our position, "Well then I guess I'll just have to trust you. Which, considering the circumstances, is not the easiest prospect."

"What circumstances?" Maria questioned as she took another, defensive step toward him.

He gestured over our shoulders toward the truck and then back up the road in the direction that we had approached the preserve from, "Everything that just happened, Maria. The way the machines were just waiting for us. The way they hemmed us in? It's not that they got lucky. They knew where we were and they almost had us dead to rights. If not for a whole shitload of good fortune on our parts this whole adventure if you can even call it that would have been over. It's not often a single truck wins a battle against a whole Caravan much less an army of them. Hell, I wouldn't be surprised if it's never happened before tonight though I have no factual basis to back that up."

I nodded. The idea that we had escaped certain capture or death given the way the deck had been stacked against us did seem *slightly* unrealistic, sarcasm fully intended.

"They *knew* where we were going to be," he repeated, "or else they wouldn't have dispatched that gunship to wait for us where it was waiting for us. And the ones that moved on us from behind? They were following us but they were doing so quietly. They waited until we were in position before they moved up and attacked. The whole damn scenario reeks of a tip-off. So when I talk about *circumstances*, Maria? That's what I'm referring to."

"So you *are* calling us traitors?" she defended loudly as she moved even closer to Jeff. In response, I tightened my grip upon her arm and gently pulled her back toward me. At first, she hesitated, but after a tense moment she obliged and stepped away from Jeff with a grunt.

"I'm sorry," she said as she lowered her head, "I'm sorry, Jeff. *And* William. I'm just not used to being accused of sympathizing with the *fucking Administration*."

"Mia," I pleaded but stopped as Jeff took a few steps toward us and placed the hand not holding his pulse rifle upon Maria's shoulder.

"Relax, Maria," Jeff continued, "no one's accusing you of *anything* like that. To put your minds at ease, I don't think that you *or* William is a traitor if for no reason other than this: You're young. Smart but young. Pat saw that and I see it too. You've got good instincts but you're not pros. It takes a seasoned one of those to be able to insert him or herself into a group like ours undetected. I'd go so far as to say it takes… an *Infiltrator*."

"A *what?*" I asked. I had never heard the term before but from the way Jeff spoke it—low and with a "hiss"—I sensed a very negative connotation.

Our companion nodded, "An Infiltrator, William. A human in the employ of the machines, contracted by the Administration to subvert groups like ours. They're about the lowliest of Administration cronies in my book but they're *also* the most dangerous. They've learned over years of betraying their fellow kind to flawlessly infiltrate and achieve a goal or goals given to them by their superiors. The problem is they could be anyone at any given time. Shit, *I* could be one though you'll just have to trust me when I tell you that I'm not."

I nodded. While the idea of trusting anyone save for Maria was a daunting prospect I understood that of all of my traveling companions, Jeff was the most trustworthy. As for how I knew that he was I cannot, to this day, say, but I did. We'd known him the longest… had been through the most with him. It was the only justification I could come up with and I silently prayed that it would not backfire on me.

"Anyway," he continued, "common sense dictates that someone, be that someone an Infiltrator or otherwise has undermined our trust and is currently feeding information in one way or another back to the Administration. And were I a betting man, William and Maria? I'd wager that your secret has something to do with that. And if I'm right? Then despite what you may be thinking I'm accusing you of understand this: *Your* concerns are the same as *mine*. We *all* need to be on our guard. I'm not going to talk to anyone other than you two about this for obvious reasons. We'll leave the others out of the know for the time being and let them form their own opinions and conclusions. After all, who knows which of them the guilty one is? Sound good to you?"

I nodded, removed my left hand from Maria's shoulder and extended it in Jeff's direction, "Agreed," I said. Jeff looked down at my extended hand, smiled, and grasped it in his own. He pumped it twice and then released it.

I turned back to Maria and saw that she was still visibly agitated. I wanted to pull her aside and remind her that while Jeff had sensed one of the secrets that we had been keeping from the group he had not addressed the other, specifically the Artifact that I carried within my right front, jean's pocket. Somehow, I felt that the presence of a traitor or—I swallowed—an *Infiltrator* within our midst was not as crucial to our future as the letter that Alex had entrusted me with. Somehow I knew that the letter was the real secret.

But what if the letter is the reason why the Infiltrator's here? My coldly rational voice asked. The prospect caused a new wave of nervousness to rush through my system and no answer was forthcoming from my mental peanut gallery. The one time I needed them to speak up they were silent.

Fuck, I thought as Jeff fell silent, turned back to the road and hefted his pulse rifle, *apparently nothing more needs to be said.* I pulled Maria to our right soundlessly and we took up position directly next to him as the night moved onward without check over and around us.

Sometime later we heard boots crunching on the gravel behind us. I turned in unison with Maria and Jeff and saw Matt and Tim approaching. Jeff stepped away from the road.

"So what's the scoop?" he asked. They were the first words he had spoken since our earlier conversation.

"The tire's changed out," Tim said as he rubbed his hands together, "it's only a doughnut but it *should* get us the rest of the way to Hempstead. Unfortunately we may have another, bigger issue to deal with."

"'*Vanderful!*'" Matt exclaimed in yet another, unfamiliar accent that caused Maria to squeak in surprise and both of us to jump in unison, "'*Ogan, 'vat are 'vee going to do?!*'" He smiled and Jeff and Tim both chuckled. He turned to Maria and me and apologized for startling us before he continued, "In all seriousness, Tim: *Tell 'em.*"

Tim sighed, "The battery. It's pretty much drained. I don't know if it was the water from the river or the sheer amount of stress the truck endured but we've *maybe* got enough charge left to get us 50 or 60 kilometers further. We've got the charger hooked up to it now. It might buy us a little more time but I don't know. I've got no idea how badly it's damaged or if it can even hold a fresh charge."

Great, I thought, "Does anyone have any idea how far from Hempstead we are?" I asked.

Matt shrugged, "No clue. But I'd wager it's more than 50 or 60 kilometers." He looked passed us and up at the sky. He paused as he seemingly noticed something and I inquired as to what he was looking at. He raised his right hand and pointed in the direction that I surmised we had been traveling in before our detour to repair the Suburban's tire: East.

Nothing but Fool's Gold there, Billy Preston's voice spoke in my mind, *can you speak amen, my brother.*

"If my sense of direction is right," he continued, "the eastern horizon's red." He lowered his arm and hand to his side and turned back to us, "not a good sign. 'Red sky at night…'"

"'Mariners take flight,'" Jeff continued, "I noticed it earlier, too. Or maybe it's 'fright' and not 'flight.' Either way…"

"It means bad weather ahead," Tim concluded, "my mother used to tell me that one, too. It may not have rained here in a while but something tells me that's going to change real soon."

Matt nodded. I turned and saw that Jeff had lowered his head and was staring intently at the gravel beneath his boots. I turned from Jeff to Maria, saw concern emblazoned across her expression, and then averted my glance to the eastern horizon that Matt had indicated. I could see a deep, red tint there that I had not noticed before. I was unfamiliar with the rhyme that Matt, Jeff and Tim were familiar with. I had never heard it before that moment and was unsure whether "flight" or "fright" was the correct word, but for me the red sky signified something more malignant… more base than a little (*or a lot of,* I considered) rain.

Blood, I concluded and felt a shiver traverse my spine, *there's blood ahead.* Whether anyone else assembled by the roadside experienced the same inclination as me I do not know but the silence that descended over our gathering? You can draw whatever conclusions you choose to from that. Amidst that silence visions from my reoccurring nightmare returned: The beach. The storm. The firefight. And the diminished figure of Maria Markinson, her one, brown eye glaring back at me from within a mass of macerated flesh and her own blaster raised to her temple.

To the end, William. To the end. Not alive. We can't let that happen. They won't take us alive…

One way or another, I understood for the first time at that moment that the end was fast approaching.

CHAPTER TWENTY FOUR

We did not dawdle long by the roadside. Save for the red tint upon the eastern horizon which seemed to be creeping closer and closer to us with each passing moment, nothing stirred above us or upon the road surface before us. We heard nothing in the distance. The world surrounding and including the once-Lakota Wolf Preserve was eerily silent. We made our way back to the truck and rendezvoused with the rest of the group. Steve, Carole and Caren's search of the interiors of the three, crumbling buildings that flanked the parking lot had yielded nothing of consequence.

"A lot of dust and some old, petrified animal shit but that was it," Steve lamented, "anything that *was* here was either destroyed by the Scourge or disappeared over the years since. This place is as dead as the rest of the Eastern Territory."

Matt nodded, "Kind of what I think we *all* expected, Doc. Okay, then. We should probably get our asses moving again. We've been here long enough. Tim, how's the battery?"

Tim, who had, upon returning to the truck, stuck his head beneath the opened hood of it to examine said battery, emerged and shook his head, "Not much better, Matt. Like I said: We may have a little more juice but I'm still 'gonna guess no more than 70, and if we're lucky 80 kilometers. After that..."

"We're dead in the water," Jeff interrupted and shook his head.

"Don't sound so skeptical, Jeff," Steve said as he handed Matt back his pulse rifle. Matt took it and shouldered it with a nod, "think about it this way: If the damn thing dies on us we'll get a good work out walking the rest of the way to Hempstead."

"Let's hope that another solution presents itself," Matt said seriously as he moved toward the front, driver's side door, "not much chance of us evading the machines on foot for long but it's another risk we're just going to have to take. Saddle up, everyone. Time to hit the road again."

In response to his statement we filed into the Suburban one, final time in the same order that we had filed into it multiple times before save for Matt and Jeff who once again switched places. Once inside, Matt turned on the truck's one, lone headlight and slowly pulled away from and out of the old wolf preserve and back onto the side road that we had traveled to get there. A moment later we arrived at the turn with the wasted and faded wooden sign that advertised "Lakota," and a moment after we turned back onto that road we arrived back at the ramp to the Highway. Matt piloted the vehicle up the ramp and onto the crumbling super road beneath the slowly encroaching, blood-red sky that marked the eastern horizon before us. He asked Tim if he was still jamming all scans and Tim affirmed that he was. He informed the rest of us, specifically those of us sitting near windows and, in my case, a gaping hole where a door had once been, to be on our guard and we acknowledged that we would be.

In response, I positioned myself a bit closer to the opening. The stagnant, humid air that rushed by the Suburban buffeted the left side of my body and my right cheek which I had craned just slightly so as to view the road behind us and the sky to our left. Matt tasked me, Jeff and Tim to keep an eye on the road and notify him at the slightest sign of movement. We all agreed that we would. But nothing stirred at any point of the compass in those early moments of our renewed journey, and the only sound that graced our ears as we slowly progressed down the Highway was that of the air rushing by the truck and the sound of its tires crunching across the progressively worsening road surface. No one spoke after that... no one even stirred as the night and our trek eastward into the unknown moved ever onward.

At first I began to notice a few, subtle differences in what little of the landscape I could see passing us by. That same, God-be-damned, piss yellow "grass" dominated not only the area beyond the shoulder of the super road but also seemed to be encroaching upon the Highway itself more and more with each passing kilometer. The super road's surface, as well, continued its deterioration (*as if it could get any worse,* I thought at one point), so much so that I actually reversed my course and moved inward and away from the gaping hole that had once been the driver's side, second row door for fear of us hitting a bump or a pothole and me tumbling out.

We further appeared to be coming out of the hills that we had been travelling through indefinitely. The land that stretched away on either side of the truck was flat and, for the most part, barren. Occasionally we would pass over a bridge and another dried creek or river bed, but we passed by little in the way of any trace of former or current habitation.

Current habitation, I thought, *what a laugh.* Until, that is, we passed over one final, surprisingly large and empty ravine and the appearance of the world that surrounded us completely changed.

Were it not for the red glow of the sky above us and the small amount of light cast by the Suburban's lone, functioning headlight before us I would not have noticed any change but said glow provided just enough light that I could make out some… *things* a bit of a distance away on either side of the Highway. There weren't many of them and they were spaced at varying intervals. I squinted in an attempt to determine what they were and realized with a loud and audible gasp that…

Yes. They *had been* buildings. The structures looked like little more than broken and jagged fingers that stretched up crookedly into the red sky overhead and my skin began to crawl as I realized what I was seeing: A once population center turned into a lifeless wasteland. A broken and crumbling diorama of the world as it had once been fashioned by an insane genius. Twisted and in some places melted steel poles curved up and over our heads like a set of skeletal ribs and I considered what they might have once been as the sound that emanated from the road surface below us shifted to a more hollow roar. The ruins on either side of the Highway gave way to another, larger ravine and I suddenly realized the origin of the "ribs" that vaulted overhead. My stomach wretched. I dry swallowed and tasted nothing but bile.

Another bridge, I realized. We were driving over what had once been a reinforced steel bridge but had, over time, turned into little more than a slab of suspended concrete held in place by the few supports that had survived the Scourge. Even before I averted my gaze forward and saw, silhouetted against the blood red sky, a highly concentrated collection of shadowy ruins a bit of a distance away I understood.

My God, I understood so much.

Now you know why they call it "The Scourge," Vato, Pat's voice lamented and confirmed in my mind, *now you know why they call this the Scorched Land.*

And I did. At that moment, as we drove beneath the last of the overhanging, once-steel supports and emerged on the other side of the bridge? I finally "figured it out." All that I had seen up until that point in our journey had been little more than a glimpse of what had happened in the Eastern Territory… a taste of the grand travesty that had been inflicted upon it. The scene surrounding me and before me at that moment? *That,* I realized, was the real casualty. The "main course" if you will.

How many people died here? I thought, *how many hundreds, thousands… hell, how many millions died here? How many of Pat's haints walk amidst these ruins?* The scope… the potential numbers involved with the answer to that question staggered me and I lowered my head to my chest. I closed my eyes against the hot tears of regret that threatened to flow down my cheeks and silently repeated my earlier proclamation to the almighty… to *any* deity that would listen.

My God, I asked, *why?*

No answer came. My mental peanut gallery had fallen silent.

"'Son of man," Tim spoke suddenly from beside me. I raised my head, opened my eyes, brushed the back of my hand across them and I turned to face him.

"Sorry?" I asked.

Tim turned and looked at me, "'Son of man, you cannot say, or guess, for you know only a heap of broken images, where the sun beats and the dead tree gives no shelter, the cricket no relief, and the dry stone no sound of water. Come in under the shadow of this red rock, and I will show you something different from either your shadow at morning striding behind you or your shadow at evening rising to meet you.

"'I will show you *fear*," he concluded, "'fear in a handful of dust.'"

"What is that?" Maria asked from beside me, her voice choked and little more than a whisper.

"A poem," Tim replied, "written by someone a long, long time ago. Sounds like he was here when he wrote it, doesn't it?"

Yes it does, I thought sadly as another crooked, warped and likely green sign, blackened around the edges loomed overhead. It was difficult to make out all that was written upon it but one thing stood out in perfect relief against the backdrop: A reflective, white-tinted-red-because-of-the-sky number "9."

Our exit, I thought. We had made it. Yet no one spoke. I heard a steady "click, click, click" from beyond the front seat. I looked forward and saw that Matt had instinctively turned on the truck's right turn signal. A moment later, he taxied the Suburban onto another fractured and curved exit ramp and we left the Highway behind us once again.

For the last time? I thought yet somehow, that thought seemed premature. We began what we hoped was the last stage of our journey on little more than a gravel road toward freedom in complete and utter silence as the residual framework of the world that had once-been continued to span the area that surrounded us.

CHAPTER TWENTY FIVE

In time, we left the majority of the ruins behind us. *Thankfully,* I thought. Slowly, the land that surrounded us once again grew vacant of any once or current habitation and I breathed a sigh of relief.

I'd rather nothing than a graveyard, I thought, though my thought was, I understood, inaccurate.

You should have thought I'd rather less of a graveyard than MORE of one, my cold and rational voice corrected me, and it was correct. I knew that the entire area that we passed through was one, massive tomb. The only difference between what we had seen previously and what we were currently passing through was, as I mentioned before, the scope of the catastrophe that had befallen the once-inhabitants of the Eastern Territory, otherwise known as the Scorched Land. None of mine and Maria's companions spoke. All seemed dumbfounded by what we were seeing. My thoughts briefly returned to the dense collection of shadowy ruins that I had beheld in the distance.

A city? I considered. It must have been, I reasoned. I saw no other explanation. But what it was... shit, what it had been was irrelevant, I understood.

That world is gone, Pat's voice mentally reminded me, *and this world is your world now, William. While accepting that may not be the easiest task it is one that you need to accept if you want to survive in it.*

I know, I responded as time moved onward without check and the remains of the road once-designated as "9" continued to unfold in the darkness before us.

To Tim's, Matt's and Jeff's credit (since all had, at one point or another, worked on the Suburban), our oft-times recharged and repaired truck held out longer than it should have, especially considering the terrain over which we traveled. The only thing that separated 9 from 61 was the absence of sinkholes. Either Tim's distance estimates had been wrong or the minimal charge that we had gained while stopped at the wolf preserve had been enough to get us a good 30 or 40 kilometers further than we had originally anticipated getting. While I didn't and still don't know how far we made it before the solid, red battery light that had appeared on the dashboard of the truck some time before began to blink I assumed, perhaps optimistically, that we were at least 50% of the way down 9. Which left...?

What? I wondered, *50 or 60 kilometers to go until we arrive at Hempstead?* It was still a long way to walk. I refused to think about where the pursuant army of machines was as, with a loud sigh, Matt slowed the Suburban to a crawl and taxied it onto what remained of the right shoulder of the road and the spoiled ground and dried reeds beyond it. It came to a rest about three meters away from the road surface as the blinking, red battery light disappeared entirely and we were plunged into complete darkness.

Complete, save for the glowing, angry red sky overhead.

"Tim," Matt said quietly, "light?" It was the first any of us had spoken in what felt like ages.

I heard Tim grunt an affirmative as he shuffled and, eventually, removed his satellite phone from his pocket. The series of pulses that had danced across its screen continued to do so. I heard a series of taps before bright, white light stabbed through the gloom. I squinted at its sudden appearance.

"Note to *all*," Tim said, "I've got maybe a few moments of battery life left on this thing. We should use it sparingly. Who knows when we'll need it?"

"Good thinking," Steve said earnestly from behind me as he leaned forward over the second row seat back and into my peripheral vision, "as much as I hate to say this, shouldn't we shut off the jamming frequency?"

"We should, Doc," Matt said and asked Tim to do so. He did without hesitation.

"Might as well kill the flashlight too," Matt added, "what illumination there is outside will have to be enough."

Tim nodded and did as Matt had requested. Darkness once again descended over the interior of the Suburban.

"Well then," Steve continued after a moment, "what now?"

"Isn't it obvious?" Matt said, "We push this baby as far off of the road as we can, grab what we can carry and start walking. Any objections?"

No one had any. We quietly piled out of the truck and onto the hardpacked soil upon which it sat as the first drops of rain began to fall out of the overarching red sky and a slight... not humid but surprisingly cool breeze blew across our stubble-covered and dirt-streaked faces.

Matt shifted the truck into neutral and with Steve's and Jeff's assistance pushed it another five or six meters into the tall reeds before it stopped moving. Tim, Carole and Caren proceeded to empty what supplies they could salvage from the secret compartment beneath the third row of seats into our backpacks. Maria and I stood with our weapons drawn by the roadside and watched for any sort of movement. There remained none as the sporadic drops of rain that had begun to fall a short while previously intensified into a light drizzle. A few moments later, the rest of the group joined us by the roadside, backpacks in hand (they handed me mine and Maria hers) and informed us that we were ready to move.

"I'll take point," Matt said as he moved down the shoulder of 9 a meter, "Jeff, you've probably got the best eyes of any of us *and* the other pulse rifle so why don't you bring up the rear? Everyone else stay between us. Walk in single file. Keep the person in front of you within sight and your eyes peeled. At the *slightest* sign of anything out of the ordinary let the rest of us know no matter how trivial it seems. Then break as far as you can off the road and *get down*. Hopefully we'll be able to get under cover before anyone or any*thing* spots us. Capice?"

"Cap… *whatever*," Steve said with a chuckle as he removed his blaster from its holster and clicked "off" its safety. The rest of the group followed suit. Matt nodded within the dim, red light that emanated from the sky, turned away from us and extended the barrel of his pulse rifle out before him. He started to move cautiously down the road. Caren followed closely behind him and was followed by Steve and Carole. Maria came next and I followed directly behind her. Tim took up position behind me and Jeff assumed his designated spot at the rear of our party. As the light drizzle that had broken out continued to fall upon us and a slight, humid breeze continued to cool our damp brows we started south along the shoulder of 9, unsure of how much longer we had to travel until we reached our destination… unsure of what resistance waited for us in the shadows beyond our limited range of vision.

Time passed. No one spoke. The scene surrounding us remained the same. You've seen me write those words or a variation thereof multiple times over the course of this chronicle. I'm not being intentionally repetitive. Those words define much of what remains in the Eastern Territory to this day. It is difficult to describe it as anything *but,* but I promise you that before my story is done you will… well, to quote an old poet whose name I still do not know, "see something different than either your shadow at morning striding behind you or your shadow at evening rising to meet you." As for "fear in a handful of dust"

Well? I leave that for you to decide.

After a while, the light drizzle intensified into a steadier rain. It did not take long for said rain to soak through the tattered clothes that my companions and I wore. Were it not for the heat and the rising humidity we might have all begun shivering but as it had Maria's and my second night on the road, the falling rain surprisingly soothed us. I felt a few of the nagging aches and pains that racked my body, specifically my still-ailing left shoulder dissipate as our trek southward continued. Sometime after we had left our abandoned transportation behind us I heard something unusual and out of place, carried back to me on the slight, warm breeze that buffeted my cheeks and blew my lengthening hair back in waves behind me. The sound was not threatening... it was far from it. The sound that I heard was humming. There were no lyrics at first but I soon heard someone in front of me—*Steve*, I realized—singing in a low baritone.

"*Sixteen tons, what do you get? Another day older and deeper in debt. Saint Peter don't you call me cause ALL I KNOW...*"

"*I OWE my soul to the company store,*" someone—*Tim*, I realized—sang from behind me.

"*DO, do, do, do, duBEEe-do-DO,*" Steve continued, and sang something else that I could not make out before he reprised the portion that he had already sung. The second time through, however, others in our group picked up Steve's chorus until everyone save for Maria and I were singing along. While I had never heard the lyrics before that moment they were, admittedly, catchy and I quickly figured them out so that by the time the third or fourth reprise began I was singing along with the rest of the group. Maria was, as well. Those few moments upon the shoulder of 9 were the first moments of real levity that I had felt since mine and Maria's rendezvous in Centralia. I closed my eyes briefly as another surprisingly cool breeze blew past me and caused me to shiver...

I opened my eyes quickly and stopped dead in my tracks. Tim came within a hair of bumping into me, broke off mid-"company store" and exclaimed "*William, what the...!?*"

At the slightest sign of anything out of the ordinary, no matter how trivial, Matt had cautioned us before we had set out.

Well, I considered, *isn't a cool breeze in contrast to the hot and humid one that has been blowing all evening out of the ordinary?*

Captain Obvious, Maria mentally scolded me. Physically, she stopped about a meter away from me and turned around in response to Tim's outburst to see what had happened. Upon seeing me standing still behind her she mentioned my name at the same time that I shouted Matt's. I saw the shadows in front of Maria pause their passage south along the roadside...

saw them move north toward where I stood. Their features became more visible as they closed the distance between us. Another stronger breeze, also cool again blew past me before I could say another word, seemingly paused upon my position, swirled around me…

And resolved itself into the black-clad shape of another, newer shadow directly to my right. I speedily turned to bring my weapon to bear upon it…

And froze as the sharp tip of something manifested itself and pressed upward directly beneath where my chin met my neck. I gasped in a combination of surprise and pain as a gravelly, toneless and unfamiliar female voice whispered in my right ear.

"Do it," the strange, female voice drawled, *"please."*

I watched helplessly as the shadows on either side of my companions both before me and, if Tim's and Jeff's gasps were any indication behind me resolved themselves into similar, black-clad shapes. All were hooded, their faces indistinguishable, and all carried some variation of firearm or other, hand held weapon. Swords, knives…

Any color that you like, Vato, Pat's voice whispered in my mind. Said whisper was followed by that then-unfamiliar-but-now-familiar voice speaking one, singular word that resounded in my mind as the steadily falling rain intensified suddenly into a downpour.

Mercs, it said, though little confirmation was required, sarcasm *fully…*

Well, you get the point.

"Your blaster," the figure to my right whispered in my ear. The sharp tip of whatever weapon she carried did not waver, "hold it out in front of you. *Slowly.*"

I did not speak. I barely breathed. Per her request I extended my blaster outward and was careful to keep my index finger as far away from its trigger as possible. *No point in provoking her,* I thought. I watched helplessly as a white forearm, beaded with rainwater emerged from the shadows to my right.

No, I realized, *not just shadows.* Her hand and forearm had emerged from the sleeve of some sort of cloak or robe. She deftly plucked my blaster from my hand. I sensed rather than saw her glide across the area to my right and reappear in front of me. I realized per the distance between us that the tip of the blade held against my neck was the tip of a slim and slightly curved sword.

And sharp, I considered as I shifted slightly and felt the blade press harder against my neck. I still could not see her face nor could I determine her height, and she was too far away for me to even entertain the prospect of moving against her.

And why would I? I thought comically, *after all, I didn't even see or sense her coming. What a neat fucking trick.*

"That goes for the rest of you," she said without turning and interrupted my thought process, "hold your weapons out in front of you. If you as much as *flinch,* you're dead. Any questions?"

No one objected nor replied. I watched as each of my companions held out their weapons in turn and had them taken away. Maria spared me a concerned glance as her own blaster was plucked from her hand by the shadowy, hooded figure that stood on her right.

It'll be okay, I mentally comforted her. Whether she sensed my thought or not, I never found out. Once we were sufficiently disarmed, the woman that had accosted me slowly lowered the sword that she held to my neck so that it was perpendicular to my midsection, reached up with her empty left hand (*where the hell did my blaster go?* I thought) and pulled back the hood of her cloak.

Her appearance was, to say the least, a surprise. *God damn,* I thought, *she actually looks pretty normal.* She stood about Maria's height, a head shorter than me. Her short and straight, lightly-colored hair framed a face that was smooth, not grizzled or gravelly like her voice. She smiled and accentuated two, small dimples, one on either cheek. Upon the bridge of her nose rested a pair of thin-framed spectacles which were quickly beading with rain water now that she had removed her hood. I could not tell the color of her eyes though her complexion combined with her appearance immediately made me think of something light. As if sensing my observation her smile widened and she cocked her head slightly to the left.

"A young one," she said, seemingly amused after a moment. I nodded but did not speak.

"Which one of you is in charge?" she asked. She had not shouted but her voice had, seemingly, carried across the entire area.

Another neat trick, I thought, *like the one that Pat used back in the clearing.* That thought inevitably led to another: Were these the mercs that Pat had been talking about? If so, they seemed less than receptive to me and my companions, contrary to his reassurance that we would be able to trust them. I glanced longingly at the tip of the blade that hovered a hair away from my stomach.

Trust you? I thought, *maybe when your sword isn't a sneeze away from spilling my guts.*

I heard someone clear his throat toward the front of our group. It was

Matt. The newcomer's smile faded. She returned her head to an upright position and turned it slightly to the right.

"And you are?" she asked. Matt introduced himself.

"Well, *O'Brien*," she said, "it's a… *pleasure* to make your acquaintance." The word "pleasure," as intoned by her, sounded far from it.

"And *you* are?" Matt inquired. His voice did not carry nearly as well as hers had but she had, by her response, heard him perfectly.

"Amy," she said, "and that's *all* you need to know. This isn't Howdy Doody Time, after all." I thought about asking her who Howdy Doody was and what his or her time had to do with anything but decided against it as she continued.

"Seems that you and your people have a death wish," she said.

"How so?" Matt asked immediately from the front of our group. I could detect a hint of annoyance in his tone, "and there I was thinking that we'd actually managed pretty fucking well up until this point… *Amy*."

She chuckled, a low and dastardly sound, and after a moment continued. "I don't equate *luck* with *well*, O'Brien. They're two entirely different concepts. Singing? Really? You're not very skilled at avoiding attention. We heard you coming even before we smelled the cigarettes on the one wearing the purple shirt with the coke-bottle eyeglasses."

"I think she's talking about you, Marine," Steve responded and I heard him gasp as someone asserted his or her dominance over him. He followed his gibe with, "alright Lurch, don't get your panties in an uproar."

"Either way," Amy continued, "you should have kept quiet. As-is, you got lucky… *again*. We've been following your movements for a while and we know about what happened in the Water Gap. The machines that have been following you are still a ways away but they have your trail. They *are* coming. You should know that the Administration doesn't fool around. They obviously want you pretty badly though…" she paused as she looked at me from my tips of my toes to the top of my head, once again found my gaze and smiled before she continued, "though *what* they want from a couple of runners and a group of ex-pats is beyond me."

I thought about the Artifact that I carried and instinctively, my hand shifted slightly toward the front, right pocket of my jeans. I paused, and prayed that the movement had been imperceptible enough. Judging from Amy's response (*or lack thereof*, I thought), it was.

"Still," she continued, undaunted, "it's not my business. We were sent to collect you and that's what we're going to do."

She reached beneath her robe with her left hand and removed, from within it, something smaller than Tim's satellite phone. She placed it to her ear and depressed the button on the side of it. I heard a muffled "beep" and then a male voice asking her to "report."

"We have them, Pete," she responded, "bring up the transport."

The voice on the other side of the communicator said "copy that," and I watched as she simultaneously replaced the communicator beneath her cloak-robe and four bright, white lights—two large ones on top and two smaller ones beneath and at an inward angle—appeared roughly a quarter of a kilometer south down 9 from our position. They grew in size as the transport moved slowly toward us until they and it stopped no more than five or six meters from where Matt stood. I could see my companions clearly... could see the steady rainfall that had broken out over the area. And I could see the collection of cloaked figures standing around us all. No one but Amy had removed their hood. I redirected my attention to her and saw that she once again gazed at me. She was smiling.

"What?" I asked instinctively, a noticeable edge to my voice. Amy once again cocked her head slightly to the right. She slowly lowered the point of her sword from where it had been hovering and stepped toward me.

"You have... *nice eyes*," she said tentatively as she moved to within a step of me, "innocent. Unblemished. Too bad, really," she said as her left hand flashed toward me in my peripheral vision. I saw that it held something though I could not make out what it was until it collided firmly with the side of my head. As white hot pain exploded in my left temple and the world around me wavered I realized that she had hit me with the butt of my own weapon.

Well isn't that ironic, I thought as I helplessly dropped to my knees amidst the cries and shouts of my companions. I could hear Maria's voice most clearly. It was choked with tears and was pleading with Amy... with anyone that would listen to *"leave him alone!"* But none of that mattered, I realized, as the butt of my confiscated weapon once again collided with my left temple and I fell face first on the shoulder of the road. The last sensation I was afforded before darkness overtook me was one of liquid warmth running down my left cheek. The taste of the acidic rain that had puddled upon the shoulder of the road mingled with the metallic taste of my own blood upon my lips as I gasped one, final time...

And blacked out.

* * *

I was someplace unfamiliar. *No,* I thought, *not entirely unfamiliar. I've been here before though admittedly, I never thought I'd be here again.*

The short, cement walkway began at the tips of my boots and stretched away and up a small hill for a short distance before it terminated at a cracked set of steps. *Three,* I counted as my gaze traced the steps up toward the onset of the covered, wooden porch that I had spent many nights sitting upon. Sometimes I had sat silently, looking out and over the houses across the street at the stars and, occasionally, the moon (when its position was right). Others I had sat with a cigarette cupped in one hand so that no one passing by— human *or* machine—could see it and a phone in my other talking quietly… almost whispering to my oldest, dearest and truest friend, Maria Markinson. Those times, normally post-the Administration imposed curfew, were the most memorable. Rarely had I been joined upon the porch by another member of my family. Not even my little sister Kaylyn had disturbed my privacy. Save for my bedroom, the front porch of my old house in Jefferson, MWT had been my lone retreat.

And yet there was something different about not only the porch but the house beyond it. I looked up at the sky and realized that it was twilight.

Or sunrise, I thought. There really was no way to tell the difference. I looked back at the porch and re-evaluated its… *strangeness.*

Yes, I reasoned, *it is different.* The familiar, dirty white, plastic furniture that had sat upon it for as long as I could remember was not plastic but wicker. And the house's siding? Not the dull and faded green that I recalled but light yellow and new. There were no gaps anywhere showing the black, vinyl surface behind. I took a step… two steps up the walkway toward the porch.

There were other dissimilarities, as well. The gate which had often hung opened and on a slight angle due to years of neglect and general disrepair was closed and upright. The once-weathered and faded wood that had comprised the porch itself stood in stark contrast to the siding: Deep and brown, it looked like it had recently been refinished. The tattered, bamboo shade that had hung crookedly from the overhang of the roof was gone and had been replaced by a pristine white one. As I gained the foot of the staircase that led up to the closed gate I determined that even the porch light was different. Not the dirty, faux-brass fixture that it had been but a striking, black iron one. The light bulb within it was currently dark but I knew it would not be for long as I once again glanced up at the sky and realized that it had grown darker.

Twilight then, I understood, and reached out my left hand to unhook the latch that held the gate closed.

"'Something to behold, isn't it, William?" came a familiar, male voice from behind me. I turned and instinctively raised my right arm but the weapon that I had been armed with wasn't there...

Of course it isn't, Willy, Maria's voice spoke in my mind, *a merc named Amy just clocked you upside your stupid head with it...*

And gasped. Alex Parker stood upon the walkway. He appeared as he had the last time I had seen him in Freeworld One, dressed in a dark blue, button down shirt with a white t-shirt or undershirt beneath it, the top of which was visible at the collar. The button down was tucked into a pair of tan pants, the cuffs of which hung over a pair of black boots. His wavy black hair remained untrimmed and hung loosely just above his shoulders. His clear, marble colored eyes stared back at me and he grinned brilliantly. He, too, was not wearing a weapon.

"My," I began, paused, and continued, "I grew up here, Alex. And yet it looks so... so..."

Alex took a step forward, *"Different?"* He stopped and turned his head first to the left, then to the right, then up and then down before he settled his gaze back upon me, "Yes, William. I suppose that it does. Why do you think that is?"

I turned from Alex and looked at the house again. *My home,* I thought but knew despite said thought that it had ceased to be my home the moment I had decided to run... the moment I had shimmied down the drainpipe which still stretched from the roof, past the second floor window of my once-room and to the ground. The moment I had walked away from it at first alone, and later with Maria beside me. My only home, I knew, was the road. *The Highway.* At least until, God, gods or whatever deities governed the universe willing, I reached Free Caymen.

"I don't," I began, "I don't know, Alex. The porch, the furniture, the siding... *everything* is different. I don't get it. Did they renovate it or something?"

"I wouldn't say renovate," Alex continued, "though when last I checked there *was* an extension on the back of this, particular house that didn't exist on... well, maybe I'm getting ahead of myself. I have a knack for doing that. As odd as this all seems, William, there is a reason why though... well, I honestly don't know how much of that reason you'll comprehend."

Understanding filled my mind, "The car in Centralia. The *red* one. That *was* the car from my dream, wasn't it?"

Alex's smile widened and he shrugged, "Yes. And no, William."

Oh Christ, I thought, "You're talking in riddles, Alex. Either it is or it isn't. Which one?"

"Not everything needs to be as cut and dry as yes or no, William," Alex continued, "*I'm* here, aren't I?"

I nodded.

"But I'm dead," he said, "I died in Freeworld One. How can I be dead there but here with you, now?"

"Because you're a ghost," I answered, "one of Pat's *haints.*"

"Am I?" he asked. Surprisingly, I found that I was unable to answer him.

"William," he said as he took a step toward me and laid a hand (*he feels solid enough,* I thought) upon my right shoulder, "you're going to find that things like life and death don't mean as much in the *grand* scheme of things as you think they do. That which is gone doesn't always remain so. Confused?"

"Immensely," I responded, closed my eyes, and shook my head back and forth.

"'Think you can handle an explanation?"

"Try me," I said as I opened my eyes, and looked into his.

Alex nodded, removed his hand from my shoulder, and took a step back, "Okay then. You asked for it. Metaphysics 101, brought to you by Alex Parker." He gestured to his right, "Do you see that big oak tree over there?"

I turned to follow Alex's indication and saw it. Where there had once been nothing in my neighbor's front yard there currently existed a sprawling tree. I glanced at the dense trunk, better than three times my own girth and up. The first of the tree's limbs began roughly two or three meters above the ground. As the tree reached upward into the night's sky one limb became two, then two became four and four became eight. Eight became a dozen and a dozen became two. I could not see the top of the tree but I counted at least forty or fifty limbs at the edge of my sight. Most were covered with leaves though in one or two spots I could see the first of the night's stars through gaping holes in the foliage. I looked down and back at Alex.

"Tough to miss it," I said, "though I've got to tell you, Alex, I don't re-member *that*"—I gestured to the tree—"from when I lived here, either."

Alex's smile widened, "That's because you *didn't*, William. At least, you didn't live *here*. Yes, it looks like your house in Jefferson but it's really not. Just like the car in the garage in Centralia. It *looks* like the car from your dream but it's really not. This house? It's some*place* else. Not Jefferson in the Administration-designated Mid-Western Territory but Jefferson... *elsewhere,* if that's even what it's called here. Same thing with the car: It exists simulta-neously there, and *here*. But that's not what we should be focusing on, at least not yet. We *will* but for the moment, let's get back to the tree."

"Okay," I responded, thankful. My mind was spinning.

"Notice," Alex continued, "how it starts out at the bottom, closest to the ground. One singular, thick tree trunk. Move a little higher and one trunk becomes one trunk and one branch. Move a little higher? Three branches. Then a little higher? Ten, twenty, et cetera et cetera. Each branch grows its own branches and onward and upward. Think of this tree as... well, think of it as a *metaphor*. You know what a metaphor is, don't you?"

I shook my head. At the time, I did not.

Alex nodded, "A metaphor, William, is something that at some point of comparison is the same as something otherwise unrelated. An example would be that poem that Tim recited in the truck a short time ago. The poet wrote it as a metaphor of a culture... *his* culture that was, in his opinion, dying. Tim? He used it to describe the ruins that you were driving through. This tree? Well, it's the same way. Down here where we're standing"—he gestured to the ground upon which he stood—"it's singular. Simple. Not difficult to understand, is it?"

"No," I responded, "it's just a tree trunk."

"*Correct*," Alex said enthusiastically, "but move a little bit higher and it becomes more than 'just a tree trunk.' It evolves. It becomes complex. Now consider *this*, William. Consider that *once upon a time...*"

"'Cause all good stories begin as such," I interrupted and Alex chuckled.

"Yes they do," he added, "yes they do, William. You've got a lot of Pat McClane in you, do you know that?"

I shook my head. I had not considered the possibility that in my limited exposure to him I had adopted a portion of the former resident of Greentree, MWT's personality. But it felt like a compliment and I thanked Alex for saying it.

"My pleasure," he responded, "Pat was a good friend of mine for a long, *long* time. I'm glad that some part of him still exists in you. I wish I could tell you more about he and I... about all that we went through together. It's quite a story. But my time here, like his was, is short. Maybe someday but for *now*? I digress."

I nodded, "I understand, Alex. Please continue."

He did. "Consider that once upon a time there was a place of perfection, William. Different spiritualties, different creeds have called it different things throughout the ages. You may have heard a couple of the names and you may have not. I'm not going to belabor your mind with all of them here and now because I quite frankly? Every one of those names from 'Nirvana' to 'Shangri La' to *whatever* is inaccurate. It… well, it really doesn't *have* a name but regardless of that fact every one of them got one thing right. That place, William? It *did* exist and it was paradise.

"My particular creed? We called it 'Edona.'"

I nodded. *Edona,* I thought. I had never heard the term before yet like so much else that I had encountered it seemed somehow familiar despite its unfamiliarity. As if it was something that existed deep down within my subconscious mind and only manifested itself occasionally. Perhaps in passing…

Or maybe in dreams, the once-unfamiliar voice that I have since identified as the voice of my older self spoke.

"But over what passes for time both in the world that you know and elsewhere, William," Alex continued and stirred me from my introspection, "that place was lost. Every branch that grew from it was one more road… one more proverbial *highway* leading away from it. Eventually we all ended up here and for many of us? That path was lost like so much else that has been lost. Trumped by a little place that you, me and everyone that we cared for and continue to care about endearingly referred to and will continue to refer to as…"

"Endworld," I said without hesitation. Alex nodded.

"And all the shit that comes with it," he confirmed, "that term is more than just the name that people like you and me have chosen to call the place… the *Skew* that we reside in."

"*Skew,*" I said as my heart skipped a beat and my eyes widened.

"Yes, William," Alex said, "*Skew.* The place that we love, fight and die in? It's just one branch… one skewing of the tree. There are others. Other branches growing out of the tree trunk. Dozens, hundreds, thousands, millions and some might argue *billions* though I've never seen anything that would lead me to believe that there are that many. Each borne of a single, simple decision. Like a Choose Your Own Adventure book: If 'yes' follow *this* branch. If 'no' follow *that* one."

Realization began to dawn in my mind despite my unfamiliarity with what a "Choose Your Own Adventure Book" was. In truth? It had been building there for some time. I remembered my dream of Jefferson-not-Jefferson: A hazy, hot and humid afternoon, a road that wasn't the Highway and a red, long-nosed car that vaguely resembled the one from Centralia that Maria and I had consummated our feelings for each other upon.

Something was supposed to happen but it didn't, I remembered thinking, *and the repercussions of that something not happening?*

"Jesus," I spoke aloud, "Jesus, Alex. What the voice on the radio was talking about in my dream… that was *it*, wasn't it?"

"Was *what*, William?" Alex asked, but the grin that eclipsed the corners of his mouth betrayed him.

"*It*," I replied, "the moment that they became self aware. The *machines*."

Alex's smile widened and he nodded, "You most certainly are a quick study, William. And you're correct. But in *that* Skew? It never happened. One reality skewed into two. *That's* the core of this idea. Two completely distinct realities, separated only because once upon a time, someone chose 'yes' and not 'no.' But when you trim back all the branches? All the *Skews*? You find the original tree trunk that began it all. That trunk? We call it the *Unum Verum Iter*."

Latin, I understood, and inquired about its meaning. Alex took a step forward, and laid his hands back on my shoulders.

"The *One, True Path*," Alex stated, "it means the One True Path. Kind of rolls off of the tongue, doesn't it?"

I nodded and Alex chuckled.

"It *does*," was all that he said as he removed his hands from my shoulders and took a step back, "now reverse your thinking. Follow each branch from its tip back to the trunk of the tree. Then follow it down. You end up right back where you began, don't you?"

"At the bottom," I replied, "at… *paradise? Edona?*"

"Correct," Alex responded, "because it's all interconnected, William. All *one*. And if it's possible to travel from the base of the tree to the furthest, most expansive limb upon it…"

"Then it's possible to travel *back*," William interrupted, "that's what you're trying to say, isn't it?"

Alex did not speak. He did not nod nor move. His smile did not waver. He did not have to.

"That mark on your forearm," I said as I stepped toward Alex, "the same one on the letter…"

"The *Artifact*," Alex corrected, "that's not just what we call it, either. It's what the machines… hell, what almost *everyone* calls it."

I nodded, "the Artifact. The mark on *it* and the mark on *you*. The figure eight and the arrow. What does it mean, Alex?"

Alex cocked his head to the left, "You noticed that?" he asked, "I'm not surprised." He held up his left arm, underside out, and pulled back the sleeve. There upon his skin was the same sigil that I had seen in Freeworld One… the same sigil that was stamped on the seal upon the Artifact.

"*Explorator*," Alex said without hesitation and a definitive amount of pride, "it's Latin too. It means 'Pathfinder.' *Pathfinders*. My creed, William."

Pathfinder, I thought, but my thought was interrupted as I heard a door open behind me. I turned from the tree and from Alex back to the enclosed porch upon which I had sat so many, many times previously and beheld…

My breath caught in my throat and I paused. I gasped in shock and awe as I saw the figure that had emerged from within the house. Said figure stood roughly as tall as me with straight, brownish-black hair and a clean shaven, slightly rounded face. He was of medium build and was slightly overweight. Previous to exiting the house he had turned on the porch light which casted his features in stark relief against the yellow backdrop of the house. By that light I could see the newcomer's eyes: They were cloudy and blue. Deep, deep blue.

Like mine, I thought, and on the coattails of that thought another.

Exactly like mine. The figure that had emerged from the house?

It was me.

I watched, dumfounded, as the newcomer…

As I, I corrected…

…moved across the porch to the wicker chair furthest from the door and removed from within his front, right jean's pocket a pack of cigarettes. He placed the filtered end of one in the corner of his mouth as he sat down. He replaced the pack in his pocket and reached into his left one. His hand emerged holding something that glinted in the white light being cast across the porch and my eyes opened widely.

It was a simple, silver Zippo lighter… *my* Zippo which he opened and lit with a practiced motion. He touched the orange flame with the blue center that emanated from it to the tip of his cigarette and he dragged deeply. The end lit up like an orange-red cherry and faded. He exhaled a thick, blue-gray cloud of smoke and watched as it drifted up and clung to the underside of the porch roof. He replaced the lighter in his left, front jeans pocket and removed from within the same pocket a phone that was vaguely reminiscent of my companions' satellite phones though somehow I knew that it, like the entire place wasn't quite the same. He pressed a button on the top of it and the screen lit up. He tapped the screen a few times before he held it up to his ear. All at once, a smile broke out across his face. I watched and listened as best I could to the conversation that ensued.

"Sorry about cutting you off, Mia," he said, "Mom needed to go over a couple of last minute things with me." He paused for a moment and took a deep drag of his cigarette before continuing, "Yeah, we're leaving early in the morning tomorrow. *Real* early. 'Gonna try to be on campus by eight or so. You know, before the mad rush gets there."

He paused again, seemingly listening to what his Mia was saying. He took another drag of his cigarette, followed by another, "of course I'll call when I get there. I wish you could come but work's work. I understand."

I turned back to Alex as the conversation continued behind me. Alex once again stood a few steps away from me at the beginning of the walkway. He had replaced his sleeve over his left forearm. I could no longer see the sigil of the...

Explorator, I thought, and on the coattails of that, *Pathfinder.*

And on the coattails of *that*? *Unum Verum Iter, The One, True Path.*

Helplessly, I shivered.

"What *is* this, Alex?" I inquired as I took a step away from the onset of the porch and down the walkway toward the once-Steward of Freeworld One, "how can my house... the car... how can *I* be *here* and... I mean, it's not possible. It defies *logic.*" I paused and turned back around to face the porch and the house beyond it and added, *"Doesn't it?"*

Alex shrugged, "Someone once wrote that 'there are things known and things unknown and in between are doors.' That someone... well, his name is irrelevant but we Explorators, Pathfinders or whatever you want to call us don't call them doors, William. We call them *Gateways.* I know you've heard *that* word before, as well."

I nodded. *Skew, Pathfinder* and *Gateway.* In my mind the trifecta from my dream of Jefferson-not-Jefferson was complete.

"Some of the decisions that were made," he continued, "the ones like the one that you witnessed in your dream? They were monumental enough to not only cause a skewing of the Unum Verum Iter, but were *game changing* enough to leave a residue behind at the exact spot that they were made. That residue? It's accessible by certain... *parties* if they have the right skills and if they know the right *praecantatio.*"

"'Praecantatio?" I asked.

"Latin for *magic,* William. Those people?"

"Pathfinders," I said definitively.

Alex nodded, "At its onset each Skew was similar too but slightly different than its closest counterpart. Over time, though? Said Skews became more and more distinguishable from each other. It's kind of mind boggling to think that something as simple as turning right and not left can mean the difference between Endworld and *this* world"—he gestured around himself—"but it happens. Or, I should say, it *happened.*"

"But no longer," I responded, had an epiphany, and added, "*'there aren't many of us left.'*"

Alex's nodded again, "I wish I could tell you more about them, William. Heck, about *everything* but my time here is unfortunately almost up and this is, after all, nothing more than a beginning. Some things can't be told. Some things need to be learned and trust me when I tell you that you'll learn about *all* of these particular things soon enough whether you want to or not. But before that happens? You've got other business to attend to."

Alex's smile waned and he paused.

"You mentioned 'logic,'" he said after a moment, "Logic, William? Logic is a staple of a machine's programming, not a human's. Imagination, though? *That's* a human staple, not a machine one. Pat, Billy Preston… they're *all* right. Our ability to grasp the ungraspable is what sets us apart. It's why that despite their best efforts, the Administration has been unable to eradicate us and fully pollute the Iter. They've tried, and they've had *some* success but there are other places… other *Skews* like this one where they have failed, and others still that they don't even know exist. They never can, William. *Ever.* While you confront and deal with what waits for you back in *your* world… *Endworld*, keep the following in mind: There's more at risk… more at stake than freedom. Yours, Maria's…. *everyone's.* There always *has* been. The Artifact? So much relies on it finding its appropriate recipient and not falling into the wrong hands. Not just the hands of the Administration, either. There are others that have sought it for much, much longer than the Lord Cornelius I and those others? They're even more dangerous than the machines if you can believe it. If that happens, William? If it falls into *their* hands, then it's not just Endworld that's at risk. It's not just the Skews closest to it, either. All of *this*"—he gestured to the area surrounding him—"*every*thing is in danger. The 'All,' if you will. Despite what's happened to you this far and all that's poised to happen to you when you wake up, never forget that anything is possible if you're simply willing to put what you've grown over time to believe is real aside, and allow yourself to believe that what you're seeing here… what you're experiencing *right now* as I'm talking to you is just as real as the hand that's caressing your cheek… *back there.*"

I moved to question Alex further but held back when I realized that he was right: I could feel the gentle caress of someone's hand upon my cheek. There was pain there, I understood as it began to creep back into my joints and I hesitated. I glanced back longingly at the porch and the person that sat upon it.

Me, I understood, *but not me?* For the first time since leaving Jefferson with Maria by my side so many, many nights before I longed for the security of my childhood home. I missed not only my porch but my room... my sister... even my parents. Simultaneously I turned back to Alex as the figure sitting upon the porch laughed and pleaded with his Mia "not to call me Willy." He removed a fresh cigarette from his pack and lit it from the smoldering remains of his previous one.

My God, I remembered as the scene that surrounded me began to waver and fade, much as the scene in Centralia had at the cessation of the Pat-specter's visitation. The scene playing out upon the porch was one that I was incredibly familiar with, everything from the statement "don't call me Willy" to the lighting of a new cigarette from the smoldering ashes of a previous one. I had said the same things... had done the same things more times than I could count, back when I and Maria Markinson had lived in a little town called Jefferson, MWT...

"And no one lived anyplace else," I vocalized as I looked up and into the clear, marble eyes of Alex Parker. His eyes were, I realized, all that remained of him as the once-Steward of Freeworld One's figure grew transparent and began to fade.

"Alex," I began, but I knew that my words had fallen upon deaf, if not non-existent ears. Alex's eyes began to waver. But before they vanished entirely, I heard him speak despite his lack of a mouth four incredibly familiar words. They had been a mantra for me... had repeated themselves in my mind multiple times since I had left Pat within the clearing by the shifting and undulating light of the fire that had consumed his once-truck. I had never understood the meaning of said words but understand them from that moment forward—as solidity departed the dream and I opened my eyes—I did, despite the fact that Alex, as far as I could remember, had never translated them for me. Neither had Pat.

No one had.

"Unus est vera semita," Alex had said as the dream had collapsed and I had slowly awoken to a dimly lit world filled with pain, "There is..."

CHAPTER TWENTY SIX

"William…"

Only…

"William? Open your eyes, William. *Please* open…"

One True Path, Alex's voice completed in my mind. It was replaced by Jeff's voice first, speaking my name, and then Maria's voice doing the same. Both echoed through the cramped interior of wherever we were. I opened my eyes per their requests. Above me, a light flickered and casted a ghoulish glow over the area. I closed my eyes against its glow and re-opened them more tentatively. I glanced over and saw a familiar, snow-white hand caressing my cheek. My gaze slowly traced the length of the hand, the forearm attached to it and the body beyond it and fell upon Maria's deep, brown eyes. I was lying in her lap and she looked down at me, her expression veiled with concern. I could see liquid residue glistening in the dim light upon her cheeks. *Tears,* I considered, *or rainwater? Both?* I did not know. Instinctively I tried to sit up and the room spun. My stomach clenched. Simultaneously another, larger hand appeared in my peripheral vision and pressed gently upon my chest.

"No, William," I heard Jeff say as his own face appeared directly in front of mine, "don't. Lie back. *Rest.*"

I did as Jeff had asked. Simultaneously I saw Maria's other hand move towards the left side of my head. In it was something and I cringed, my memory of Amy hitting me with the butt of my own weapon fresh in my mind.

"Relax, William," she said as she paused, "it's an ice pack. It'll help with the swelling and the pain."

I sighed but did not speak (*she hits me in the head with my own weapon and then gives me an ice pack for the pain? What fucked up kind of rationale is that, merc or not?*) as Maria placed the ice pack gently against the left side of my face and temple. I closed my eyes against the sensation. It was soothing but did little to ease the pounding in my head and my jaw.

Not to mention my still sore shoulder, I thought, *Christ I'm a train wreck.* I stifled a chuckle. Laughing, I realized, would do little to alleviate my pain. I opened my eyes again and allowed myself to look around. We were in a small enclosure, featureless save for the lone, flickering light above our heads. A bench lined the wall upon which Maria sat and I reclined. A matching one lined the wall across from us where Matt, Tim, Carole, Steve and Caren sat. All surveyed me with equivalent looks of concern and...

Confusion? I watched as Jeff moved back across from me and Maria to the opposing side of the enclosure and sat beside Caren. I shifted my gaze to the front wall which was empty save for what appeared to be an opening or a window, closed. I could not see the rear wall but I judged from the size of the enclosure and the sensation of movement beneath me that we were in transit.

In the transport, I concluded, and spoke.

"How..." I began, my voice still muffled, "how long?"

Caren's gaze wavered and she shook her head, "Not very. No real way to be sure considering..."

"We can't see where the hell we are," Matt concluded as he gestured to the barren walls of the enclosure, "but something tells me that we're still moving south."

"Seconded," Jeff said as he crossed his left leg over his right thigh, "definitely south. And straight. I don't get the impression that we've even turned since they herded us in here."

Steve added, "Like cattle," to Jeff's statement with a noticeable hiss. In my peripheral vision I saw Tim, Carole, Caren and Jeff all nod in unison. Silence descended over the enclosure before Carole, an indefinite amount of time later, broke it.

"And *these* are the people that are supposed to be *helping* us?" she asked, "They have a funny way of showing it."

No one added anything to Carole's statement. Most everyone's gazes averted from me as silence descended once again over the interior of the enclosure within which we sat or in my case, reclined. Our trek toward wherever we were being herded continued indefinitely, the only common denominators the feel of the ice pack that remained pressed against the one side of my face, Maria's hand upon the other, the pain in my head, the sound of the rutted and deteriorated road that passed beneath us and the steady "pitter-pat" of rain against the fuselage of the transport. Occasionally, I felt the vehicle shift briefly, suddenly either left or right but I equated said movement to my own dizziness and nausea. Matt, however, addressed it after one uncommonly violent shift.

"Wind," he said simply, "if I press my ear up against the wall I can hear it howling out there. Weather's worsening."

All assembled nodded but no one spoke. The weather was, apparently, the furthest thing from our collective minds. Sometime later, the transport seemed to slow before I felt easily the most noticeable shift in direction that I had experienced since I had awakened.

Left, I thought, *we just turned left.* Did left mean east? The vehicle within which we were gathered…

Or imprisoned, I thought…

…picked up speed and the shifting of the car first left and then right increased exponentially. I could hear the wind howling outside, even with my left ear cushioned by the ice pack and my right cushioned by Maria's jean-clad thigh. Beneath that I could hear something else: An unfamiliar and comforting sound that I was initially unable to associate with anything. After a moment, however, I figured it out.

Splashing, I realized. It sounded like water splashing against something solid. *A lot of water,* I understood, and it continued for a short while before the vehicle's trajectory seemingly lowered and it vanished. It was replaced by only the sound of the road surface beneath us, the sound of the wind around us and the sound of the rain that pelted the exterior of the transport.

I felt us turn a few other times after that. One time right, and then left shortly thereafter. A moment later, I felt the vehicle begin to slow and eventually, stop. Despite my still pounding head and the dizziness and nausea that threatened to overcome me I gently pushed Maria's hand and the ice pack aside and slowly sat up. I groaned at the sensation that racked my body as Maria's hand fell upon my shoulder and she bent toward me. She spoke my name. I lowered my head, raised my left hand—my still sore, once-dislocated left shoulder throbbed in protest—and shook my head slowly from side to side.

"It's okay, Mia," I said as the sensation faded slightly. I rose my head back up and looked first at her and then across the enclosure at the others, "I'll be okay."

Matt nodded and elicited a low and obviously sarcastic chuckle. "We're here, folks," he said, "wherever *here* is. I guess we're going to find out soon enough. Look sharp."

"Easier said than…" I managed before another wave of vertigo washed over me. I groaned and re-lowered my head. Maria's hand that had rested upon my shoulder shifted to the back of my neck and her fingers tousled the hair there.

Nice try, kiddo, I thought. I admired her for her attempt to comfort me but knew that it would take a great deal more to make me feel even remotely normal again. I heard a door open toward the front of the vehicle and quickly close. I heard other sounds, as well: Other doors opening and closing, along with the incessant sound of the rain pounding the fuselage of the vehicle and muffled conversation. I could distinguish Amy's voice despite the walls that separated us along with other, unfamiliar voices that I assumed to be the other, cloak-clad figures that had accosted us upon the shoulder of 9.

One such male voice seemed to stand out from the others if only for the way it projected itself across not only the area outside the vehicle but seemingly into the vehicle, as well. Said voice seemed to not be engaged in the conversation but leading it as it calmly ordered a series of unfamiliar names to do various things. The bulk of his directives were unfamiliar to me and the one or two that I managed to catch did little to answer any of my or my companions' questions. After a few, hectic moments the conversation outside lessened and, eventually, faded. Silence once again fell throughout the interior of the enclosure. I glanced across the faces of my traveling companions and eventually, back to Maria and saw confusion mingled with anticipation in their expressions.

Now what? I thought. My inquiry was promptly answered as the same, male voice that had distinguished itself from the others echoed through the interior in which we were gathered. *It's as if he was in here,* I thought and once again marveled at the trick that so many associated with Pat McClane seemed able to perform.

So much for originality of thought, Vato, Pat's voice spoke in my mind and I groaned again.

"LET THERE BE LIGHT!" the voice exclaimed and caused us all to start in surprise. Simultaneously, the rear wall of the enclosure which was actually a double door opened wide and per the male voice's statement, light flooded in. It was not the natural, ambient light of the sun. It was definitely artificial but given my diminished tolerance for any extreme—be it visual or auditory—I squinted at the sudden increase in illumination. A breath or two later, I opened my eyes against the glare and saw what awaited us outside of the vehicle.

The black-clad figures that had accosted us upon the shoulder of 9...

And others, I reasoned, *there's more here than there were there, I think...*

...had formed into an ad hoc honor guard on either side of the vehicle.

There appeared to be two dozen or so, roughly 12 on either side of the transport's rear entrance. The nearest two held the transport's rear, double doors open and the farthest from us stood almost directly in front of what once upon a time might have been a sign but had, in subsequent years, been reduced to little more than a few, meaningless letters: A highly stylized "W" followed by an "I" and an "L," followed by a sizable gap followed by two "O's" and a "D."

WILOOD? I considered, *what the hell is a "wilood?"* Behind the honor guard and on either side were what appeared to be portable floodlights. I counted four in all and all were on and pointed toward the rear of the vehicle and, subsequently, us. Said figures stood with their hoods still over their heads and their hands either down at their sides or folded in front of them. None held a weapon of any sort though who knew what they concealed beneath their cloaks or robes?

Learned that the hard way, my coldly, rational voice spoke in my mind and simultaneously, a fresh bolt of pain traversed my head. From within their midst and down the aisle that they had created across the cracked…

And painted? I considered, *is that painted…*

…cement emerged a man, roughly as tall as me, with spiked, lightly-colored hair and a well-defined jawline. He was flanked on his right side by Amy and on his left side by an unfamiliar female. He, unlike his counterparts and the woman on his right was dressed not in a cloak but in an ankle length, black trench coat that glistened in the artificial light that emanated from the flood lamps. I could not make out the color of his eyes because of the glare but I could see that he sported what appeared to be a genuine smile upon his stern face. Though his figure was an enigma because of the jacket that he wore I was still intimidated.

Something in that gaze and in that smile, I thought. Something in both marked him as a man not to be reckoned with despite his unknown, physical prowess. As if he had heard my thoughts his gaze immediately shifted to mine. He raised his arms up and over his head and faced the palms of his hands toward us. His smile did not waver.

"Welcome!" he said in the same, booming-but-calm voice that had a moment before echoed through the interior of the transport. I cringed as his eyes locked upon mine, "welcome, weary travelers to the town of Hempstead. My name is Ed Wilkinson but you can call me Ed. You already know Amy"—he pointed to the figure on his right who mimed what I assumed was a sarcastic curtsy—"and this *strikingly* beautiful woman on my left is my wife, Molly."

I glanced at Molly. She was shorter than Ed… hell, shorter than the shortest of my companions. She had long, dark hair, a slightly elongated face and jaw line and, like her husband, had unreadable eyes and was dressed in what appeared to be a black trench coat, the bottom of which terminated directly above her knees. Her gaze traced across the faces of my companions, fell upon me, paused for a moment and then returned to Ed's. Amy's gaze focused on the tall and lanky figure standing a few meters away from the transport's rear exit, as well. Rain continued to pour down around him and the others assembled but he and all of his…

Followers? Counterparts…

…were seemingly unfazed. A howling gust of wind blew across the exterior of the transport and kicked a spattering of rain into the enclosure. I felt it land upon my face and I shivered. *Warm,* I thought, as Ed lowered his arms and turned to his left. He gestured to someone there and one of the hooded figures moved toward him with something in his or her hands. I recognized it almost immediately.

It was my backpack.

The figure handed it to Ed and Ed replied with, "Thank you, Pete." I heard the figure say something that sounded like "no problem" before he turned and rejoined the line to my right. Ed turned back to face us and held the backpack up in the air.

"Which of you was carrying *this*?" he asked. His voice echoed across the area both within and outside of the vehicle, "Speak *now*." It was not a request but a directive.

I slowly shifted toward the exit of the car and raised my right hand despite the cautious way that Maria grasped my right shoulder. Her gesture seemed to say *don't, William* but I knew that I had no choice as another wave of nausea overtook me. Admittedly? I did not and still do not think said nausea was caused at that, particular moment by my pounding head. It was sickened by the situation and feared the worst, even before his gaze once again shifted and met mine. He lowered the backpack. His confidant smile widened and he nodded.

"And you are…?" he asked. I introduced myself as I had many times previously.

"William MacNuff," he said as he unzipped the backpack and reached into it. His gaze never left mine as he continued, "formerly of Jefferson, MWT. Ah *yes*! The Jefferson runner. That means that the striking young lady behind you is Maria Markinson, I presume?"

Maria's hand tightened upon my shoulder as she answered him with a whispered, "Yes."

Ed nodded, paused for a moment as he seemingly considered what to say next and finally continued, "On behalf of Amy and every one of my counterparts I apologize for the severity of your treatment. Understand that it is difficult to know who we should and *should not* trust with affairs the way they are currently and... *ahhh,"* he intoned as the hand which he had plunged into the backpack paused its movement. A moment later, he removed it and simultaneously dropped the bag to the wet and puddle-covered ground. His hand was clenched upon... *something* and the nausea that I had been experiencing increased in severity. My stomach clenched. I almost gagged as Ed took another step toward the open, rear exit of the transport—Amy and Molly kept pace and remained directly beside him—and opened his hand as he spoke.

"Of course, when a solution or rather, an explanation to the concerns that vex us presents itself we are, more often times than not, pleasantly surprised," he concluded as he finished opening his hand and revealed what he had removed from my backpack.

I did not recognize it at first: A small, black square that appeared smooth to the touch. He shifted it to between his index finger and thumb and held it out toward me as a few drops of rainwater beaded upon its surface. I heard a series of gasps from my companions. I turned, and saw them all staring back at me with looks of horror and understanding upon their faces. I watched as Ed dropped the cube to the ground directly outside and, without averting his gaze from mine, brought the heel of his boot down hard upon it. I heard it crack. Said cracking was followed by an unmistakable burst of electrical static that was audible over the rain and then? Silence. I *gulped* and once again tasted only bile. I did not need anyone to tell me what the cube had been. I knew it, even before Tim spoke.

"That's... it *was* a tracking device," he said quietly.

"Administration make," Carole answered him, "easily concealed. And *very*, very powerful."

"You've been transmitting a sub-wave, Administration frequency since we first picked you up in the Water Gap," Ed said definitively, "and likely *have been* transmitting it for some time. They're generally undetectable but thankfully, we have one of the best once-Operators in our ranks and he caught it relatively quickly. Tracking devices like *that* one"—he gestured to the shattered fragments lying upon the ground—"are the tools of a traitor."

His smile faded.

"Or an Infiltrator, William."

No, I thought as Ed turned to Amy and forcefully ordered her to "get him out of there *now*." Amy nodded her head and gestured to two figures in the line to my left. They nodded back as they moved forward and into the interior of the transport in a flash with Amy directly behind them. I heard Jeff begin to protest… heard Maria's shouted *"NO!"* as her hand slid from my shoulder, but any objection or debate was cut off immediately as Amy looked over my shoulder at my companions and stated, quite conclusively that they not "make this difficult." The two figures that she had summoned forcibly grabbed either of my arms.

I did not struggle as I was lifted easily from the bench upon which I had been sitting and thrust out the rear entrance into the pouring rain. I couldn't. I lowered my head to my chest for it was all that I could do to protect myself against the downpour. My left shoulder screamed in response and my head pounded with every step as I was dragged to within a breath of where Ed stood. I saw the tips of his boots directly in front of mine and I raised my head defiantly. Rain pounded my forehead and blurred my vision but beyond it, I could see Ed's eyes staring back into mine. They were, I finally realized, gray.

And clear, I thought, *crystal clear*.

"You're making…" I gurgled as a steady stream of rain rolled from the front of my lengthening hair into my mouth, "a mistake."

"Maybe," Ed responded as he cocked his head slightly, "but I don't have the luxury of due process, William. Especially not now." He looked over my shoulder at the two figures that supported me between them and Amy, who, I sensed, was directly behind me. Somehow, I knew that her sword hand was beneath her cloak. Somehow, I knew that her fingers were dancing within a hair or two of the hilt of her weapon.

Just in case, I thought. In her eyes and the eyes of the mercs I was, after all, a traitor.

But I knew the truth. I had been set up. The true traitor within our party? The Infiltrator? He or she had done their job very, very effectively.

"Take him to the Ghost Ship," Ed said, "lock him in the galley. Amy, meet us back at the deli when he's secure. We'll keep the others with us."

Amy spoke an affirmation from behind me. I felt one of her hands press in between my shoulder blades as she non-verbally coaxed me to move. I did as she had requested and began dragging my feet up the cracked and painted cement walkway toward the "wilood" sign. I noticed, as I gained the area directly in front of it, that the once-cement walkway had transitioned to one made of wood. Faded and weathered boards that creaked as I walked over them were spaced evenly apart and stretched to both my left and my right.

I glanced up at the sign and noticed that the gaping space between the first "L" and the first "O" that I had glimpsed previously was not entirely empty. Two other letters lay upon the walkway: An equally large "D" and another "W."

I filled in the blanks. *Wildwood,* I thought as Amy's hand once again materialized between my shoulder blades and she ordered me to turn left. I did as she had requested. As I did, two things happened simultaneously. The first thing was the emergence of Ed's voice from behind me which boomed across the entire area.

"Friends!" he addressed his counterparts, "our time is short. We have incoming Administration forces. While their means of pinpointing our exact location has been neutralized, they likely can extrapolate per the information that they have and the location of the last transmission where we are. We must make ready as if they will be here any moment and we must make ready *quickly!* Report to your designated posts… summon our reserves from their homes and prepare for engagement!"

A flurry of affirmatives from the black-cloaked figures assembled around Ed echoed through the rain and the wind as I continued my forced passage down the…

Wood walk, I thought, *board walk, maybe?* It was the best that I could do to distract myself from what was occurring. Any attempts to distract myself were forgotten, however, as the second thing registered. I could hear something off to my right. The sound that I heard was unfamiliar but surprisingly soothing considering the gravity of my situation: Water, crashing against something solid and then fading from my hearing, then crashing again before fading… *fading,* once again.

"What…" I began as we continued our passage down the wooden walkway, "what sound is that? Over to the right?"

The two figures that supported me on either side chuckled in response—*males,* I understood from the sounds of their voices—but Amy did not. Amy answered me without hesitation.

"The Great Sea," she simply said before she forcibly shoved me forward and caused me to briefly stumble, "Keep moving."

Despite the aforementioned "gravity of my situation" I helplessly smiled. *Made it,* I thought as the storm continued to rage around me and the night moved onward without check over Hempstead and a place that I had only ever heard of and dreamed of before.

Not theoretical anymore, I thought, and believe it or not? My smile widened as I was led through the downpour, down the old, wooden walkway toward...

I squinted against the pounding rain and observed a collection of shadowy, geometrical structures in the distance. They were seemingly constructed upon an extension of the walkway that jutted out toward where I assumed the Sea lay. From my vantage point I could not make out any details but I knew, however reluctantly, that I would be able to soon enough.

CHAPTER TWENTY SEVEN

Maria Markinson watched helplessly as William disappeared from her view and the doors to the enclosure were simultaneously closed. A moment later, she heard the front doors of the transport open and close again. The vehicle's engine sprang to life and she felt the unmistakable sensation of movement beneath her and around her.

Here we go again, she thought, but where to this time? Her gaze traced across the faces of her and William's travelling party. All stared off expressionlessly in various directions. She was distraught as she wiped a stray tear from her cheek and fought to catch her breath and her companions offered no solace... no alternative. There was nothing in any of their gazes that gave away a betrayal.

And why would there be? She thought. Whoever had planted that tracking device on William had done his or her job perfectly.

An Infiltrator, she thought. She shivered. It could be any of them. Even Jeff though she had believed and continued to believe what he had told her and William by the roadside during their brief stopover at the wolf preserve.

Jeff, she thought. She affixed her gaze upon him. Apparently sensing her gaze, he refocused his own from the closed entrance/exit to the enclosure upon her and managed a forced smile. She could not read his expression, not like she could read William's, but she hoped and prayed that his smile offered some sort of solace... some sort of solution to the problem that faced them.

Do you have a plan, Jeff? She thought but received nothing in response save for the same smile and the same unreadable stare. She sighed as she looked away from him and forward to the closed cab of the transport and felt the vehicle turn right. It was, she understood, hopeless as the vehicle within which they were being held continued its trek toward wherever it was taking them. Hot tears once again threatened to fall but she held them back.

Be strong, Mia, William's voice spoke in her mind, be strong for me.

I'll try, she thought back as the transport hit a bump or a pothole and she was jolted briefly upward. She heard what she thought was a similar sound from the cab of the vehicle—someone being jolted upward and then landing upon the bench, the seat or whatever they sat upon—but said thought quickly vanished as she heard an-other sound: Another, louder bump followed by a gasp and a grunt. Simultaneously and without warning, the transport veered violently to the right and she was thrown forward as her companions surprisingly tumbled across the enclosure's interior. Shouts of "What the hell!?" and more colorful profanities graced her ears as the vehicle suddenly and noticeably picked up speed.

What the...!?

Her thought was cut off as the transport's trajectory abruptly ceased. Thankfully for her she had already come into contact with the front of the enclosure. The others? They weren't quite as lucky. She watched as their momentum carried them in a tidy heap up the enclosure's center aisle. They pig-piled into the front of the enclosure as Maria felt the rear of the vehicle lift briefly off of the ground, and then lower with a subsequent smash. Something exploded beneath them (the tire or tires, she thought) and silence descended over the vehicle. Silence, broken only by the sound of the rain that pelted the transport's fuselage...

And that of a door opening and closing. Passenger side, she thought as her com-panions sought to untangle and right themselves. She heard footsteps on the pave-ment outside and on the vehicle's right. They circled around to the back of the vehicle and stopped. She heard something click within the double door exit/entrance and a rustling of cloth but that was all. As she watched, something slid beneath the small gap between the floor of the enclosure and the doors. She could see water glistening beyond it and outside but her eyes were intently focused upon...

She spared the others a glance before she slid down the length of the bench and gained the doors. She picked up the folded piece of paper and turned it over in her hands. She began to unfold it. She heard someone move up behind her as someone else—Steve, she realized—asked "what the fuck just happened?" and was promptly answered by Tim: "We crashed, you 'idget." Carole and/or Caren laughed nervous-ly. She heard Matt mumble something like, "Tim, move your hand," before Jeff spoke from directly over her shoulder.

"What the hell is that?" he asked.

"I don't..." Maria began as she managed to get it opened and glanced at it. It was a map. It was old and faded and the heading at the top of it was a simple one: "Wildwood, NJ: America's Playground." She asked Jeff if the term had any signifi-cance for him and Jeff paused briefly and considered it before he finally shook his head.

"It sounds familiar yet I can't say where or when I've heard it before," he said, and sighed, "I grew up far west of here... farther west than Jefferson, even, so I'm not that familiar with the eastern part of the continent."

He said nothing further and Maria did not press him. Beneath the heading was a long either brown or red pathway that stretched from right to left. But that was not what caught her and, subsequently, Jeff "Jeebus" Howard's eye. What caught their eyes was the area labeled "Mariners Landing" and the… what looked like a boat that someone had circled in dark ink within it. Maria squinted and could not make out the words that had once been printed beneath it but she understood.

"'Take him to the Ghost Ship,' Ed said," she said, "the Ghost Ship, Jeff."

She smiled. As evidenced by Jeff's subsequent smile he understood, as well. He moved past her and in the process patted her gently on her shoulder. He rested his hands on the surface of the double doors and pushed. They creaked but did not budge. He called for help and Matt and Caren moved quickly down the aisle and joined him by the doors. Maria did so, as well. All four of them laid their hands upon the smooth surface of said doors and on the count of three, shoved. For a transient moment Maria did not think that they were going to open but eventually, something gave within the superstructure. They swung open and slammed hard into either side of the transport.

Maria quickly scampered out into the pouring rain and glanced around. They had come to rest perpendicular to a crumbling and deserted street which was flanked by old and mainly deteriorating buildings. There was no sign of whomever or whatever had unlocked the double doors and slipped the map underneath them.

Strange, she thought as her toe caught on something. She looked down and saw a discarded, black robe lying at her feet.

Really strange, she thought again. She glanced forward up the body of the transport and saw what it had come into contact with: A large, seemingly wooden pole that had cracked near where the grill of the vehicle had hit it. It was precariously hanging on an angle over the roof and was swaying in the wind. Fearing the worst, she shouted for everyone still inside to exit and they did so quickly. They gathered around her on the pavement. No sooner had the last person exited than the pole snapped with a deafening crack and fell upon the roof of the transport. The force of the impact caused her and the others to jump backward. The respective roofs of both the cab and the enclosure buckled under the force of the falling projectile and caved inward.

Jesus, she thought, had we waited any longer we would have been crushed.

There's something to be said for that, Mia, William's voice spoke in her mind and despite herself, she smiled and looked at the map. Her gaze returned once again to the circled ship and the label: "Mariners Landing." She glanced up from it and saw that Matt had moved around to the driver's side of the cab. She watched as he looked within it and quickly turned away with a disgusted gag.

"Pulverized," he said. He turned back, reached his hand in and seemingly felt blindly around for something. Maria could hear cloth rustling for a moment before

Matt triumphantly "ahh'd" and emerged with first, a blaster which he shifted to his other hand and second, a slightly curved sword. He held up the former and glanced at the handle. He nodded. checked the safety of the blaster, and shoved it into the waistband of his slacks. He turned back to the group and asked who wanted the sword. Jeff immediately stepped forward.

"I'm not as good with one as Pat was but he taught me a few things," Jeff said as he held the sword up, swung it in an arc and then lowered it to his side, "I'll try to hold my own. That it?"

"That's it," Matt repeated as he stepped away from the cab and back toward the rest of the group, "it'll have to be enough for now. Any sign of whoever or whatever sprung us?"

Maria pointed to the crumpled robe that lay at her feet and shook her head, "I was the first one out. Other than that, the street was deserted."

Matt shrugged, "Well I guess we'll just have to thank our mystery benefactor the next time we see him or her... if we ever see him or her. In the meantime, did I hear someone say something about a map?"

Maria and Jeff both nodded and simultaneously answered Matt's inquiry with "yes." Matt requested to see it and Maria obliged. She handed it to Matt and he glanced at it in the minimal light provided by the stormy, red sky overhead. Jeff moved up on Matt's left and pointed to the part that was circled.

"I'm thinking we need to go that way"—Jeff pointed to the map and then to his right—"I honestly have no idea where we are with respect to this"—he pointed to the brown or red pathway—" but we'll know better once we get off of this street and into the open."

Matt nodded, "Ed did say 'Ghost Ship.' That certainly looks like a ship to me."

"Wait a second," Tim said as he moved up, reached out and snatched the map away from Matt, "Are you serious? You're not actually thinking about going after him, are you? He betrayed us. We wouldn't be here right now if it wasn't for him and you want to... what, go and rescue him?"

"That's exactly what I want to do and what I'm going to do," Jeff said calmly as he took the map back from Tim and took a step toward him. Maria sensed Jeff's grip tighten upon the hilt of the sword, "if you don't like it... Marine... you don't have to come. None of you do. But I'm going. End of discussion."

"Well I don't like it," Tim said, "and I won't come. I vote we find a place to hole up for the duration of whatever 'engagement' that Ed and his black-cloaked cronies are planning for. No one's going to attempt an extraction if there's a battle raging in town. Leave the traitor to rot."

"Tim!" Steve exclaimed, and Carole placed a hand on his arm. She turned to Jeff.

"He's right, Jeff," she said, "Think about this for a second. Use your common sense. Tim's right: He's a traitor. They caught him red-handed…"

"William MacNuff is NOT traitor!" Maria exclaimed angrily as she aggressively stepped toward Carole and raised her fist up, "and the next person who accuses him of that…!"

"EVERYBODY CALM DOWN!" Matt shouted as he stepped between Maria and Carole and held his hands out, "Jeff's right. You don't have to come if you don't want to. But he's going, I'm pretty sure Maria's going…"

Maria, whose angered eyes remained locked upon Carole's, nodded defiantly.

"And I'm going," he completed. Carole sighed and Tim muttered what sounded like "'idget" before Matt continued.

"Anyone else?"

"Me," Caren said without hesitation and moved across to where Matt stood.

"You?" Tim exclaimed, "You're the one person out of everyone that I figured would agree with me. After all, you pistol whipped him the first time you met him."

"I did," she responded, "and he repaid me by saving my life… potentially all of our lives on Halmier's Pass. You think someone that would do something like that would betray us, Tim?"

"He had an Administration tracking device on him!" Tim rebutted, "Doesn't that count for something?"

"Yes," Caren said defiantly, "it means someone set him up. I don't know who did or when but someone did. Maybe it was you, Marine!"

"And maybe it was YOU, Missus O'Brien!" Tim replied.

"Okay!" Carole exclaimed, "Enough! I've heard enough! Fuck it: I'm in. But if he so much as looks at me askance, Matt…"

Matt nodded, "Let's put it to a vote. All in favor?"

"Me," Maria said.

"And me," Jeff replied.

"Me," Caren said, "Matt?"

"Yes," Matt answered, "what about you, Doc?"

"In," Steve said, "Carole?"

Carole looked from Steve to Caren and then at Tim. She slowly nodded her head.

"Tim?" Matt asked. Tim paused, seemingly contemplating his answer before he threw his hands up in a gesture of futility.

"Oh for CHRIST'S SAKE!" Tim exclaimed, "Am I the ONLY fucking person with any sense in this group? ALRIGHT already. I'm with you. Jesus. I just hope to fuck you're right."

Matt smiled and nodded, "Me too, Tim. Me too. Settled, then. Let's move before either the mercs or the machines get here."

I'm not sure which is worse, Maria thought as Matt asked for the map and Jeff handed it to him. He glanced at it briefly, and then back to the right again before he started off in a trot toward the nearest side street and turned right down it. The others followed him. She was the last to move and as she did, she turned her head to her right in the direction that Jeff had indicated and sent in what she assumed was William's general direction, we're coming, William. We're coming. She then looked up at the blood-red, stormy sky. Rain continued to pour incessantly from it. She attuned her ears and heard nothing but the sound of it and the wind.

Nothing, she thought, but knew that the "nothing" that she heard was only temporary. The machines were coming. Ed had been right about that. The question was not if but when. And would they have enough time to get William out before the machines got there?

Time, Maria mused as she turned down the side street and followed her companions into the swirling blackness, what a bogus concept.

* * *

We continued our trek down the wooden walkway. An indeterminate amount of time later I glanced to my left and saw the onset of a seemingly unbroken row of abandoned structures. All were boarded up and, per the amount of weathering upon both the wood and the structures, had been boarded up for ages. I say "seemingly unbroken" because after every six or seven distinct structures, and proceeding the next six or seven, there was a break. It was difficult to make out what lay beyond them because of the darkness and the veil of rain that fell upon the area, but in one or two cases I could see a ramp or the remains of a staircase that led down from the surface of the wooden walkway to the surface of what might have once been a road but had since been reduced to little more than cracked asphalt, gravel and dried weeds. I gave little credence to these structures and refocused my gaze forward as our path brought us to within a few meters of...

Upon seeing the structures that I had observed from a distance up close, I quickly wished that I had never noticed them in the first place. The ruins that I had seen at the cessation of the Highway and at the onset of 9 had been daunting in their scope but in the end they had been easily explained as aftereffects of the Scourge. Most of what I had seen since entering the Eastern Territory was justifiable by the same. But the ruins that towered over me in Hempstead upon what, in fact, was an extension of the wooden walkway upon which I trod with one merc on either side of me and Amy directly behind me? They didn't really seem to be ruins at all. Most of the… *attractions* assembled upon the extension seemed to be relatively intact.

Relatively, I thought, *but I wouldn't want to take a ride on any of them.*

At the entrance to the extension was an arch. It spanned overhead for two or three meters and was anchored on either side by once-habitations not much larger in size than the ones that had comprised the town proper of Freeworld One. Said structures were also boarded up, but my eyes did not linger long upon them. My gaze returned to the arch and, subsequently, the raised words spelled out upon it.

Mariner's Landing they said. I could see what appeared to be broken light bulbs within the sign's interior. I did not speak nor question what I was seeing to my captors as Amy prodded me and told me to "keep moving" beneath the arch and onto the…

Landing I thought, *is that what this is called, then? A landing?*

I took in the scene beyond the arch as we continued our passage through the downpour. Numerous, free-standing structures of the same make as the ones that had marked the onset of the landing dotted the wood-planked surface of it. But the other structures… the geometric ones that I had seen from a distance were the ones that held my attention. One particular structure which towered above the rest looked like a very, *very* large wheel with…

Benches? Seats? I considered, spaced evenly apart upon its surface. There were gaps and in one or two places, the bench-seats hung loosely from one of its supports. As I watched, a swift gust of wind blew across the area and caused the two mercs who supported me, and by association me, to stumble. Simultaneously, one of the bench-seats which had been, to employ yet another old cliché "hanging on by a thread," broke free with a screech and tumbled to the surface of the landing. It hit it with a dull *thud*, the sound muffled by the wet wood with which it had impacted. I felt the two figures that held me jump and their grips upon my arms briefly relaxed. I considered an attempt to break free of them but the sound of rustling cloth, the pain racking both my head and my shoulder, and the feel of something pointy and sharp between my shoulder blades convinced me otherwise.

"Don't," Amy spoke with a hiss from directly behind me. No other convincing was required as the two mercs tightened their respective grips upon my arms and the tip of Amy's sword pressed harder. I clenched my teeth as I felt the skin beneath my water-logged t-shirt break.

"Forward," she continued and without any thoughts to the contrary, I did as she had requested. We moved past the large, iron wheel and a few other, unfamiliar and abandoned structures that stood and likely had stood

sentinel over the landing for ages. As we passed beneath the shadow of what in the dim, red light emanating from the sky resembled a sprawling, iron python (sarcasm *fully* intended) the Ghost Ship that Ed had referred to materialized before us.

It was just that, I reasoned: A once-water going vessel that had been moored to the landing. Its top was not visible because of the darkness and the downpour but I could see two, faded words painted high upon its surface: *Ignis Fatuus*. There were multiple holes in the ship's fuselage beyond which only darkness loomed and... what appeared to be a shadowy entrance facing us that we were quite obviously walking toward. A moment later, we crossed beneath the entrance/exit and into the relatively dry but pitch-black interior of the vessel.

The rain that had been falling incessantly upon us ceased. The area beyond the entrance was little more than a left-to-right hallway, and it echoed with the combined sounds of our boot falls, water dripping into puddles and the ceaseless rain that pounded the exterior as we began walking right down it. I could see nothing until I heard a rustling behind me. A beam of white light shot forth and reflected off of the featureless wall. Featureless save for a few, rusted rivets spaced evenly apart from top to bottom.

Let there be light, I thought and stifled a hysterical chuckle. Amy prodded me and I obeyed. We proceeded silently down the hallway for a short time before she ordered us to "stop" and we did. I watched her circle from behind me to my left, light in hand. It was not a satellite phone but a standard, battery operated flashlight. Once into my peripheral view she indicated a door a step or two away from us and on the left. I squinted as her light fell upon it and saw, painted upon the surface of it, black letters that spelled out a single word: "Galley." She looked over at me, smiled with what I assumed was sarcasm, and walked the last of the distance toward the door. She pulled it opened with a "screech" that rattled my teeth and made me cringe before it echoed up and down the hallway. She motioned for the two mercs holding me between them to move forward and they did. I did not struggle as I was brought to within a hair of her position. She looked up at me, her smile unwavering, and surprisingly winked.

"Inside," she commanded. Simultaneously, the two figures on either side of me forced me forward and through the doorway. I stumbled as I entered but I did not fall. I caught myself just before I tipped over and turned defiantly to face my captors.

"Thanks for the hospitality," I managed, though with the way the side of my face and subsequently, my jaw was growing progressively more and more swollen it sounded more like "'tanks 'foo 'da 'hofpitality." I considered adding "bitch" to my rhetoric but decided against it.

Amy shrugged and her smile faded, "'Least we can do. But just to show you that we're not entirely without mercy, *here."* She flipped the flashlight over so that the beam was facing out toward her and extended the shaft of it in my direction. I hesitated for a moment (*no weakness,* I thought, *don't show any weakness*) before I realized that "weakness" and "common sense" were two completely different entities. I reached out, took the flashlight and reluctantly thanked her, though what emanated from my mouth sounded like "'tank 'oo."

"Might want to preserve it until your machine buddies get here," she said as she stepped back, her other hand still on the door, "when last I checked that battery only had a little bit of charge left."

You're too kind, I thought as I held the flashlight down at my side and switched it off. Darkness descended over not only the galley but the hallway outside of it. A moment later, I heard the door once again screech loudly before it latched shut with a hollow *boom.* I heard something *click* within it.

Simultaneously, I turned on the flashlight and shined it in the direction of the closed door. The surface was featureless save for a small, metal plate that was, I reasoned, welded over the spot where the handle should have been. I could hear muffled voices outside in the hallway. Amy's voice ordered the mercs to stand guard and they acknowledged her directive with what sounded like affirmatives. I then heard boot falls echoing away, down the hallway in the direction we had come from. They grew quieter and more distant until they vanished entirely and were replaced by the same, dual sounds that I had heard earlier: Water dripping and rain pounding the Ghost Ship's surface.

I turned from the door, the flashlight still on, and took in the interior of the galley. It was a relatively small but long room, maybe two meters wide by five or six meters long with walls that were lined with empty shelves, cabinetry and in one or two places what looked like an old stove or a sink. I strolled slowly down the length of it and saw that anything functional had long since been plundered. I thought about searching the cabinets but decided against it.

Save your strength and your flashlight battery, my coldly rational voice tasked me as I turned back to face the door, realized that there was no place to sit, sighed with resignation and slowly lowered myself into a sitting position. I leaned my back up against the nearest cabinet, glanced longingly at the flashlight, sighed again and turned it off. I was immediately plunged into complete darkness. Despite it, I closed my eyes against the pain in my head and behind my temples as the rain continued to pound the fuselage of the Ignis Fatuus. I resigned myself to the inevitable truth inherent in my situation. My mind began to wander...

We're coming, William. We're coming...

Did I open my eyes? I thought I did but there was no way to be sure as the darkness surrounding me remained utter and complete. I fumbled across the smooth surface of the flashlight which I still held in my hand and found the button that turned it on. I pressed it and a sharp beam of white light shot across the floor, a lit upon the dulled, metal surface of one of the cabinets, reflected back at me and caused me to squint.

Maria, I thought, *that was definitely Maria's voice.* I was sure that it had been though I did not rule out the possibility that it had been little more than wishful thinking. Still, I returned my gaze and the beam of light to the door and gazed at it longingly.

Well if you are coming, Mia, I thought back, *get here soon. And watch out for the two goons guarding the room I'm in.* Simultaneously with my thought the beam of light that emanated from the flashlight flickered and dimmed before it re-established itself. Reluctantly I turned it off, reclined backward against the cabinet behind me, closed my eyes again and waited.

I waited.

* * *

"Goons," Maria spoke aloud as she ran down the street toward wherever Matt was leading them through the blinding rain and the howling wind. She had no idea where they were going, though conditions seemed to be worsening the farther they ran. Shadowy, towering structures loomed up on either side of her but she could not see their tops.

Anyone or anyTHING could be lurking up there, she thought.

"What?" the person in front of her—Jeff, Maria recognized—said.

"Huh?" she asked. Jeff turned his head to look at her though he did not slow his pace.

"You said something, Maria," he responded between breaths, "'toons' or something. I didn't quite make it out."

Maria nodded as she ran, "Goons," she said, "two of 'em. They're guarding the room that William is being held in. Don't ask me how I know, Jeff. I just do."

Jeff, who had likely opened his mouth to ask her how she knew, closed it and smiled. He looked away from her and forward. He called Matt's name. Maria heard a loud "what?!" echo back to her on the breeze that buffeted her cheeks and she saw shadows paused a few steps away from Jeff. Jeff slowed his own pace and stopped. She followed suit as she realized that the shadows were, in fact, her companions.

"William," Jeff said as Matt took a step toward him, "Maria thinks he's being guarded by a couple of mercs."

Matt nodded, "Noted. I'm not even going to ask how Maria knows. Sorry, Maria. How you know. No offense."

"None taken," Maria said as Matt turned and re-established his pace. The others followed closely behind him as the street upon which they had been running sloped slightly upward...

And, Maria observed, terminated at what appeared to be a meter wide wooden staircase that led from the street level to what appeared to be a raised walkway of some sort. The steps were in places splintered and in others, missing entirely. Matt arrived at the bottom step, removed from his waistband the blaster he had liberated from the dead merc and held it out in front of him. He glanced at the handle as Maria arrived at the foot of the steps, checked the safety, lowered it to his side, turned back to the group and nodded.

"Let's go," he said. He began to make his way slowly up the steps and across the gaps. He was followed by first, Caren, then Tim, then Steve and Carole and finally, Jeff and Maria. The steps creaked as they made their way up and across them. Jeff held the sword he had acquired down at his side and on an angle. Maria watched as the rain beaded upon the weapon's steel surface, ran down it and dripped off of the tip. Occasionally, Jeff loosened and re-tightened his grip nervously upon the hilt as they made their way up toward the raised walkway. They gained the top, one at a time, and glanced expectantly at the area before them.

Maria looked down. They stood at the onset of an expansive, wooden walkway. On either side of them antique, one-level buildings sat quietly in the shadows. Across from them, though...

Maria gasped.

The structures that towered overhead and on an extension of the walkway looked like the skeletal remains of a once-creature that had expired many, many ages before, their tops lost in the bank of red clouds that swirled overhead. She glanced from them to Matt and saw that he had unfolded and was once again reading the map by the dull glow of the sky. He glanced up from it at the structures...

Ruins? She thought, are they ruins?

...and then back to it again. After a moment, he refolded it and replaced it in the back, left pocket of his slacks. He turned back to the group and raised his right index finger to his lips. Quiet, Maria thought, and instinctively nodded. He pointed to Jeff and motioned for him to take a step back. Jeff did as had been requested of him and stepped behind Maria. He motioned to her and the rest of her companions to *move forward as he did the same and they did. They made their way slowly across the wooden walkway toward the onset of the extension. Maria's head rotated first left and then right but nothing impinged upon their position from either direction.*

Nothing that you can see, Mia, William spoke in her mind, there be haints... a lot of haints here. She nodded and resigned to remained on her guard. Her gaze swung forward again...

And paused.

The area beyond the tarnished railing that marked the termination of the wooden walkway was dark but she could hear... something in that darkness. It sounded like water, crashing against something solid before it faded from her hearing, only to crash again and fade again... and again... and again. She thought to inquire of her companions what the sound was but realized that she did not need to. It was unmistakable, and though she had never heard it before that moment it matched what she had always believed it would sound like.

The Great Sea, she thought, and was filled with a momentary burst of elation that quickly and sadly faded. They continued through the rain across the wooden walkway and eventually gained the entrance to the extension. A large sign arched overhead, suspended between two, low-lying and boarded up structures that looked like the structures that had lain throughout Freeworld One. It advertised "Mariner's Landing." Maria felt a quiver of anticipation that mingled with her fear. They passed under it, one at a time, and moved onto the...

It's called a landing? Maria thought but dismissed said thought as irrelevant.

Their progress carried them passed multiple structures and what looked like a large wheel. They moved beneath what looked like the twisted skeleton of a snake in its death throes and it materialized out of the darkness before them: A large, once-sea going vessel that had been subsequently grounded for obvious reasons, not the least of which were all of the holes in its hull. It was moored to the landing. The words "Ignis Fatuus" were printed high atop the vessel's hull and almost disappeared into the swirling clouds overhead. Matt's passage paused as did the passages of the rest of her companions. Maria's did, as well. Matt turned to address the group. As he did, Maria caught a glimpse of something peculiar over his shoulder: A shadow that seemingly detached itself from the fuselage of the vessel and moved quickly toward a large, gaping hole that she immediately associated with the entrance/exit and disappeared into it.

My God, she thought, I've never seen anything move that quickly before! What the hell was that? Sadly, no answer to her inquiry came.

"Okay," Matt began, "we're going to move in single file, real slow, with me and Jeff in the lead..."

"Um, Matt?" Maria began. Her eyes remained fixed on the entrance/exit that

the shadow had disappeared in to. No, she thought, "disappeared" isn't the right word. It had... dematerialized was the best way that she could describe it.

"Yeah, Maria?" Matt replied. He took a step away from the Ghost Ship and toward her. Simultaneously with his movement, Maria heard a male shout from within the vessel which was followed by a scream and the sound of a blaster repeatedly discharging. She started, as did the others, as the sounds reverberated through the Ghost Ship and out into the night air. The echo did not make it far before it was blocked by the wall of rain water that fell around them but she had heard enough. She felt her heart sink into her stomach as she took one... two... three steps toward the ship and broke into a run. She heard shouts from behind her of "Maria!" and "wait!" as she ran passed her companions but she was undaunted as she gained the entrance, turned right, and fled blindly into the blackness. Her lone thought was of him.

Oh God William, she thought as she forced herself to stop and take a deep breath, please be okay! She started to move again, more slowly than before. She trailed her fingers across the cold, metal surface of the wall as she descended blindly, ever onward toward...

* * *

I heard something outside the closed door to the galley and I immediately opened my eyes though I left the flashlight off. It was a peculiar sound: A low *thump* that seemed to echo through the ship. Said thump was followed by an all too familiar sound: Shouting, followed by screaming and then, as if the thumps, shouts and screams were not enough, I heard the unmistakable sound of a blaster discharging once... twice... and a third time before I heard something crack (*my God*, I thought, *that sounds like bone!*) and another *thump* low to the floor. Thereafter? I heard nothing but silence.

My heart pounding, I fumbled with and found the button that turned on the flashlight and I slammed my thumb against it. Bright, white light shot forward from it and once again illuminated the metal cabinet across from me as I stood as quickly as I could manage and turned the flashlight upon the door. Nothing about it had changed. It remained as featureless as it had before but as I watched and listened, I heard something *click* within it. Simultaneously, I heard footsteps in the hallway outside echoing not toward the door but away from it, and not in the direction that Amy, the mercs and I had approached from but in the opposite direction.

I took a cautious step toward the closed door. My boots shuffled across the floor as I gained its smooth surface. I shifted the flashlight from my right to my left hand and laid my right upon the door. I pushed against it. At first, nothing happened, but as I applied more pressure the door began to creak on its hinges until, after a moment's struggle, I felt something give within the interior and the door swung slowly opened with a *screech*. The two mercs that had, I assumed, been standing on either side were no longer there. Instinctively, I shined the flashlight down upon the floor of the hallway...

I gasped.

Two black, cloaked figures lay beside each other. Their hoods had been removed. One lay with his face down against the floor. I could see the back of his lightly colored hair which was tightly trimmed so that I could see a glimpse of the scalp beneath it. He did not move. The other figure was less fortunate. He too lay on his stomach but someone or some*thing* had turned his head all the way around so that his wide-opened eyes stared up into mine in horror. His mouth was contorted in an eternal grimace of pain and surprise. I helplessly retched and looked away, but not before I noticed the blaster that lay beside him. I forced myself to turn back and, without looking at his face, I knelt down and picked up the weapon. I glanced at its handle and saw that four of the five charge bars there were lit. I checked the safety by the suddenly flickering light of the flashlight, saw that it was in the "off" position, and felt a momentary rush of relief. I turned to search the other body...

And heard footsteps approaching cautiously down the hallway from the direction that I and my escorts had originally arrived from. That, along with what sounded like fingers trailing along the wall. Without thinking I found and pressed the button on the flashlight again, turning it off. Though I could not see where I was I estimated my position relative to the galley and as quietly as I could manage shifted backward. My ass came into contact with the right door jamb and I shifted slightly to the left. When I was clear I took a shuffling step backward and simultaneously raised my new found weapon and the flashlight up to my eye level. I waited as the footsteps moved closer... *closer*...

I judged as best I could the newcomer's position relative to my own. The footsteps paused directly outside the door as the newcomer's shoes or boots came into contact with something soft. I heard what sounded like a female's voice intone "'wha?" and pushed the button on the flashlight with my left thumb simultaneously. My right index finger hovered precariously close to my acquired weapon's trigger as I beheld...

I stopped. The subtle pressure that I had been applying to the trigger vanished entirely and what little strength I had managed to summon from my dwindling reserves left me entirely at the sight of the newcomer's long, black, rain-soaked hair, her white face which was beaded with water that, along with the darkness, all but disguised the small spattering of brown freckles across each cheek and her deep, brown eyes.

Maria.

Upon seeing me standing a step or two away from her, and even with my blaster trained upon her position she smiled slightly. I quickly lowered the weapon to my side and stepped out of the galley toward her. She took a step toward me. An awkward silence fell between us and she reached out to me as if to verify that it was really and truly me. But said silence was promptly broken as I heard voices echoing down the corridor from the direction she had approached from. Recognizable voices calling her name. Someone—Steve, I think—shouted "I see light ahead!" and was answered by someone else—*that's Tim*, I thought—shouting "no *shit!*" Tim's retort was answered by Steve: "Shut the *fuck* up, Marine!"

Maria lowered her hand and her smile faded. A moment later, our companions emerged from the shadows and stopped a meter or two away from where we stood. Matt was in the lead and the weapon that he held—a blaster similar in model and make to the one that I held—immediately trained upon my position. Jeff moved up beside him. In his left hand he held a sword, similar to Amy's, down at his side. His hand tensed upon its hilt as he saw me. The others, unarmed as far as I could see filed in behind them. Tim glared at me with a mixture of what looked like reprehension and hatred upon his face. I opened my mouth to speak…

And paused.

Which one of them? I thought as I scanned their faces, *which one of you betrayed me… betrayed us?* My grip tightened upon the blaster that I held and my index finger once again hovered precariously close to the trigger.

Maybe I should be the one targeting them, I thought.

No, William, my coldly, rational voice spoke in my mind, *that's not the answer and you know it.*

Then what is? I asked that voice. Said question had a noticeable edge to it in my mind but I knew, even as I thought it that it was rhetorical.

You know what you have to do, Pat's and Alex's voices spoke in unison in my mind. Their voices were followed by another voice: The aforementioned unfamiliar-then-but-now-familiar voice of my present self that sits within the abandoned darkness of my "home" here in Bumblefuck by the light of my almost-diminished candle and tries desperately to complete this chronicle before the candle burns down to nothing and winks out.

There is little left to tell. I wish I could end it here, reunited with my companions. I wish I could tell you that any doubt or suspicion that hung in the air between us vanished… that we all dropped our weapons and embraced each other. I wish I could tell you that we exited the Ignis Fatuus arm-in-arm and discovered that the rain had stopped, that the night had ended, that the sun had arisen and that our transport off of the continent and to freedom was waiting for us. I wish I could tell you that we all lived happily ever after, away from the tyranny of the Administration because let's face it, the best stories end as such.

But sadly? I can only tell you what happened. The truth. Not that revisionist bullshit that the machines spoon feed you.

That moment, as Maria and I stood across from people that I had grown to think of as not just my companions but my brethren was another watershed moment for me, similar to the one that I had experienced upon the bank of the Shenango River so many, many kilometers and so many, many experiences, both good and bad before.

So much death, my unfamiliar-then-but-familiar-now voice spoke in my mind, *so much. Yours is not to add to it. Yours is to preserve what life you can.*

The vision of the sigil upon Alex Parker's forearm... the same sigil imprinted upon the seal of the letter that I carried in my front right, jean's pocket suddenly appeared in my mind.

Explorator, the once-Steward of Freeworld One spoke in my mind, *Pathfinder. Unus est vera semita. There is only One True Path, William MacNuff, and this? This is not the way to find it.*

I lowered my right hand to my side. I placed the back of it against my pocket and felt the shape of the Artifact within. I was reassured. My head stopped pounding, the pain in my shoulder disappeared, my mind cleared and I breathed in deeply the smell of the Ghost Ship: Mildew mixed with dust, mingled with the smell of metal, tar and oil and other scents that I did not recognize... fresh, foreign scents that seemed to be carried upon the wind that, despite our proximity to the outside, still blew slightly down the hallway.

That's a neat trick too, I thought and mentally shook my head. I could smell Maria's natural scent directly next to me and my mind hearkened back to our first encounter on the bank of the Little Shenango River in Freeworld One and forward to our rendezvous in Centralia. I moved my left hand away from my thigh and brushed it against her right hand which she held down at her side. *I'm here, William* that slight touch seemed to say, *I'm with you.*

And I knew at that moment that she was, even if no one else was. *You and me, kiddo,* I thought as I surveyed the expectant faces of our traveling companions, *it's always been you and me. Always has been and always will be. Nothing else... Not the One, True Path nor Edona nor any Skew or Gateway matters as much to me as that.*

"You can believe what you want to believe," I said as I continued my purveyance of the figures assembled before me and my grip upon my weapon loosened. My finger retired from the trigger, "I'm not going to try to convince you otherwise. Whether you believe that I betrayed you or not is irrelevant. What matters is not what happened *before* this moment but what happens from this moment forth. We're here. We've made it to the end. If Alex kept his word and sent someone ahead to notify the Free Caymenites that we were coming... and none of us have any reason to believe that he didn't... then we need to move and we need to move *now*. They're coming for us. And considering that our 'help' here apparently trusts us about as much as the Administration does... well, the way I see it? There's no place for us here, anymore. Not in Hempstead, not in Centralia. Not in Freeworld One or Greentree or even Jefferson. You can believe me a traitor or an Infiltrator or whatever the fuck you want to be believe me if you want but all you need to know is this: I... *we*"—I gestured to Maria—"started this journey long before we met any of you. And we started it with one goal in mind: Freedom. I think I speak for both of us when I say that we've come this close and we're not going to stop now, or let our suspicions get the best of us. You can either trust me..."

I moved my thumb to the safety of my weapon and clicked it into the "on" position. I released my grip upon it and let it tumble to the ground. Maria gasped beside me but I was undaunted.

"...or you can shoot me. It's your decision."

I held out my arms as if to say *go ahead,* raised my head and closed my eyes. I did not realize at the time that I had unknowingly assumed the same position as the figure that had been pictured upon the reliefs in the church in Centralia but assume it I had. Another of Alex Parker's metaphors? I leave that for you to decide. I could hear shuffling before me as my companions seemingly wrestled with all that I had just said to them. I waited for the shot or the stab... someone, I knew, would do it. But what passed for and passes for time here in Endworld elapsed and nothing happened.

After an indeterminate amount of moments I lowered my arms and my head and I re-opened my eyes. The fleeting strength that I had gained had diminished and my head and shoulder once again pounded. My companions stood as they had before. All gazed at me by the dim, flickering light of the flashlight with a mixture of emotions. As I watched, Matt slowly lowered his own weapon to his side and clicked "on" his safety. He flashed me a grin. Jeff relaxed his grip upon his sword. The intense expressions of my counterparts relaxed slightly. Even Tim who had glared at me with the most suspicion seemed to have relaxed his stance a bit. He nodded quickly and briefly as my gaze met his and looked away. No one spoke. That is, until Matt did.

"Pick up your weapon, William," he said as he took one... two... three steps toward me and rested his right hand upon my right shoulder, "you're probably going to need it. That goes for the rest of you," he continued, "see what, if anything, you can find on these two bodies. Even a pocket knife would be helpful. By the way, William: Did *you* do this?"

I shook my head and responded with, "I didn't and I have no idea who did. I was locked in there"—I gestured to the galley—"the whole time. I heard a commotion out here and then someone unlocked the door. When I got out here, *this* is what I saw."

Matt guffawed and shook his head, "Sounds like our mysterious benefactor is two for two."

I thought about inquiring as to what he was talking about but decided against it for the moment. I looked passed Matt at the others and all nodded in turn. Slowly, I knelt and picked my discarded weapon up off of the ground. I glanced once again at its handle and saw the same four bars as I had before. I grinned despite the pain and sudden exhaustion that racked my body and clicked back "off" the safety.

Be prepared, my coldly rational voice cautioned me, *a nice speech like that doesn't change the fact that one of these people betrayed you.*

I will, I responded and from that moment forth? I vowed to never let my guard down again.

"Okay," I said as I averted my gaze from my companions to Maria. By the fading light of the flashlight that I still held she smiled at me, though beneath her smile I could see... *something.* The same something I had seen previously on more than one occasion. I wrestled with it for a moment... considered addressing it but decided not to as Matt moved away from me and the others moved toward me to search the bodies. I moved a step closer to Maria instead and said, "Ready to light out one more time?"

Whatever had lain behind her smile vanished and she nodded, "You bet your ass I am."

I smiled and bent into kiss her, but my attempt to do so was interrupted as something rocketed overhead. I heard it whistle as it approached and whistle past us. Said whistle was followed by a deafening explosion that shook the ground beneath my feet and the entire Ghost Ship. I heard a loud, ear-splitting *screech* as something large... something *very* large broke free of its moorings and crashed to the surface of the landing. Another, more violent tremor shook the area and I and my brethren struggled to remain upright.

Beneath the chaos I could hear something else, as well: What sounded like engines kicking dust, debris and water into a frenzy that pelted not only the exterior of the Ghost Ship but everything else that lay around it.

And it was clearly moving closer.

"Oh, fuck," Steve said as he stood from his perusal of the body with the closely trimmed, lightly colored hair. He had discovered another blaster and he held it in his left hand but his eyes glanced upward at the ceiling of the hallway. Caren, who had been searching the less fortunate corpse, did not stand. She continued to kneel but she, too, gazed up worriedly at the ceiling.

We all did.

"That sounds like a…" Caren began.

"Yeah, dear," Matt interrupted as he raised his weapon up to his eye level and clicked the safety back "off," "I think you're right."

The sound of the approaching engines and the subsequent storm being kicked up by them grew even louder. It did not take me long to realize what was happening. Amidst the growing din I heard Maria's voice speak in my mind. It was not the Maria that stood before me by the flickering light of the flashlight that I held. It was the diminished Maria from my reoccurring nightmare and the words that she spoke? I knew them all too well.

To the end, William. To the end. Not alive. We can't let that happen. They won't take us alive. They won't…

Gunship, I thought as the flashlight which had been threatening to die on me flickered and did so and plunged me and my companions into complete and utter blackness again. The Administration's forces had, quite obviously, arrived in Hempstead.

CHAPTER TWENTY EIGHT

"Report!" Ed Wilkinson shouted as he entered "Wilkinson's Deli" at a trot with Molly and two other, cloaked mercs on his heels. Wilkinson's Deli was a sprawling, one-story building situated two blocks away from the once-boardwalk and by association the beach and the Great Sea. The marquis that had once advertised it as such had long since disappeared: A victim of countless years of disrepair and countless storms like the one that had raged over Hempstead for the last few, pre-Administration hours and was showing no signs of stopping. Its windows and what had once been its front, double door were boarded over. To the casual passerby or worse it looked like just another, abandoned, burnt out husk of a once-prosperous eatery from the pre-Administration era. But once through the lone entrance or exit—what had once been the back door was concealed from view by not only the building in front, but also by a crumbling ruin of a residence that had once been Ed and Molly's home—an entirely different scene presented itself.

All evidence of the deli that had once filled the interior was gone save for the long, wooden countertop upon which multiple, flat-paneled computer monitors sat. They were powered by the generator that lay concealed in the basement of the deli. Numerous cloaked figures stood before them or sat upon stools in front of them. One such seated figure had removed his hood and was revealed to be a man in his early thirties with wavy black hair that hung past his ears, a round face, a black goatee and a mustache. Said man turned to Ed as Ed removed his long, black trench coat and threw it in an empty spot on the counter. Beneath it, he wore a long sleeved, black shirt which was tucked into a pair of black jeans. He wore a blaster in a holster on either side of his ribs and a sword in a sheath upon his back. His overall appearance was complimented by the shin-high pair of black boots that he wore upon his feet. He was thin but chiseled: William's impression of his physical prowess had been correct.

"We have incoming," the man with the wavy black hair and the black goatee and mustache stated, "Administration gunship on approach. Current position"—he reached in and tapped the screen of the monitor in front of him—"roughly one half kilometer north of Mariner's Landing and slowing."

"What about the main force of machines, Pete?" Ed asked as he moved up behind

him. He bent in and glanced over his shoulder. Behind him, Molly removed her own coat and revealed similar attire to Ed's: A form fitting, black body suit top and a pair of black jeans, complimented by a pair of black, knee-high boots. She had a blaster holstered on her left hip—a smaller make and model than the ones her husband was wearing—and... not a sword but what looked like a wide, quarter moon-shaped blade with a short hilt upon her right. Said hilt had four dainty finger holes inset within it. As she moved up behind Ed and Pete she reached down with her right hand and brushed her finger tips across the blade. Her deep, brown eyes sparkled and she smiled. Anyone that did not know her and witnessed the glint in her eyes would have thought her insane but she was not. None of the mercs were. Far from it: They were by their nature intently focused and very deadly.

Pete tapped the monitor before him a few more times and ran his fingertips across the screen and to his right. The picture upon it shifted in time with his touch. He ran his fingertips down the length of the screen before he paused and tapped it one final time. A red circle began to blink in the upper, right hand corner of the monitor.

"There," he said as he gestured to the mark, "they're coming up on the bridge now. Their forward vanguard will be over it and at the town limit in moments."

Ed heard the sound of a door opening and beyond it, the sound of the rain pelting the ground outside. A warm breeze blew passed him as he heard the door close and he turned from his perusal of Pete's monitor to see Amy and another, hooded mercenary entering the once-dining area.

"Report?" Ed asked her immediately.

"MacNuff is secure for the moment," she said confidently, "but we have another... concern."

Amy turned and gestured to the hooded figure beside her, who recounted his tale for Ed in much the same fashion as he had originally told it to Amy. He and his counterparts had come upon the transport that had been ferrying the other fugitives back to the deli. It had crashed and save for the driver who had been sufficiently eliminated by the impact, the vehicle's other occupants were gone. Not just the fugitives but the mercenary that had ridden shotgun, as well. The driver had been looted of both his blaster and his sword and the one that had ridden in the passenger seat had been de-cloaked.

A prisoner, perhaps? Ed thought, someone to use as a bargaining chip for MacNuff's release? He highly doubted it. Such a strategy did not correspond with what little he knew of Matt O'Brien and his band of travelers via the limited intelligence he had managed to accrue. Whether by luck or skill they had made it further than most and nothing save for the transmitter that they had discovered on MacNuff labeled any of them as a threat.

The actions of the "one" do not damn "the whole," Ed thought in the words of *his once-mentor. The man who had taught him all that he knew. The man who had taught him to lead other men and women. The man who had taught him to fight and to avoid fighting. He wished that man was there at that moment but he knew that such a prospect was...*

Impossible, he thought. Circumstances prevented it. Besides, he thought, today is not a day to avoid confrontation. It is coming whether I want it to or not. And I will fight. We all will.

"They are irrelevant," Ed said as he looked away from Amy and back at the monitor, "they will try to free MacNuff but will likely end up lost within the proverbial maze of streets near the landing. And if that doesn't dispose of them then the gunship will. Was MacNuff under lock and key?"

"Yes," Amy said.

"Good," Ed replied, "head back to Mariner's Landing, extricate the guards from the Ghost Ship and report..."

A loud and thunderous explosion echoed from the direction of the once-boardwalk and caused the ground, the countertop and the monitors atop it to shudder and briefly wink out before re-establishing themselves. Dust fell from the ceiling and landed upon Ed's cheek. He absently brushed his hand across his face and turned toward the front of the deli. He could see something bright through one of the small gaps between the boards that covered the windows. He moved quickly across the floor toward what he had seen and glanced out.

Per what he could judge through the crack, something large on Mariner's Landing was in flames. A second later, he heard a loud, metallic screech from the same direction which was followed by a second, thunderous boom. The ground and the building once again shook. He turned away from the scene that unfolded before him and moved back across the floor toward where Molly, Amy, the two hooded mercs that had arrived with him and the additional hooded merc that had arrived with Amy were all assembled around Pete. He stopped directly before the once-Operator.

"What was...?" Pete began but Ed held his hand up and shook his head.

"What that was, is irrelevant too, Pete," he said, "but Amy, it seems you can belay my directive about extricating the guards from the Ghost Ship."

Amy nodded but said nothing. Ed leaned back over Pete's shoulder.

"Status?" He asked.

Pete reluctantly turned back to the monitor. His hand was visibly shaking as he touched the screen and the flickering picture stabilized. The red circle was still blinking angrily at them.

"On the bridge, now," he said. His voice wavered but his hand steadied. Ed laid a comforting hand upon Pete's shoulder and spoke.

"Can we still blow it?" he asked Pete. Pete looked back at the monitor, pinched the red circle between his right index and middle finger and separated said fingers. The circle widened and grew as he dragged his fingers across the screen and as Ed watched, an overhead, real time view of the bridge beamed down to them from one of the last, functioning satellites overhead. The picture was clear which meant that the satellite's orbit had carried it close to their position. Ed watched as MDU after ATT after HIT after assault bike moved across the screen from top to bottom. Pete shook his head.

"The main force is already on it or over it," Pete replied, "you might take out a few of them but the majority…"

"I do not care," Ed said as he removed his hand from Pete's shoulder and stood up straight. The old merc's voice was cold and purposeful, "blow it, Pete. Even one less to deal with is a strategic advantage."

Pete hesitated for a moment. He turned on his stool and looked up at Ed but saw no reprieve in his gaze. His face remained stern; it did not falter as he reiterated his command. A ghost of a smile eclipsed Ed's face and Pete shivered at the sight of it. He turned away and back to the monitor as a series of HITs moved across the screen. He shuddered.

"Huma…" he began but Ed interrupted him before he could speak the entire word.

"In war, Pete," Ed said, "choices must be made. Those that you refer to are no longer human. Whether by their choice or not they are as much our enemy now as the machines that command them… that control them. If we are to survive this night we must not distinguish between the two. Understood?"

Pete turned from the screen to look at the old merc and nodded slowly. Simultaneously, Ed turned toward and removed his coat from atop the countertop. Pete watched as Molly removed hers from beside Ed's and slipped it on. Amy glanced emotionlessly at Pete one, final time before she motioned to the three hooded mercs that had arrived with Ed, Molly and her and turned away. Pete reluctantly turned from them back to the monitor and watched as another HIT moved from the top of the screen to the bottom. His hand once again shook as he reached toward the bottom of the screen and tapped it. A taskbar appeared there. Upon it were multiple icons but the one that caught his attention was the red "X." Beneath it were the words: "Bridge Destruct Sequence. Press to activate."

Choices must be made, Pete thought as he slid his finger across the taskbar toward the "X." It hovered shaking over it as Ed spoke.

"Make haste to your designated positions and prepare for battle," he said. Pete heard affirmative murmurs from Amy, Molly and the three mercs followed by the sound of them departing the deli. He heard the door open… heard the sound of the rain that fell upon the rutted ground beyond it. He heard the door close and simultaneously, he slowly lowered his finger to the icon and reluctantly but assured that said course was, as Ed had reassured, the correct one...

He pressed it.

* * *

SLNyxV4.0's MDU had fallen back from the front of the army's forward vanguard. It had been the first to gain the bridge and subsequently had been the first to arrive at the other end but it had slowed its pace upon doing so. It watched out either side of the reinforced cockpit of the vehicle it was embedded in as the army moved passed it on either side and toward the center of town where the largest concentration of life signs had initially been reported.

Initially, it thought. The numbers were disconcertingly in flux. One minute, there appeared to be hundreds and the next? None. The Supreme Leader was unsure of what said anomaly meant. Nothing was jamming them as near as it could tell. It warned its forces to remain on their guard as they progressed further into the town of Wildwood, ET. Its forces answered it with affirmatives.

It had pursued the fugitives south down the road designated "47," an old tributary of the Highway that ran parallel to the road designated "9" that its quarry had been travelling upon. When the tracking signal that it had been following had been lost, it had triangulated the location of the final transmission and had determined the fugitives' location: Wildwood, ET. Current intelligence revealed that the town had recently been repopulated by an unknown group of humans who had renamed it "Hempstead," but said intelligence was spotty, and information on the "unknown group of humans" was even more so. A less-enlightened mind would have considered this fact disconcerting, but SLNyxV4.0 did not.

It is irrelevant, the Supreme Leader thought. Occupied or not the town remained, per its extrapolation, the most probable location of its quarry. It had ordered the gunship to break off pursuit, turn east, and move on the town from the north. It had calculated the time it would take at the army's current speed to get in to position and had coordinated its arrival with that of the gunship. Any resistance facing it would be immediately sandwiched between its forces and the gunship.

We will not fail again, it thought, and requested that its rear vanguard report its position...

Concurrently, it heard a loud explosion well behind it and near the rear of its force. It shifted its head backward and saw that a plume of fire and smoke had emerged from the end of the bridge opposite the land mass that the majority of its army moved upon. Said explosion was followed by another, and another as similar plumes of fire and smoke blossomed into the air and moved steadily closer to its position. Warnings entered its neural net from the forces at the rear of its column. Shouts and screams from the humans in the HITs assaulted its auditory processors. Said warnings, shouts and screams were quickly silenced with each subsequent explosion.

SLNyxV4.0 commanded the army to quicken its pace but said command fell on deaf, if not deactivated "ears." By the time the last explosion had occurred and the remnants of the long, raised bridge over the inlet from the termination of 47 to Wildwood, ET fell into the water, better than a quarter of its army had been rendered immaterial.

Perhaps I underestimated them, it thought, but "doubt" was not a tenant of its programming. Rather than order the army to decrease its pace and proceed with caution it did the opposite: It ordered the MDUs to move into their designated assault positions at the back of the column and the ATTs, HITs and assault bikes to move into their designated positions near the front. The juxtaposition happened immediately as the Supreme Leader's MDU slowed even further and allowed the rest of the vehicles to move past it.

"At the first sign of resistance, engage unknown hostiles per your pre-specified directives," SLNyxV4.0 ordered its army. Affirmatives once again entered its neural net from the column as the Supreme Leader's MDU turned a corner, and found itself at the rear of the army in the center of town, surrounded on either side by low-lying, abandoned structures within which anything... or anyONE could be waiting.

* * *

From within the old deli and behind his computer screen, Pete Daley heard the earpiece that sat beside his computer monitor crackle with static.

Shit, he thought as he picked it up and jammed it into his ear.

"Daley, here," he said once he had the prosthetic positioned.

"Pete," Ed's voice crackled through the static, "can you hear me?"

"Loud and... well, not so clear," he said as he tapped his computer monitor a few times, "trying to boost signal. I'm running a pretty rough encryption." His hands moved quickly, almost imperceptibly across the screen, "How's that?"

"Better," Ed said as his voice noticeably cleared, "We are in position now. I need your eyes."

Pete nodded, "Getting there now," he said as he quickly and deftly repositioned the satellite that had been surveying the recently demolished bridge (he shivered again at the knowledge of what he had done). His monitor filled with static for a brief moment before it stabilized. It showed the center of town: Low lying buildings on either side of a broad and rutted throughway which was, presently, clogged with a collection of slow moving vehicles. He pinched his index and middle finger together and touched them to the screen. He separated them and the view expanded. His gaze traced across the assortment of Administration vehicles: ATTs and HITs encircled by a swiftly moving oval of assault bikes.

"Looks like a typical deployment, Ed," Pete said, "transports in the middle, speed and agility on the perimeter. And if I'm right"—he brushed his fingers to the left across the screen; the view shifted and he saw that he was—"armor at the rear. I count at least a dozen MDUs."

"Understood, Pete," Ed replied, "where's the gunship?"

Pete tapped the top, right corner of his screen and a separate view box appeared. He tapped it again and instinctively tried to bring up the camera that was positioned atop the old Ferris wheel. He quickly realized that said camera was, if Ed had been right, no longer functional and shifted to the back-up that was positioned atop the old roller coaster. Static filled the small view box before a picture appeared within it. He could see, near where the screen terminated at the bottom, the remains of the Ferris wheel...

I guess he was right, Pete thought...

...and steadily diminishing flames licked the steel superstructure of the fallen once-attraction amidst a haze of rising steam. Pete could see the rain that fell in torrents upon it and the surrounding landing clearly. He could also see, positioned directly above it on his monitor, the side of the Ignis Fatuus that faced the camera. The flames reflected dully off of the tarnished, rusted siding of the retired vessel. The entrance/exit loomed darkly amidst the equally dark, gaping holes that dotted the fuselage but nothing within it or any of the holes moved.

Strange, he thought. With all the commotion, he had half expected to see the guards that Amy had left behind...

He caught something out of the corner of his right eye and quickly shifted his gaze in that direction. He squinted.

Did something just move there? He asked himself. He considered the possibility as he pinched his index and middle finger together again and separated them to the far right of the screen. The camera zoomed in and Pete observed the area closely. The light from the flames shifted and caused the abundant shadows to undulate steadily. He waited...

And practically jumped as one of the shadows that he observed looked at him.

Not at me, he thought, at the camera. He knows it's there. He could clearly discern an eye and the rough outline of a chiseled, bearded and unfamiliar face but that was all. A breath after he had seen it the shadow-face shifted right and quickly off of the monitor.

Jesus, he thought, I've never seen anything move that fast. Not even Ed! He considered rotating the camera right to follow its progress but Ed's voice in his ear overruled the idea.

"Pete!" he said in an urgent whisper, "report: What is the gunship's status?"

Pete blinked twice in rapid succession, opened his eyes wide and spoke, "Sorry, boss. Um… Technical difficulties. Hold a tic." He manipulated the camera back to its original position and shifted it with an upward swipe of his fingers…

He saw it's unmistakable outline hovering just beyond the vessel moored to the landing: Streamlined wing tip to wing tip with no, visible cockpit and with two plasma canons beneath either wing, it's girth stretched from the low lying, wooden buildings that faced Mariner's Landing to the breakwater of the Great Sea. The vertical engines that lined the underside of the ship kicked up a secondary maelstrom of dust, water, sand and debris that pelted everything from the Ghost Ship to the buildings that faced the landing.

I sure as hell wouldn't want to be in the middle of that, he thought. He considered the two guards in the Ignis Fatuus… considered MacNuff and the other fugitives. He knew where the Jefferson runaway was. But where were the others? He did not, he knew, have time to muse about such things. They were beyond his control.

Focus on what you can control, an unfamiliar but stern voice spoke in Pete's mind and he nodded.

"Still stationary, just north of the landing," he said, "and not moving."

"They're waiting for us," Ed whispered back, "well, then. No sense in keeping them waiting. Patch me through to the others, Pete."

Pete tapped the bottom of the screen and the taskbar reappeared. He found the icon in the shape of a microphone, tapped it once, adjusted the settings via the dialogue box that popped up to "communicate ALL" and heard an audible click in his own earpiece. Said click was followed immediately by Ed's voice which spoke a simple, three word command. Little more was required. The dozens… the hundreds of mercenaries listening from within various cracks, crags and crevices around Hempstead knew what they had to do next.

"All forces," Ed spoke definitively, "attack."

Here we go, Pete thought, and watched his monitor as all hell broke loose.

* * *

"Report," SLNyxV4.0 commanded. It gazed out from behind the reinforced glass cockpit of the MDU within which it was sequestered at the army deployed before it. As it watched, the ATTs and HITs stopped moving. The assault bikes continued their perusal of the perimeter as both machines and humans alike began to disembark from their respective transports onto the street.

"SCANS SHOW NO LIFE SIGNS, 2.4 KILOMETER RADIUS," the Surveillance Mark behind it reported.

"Unfeasible," the Supreme Leader stated, *"rescan. And account for current weather conditions, as well."* It was the third rescan that SLNyxV4.0 had commanded though it was the first that included the weather conditions. Might the storm raging over Wildwood, ET be inadvertently scrambling their scans? While the Supreme Leader thought the possibility remote it refused to rule it out. The previous two scans had been equivalently negative. It glanced from the collection of structures on its right flank to the ones on its left. It cycled its visual processors from "standard" to "filtered" and back again. Zoomed in. Zoomed out. Nothing moved within them. Yet it recognized the terrain before it as a classic bottle neck and ordered its forces to remain on their guard as they continued their deployment across the street and toward the structures on either side of it.

"SCAN SHOWS NO LIFE SIGNS, 2.4 KILOMETER RADIUS," the Surveillance Mark behind it repeated shortly thereafter, *"CURRENT WEATHER CONDITIONS: RAIN ACCOMPANIED BY WIND. WIND 45 TO 50 KILOMETERS PER PRE-ADMINISTRATION MINUTE GUSTING TO 75... TO 80... TO 85..."*

The SM continued to count up passed 100 as the Supreme Leader listened intently, before it dropped back to *"GUSTING TO 75... TO 80... TO 85..."* and repeated the litany again.

Was it malfunctioning, SLNyxV4.0 considered? It redirected its gaze to the area directly in front of the MDU and saw a swirling gust of wind, rain and debris blow across the rutted road surface. It kicked against the side of the MDU and howled around and through the edges of the top hatch into the vehicle's cavernous interior. The vehicle actually shook. Were it human, the Supreme Leader might have recognized the sensation that passed through its neural net as "surprise" yet its surprise at a sudden, chilled gust of wind strong enough to shift a Mobile Defense Unit was nothing compared to what happened next. Said wind seemed to hover around the vehicle for a moment before it suddenly resolved itself into a series of black, cloaked figures visible directly beyond the reinforced glass cockpit. The figures materialized primarily on the street but two in particular appeared perched on the sloping nose of its MDU.

Inconceivable, SLNyxV4.0 thought as it noticed that the black-clad figures held between them what looked like a portable version of the plasma canon perched atop the vehicle within which it waited. As it watched, the hole at the termination of the weapon's barrel a lit and the light that had appeared there began to rotate counter-clockwise. The Supreme Leader had little time to respond to the warnings from the rest of the army that entered its neural net as the force opposing it materialized synchronously, in totality across not only the bottle neck in which it and the majority *of its force was contained but behind and before it, as well. Hundreds of similarly attired hostiles.*

Its hand instinctively tightened upon the hilt of the sword it had recovered at the termination of Halmier's Pass. It ordered its MDU… ordered all of the MDUs to take evasive action. The driver of the vehicle it was in barked back a toneless affirmative and its idling engine roared as it suddenly swung left. Simultaneously, the two humans perched upon its nose were thrown to the right and tumbled to the street. The plasma canon that they held between them discharged and the shot flew harmlessly up and wide of the cockpit. Yet the night on either side of it a lit with explosions as other MDUs within its army were not as fortunate as it had been.

But it was no matter. SLNyxV4.0 had survived.

"All units," it commanded tonelessly as it "felt" the leather-wrapped hilt of the sword it held at its side, "engage."

* * *

Ed Wilkinson watched from his position at the front of the machine column behind the crumbling retaining wall of what had once been either a hotel or a condominium complex (he could not remember which) as his forces materialized around and amidst the force of machines and humachines that had invaded his and his counterparts' home. He watched as a half a dozen of the dozen MDUs at the rear of the column exploded in respective, sizzling white fireballs. His gambit was not entirely successful: A few of the MDUs managed to either shift their position and throw the two mercenaries holding the plasma canons off of their noses before they could fire or were close enough to either the machine infantry or the assault bikes that ringed the army's perimeter that said infantry or assault bike had just enough warning to eliminate the threat before the mercenaries could cause more damage.

Still, it was successful enough, he reasoned. The machines were caught off guard as was evidenced by the haphazard way in which the remaining forces began moving and engaging randomly.

Had his gambit taken out the Supreme Leader? He could not tell. A few, stray shots found their marks in the early moments of the battle that raged within the downpour that fell upon Hempstead, ET and the wind that howled across the stretch of road where Ed had opted to make his stand. A handful of his colleagues were killed by the subsequent explosions of the MDUs but Ed was undaunted… his resolve was unwavering.

In war, his once-mentor spoke in his mind, there are always causalities. And the machines would soon recompose themselves, he understood, regardless of whether his initial attack had gotten their Leader or not. He stood from his crouch within the rubble and reached beneath his long coat. He removed both of his blasters from their holsters with a swift, cross-armed gesture and held them out on either side of him. He clicked "off" their safeties with his thumbs and heard the mercenaries assembled on either side of him, Molly and Amy included, do the same.

He raised his weapons up over his head and let out a thunderous cry that echoed not only across the street before him but across all of Hempstead and even across points beyond the town limits. The cry was taken up by not only the people assembled behind and around him but by the forces that had already engaged the machine column before him. Without a thought to the contrary he leapt from the ruins within which he had been sheltering and onto the crumbling street.

He targeted the Administration pawn nearest him—an assault bike that was in the process of turning to greet his approach—and fired. The shot from his weapon came within a hair of hitting the reinforced, curved glass window behind which the bike's pilot crouched, but slipped past it and impacted squarely with the unarmored side of the 78A's head. Sparks exploded from the exit wound on the other side as the bolt from Ed's blaster sliced through the last of the metal, impacted and sizzled against the wet road surface. The bike accelerated quickly and careened across the street before it flipped onto its side. It impacted with one of the piles of bricks that clogged the shoulder of the road and lay still.

A second shadow and a third moved into Ed's peripheral vision and he turned with almost inhuman speed to face the oncoming threat: Two humachines, both with pulse rifles. Their bare torsos and chests were slightly visible beneath their armor (little more than plates, Ed thought) that they wore upon their bodies and Ed targeted with pinpoint accuracy the places where he could see skin and fired with no remorse once... twice in rapid succession. The humachine on the left fell with a black burn hole to the left of its stomach, and the one on the right fell directly beside it with a matching one upon its upper, left chest.

Molly and Amy moved up on either side of him, weapons drawn, and began firing as the forces nearest them converged upon them en masse. Ed fired once... twice... three times, and each time his shot found its fatal mark. But there were more machines and humachines than he had initially anticipated and as his blasters grew warm in his hands despite the rain falling upon them, he felt any advantage that he had briefly enjoyed slowly begin to slip away as he and his counterparts were helplessly driven back toward the old, crumbling structure from which they had emerged.

He heard something moving speedily toward his position from his left side and another something moving toward him from his right. Assault bikes, he understood. He knew, however reluctantly, that his blasters had suddenly grown obsolete. As the others surrounding him kept firing, he cast both weapons down to either side of his body—they landed upon the wet, road surface with dual clinks—and quickly ripped his coat off of his back. He reached behind him with his left hand and felt the hilt of his sword against his fingertips. He smiled as he wrapped said hand around it and removed it from its sheath as the first assault bike moved into his left, peripheral vision. He turned slightly in that direction, closed his eyes, embraced the wind...

And moved imperceptibly across the area between him and the vehicle just as the assault bike's pilot targeted his position and fired. Its shot flew wide and impacted with the windshield of the assault bike that had been moving up on Ed's right, whose pilot was temporarily stunned. Amy took advantage of it and fired a single shot from her weapon that snuck around the side of the reinforced, glass cockpit and impacted with the side of the 78A's head facing her. Ed rematerialized directly before the assault bike that had been moving up on his left, took a leaping step to the side and brought his sword across the tendons of the pilot's exposed neck.

The pneumatic cylinders audibly popped and hissed as the bike tilted to the right and fell upon the ground. It screeched upon the road surface as it spun and came to a rest no more than a meter from where Molly stood. Molly looked up at Ed, cocked her head inquisitively, smiled and threw her blaster down to the ground as a 78A emerged from the veil of rain that fell around them, raised the business end of its pulse rifle's barrel until it was pointing directly at her...

And fired as Molly grabbed the hilt of the mini-scythe upon her belt, removed the weapon in a flash, closed her eyes...

And vanished from the street in a cold gust of wind.

The shot flew passed where she had stood and, sadly, hit the mercenary that had been standing directly behind her squarely in the chest. Said mercenary was thrown backward and collapsed upon one of the piles of rubble at the foot of the ruins within which they had sheltered. Molly Wilkinson, never one to be outdone by her husband, materialized directly behind the 78A that had fired upon her and slashed once... twice across the exposed tendons near the 78A's shoulders, brought her blade across the 78As neck from behind, directly beneath where its head armor ended and its chest armor began and sliced deeply.

Pop. Hiss. It fell sparking to the ground directly next to its discarded pulse rifle with its head hanging back behind it on a lone, fiber optic cable. Simultaneously, Ed heard a familiar sound: A detonation, followed by a whistle that moved quickly toward his, Molly's, Amy's and their counterparts' position.

The sound of inevitability, he thought.

"Time to relocate," he said loudly. His voice echoed across the area directly surrounding him and he barely caught a glimpse of Amy, Molly and the rest of his band agreeing with him before he closed his eyes, once again "became" the wind...

And vanished along with the rest of his counterparts as the incoming plasma canon shot impacted with the ruins within which they had been sheltering before the battle broke out and sent white-hot rivulets of concrete soaring in a firestorm in all directions. A stiff, swirling breeze—cool, contrary to the warm, humid wind that blew incessantly through town—blew down the center of the machine column as time moved onward without check and the battle for Hempstead, formerly known as Wildwood, continued amidst a cacophony of pulse rifle, blaster and plasma canon fire, interspersed with the screeching sound of metal upon metal and the endlessly howling storm that raged across the ruined town.

* * *

Pete Daley watched the battle that raged across the center of town from a different vantage point a mere three blocks away. It was difficult to make out what was happening per the satellite feed upon his monitor which he was constantly shifting in response to Ed or someone else's request, but it was even more difficult to determine who was winning. He could hear the battle… the resounding plasma canon fire and the more muted pulse rifle and blaster fire but little else.

Simultaneously with Ed's proclamation to "relocate" an alarm began beeping over the monitor's speakers. His eyes opened wide and he shook his head.

What the fuck now? He questioned as he tapped the screen and brought up the task bar. He tapped the icon labeled "PIP" and the screen that he had been observing shrank and relocated to the upper, right corner of the monitor. He tapped the icon labeled "MAIN" and watched as the familiar, main screen appeared before him. He squinted: The "PROXIMITY ALARM" icon on the taskbar was blinking an angry red color. He tapped it and an overhead, relief view of not just the area directly around his location but of the entire town of Hempstead appeared before him. The view extended beyond the boardwalk, over the beach and three kilometers out over the Great Sea. He brushed his fingers down and the screen shifted slightly higher: Five kilometers out…

And he saw them. Two, red dots moving rapidly over the sea toward the shore. Behind them (beneath them, he thought) were three other dots. They were moving much slower but in the same, general direction as the two, leading dots. He frantically tapped the screen of the monitor with his fingers and triangulated the general direction in which they were heading…

Towards Mariner's Landing.

Pete felt his heart drop into his stomach as he pressed the "aux" button on his head set and spoke in a shaky voice, "uh… Ed?"

The resultant static was followed a moment later by Ed's distinctive and surprisingly harried voice, "I am slightly busy at the moment, Pete. Report?" Behind it he could hear the sounds of the battle that raged in the center of town along with something he did not want to hear: Screaming. Human's screaming. He was filled with dread as the realization of what was occurring filled his mind.

We're losing, he thought, as the unmistakable whistle of a plasma canon burst screeched across his headset. More static before Ed's voice re-established itself, "Pete! Report?!" He sounded furious.

What I'm about to tell him isn't going to help his mood, Pete thought.

"Uh… Ed?" he began, "new contact roughly four kilometers out over the Great Sea and closing fast. Two airborne marks and three sea-borne bogies. Look sharp.

"We have additional…"

* * *

"…INCOMING," the SM directly next to SLNyxV4.0 intoned, "REPEAT: UNIDENTIFIED INCOMING CRAFT."

The Supreme Leader turned from the battle unfolding around it to look at the Surveillance Mark. "Distance?" It asked.

The robot's response was virtually immediate, "FOUR KILOMETERS OUT OVER THE GREAT SEA AND CLOSING RAPIDLY. ESTIMATED TRAJECTORY GRID…"

SLNyxV4.0 listened intently. The unidentified craft appeared to be heading to an area north and east of its position near where the gunship was positioned. Inconceivable, it considered, for the battle is here. What reason would they have to…?

Recognition sparked its neural net. They are not a part of the force that we are currently engaged with, it understood, they are here for a different reason entirely: Extraction. Specifically, it determined, the extrication of the Jefferson and the Freeworld One fugitives.

And with them? The Artifact that it had been tasked to recover.

"All forces," it commanded instantly, "break off hostilities. Artillery: Lay down a suppressing fire. Infantry: Create a perimeter. All other forces move northeast 0.6 kilometers to where the gunship is stationed and prepare to engage unidentified incoming."

* * *

"PETE!" Ed's voice exclaimed over his head set and caused him to cringe. Pete almost yanked it from his ear and dropped it on the countertop instinctively but upon second thought realized that doing so and cutting off his lone line of communication to what remained of the mercenary force was inadvisable.

"Ed!" He exclaimed, his voice a mixture of elation and terror, "Ed? Can you hear me, boss?"

"I can," Ed said immediately, his voice surprisingly restrained, "The Administration's army is dispersing hastily and heading in the direction of Mariner's Landing. Seems that their attention is no longer affixed upon us but upon the 'additional incoming.' Which means...?"

"They're friendlies?" Pete interrupted Ed's statement, "but... how? How would they know... and how would the machines know..."

"It is irrelevant," Ed continued, "and not our concern. We've lost too many of our number already. Patch me through to what remains of our forces."

Pete did once again as Ed had requested and heard the familiar, audible click in his ear which was followed immediately by Ed's voice.

"All forces," he said, "fall back to the deli and regroup. Pete, you and your people commence backing up all of our systems and prepare to evacuate.

"We are leaving."

Ed Wilkinson's voice fell silent. A flurry of affirmatives entered Pete's ear from the remaining mercenaries. Pete added one of his own and once again clicked the "aux" button on his headset. He glanced at the monitor that rested upon the countertop before him for another breath... glanced at the two, rapidly approaching red dots before he turned to the others that were gathered in front of their own, respective monitors down the length of the old, wooden countertop. All gazed back at him with a mixture of confusion and resignation.

"You heard the man!" Pete said as forcibly as he could, "let's move our asses and have it done by the time he gets back here!"

His fellow once-Operators nodded and turned back to their computer screens. A few reached beneath their cloaks and removed either satellite phones or portable hard drives which they deftly and skillfully hooked up to their terminals and began backing up their records. Pete did the same and removed from within the rear pocket of the jeans he wore his own apparatus: A highly modified sat phone that was also usable as a portable computer terminal. While it lacked the processing power of the machine that glowed black and white before him it was ample enough to use for many of the same tasks that he had been using his countertop model for.

Operating on the move, he thought to himself as he hooked it up to the side of his monitor and with a few, quick taps and movements of his fingers across the screen began backing up the majority of the intelligence that Ed Wilkinson and his group of mercenaries had managed to accrue over the course of their time in Hempstead, ET.

Sadly, Pete understood, that time had come to a close. As he worked quickly and efficiently, his thoughts returned not to Ed, nor to the battle that raged across Hempstead nor to the guards that had been watching the fugitive in the Ghost Ship but surprisingly to the fugitive himself: William MacNuff.

If he's still alive, Pete thought, he may not survive the army that's heading in his direction. Sadly, he could not belabor his mind over the fugitive's fate but somewhere deep within his heart and mind and for no apparent reason he made a wish… something he had not done in many, many years. He wished for reasons unknown to him then, reasons that he knew would remain unknown to him indefinitely, for MacNuff's survival as his sat phone beeped to signify the completion of the download. He removed it and replaced it in his back pocket.

God speed, he thought to himself as he turned off his monitor, and moved down the counter to assist the once-Operator closest to him.

God speed.

CHAPTER TWENTY NINE

We stood huddled around the interior of the entrance/exit to the Ignis Fatuus in the darkness and patiently awaited Jeff's return from his reconnaissance. The wind-driven rain and the gunship-driven maelstrom that raged outside and just behind our position, combined with the smoldering remnants of the felled, large wheel that lay upon the surface of the landing disguised all details of the landscape from our view. We could not see more than two or three meters out into the darkness. Tim had given Jeff his satellite phone and had turned on its jamming function before Jeff had slipped out into the darkness. I did not know how much battery life it had left.

Very little, I reasoned which meant that Jeff's position was more than precarious. I raised my left hand to my left temple with a cringe and briefly closed my eyes. As I opened them, I saw a shadow move toward the entrance outside from my right... a shadow which quickly resolved itself into Jeff's familiar figure. He slipped around the corner of the entrance/exit and into our vicinity. I breathed a sigh of relief and loosened my grip upon the hilt of my blaster.

"Well?" Matt asked with an audible sigh. He, too, seemed relieved that it was only Jeff.

Jeff shook his head as he gave Steve back the weapon he had procured and took back his sword. Droplets of rain water spattered against our collective cheeks, "Not good. The gunship is positioned no more than 10 or 20 meters behind us and up the boardwalk..."

Boardwalk, I thought, *so that's what it's called...*

"...and it didn't show any sign that it saw me which means *this* thing"— he pointed to the phone in his right hand with the hilt of his sword before he handed it back to Tim—"was working."

"*Was?*" Carole asked as she took a step forward.

Tim took the phone from Jeff, tapped its screen once and sighed. He held it up so that Carole could see it, "Dead," he said, "battery's kaputskie."

"Then how are we still here?" Caren asked as she, too, took a step forward out of the shadows, "I mean, wouldn't the gunship… wouldn't the *machines* be able to detect us, now?"

Jeff shrugged, "No idea. It died on me while I was out there and I froze. I thought that I was a dead man. But nothing happened. Might be that…"

"Someone *else* is jamming it?" Matt interrupted and flashed a ghost of a smile, "I wouldn't be surprised."

"Meaning?" I asked. I looked at Maria. *What the hell are they talking about*, I mentally asked her. She must have sensed my thought because she opened her mouth to respond. Matt, however, beat her too it.

"*Meaning*," he emphasized, "that our Mystery Man or Woman has done it again. That's three we owe him or her. God *damnit*."

What the hell are they talking about? I mentally asked Maria. Maria flashed me a lukewarm smile and mouthed, *I'll tell you later*. My mind flashed back to the scene I had beheld upon first escaping the galley: Both of my guards lying dead on the cold, steel floor of the Ignis Fatuus. I had not done it. I hadn't considered the "who" since because of everything else that had happened but suddenly and without warning, I considered it again.

There's more to this than you know, Alex's voice spoke assuredly in my mind, *other parties with a vested interest in the outcome. I told you I was sending someone ahead. Someone trustworthy. Not just to notify the people of Free Caymen that you're coming but to protect you and to protect our shared interests.*

There's too much at risk here, William. Much too much, it concluded and my weapon's hand instinctively and for no other conceivable reason went to the front, right pocket of my jeans again. I could feel the Artifact with the back of my hand. I felt another rush of strength flow through my body that passed immediately as I re-removed my hand from my side, held my weapon out in front of me and pointed it directly at and out the entrance/exit again.

"Whatever the case," I said as a fresh bolt of pain shot across my head and made me gasp, "We can't just run out into the open with no…"

Simultaneously with my "no" I heard something approaching despite the seemingly ceaseless din of the rain, wind and debris that pounded against the Ghost Ship's exterior. It was an unusual sound that started distant but rapidly moved closer with each passing breath: A low rumble that quickly grew into a thunderous one. I averted my gaze from the scene on the landing to the area over my head and raised the barrel of my weapon instinctively until it pointed upward. Said noise, I realized, was not coming from the landing but from the air above it… above the Great Sea and above Hempstead.

What the hell? I thought before the entire area... well, the best way that I can describe it is it *split* with a thunderous *boom* that shook the walls on either side of me, the ceiling above me and the ground beneath me. The pain in my head intensified tenfold and I almost screamed as another *boom* passed overhead and segued into another sound: An audible *click*, followed by the sound of something being fired followed by the distinctive whistle of an approaching weapon's shell followed by the sound of one... of *two* detonations in the air above us and behind the Ignis Fatuus.

"That was the *gunship!*" Matt exclaimed suddenly as he broke from our group and dashed out into the night blindly. Multiple people shouted a warning at him but he was undeterred.

"Ah *fuck!*" Steve screamed as he ran out into the night after Matt. He was followed by Caren and Carole, then Jeff and Tim. Maria and I stood staring at each other, confused, as the two explosions that I had heard behind and above the Ghost Ship segued into another sound: That of something large... something *incredibly* large moving toward us quickly. Not thinking, I grabbed Maria's hand and pulled her out into the downpour. Rain mixed with something hard pelted us as we ran and I could barely make out the figures of our companions as they ran through the driving rain toward the smoldering wreckage of the Ferris wheel. I ventured a glance behind me...

And almost screamed in terror as I saw the gunship, in flames, descending rapidly toward our position. I urged Maria with all of my might to move faster... *faster*... and I sensed rather than felt her pace quicken as we gained the leading edge of the smoldering wreckage and dashed passed it. I glanced back and watched helplessly as the gunship's left wing broke away from the fuselage and spiraled downward toward the ground. The remnants of the machine banked to my right suddenly. The nose headed straight for the old Ghost Ship and the landing as we gained the far edge of the wreckage, vaulted over a twisted and blackened bench...

I did not see the gunship hit the landing, nor did I witness the explosion that lit-up the night behind us. I felt the damp, wooden planks beneath my feet tremor violently. In the light afforded by the explosion I could see, a few meters away, the fence that marked the termination of the landing. As for what lay beyond it? I could not determine it nor did I have a chance to consider my course of action. I could see my companions as they gained the fence... could see the one in the lead vault over it and plummet to whatever lay below. Someone else followed his lead but that was all. The heat of the shockwave from the explosion hit mine and Maria's backs with the force of a hundred... of a thousand moving vehicles. I lost my grip on her hand as we were promptly lifted off of our feet and sent spiraling head first, then feet first in a storm of bodies over the fence and into the unknown. I fell for a moment and I considered the possibility that our luck had finally run out and that we had reached our end *so close to the end...*

I'm sorry, Mia, I thought, *I'm so sorry but I tried, damnit, I tried...*

I braced for a jarring impact that never came. Instead, I landed face first a breath later in a soft pile of something grainy. My left shoulder screeched in pain...

Well that's dislocated again, I knew without a doctor's diagnosis...

...and I cried out. Simultaneously, I felt someone pull me backwards by my feet and under something as burning hot fragments of steel and wood began to rain down upon the place that I had, briefly, lain. I turned over with a grunt onto my back and found myself looking up into Jeff's face. The flames from the explosion on the landing above shined through the gaps in the boards overhead and played across his visage like cell bars. Despite the minimal light he smiled and asked me if I was okay. I nodded but quickly gritted my teeth and reached for my shoulder. The pain was excruciating. I still held my weapon firmly in my right hand and I felt its cold, steel touch against my wet t-shirt. I considered inquiring about Maria but quickly realized that such an inquiry was unnecessary as her face appeared next to Jeff's over mine. She looked terrified.

I understand, I thought as I heard someone groan in pain from a few steps away. I directed my gaze toward the sound and could barely make out Tim lying on his back with Steve and Carole on either side of him. Steve was in the process of doing something to his left leg. Tim shouted out in pain. I heard Steve say something that sounded like "broken" before the sound that had preceded the two explosions, the subsequent, fiery crash of the gunship and my subsequent plummet into the unknown echoed overhead once again. The air split again. A loud *boom* echoed across the area and was followed by another one as I felt the ground beneath my back shudder.

"What the hell *is that?!*" I asked Jeff through gritted teeth. Jeff surprisingly smiled.

"That, William MacNuff," he said as he patted me on my good, right shoulder, "is a sonic boom. It's the sound of our ride. Sounds like Alex kept his promise. We're almost home free, kid."

That's usually when the bottom falls out, I thought to myself as the pain in my head and my shoulder briefly waned before it re-intensified. I closed my eyes against it and briefly drifted.

Little did I know how right I was.

"Well isn't *this* a pickle?" I heard Jeff say a few moments later. His voice snapped me back from the border of unconsciousness, back into a world of seemingly endless pain. I opened my eyes slowly.

The first thing that I saw was him. Jeff stood a few steps away from me, glancing down at Tim whose leg Steve... likely with Carole's assistance... had placed in a splint fashioned from a plank of charred wood. He had completed it with both his own and Jeff's belt. Jeff moved past Tim toward where I lay and hiked up his pants as he did so. Rain and something hard continued to pound the sand directly beyond our shelter. The wind continued to howl and occasionally spattered our faces with rainwater. Occasionally the night brightened with a distant strike of lighting and I could hear a rumble of thunder but that was all. Said lightning and thunder did appear to be increasing in frequency and moving closer.

The worst is yet to come, I thought, *physically... and proverbially* and I shivered. I had not heard the *boom* that had rattled the area in some time.

"You already said that... *Jeebus,*" I said as I managed to prop myself up on my right arm and look at him. Maria placed her own hand upon my right shoulder to steady me. In the dwindling light that emanated from the fires that burned a top our position on the landing I saw him smile, and wink in his characteristic fashion.

"Did I?" he asked.

I nodded, "You did. Right before Freeworld One. Remember?"

Jeff "ahh'd" and his smile widened despite the obvious precariousness of our situation.

Not even a "don't call me Jeebus," I thought and stifled a nervous chuckle.

If I wasn't mental before, I thought as Matt suddenly stood from his position beside me, took a step toward the beach and spoke.

"We need to move," he said, "it's quiet. *Too* quiet. I get the feeling that..."

"Something's moving out there," Caren said hectically as she stepped back within our midst, Steve's blaster held out before her. She had been positioned a meter or two away from the rest of our party in the direction of the boardwalk, "I can't make much out but there's definitely movement *up there.*" She pointed with the weapon to the shadowy walkway that seemingly stretched endlessly from our left to our right.

"Maybe it's your eyes playing tricks on you, dear," Matt ventured as Caren handed Steve back his blaster. Steve took it with a nod.

"Wishful thinking, Pancho," Steve said as he instinctively checked the safety.

"Right," Matt replied, "okay, then. Wishful thinking or not we need to head for the water. If there *is* an extraction team out there then *that's* where it'll be looking for us, especially now."

Murmurs of "yes" and "okay" echoed across our shelter. All affirmatives and one…

"No," Tim said. His pained negative was unexpected and we all redirected our attentions immediately toward him.

"Sorry?" Steve said as he took a step backward away from him, "what do you mean 'no?'"

It sounded like Tim chuckled, though I could not be sure, "I mean *no*. At least for me, Doc. You don't mind if I call you Doc, do you?"

Steve shook his head in response and Tim continued.

"I can't move on this thing myself," he said as he gestured to his leg, "You know that. I'll only slow you down. One of you leave me your weapon. I'll cover you as long as I can. At least until whatever is coming overwhelms *me*. Then I'll either let them finish me off…" he paused for a moment before he added, "or I'll do it myself."

To the end, the Maria-specter from my recurring dream spoke in my mind, *not alive…*

I looked from Tim to Matt and Matt shook his head, "Negative, Tim. There's no way in hell we're leaving you here to fend for yourself against whatever's out *there*"—he gestured toward the boardwalk.

Tim chuckled (*definitely a chuckle that time,* I thought), "You're not, Matt. You're doing me a favor. I'm tired. There's nothing for me here and there's nothing for me *out there*"—he gestured toward where I assumed the Great Sea began—"either. I'm tired of running… tired of fighting. I sometimes feel like I've been doing it for my whole life. I've seen things… *done* things back when I was a member of the Marine Corp that I'm not proud of and that I'll never be proud of. Then I met Alex Parker and he taught me that I hadn't lost my humanity… not entirely, at least. He gave me a second chance… gave me a shot a redemption. I did the best I could with it but that's gone, now. *He's* gone. All that he was and all that he stood for. Free Caymen may exist just like Freeworld One did but it won't remain 'free' for much longer. Won't exist. *No place will.* That said, I'm *ready*."

There was finality in his last statement inherent in the way he placed an intentional emphasis on "ready" that I did not want to accept. But I understood him. It was not just the echo of my once-classmate's words as he walked away from me upon the grounds of Jefferson Prep so many, *many* days and nights before in Tim's.

Our time here is through, said once-classmate's voice reminded me, and my right hand instinctively fell to my right front, jean's pocket and caressed the Artifact within it. I considered saying something, then. Considered telling Tim that he was wrong... that a vestige of what Alex had been and what he had stood for remained. That what I carried was proof that we weren't finished. That other times... other *Skews* existed and would continue to exist so long as...

So long as the Artifact doesn't fall into the wrong hands, Alex's voice reminded me, *and that doesn't just mean the machines.* Whether out of instinct or simply out of fear at the once-Steward of Freeworld One's caution, I paused. My hand retreated from my pocket and simultaneously, I looked down at the weapon clamped tightly in my right hand, verified that the four bars upon its grip were still a lit, clicked the safety into the "on" position and tossed it toward Tim. It landed with a soft *thump* in the sand directly before him. He reached down without hesitation, plucked it up and off of the ground and gripped it in his left hand.

"Thanks for checking the safety," Tim said with what I could tell was a forced grin.

"Didn't want it to go off and accidentally shoot through a door," I responded with the same and Tim briefly but earnestly guffawed. His forced smile widened and he nodded his head to me.

"Or one of you," he stated. He then paused for a moment before he continued with, "William? I'm sorry. I *still* don't know if I believe you... *still* don't know how the hell that tracking device ended up in your backpack but at this point? I really don't care. Can you... *will you* do something for me?"

I looked back at my companions, shrugged, then turned back to Tim and nodded my head, "Sure, Tim. What do you need?"

He did not speak. His smile did not falter. He simply wrapped his hand around the cross that hung from his neck and jerked. Without a word the cross broke free. He held it out in my direction and said, "Take this. I've had it since I was an altar boy, way, *way* back before the Administration. Those were simpler times then... *better* times. It's the last thing I have from those days. It survived the Corp... survived running and survived being a fugitive. Take it, and bury it somewhere nice on Free Caymen for me? Preferably someplace that can always see either a sunrise or a sunset? I used to love them both back... back *before*. Can you do that for me?"

I looked from Tim to the cross and then back to Tim. I surveyed his face for something questionable but there was nothing upon it. Nothing save for a grin, a spattering of freckles and a pair of gaudy black glasses, the lenses of which sparkled with the barred reflection of the fire still burning upon the landing. And sincerity. I judged that the ex-Marine was sincere in his statement. I shifted through the sand toward him, reached out, and gently took the cross from him. He sighed as he released it, seemingly resigned to the fact that said gesture was, in all likelihood, one of his last.

"I will, Tim," I said reassuringly as I dropped it into my right pocket and felt it come to rest next to the Artifact, "I promise."

He nodded and spoke no more words. None, I realized, needed to be spoken. Not from him and not from any of our companions. There was, I understood, no dissuading him from his chosen task.

His fate, my coldly rational voice spoke in my mind, *we all have a destiny, William.* Even then a part of me knew that Tim was right. Eventually, you simply grow tired. Tired of running… tired of fighting. I didn't believe that as much then as I do now. But now? I sometimes wonder at what keeps me from simply giving up. I nodded back and averted my gaze from him to Jeff.

"Help me?" I asked. Jeff did not hesitate. He reached his non-sword hand down to me and I took it. Matt moved up on my left and offered his own non-weapon hand in assistance. I took his, as well, as Maria moved up behind me and gently pushed upon my back until I was in a standing position. I briefly swooned before I recomposed myself and looked across the expectant faces of the group.

My companions, I thought. *My brethren. My…*

"Let's go," I said as the grayness faded and the world, which had momentarily wavered, re-solidified, "what passes for time here is wasting."

Matt nodded, his expression stern (*there's nothing humorous about this,* I thought again) and stepped away from me toward the termination of our shelter and the onset of the beach. He raised his weapon and pointed it out into the rain. Jeff moved up behind him with his sword held down at his side and Caren moved up behind him. With a bit of assistance from Maria I moved up behind Caren and Maria remained directly beside me. I reached down with my left hand and grabbed Maria's right. She accepted it. I heard a shuffling in the sand behind me as Carole took up position there and Steve…

I glanced over my shoulder. Steve had hesitated for a moment by where Tim lay. As I watched he knelt down and placed a hand upon Tim's chest. He genuinely smiled. Tim's once-forced grin, which had never really disappeared, intensified into something natural.

"'Something to say, Doc?" Tim cocked his head and said, "You don't want to miss your ride, do you?"

Steve shook his head and smiled, "Good luck, Marine," he said, "and *thank you. From all* of us."

Tim nodded, "You're welcome. Now *go already* you 'idget. Enough with the mushy shit. I *hate* mushy shit."

Steve needed no further encouragement. He removed his hand from Tim's chest, stood from his crouch and took up position behind Carole. He shifted his weapon from his left hand to his right, held it out before him and said, "Ready?"

"Ready," Matt responded, "don't look up the beach and"—he paused— "and *don't look back*. Whatever you do, *don't look back*. Run like hell for the breakwater. William and Maria, if we get separated for whatever reason follow the sound. You know what I'm talking about, don't you?"

I nodded, as did Maria. *The sound of the waves breaking on the beach,* I thought. Apparently Maria had heard it as well.

Almost there, I thought again, but knew that the success of our endeavor was far from sealed.

"If... no, *scratch that*," he continued, "*as soon as* whatever is lurking around up there by the boardwalk sees us or detects us they'll be on us before we can react." He paused for a moment and added: "And pray that our ticket off of the mainland isn't too far away, *knows* we're coming and is looking for us. Everyone got it?"

We all either nodded instinctively in approval or murmured in agreement.

"Okay then," Matt took a deep breath and began, "on three. One..."

Maria's grip tensed upon mine....

"Two..."

Lightning struck not far from our position. Thunder split the air and caused me to cringe...

"THREE!"

Without a thought to the contrary we dashed out from beneath the overhang of the landing and into the driving rain, hail and wind as lightning once again a lit the steadily swirling sky and a rumble of thunder shook the air around us and the ground beneath us. Simultaneously with our gambit an alarm screeched through the air from the direction of the boardwalk and a flurry of unmistakable pulse rifle...

That answers the "machine or merc" question, I thought...

...and occasional blaster fire immediately erupted, obviously aimed toward our position from all points of the compass. The shots quickly began to impact with the ground around us but lacked any sort of sustained accuracy, likely a result of not only the rapidly deteriorating weather conditions over Hempstead and her surrounding areas, but also whatever Matt's aforementioned benefactor was doing to assist us. I heard a shout from beneath the landing where we had sheltered… heard the once-member of the Royal Human Marine Corp (*a humachine,* I thought and cringed) turned runner turned spotter turned my reluctant but accommodating travelling companion, Tim Redfield, begin returning the army's fire with a scream despite his precarious and completely vulnerable position. As Matt had instructed, I did not look back, not at the landing and not at the boardwalk. Rather, I continued to run with Maria's hand grasped firmly in mine toward the steadily increasing thunder of not the storm, but the Great Sea crashing against the shore.

A shot coughed up a hot mini-explosion of sand next to my right boot and forced me to my left. My feet tangled. I ran briefly into Maria and almost toppled us both but felt a surprisingly strong hand steady me from behind. I knew without looking that it was Steve's.

"*KEEP MOVING!*" he shouted as another shot sizzled through the air just wide of my right ear. It was followed by another that cut through the rain and hail directly between Maria and I. Yet I was undaunted. I ran onward and silently urged Maria to do the same as the shadows of my companions before me continued running and the sound of the…

Breakwater, Matt had called it…

Drew closer… and *closer…*

Simultaneously with the recognition that a large hill of some sort loomed before us I heard a thunderous explosion from the boardwalk or just beyond it which was followed by a familiar whistle that increased in volume with each, passing breath that rapidly escaped from my lips. Said explosion was followed by another… and another whistle… and another explosion… and *another* whistle, as the MDUs that had taken up position either on the beach or on the boardwalk or beyond it *all* fired their plasma canons upon our position. We had little time to react and every one of my companions knew it. I watched as one by one, they arrived at and ducked behind the large, sand-constructed hill that loomed before us. I quickened my pace and virtually yanked Maria along behind me as the approaching whistle shrieked louder and the sand hill…

Dune, William, I remembered from my reoccurring nightmare, *it's called a dune…*

…drew closer. We gained the left edge of it simultaneously with Steve and Carole gaining the right, and without hesitation I dove right and pulled Maria behind me. I heard her shout and to this day, I am unsure if her shout was one of surprise, one of objection or one of pain. Whatever the case, I landed on my right side in a puddle and Maria landed squarely a top my left arm and shoulder. I screamed as a fresh bolt of pain shot down my arm and across my chest and rolled away from her as the first burst fired by one of the MDUs impacted with the beach surface two or three meters beyond the boardwalk-facing front of the dune, and a white hot storm of sand rivulets careened over top and sizzled down onto the wet sand around us. A second burst impacted not far from where the first one had; another storm engulfed the air above us and on either side of the dune. It was followed by *another…* and *another,* as someone… I have no idea who… pulled me forward and deposited me against the Great Sea-facing back of the dune. I glanced to my left and my right and saw the remainder of my companions gathered, either sitting or standing with their backs similarly against the hill. I struggled up and into a sitting position. Simultaneously, pulse rifle and blaster fire began to shred the top and the sides of the dune. Hot particles landed upon my saturated clothes and exposed skin and quickly smoldered.

Fuck, I thought hopelessly, *pinned down. Just like in my…*

An ear-splitting roll of thunder cascaded across the sky accompanied by a strike of lightning which illuminated my surroundings and I gasped in shock at what I saw. The lightning strike was brief… the aftereffects of it lasted much, much longer but what it revealed was unmistakable. Not 10 meters from where I and my companions sheltered sat the largest body of water I had ever seen. I could see it undulating and crashing violently against the surface of the beach before it rolled back out in a maelstrom of what had to be foam and spray.

The Great Sea, I thought. But even the majesty of that sight, one that I had waited a long time to behold did not hold my attention. What did hold it was what I had seen beyond the…

Now I know why Matt called it a "breakwater," I thought: Three formed and unmistakable shadows floated upon the Great Sea. They were some distance out still—maybe a quarter of a kilometer—and at first, I thought said shadows little more than a product of my seemingly insatiable desire for hope or my naive propensity toward wishful thinking. But a second burst of lightning, more sustained than the first quantified what I had seen and caused what little hope I had retained to spring anew.

I started to call out to my companions but my call was cut short. As the lightning faded, I saw something else move swiftly through the air above the floating shadows and in our direction: Two shadows, each with two sets of two lights a piece spaced evenly apart. They closed the distance between where I had initially seen them and our position behind the dune quickly and rocketed low overhead with a pair of loud and complimentary "booms." My teeth shook within my mouth. I did not hear "clicks" as they passed overhead and I did not need to. What sounded like automatic rifle fire echoed down toward where I sat and seemingly cut across and through the Administration forces that were advancing upon our position. The pulse rifle and blaster fire that had been shredding the top and sides of the dune momentarily subsided. I did not chance a look over it. I heard explosions... heard gasps from my companions that had chanced to look over it and the area over which we had recently ran noticeably brightened (I could see it glowing around either side of the dune) but I did not see anything first hand. Not yet, at least.

"*Now THAT'S what I'M...!*" Steve began but his exclamation was cut short as one... two... *three* of the MDUs fired. One of the whistles that followed—the second—seemed to be moving in our direction again but the other two? One cut-off quickly and I heard a thunderous explosion echo through the air above followed by the sound of something shrieking... falling quickly, followed by the sound of something crashing into either the boardwalk or one of the structures that lined it. The other continued to whistle and faded simultaneously with the plasma canon burst that impacted with the beach little more than a meter or two away from the front of the dune. Another fresh cascade of particulates descended upon the ground that immediately surrounded us and simmered upon the wet sand. Thereafter, pulse rifle and blaster fire once again erupted from the beach—*nearer now,* I understood—and the top of the sand hill once again became little more than a hastily prepared and deteriorating shield for us to hide behind.

"*Ah SHIT!*" Matt exclaimed as he crouched lower.

"*MATT!*" Caren shouted over the deafening din of weapon's fire, thunder and wind, "*we CAN'T STAY HERE!*"

I turned to Matt and Matt nodded, "*NO!*" he shouted, and opened his mouth to say something else. As he did so, however, a surprising yet comforting light appeared near where I had originally diagnosed the breakwater was. *A floodlight,* I understood, and by it and on either side of it I could see figures that appeared to be disembarking from some sort of water bound craft. While I could not visually verify whether they were machine or man, the fact that they immediately began firing their weapons up the beach and past our position told me more than their shadows.

Human, I thought. As soon as it had appeared, the light vanished, but I had seen enough. I knew that our extractors had arrived.

"*OKAY, THEN!*" Matt shouted as he, apparently, noticed it as well and crouched lower beneath the diminishing dune, "*if we're going to do this then we're going to have to do it NOW! Everybody GET READY! WE GO ON THREE!"*

I nodded and forced myself into a standing position though I remained crouched behind the sand hill, as did the others that had been sitting. Matt began to count but never made it past "one." An MDU, surprisingly close to our position and up the beach fired its plasma canon. Apparently, *it* had seen the floodlight, as well. The whistle only lasted for a breath or two. It impacted with the surface of the beach near where I remembered seeing the transport waiting and momentarily blinded me. As the dust and the smoke cleared I saw the result of the detonation and I felt my heart sink into my stomach: The figures that had disembarked from it... the ones that had been covering us lay motionless and in flames on either side of it, their weapons beside them and our transport? I could barely see it by the firelight, bobbing in the breakwater.

"FUCK!" Matt shouted hopelessly. I turned to him in search of a glimmer of optimism yet there was nothing. He crouched low as blaster fire sliced through the dune top over his head, his blaster held down at his side, almost invisible behind a veil of rainwater.

"MATT!" shouted someone from behind me. I turned instinctively in response to the familiarity of the voice...

Maria's voice.

I felt Matt's gaze avert from the sand beneath his boots, passed me and to her. I gazed into her deep, brown eyes and felt a shiver traverse my spine. The look within them? It was not hopeless nor was it frightened. It was determined.

Suicidally so, I thought and knew, however reluctantly, the statement that was about to emanate from her lips. I had heard it more times than I could count in my dreams. It echoed in my mind that timeless moment there, upon the shore of the Great Sea in Hempstead within sight of the freedom that we had left Jefferson so many, *many* days and nights before in search of.

To the end, William. To the end. Not alive. We can't let that happen. They won't take us alive.

No, the unfamiliar-then-but-familiar-now voice of my adult self spoke in my mind as a pulse rifle shot sizzled not over the dune but through it and cut through the air between Maria and me. Dream and reality intermingled and became one as a spattering of smoldering sand cascaded against my cheeks and fledgling beard and sizzled upon both. The cascade appeared to do the same upon Maria's face yet was indistinguishable amidst the familiar collection of freckles that was just visible by the light of the fire burning by the breakwater.

She smiled then, and I swear that I heard her think: *It's the only way, William. The only way.* I will never forget that smile as she opened her mouth to speak…

And I instinctively did so for her.

"*No,*" I whispered and she froze mid-breath. She gazed at me curiously. *No?* Her gaze asked.

"*NO!*" I shouted so that everyone else could hear me, "*no GODDAMN way!*" I turned from Maria briefly to Matt, "*Matt! Give me your weapon NOW and get ready to RUN!*"

My gaze averted from him to Maria's. Her confusion gave way to surprise before it gave way to rejection. She shook her head.

"*YES, Mia!*" I shouted so that she could hear me, "*this is the ONLY WAY!*"

"*NO!*" she screamed and moved toward me, "*it's NOT THE ONLY WAY, WILLIAM! YOU SAID IT YOURSELF, DAMNIT! THAT FIRST NIGHT ON THE ROAD, 'WE…!'*"

I reached across the area that separated her and pulled her toward me until she was a breath away from my face.

"*It doesn't MATTER what I said then, Mia!*" I shouted. Could the others hear me, as well? It did not matter. What I had to say was for Maria and Maria only and if they overheard it? Well, perhaps they would not attempt to convince me otherwise. I knew my course of action. Subconsciously? I had known it since mine and Pat McClane's conversation our first night on the road together. The content of that conversation echoed in my mind as I gazed at Maria through the veil of rainwater that fell around us.

This is the part that you really need to hear, Pat's voice reminded me, *and the bitch of it is that it's the toughest part to tell but you wanted a story and I wanted to tell you one. I needed to. Not all stories start with 'once upon a time' and end with 'and they lived happily ever after,' Vato. Always remember that…*

If given the choice, his voice continued, *of her freedom or mine I'd have chosen the former with no questions asked. I'm not saying that you're going to have it with Maria. Hell, I'm not saying that you're going to have any choice. It might come down to something as simple as capture of kill with no choice 'C.' Or you may defy the odds and make it all the way to Free Caymen. But if you do? Heed my advice, Vato: Don't hesitate. Take it. Part of loving someone is having the strength to set them free…*

Part of loving someone, it repeated, *is having the strength to set them free.*

"*Things,*" I began, "*EVERYTHING has changed and someone needs to stay back and cover our retreat! I'm VOLUNTEERING, Mia! I'll follow you if I can but YOU have got to LIVE Mia! FOR ME! And this is the ONLY way to ensure that happens!"*

"*NO!*" she shouted again as she balled her fists and pounded them repeatedly against my chest. My left shoulder screamed in agony from her barrage yet I was undeterred as she buried her head against my right shoulder. I could feel hot tears cutting through the rainwater that had inundated my shirt, "*I don't WANT to live if I can't be with YOU, William…!*"

"*And I can't live knowing that YOU AREN'T alive, Mia!*" I responded. She did not respond but continued to sob on my shoulder.

Oh, Mia, I thought, *oh God, I am so sorry but this is the only way.*

"*There's something…!*" I began, and could feel hot tears building in my own eyes. I looked away and down the beach toward the transport which still bobbed in the breakwater. In truth, they had been building there for quite some time. I softened my voice and spoke… albeit *whispered* her surname in her ear. She pulled slowly away from me and looked into my eyes, her brown against my blue. Her chest heaved as she continued to sob and tried to control her breathing.

"There's something I need to tell you, Mia," I said, my voice controlled as weapon's fire continued to erupt around us and drew closer, "something that I may not have another chance to tell you. People say it every day yet few of them actually mean it when they say it. Most people just use it to get what they want but some people… people like you and me, kiddo? We *know* it. We feel it deep in our hearts, deep in our minds and deep in our souls. *Nothing* can ever take the place of that, Mia. Nothing can stop it. You taught me that, kiddo. *You.* No one else. You've been there… been *here* beside me my whole life. I just wish"—I paused—"I just wish that I'd realized it sooner. I… I…"

Another explosion and another whistle. The shot from the MDU impacted wide right of the slowly disintegrating dune behind which we sheltered. I could sense my companions growing restless… could sense their desire to go but they were inconsequential at that moment. For one, brief moment what passed passes and likely always will pass for time in Endworld stopped. There was only me and Maria Markinson: My oldest, dearest and truest friend.

Maria Markinson: My oldest, dearest, and truest…

Her hands moved up from her sides and fell upon either side of my face. She continued to gaze into my eyes and I continued to gaze into hers as the battle mingled with the rain, hail and the wind that raged around us. But everything was muffled. Everything, to employ yet another old cliché "faded to gray." There was only me and her. She pulled my face toward hers… my lips toward hers. I closed my eyes…

And we kissed. We kissed as we had upon the bank of the Little Shenango River in Freeworld One. We kissed as we had in Centralia. We kissed and I savored our embrace, for I knew deep within the darkest recesses of my mind, my heart and my soul that it would likely be the last time we ever would.

One more thing, William, Alex's voice whispered in my mind. It did not need to. I knew it already. Without thinking and acting purely on instinct I reached into the front, right pocket of my jeans and felt the two items within it. My fingers brushed across the edge of Tim's cross and found the Artifact. I ran my fingers over its edges… over its raised seal, imprinted with a figure eight and an arrow crosscutting it (*the sigil of the Explorator,* I thought), paused upon the edge nearest the top of my pocket and removed it. I felt its power wash over me one, final time as I held it close and shifted my body slightly so that it was hidden from my companions' views. They could not see what I was planning to do. I palmed it, gently wrapped my hand around Maria's waist so that it was touching the small of her back, pulled her closer to me…

And slipped the Artifact as deftly as I could manage into the rear, left pocket of the jeans she wore. She startled… I felt her lips tense against mine and my eyes opened in time with hers. Our embrace broke and we pulled away from each other slowly.

Keep it safe, Mia, I thought. Whether she understood or not I am sorry to say I never found out. Another MDU shot exploded directly in front of the dune. Matt's restless voice cut through the sensory cacophony that surrounded us.

"WILLIAM!" he shouted but there would be time for that… time for him and time for all of them later, I knew. At that moment there was only…

"I love you, Mia," I whispered, "I always have and I swear to you: I always will. No matter how much distance separates us know this now. I do. You are my everything, kiddo. *Everything.* Always."

She nodded her head and a ghost of a smile eclipsed her face, "I love you too, William MacNuff. And I promise *you,* I always will, too."

Without turning from her I reached my right hand behind me and gestured for Matt's weapon. A breath later I felt the slippery hilt of it against my palm and I closed my fingers around it. I positioned my index finger over the trigger and slowly with Maria's assistance stood.

I turned to face my companions. All gazed back at me with a mixture of sadness and understanding upon their faces.

What can I say to them? I wondered.

They're likely wondering the same thing, my coldly, rational voice determined. An all-to-brief moment later I realized what I needed to say and I forced a half-hearted smile.

"Take care of her!" I shouted, and followed it up with, *"I'll be along! In one way or the other! NOW GO!"* Did I realize at the time that my words were reminiscent of Pat McClane's final, living words to me? Somewhere deep within my subconscious, *yes,* I did.

Matt looked at Caren and Caren looked at Steve. Steve looked at Carole and Carole looked at Jeff. Jeff gazed at me, opened his mouth to say something, seemingly realized it was pointless and reached his non-sword hand out instead to Maria. Maria paused briefly before she stepped forward and took his hand in hers. He pulled her toward him, turned back to me, and spoke.

"We will, William!" he shouted, *"and we know!"*

He turned from me then and I turned to face the dune. From my crouch I had very little clearance over it yet I knew that I had no choice. I moved a step closer toward it, glanced down at the blaster that I held in my hand, made sure that the safety was "off" and held it down at my side. I glanced over my shoulder at my companions. All had refocused their gazes down the remainder of the beach between them and the breakwater within which the transport bobbed empty and waiting but Maria? Maria continued to look back at me despite Jeff's grip upon her hand.

I heard someone—*Matt,* I understood—shout *"ON THREE!"* I heard him count in sequence up to it yet my eyes remained fixed upon Maria's as a blaster bolt flew very close over my head and singed the hair there. As Matt screamed *"THREE!"* and they bolted for the water in tandem, Maria mouthed something to me that I could just barely discern by the light of the floodlight. I had heard it before: In Centralia as I had dozed off to sleep atop the hood of the red, nameless car…

Je'taime, she mouthed. *I love you.* Then, in a flash of lightning and a roll of thunder she disappeared into the night and I, simultaneously, turned and raised my weapon up over the diminished top of the dune. I could see the machines encroaching upon my position… could see the nearest vanguard no more than seven or eight meters from where I was and I immediately targeted them, inhaled deeply, focused as I had over Halmier's Pass…

And began firing. I began to scream with each shot as 78A after Surveillance Mark after Leader after humachine dropped to the beach amidst the pouring rain, the pelting hail and the howling wind, interspersed at times with blinding lightning and rolling thunder. I did not discriminate and I will not lie: The process… the *killing* was borderline hypnotic and I found myself quickly lapsing into what I could only then and can only describe now as a void: A nothingness that engulfed my aching body and made me quick. The dune behind which I and my companions had sheltered and behind which I remained quickly depleted via the increased accuracy of the Administration forces that encroached upon my position as they diagnosed and visually verified my position.

So much for our benefactor, I thought.

My right palm was growing hot yet I dismissed it. The heat was not a part of the void. Within the void things like heat and pain were irrelevant. Yet as it continued to build and the trigger of my weapon began to stick my focus shattered. I waited for a break in the barrage of weapon's fire and when I got it, I quickly dropped back behind what was left of the dune.

I cocked my head and gazed at the blaster. *Christ,* I thought with a touch of sarcastic humor as I dropped the useless weapon into the puddle at my feet. The water immediately began to smoke. With little consideration to the contrary, I leapt up and out of my crouch and took off in a sprint for the breakwater.

Maybe they're still there, I thought optimistically, *maybe I can still make it.* Through the downpour and the haze that had fallen like a thick and cloying mist over the beach I could still see the transport, bathed by the fire's shifting light. It was still stationary in the breakwater and there were shadows moving upon and around it. With a rush of adrenaline I pumped my legs harder as weapon's fire once again erupted around my feet.

I can still make it, I thought hectically, *I'm COMING Mia… wait for me… WAIT FOR ME…!*

Silhouetted against the floodlight, a dark figure ran into my view and sprinted in my direction. I felt my heart leap as I beheld his visage. He was not taller than, but roughly the same height as me. Thin but chiseled, I knew despite the shadows that surrounded him that he had no facial hair and although I could not see them I knew he also had a set of piercing blue eyes. His hair was cut tightly to his scalp but what he wore was indistinguishable. In his right hand he held a blaster—*Steve's,* I understood—and in his left he held a sword. Despite the situation, my heart leapt for joy at the sight of him. Jeff "Jeebus" Howard had not given up, either.

Jeff "Jeebus" Howard was, despite his once-posturing to the contrary, coming back for me.

"*JEFF!*" I shouted, "*Thank GOD you…!*"

"DOWN, WILLIAM!" he screamed in warning as he raised his blaster… *Steve's* blaster I self-corrected and pointed it in my direction. Without hesitation I heeded his warning and quickly threw myself to the wet and sandy ground. A pulse rifle burst sizzled through the air where my head had been. I heard Jeff return fire from before me… heard something explode behind me and white hot, metallic debris exploded over my head.

I looked up from where I lay and saw Jeff still sprinting up the beach toward me. A small smile graced his face and he winked. God be damned, that sonofabitch winked at me. I shouted his name again as I quickly stood and began to run toward him… shouted *"thank GOD you…!"* again before thunder without lightning exploded from the area behind me. Said thunder was followed by a familiar whistle as the plasma canon burst from the nearest MDU shot over my head and impacted with the ground between me and Jeff. My momentum was quickly halted as the shockwave from the impact picked me up and threw me end over end in no discernible direction. I slammed head first into the soft ground and felt the world waver around me. There was little that I could do to ward off the grayness that overtook me as the sounds of the battle and the subsequent screams of either pain or dread that emanated from nowhere and everywhere at the same time followed me down into the darkness.

I embraced it. It was all that I could do. *Finis,* I heard Pat's voice lament in my mind. *Finis, William MacNuff.*

Finis? It too is Latin.

It means *the end.*

CHAPTER THIRTY

A dreary sunrise arose over Wildwood/Hempstead, ET, the beach near Mariner's Landing and the gray-as-slate Great Sea that crashed against said beach. A light drizzle fell upon the area and a gentle breeze blew across it. A low, ground haze consumed everything, a combination of the battle that had raged upon it and the weather that had pummeled it the previous evening.

From within the thick haze, a figure emerged. Said figure was limping as it made its way slowly down the beachfront toward the breakwater. It... he was unremarkable to look at upon first glance. He was short and stocky, and his once-dirty blonde hair was trimmed tightly to his scalp and interspersed with streaks of white. While his attire was difficult to discern per the minimal light that filtered down upon the beach and the breakwater through the overcast, one could discern that the man wore arguably the gaudiest pair of glasses ever manufactured. They were black with rims the size of a normal person's pinky finger and about two sizes too big for his heavily freckled face. He wore a dark-colored t-shirt that bore what appeared to be the countenance of a smiling, cartoon tiger upon its lapel. His right arm was covered by what appeared to be a hastily prepared, dirty bandage (what passes for 'triage' in the field) but his left was unhindered. In it he held a blaster. Tim Redfield, once member of the Royal Human Marine Corps turned runner, turned spotter and turned fugitive, paused within a few meters of the two bodies that lay motionless halfway between a blackened and diminished dune and the sea. He sighed.

He heard something behind him and he turned instinctively...

As a single Leader, armed with only a sword and two weaponized, model 78A protocol droids emerged from the drizzle and the haze and brought their respective firearms to bear upon his position. Behind them was a lone Surveillance Mark. The inset radar dish upon its chest rotated smoothly. Whatever interference Matt's Mystery Man or Woman had created at the height of the battle had, seemingly, disappeared.

Tough break, Tim thought as he sized up the newcomers.

"HUMAN IDENTIFY," the 78A on the right spoke tonelessly as the mist licked around the barrel of its weapon. The one on the left repeated the request. The Leader remained silent.

More like a directive, Tim thought as he smiled despite the pain in his broken, right leg, well? I guess this is "it," then.

He held up his left hand and let his blaster fall from his grip onto the sand with a gentle thump. He showed his open palm to the 78As and said, "May I?" The 78As turned to each other simultaneously. A series of audible clicks and whirs issued from their superstructures. They turned to the Leader who, in turn, turned to Tim.

"Proceed," it spoke, and shifted its grip upon the sword it carried. Tim nodded and reached into his right, front pants pocket. His fingers fell upon the cold steel of the blade that rested within it and he removed it, hilt first. He brought the point of it cautiously to his left hand which he opened…

And sliced deeply into his palm. He did not wince. Warm, red blood immediately began to flow from the self-inflicted wound. It dripped from his extended fingers and onto the sandy ground below him yet he felt no pain. He motioned to the SM with his knife hand and said, "Come on, sweetheart. We haven't got all day."

The Surveillance Mark stepped forward and reached out its arm. It opened its palm and Tim placed his own, bleeding palm in it as if he was shaking the machine's hand. The SM's grip tightened around his own but Tim did not flinch. He glanced unblinkingly into the emotionless, red eyes of the robot as a series of sounds emanated from its superstructure. The Leader and the 78As watched intently and Tim waited patiently, his weight supported by the long, charred plank that he was using as a crutch. After an eternal moment — 21 pre-Administration seconds to be exact — the Surveillance Mark revealed its findings to the Leader and the 78As in its own, toneless voice. The other machines acknowledged said findings. They turned back to Tim…

And lowered their weapons.

"DNA SIGNATURE VERIFIED," the 78A on Tim's right spoke.

"INFILTRATOR," the one on his left continued.

"Report," the Leader concluded tonelessly.

Tim's sarcastic smile widened and he removed his glasses. Finally, he thought as he dropped them to the ground and brought his left heel down upon them. They shattered instantaneously.

If I never see those damned things again, he thought as his eyes sparkled and changed color in the dim, gray glow that had befallen the beach. Pat McClane would have immediately recognized them. Confused eyes, one minute blue, the next green, the next brown and the next hazel. Gray, black… any color that you like. He gestured to the sword that the Leader held as he placed his knife back in its customary place in his pocket, "Think I can get that back now, Nyx? I earned it. I killed

McClane, not you."

SLNyxV4.0 appeared hesitant for a moment before it stepped forward and extended the hilt of the sword that was once Pat McClane's in Tim's direction. Tim bent down to the machine's level and took it in his bloody left hand. The feel of the cold and damp leather of the hilt soothed his cut. He squeezed it tightly and a spray of red droplets escaped from his hand. He gestured over his shoulders at the two bodies lying motionless upon the beach, "Shall we go check those two, now?"

The Leader nodded its loaf of bread shaped head, "Affirmative, Infiltrator. Commence search."

Tim knelt down on the knee of his unbroken, left leg with a gasp and reclaimed his blaster from the sand. He wrapped his right hand around its handle and thought of MacNuff. So gullible, he thought as he glanced at the weapon. The Jefferson, MWT fugitive had voluntarily given it to him in a gesture of solidarity... a gesture of trust... a gesture of friendship.

He turned and began to limp down the beach toward where the nearest body lay. A slight gust of cool wind blew passed him as he reached the first figure which lay contorted and face-down in the sand, and turned said figure the rest of the way over with a nudge of his boot. He was greeted by a blank, blue-eyed stare and a thin but chiseled face. The figure's mouth was closed though a very, very slight grin touched the corners of it.

And would eternally, Tim thought as his gaze took in the figure's hair which was cut tightly to its... to his scalp. His gaze traced its length down the figure's body and he saw a jagged hole on the left side of his...

Of Jeff Howard's chest.

The area around the wound was thick with congealing blood and wet sand but Tim did not find the sight revolting. Rather, he found it soothing.

Only human, he thought as he took a step back in the direction that he had come from, raised his blaster and fired a lone shot at close range that sizzled and sliced through the center of Jeff's chest that all but ensured the former resident of Greentree, MWT's demise. Jeff's body jerked once from the impact and fell still.

Just in case, Tim thought, and on the coattails of that, another...

One down.

He stepped over Jeff's motionless body and limped across the last of the distance toward the second body. He arrived beside it a moment later. It lay upon its left side and its back was turned toward him.

Only one way to be sure, he thought, lifted his broken, right leg with a "hiss" and laid the heel upon the figure's chest. He pulled it toward him...

And gasped. It's... his eyes were closed and his mouth was slightly pursed beneath his fledgling, proto-beard. His head lay at an awkward angle from his neck and his wet, brownish-black hair was bespeckled with sand. His left arm lay across his body at an equally, if not more extreme angle than his head did from his neck.

MacNuff, he thought as he once again knelt down on the knee of his good, left leg. He positioned his body so that the machines could not see what he was doing, reached deftly for the right, front pocket of the Jefferson fugitive's jeans and slipped his fingers inside. He expected to touch thick paper...

And instead touched something cold. He felt his heart drop into his stomach. He fumbled with it and removed it quickly.

It was his cross.

"No," he murmured as he dropped the cross in the sand beside him. He heard a beep from behind him and one of the machines — the SM, he assumed — stated, "TRACKING DEVICE LOCATED." But the significance of the cross as a back-up tracking device that Tim had planted on MacNuff in an attempt to fulfill his Administration sanctioned mission was inconsequential. He had failed to infiltrate the Rebellion and, by association, he had failed to lead the machines to Free Caymen. He knew that he would be forced to pay a price for his failure. But the real crime? Not the loss of the Rebellion, nor the location of the refugee camp, but the loss of the Artifact. He knew this. As far as his Administration overlords had known he had not been aware of their goal despite the fact that their goal?

Ultimately... Secretly, that goal had been his goal, as well.

Not just my goal, Tim thought angrily, my destiny.

He reiterated his negative, louder than before and reached into MacNuff's left pocket. Maybe he shifted it, he thought. His fingertips sought for but found only damp cloth. It was no use.

The Artifact was gone.

Unchecked rage built quickly within his mind. He could feel a primal scream on his lips yet he literally bit it back. Warm blood escaped from the puncture wound within his lip, ran down his tongue and into his throat. He stood slowly. His broken, right leg blazed with pain but he did not hesitate for an instant. He brought his blaster up from his side and pointed the barrel of it directly at the bastard's head.

William MacNuff, he thought with a sneer, this end is too good for you.

He thought of the knife within in his pocket. How much more poetic... how much more Shakespearean that would be, he thought but he did not shift his focus. In truth? He longed for it to be over. He was tired but for different reasons then he had explicated to his once-counterparts. Somehow, despite his many, many years of experience he had been deceived, not only by the boy lying motionless before him but by the universe... by all of the Skews themselves. He could not lash out against the "All" but the boy? The boy was his scapegoat. Not the machines watching him from a meter or two away, but the fucking child. MacNuff. Whether he had known it or not, in Tim's mind? The child had deceived him.

And the repercussions of that transgression? Well, Tim reasoned, they will be immediate.

"'Some rise by sin and some by virtue fall,'" Tim spoke. His voice shook with rage as his finger tightened upon the trigger of his weapon, "goodbye, William Macnuff." His finger tensed as he began to pull the trigger of his... of William's old weapon...

Well at least that's relatively poetic, he thought...

And another cool breeze blew passed him and up the beach in the direction of the Supreme Leader, the two 78As and the Surveillance Mark. He had thought nothing of it the first time it had engulfed him but recognition suddenly occurred in his mind as he turned in a flash from his quarry. He remembered 9. Remembered what had transpired upon it. He saw something, little more than a shadow appear directly behind the Nyx... saw something sharp that glistened in the dim, early morning glow slice quickly across and beneath what passed for the Leader's chin. Said machine collapsed in a flurry of sparks and electricity as the 78As brought their pulse rifles quickly to bear upon the new threat...

And received complimentary blaster bolts at close range through their optical processors in response. Both machines fell to the ground directly next to the Leader in a similar flurry of sparking fire, smoke and ozone without firing a single shot.

Tim screamed in anger and raised his own blaster toward the shadow that quickly and systematically disposed of the defenseless SM with a well-positioned shot through its inset, rotating radar. Tim fired once... twice but he was too slow, and the shots sizzled through the falling drizzle and impacted with open air. The shadow had vanished. Another cool gust of wind blew passed him and away up the shoreline and a breath later, two blaster shots fired without warning from the area directly to his right. The first sliced through his good left leg at the bottom of his thigh and the other did the same through the meaty part of the thigh of his broken right leg. He shrieked and fell to the ground as a third and final shot impacted squarely with the upper, left side of his chest near his shoulder. All strength left his arm and he helplessly dropped his blaster as he landed hard on his back. He could smell charred flesh... could feel his blood pouring out of the exit wounds upon his back and his legs. It mingled with the sand beneath him and spread in a red puddle upon it. Tim could see it doing so in his peripheral vision.

He reached for his discarded blaster as yet another cool breeze blew passed him, reversed itself and paused upon his position. Simultaneously, he watched as the shadow which, Tim understood, really wasn't a shadow rematerialized directly where his blaster lay in the sand. A heavily booted foot appeared and kicked said *weapon away from his reach and Tim moaned in resignation.*

His grip tightened upon the sword that he held in his left hand. Despite the pain that raged through his body he glanced up the length of the figure that had appeared beside him from boot to torso and torso to chest and beheld an oddity. The man that gazed back at him did so from beneath a long, curly mane of black hair and a curly black beard with a synthesis of determination and sadness in his expression. The newcomer's appearance was dominated by a pristine, white patch which clung tightly to one eye. The other eye was uncovered and appeared clear and blue.

Chuck, Tim understood, Alex Parker's silent crony. The purveyor of his armory. But that, Tim understood, was not entirely true. There was something in the figure's lone, visible eye. He had never looked as closely at that eye as he did in that moment but there was something else in it. Something even more familiar than the man that had ceaselessly stood by Alex's side and had guarded the weapons depot in Freeworld One.

A clear, blue eye...

Tim's stomach wretched in realization as Chuck raised his blaster up from his side and into his sightline. It couldn't be, he reasoned. He...

"I..." Tim managed, "I... you. YOU. How can you be...?"

Chuck did not speak. He didn't have to. That's because he's not Chuck, Tim thought as he closed his eyes against the truth...

Not that revisionist bullshit that the Administration preaches, he thought...

...that was slowly overtaking his mind and surprisingly? He began to chuckle. His chuckle segued into a laugh which segued quickly into full blow hysteria. He opened his eyes again as tears of laughter began to cascade down his cheeks. He was growing weaker by the moment, he understood. The world around him was beginning to fade. Yet he continued to laugh, his hysteria undaunted, as he gazed up at the man that towered over him.

Not just any man, he thought, and his hysteria redoubled.

"Go ON!" He shouted and coughed. Blood mixed with spittle flew from his lips, "DO IT you BASTARD!" DO IT, GODDAMN YOU! I killed you ONCE and I'll DO IT AGAIN if you don't DO IT NOW...!" Cough. Laugh. Rinse and repeat.

Instead of the fatal shot that Tim had anticipated he felt something solid collide with his left temple. Said impact was followed by another against the side of his face and the grayness that had threatened to overtake him engulfed him as his head whiplashed to his right. The sound of his own laughter followed him down into the darkness as the second impact was followed by another against his arm, and another against his torso. His last sensation was of the damp, leather hilt of the sword that he still held in his left hand. And Tim Redfield, alias the Infiltrator that had permeated William MacNuff's traveling party and had been involved in dozens of other, covert *initiatives over his years in the employ of the Administration… the infamous he of the confused eyes and the lengthy and sordid history known only to him and to no one else in Endworld that he knew of helplessly and without pause blacked out, his final thought not of his successes but of his failures…*

Specifically of one, particular failure.

Thereafter, there was only silence.

* * *

Chuck looked down at the broken and bleeding figure that lay in the sand before him and paused mid-kick. The same sadness he had felt as he had watched the scene above the breakwater transpire from his position behind a collection of tall, dry reeds a short distance down the beach, before he had decided to intervene welled up in his heart and he closed his eyes. He willed himself to relax and he felt his heart rate slow. His breathing, which had been heavy with fury equalized as he opened his eyes again and glanced down at the traitor.

He knew that the machines would soon come to collect him. He knew that the patrol that had been dispatched to search the breakwater would eventually be missed. He watched as the beaten figure breathed shallowly.

He teeters on the edge of oblivion, Chuck thought compassionately, *but for what his life is worth he will live. There has been enough killing upon these shores for one day.* His eyes fell briefly upon the sword that the traitor held tightly in his left hand before sighed, and redirected his attention to the figure that lay motionless upon the beach, closer to the onset of the Great Sea.

The Atlantic Ocean, he thought as his compassion was replaced by another rush of sadness for all that had been lost over the years. It welled up within him. Chuck glanced down at the seemingly lifeless figure of William MacNuff, formerly of Jefferson, MWT that lay at his feet. He knelt down beside him and rested his right hand upon William's forehead. In the process of doing so the sleeve of the dark-colored and wet, black jacket he wore retreated and revealed a familiar sigil upon his forearm:

A figure-eight, cross-cut by an arrow that pointed to his palm.

The sigil of the Explorator. The Pathfinder.

He closed his eyes and worked his "praecantatio." He realized that yes, the boy lived albeit barely, though to the common passerby such an eventuality would, he realized, go unnoticed without a thorough life scan. But Chuck? He knew better. He had seen more than even the most enlightened… the most "evolved" machine had seen.

If I leave him here, he thought as he opened his eyes…

He resolved himself to his course of action. He extended his arms under William's back and lifted him from the surface of the beach as if he weighed little more than a piece of paper. He stood without effort and simultaneously closed his eyes. He "became" the breeze as he had been taught so many, many...

How many? My God how many, Chuck thought...

...years before and he felt it engulf him. The process was not a physical one. While it depended upon certain, physical attributes the process of "becoming the wind" was primarily spiritual. Ed Wilkinson knew that, Chuck recognized. But what Ed and his mercenary counterparts knew was a fraction of the truth. Merely a taste of the infinite, the "All" he thought as he pinpointed his destination — near to where he stood but far enough away that the remnants of the army that mulled about the area would not be able to find him... to find them — and he went there. He went.

A moment later, he opened his eyes and physically saw the exact place he had envisioned. He turned with William still in his arms and beheld, beneath the gray sky overhead and the drizzle that fell from it a few meters away, a twisted and abstract tree stand that choked the tops of a series of towering dunes. Said trees diminished the further down the fronts of the dunes his gaze travelled though in one or two places, a root or a once-fledgling turned barren sapling reached its jagged fingers out from the sand, into the open air and in his direction. Chuck glanced to his immediate right and there saw a landmark that he remembered from his long ago youth: A lone tree, about halfway between the bottom of the closest dune and the slowly rolling breakwater of the bay. Little Atlantic, they had once called it yet that name, like the name of its once-big brother the Atlantic Ocean, had vanished over time.

Time, he mused as he took a step... two steps toward the tree and paused within arm's reach of it. He gazed longingly at the faded piece of driftwood nailed to its front, water-facing surface about three quarters of the way toward its top. While the letters that had been carved into it once were long faded he remembered their content as if he had just seen it for the first time yesterday. "Voodoo Tree," it had once said. It was at the base of the Voodoo Tree that he gently laid William MacNuff. He stood as he relinquished his hold upon the Jefferson runner and closed his eyes again.

One more thing left to do, Chuck thought. He once again "became" the breeze and vanished from the area. A moment later he rematerialized on the beach head with Jeff Howard in his arms. He laid Jeff down upon the sand a short distance away from William and the tree beneath which he lay and closed the former resident of Greentree, MWT's eyes. He closed his own eyes and laid his hand upon Jeff's forehead. He muttered something indistinguishable — a prayer in a long forgotten language that others of his Creed would have recognized immediately as Latin — before he opened his eyes, removed his hand from Jeff's forehead and stood slowly.

He turned back to where William lay. The boy's lightly bearded face appeared serene in the diminished glow that engulfed the beach. *So young,* Chuck thought as he glided across the area between where he stood and where William lay and knelt down beside him.

Young no more, he added as he closed his eyes and laid his hand upon William's forehead. He spoke another series of Latin words before he removed his hand from William's head and opened his eyes. He stood from his position beside William, turned and glanced out over the steadily undulating water of the bay.

Still so beautiful, Chuck thought and felt something warm and small caress his right cheek. He had not felt it for many, many ages but at that moment? He welcomed it. It reminded him of the person he had once been rather than the person he had grown in to: A scarred product of his extensive experiences... a shell of the child that had once stood upon the same beach that he stood upon presently—Higbee, he remembered, it used to be called Higbee Beach. He had leaned upon the Voodoo Tree then and had glanced out and over the rolling water. He had dreamed... dreamed of and had wished for more. He had gotten his wish but he had paid a price for it. A lofty one, he thought as the tear that rolled slowly down his cheek paused for a breath upon the edge of his beard, detached itself and gently fell upon the coarse sand at his feet. *Said tear?* It reminded him, ever briefly and bitter sweetly of his humanity.

But what of the Artifact? Chuck thought as he gazed out over the water, *what of it?* It was, he understood, an extremely valid question and his thoughts lingered upon it for a moment. He knew that William no longer had it for he could no longer sense its presence. But he also knew that the Administration did not have it. He had not given them enough time to recover it before his intervention upon the beach. And while the latter mattered greatly, his lack of knowledge about the Artifact's whereabouts was disconcerting. It stood to reason that William had entrusted it into the care of one of the survivors who had escaped but he did not have and would not get confirmation of that fact, he realized. His place was not there. No. Not in Free Caymen.

I have no home any longer, Chuck thought reluctantly, *Freeworld One was my last and Alex? The last of the only family I have known for as long as I can remember. I dwell now in the shadows. They are my home. My family. Non multa nostrae solitudini. There aren't many of us left.* No truer words had ever been spoken, he understood.

I may be the last, Chuck thought reluctantly, and audibly sighed.

He held up his right arm, pushed the sleeve of his jacket back and glanced at the underside of his forearm. The mark... the sigil imprinted there stood out in stark, black relief against his too-pale skin. *After me,* he considered again, *after me...*

And shook the thought away. *It is better this way,* he concluded as he secured his sleeve around his upper arm, turned away reluctantly from the bay and began to make his way up the beach head toward the dune line. Better that its whereabouts remain unknown to all including me until such time as the rightful owner of it... until he is ready to step forward and claim it. Whoever has it, wherever it is, please keep it safe.

Chuck stopped and turned within a step of the bottom of the nearest dune and spared the motionless figures of William MacNuff and Jeff Howard a final glance. Would it be the last time he saw them? He did not know, but he highly doubted it. There are, he thought, no certainties here in Endworld or any world... any Skew for that matter as his gaze averted over them and back to the Little Atlantic. Not everything dead need remain so. He knew that fact better than most.

So beautiful, he thought again. He smiled as he closed his eyes and reached out with his mind. He could feel it close to where he stood. He could hear it, too: A low, monotonous hum, not discernible upon casual observation but there if you knew what to look for. And he did. He had been trained to seek it out.

"There is a hum that underscores everything, and it is the key that unlocks the secret. The 'All.'" He remembered those words, and spoke them aloud. The words of the man... the great man who had taught him and so many others to be what he was now, what he had been for as long as he could remember and likely what he always would be. One of, if not the last of the Explorators.

No, he thought, not unlock but...

"Unglew," Chuck spoke authoritatively as he extended his arm with the sigil upon it up and out, and the hum that he had detected steadily began to increase in volume. He felt a rush of air swirl past the outstretched and splayed fingers of that hand and he slowly opened his eyes. The swirling wind was coming from the rotating hole in the air, ringed with rain water that had appeared a few meters away from him, a hole that was growing in size with each passing breath. Beyond the edges of it, large enough for a man or a woman to step through but little more, was darkness.

Yet he knew better. He knew that the darkness was deceptive. He did not know what lay within the Gateway that lay before him despite his familiarity with it from his past. Such things had grown difficult over what passed for time in Endworld to discern, but Chuck knew that he needed to be on his guard. He reached down and caressed the hilt of the blaster that was holstered upon his right hip. He reached back and felt the hilt of the sword that he wore upon his back. From within the darkness he could smell lingering, familiar scents that hearkened his mind back to the days that he had spent as a youth upon Higbee Beach's shore: Salt and flowers, primarily, but there were other smells within, as well—some refreshing and reminiscent, but others base and decrepit.

Death smells, Chuck thought, as he lowered his arm and took a step toward the Gateway. His heart pounded but he was undeterred. He knew what he had to do. He *knew where he had to go.*

"Wha...?"

He heard a weakened, male voice speak from behind him and he quickly turned and brought his weapon to bear upon...

William MacNuff, formerly of Jefferson, MWT lay on his side beneath the Voodoo Tree and gazed back at him, his eyes opened widely. The man smiled as he lowered his blaster...

* * *

...and spoke to me.

"Unus est vera Semita, William," the shockingly familiar man who stood a few meters away from me, silhouetted against what appeared to be a dark and twisting hole in the air said in a deep voice. I heard myself speak his name as he turned from me and stepped into the shadows that shifted beyond the opening...

The Gateway, William, that's a Gateway...

...for I had recognized him as soon as I had opened my eyes. I had never considered the prospect that he had survived the melee in Freeworld One. I had never considered that the person Alex Parker had sent ahead to notify the people of Free Caymen that we were coming was him despite the fact that he had been conspicuous in his absence. But it had been, I understood at that moment.

"*Chuck?*" I spoke again, more urgently than before. He did not turn though his head seemingly cocked in recognition and he paused in his passage. He raised the hand that held his blaster up and over his head in a gesture that I presumed to mean "goodbye." I watched helplessly as he took another step forward into the darkness beyond the opening...

The Gateway...

...and then another step before he was engulfed wholly by the shadows. The Gateway that he had created seemingly spiraled in upon itself immediately and disappeared with an audible *pop*, but before it did I heard him say one more thing. One more statement that I have carried with me ever since. Its significance was undeniable.

Its repercussions far reaching.

"To some," Chuck's voice had begun. *To some...*

"Vato."

I stared longingly at the place where the Gateway had been for an indefinite amount of time, flabbergasted by what I had just seen and heard. Overhead, I heard something *caw* yet I disregarded it. I simply continued to stare at the patch of air where the Gateway had been and the steep dune... almost a cliff, behind it. In time, I managed to get myself up and into a sitting position, and upon surveying my unfamiliar surroundings, I discovered the motionless body of Jeff "Jeebus" Howard lying a few meters away from me. I managed, despite the pain that racked my body, to make my way over to his position. Upon arriving, I discovered that his eyes were closed and a slight smile graced the corners of his mouth. His cheeks had grown pale and were beaded with rainwater. I traced my gaze down the length of his body and saw not one but two fatal wounds: A jagged burn hole which was surrounded by dried blood and congealed sand and the fresher of the two? A burn mark upon the center of his shirt, likely the result of either a pulse rifle or a blaster shot.

My observance of him broke off as I heard the same *caw* above that I had heard upon first waking up. I glanced from Jeff's motionless figure to the sky above me and saw an unusual bird glide effortlessly past my sightline upon the breeze, its wings extended outward. Its body was grey and oblong and its head and wings were white. After a moment, I returned my glance to Jeff's motionless body and fresh tears began to flow from my eyes. I draped my arms over him and lowered my forehead to his chest. I could smell the singed fabric of his shirt and beneath it, I could smell burnt hair and flesh. My tears quickly segued into sobs and I remained like that indefinitely as time moved onward without check over the living and the dead here, there, and all over what I and my companions... my brethren...

My *friends*...

Endearingly referred to then and will always refer to as Endworld.

EPILOGUE

Alone Again

"I was neither living nor dead, and I knew nothing looking into the heart of light, the silence."

That occurred some time ago here in Endworld. At least that is my best estimate. "Some time ago." Time has never held much significance for me, and if I haven't made that point yet? Well, I'm pretty sure that I've made it. Perhaps exhausted it. Some of you will likely accuse me of, to employ an old, pre-Administration cliché, "beating it into the ground." I apologize to those of you that feel that way. My goal was not to confuse or exacerbate your experience. Once upon a time (*'cause all good stories begin as such, Vato,* Pat McClane's voice echoes in my mind), I told you that I did not fancy myself an author, nor a poet, nor anything save for a guy who needed to tell a story. I further told you that my decision to write the previous account was not done to heal the ills of a sick and twisted world. Rather, it was undertaken in an attempt to heal myself. Now, as the flickering light from my diminished candle, unfortunately the last of my supply playfully dances across the faded mural of a forest at dusk that dominates one of the walls of my temporary home, I muse upon the success or failure of my endeavor. Am I healed? Well, I don't think that I ever will be. Vindicated? Not likely. Enlightened? I think I'm more confused than anything else. But do I feel better for having written all that I have?

Maybe not better. But I may actually sleep a bit today… or tonight. I'm not even sure what time of day it is right now as time…

Ah, fuck it. I'm sure that you get the picture.

I buried Jeff "Jeebus" Howard that same morning, afternoon, or evening directly beneath the dune line at the top of the unfamiliar beach upon which I had awoken. I had wanted to bury him beneath the strange and stunted tree, next to which I had seen… whatever I saw that day, but I knew via no real knowledge, simply instinct, that it was too close to the breakwater. The soil beneath the dune-cliff, I discovered, was a bit more rugged. It had taken time… a great deal of it, and I accomplished the majority of the work with my hands and the few shells and detritus that I uncovered upon the beachhead large enough to manage the task. As the gray haze that hung over me segued into a deep, blue twilight I threw the last of the sandy soil that I had accumulated upon the once-resident of Greentree, MWT's grave and stood slowly. My injured extremities screamed and creaked in protest.

You need a marker, William, my coldly rational voice advised me and I began to search the area for one. I found what I was looking for a few meters away above what I assumed was the tideline. It wasn't exactly a shell but it was rounded like one. It was brown and vaguely resembled a jointed carapace. I picked it up, turned it over, and found what I assumed to be the bottom of it hollowed out. I turned, walked back to the grave and placed it atop it.

Thereafter, I thought about retreating back down the beach toward the strangely beautiful tree beneath which I had awoken, but could tell from the position of the tideline that the water was moving higher. *If I go back down there I'll be drenched, or worse, washed out to sea,* I thought. Instead, I collapsed on my back a few steps away from the grave that I had just dug and within moments, I fell asleep.

I don't honestly know how long I slept for. All I know is that some time later, I awoke and cried out. My entire body was a receptacle of pain. I saw that an almost-full moon was peeking through the clouds overhead and I stared at it for an indefinite amount of time. I watched the clouds play across its face and then disappear and I willed the pain that I was feeling in everything from my shoulder to my head to dissipate.

I tried to think but could not. I knew I had to move… knew that I couldn't stay where I was. I didn't know how far away from the beach in Hempstead I was, but I thought it best to err on the side of caution in the event that the machines *or* Ed Wilkinson and his mercs were looking for me.

But what about the others? My coldly rational voice reminded me, *what about Maria, the O'Briens and the Wetherhills? Might they be looking for you, too?* It was a valid point, and I found myself helplessly caught between the two possibilities. In the end, the desire for self-preservation outweighed the desire to be rescued.

The only one I can count on right now is me, I thought to myself. A short time later, I judged the pain to be tolerable, stood and began to make my way down the shoreline by moonlight. A short distance from where I had been I found a path that cut through the dead tree and dried shrub covered dunes. I took it and left Jeff, the water and the Gateway behind me.

But Chuck's final word? It followed me through the shadows into the unknown. It still follows me to this day. Across the seasons I wandered aimlessly, rarely aware of the direction I was heading in, the only constant in my travels the Highway. Eventually, my wayward wandering carried me here, to a little, nameless town nestled between a nameless river and the Highway… a place that my brethren would have called "The Center of Bumblefuck."

Occasionally, I stand by the lone window of my temporary home and I wonder about my companions… my brethren…

My friends.

I can see their faces reflected back to me in the glass yet they are ethereal… wispy. Little more than my own, personal haints. But see them I can. From beginning to end their faces materialize before me: Pat McClane silhouetted against the flickering flames of his once-truck in his "hero pose" with his sword held out in his left hand and his blaster held out in his right…

Alex Parker standing on the bank of the Little Shenango River, smiling at me as the community he endeavored to build and protect burns behind him…

Steve and Carole Wetherhill as they had appeared when I had first encountered them in Freeworld One, Steve with his arm around a blushing but radiant Carole…

Caren and Matt O'Brien as they had looked, sitting in the shadowy corner of the old, abandoned church in the eternally-burning, once-mining town turned ghost town of Centralia where we had sheltered for a night.

I even see Ed Wilkinson and his wife Molly occasionally, along with their right hand woman, Amy, standing amidst the wind-driven rain a few steps away from the exit/entrance to the transport that had carried us that last of the distance to our final destination, eastward toward a hypothetical freedom that I, sadly, never got to experience and likely never will. Because I made a choice. I chose to stay behind. Daily and nightly, I live with the consequences of that choice.

Yet I live, which I sadly cannot say of others. Particularly one who was my companion for longer than any other save for one. I see two different representations of him. In the first he is running up the beach toward me, a blaster held out in his right hand and a sword held out in his left. He is smiling a cocky smile that reminds me so much of Pat McClane's. In the second he lays motionless, his eyes closed upon an unfamiliar beach. It is the second that, unfortunately, lingers, as my eyes move from his eyes to the gaping wound upon his upper, right chest and the burn mark upon the center of the same and I realize, however reluctantly, that his lone wish—a wish that he had conveyed to me during a humid and dreary twilight encounter upon Pat McClane's wrap–around balcony at his once-home in faraway Greentree, MWT—remains unfulfilled and will always remain so.

Or does it? Who knows what lies beyond? Not I. And the glimpses that I have caught do little more than confuse my already confused mind further. As for the ones that may? Sadly, I have not seen nor heard from any of them in quite some time. Pat? Alex? All of the members of my mental peanut gallery have given way to the silence that hangs like the water damaged, drop ceiling over my head as I write these, the final words of this chronicle. I am left with only their words to remind me that they ever existed.

I am unabashedly alone.

And what of Chuck? Can I even call him that at this juncture? I find it difficult to grasp the alternative. *Vato*, he said. I wonder if it was, perhaps, nothing more than a coincidence: Someone other than Pat McClane using said surname to refer to another. That's the easiest truth, revisionist or not to grasp. But then I think of all that Alex told me in my dream of him, the tree, Jefferson-not-Jefferson and the one, true path. About dead not necessarily meaning *dead*. In this brave, new world full of Skews, Gateways and Pathfinders? Nothing is certain. I understand that now. It may be the only thing that I fully understand at this juncture.

Unus est vera semita, William, a voice speaks in my mind. I think of what I saw sitting upon the porch of my once-home in Jefferson, MWT and I consider the possibility. *If there are two of me, two of the red car, why couldn't there be two of him? Or more than that? If that is the unabridged and un-revisionist truth than really, does "death" have any meaning anymore? Any significance in this or any Skew?*

Questions without answers. Like the fate of Tim Redfield, who stayed behind to cover our initial retreat as the Administration forces that had been following us indefinitely converged upon us. I neither saw nor heard from him again. Perhaps that was, is, and will remain all the validation that I need of Tim's fate. But frankly? It doesn't feel right. My instincts tell me otherwise.

Said thought helplessly transitions into another: I never discovered the identity of the traitor… the Infiltrator within our ranks. While the identity of that person remains a mystery to me I pray daily and nightly that my surviving companions are safe. Especially…

It is the last face that appears in the window. Always the last. It is the face that my heart, soul and mind linger upon every time. Picture this, if you will: Straight, black hair the color of a raven's feathers; deep brown eyes filled with a warmth that only a few lucky souls can see; a face, pure whiteness, like the face of an angel; a spattering of light brown freckles on either cheek; lips naturally full and red without adornment. In truth, perhaps the most beautiful face that I have and likely ever will encounter. It is the face of Maria Markinson, my oldest, dearest and truest friend.

It is the face of Maria Markinson, my oldest, dearest and truest love.

That which I imparted upon her? The Artifact? I pray that it remains safely in her possession. A secret to all that might inquire about it save for her and I. I pray that she will succeed where I could not… that she will find the man that said Artifact belongs to, whatever its contents. Most importantly, however? I pray that my decision to give it to her has not placed her in danger. Sadly, there is no way that I can be sure, but I wonder.

Daily and nightly, I wonder.

* * *

"Open your eyes, Infiltrator."

Tim Redfield was reluctant to do so but at the gentle insistence of the voice that spoke to him in the darkness, a voice that sounded almost but not quite human, he did as had been requested of him. His vision was immediately assaulted by the bright, fluorescent light positioned directly overhead and he closed his eyes again with a gasp. As he had so many times previously, he rued the fact that he had been born as an imperfect vessel so many, many years before. So human, he thought and a low, almost imperceptible "hiss" echoed from between his closed lips.

"Drone," the voice spoke simultaneously with his "hiss," "Turn off the lights. He is uncomfortable."

Beyond his closed eyelids, Tim sensed the overhead light disappear. He cautiously opened his eyes again and was relieved to discover that his sense had been correct. A dim, gray light emanated from a window inset within the wall across from the bed in which he lay. He shifted his head to the right and saw a featureless wall and door, closed. Silhouetted against it and on either side of the door frame were the unmistakable shapes of two model 78A protocol droids. They stood still, fully armored, with their pulse rifles down at their sides.

Guards, he considered. For me? He didn't understand it. He was one of them, wasn't he? An ally in the employ of the Administration? What he truly was, was irrelevant. Appearances are everything, he thought, not for the first time and, he knew, not for the last. Said thought was interrupted as the gentle, human-not-human voice that had tasked him to "open his eyes" spoke again from his left.

"You have failed us, Infiltrator," the voice, unwavering and without hesitation, spoke, "failed me. We do not have access to the People's Rebellion for Freedom and Equality. We do not know the location of the refugee camp, Free Caymen. You were given two, distinct tasks. The first you fulfilled, but the second? You failed to carry it out. What is your explanation?"

And that's not all that you don't have, Tim thought.

"JUSTIFY," one of the 78As added and took a step toward him. It raised the pulse rifle it carried slightly so that its barrel was pointed directly at him. Tim did not turn away from the encroaching protocol droid. His eyes remained fixed upon its burning, red gaze. He did not flinch. It was not in his nature. I'll remember you, he thought and stifled another "hiss" that threatened to escape his lips, I'll teach you all about justification one day, drone.

Tim directed his response to the 78A, "When I encountered MacNuff's corpse on the beach I found the tracking device that I had planted on him still on his person and his fellow fugitives gone. The other device was destroyed by Ed Wilkinson back in Hempstead err... Wildwood. There was another corpse on the beach with MacNuff. That of Jeff Howard."

"Did you verify that MacNuff and Howard were deceased?" the gentle human-not-human voice responded immediately from his left. Toneless, Tim thought, just like the rest of them. So predictable a trait. He did not remove his own gaze from the gaze of the 78A... did not turn to look at the owner of the voice. He answered immediately.

"Howard, yes. But MacNuff? I was unable to do so as I was... accosted by a... an unknown party as you may or may not be aware," he said. He recalled how the two blaster bolts had sizzled through his pant legs. He recalled the pain that had exploded across his left side as another bolt had ripped through his left shoulder and had caused him to drop his blaster before he could ensure MacNuff's fate. He remembered the face that had loomed over him as he had writhed in pain upon the beach: Chiseled and grizzled with an eye patch covering one eye. He remembered the realization that he had come to upon beholding it but he did not reveal that knowledge.

No, he thought, I will not. That knowledge is for me, and me alone.

How much do they really know, Tim ruminated, not just about the Artifact and what it contains, but about the secret battle happening right beneath their metal noses? Do they even have the slightest clue of how much is at stake? Of what the Artifact means if placed in the right hands?

He did not know and did not desire to. He remained vigilant in his resolve to keep that information close to his belt, and instead spoke to his questioner about how the shooter had pointed his blaster at him and he, despite the pain that had surged through his body, had laughed. He had laughed so hard that tears had begun to cascade down his cheeks. Said tears had mingled with the still-falling rain. He had tasked the stranger to finish him. Yet instead of the fatal shot that Tim had anticipated, the shooter had dealt him a series of painful kicks and Tim had blacked out. He had awakened an indefinite amount of time later in the back of an Administration transport.

"I was unable to feel my legs," he concluded. He had known, even then, that his legs were lost. He still could not feel them, yet there was the sensation of something below his waist. He averted his eyes slowly from the gaze of the 78A (it remained still, a few steps away from him with its pulse rifle trained directly upon his position) and down the length of his body.

He gasped in astonishment.

In the dim light that emanated from the window he could see the shape of his legs beneath the heavy sheet that covered them. No, he understood, that is not entirely true. There were shapes there but said shapes were different. Not malformed and flawed but smooth. Not human but... but...

Without thinking and still without turning to his left to see the owner of the human-not-human voice he reached down and pulled the sheet back. He gasped again as he caught his first glimpse of the profiled, metallic limbs that had replaced his once-legs from his mid-thigh, directly above where he had been shot, down. Said legs were jointed at the knees and at the ankles. They were impressive to look at but were they functional? He tried to move them instinctively but they did not budge.

"You need to think it, Infiltrator," the calm voice spoke again from his left, "the muscles... the tendons that you once utilized are no longer viable. Think it and allow the technology to work for you and not against you."

Tim closed his eyes and thought: Move my left leg up. Something seemed to click both within his head and his leg. He opened his eyes and looked down the length of his body once again. His left leg, which had a moment before lain docile upon the bed, had shifted upward. He smiled. Move left leg down, he thought and with another, audible click his leg lowered slowly to the surface of the bed. It landed there softly. His smile widened.

"Thank..." he began calmly but paused. His curiosity overwhelmed him and he finally turned his head to his left to glance at the owner of the human-not-human voice. The face of the speaker swam into view. It was a strange face, undoubtedly machine yet surprisingly human looking. Its two, red eyes were inset in its head beneath a protruding brow. It's facsimile of a nose, little more than a slight hill upon the landscape of its face, was positioned directly above its tapered jaw. Said jaw terminated in a chin directly beneath its jointed mouth, the top of which was engineered in an eternal sneer. The body attached to and beneath it appeared refurbished. It glistened a polished silver in the dim light that emanated from the window and was sleeker than the bodies of the 78As guarding the door to the room but not as sleek as the body of a Surveillance Mark.

Lithe yet deadly, Tim thought. Perfect. In stark contrast to its head which appeared... antique? What was this hybrid creature that was speaking to him? It looked like a living Rock 'Em Sock 'Em Robot. Tim realized the answer to his question even before it spoke and confirmed his suspicions.

"Do not thank me, Infiltrator," it spoke, "succeed. That is all that your Lord and Master Cornelius asks of you. You have been given a gift that few humans are granted. You have been upgraded. If you desire to be further improved upon you will not fail me again. Are we in agreement?"

Tim did not smile. He did not frown. He closed his eyes and slowed his breathing. A wave of calmness flowed through him and he nodded his head as he once again opened his eyes.

Yes, my Lord Cornelius, he thought, we are in agreement...

For now.

Lord Cornelius I, seemingly satisfied, nodded and turned from Tim's bedside. "MacNuff lives," it spoke with its back to him, "his whereabouts are currently unknown. We have some intelligence yet none that is currently feasible. We will continue to collect information on his movements... will continue to look for him... will deploy other Infiltrators to find him and we will continue to pursue him until you are mended. When you are mended, the task may once again be yours but only if I deem it so. That is all I can and will promise you. Your failure in this was monumental."

"His companions," Tim added, "if they know he is alive they will return for him."

"They will," the Lord Cornelius I replied without turning around, "soon they will know. I intend to make sure of it. And when they try to come back for him we will be ready for them, whenever that is. I expect that you will be, as well."

"If you deem me up to the task," Tim stated tonelessly, "I will not fail you again."

The Lord Cornelius I turned back to him then, "We shall see. For now, recover. If you need further encouragement to heal consider this it."

The Lord Cornelius I raised its left hand and arm up into Tim's view and Tim saw what it held within it. The blade of the sword was slightly curved and its hilt was wrapped in freshly bound, red leather. Said hilt ended in a tarnished metal ball and the wrist guard sparkled dully in the minimal light provided by the gray day outside the room's lone window. Each end of the wrist guard terminated in what appeared to be a cross.

Tim recognized it immediately. He cringed as he reached out with his sore left arm and hand. He opened his fingers and the Lord Cornelius I gently placed the hilt of Pat McClane's once-sword upon his palm. He tightened his grip around it and simultaneously felt a wave of strength rush through his body. He shifted his arm toward him painfully and laid it down beside him upon his cot. He did not relinquish his grasp upon it.

"We appear to have an accord," Lord Cornelius I stated. Tim nodded. To heighten the impression of gratitude that he was feigning, he forced a few tears to flow from his eyes. It was not difficult. He had done it many, many times before. All part of the program, he thought.

"MacNuff," Lord Cornelius I continued, "is our link. He is the key to discovering the whereabouts of the refugee camp, the stronghold of the People's Rebellion for Freedom and Equality... potentially..."

"Others," Tim interrupted. His thoughts returned to the Artifact again. Did they... did it know that he, too, was searching for it? He was unable to gauge a reaction either way from the Lord Cornelius. Instead of pressing the issue and potentially giving away his true motive...

My destiny, he thought again…

…he completed his statement with, "there are always other concerns, my Lord."

"There are," the Lord Cornelius stated and fell silent. Tim nodded in response but intentionally did not speak. *I've already said too much,* he thought. The Lord Cornelius, apparently satisfied with the responses of its Infiltrator and seemingly content in the knowledge that the two of them "had an accord" moved speechlessly from Tim's bedside toward the door. Tim turned his head and watched as it motioned to the nearest 78A. Said protocol droid lowered its weapon and turned without hesitation. It moved back to the threshold of the door and pressed a button upon the wall. The door slowly opened with a swoosh of recycled and sterile air. Lord Cornelius I gained the entrance/exit to the room, turned right and disappeared without another word. It was followed by both 78As. Simultaneously with the departure and subsequent disappearance of the last machine the door slid closed.

Tim was left alone. He turned back and glanced at his new legs… his "upgrade" again. To the common passerby it sounded like he was crying. But Tim Redfield was not sad. He did not sob. He chuckled. And his chuckling quickly grew into a laugh as he raised his left arm and hand up and glanced at the way the slightly curved blade of the sword sparkled in the dim daylight. One, lone thought reverberated in his mind, and whether said thought was justified or not, to Tim Redfield? It did not matter.

The devil can cite scripture for his purpose, Tim thought, *but me? I rely on myself for the same.*

You took my legs, MacNuff, he thought despite the fact that he knew it was untrue. The Jefferson runner remained his scapegoat, and his laughing echoed through the hallways of the hospital within which he was sequestered, *so help me, one day? Artifact or not, one day you will pay with your head.*

* * *

"You can open your eyes, Maria. We're done."

Maria Markinson did as had been requested of her and opened her eyes. Above her, the dim, hanging lamp that a lit the room glowed back at her and she squinted and closed her eyes, again. *Slower this time,* she thought, and reopened them.

Better, she thought as she raised her fists to her face and rubbed her eyes once… twice. She turned her head to her right and there saw Steve Wetherhill. He grinned at her: His black goatee and mustache glistened with sweat upon his thin, tanned face. His long, black hair was held back in a ponytail and he wore a white lab coat over his customary ripped jeans and t-shirt. An apparatus (stethoscope, she thought, it's called a stethoscope) hung around his neck. He held something in his right hand. It looked like a pen but that was all that she could determine. She could see a shorter *figure behind him with long, brown hair and a shapely body that was shockingly visible beneath a loose-fitting, white button down shirt and a pair of khaki shorts. Said figure grinned at her, as well, a gesture which accentuated two almost perfect dimples upon either freckled cheek. Not as perfect as Caren's, Maria reasoned, but familiar and comforting. Steve's wife, Carole Wetherhill, moved across the room and over to her bedside. She reached down and took Maria's hand in hers.*

"How do you feel?" She asked.

Maria forced a smile and responded with a simple, "Okay. How long 'till we know?"

"Only a moment or two," Steve said as he turned away and moved across the room to where the sink was, "do you need anything?"

Maria shook her head and sat up. Carole relinquished her grasp upon Maria's hand and stepped back as Maria swung her legs over the right side of the bed upon which she had been reclining and felt her feet touch the soft, carpeted floor. She stood slowly, moved passed Carole and took up position beside the open window across from her.

She gazed out it at the scene beyond it. Beneath the diminished, afternoon light that bathed the world in a familiar but eerie, golden-red iridescence she could see, less than 20 meters from her position, the termination of the Great Sea and the beginning of the beach. Directly beyond the beach and the strange, fruit-bearing trees with large, floppy leaves that marked its border (palm trees, Maria thought, they're called palm trees) there was a patio, within which sat a once-pool turned empty, tiled crater in the otherwise beautiful landscape.

Upon their arrival in Free Caymen she and her companions had been escorted to the place in which they currently resided. Their guide, a young, blonde woman named Kim, had told them that the structure was an old "resort." Whatever that means, Maria had thought then and thought again. Her room—the same room in which she waited by the window with Steve and Carole behind her—was on the second floor.

A warm sea breeze that smelled distinctly of salt blew past her cheeks and temporarily cooled her despite the oppressive humidity that always dominated the Free Caymen climate. She closed her eyes and ran her fingers through her shortened, black hair. She had cut it just above her shoulders shortly upon arriving in Free Caymen. The decision to do so had seemed logical at the time: A cleansing ritual. Not just from what she had been through...

But for what she had done.

No one knows the truth, here, she reminded herself as she had so many times previously. As far as she knew, no people knew the REAL truth. People, she thought, but non-people? Machines?

Somewhere, someone… someTHING did.

She could feel hot tears burning against her closed eyelids but she did not allow them to flow. She couldn't. Tears would betray her to the Wetherhills. She thought back to her and William's first night on the road. She remembered their conversation from within the dark and dusty basement of the once-pharmacy turned vermin hotel. She remembered leaving him, returning home and packing a bag. She had not been noticed by her family, nor had she been noticed by any of her neighbors as near as she could tell. She had made it out of her house and back up her street. She had been, by her reckoning, half – way back to where she had left William when…

Maria shivered despite the warmth and humidity that encapsulated her. She remembered how the darkness that had surrounded her had shattered and been replaced by a blinding floodlight. She remembered how the joy she had felt upon leaving her house for the second time had faded as the familiar figures of two 78A Model Protocol Droids and a taller, leaner Surveillance Mark had approached her. She had not seen them coming. She had frozen her passage as the fully weaponized, 78As had leveled their pulse rifles upon her position. One had started to question her but its rhetoric had been cut off almost instantaneously by the lower, calmer voice of the Leader that had been hiding behind the Surveillance Mark. Upon beholding her, it had stepped forward.

"Identify," the Leader had requested tonelessly. Maria had not spoken.

"Identify, or perish," the Leader had insisted, and Maria had seen no other alternative. She had done as it had requested.

"Maria Markinson," the Leader had spoken, "you are in violation of curfew and your action this evening can only be construed as an attempt to run, a well-documented Crime against the Administration. Crimes against the Administration are, as you well know, punishable by…"

She had started to cry, then, and her crying had continued unabated for a few moments. She had, at first, pleaded with the Leader to spare her. She had told it that she would return home immediately. She had not given up her true reason for being out passed curfew. Not at first. But further questioning… further threatening had brought the real truth of her post-curfew "stroll" to light. She had not considered herself weak at the time for giving herself and William up. She had been concerned: Concerned for her family and for her friend (not to mention his own family) who, she remembered then, was waiting patiently for her. Waiting, and likely oblivious to her… their current situation.

"You will tell William MacNuff that you encountered a patrol but were able to avoid notice," the Leader had told her, "that is all. You will then leave with him east down the Highway as you had planned. I assure you that you will not be accosted. You will carry this"—it had gestured to the Surveillance Mark behind it and

said SM had stepped forward. It had opened its hand and Maria had beheld, within it, a small, black, nondescript and unrecognizable cube. Unrecognizable then. She knew, presently, that the cube? It had been the same type of tracking device that Ed Wilkinson had found in William's backpack in Hempstead.

"Machine make," she heard Tim's voice speak in her mind, and then Carole's: "Very powerful."

"You will carry this with you," it had continued, undaunted, "do not ask why for our reasons are our own. Merely do. Any failure to carry out this order... any failure to fulfill this task will result in not only yours and you co-conspirator's termination, but the extermination of both of your families in totality. Is this debatable?"

She had shaken her head and more tears had cascaded down her cheeks. She had reached out and had reluctantly taken the slick surfaced, black cube in her hand. She had glanced down at it and had seen the red light blinking upon its side. Active, she had thought, that must mean it's active, already.

"Place it in your backpack where it will not be noticed," the Leader had commanded her and she had done so without hesitation. She had asked then to be reassured that she and William's families would be spared and the Leader corroborated its earlier statement that they would be, in the event that she successfully carried out her designated task. She had asked for a guarantee that her and William would also be spared and had, to her chagrin, not received one in response.

"You will fulfill this task and then we will see what happens to you and William MacNuff, Maria Markinson. You still stand guilty of a viable Crime against the Administration. Your cooperation does not necessarily change that. Is this debatable?"

She had slowly shaken her head, for she had known that her options had been limited. The alternative? Had she not agreed to betray William she would have been summarily executed, along with him, his family and her family.

This is the only way, she had thought as the two 78As, the SM and the Leader had turned and left her without another word. She had composed herself and had proceeded back to the once-pharmacy where William had been waiting for her. Upon reuniting with him, she had told him that she had narrowly avoided a patrol... had even formulated a joke about "too much lube." She had hoped that he would fall for it. Per his reaction at the time, he had.

Maria sighed as another warm and humid breeze blew past her face. She had carried the tracking device with her all throughout her encounter with Pat and Jeff, and had had it on her person in the truck as she, William, Pat and Jeff had left Greentree and made their leisurely way through the easternmost portions of the MWT, She had had it with her when they had been cornered by the Caravan near the border and had carried it with her when they made their blind run through the woods. Thereafter, though? Thereafter she had lost it when William had pulled her from the truck, seconds before a blast from one of the pursuant MDUs had reduced the truck and, by association, her backpack and the tracking device within it to cinders.

When she had awoken in Freeworld One, she had realized what had happened. She had immediately feared the worst for not only her and William, but for their families, as well. News, she knew, was not forthcoming. The knowledge of what she had potentially caused had been a constant distraction throughout everything that had happened to her since. But in her mind? In Maria Markinson's mind, her rationale had been sound.

I didn't want to believe that we might not make it, she thought as a low hum of conversation between Steve and Carole commenced behind her, *I thought that we'd escape... that we'd make it to freedom, despite what I had agreed to. I wanted that to be true.* The hot tears that she had been holding at bay threatened to overflow her closed eyelids again and she felt a gasp growing in her throat. She willed herself to be strong but if was difficult. She thought of their kiss upon the riverbank in Freeworld One... thought about their tryst in Centralia.

I never told him, she thought to herself, *I knew the whole time but I couldn't. I'd just.... I'd just wanted to forget. God, how I'd just wanted to forget. If he ever found out... if any of them ever found out it would be the end of everything. The end of us.*

And she couldn't have that. She loved William with all of her heart, soul and mind and presumably? She had at the time when she had agreed to do what the Leader had asked her to do as well, she had simply never acknowledged it. Whether love had been her reason for doing it or not was, she knew, irrelevant. She had betrayed him... had betrayed all of them, and because of her betrayal? Freedom remained as alien a word to her as it had before she had left Jefferson. Before she had run.

Freedom is a state of mind, and in my mind? I'm still trapped, she thought with an audible sigh. Instinctively, she reached out with her mind and thought his name as she had so many times before. *William,* she thought, *William MacNuff. Are you out there? Can you hear me?*

She received only silence in response.

If he lives, she thought, *wherever he is he is beyond me. And if he doesn't...*

Maria Markinson refused to accept that particular eventuality, regardless of what she had done. *No one knows for sure,* she thought, *and everyone who thinks it? Well, they'd best stop trying to convince me otherwise. He isn't dead or captured. He can't be. Because then...*

No. Until she received confirmation of his whereabouts for good or ill Maria would never give up hope. *Some may think that it doesn't exist anymore,* she thought, *but it's all that I have... all that keeps me going, now. I can't concede that BLANK died the day hope did, William. That's not how I work.*

She heard the muttered conversation behind her break off... heard someone approaching her from behind. Instinctively and without opening her eyes she reached down and touched the right, front pocket of the shorts that she wore. She could feel it within said pocket: The square outline of the item that William had given her and the raised seal upon its surface. A seal imprinted with a figure eight, cross-cut by an arrow. The Artifact. But what did it mean and who was it intended for? She did not know and wondered if she ever would. She knew only that per William's instructions she needed to keep it safe. And she had. If she had achieved nothing else, she had fulfilled that promise to him. And while that did not cancel out her other transgression?

Well, she thought, it'll simply have to for now.

The letter had another purpose, she understood, as she felt a wave of power rush through her body. Give me strength, she thought, a familiar mantra. Her doubts temporarily subsided. She opened her eyes—clear, and not tear-filled—and turned to see Steve standing a step or two behind her. In his left hand he held the pen-like object. He smiled as he held it out to her and spoke five words that, she knew, would echo in her mind not just for that moment...

But forever.

Ever after.

"It's positive, Maria," Steve Wetherhill said demonstratively.

"You're pregnant."

The hand that had caressed the Artifact within her pocket shifted immediately to her slightly protruding belly and she rubbed it across it. She felt the momentary strength that she had experienced leave her in a rush as she reached out and took the pen-like object from Steve. She glanced at it as tears welled up in her eyes and this time? She let them come. A breath or two later she fell into Steve's embrace and sobbed. Carole moved across the room and rubbed a hand across her back as another breeze blew in from the window and caressed the nape of her neck.

Ever after, William, she thought again between sobs, ever, ever onward. If you're out there, go east. East. Find me. Find us.

They remained like that indefinitely, three strangers turned companions turned brethren turned friends, silhouetted against the sun that had begun to set over Free Caymen and the Great, undulating Sea beyond.

* * *

Movement.

Yes, definitely movement in town. The first I have seen in a while. From my vantage point atop the hill upon which my temporary home is situated it is unmistakable. I open the door a crack and the chill outside slaps me despite my heavily bearded face. I can hear a collection of all-to-familiar sounds echoing through the cold and overcast day: Servos grinding. Treads trundling across the rutted road surface. The sounds of the present... *my* present... *Endworld's* present.

The signature sounds of the Administration.

My time has grown short. This place which has sheltered me indefinitely is no longer safe. The faces of my companions both living and deceased once again parade through my mind as I move hastily to finish my account. I hope... I pray that I will live to know the outcome of this manuscript. It lies before me now, written in shaky long-hand upon a ream of faded, yellow paper by an 18 year old boy turned man against his will. Said thoughts quickly turn to thoughts of Maria. *Mia*. Sadly, the pages of this composition are not enough to explicate how much I love her...

How much I will always love her.

There are many lessons to be learned from my experiences and you can take what you desire to away from this. Mine is not to question what you decide. But if there is a moral to my tale for me it is this: You cannot and should not attempt to put a word or words on a feeling, especially when your back is against an open expanse of countryside, your only salvation a theoretical freedom that lays waiting for you an undetermined distance... an undetermined day, an undetermined month and an undetermined year away from your current position across a Great Sea that you've only ever glimpsed but never touched. You can't BLANK because as a wise, once-revolutionary turned recluse turned friend turned martyr turned omniscient specter turned potentially Skew-hopping stranger once said to me, "BLANK died the day hope did." No truer words were ever spoken, Vato. But perhaps she is thinking about me. Perhaps she is attempting to find a way to return to me, if she even knows that I live.

Perhaps.

I watch as an MDU moves across my sightline, parallel to my position on another street roughly a half a kilometer down the hill from where I am positioned. It is followed by an ATT (or a HIT: I cannot tell from my position whether the bed is enclosed or not) and a series of machines or humachines on foot. I gently close the door as the first flakes of snow begin to fall from the familiar, gray-as-slate sky overhead and I shoulder my backpack and remove my recently acquired satellite phone from the dirt-encrusted, front pocket of my jeans and I power it up and tap it and watch as a familiar series of pulses begin to undulate across its screen and I sigh... I sigh with satisfaction as I instinctively close the blind overlooking the town and...

* * *

William MacNuff retired quickly through the warped, wooden door that separated the office that had been his surrogate "home" from the warehouse. He did not pause to glance at the pictures or the mural of the forest at dusk upon the walls. He knew enough about "Teamwork," "Excellence" and "Leadership" to last him a lifetime. He ran across the cracked, cement floor of the warehouse and gained the rear entrance quickly. He slipped outside into the darkening, late afternoon and peeked around the side of the building. The machines had moved out of his view in the direction of the river yet he could still hear them. Grinding. Approaching. Without a thought to the contrary, he began to run up the hill.

Will I ever see you again, Mia? He thought to himself as he blindly fled through the ruined, once-properties above town and blessedly gained the trees beyond. His optimism… His idealism…. everything that he had been was quickly being replaced by something else. Something as cold as the bare branches that scratched his heavily bearded cheeks like jagged nails, and the steadily intensifying snow that settled upon the top of his head before it melted, and ran down his cheeks. It mingled with his tears and both froze almost immediately upon his skin.

Don't let it, Mia, he thought as he reached the top of the hill and began his stumbling trek down its far side, don't let it end without a final glimpse of your face.

He reached a break in the undergrowth and stopped. He looked out over the eight lane, asphalt super Highway distant and below. It was the deepest, darkest black that he had ever seen. It stood in contrast to the browned countryside on either side of it which was quickly whitening. Reluctantly, he proceeded down the last of the hill toward its threshold.

Ever after, William, a familiar, female voice suddenly spoke in his mind, ever, ever onward. He paused in his passage, shocked at not just the voice's presence but its familiarity. He listened intently. A moment later, he gazed in the direction that he believed was east and nodded his head. He resumed his passage down the hill and through the trees. Time moved onward without check, as time always does in Endworld. The Highway stretched off endlessly in either direction before him beneath a darkening, twilight sky in the midst of a thickening snowfall like a huge, dreaming python and William MacNuff felt the cold, steely hands of inevitability clamp down upon his heart.

Another day in Endworld had passed.

Made in the USA
Charleston, SC
15 May 2013